Dying To Win

Patricia H. Rushford

MW00782525

Jennie McGrady Mystery Series

Helen Bradley Mystery Series

9610

Dying To Win

Patricia H. Rushford

BETHANY HOUSE PUBLISHERS
MINNEAPOLIS, MINNESOTA 55438

Copyright © 1995
Patricia H. Rushford

Published by Bethany House Publishers
A Ministry of Bethany Fellowship, Inc.
11300 Hampshire Avenue South
Minneapolis, Minnesota 55438

Printed in the United States of America.

Library of Congress Cataloging-in-Publication Data

Rushford, Patricia H.
    Dying to win / Patricia Rushford.
        p.   cm. — (Jennie McGrady mystery series ; 6)
    Summary: When sixteen-year-old Courtney, the
daughter of a pharmacist, calls for help, Jennie sets off to
solve a mystery involving drugs, sports, and competition.

    [1. Drug abuse—Fiction. 2. Christian life—Fiction.
3. Mystery and detective stories.] I. Title. II. Series:
Rushford, Patricia H. Jennie McGrady mystery series ; 6.
PZ7.R8962Dy   1995
[Fic]—dc20   95-33332
ISBN 1–55661–559–0   CIP
                                                         AC

For David

PATRICIA RUSHFORD is an award-winning writer, speaker, and teacher who has published over twenty books and numerous articles, including *What Kids Need Most in a Mom*, *The Humpty Dumpty Syndrome: Putting Yourself Back Together Again*, and her first young adult novel, *Kristen's Choice*. She is a registered nurse and has a master's degree in counseling from Western Evangelical Seminary. She and her husband, Ron, live in Washington State and have two grown children, six grandchildren, and lots of nephews and nieces.

Pat has been reading mysteries for as long as she can remember and is delighted to be writing a series of her own. She is a member of Mystery Writers of America, Society of Children's Book Writers and Illustrators, and several other writing organizations. She is also co-director of Writer's Weekend at the Beach.

1

"Were you shocked to discover who had abducted the children?" Nancy Edwards, one of the television news reporters, directed her question to Jennie McGrady.

"Yes." *Of course I was*, Jennie wanted to say, but didn't. If she'd known who had taken the children, she'd have been able to rescue them immediately, instead of going through the terror of being abducted and nearly killed herself.

Jennie gazed out over the herd of reporters and cameras. She and her mother had been answering questions for over an hour. Her cobalt blue eyes had long since glazed over. Her jaw ached and Jennie figured it would probably take a week for her camera smile to fade.

Any other time Jennie might have enjoyed the media attention. She'd helped solve several criminal cases of late, and though she had no delusions of being an internationally known amateur detective, she did relish these brief snatches of fame. Now, however, she just wanted to go home.

Her excitement over rescuing her little brother, Nick, and his four-year-old friend, Hannah Stuart, had long since turned to exhaustion. Jennie lifted her long, nearly black hair from the back of her neck, wishing she'd braided it. She'd worn a white cotton dress, but the heat from the lights had turned the podium area into a sauna.

Susan McGrady slipped a comforting arm around her

daughter's waist. Her auburn hair tickled Jennie's chin. "We were all surprised, and disturbed," Mom said, her voice lacking expression. "We're also very tired. I think it would be a good idea to conclude the press conference." She glanced to her left where Nick and Hannah sat on separate chairs, both asleep and leaning against each other like limp rag dolls.

Several of the photographers followed her gaze. They must have thought the photo opportunity too great to pass up. For the next few seconds, lights flashed at the children, cameras popped and whirred, then focused back on Jennie and her mother.

"What's going to happen to Hannah?" another voice from the crowd asked.

"It's too soon to say," Mom answered. "Children's Services has granted me temporary custody."

Other questions erupted. Mom held up her hand and shook her head. "No more questions, please." She glanced up to meet Jennie's eyes. "Why don't you take Nick? I'll carry Hannah." Mom turned to Gram and J.B., who were seated behind them on the platform. "Would you mind finishing up here?" she whispered. "Give us a chance to escape?"

J.B., otherwise known as Jason Bradley, went to the microphone and motioned for Gram to join him. Jennie had come to love J.B., but still had trouble imagining the silver-haired Irish FBI agent as her grandfather. He seemed a more likely candidate for a James Bond movie. Actually, so did Gram. As a travel writer, ex-police officer, and part-time agent, Gram lived the kind of life others only dreamed about. Maybe that's what made them such a perfect couple—and just about the most interesting people Jennie knew.

Holding the press conference at the Hilton in downtown Portland had been J.B.'s idea. That way, he'd explained, they could answer all of the reporters' questions at one time. It had also given the family time to celebrate Nick and Hannah's homecoming privately.

"Ladies and gentlemen," J.B. began. With his Irish accent and firm, mellow voice, he appeased the crowd with a promise to answer a few more questions.

The thought of leaving revived Jennie. She tossed her grandparents a genuine smile and scooped Nick into her arms, then followed her mother through a side door. The door led to a hallway, which would eventually take them to the street and their car.

To guarantee their privacy, J.B. had arranged for security guards to be posted at the pressroom door as well as the hotel entrance. Halfway down the hall, Jennie heard a ruckus and turned around. Apparently, one of the reporters had decided to follow them because the guards blocked the doorway and were talking to a young man with a camera.

Jennie shook her head and continued. Reporters could be relentless. She'd nearly reached the exit when she heard footsteps behind her.

"How does it feel to be a hero, Jennie?"

She groaned and kept walking. "Don't you people know when to quit? The press conference is over. How did you get past security?"

"I told them I was your boyfriend." The reporter nearly ran into her when she stopped.

"My what?"

Nick moaned and turned his head, letting it come to rest on her left shoulder.

"Well, I am a friend—sort of."

The tall, lanky young man looked familiar, but her mind refused to come up with a name.

"Help me out here, Jen. This could be my big break."

"Gavin?" Jennie finally recognized him. Gavin Winslow worked on *The Forum*, Trinity High's school paper. He was forever following people around with his camera and tape recorder. "What are you doing here? School doesn't start for a month and a half. This story will be old news by then."

"I got a summer job with *The Oregonian.* So far I've only been able to do small stuff. When I told the editor I knew you personally, he gave me the assignment. He wants me to do a feature story on you and your little brother—you know, the human interest angle." Gavin reached up and brushed several strands of straight hair, almost as dark as her own, from his forehead. When he pushed his glasses back he reminded her of Clark Kent—without the muscle.

"Me?" she asked. Nick stirred in her arms again. Jennie shifted him to her right arm and supported some of his weight with her hip. "Why would you want to do a story about me? The press already knows more about me than I know about myself."

"You're a hero, Jennie. Two kids were kidnapped and you risked your own neck to save them. The boss wants your story."

Jennie rolled her eyes and started to walk away. "No way."

Gavin stepped in front of her. "Please, Jen. This is extremely important to me."

Exhaustion washed over her again. Seeing the disappointment in his blue-gray eyes, her reserve crumbled. "Okay," she heard herself say. "You can come by tomorrow afternoon."

"Great! I'll be there at one." Gavin's eyes flashed to high beam. "You won't regret this, McGrady."

Jennie watched as he loped off. Some of his excitement and exuberance had worn off on her and she found herself looking forward to the interview almost as much as she dreaded it.

2

When Jennie reached the sidewalk, her mother already had the car running and, thankfully, the air conditioner. She secured Nick into the seat belt beside Hannah and climbed into the front passenger seat of the Oldsmobile. Being in a car—any car—brought back memories of her dearly departed white Mustang. During the search for Nick, the car had tangled with some trees and lost.

"What took you so long?" Mom asked as she shifted into drive and pulled away from the curb. "I was about to send in reinforcements."

"I ran into a guy from school," Jennie answered, pushing away the depressing thoughts of losing her car. "He wants to interview me."

"You told him no, didn't you? We've had enough excitement for a while. I just hope those reporters don't decide to set up camp in our front yard." Mom stopped at a red light and glanced at Jennie. "You agreed to the interview?"

Jennie nodded, wishing she could avert the forthcoming lecture. "He's a friend, Mom. He goes to Trinity High *and* to our church."

"I don't care if he's the Pope." Mom sighed as the light turned green. Dividing her attention between the late Sunday afternoon traffic and Jennie, she began what promised to be a long lecture. "Honey, I know all this attention is excit-

11

ing, but you have to know where to draw the line."

"I know. . . ." Jennie rubbed at the goosebumps on her bare arms and reached forward to turn the air conditioner down.

"It's not that I don't want you to talk to the press. You deserve the recognition. It's just that we . . ."

"We have to think of the children," Jennie finished.

Mom smiled. "Are you telling me I've said this before?"

"Only about a dozen times since yesterday. Don't worry so much, Mom. In another couple of days the press will move on to something else. Right now the kidnapping is big news. People want to know what happened. Tomorrow they won't remember our names."

Mom lifted her eyebrows in an I'll-believe-it-when-I-see-it look. "So, who's the *friend?*"

"Gavin Winslow."

"Really." Mom raised her eyebrows again. Tossing Jennie a conspiratorial smile she added, "Giving Ryan a little competition?"

"Mom, p-lease." Ryan Johnson, her long-time friend, lived next door to Gram in Bay Village on the Oregon Coast. Just when their relationship had begun to grow into something more interesting, Ryan decided to spend the summer fishing in Alaska to earn money for college. When he heard about Nick's disappearance, Ryan left his fishing job and flew to Portland to be with her.

With the kidnapping ordeal over, he'd gone back to the beach to spend a couple days with his mom and stepdad. He'd be back tomorrow and had promised her a real date—with dinner and a movie. Sadly, the following day she'd be dropping him off at the airport. Their on-and-off romance was definitely on at the moment and Jennie didn't want anything or anyone to get in the way.

She shook her head. "Trust me on this one. There is no way Gavin could compete with Ryan."

"Oh, I don't know. He's intelligent and rather good-looking, and, according to my source, he's going to be the next Peter Jennings."

Jennie didn't like the direction the conversation was heading. One of the problems with going to a private school was that parents usually knew one another and the kids. Mom's *source* was probably Gavin's mother. Jennie had no intention of dating anyone but Ryan, especially now that she knew how he felt about her.

"Speaking of someone being interested in someone," Jennie said, abruptly changing the subject, "are you and Michael getting back together?" Michael Rhodes was Mom's ex-fiance. Jennie regretted asking the question the moment it came out of her mouth. "I mean, he came with you to pick us up at the hospital last night—I thought maybe—"

The teasing grin on Mom's face faded into a pained expression. She didn't answer.

"I'm sorry," Jennie said. "I shouldn't have brought it up."

"No, it's all right." Mom frowned and bit her lip. "We've decided it might be a good idea to see other people for a while. It was Michael's idea. He thought maybe dating others would help us evaluate how we really feel about each other."

"So are you going to?"

"Maybe."

The conversation stalemated as Jennie sank into her own thoughts and Mom into hers. Thinking about Mom and Michael naturally brought back memories of her father, Jason McGrady. He'd disappeared five years before in a mysterious plane crash. Jennie had never accepted the theory that he'd been killed, and on her sixteenth birthday decided it was time to solve the mystery of his disappearance once and for all. She'd managed to accomplish her goal, but the dream of seeing her parents reunited fizzled like a fire in a rainstorm.

Dad wasn't coming home.

As an agent for the Drug Enforcement Agency, he'd made

too many powerful enemies in the drug world. In order to protect himself and his family, he'd changed his identity. Jason McGrady no longer existed—the government had declared him officially dead. Only Jennie, Gram, and a few top-level officials knew the truth.

At first Jennie thought keeping Dad's secret would be easy. Now she wasn't so sure. Mom deserved to know. *But you made a promise, McGrady*, Jennie reminded herself.

She closed her eyes and pictured the last few moments she had shared with her father. A flood of emotions tumbled inside her like clothes in a dryer. She'd been so proud of him, bringing down drug lords and curbing drug traffic into the United States and abroad. At the same time, Jennie resented his absence—especially during the last few days.

You had to have known about Nick, she mentally accused him. Every television station and newspaper in the country had carried the story. *You should have been with us.* Jennie searched for excuses that would vindicate him, but could find none. She sighed. *Oh, Dad, why couldn't you have at least called? We needed you.*

"Are you okay, honey?" Mom asked as she reached over to take Jennie's hand in hers. "You look—I don't know—angry, sad."

"I was just wishing Dad could have been here."

Mom squeezed Jennie's hand. Tears gathered in her eyes. "I wish I knew what to say. You don't know how many times I've felt the same thing—even before the crash. He never seemed to be there when we needed him. I think the worst time was not having him with us when Nick was born."

Or when Nick was growing up, Jennie added silently, remembering the pain in Dad's eyes when he'd talked about the son he'd never known.

"I didn't feel that way this time," Mom continued. "Maybe because of Michael's support." Mom wiped the moisture from her cheeks with her fingers. "Mostly, though,

I think it's because I know now that your father's really gone. He was a good man, Jennie. In his own way he loved us."

Loves us, Mom, Jennie wanted to say, but couldn't. Dad did love them. She'd seen it in his face when he told her he couldn't go home. So why hadn't he called? *Because it's too dangerous, McGrady,* she reminded herself. *Dangerous for him and for the family.*

When they arrived at the house, Jennie pushed her disappointment and resentment away and helped her mother settle the children into bed to finish their naps. With the ordeal they had gone through, Jennie could have used a nap herself. Instead she decided to change clothes and read until dinner.

A few minutes later, wearing a comfortable oversized pink cotton T-shirt and knit white shorts, Jennie stretched out on one of the lounge chairs on the porch and began to read the new mystery she'd gotten from Gram.

Afternoon faded into dusk, then night. Somewhere in between, Nick and Hannah woke up and wanted to play dragons. They'd eaten a dinner of salad, spaghetti with meat sauce, and garlic bread, then watched the news. The hour-and-a-half interview had been condensed to a two-minute segment as the newscaster related a happy ending to a tragic story.

Ryan called at nine-thirty as dark clouds, hovering on the horizon, devoured the sun's last rays.

"How's the hero business?" Ryan teased when Jennie answered the private phone in her room. "Been offered any movie contracts yet?"

Jennie chuckled. "Sure. My agent and I are trying to decide between Spielberg and Disney. Then, of course, I have to find someone to play me."

"Oh, that's easy," Ryan said. "Connie Selleca."

"Really?" Jennie carried the phone to her dresser and studied herself in the mirror. She'd never seen herself as especially pretty. Compared to beauty contest winners like her redheaded cousin, Lisa, and their elegant and sophisticated friend, Allison Beaumont, Jennie considered herself average looking. But Ryan's comment made her feel attractive. With her long dark hair and cobalt blue eyes, she did resemble Connie—just a little.

"So tell me honestly," Ryan said, becoming more serious. "How are you doing? I caught the news earlier. You looked great, but I could tell you were pretty bummed out."

Jennie moved away from the mirror, wandered back to her bed, and sat down. "That's putting it mildly." She told him about the long press conference and the scheduled interview with Gavin Winslow. "Oh no. I just realized I have him coming about the same time you are."

"Hey, don't worry about it. Mom and I probably won't get to Portland until around two. If he's still there, I'll just come in and make faces at you."

They talked for another five minutes about friends, Alaska, and their date the next night, then hung up. Jennie spent the next hour or so at loose ends. She wandered around the house enjoying the quiet, yet wishing she could talk to someone. Mom, a CPA, was holed up in her office catching up on some paper work. After trying a few friends and finding no one at home, Jennie curled up on the couch and finished reading the book she'd started earlier.

She finished the book at eleven and went in search of her mother. Jennie found her, still in her office, hunched over a pile of ledgers. "Mom? I just wanted to let you know I'm going to bed."

Mom glanced at her watch and frowned. "I'll be up in a while. I just need to make a few more entries."

Jennie kissed Mom good-night and headed upstairs, stopping off at Nick's room to check on him and Hannah. She watched them for a few minutes and, not being able to resist, knelt beside Nick. She brushed his dark wavy hair aside and pressed her lips to his forehead. " 'Night, little buddy," she whispered.

Stopping at Hannah's temporary bed, Jennie gently removed a Madeline book. Eventually, Hannah would have her own room, but for now, Nick insisted on taking care of her.

With the back of her fingers she stroked Hannah's cheek, and sighed. An overwhelming feeling of sadness washed over her. "You're going to be all right, little one," Jennie promised. "We'll take good care of you."

Jennie rose to leave, pausing in the doorway to look back at the children she'd helped save. After sending up thanks for the umpteenth time, she closed the door.

Jennie brushed her teeth, changed into her lightweight cotton pajamas, and turned out the light. The room was stuffy and warm so she opened the windows, then sat in her window seat. Cool summer air wafted in, smelling of roses. She leaned against the cushions and watched the moon play hide-and-seek behind the clouds.

Tomorrow would be a busy day. She'd promised to help her mother clean the house, wash the car, and mow the lawn—all before Ryan came. She remembered her appointment with Gavin and groaned. Why had she agreed to it? Before she could think of a way out of the commitment, her phone rang. Jennie glanced at the clock. Eleven-thirty. Probably Lisa calling to let her know how things went.

"Hello?" Jennie answered, cradling the receiver against her shoulder.

No one answered.

"Lisa, is that you?"

Still no answer.

"Who is this? Look, I know you're there. I can hear you breathing."

"Um . . . Jennie, this is Courtney Evans. You probably don't remember me. I go to Trinity."

A picture of the tall slender girl appeared in Jennie's

mind. She and Courtney had a similar build, but there the resemblance ended. Courtney's short, shaggy haircut varied in color from cream to burgundy, depending on her mood. She wore colored contacts—green one day, purple the next. She must have had a dozen shades.

Courtney had been expelled from school twice for wearing "inappropriate dress." Her *dress* ranged from studded leathers with pants so tight they probably had to be peeled off, to layers of clothes that looked like rejects from a thrift store.

"Of course I remember you," Jennie said, hoping she didn't sound too critical.

"The reason, um . . . the reason I'm calling is . . . Look, never mind, I shouldn't have bothered you."

"No, hey, it's okay. Really."

"I saw you on the news tonight and thought maybe you could help. . . ." Courtney hesitated again. Jennie heard a shuddering sound and wondered if she'd been crying.

"Are you in some kind of trouble?"

"Yeah, I guess you could say that. Look, could you meet me at the mall tomorrow afternoon?"

"Tomorrow?" With Gavin coming—and her date with Ryan, there was no way. Still, Jennie couldn't ignore her plea for help. "Maybe late. I have an appointment. . . ."

"Right. Forget I called, okay? I shouldn't have bothered you."

"Courtney, wait. Courtney!"

3

Jennie had been kissing Ryan and suddenly his summer sky eyes faded to gray, glasses appeared on his blue face, and his hair turned dark.

"No! Go away and leave me alone." Jennie recognized the voice as her own as she fought her way out of the strange and annoying dream.

Gavin had been following her. No matter what she did, Gavin was there. Jennie tried to scream, but nothing came out. She tried to run, but her feet wouldn't move. Even in her sleep he sat beside her—watching. He kissed her hand—then licked it. Gross!

She shoved her wet hand under her pillow. "Leave me alone."

A snuffling, whining sound roused her more fully. Someone pulled at the sheets. She grabbed them back.

Wait a minute, McGrady. This isn't a dream. Someone's in your room. She yanked the covers off and bolted out of bed. Jennie fully expected to see the would-be reporter sitting in the chair, pad and pencil in hand, poised for an interview. The intruder, however, was not Gavin Winslow, but Nick's St. Bernard puppy. Sinking back onto the bed, Jennie willed her heart rate to settle back into its normal rhythm.

"Bernie." She ruffled the dog's silky brown and white fur. "Am I glad to see you. You would not believe the crazy dream I just had."

Remembering the interview she'd promised Gavin, Jennie grimaced. "I just hope he doesn't turn out to be that obnoxious in real life."

Bernie joined her on the bed and planted another slobbery kiss—this time on her face. A moment later he bounced to the door, turned around, woofed, then disappeared. When Jennie didn't follow, he came back in and looked up at her with huge, pleading brown eyes.

"Let me guess. You're hungry."

Bernie pulled in his tongue and stopped panting long enough to woof again, then headed for the door. Jennie glanced at the radio alarm beside her bed. Six a.m. "Why me?" She rolled her eyes and looked longingly at her pillow. "Mom bought you. You're Nick's responsibility. Okay, okay, I'm the only one who forgot to close my door."

Resigning herself to the task at hand, Jennie pulled on her bathrobe, then followed Bernie down the stairs and into the kitchen. At the pantry, Bernie stopped and let her get ahead of him. His tail swished wildly from one side to the other as she pulled open the bi-fold louvered doors and scooped about a pound of Puppy Chow from the 100-pound bag. "I'm surprised you haven't figured out a way to get into the pantry yet." When Jennie finished pouring the food, he nudged her out of the way and buried his nose into his dish.

She refilled his water bowl, then set a cup of water in the microwave for herself. While waiting for the water to heat, Jennie raided the refrigerator, surfaced with a carton of yogurt, and topped it with granola. A few minutes later, with tea and breakfast in hand, Jennie made her way back through the house and out the front door. She settled into the white porch swing to enjoy the freshness of the morning. A heavy rain had washed away the dust and summer heat.

Her annoyance at being awakened so early disappeared in an overwhelming sense of gratefulness. Off to the east the sun was just getting up. The clear rose-colored sky held a promise of a bright, new, wonderful day.

The children were safe, Ryan would be coming that afternoon, and Gavin's annoying presence had only been a dream.

On a slightly depressing note, the dream held a tinge of reality. Ryan would be leaving tomorrow. Jennie would be taking him to the airport where he'd catch a flight to Alaska for another month of fishing. She hated saying goodbye again, but at least this time she knew he loved her.

Jennie leaned her head back against the post and frowned as Ryan's image faded from her mind and Courtney Evans' face came into focus.

The disturbing phone call she'd gotten from Courtney last night drifted into her memory like a black cloud marring an otherwise clear day. She'd tried to call Courtney back right away, but no one answered.

Let it go, McGrady, she told herself firmly. *If it's really important she'll get hold of you. But what if she can't?* another part of her wondered. *What if she's in trouble?*

Okay, so maybe she wouldn't forget it. She'd try calling Courtney again later that morning. A greeting from the paper boy and the thump of *The Oregonian* hitting the porch step brought Jennie out of her reverie.

Jennie finished her yogurt and tea, scooped up the paper, and wandered back into the kitchen. She deposited the paper on the table and her breakfast dishes in the sink. By eight o'clock Jennie had gotten dressed, cleaned her room, done a load of laundry, and made breakfast—French toast, ham, and pineapple-orange juice for Mom and the kids. Mom stumbled into the kitchen just as the coffee machine sputtered its I'm-ready signal.

"Good morning, Mother," Jennie chirped. She set coffee and the morning paper on the table and steered her mother to the chair.

Mom stared at the table and yawned before lifting the cup

to her lips. "Okay," she mumbled, still holding the cup, "what have you done with my daughter?"

Jennie grinned. "Couldn't fool you, could we? I am an alien being. My spaceship landed in your backyard last night. We climbed through an open window and captured Jennie. My colleagues are extracting information from her brain as we speak. I have taken on her persona. My alien friends are likewise taking over the bodies of certain key people we see as highly intelligent beings. Soon we will rule the world."

"Highly intelligent beings? Taking over the world? Hmmm. That sounds plausible. For a moment I thought you were going to tell me you got up early, were in a good mood, and decided to make everyone breakfast."

"Not even I would have believed that story." Jennie dished up a plate of French toast and ham and served her mother. "There will be differences, Mrs. McGrady, but in time you will come to accept me. Now relax and enjoy your breakfast while I get Nick and Hannah up."

"We're already up, Jennie." Hannah appeared in the doorway, took her thumb out of her mouth to speak, then plugged it back in.

Nick raced past her and pulled out a chair. "You sit here, Hannah. This can be your place."

Hannah obediently climbed into the chair Nick indicated and watched intently as he took the one next to her. Jennie's throat tightened. She wondered how long the kidnapping would bother her. Swallowing back the rush of emotions, Jennie dished up their plates.

Nick shoveled a piece of French toast into his mouth. A trail of syrup ran down his chin; he tried to catch it with his tongue.

"Use your napkin," Mom said as she cut up Hannah's ham.

Jennie pulled out a chair and was about to lower herself into it.

22

Mom opened *The Oregonian* and almost spilled her coffee. "Did you see this?"

Jennie shook her head. "No, why?"

"The entire front page is dedicated to the kidnapping." Jennie peered over Mom's shoulder. Under the heading "He's Her Brother" was a large color photo of Jennie carrying Nick. The caption beneath the photo read, "Sixteen-year-old Jennie McGrady risks life to save abducted children."

"Here's an article by Gavin Winslow," Mom murmured.

Jennie leaned in closer. He wasn't interviewing her until this afternoon. Apparently, he'd written up the results of the press conference.

"He calls you 'a rising star in the field of law enforcement.' " Mom reached up and tucked a strand of hair behind Jennie's ear. "Sounds like you made quite an impression on him."

Embarrassed by the accolades, Jennie wrinkled her nose. "It doesn't take much to make an impression on Gavin."

Mom stood and took her dishes to the sink. "Oh, honey, stop being so cynical. Gavin seems like a nice young man. I'm not too crazy about him encouraging you with this law enforcement business though, *and* his tactics to get an interview might have been a little underhanded, but getting a story on the front page is impressive."

Jennie nodded. "I suppose you're right. I just hope the interview with him this afternoon is the end of it. Being a hero has its moments, but enough is enough."

After breakfast and dishes, Jennie volunteered to take the kids to the park so Mom could work. Being a CPA, she often met clients in their offices or had them come to her home. Mom sent Nick and Hannah up to clean Nick's room and began straightening the living room. "I hate to ask after all you've done this morning, Jennie, but how about vacuuming the downstairs for me?" Mom folded the afghan on the couch

23

and fluffed a pink throw pillow. "I have a new client coming today. Frank Evans."

At the mention of his name, Jennie snapped to attention. "Frank Evans? Isn't that Courtney's dad?"

Mom nodded. "He's a pharmacist. Owns Evans' Pharmacy near Oregon City. A couple of Sundays ago, at church, he asked me if I'd do his books for him. His regular bookkeeper recently died."

Jennie considered telling her mother about Courtney's call, then decided against it. No point in alarming Mom or Courtney's father unnecessarily. "Um . . . when's he coming?"

"In an hour. I'd like to get the house cleaned—and I need to do some work in the office." She sighed and glanced around. "And I suppose I should shower and get dressed."

Glancing down at the tangle of shoulder-length auburn hair, Mom's bare feet, and the floral print cotton bathrobe, Jennie teased, "Why? You look great."

Mom cast Jennie an incredulous look. "Keep that up and I'll think you really are an alien."

Jennie chuckled as she retrieved the vacuum cleaner from the hall closet. Mom disappeared upstairs and Jennie wondered what, if anything, she should say to Mr. Evans. She had tried calling Courtney earlier and left a message on the answering machine. Jennie finally decided a few innocuous questions like, "How's Courtney?" wouldn't hurt.

Unfortunately, she didn't get to talk to him. Mom shooed Jennie, Nick, and Hannah out of the house half an hour before his arrival so she could "tidy her office." Judging from her mother's nervous behavior and the careful way she'd applied her makeup, Jennie had the unsettling feeling Mom viewed Frank Evans as more than just a client.

Jennie didn't much like the idea of her mother dating. After finding and talking with Dad, Jennie had been nearly ready to accept Michael as a stepfather. In her heart, she preferred having Mom and Dad get back together, but like Dad had said, "Things don't always work out the way you want them to."

Two hours later, Jennie extracted Nick and Hannah from the playground equipment and headed home. When the weary children lagged behind, Jennie suggested piggyback rides, which brought an immediate round of cheers. Since she had only one back, Nick did the gentlemanly thing and offered to let Hannah ride on Jennie while he walked Bernie.

Bernie, probably more interested in food than his family, strained at his leash as they neared the house. Jennie picked up her pace as well when she saw a teal green Lexus still parked in the driveway.

"Looks like Mom's client is still there," Jennie said to no one in particular as they neared the yard.

"What's a kwient?" Hannah asked.

Jennie was about to respond when the door opened and Mr. Evans and Mom stepped onto the porch. They were laughing. "Well," Frank said, "I'd better get back to work. I left Courtney in charge. She's a great help, but with that new look of hers I'm afraid she might scare off some of my more conservative customers. I guess I'll see you Friday night." He leaned toward Susan slightly, as if he were thinking about kissing her.

No, don't let him, Mom, please, you can't, Jennie wanted to yell, but didn't. Suddenly feeling confused and angry, she wanted to stop whatever was happening between Mr. Evans and her mother.

"Mommy, Mommy, guess what we did?" Nick raced across the yard and bounded up the steps.

Mr. Evans stepped back, then cleared his throat and smiled. Bending at the waist, he ruffled Nick's dark hair. "You must be Nick."

Nick backed away and wrapped his arms around Mom's leg.

"Jennie," Hannah whispered in Jennie's ear. "Don't squeeze me so hard."

"Oh, Hannah, I'm sorry." Jennie released her grip on Hannah's legs and lowered her to the ground. "Did I hurt you?"

Hannah shook her head, rubbing her blond curls against Jennie's arm.

With Hannah clinging to her hand, Jennie walked toward the steps. "Hi, Mr. Evans." She shoved her confused emotions temporarily aside. "I'm Jennie."

"I know. I was just telling your mother that I wished you and Courtney could get together. You'd be a good influence on her, I . . ." His voice trailed off.

Oh, great. Just what she always wanted to be—an influence. Was that why Courtney had called? Had her dad been bugging her about her choice of friends? No, being bugged didn't explain the fear Jennie had sensed in Courtney's voice.

"Maybe we could have you and Courtney over for dinner one night," Mom said, interrupting Jennie's thoughts. "That would give the girls a chance to get to know each other."

"Wonderful idea, Susan. I'll talk to Courtney." Mr. Evans turned back to Jennie. "Courtney's really a sweet girl—at least she was before . . ." he paused and glanced at Mom, then at Nick and Hannah. "I think perhaps I'd better save that story for another time."

Frank Evans said goodbye and left. Whatever he'd been about to say couldn't be said in front of the children. Jennie felt like she'd come to the end of a suspenseful chapter in a mystery, only to find someone had torn out the rest of the pages.

4

Over a lunch of toasted cheese sandwiches, tomato soup, and Jell-O, Jennie brooded about Courtney's phone call and Mr. Evans' unfinished sentence.

"You'll never guess who called while you were out," Mom said when they were nearly finished eating.

"Lisa?"

Mom shook her head. "Don't slurp your soup, Nick. Use your spoon."

"Courtney?"

"No. Marge Thurman, from the insurance company."

Jennie's thoughts about Courtney and her dad vanished. Marge would only be calling about one thing. Her car.

Jennie felt a twinge of sadness over losing the white Mustang. Being run off the road and landing in a stand of fir trees had done terrible things to it. Jennie had fought to have it restored, but the insurance adjuster insisted the car be totaled. "What did she say?"

"She's found a car for us."

Jennie frowned. "I don't understand. I thought they were just going to send us a check."

"Ordinarily they would, but with all we were going through, Marge offered to go a step further. She knew how much you liked the Mustang and said she'd do her best to find one like it."

"Really?" Jennie wiped her hands off on the napkin. "When do I get to see it?"

A horn sounded outside. Mom glanced at her watch, and the smile on her face broadened. "I think that's her."

Jennie excused herself and ran outside. Parked in the driveway was the most beautiful car she had ever seen. Marge Thurman stepped out and waved. "Do you like it? It's three years newer. I know the other one was white, but when I saw this one . . ."

"I love it." Jennie crossed behind the car, touching the glossy fire-engine red finish as she made her way to the driver's side.

Mom appeared on the porch with Nick and Hannah. "It looks expensive. Are you sure the insurance money will cover it?"

"Absolutely," Marge assured. "It was recently repossessed, so we got a great buy on it."

Another car, this one a cream-colored Cadillac, pulled into the driveway. "My husband," Marge explained, dropping the keys into Jennie's hand. "The papers are in the glove box." She patted the Mustang's trunk. "It's all yours, Jennie."

"Thanks!" Jennie resisted the urge to bounce as she gripped the keys. She waved goodbye and turned back to the car. Excitement pulsed through her, probably sending her adrenaline to dangerously high levels. Climbing into the driver's seat, she felt like a princess who'd just had a visit from her fairy godmother. "Wow," she murmured, running her hand over the black leather seats. "Radio, tape deck, air conditioner—everything."

Remembering the rest of her family, Jennie got out, leaned her arms on the roof, and offered them a ride.

"I'd love to, hon, but I think it will have to wait." Mom glanced toward the street. "Here comes Gavin. Maybe he'd like to go with you."

Images of the dream she'd had that morning threatened to cloud her day. *Come on, McGrady. Be fair. You promised Gavin an interview. You can enjoy driving the car later—with Ryan.*

Jennie took a deep breath and managed a smile as Gavin jumped off his bike, removed his helmet, and walked toward her. Bony legs extended from a pair of khaki shorts. His hair had a funny kink in it where the helmet had crushed it and his white polo shirt looked like he'd taken a shower with his clothes on. On his back he carried a dull reddish brown leather backpack that looked like it had survived a war.

After introducing Gavin to her new car and her family, Jennie offered him a seat in one of the wicker chairs adorning the front porch.

"Would you like something to drink?" Mom asked. "We have iced tea, lemonade, root beer, Coke. . . ."

"Thanks, Mrs. McGrady, but I'd prefer some ice water." He nodded toward his bike. "And maybe I could wash up?"

Jennie fixed a tray of drinks and dug some chocolate chip cookies out of the ceramic lamb cookie jar. She set them on the white wicker table. While she waited for Gavin, she imagined herself and Ryan driving through the woods.

"Bet you're anxious to drive it," Gavin said, pulling Jennie out of her daydream.

"I am. But . . ." Jennie glanced back at Gavin, surprised at the transformation. He'd changed his shirt and now wore a salmon-colored polo. He'd wet and combed his hair and looked—well, almost handsome.

"The interview?" Gavin grinned. "We can do that anywhere."

"Really?"

"Sure." He reached for his water and gulped it down to nothing but ice.

Jennie didn't need any more encouragement. After telling her mother where they were going, she and Gavin climbed into the car and headed west. With the windows down and the radio on, Jennie took the nearest route to Washington Park.

"So, do you want to interview me while I'm driving?"

"Yeah. Why don't you start by telling me your life story?"

"Not much to tell." Jennie started with what she thought was the most interesting part. About being born into a family of law-enforcement people. How her grandfather Ian—Gram's first husband—was a secret service agent, and had been killed in a bombing in Beruit. How her father had been a DEA agent prior to the plane crash. How her parents and Lisa's parents got together. "My mom's brother, Kevin Calhoun, is Lisa's dad—you know Lisa, don't you?"

When Gavin nodded, she went on. "Anyway, Dad and Uncle Kevin met in the Air Force—they were both pilots. When they got out, they stayed friends. Kevin fell in love with my dad's twin sister, Kate, and Dad fell in love with Kevin's younger sister, my mom. They had a double wedding a few months later."

"Whew," Gavin shook his head. "Sounds confusing."

"We're used to it." When Jennie's gaze met his he quickly glanced away, as if embarrassed at being caught. But at what? Looking at her? Jennie hoped that by agreeing to the interview or taking him for a drive he wouldn't think she was leading him on.

She sneaked a peek at him again, and this time it was her turn to be embarrassed. He'd been watching the road, then turned to catch her watching him.

He pressed his wire-framed glasses against his nose. "Driving around has been fun, Jennie, but do you think we could stop somewhere so I can get some photos? Also, I need part of the interview on tape."

Jennie parked in a wooded lot and she and Gavin found a shady spot near a pond. Once they were seated on the cool lawn, Gavin retrieved his camera, a tape recorder, and a notepad from the worn leather pack and began his interview.

After a few dozen photos and what seemed like a hundred questions later, Jennie called a halt to the interview. As they walked back to the car, she told him about Ryan and how he'd helped her in the kidnapping case.

"He sounds like a great guy. I'd like to meet him. Maybe I could ask him a few questions too." Gavin set his backpack down and folded himself into the passenger seat.

Gavin's response settled Jennie's mind about his possibly being interested in her as a girlfriend. She was beginning to feel much more at ease with him. "I'm sure Ryan won't mind." Jennie started the Mustang and shifted into reverse.

As she drove through the park and merged onto the Sunset Highway, an idea began to take shape and form. Being a reporter, Gavin just might be able to answer some of the questions she had about Courtney Evans. The trick would be to extract that information without arousing suspicion. "You're a good interviewer, Gavin."

"Thanks. You're an easy person to interview. Actually, it's my favorite part of being a reporter. I love to talk to people and listen to their stories."

"Have you ever interviewed Courtney Evans?" *Way to go, McGrady. So much for the subtle approach.*

Gavin frowned. "Courtney?"

Jennie had struck a nerve. She could almost see a wall go up between them. He seemed agitated. Why?

"Yeah," Jennie continued on as if she hadn't noticed his discomfort. "You must know her. It would be hard for anyone not to. She's one of the most, um . . . interesting kids in school."

"I know her." Gavin pushed a hand through his hair. "Why are you asking?"

Should she tell him about the phone call? Jennie played a mental tug-of-war with herself for a few seconds before coming to a decision. "Courtney called me last night and asked for my help. She wanted to meet me at the mall today. When I tried to explain that I had an appointment, she said to forget it and hung up. I tried calling her back, but . . ."

Gavin shook his head. "I wouldn't worry too much about it, Jennie. Courtney tends to be sort of melodramatic. And to answer your question, I did interview her—last May. You didn't see my article in *The Forum*?"

"No, I'm sorry. With finals and everything—I was getting ready for a trip to Florida with my grandmother."

"It was one of my best pieces. I titled it "Rainbow Girl" because of how she's always changing the color of her hair and eyes. A lot of people don't understand Courtney."

"She's not easy to understand. Those outrageous clothes and hairstyles. And her attitude—like she'd rather eat nails than talk to you. That's why I was so surprised when she called."

"You want to know about Courtney? Why don't you read the article I wrote? That will give you a better picture than anything I could say right now."

"You sound like you're upset with her about something."

Gavin folded his arms over his chest and sulked. After a few seconds he straightened and sighed. "You'll find out anyway, so I might as well tell you. After I interviewed her, Courtney and I became friends—we dated a few times. I thought we had something going, you know? After the article came out, she went from being an outsider to being Miss Popularity. Then she dumped me for a jock."

"Anyone I know?"

"Everyone in town knows him. Joel Nielsen."

Jennie raised her eyebrows. Joel would be a senior this year. He was captain of the football team and Brad's best friend. In a way, Jennie could understand Courtney's choice.

"I'm sorry, Gavin."

"I don't know. I should be used to it by now. It doesn't matter how intelligent or talented you are in this world. If you don't have a great *bod*, you might as well pack it in."

"Not all girls feel that way." Jennie pulled into the driveway. Ryan was there—stretched out on the chaise lounge on her front porch. "That's Ryan," Jennie said, a smile stretched across her face.

Jennie and Ryan talked with Gavin for about an hour. When Gavin left, Jennie was certain he felt better about himself. She gave Ryan credit for that. Not being much of a jock himself, Ryan had empathized with Gavin, then encouraged him to be himself.

"Eventually," Ryan said as they walked Gavin to his bike, "you'll find a girl who appreciates you."

Gavin snorted. "Sounds like something my mother would say."

Ryan laughed. "It is. My mother told me that all through my freshman and sophomore years. Turned out to be right." Ryan settled his arm around Jennie's shoulder and hugged her to him. "Case in point," he said, looking square into Jennie's eyes. "You can't do much better than this."

Wow. The butterflies in Jennie's stomach took off at warp speed. When Ryan looked away, Jennie let her focus shift back to Gavin.

He snapped the chin strap of his helmet into place and shrugged on his backpack. Looking from Ryan to Jennie, he said, "Thanks again for the interview. I'll bring a copy of the article by tomorrow afternoon."

Jennie agreed, but the moment Gavin's bike disappeared around the corner of Magnolia and Elm, she forgot he even existed. Her long-awaited date with Ryan had officially begun.

5

On Tuesday morning, Jennie overslept.

She managed to get Ryan to the airport twenty minutes before his flight. Just time enough to drop him off at the curb and say goodbye. "I'll miss you," she whispered in his ear when he hugged her.

"Me too." Ryan chuckled. "I mean . . . I won't miss me. I'll miss you." He released her and took a step back. "Hey, promise me you'll stay out of trouble while I'm gone."

Jennie laughed. "I'll try." She waved goodbye until he disappeared through the revolving door. She hated seeing Ryan go, but he'd be back in four weeks.

Stay out of trouble? He was teasing, but also serious. Jennie wondered what Ryan would have said if she'd told him about Courtney.

On the way home, she stopped by Lisa's. It seemed odd that Lisa hadn't called after her date with Brad. In fact, Jennie hadn't seen or talked to her cousin since Friday—nearly four days ago. Up until now Jennie had been too busy to worry. Lisa usually kept her informed of everything from the latest happenings around town to her newest nail color. So why hadn't she called?

When no one answered the door of the two-story English Tudor, Jennie wandered around to the back of the house to Aunt Kate's studio where she did her artwork and conducted her interior-design business. The door was unlocked so Jennie went in.

She loved the wild splashes of color and natural light streaming in from the skylights and large picture windows. The scent of plum potpourri mingled with linseed oil, paint, and a touch of turpentine. On an easel in the middle of the room sat an unfinished portrait of Gram and J.B. Jennie hadn't seen it before and marveled at how lifelike Kate had made them. The silver in Gram's salt-and-pepper hair glistened in the light. Jennie wondered if Kate was doing it as a wedding present for them.

Jennie knocked on the bedroom door before opening it. Gram and J.B. had been staying there the last few nights and she hoped Gram would be there. She wasn't. Jennie left a note on the front door of the main house asking Lisa to call or come over, then headed home.

Jennie felt the chaos the moment she walked in the front door. Four large mailbags cluttered the entry, their contents spilling out onto the tiled floor.

Nick and Hannah charged at her, nearly knocking her over.

"Look at all the mail, Jennie," Nick cheered. "We got lots and lots, and Mommy's pulling her hair out."

Mom appeared in the kitchen doorway, her thick auburn tresses still intact. "Thank goodness you're back. The phone hasn't stopped ringing since you left."

"What's going on?"

"These, for one thing." Mom pointed to the mail. "I started going through them and gave up. Kate and Lisa are coming by later to help out. And I've taken about twenty phone calls asking for you."

"When is Lisa coming? I stopped by the house on my way home, but no one was there."

"I'm not sure—Kate said something about a doctor appointment. Apparently Lisa's not been feeling well."

Jennie frowned, concern over her cousin's health mingled with relief that she'd be seeing her soon.

Mom handed her a notepad with two pages full of names and numbers. "I was tempted to just say no to most of these. But I decided you might want to do that yourself."

Jennie glanced at the list. "Someone wants me to help them find their dog?"

Mom smiled. "That's only the beginning. Dogs, birds, cats, jewelry, and—" she paused. "One woman thought you might be able to help her locate her missing child." Tears filled her gray-green eyes. "I almost feel guilty at our success in finding Nick so quickly. I wish there was something we could do for them."

"Maybe I could—"

"No," Mom interrupted. "Despite what the media says, you are not a detective. You attract enough trouble on your own without looking for it."

Jennie wanted to argue the point, but didn't. After what she and her family had just been through, she wasn't in the mood to do anything remotely dangerous.

"Besides," Mom went on. "I doubt any of us can help in this case. It's been over three years since her child disappeared."

"Oh, Mom, that's so sad." Jennie looked down at the list again. "What am I supposed to tell all these people? That my mother won't let me help them?"

"Sounds good to me."

Jennie had gotten halfway through the list when Aunt Kate and Lisa arrived.

"Just don't, okay?" Jennie heard Lisa say before they entered the kitchen.

Don't what? Jennie wanted to ask, but didn't. She'd find out later. Aunt Kate appeared first, giving Mom, then Jennie a hug. "Where do you want us, Susan?" Kate reached into the cupboard and retrieved a cup, then poured herself some coffee.

Watching Aunt Kate was like looking in the mirror—not unusual when you considered the fact that Kate was Dad's twin and that Jennie carried the McGrady genes. People were always confusing them as mother and daughter. Today, they looked almost like twins—both wore white shorts and shirts with their long, dark hair in ponytails.

Lisa, on the other hand, looked like Mom—flaming red hair, freckles, short, with a great figure. At least she used to. Jennie shifted her focus from Kate to Lisa, and felt like she'd been punched in the stomach. Lisa's beautiful round face was now pale and gaunt. Deep shadows lined her once sparkling green eyes. She looked sick—really sick.

Concern and shock coiled themselves around Jennie's heart. "Lisa, what's wrong? You look awful."

"Thanks a lot," she countered, then offered a wane smile. She threw her mother a warning glance.

Aunt Kate sighed. "Lisa, honey, tell them. They know something is wrong and they're just going to think the worst."

"I can't." Lisa sank into a kitchen chair and stared at her clasped hands. "I should have known it would be impossible to keep a secret in this family."

Jennie's heart ached as her brain came up with the worst possible explanation. Tears formed in her eyes. "It's cancer, isn't it? Is that why you won't tell us?"

"No. It's . . ." Lisa glanced up at her mom. "You tell them."

Kate took a sip of her coffee. "Lisa is anorexic."

"What?" Jennie and her mother chorused.

Jennie rushed to her cousin's side and dropped into the chair next to her. "I can't believe that. You seemed fine last week."

Lisa continued to stare at her hands. "I was getting too fat. I decided to go on a diet after school let out in May—

while you were in Florida with Gram. At first everything went great. I lost five pounds for the cruise and felt so good I decided to keep going."

Jennie had noticed the weight loss, but hadn't thought much about it. Lisa often dieted for a week or two at a time, but had never been obsessive about it. "Going on a diet once in a while doesn't make you anorexic." Jennie glanced at Kate. "Does it?"

"No. And she doesn't have the chronic type—at least not yet. But she took her dieting too far this time." Kate slid a hand across Lisa's back, then let it come to rest on her shoulder. "The doctor said that she's messed up her electrolytes and metabolism. It's all very complicated, but the dieting along with not eating proper meals have worn her out. That last flu bug she got made matters even worse. Anyway, the good news is she's going to be okay."

"Don't look at me like that." Lisa glared at Jennie for a moment then glanced away. "I didn't mean to. I tried to stop." She folded her arms across her chest. "Anyway, you don't know what it's like to be overweight. You never have to worry about whether or not guys are going to like you."

"Lisa, I don't get it. You're not fat. You never have been. I've always thought of you as the pretty one with a gorgeous figure and you've always had dates. I'm a stick. I haven't even graduated to a B cup." Jennie stopped. *Way to go, McGrady*, she chastised herself. *She really wants to be reminded of how thin you are.*

"I just wanted to look good for the summer and—" Lisa paused to look up at Jennie. "Cheerleader tryouts are coming up. I knew I wouldn't make the rally squad unless I dropped some weight."

"Lisa, you need to forget about rally squad." Kate picked up her coffee cup. "The doctor said no strenuous activity for two weeks."

Mom put an arm around Lisa's shoulders. "I know exactly what you're going through. I've struggled with my weight too."

Lisa was crying now. "I don't want to die, Aunt Susan." She wrapped her arms around Mom's neck. "But I hate this."

"I know, honey, I know." Mom held Lisa close and patted her back.

Jennie had never seen this side of Lisa and it unnerved her. Her cousin had always been so bubbly and cheerful. As she thought back on it, looking good had always been important to Lisa. Jennie just hadn't realized how important until now.

Aunt Kate signaled to Jennie to follow her out of the kitchen. "I think it might be better if we let your mom handle this one," she whispered when they reached the entry. "I've been trying to get Lisa over here for two days. If anyone can help her through this, Susan can. I've tried to be supportive, but I have a hard time understanding why she's so down on herself."

Jennie nodded. "I feel terrible. Why couldn't I see it? I might have been able to help."

"I missed it too. I knew she'd dropped some weight, but it wasn't until she got the flu last week that I really noticed how frail she'd become." Kate sighed and offered Jennie a halfhearted smile. "But don't worry. She'll come out of it. I think there's just been too much going on lately, her breakup with Brad, the cruise, getting ready for cheerleading . . . at any rate, I think Lisa's weight loss has a lot to do with Brad."

"Lisa never called me to let me know how their date went. Do you know?"

Kate shrugged, then stooped to grab one of the mail bags and drag it into the dining room. "Ugh. You could get a hernia toting these things around." She scooped out a bunch of mail and sat in one of the six chairs surrounding the large antique rosewood table.

Jennie brought in the other bag and, following Kate's lead, began opening the mail.

"I'm not avoiding your question," Kate said, finally. "I don't really know. According to Lisa, everything is fine and she and Brad are going out again this Friday."

"You say that like you don't believe her."

"It's an intuition thing, you know. Something just doesn't feel right. I'm sure part of it is the way the anorexia has altered her personality. I have a feeling something else is going on. Maybe she'll tell you."

Kate paused to read the card she'd opened. "Oh, this is so nice. It's a congratulations card and there's a check for fifty dollars enclosed to help with expenses for Hannah."

Jennie hoped Lisa would talk to her, but a wall of secrecy had somehow come between them. They no longer told each other everything. *Later, McGrady*, Jennie promised herself. *Later you and Lisa will go up to your room and talk. It will be just like always. After all, you and Lisa are more than cousins— you're best friends*. That hadn't changed, had it?

Jennie set aside her nagging doubts and opened an envelope. She read the note and set it in the discard pile. It was from a guy in Minnesota asking her to marry him. This hero business was definitely turning into a major pain.

By the time Mom and Lisa joined them, Jennie and Aunt Kate had sorted through at least a hundred pieces of mail. Several people asked for Jennie's help in locating missing family members and animals. Most offered congratulations and encouragement. A few sent money.

Neither Lisa nor Mom brought up Lisa's problem, but Jennie hoped Lisa would still confide in her. She had a lot of questions and even more concerns.

They spent the entire afternoon opening and responding to the mail. At five, Mom called it to a halt and suggested they all go out for pizza. While Kate called Uncle Kevin, Jennie invited Lisa upstairs.

Lisa fell onto Jennie's bed, grabbing a fluffy white stuffed bunny as she went down. Jennie curled up on the window seat and leaned her head against the window. Neither of them spoke.

After about five minutes, Lisa broke the silence. "You think I'm a total nut case, don't you."

"I think . . ." Jennie began, weighing her words carefully. Then deciding to be honest, said, "Yes. I can't believe you would starve yourself like that. I thought you knew better."

"I don't have to listen to a lecture from you too, do I?" Lisa twisted around to a sitting position and stroked the bunny's ears. The beginnings of a smile appeared on her lips, then faded.

"I wish you had told me what was going on." Jennie left the window seat and plopped down on the bed next to Lisa.

"What would you have said if I had?"

"I'd have tried to talk you out of it."

"That's why I didn't say anything. I didn't want anybody to tell me I looked okay. I didn't feel okay."

"Does Brad have anything to do with this?"

Lisa hugged the fluffy bunny to her chest. "Before we broke up, he told me I could stand to lose a little weight. He wanted me to start working out so I could exchange my flab for muscle."

"Let me guess. You told him where he could take his muscle."

The semi-smile came back. "He really hurt me. I know he was just trying to be helpful, but it tore me up inside. He might as well have said, 'Lisa, you're a fat slob. Lose the weight or lose me.' "

"He didn't say that, did he?"

"Not exactly, but I knew what he meant. I got mad and broke up with him before he could dump me."

"Is that when you decided to go on this diet?"

Lisa tipped her head back and closed her eyes. "I didn't mean to lose so much. It just felt so good to be skinny. Then everything backfired. I started getting sick and . . ." Lisa's large green eyes reminded Jennie of pictures she'd seen of starving children. "The most frustrating part about all this is that now Brad thinks I'm too skinny. He liked me better the way I was." Her eyes turned to liquid pools and she looked away.

Jennie hooked an arm around Lisa's neck. "I take it your date with Brad didn't go so well. Is that why you didn't call me?"

"I tried to call, but your line was busy. Then I fell asleep. We worked things out. He apologized for making me think I was fat. When I get some strength back, he wants to help me with a weight-training program. He's taking me to a health-food store Friday before we go to a movie. Wants to show me some high-powered protein stuff."

"Sounds like he's turning into a health nut."

"He is. The whole football team is—especially Joel Nielsen. And it's really paying off for them. They are looking so good. In fact, Coach Haskell says if they play as well in the season as they do in practice, we may win the state championship." Lisa smiled again and this time it reached her eyes.

"By the way," Lisa said, becoming more animated, as though someone had wound her up. Jennie hoped it was a good sign. "Joel and Courtney asked about you the other night."

"What?" Jennie's attention snapped from Lisa's health to Courtney's name.

Lisa leaned back and frowned at Jennie's reaction. "It wasn't anything bad. They wanted to know about the cases you'd solved and—"

"When did you talk to Courtney?"

"Sunday night. Brad and I doubled with her and Joel. Why?"

Jennie told Lisa about the strange call she'd gotten, then asked, "Did she seem upset about anything? Do you know why she called?"

Lisa shook her head. "She seemed fine—a little crabby, but then that's Courtney. If she was in some kind of trouble, she didn't tell me about it. Courtney is so cool. I wish I had the nerve to do some of the stuff she does. I mean, Sunday night she had purple hair. And she wore these lavender contacts. The most bizarre thing I've done lately is wear green nail polish."

"Hmmm," Jennie murmured, not really listening. "That call is really bugging me. I left several messages, but she hasn't called me back. It's weird."

"Hey, look, I'll ask her about it Friday night. We're doubling again—or, better yet, you can ask her yourself at cheerleading tryouts tomorrow."

"Yeah, I will." Jennie thought again about the desperation she'd sensed in Courtney's voice. "I just hope it isn't too late."

6

It took several seconds for Jennie to digest Lisa's words. The statement, "You can ask her yourself at cheerleading tryouts" held more hidden messages than a "Where's Waldo" picture. First, of course, Courtney planned to be there. Second, Lisa wanted Jennie to come and had used Courtney as an enticement.

Nothing short of curiosity and a chance to talk to Courtney could have dragged Jennie to cheerleader tryouts and Lisa knew it. Not that Jennie had anything against cheerleaders, she just didn't feel coordinated enough to be one. Besides, Jennie really didn't see herself as the cheerleader type.

The third and probably scariest message was that, despite orders from her doctor and mother, Lisa intended to go ahead with the tryouts.

It was this point Jennie addressed first. "You're still going? Your mom said you were supposed to rest for at least two weeks."

"I will—after." Lisa wove a long strand of hair between perfectly manicured fingers. "Don't say it, Jen. And don't tell Mom. I've made up my mind. I've been resting for four days now. I've been thinking about this and I can do it."

"I don't believe you." Jennie placed her hand on Lisa's forehead. "This diet you were on has affected your brain.

You're delirious. Cheerleading is way too strenuous for you right now."

Lisa knocked Jennie's hand away. "I have to try. You can understand that. And I'll make it, you'll see." Lisa's gaze drifted up to meet Jennie's. "Please don't rat on me, Jen. If you love me at all, you'll let me do this. I can rest later. I just have to make the rally squad."

Jennie closed her eyes. *If you really love her*, a voice seemed to say, *you'll go downstairs right now and tell Aunt Kate.* Jennie didn't move. She did love Lisa, but—

Lisa placed a hand on Jennie's arm. "Please. This is extremely important to me. I'd do it for you."

"All right," Jennie heard herself saying. "I won't say anything right now. But I'm going with you and if I think for one second you're getting worse, I'll stop you myself."

"It'll be fine," Lisa promised. "I'll eat plenty of carbs and protein."

"Jennie," Mom's voice bellowed up the stairs. "Someone's here to see you."

"You expecting company?" Lisa asked.

Jennie glanced at her watch as if it might tell her something more than the time. "It's probably Gavin. He promised to show me the article he's writing about me."

Coming down the stairs, Jennie heard her mother invite Gavin to have pizza with them.

"That'd be great, Mrs. McGrady." He glanced up. "That is, if it's okay with Jennie."

It wasn't, but Jennie shrugged and said, "Sure, why not?" Gavin's presence bugged her, and Jennie wasn't sure why. After mulling it over a few seconds, she blamed the dream.

Though Gavin hadn't replaced Ryan in real life as he had in the dream, he had managed to insert himself into her life like an unwanted bout with poison oak.

"I brought you a copy of 'Rainbow Girl,' the article I did on Courtney," he said, drawing a clipping out of his worn backpack. "In case you lost your copy."

"Thanks." Her annoyance slinked away as she scanned Gavin's article.

"Jennie," her mother interrupted, "why don't you read it later. We need to get going."

Rather than leave the article until later, Jennie took it with her. Sitting between Lisa and Gavin in the rear seat of Aunt Kate's van, she finished reading about Courtney Evans. Okay, so reading when she should have been talking to Gavin and Lisa was rude, but Jennie couldn't wait. She hoped the article would give her some clues about Courtney and the strange phone call.

She browsed through some of the initial statistics and history. Up until the first of the year Courtney had lived in Boston. *After Mom died last year,* Gavin quoted her as saying, *my father decided to move to Oregon. I guess he thought we could leave the past behind. You can't, you know. Mom's dead. She'll always be dead. Nothing's going to change that.*

Jennie bit back the urge to cry. She thought back to the comment Mr. Evans had left unfinished the other day and filled it in. *Courtney's really a sweet girl—at least she was before . . . her mother died.* Having her mom die must have been really hard on her. No wonder she had problems.

Turning her attention back to the article, Jennie read Gavin's next question. *Why do you always change the color of your eyes and hair?* Courtney responded with, *My mom loved rainbows. She always used to tell me that rainbows were a sign of hope. In fact, she even called me her rainbow girl because she'd almost given up hope of ever having a child.*

Then I came along—I'm adopted. Courtney Hope Evans, that's me. I don't know, maybe I do it to drive my dad crazy. Maybe I do it for attention. Maybe I just do it to find the hope in me.

The article ended there. Jennie looked over at Gavin. "This is really good."

He shrugged and glanced away as if the compliment had embarrassed him. "Thanks."

The article revealed a lot about Courtney Evans, but it also told a great deal about Gavin Winslow. He was a talented writer. Jennie felt much of her annoyance toward him melt into admiration.

After their pizza dinner, Kate and Lisa dropped Jennie, Gavin, and the rest of Jennie's family off at the house and went home. Lisa had been strangely sullen the entire evening. Was she upset about something, or had the day's activities simply worn her out? Jennie's goodbye to Lisa included a brief hug and a warning to be careful.

Lisa answered with the standard, "Don't worry," and a look that said, *Don't tell.*

Once inside, Mom started to take the kids upstairs to get them ready for bed.

"We want Jennie to read us a story," Nick declared half-way up the stairs. "Will you? Please!"

"Jennie has company tonight," Mom said. "Maybe she can read to you tomorrow."

"Hey," Gavin piped up, "don't change your routine on my account. Maybe we can read to the kids together. I don't mind."

"Yeah!" Hannah and Nick both squealed. "Jennie and Gavin. Jennie and Gavin." The kids continued their chant the rest of the way upstairs and into the bedroom where Mom finally hushed them with a no-story-if-you-don't-settle-down threat.

The annoyance was back. Jennie left Gavin standing in the entry. *That was rude, McGrady. He was just trying to be nice.*

She heard him come into the kitchen behind her and ignored him.

"I goofed, didn't I? I'm sorry. I should have asked instead of volunteering our services. I do that sometimes. I mean, if you want I can just leave now—"

"No." Jennie stopped him. "It's okay. I like reading to them. If you left they'd be disappointed."

Gavin offered her a lopsided grin. "Do you want to see the article I wrote about you before or after we read stories?"

Before she could answer, Nick hollered, "Jennie! Gavin! We're ready."

"Jennie and Gabin," Hannah echoed, "we're ready."

Jennie chuckled and shook her head. "I guess that answers your question, Ga-bin, we're being summoned."

In the middle of Gavin's presentation of *The Princess and the Pea*, Hannah fell asleep. Nick held out until the last page of *Little Prince*. Being careful not to wake her, Jennie lifted Hannah from Nick's bed where the four of them had been sitting and placed her in the cot against the wall.

After tucking both of them in and turning out the lights, Jennie led Gavin downstairs, into the kitchen for a Coke, then out to the porch. Jennie sat on the swing and scanned the article Gavin had titled *The New Nancy Drew*. He'd presented her as "an amateur sleuth with a big heart and beautiful cobalt eyes."

"It's too flowery," she said after reading it. "You made me sound too good, too efficient—too everything. You didn't say anything about my being scared spitless—or getting in over my head. Or that I would never have gotten myself kidnapped in the first place if I'd had half a brain."

"You care, Jennie, you're intelligent and decent. . . ."

"I'm obstinate, judgmental, opinionated, and bratty— and I can be extremely rude."

Gavin grinned. "That's true. Can I quote you?"

Jennie punched him in the arm. "I wish I hadn't agreed to let you write this. I really don't want any more publicity."

"Too late," he shrugged. "Already turned it in. I could always write another one."

Jennie punched him again.

For the next hour Gavin told her about his dreams of becoming a television journalist and engaged her in a debate over freedom of the press versus the right to privacy.

———————

The next day at cheerleading tryouts, Jennie found herself arguing again. This time it was with Lisa, who wanted Jennie to try out with her. "Just think of it," Lisa said. "We could go to all the games together."

"I really don't want to be a cheerleader. Besides, I don't know the cheers."

"Yes you do. You helped me learn them. You'd be great."

She'd helped Lisa learn the routines months ago before school let out for the summer. But bouncing around in the backyard was a whole lot different than being in front of the entire school. "Forget it. Look, Lisa, you've got the personality for it, I don't. Now quit bugging me or I'll go call your mom. I'll bet she'd love to know where you are right now."

"You wouldn't." Her eyes widened. For a second, Jennie thought Lisa would hit her, but she backed down. "I just thought it would be fun to do it together, that's all, but if you really don't want to. . . ."

"Don't let her wear you down, McGrady." B.J. thumped Jennie on the shoulder. "Allison's been on my case for a week."

Before Jennie could respond, Gavin climbed up the bleacher seats and dropped down beside her.

A shrill whistle sounded. "Okay everyone, let's get started."

Allison and Lisa bounded down the bleacher steps and hurried toward the voice. A slender woman in a white camp shirt and shorts and a Hawaiian tan stepped onto the field. Short dark hair framed a heart-shaped face.

"Who's that?" Jennie asked.

Gavin answered, "New women's coach and PE teacher.

49

Name's Diane Dayton. DeeDee for short."

"I thought the school was hurting for money. How could they afford to hire her? The last I heard, the school board was thinking of dropping the athletic program altogether."

"You have been out of touch, haven't you?" Gavin lifted his camera and snapped several photos. "Maybe that's what motivated the guys to work harder. That and Joel's dad." He lowered the camera and looked back at Jennie. "Buck Nielsen is a major contributor to Trinity High and when he talks they listen. Anyway, Nielsen volunteered to come in as an assistant coach last year and really turned things around for all the major sports. We went from being a losing team to being one of the contenders for the league championship."

Joel's father had been a quarterback for one of the top NFL teams a few years ago. After retiring he developed his own line of athletic equipment. "I knew about Joel's dad and getting bumped up in the standings, but how does that translate into more money?"

"More students are enrolling this year, and the sporting events are drawing bigger crowds. I think what topped it off though was the grant Nielsen's company offered. The board decided that with sports generating all that extra money, and Haskell putting so much more energy into coaching the guys, they could hire someone to take over the girls' athletic program."

Gavin raised his camera again. About a dozen girls and two boys gathered around the coach as she blew the whistle again. She separated the girls into groups of threes and fours and told them to begin working through routines.

After their names were called, Lisa, Allison, Courtney, and Annie Koler walked over to their designated space and started stretching. Annie had long straight hair about the same coppery color as Lisa's. She wore it back with no bangs, which seemed to accentuate her oval face and clear, creamy skin. Annie and Lisa could have passed as sisters if Lisa hadn't been so thin and pale.

Another group of girls ran out onto the field, purple and gold pompons waving: Lori Chan, Corky Simmons, Tracy Parouski, and Cassie Nielsen, Joel's sister.

Cassie seemed more the type to play the game than to cheer the teams on. She matched Jennie in height and had the angular build of a weight trainer—the type who'd be good at just about anything.

Tracy and Corky had been on rally squad last year and obviously planned to do it again. Tracy's sun-bleached hair swayed back and forth across her shoulders as she and Corky practiced a yell.

"So who do you think she'll pick?" Gavin asked.

Jennie had no idea. She shifted her attention to Lisa's group. Courtney did a series of backflips, looking like a practiced gymnast.

"Courtney. Definitely." B.J. nodded toward the group. "Allison's looking good too, but Lisa's . . ." B.J. gasped.

Jennie's focus snapped from Courtney to Lisa.

Lisa tossed her brightly-colored pompons into the air and reached out to capture them again. Her knees buckled. She crumpled to the ground. The pompons drifted to earth and settled over her limp body.

7

"I didn't make it, did I?" Lisa stared at the ceiling tiles above her hospital bed. A tear slid from the corner of her eye and trailed into her hair.

Kate soothed back Lisa's matted hair and sighed. "Oh, sweetie, I know how much you wanted this, but . . . no, of course you didn't make it. You shouldn't have even tried."

Lisa took a deep breath and asked, "Who did?"

Their attention shifted to Jennie who was standing beside her aunt.

Jennie avoided Aunt Kate's eyes. She didn't want to see the accusations she knew would be written there. If she had told Aunt Kate about Lisa's plans to go ahead with the cheer-leading tryouts, this wouldn't have happened.

"Jennie?" Lisa's voice interrupted Jennie's guilt trip. "Please tell me. Did Allison make it? And Courtney?"

Jennie wouldn't have known the answer if she hadn't just spent the last hour in the hospital cafeteria bringing Allison, B.J., and Gavin up to date on Lisa's condition, which wasn't good.

Jennie stared at the IV tubing, following it to the spot where it entered Lisa's wrist. "They both did—and Annie Koler and Lori Chan." Jennie didn't bother to tell her about the boys—only two had turned out and they were both gymnasts.

52

Lisa nodded, her lips curling in a weary smile. "They'll make a good team." Lisa closed her eyes and opened them again. "Tracy must be furious. She was really rude to Courtney and Allison during tryouts. I bet that's why DeeDee eliminated her." Lisa's eyes drifted closed again and stayed that way.

"We'd better go," Kate whispered. "We should let her rest for a while." She gave Jennie's shoulder a gentle squeeze and guided her out of the room.

While Aunt Kate made some phone calls, Jennie slumped into a waiting room chair. She'd chosen not to tell Lisa about the fight that had erupted between the girls after DeeDee had made her selection.

According to B.J., Tracy had acted fine until the coach left, then blew up at Courtney, saying the coach had to be color blind to let a girl with purple hair represent the school. B.J., who seemed to enjoy conflicts, had mimicked Tracy saying, "I'm going to be on rally squad this year and I intend to do whatever I have to to change Coach Dayton's mind."

Jennie sniffed and reached into her bag for a tissue. She finally found one, but dug up something else in the search— a white piece of paper. She frowned as she unfolded it, wondering where it had come from. The note had been hand written on a square paper bearing the name, DIANABOL. Jennie suspected it was some sort of drug. The paper had apparently come from a doctor's office—or a pharmacy.

I'm in over my head, the note read. *Call me. Courtney*.

Jennie tried to remember how and when Courtney could have slipped it to her. The last time Jennie had seen the rainbow girl, they'd all been watching the paramedics load Lisa into an ambulance. Courtney had come over to see how Lisa was doing. Then she'd said, "About the phone call, Jennie. . . ."

Before Courtney could finish, Cassie joined them. "You think Lisa's going to be okay?"

"I don't know," Jennie answered.

"You'll keep us posted, won't you?" Cassie seemed genuinely concerned and Jennie promised she'd call later.

"I need to talk to you for a minute," Cassie said as she drew Courtney away from the ambulance. Jennie had watched them walk away, then swung her attention back to Lisa. *How are you going to explain all of this to Aunt Kate, and Mom and Gram?* The question had torpedoed through her mind and exploded in her stomach. She could still feel the effects of it.

Jennie fingered the note from Courtney and forced her attention back to it. She didn't feel like dealing with Courtney Evans at the moment. If it had been anything serious she'd have said something earlier. She tucked the note into her pocket and made plans to call the rainbow girl when she got home.

———

Jennie couldn't make the call to Courtney until nine that night. After dinner Mom asked her to stay with the kids so she, Gram, and Uncle Kevin could go visit Lisa. Jennie and Kurt, Lisa's eleven-year-old brother, finished feeding Nick and Hannah, gave them baths, and put them to bed. Jennie left Kurt to finish reading *The Little Mermaid* and went up to her room to call Courtney.

Mr. Evans answered. "She's not home. She's gone out with Joel. They were going to pick up Brad and go to the hospital to see Lisa."

Jennie asked him to tell Courtney she'd called. He hesitated for a moment. "Jennie, have you noticed anything strange about Courtney? I mean . . . she's been edgy lately—more so than usual."

Everything about Courtney is strange, Jennie started to say, then stopped. "I don't really know her that well, Mr. Evans. She seemed fine at tryouts today."

He hesitated again, "Is Susan . . . is your mother there by any chance?"

"She's at the hospital too. Want me to have her call you?"

"No, I'll talk with her later. It's just a bookkeeping problem I'm having."

Mom, Gram, and Uncle Kevin arrived as Jennie hung up. She raced up the stairs, nearly colliding with Kurt as he stepped out of Nick's bedroom.

"Your dad's here," she explained and helped him regain his balance.

Even with his thick chestnut hair adding nearly two inches to his height, Kurt barely reached her rib cage. He gazed up into Jennie's eyes, his face round, freckled and healthy looking, like Lisa's used to be. "Do you think Lisa's gonna die?"

His question hit Jennie with the impact of a freight train. "No." Her answer came out more harshly than she had intended. "Why would you think that?"

Kurt shrugged. " 'Cause everybody's so sad."

Jennie rested a hand on his shoulder and walked with him down the stairs.

"How's Lisa?" Jennie asked as she and Kurt joined the rest of the family in the kitchen.

"Better," Uncle Kevin said.

"Her blood sugar level and electrolytes are almost back to normal," Mom added as she measured coffee into the filter. "She's been keeping water and apple juice down so it looks like they'll be able to take out the IV in the morning."

Jennie eased into a chair beside Gram, who'd been staring at the table. She glanced up briefly and patted Jennie's hand.

The distant, sad look in Gram's blue eyes shook Jennie. "Are you sure Lisa's going to be okay? You look worried."

"What?" Gram asked, running a hand through her bangs.

"Lisa. Are you sure . . ."

"Oh. No, dear, Lisa's okay, it's . . ." Gram glanced over

at Mom and back at Kevin. "I'm just worried about J.B. He's been called away and—" Gram stopped and shook her head. "Listen to me. Going on like that. I'm getting paranoid in my old age. J.B. is perfectly capable of taking care of himself."

———

Jennie spent a sleepless night worrying. It didn't help that Bernie had chosen her as his designated feeder. Or that she'd forgotten to shut her door all the way again.

At six-thirty, the oversized pup climbed onto her bed, nudging and licking until she got up. Unable to resist his sad brown eyes, Jennie followed him downstairs and fed him. "There," she said, setting the half-empty bag back in the pantry. "I hope you're happy."

Bernie woofed what sounded like a "thank you" and began eating.

She yawned and mumbled, "I'm going back to bed."

Mom stopped her at the foot of the stairs. "I'm glad you're up, honey," she said. "We need to talk."

Jennie groaned in protest, then deciding she probably wouldn't be able to go back to sleep anyway, followed her mother back down the hall and into the kitchen.

After pouring herself a bowl of granola, Jennie reached for the milk. "What did you want to talk to me about? If it's Lisa, I already said I was sorry."

"It's not Lisa. I think you've learned your lesson there." Mom lifted her coffee to her lips and blew on it before taking a tentative sip.

"Then what?"

"How would you feel about my accepting a date with Frank Evans?"

Jennie's mood dropped about twenty degrees. *Lousy.* She shoveled a spoonful of granola and milk into her mouth and chewed on it before answering. Mom's dating Frank presented all sorts of problems Jennie didn't want to think about. Dating could lead to an engagement, which would lead to marriage. Marriage meant having Courtney as a step-sister.

Worse, marriage would eliminate any chance of Mom and Dad getting back together again. "I hate the idea," she finally said.

"Why?" Mom asked. "Is there something you don't like about him, or are you just opposed to my dating anyone?"

Because Dad's still alive. Jennie swallowed back the response and shrugged instead. "I don't think you should jump into anything. I mean, you and Michael just broke up."

"It's only dinner." The toast popped up and Mom pulled out the two slices and buttered them. "I'd like to go. He seems like a nice man."

"Sounds like you've made up your mind, so why ask me?"

Mom slathered strawberry jam on the toast slices and handed one to Jennie. "Believe it or not, I value your opinion. I know we don't always agree, but I do want to know what you think."

"Well . . ." Jennie paused to catch a drip of jam with her tongue. "I told you what I think. Are you going out with him anyway?"

Mom nodded. "Probably." She peered over the rim of her cup and took another drink. "Don't worry. I'm not planning on getting married any time soon."

"Mr. Evans called last night," Jennie said, remembering the phone conversation she'd had with him the night before. "Something about a bookkeeping problem."

"That doesn't surprise me. His records are a mess."

Jennie finished breakfast while she listened to her mother talk about people who dump a year's worth of receipts on her desk and expect her to work miracles. As soon as Jennie could make a break for it, she excused herself and headed upstairs. "I gotta take a shower and get dressed."

"Okay, but don't be too long," Mom called after her. "I'll

need you to take care of the kids for a while this morning while I get some work done."

Jennie took her time showering. The warm water washed away tension as well as soap. On the way back to her room she stopped at the bedroom next to hers and peeked in. Good. Nick and Hannah were still asleep.

Jennie needed some time alone. After getting dressed and braiding her hair, she straightened her room, then pulled a box labeled *Dad's Things* from a closet shelf.

It had been a long time since Jennie had gone through them. The memories assaulted her. She pulled out the tweed hat and scarf, the wooden horse she'd given him as a Christmas gift, and his golf trophy from college, then set them on her bed. She held up the model airplane they'd assembled one winter. Its wings had been broken and hung limply against the plane's side. She'd have to fix it.

Jennie set the plane aside and sorted through the collection of rocks and shells that littered the bottom of the box. Most of the shells lay in pieces. Jennie picked up the shell fragments and after holding them for a long time, threw them away. Some things were too broken to be fixed.

Some things were too broken...

The thought buried itself in her mind. *Too broken to fix.* A light clicked on in Jennie's head. She'd spent a lot of time over the last few years trying to fix things—like her parents' marriage. Maybe their relationship, like the shells she and dad had collected over the years, was too broken. Maybe she needed to let it go, as she'd done with the shells. Let Mom live her life and Dad live his—separately.

Jennie closed her eyes and took a deep breath. She pictured herself standing between Mom and Dad, holding tightly to them, then being split apart as they walked away from each other. If she didn't let go, she'd end up broken too. Jennie imagined herself releasing one, then the other. Tears gathered in her eyes and she hugged herself to lessen the loss.

Jennie kept the picture in her mind while she gathered up her treasures and set them back on the shelf. Maybe she'd leave the airplane too—at least for now. Giggles from the next bedroom told her Nick and Hannah were awake.

A car door slammed from somewhere outside and a minute or so later, the doorbell rang. Maybe it was Aunt Kate with an update on Lisa. Ordinarily she'd have raced down the stairs to answer the door, but decided to let Mom or Nick get it. Jennie didn't feel like talking to anyone just yet.

Before going downstairs, she eyed herself in the mirror. The white shorts and pale pink T-shirt felt as comfortable and cool as they looked. She paused briefly to admire her long tanned legs and suddenly felt guilty. How often had she heard Lisa say, "Jennie, I'm so jealous. You have legs to die for."

She shrugged the guilt aside and turned away from the mirror. *You didn't cause Lisa's illness, McGrady*, she reminded herself. After lunch, when the kids went down for naps, she'd drive over to the hospital to see Lisa.

Before heading downstairs, Jennie placed another call to Courtney. The answering machine picked up. This time Jennie didn't leave a message. Maybe she should add Courtney to the new "Too-Broken-to-Fix" list.

Jennie skipped down the stairs and stopped by the living room to greet Nick and Hannah who were making a "house" out of blankets and sheets. Bernie woofed and shook free of the baby blanket Hannah was trying to wrap around him.

"Bernie, stand still," Hannah ordered. "You s'posed to be the baby."

Feeling sorry for the dog, Jennie suggested an alternate plan. "Why don't you let Bernie play the rescue dog and Hannah's doll can be the baby."

"Okay," they both echoed.

Hearing voices in the kitchen, Jennie headed that way.

"Have you called the police?" Mom asked as Jennie wandered in.

Jennie stopped midstep.

"This morning." Frank Evans was sitting at the table next to Mom. "They think she may have run away."

"Who?" Jennie knew the answer but asked anyway. Instead of joining her mother and Frank at the table, she snagged a barstool and sat at the counter. Somehow it seemed important to keep her distance.

"Courtney's missing," Mom said. "Frank said she didn't come home last night."

8

Jennie was beginning to wonder if her stomach would ever be normal again. Recent events had tied it up in knots the size of basketballs. "Maybe she and Joel decided to do something crazy—drive to the beach, or . . ."

"I called Joel last night around twelve-thirty. He said they'd had an early night. Claims he dropped Courtney off at the house around ten. Brad and Joel's sister Cassie verified Joel's story this morning. I was at the pharmacy until midnight. If she did come home, she must have gone out again. Either that or the kids are lying."

"I doubt that," Jennie jumped to their defense.

"I just can't believe Courtney would run away. We don't always get along—especially since her mother's death, but we have a pretty good relationship." Frank Evans pushed the coffee cup back and forth between his hands. "I've always felt I could trust her."

"She's a teenager, Frank," Mom said as if that was supposed to explain everything. "Even well-adjusted kids," Mom nodded toward Jennie, "—like this one—can have their moments. Maybe Courtney needed to get away for a while."

Jennie didn't know what to say. She could imagine Courtney running away, but not after just having made the rally squad.

"Could you tell if any of her things were missing, an over-

61

night bag, makeup, clothes—that sort of thing?" Jennie asked.

"The police asked me that too. Courtney had enough makeup in her bathroom to start her own cosmetic company. She had so many clothes it's hard to tell. There's a green canvas bag missing, only it's mine. I thought maybe I'd left it at the gym, but I stopped by there this morning and no one had seen it."

Maybe she had run away after all, but why? The phone call and note indicated Courtney was in some kind of trouble. Did that have anything to do with her disappearance? Should she mention the note and phone call to Frank? Yes. The information might provide police with a link. Jennie told Frank what she knew. What she didn't say was that she intended to do some digging of her own.

———

That afternoon at the hospital, one of the knots in Jennie's stomach began to relax. While Lisa still looked like a poster child for a feed-the-hungry campaign, her cheeks were flushed. Sitting up in bed, wearing a bright floral robe with her copper hair up in a pony tail, she seemed almost like the old Lisa again.

"It's about time you got here. Your mom said you left an hour ago."

"Well, *ex-cuse me*. I thought you might like some flowers." Jennie set the arrangement of pink roses and baby's breath on the bedside stand.

"I'm sorry. They're beautiful. I appreciate the thought, but I've been dying to talk to you about Courtney."

Jennie winced. "Do me a favor, Lisa, and don't use that phrase anymore. I don't want you to *die* for anything."

"Sorry." Lisa wrinkled her nose. "Anyway, tell me what's going on. Have they found her?"

Jennie shook her head. "Not yet. The police are checking

things out. They're pretty sure she ran away." Sinking into a brown vinyl chair, Jennie related her conversation with Frank Evans that morning then asked, "So what do you think? Did she run?"

"I suppose it's possible. When she was here last night with Brad and Joel, she seemed . . . I don't know, distant and scared, maybe. She's a hard person to read. When I asked her about cheerleading, she shrugged it off—like she didn't really care."

Jennie told her about the note Courtney had slipped into her bag at tryouts. "Did she say anything yesterday while you were practicing?"

Lisa fingered the folds of her robe. "I can't think of anything. Except . . ." Her green eyes locked with Jennie's.

"What?"

"Last night just before they left she said she needed to go home early. She had some business to take care of."

"Business? Like packing?"

"I have no idea. Maybe we should talk to Cassie and Joel. She might have said something to them."

"We?" Jennie raised an eyebrow and gave Lisa an incredulous look. "Mom said you had to be in here for another day, at least."

"Don't remind me," she pouted. "Anyway, she could have confided in them."

"I thought I'd talk to them tonight at the youth meeting." About once a month they'd head down to Pioneer Square or Waterfront Park and hand out tracts—fact sheets about drugs, sex, and AIDS. Some of the more talented kids—musicians, singers, and dancers—performed and gave their testimonies. Michael had started the practice saying he wanted to reach some of Portland's homeless kids—not to preach at them, but to educate them and let them know someone cared. Jennie planned to use the opportunity to question some of the kids in the youth group about Courtney.

Lisa sighed. Her eyes drifted closed. "I wish I could go," she murmured.

"So do I," Jennie whispered. She watched her cousin for a few moments. When Lisa didn't open her eyes again, Jennie left.

On the way home, Jennie stopped at the church to talk to Michael. She wasn't sure why. Well, that wasn't quite true. About two seconds after the secretary buzzed him to let him know Jennie was there, his office door swung open. "Jennie! Come in." He stepped aside to let her in, then closed the door behind him. "Have a seat." He pointed to two blue-and-white upholstered chairs and folded himself into the one closest to him. Jennie sank into the other.

She glanced around the office. At least two hundred books with titles like *Hermeneutics*, *Biblical Archeology*, and *Church History* lined one wall. Her gaze lingered on a metal sculpture of the crucifix sitting on his desk.

"Like it?"

Jennie nodded.

"It's a bronze. Picked it up in Jerusalem a few years ago. The first piece in the Rhode's Gallery art collection." Michael laughed. "Actually it's the only piece so far." He hesitated, his smile faded. "But you didn't come to learn about fine arts did you? Everything okay at home?"

Jennie dragged her eyes from the statue to Michael's face. "I guess. Except for Lisa." Jennie sighed. "Did you know Mom was thinking about dating Frank Evans?"

Michael cleared his throat and looked down at his clasped hands. "Yes. As a matter of fact, I introduced them."

"How could you do that? I thought you loved Mom."

"Jennie . . ." he ran a hand through his sandy brown hair. His blue gaze met hers. "I do, but I just don't think it's ever going to work between us. Your mother wants someone more . . . I don't know. I'm devoted to my work—to the youth group. If she can't accept who I am . . ." He shrugged and

64

lifted his hands in a what-can-I-do? gesture.

Jennie ran her fingers along the chair's seam. "This is stupid. I shouldn't have come."

"It's not stupid. I'm glad you're here. Like I said before, my door is always open to you." Michael stood and walked over to his desk. "In fact, I was going to call you. You know about Courtney being missing?"

Jennie nodded. "Yeah. Why?"

"I made some of these up today." He handed her a flyer. "I knew you'd want to help and thought this might be a good place to start."

The word MISSING marched across the top of the page in bold black letters. Under it was a picture of Courtney along with her age and a description. "They're offering a reward?"

"The police thought we'd have a better chance of getting information. I was hoping you and some of the kids from the youth group would help me distribute them when we do our street ministry tonight."

"You think she might be downtown?"

"Maybe. She seemed to enjoy going down there and talking to the homeless kids. Courtney has a real gift for helping people. Through her intervention we've been able to get three kids off the street and into programs where they'll get the help they need. If she did run away, my guess is that she'd go there."

Jennie agreed. They spent the next hour talking. Actually Jennie talked while Michael mostly listened. When she left, nothing had really changed—except maybe her anxiety level.

———

That evening as they boarded the Trinity Center bus, Jennie got her opportunity to talk to Brad, Joel, and Cassie all at the same time. The guys had taken separate seats, one behind the other. Cassie slipped into the seat next to Brad, which Jennie might have found disconcerting if they hadn't both asked about Lisa. She hoped Brad and Cassie didn't have something going. It would really tear Lisa up if he broke up with her now.

"She looked much better today," Jennie stopped in the aisle to talk to them. "I'm still worried about her."

"I wanted to go by and see her this afternoon," Brad said, stretching his arms out in front of him. The muscles in his shoulders bulged under his black T-shirt. "But the coach kept us over. We barely had time to get cleaned up and eat."

Now that Jennie thought about it, maybe Cassie was more Brad's type than Lisa. She was taller, sturdier. In fact, seeing Brad, Cassie, and Joel together sent a wave of empathy through her. No wonder Lisa felt so insecure. The three of them looked like perfect candidates for the cover of *Sports Illustrated*.

Joel's somber expression gave way to a smile as Jennie took the space beside him. "Hey, if it isn't our very own super sleuth." He shifted his bulky shoulders and extended a muscular arm across the seat behind her. His sleeveless T-shirt stretched across a chest that would have made Arnold Schwarzenegger proud. "So what do you want to know?"

"Excuse me?" Jennie felt like a kid with her hand caught in a cookie jar. Was she that transparent?

"About Courtney. You're on the case, right? You're going to try to find out what happened to her."

Jennie shrugged. "Well," she admitted, "I am curious. But I'm not on the case."

"Come on, Jennie, be honest." Cassie twisted around in her seat so she could face Jennie and her brother. "You think we'll tell you something we didn't tell the police." She glanced at Joel then back at Jennie. "I really wish we had some answers. Truth is, Joel and Brad picked me up at the mall at nine. We stopped at Wendy's for a snack and dropped

Courtney off at about ten. After that, we took Brad to his place and went home."

"The police think she ran away," Jennie said. "Personally, I have a hard time with that, but then, I don't know her all that well. Did she say anything to you?"

"Yeah, she did." Joel huffed disgustedly and fingered the rim of his Miami Dolphins baseball cap. He shook his head. "I'm surprised she didn't take off sooner."

"Why?" Jennie asked.

"Ask her father." Joel folded his arms and stared out the window.

"According to him they get along fairly well," Jennie countered, bracing herself as the bus turned a corner.

"He's lying." Cassie pursed her lips as though deliberating whether or not to go on. After a moment she did. "They fight all the time. He hit her really hard the other day. Here." Cassie pointed at her front left shoulder. "She showed me the bruise."

"Mr. Evans?" Somehow, Jennie didn't see him as an abusive parent, but then you couldn't always tell. She'd long since learned that appearances could be deceiving. *If he really is abusive, McGrady, that puts a whole new light on things. Maybe Courtney called to ask for help—or to warn me and Mom. Maybe Frank beat Courtney up and has her hidden somewhere . . . .* "Did you tell the police?"

"What good would that do?" Joel asked. "Evans would just deny it. Who are the police going to believe? A couple of kids or some rich dude pharmacist? Besides, she's safe now."

"How do you know she's safe?" Jennie asked. "Did she tell you where she was going?"

Joel didn't answer.

"Come on you guys, are you hiding her somewhere?"

Cassie looked Jennie square in the eyes. "No. I wish we were. We're as worried about Courtney as you are. It's just that if she ran away and if she's on the streets, she's probably okay."

"Cassie's right." Joel unfolded his arms and turned toward her, then rested his arm on the seat back again. "She asked me to come downtown with her a couple of times. I don't know, maybe it was her hair or the way she dressed, but the kids seemed to like her. So I figure if she's with them—they'll watch out for her, you know?"

The three athletes managed to shift the conversation from Courtney to sports. Jennie's mind stuck to Frank Evans and his missing daughter. At least now she wouldn't have to worry about Mom dating him. She'd have to warn Mom before . . .

The bus made a sharp turn, throwing Jennie against Joel and scattering her thoughts. His chest was rock hard against her shoulder. "Sorry," she stammered. "The turn caught me by surprise."

When Jennie tried to straighten, Joel held her in place. "Me too," he murmured. "But, hey, I'm not complaining."

His breath fluttered against her cheek like butterfly wings. Her stomach tightened. For a moment Jennie found herself wondering what it would be like to kiss him. But only for a moment. Startled at her response, she jerked back. He let her go, but not before giving her a conceited I-know-you-want-me smile.

"Cool your jets, Nielsen," Jennie muttered.

Joel wasn't her type. He was too—too bulky. And he was Courtney's boyfriend.

Wait a minute. Jennie backed up her brain and replayed the incident. *Something doesn't compute here, McGrady. Joel's girlfriend has been missing for what? Twenty-four hours? And he's making a pass at you? Either Joel knows more than he's letting on or he's a total jerk.*

Since they all seemed genuinely concerned about Courtney's disappearance, Jennie went with her second impression.

Before heading out to distribute flyers and fact sheets on drugs and AIDS, Michael gave them some last-minute instructions, which, as always, included the buddy system. They were to go out in groups of twos, threes and fours, but never alone. Instructions complete, the kids started drifting off.

Ordinarily Jennie would have paired up with Lisa. She looked around for B.J. and Allison, then remembered they'd gone to the beach with their parents. She thought about teaming up with Joel, Cassie, and Brad, but didn't see them.

Jennie was beginning to feel like the last person picked for a baseball team when Gavin tapped her on the shoulder. "Will I do?"

"Perfectly." The word slipped out before Jennie could stop it. The last thing she wanted to do was encourage him.

Gavin turned out to be a great partner. Having dated Courtney he knew her favorite haunts and remembered meeting some of the kids she'd befriended.

They didn't find Courtney, but they did talk to a dozen kids who recognized her picture and two people who had seen her the night before. Randy, a student at Portland State who worked at The Eatery, recognized Courtney's picture immediately.

"Wow," he said, "I can't believe she's missing." He reached up to shove back a straw-colored swatch of hair. "If I tell you what I know do I get the two hundred?"

"If you call the number on the flyer and if they find her, you might," Jennie answered.

"So why should I tell you anything?"

"Because I think she might be in trouble and I want to help."

He shrugged. "Courtney comes in once or twice a week. She came in last night around eleven."

"Last night? You're sure?" Jennie asked, trying to concentrate on why she was there, rather than why he'd shave his head and leave a tail hanging in his face.

"Yeah. I remember 'cause she seemed different, you know? Like nervous, maybe, or scared. She kept looking at the door like maybe she was waiting for someone."

"And did this person ever show?"

"I don't think so. The only one I saw her talking to was Tina."

They were getting close. Jennie's heart did a triple flip. "Tina," Jennie repeated. "Do you know her last name?"

"Nope. Just Tina."

"Any idea where I can find her?"

"Yep." He nodded toward the door. "She just walked in."

9

"Hey, Tina," Randy called to the girl with burgundy hair who was backing into the restaurant. "How's it goin'?"

"Been better." Favoring a bandaged right foot, Tina turned, then crutch-walked across the room and settled her small frame into a bench seat in the far corner near the window. She placed the crutches on the floor beside her and started to remove her studded black leather jacket. A bright yellow knit tank top contrasted sharply with her mahogany skin.

She eyed Jennie and Gavin wearily and shrugged the jacket back on again. Tina reminded Jennie of a little girl wearing dress-up clothes several sizes too big. Jennie remembered seeing the jacket—or one like it—on Courtney.

Randy grabbed a hamburger and box of fries from the warmer and set them on a tray along with a salad and a carton of milk, then delivered them to Tina's table. Not only routine, but gratis, Jennie noticed. He leaned on the table and nodded his head toward Jennie and Gavin. "Couple kids here asking about Courtney Evans."

Tina muttered something unintelligible and grabbed for her crutches. Her dark eyes flashed angrily at Randy.

"Wait!" Jennie hurried to the table. "Please. We're Courtney's friends. She's missing and . . ." Jennie handed Tina a flyer. "We just want to make sure she's safe."

"Don't know nuthin' about it," Tina insisted. She glanced briefly at Courtney's picture, pulled a French fry out of the box and shoved it into her mouth.

Gavin slid into the bench opposite Tina and made room for Jennie to sit beside him.

"Hey, don't I know you?" Tina asked, scooping up another fry.

Gavin nodded. "We met a couple months ago. Courtney introduced us."

"Oh yeah. The guy with the camera. You're not gonna try takin' my picture again, are you?"

"And have you ruin another roll of film? No way."

Tina chuckled and glanced toward Jennie. "Who's she?"

Gavin introduced Jennie as a friend of his and Courtney's.

Tina peeled off the wrapper of her hamburger. "Hope you guys don't mind if I eat in front of you. Low blood sugar, you know."

Jennie watched her eat, wondering how best to phrase her questions. "Um . . . Tina," Jennie hesitated. "About Courtney. She didn't come home last night and . . ."

"Like I said, I don't know nuthin'."

"But you saw her last night."

"Yeah." Tina paused to swallow. "She comes around—oh, 'bout once a week or so. Sees how I'm doing. Talks to some of the other kids. Courtney's a good person. Always helpin' people."

Jennie tried another approach. "Randy said she seemed different last night—scared, maybe. Do you know where she was going after you talked to her—or if she was meeting anyone?"

"Nope. We left at the same time. I went one way, she went the other."

Several questions later, Jennie realized she'd gotten all the information Tina intended to give. She thanked her and

Randy and left several flyers. On the back of the one she'd given Tina, Jennie wrote her name and phone number. "If you see Courtney, have her call me."

Tina didn't answer.

Out on the sidewalk Jennie heaved a long, exasperated sigh. It was nine o'clock—time to head back to the bus. "I wish I'd driven my car. I have a feeling Tina knows more than she's telling us. I'd love to wait around and follow her."

Gavin shook his head. "Wouldn't work. She's too smart for that. If she does know where Courtney is, she'll tell her we're looking for her. Courtney will either call us or not."

"I suppose you're right."

"Come on." Gavin draped an arm across her shoulders. "We'd better get back."

Jennie thought about pulling away from him, but didn't. Unlike Joel, Gavin's gesture carried no sexual overtones, only friendship. "So," Jennie said as she fell into step beside him, "tell me about Tina and how she managed to ruin your film."

"The first time Courtney brought me down here with her, I started taking photos like crazy. Thought I might do an article on homeless kids. Most of them didn't mind, but Tina went wild. Told me if I didn't give her the film, she was going to smash my camera."

"That's pretty tough talk for someone so little."

"Tina's tougher than she looks. Besides, she had some big friends and I wasn't about to tangle with those dudes. One word from her and they'd have smashed the camera *and* my head."

"Why so camera shy?"

"She's a runaway. Courtney said she is only thirteen. Her parents are alcoholics. She's been in a dozen foster homes since she was five and a few months ago decided she'd be better off living on the streets."

"That's so sad."

"Yeah. But you hang out here long enough and you hear

all kinds of stories like that. Courtney wanted to help them all." Gavin frowned and stuffed his hands in his pockets.

Before boarding the bus, they pooled the information they'd learned about Courtney. A few of the others had talked to kids who recognized her, but no one admitted to knowing where she was or whether or not she'd run away. Gavin didn't mention Tina so Jennie didn't either. If the police started asking questions, Tina might get scared off.

Michael commended them. "We'll give this to the police and hope they're able to come up with some answers."

Jennie arrived back at the house around ten. Frank's Lexus was parked in the driveway. She sat in the Mustang for a few minutes gathering her thoughts. Joel and the others had made some frightening accusations against Courtney's father. Jennie wished she had the nerve to walk in and ask him whether or not they were true.

Mr. Evans, she imagined herself saying, *my sources tell me you beat up your daughter.* Right. He'd just deny it and Mom would come unglued. No, she'd have to engage in as normal a conversation as she could and try to read between the lines. Later she'd tell Mom what she'd learned.

Jennie exited the car and strolled up the walk, wondering how best to make her entrance. At the door, she took a deep breath to steel herself—against what, Jennie wasn't sure.

As Jennie opened the door, she heard voices coming from the living room.

"I wish I knew what to do," Frank was saying. "Courtney's never run away before."

Jennie quietly closed the door and tiptoed across the entry floor. Okay, so eavesdropping wasn't the most ethical way to get information, but it could be effective.

Frank and Mom were sitting together on the sofa with their backs to Jennie. "What am I doing wrong, Susan?" Frank asked. "What did I do to drive her away?"

74

Jennie pinched her lips together. *Knocking her around might have done it.*

"Don't be so hard on yourself," Mom said, leaning toward him. The couch hid all but their heads and shoulders, but knowing her mom, Jennie suspected she'd taken hold of his hand. "It may not have anything to do with you. Not long ago, Jennie ran away. She was going through a hard time accepting her father's death and went to the coast to visit her grandmother."

Enough. Talking about Courtney was one thing, but Jennie did not want her mother telling Frank stories about her. Jennie stepped back into the entry, opened the door and closed it again. "Mom," she said, announcing her arrival, "I'm back."

She walked into the living room, leaned over the couch, and kissed her mother's cheek.

"Hi, sweetheart. How was the meeting?"

"Good." As Jennie told them about their search, she watched Frank's face. "We handed out a lot of flyers. Gavin and I talked to a couple of people who saw Courtney last night."

Frank frowned and shook his head. "God only knows what terrible things could happen to her down there. I kept asking her not to go. She just wouldn't listen. I . . ." He closed his eyes and took a deep breath. "I'll never forgive myself if anything happens to her."

Jennie couldn't tell. She honestly couldn't tell whether or not Frank Evans was sincere. He seemed broken up about Courtney's disappearance, but that didn't indicate whether or not he had been the reason for her running away.

Frank left a few minutes later. While Mom walked him outside, Jennie filled two cups with water and set them in the microwave. She'd just put them on the table and dropped in the peppermint tea bags when Mom came back inside.

75

"Tea!" Mom crossed the kitchen and gave Jennie a hug. "That's so sweet."

Jennie shrugged. "Thought maybe you could use it. Besides, I wanted to talk to you about something." She waited until her mother had removed the tea bag and taken a sip, then told her about the bruises Cassie had seen on Courtney. "He hits her, Mom. That's why she ran away."

Mom stared at the greenish brown liquid. "I don't know what to say. Frank is one of the nicest men I've ever met. I . . ." Mom shifted her gaze from the cup to Jennie's face. "Honey, could your friends have made a mistake?"

"Courtney told them she was afraid of her dad. Cassie saw the bruises."

Mom sighed. "If it's true, we should tell the police. But . . ." She stopped, her brows furrowed in thought. "I'll talk to Michael first."

Jennie placed a hand on her mother's arm. "I'm sorry, Mom. I really am."

Her mother nodded and stared into her tea again. After a few minutes of silence, Jennie moved quietly away from the table, dumped her remaining tea in the sink, and left the room.

The phone in her room rang as Jennie pulled a light cotton nightshirt over her head. Two rings later she'd managed to work her arms out of the sleeve holes so she could answer it.

"Jennie," a raspy voice whispered.

Jennie stopped breathing. "Who. . . ?"

"It's me—Courtney."

10

"Where are you?" Jennie's heart leapt into high gear.

"Never mind that." Courtney coughed. Apparently she had a cold.

"Are you all right?" Jennie asked.

"Yes."

"Why did you run away? Everyone's been worried about you."

"Can't talk here. I need to see you."

"When?"

"Now."

Jennie hesitated. "I don't know."

"Please. I have to talk to someone. You're the only one I can trust."

"Courtney, if it's about your father . . ."

"No. Whatever you do, don't say anything to him. Just meet me in South Park Blocks by the statue of Teddy Roosevelt."

Jennie weighed the options. *If you refuse, Courtney might end up in terrible trouble. If you go, you might be able to talk her into getting help.* Courtney wouldn't have to go back home.

"Okay," Jennie said finally. "But look for my car—a red Mustang. I'll drive by and pick you up. We'll go somewhere safe and talk."

Courtney agreed.

Jennie changed back into jeans and a sweatshirt. The dark hallway and narrow strip of light under her mother's bedroom door told her that Mom had gone to bed. Jennie sneaked downstairs, out the door, and into the night.

Shifting the car into neutral, she let it back out of the driveway before starting the engine. *You shouldn't be doing this, McGrady. Mom's going to kill you.* "Hopefully," Jennie mumbled, "she won't find out."

A block away, Jennie almost went back to talk to Mom, or at least write a note, then decided against it. She wanted to get to Courtney as quickly as possible.

With her windows up and the car doors locked, Jennie drove around the Park Blocks four times. On the fifth time around, Jennie stopped the car near the Roosevelt Rough Rider statue and looked into the park's shadowy depths.

"Where are you, Courtney?" Jennie asked aloud. She didn't want to give up, but had no intention of getting out of the car to look for her.

Jennie was about to drive on when headlights glared behind her. She gripped the steering wheel, then relaxed her hands when she caught a glimpse of the uniform. A police officer tapped on her window. Jennie groped for the power button to lower the window and finally found it.

The officer, a woman, lifted her flashlight, shining it in Jennie's face and into the car. "I'd like to see your driver's license, please."

"I was supposed to meet a friend down here," Jennie explained as she reached into the bag on the passenger seat and withdrew her wallet. She fished out the license and handed it to the officer.

When she directed the flashlight beam to the driver's license, Jennie could barely make out the name badge—Sgt. R.L. Brown.

Officer Brown went back to the patrol car and after a few

minutes returned. "So you're the McGrady girl. I've heard about you."

"Oh." From the flat tone of her voice, Jennie couldn't tell if that was good or bad.

"Out kind of late, aren't you?"

Jennie explained again. This time she handed the officer one of the flyers she and the others had distributed earlier that night. "Courtney asked me to meet her here. I'm worried something might have happened to her."

Officer Brown scanned the flyer. "What time did she call you?"

"Around eleven," Jennie said. "She insisted I meet her alone. I told her I'd pick her up. Didn't want to walk around in the park by myself."

Brown nodded. "Good move. Staying home and calling us would have been even better."

"I thought I could help. I don't understand why she's not here."

"She may have seen the patrol car and gotten cold feet."

Brown's explanation seemed plausible, but Jennie had a sick feeling in the pit of her stomach. Her intuition told her it wasn't that simple. Courtney had asked for help three different times. "Could you help me check out the area in case . . . I mean, someone might have attacked her or something before I got here."

Brown looked at the poster again and back at Jennie. "I'll call for backup. In the meantime I'd like you to go on home."

"Can't I go with you? She called me and . . ."

"Miss McGrady." The sergeant put her hands on her hips. "Either go home now, or I'll haul you in for breaking curfew."

"Okay. I'm going, but could you call me if you find her? I'd like to know."

Officer Brown's look of disapproval softened. "I'll think about it."

Jennie scribbled her phone number on the flyer and left.

———

When Jennie pulled into the driveway, the lights were on all over the house. That meant Mom had gotten up again. Great. *Take it easy, McGrady*, Jennie told herself. *Maybe she doesn't know you went out. Maybe you can sneak in and...*

The front door snapped open as Jennie stepped onto the porch. Mom stood in the entry, her hair as wild as the look on her face. "Where have you been?"

"Courtney called," Jennie explained, hoping to defuse her mother before the explosion came. "She asked me to meet her downtown."

It worked. Sort of. Mom closed her eyes the way she did when she counted to ten to keep from losing her temper. She waited for Jennie to come in, then closed the door.

"And you went—just like that? Couldn't you have at least told me?"

"She asked me not to." Jennie sank onto the living room couch.

"Where is she?" Mom raked her fingers through her hair, trying to restore some kind of order to her curls and probably the situation.

Jennie shrugged. "I don't know. She never showed up. I gave the information to the police and came home." Mom was not impressed.

"You shouldn't have gone alone."

"But, Mom, I had no choice."

Mom tossed her a why-did-I-ever-have-children look. "Go to bed, Jennie. It's late and I'm far too angry to discuss this rationally."

This time Jennie didn't argue.

The next morning Jennie's private phone rang at seven in the morning. "H'lo," she murmured into the receiver.

"Miss McGrady?" Jennie didn't recognize the woman's

voice. "This is Sergeant Brown—Portland police. You wanted me to call if we learned anything about Courtney Evans."

"You found her?"

Brown hesitated. "Yes, but not in the park. A sanitation crew found her in a dumpster around five this morning."

11

"A dumpster?" Jennie repeated the words she couldn't possibly have heard. "Is Courtney dead?"

"Not quite, but from the beating she took, it looks like someone wanted her that way." The officer's businesslike voice belied the horror of the words she'd spoken.

"I can't believe it."

"Any idea who might have wanted this kid dead?"

Her father. Jennie wanted to say the words but they got stuck in her throat. Fathers didn't beat up their kids and throw them away. *Some did,* a voice reminded her, but Jennie didn't want to listen to that one. Instead, she grasped another, more acceptable thought. Courtney had been the victim of a mugging.

Jennie took a couple of deep breaths to steady herself.

"Jennie?" Brown's voice penetrated her thoughts. "You still with me?"

"Y-yes," Jennie stammered. "I just can't believe it. Are you sure it was Courtney?"

"'Fraid so. She didn't have any ID on her, but you'd given me the poster. I contacted her father. He met me at the hospital and gave us a positive identification."

"Is—is she going to be okay?" Jennie asked.

Brown hesitated. "It doesn't look good. She's in a coma. We'll know more after we get a report from the doctors."

Oh, God, Jennie prayed. *Please let her be okay. Don't let her die.*

"We'll need you to come down to the station sometime today to give us a statement," Brown went on. "Looks like you may have been one of the last ones to talk to her before she was attacked."

"Um—sure." Even though she already knew, Jennie listened to Brown's instructions regarding the location of the police station and what to do when she got there.

Still dazed, she walked over to her window and folded herself onto the deep cushions. Jennie shook her head. *How could something like this happen?* Kids she knew didn't get beaten up and thrown into dumpsters. That only happened to thugs in the movies—didn't it? Only hours ago, Courtney had asked for help. What kind of trouble had she gotten into? Could it have been a random mugging? At least a dozen questions flooded Jennie's mind. Questions she intended to find answers to. She owed Courtney that much.

A gentle knock on the door interrupted Jennie's jumbled thoughts, bringing a rush of relief. She hurried to unlock the door.

"Frank just called." Mom pinched her lips together, then released them. "Courtney's in the hospital."

"I know. The police just told me."

Mom frowned. "I don't understand. Why would the police call you?" She hesitated a moment. "Does this have anything to do with your being gone last night?"

Jennie nodded, and explained the events of the night before. "I had to go, Mom. She sounded so scared."

"You should have talked to me first—and the police. You shouldn't have gone alone. Jennie, it could just as easily have been you lying in that hospital bed."

"I didn't get out of the car," Jennie began in her own defense. "I had the doors locked."

"You broke curfew."

"Mom. . . ."

"Stop. I don't want to argue with you. I know you thought you were making the right choice, but . . ." She paused to take another deep breath. "I'm going to get dressed and go to the hospital. Frank needs my support right now."

He's probably the one who put her there. Courtney's the one who needs us, Jennie wanted to argue, but didn't. "I'd like to go see her, too."

Mom hesitated. "Maybe Kate or Gram can watch Nick."

"I'll call Gram," Jennie said, feeling the need to touch base with her. Having been on the police force for ten years, Gram might have some insights.

"I'm so sorry about your friend, Jennie," Gram said after hearing Jennie's story.

"I don't want to believe that Mr. Evans did it, but after what Joel and Cassie said . . ." Jennie hesitated, hoping Gram would have some answers.

"Abuse is a possibility the police will want to pursue—especially if she's a runaway." Gram's voice, even on the phone, had a stabilizing effect on Jennie. "You said you were going down to the station this afternoon to make a statement. Would you like me to come with you?"

"Would you?" Jennie felt like a boulder had fallen from her shoulders. Until that moment, Jennie hadn't realized how much she was dreading her encounter with the police. "Oh, Gram, thank you." She almost said goodbye when she remembered her reason for calling. Gram agreed to take care of Nick and Hannah and promised to be there within the hour.

"I'll tell you what, dear," Gram said before hanging up. "It's been a long time since you and I have had time to ourselves. If it's all right with your mother, why don't the two of us have a nice lunch when you get back from the hospital? We'll do that before we go to the police department. It will give us a chance to catch up."

When Jennie and her mom arrived at the hospital, they found Frank Evans pacing across the floor of a large waiting room situated outside the hospital's surgical unit. His bowed shoulders lifted some as Mom walked toward him. He stretched out his arms and embraced her.

Jennie stared at them. Hadn't Mom believed her? Jennie wanted to scream at her, *He's the enemy. He's the one who hit Courtney.*

Frank held Mom for a moment, then fastened his gaze on Jennie. "Thanks for coming."

Jennie unclenched her fists, but didn't respond.

"How is she?" Mom asked. "They told us at the front desk that she was in surgery."

"I don't know. The doctor said he needed to remove a blood clot to relieve pressure on her brain. She has a collapsed lung and . . ." He shook his head and moved his right hand up to cover his eyes. "There's so much. She's been in there for over an hour already."

Mom reached up and touched his shoulders. "Why don't we sit down." To Jennie she said, "Can you get us some coffee, hon? I think we could both use a cup."

Jennie set her bag on the seat next to Mom and tried to push her anger aside. She walked slowly in the direction of the coffee maker on the opposite side of the room. Watching Frank twisted her insides into massive knots. Somehow he wasn't acting like a guy who'd nearly beaten his own daughter to death, but then what did she know? It wasn't as if she saw people like that everyday. He could be acting, she reminded herself. Some people were good at that.

Jennie watched Frank closely as she handed him and Mom their coffee in Styrofoam cups. His blue gaze met hers briefly as he murmured "thank you," then looked away. She took the chair opposite Frank, but after five minutes of watching him stare into his coffee cup, decided her intuition had gone on vacation.

Jennie needed something to do. Why couldn't Lisa have been in this hospital instead of the one in east county? At least then she could have visited her while they were waiting. "I can't handle sitting around like this," Jennie finally said, bouncing to her feet. "I'm going down to the cafeteria for a Coke."

Mom nodded and turned her attention back to Frank.

Twenty-five minutes later, with a blueberry bagel, cream cheese, and a soft drink still churning in her stomach, Jennie decided to head back to the surgical waiting area. Not wanting to wait for an elevator, she took the stairs.

The echo in the stairwell reminded Jennie of another stairwell in another hospital—and the terror she'd felt when cornered in a similar space by a murderer. Her heart pounded as she placed one foot in front of the other. *He'd been a nice guy too*, Jennie mused. *Nice and deadly.*

The incident had affected her more than she'd thought. She turned around, intending to go back to the elevator, then stopped. *Come on, McGrady, you are not going to let one bad incident give you panic attacks for the rest of your life. Just keep moving.*

Jennie raced up the first two floors, slowing only when her lungs and legs threatened to collapse if she didn't stop abusing them. By the time she reached the third floor her breathing had almost returned to normal. *See*, she told herself. *There's nothing to be afraid of. It's not going to happen again so just relax.*

A door opened overhead. Panic exploded in her chest. Laughter filled the empty spaces around her as two women in white uniforms came into view. They smiled as they passed, then resumed their conversation. Jennie gripped the railing, took a deep breath, and kept moving. *You're going to make it, McGrady. Only one more floor.* When she reached the fourth floor, Jennie flung open the door and stepped into the lobby.

She was still puffing when she reached the waiting room. Mom sat there alone, reading a magazine. "Where's Frank?" Jennie asked as she sat down next to her.

"Talking to the police."

"Are they going to arrest him?"

Obviously irritated, Mom closed the magazine and tossed it on a coffee table. "Jennie, I know you think Frank is responsible for this, but I don't believe it for a minute. He's devastated by what's happened. I don't know why Courtney told her friends that her dad hit her, but she must have been lying."

"Why would she do that?"

"The police told us they had found Valium in her pockets and traces of amphetamines in her blood. They think she may have gotten them from her father's pharmacy."

"Drugs? Courtney was doing drugs?"

12

Drugs.

There's your motive, McGrady. Courtney was helping herself to drugs and good old dad found out about it. Maybe he confronted her, they fought. The rest is history.

Jennie was about to relate all this to her mother when Frank returned. Michael walked in with him.

Frank looked dazed and, once again, Jennie felt sorry for him. "I don't understand any of this," he said, his gaze darting from one to the other. "Courtney didn't take drugs—I'm certain of it. She knows how dangerous they are."

"But we did find a discrepancy in your books, Frank," Mom said. "You said yourself that some of your inventory is missing."

"Yes, but not the controlled drugs." He sat down, resting his elbows on his knees. "If Courtney was on drugs, I would have known."

"Not necessarily." Michael gripped Frank's shoulder. "It's sad, but parents are often the last to know."

"But I'm a pharmacist. . . ."

"Mr. Evans?" The deep male voice came from a man in green surgical scrubs.

Frank raised his head, and placing his hands against his knees, pushed himself into a standing position. "Courtney, is she. . . ?"

"She made it through surgery. We'll be transferring her to Intensive Care shortly."

"Can I see her?"

"Not for a couple of hours. Why don't you have something to eat and we'll page you."

Frank nodded and turned to Michael. "Can you stay?"

"Sorry, I have an appointment at the church."

Jennie, definitely not wanting to hang around with her mother and Frank for the next two hours, asked Michael to drop her off at the house. "I need to go to the police station this afternoon," she added for emphasis.

"Sure." Michael glanced at Mom. "That is, if it's okay with your mother."

"Fine. Jennie, tell Gram I'll be home sometime this afternoon. I'd like to stay with Frank until Courtney's stable."

So much for having lunch with Gram.

Jennie and Michael said goodbye and left. Once in the parking lot, Michael led her to his BMW and unlocked the door. "Want to drive?"

"Sure." Jennie grinned and wedged herself into the driver's seat. Sheer luxury. Sitting behind the wheel of the sports car drained the tension from her neck and shoulders.

Once she'd merged onto the freeway, Jennie chanced a look at Michael. He stared straight ahead, seemingly deep in thought.

"What are you thinking about?" she asked.

He sighed and shook his head. "Just trying to make some sense of this thing. Courtney's a good kid. I know she comes off as tough and rebellious at times, but that's all an act. I have to admit, I find the drug thing hard to imagine. Why anyone would want to beat her up like that—"

"I think it was her dad," Jennie said, relaying the conversation she'd had with Joel and Cassie.

"They told me that too. Came in yesterday afternoon. Apparently Courtney had told them not to say anything. She didn't want to get her dad in trouble. Cassie and Joel decided they'd better tell someone. They were worried that Frank might have done something to her. If fact, that's what initiated the search. I'm not sure I buy it though."

"Why?" Jennie tried unsuccessfully to keep the irritation out of her voice.

"Courtney and her dad had their differences—all families do, but somehow I just don't see him as an abuser."

"So you think Courtney lied?" Jennie set her jaw, anger rising inside her like a geyser. "What if she didn't? What if her dad is the one who's lying?" Jennie paused in her tirade to pass an extremely slow van.

Seeing she had his attention, she went on. "Why is it so hard for adults to believe kids? It just isn't fair."

"Jennie, calm down. And while you're at it, you might want to let up on the gas pedal just a tad. I think the speed limit along here is fifty."

Jennie glanced at the speedometer and winced. Seventy-five? "Sorry." She slowed down and glanced in the rearview mirror, half expecting to see a bank of flashing lights bearing down on her.

"You're safe," Michael said. "This time."

"I really am sorry. But I meant what I said."

"I know. You've brought up some good points. I'm not accusing anyone of lying. Basically, I'm just trying to make sense of it all."

"Me too."

They didn't talk much the rest of the way. Jennie mainly concentrated on maintaining an acceptable speed limit. She took the exit off the freeway and angled down the streets leading toward the Crystal Lake area and home.

They'd no sooner pulled into the driveway when Nick and Bernie came bounding down the porch steps. Before Michael could even get out of the car, Nick had him in a head lock.

"Whoa. Take it easy, big fella." Michael laughed and extricated himself from the car, then swung Nick into his arms and onto his shoulders. Jennie blinked back the tears that always seemed to threaten when she saw Nick and Michael together. How could Mom be so blind? Couldn't she see? Michael was perfect for Nick. Almost as perfect as their real dad. *Maybe even more so.* The thought slipped in and Jennie pushed it away again.

"Me too, me too! Hannah squealed as she disengaged herself from Gram's lap and the porch swing and allowed Michael to scoop her into his arms.

While Jennie explained Mom's plan to stay at the hospital to Gram, she watched Michael roughhousing with the kids and Bernie on the grass.

"I'm sorry we have to put our plans on hold," Gram said. "Perhaps if your mother comes home early enough, I can take you out for tea at that new British Isles restaurant. I hear they serve wonderful scones with preserves and Devonshire cream."

"That would be great," Jennie heard herself saying. At the moment, food was the last thing on her mind. She dug into her bag, and after rummaging around for too long, came up with the keys to the Mustang. "I'd better get down to the police department before they decide to arrest me."

"Now don't you worry about that." Gram pulled her into a warm embrace. "You'll do fine."

Grandparents were wonderful people, Jennie decided as she maneuvered the car down the driveway and waved. You never had to prove yourself to them. They loved you just for breathing. And they believed in you. At least Gram did in her. While Mom wanted Jennie to go into anything but law enforcement, Gram took her seriously and had even coached her from time to time. She definitely needed to talk to Gram about Courtney.

By the time Jennie reached the police station the sky had turned a charcoal gray. She found a parking space two blocks away and raced to beat the downpour. Thunder cracked and lightning flashed as the sky opened up.

The drenched female reflected in the glass door bore little resemblance to the one she'd seen in the mirror earlier that morning, but he recognized her anyway.

"Hey, Jennie, you're wet." Dean Rockford, alias Rocky, chuckled and walked toward her.

"No kidding." Jennie tossed an easy grin his way. Rocky was her favorite cop. Frustrating as he could be at times, Jennie had gone from having a crush on him to thinking of him as a big brother and a good friend.

His laughing blue eyes turned serious. "I wondered if I'd run into you. Brown told me about seeing you last night. You're lucky it wasn't me. I'd have hauled you in."

"Yeah right." He might have too—if for nothing else than to protect her. He seemed to feel she needed looking after. "This isn't going to be another lecture is it?"

"Nah. As much fun as that sounds, I gotta get going. But I hope you take what happened to your friend seriously. How's she doing, by the way?"

Jennie told him.

He offered sympathies and said he'd see her later.

"Rocky?" she called as he reached the door. "Do you know who did it? I mean, do you have any suspects?"

"You never quit, do you Sherlock?"

"I just want to help. . . ." Now she *was* getting annoyed.

"Sorry, Jennie. You won't get a chance to play detective on this one. We're way ahead of you."

"What do you mean?"

"We're making an arrest this afternoon. Brown's probably collaring him right now."

"Him? Mr. Evans?"

Rocky took a step toward her. His blue eyes flashed with exasperation and admiration. "How do you do that?" He shook his head. "Never mind. Yeah. It's Evans. We got to checking for priors and hit pay dirt. Two years ago, Frank Evans was arrested, tried, and acquitted for his wife's murder."

13

Courtney lay under layers of white, looking more like snow than a rainbow.

A machine pumped air into her lungs through a tube secured to her mouth with a strip of tape. Two bags of liquid dripped into smaller tubes that wormed through a machine, joined at a Y, then disappeared under a bandage on Courtney's left wrist. White gauze covered her head, eliminating Courtney's colorful hair. They'd probably shaved it off, taking away her rainbow—her hope.

Jennie pressed a hand on the large plate glass window that separated them. A sign on the closed door read *No Visitors*.

The burden of guilt that Gram had lifted earlier in the day came back and settled on her like a coat of armor. Jennie felt a terrible sense of responsibility. *If you'd met Courtney at the mall after that first phone call, McGrady, maybe this wouldn't have happened.*

The guilt stretched beyond Courtney. Jennie shuddered, remembering the dazed look of disbelief on Frank Evans' face when the officers brought him into the police department. Jennie had just finished giving her statement. He'd seen her—or at least she thought he had. She'd expected him to be angry—he wasn't. Grief seemed to have etched deeper lines at the corners of his eyes and around his mouth. The gray in his sideburns seemed more prominent—as though he'd aged a dozen years since that morning.

Another lump made its way into Jennie's throat. Tears filled her eyes and dripped down her cheeks. "It isn't my fault," she whispered. "I didn't do anything wrong."

Curtains slid across the window, blocking Jennie's view of the room. She stepped back and felt someone's presence behind her. "Are you okay?" Michael's hands cupped her shoulders.

"No." She turned into his arms and buried her face in his shoulder. How could she be okay? She was crying her heart out over people she barely knew; and feeling like she had somehow brought it all about. Michael led her out of the ICU area, down the hall, and into another waiting room.

———

At four that afternoon, eyes dry and emotions under control, Jennie sat at a table near flouncey, white Victorian curtains. The window overlooked a quaint English garden in full bloom. She slathered rich whipped cream on a scone with raspberry jam and lifted it to her mouth. "Hmmm." She closed her eyes, savoring the taste and smells of the charming restaurant.

"It is good, isn't it?" Gram took several sips of her Earl Grey tea and settled her blue gaze on Jennie.

"Thanks for bringing me. I guess I needed to escape for a while. That business with Courtney and her dad was really getting to me."

"Such a tragedy."

"And Mom . . ." Jennie sighed. "I think she blames me for Frank's arrest."

"Oh no, Jennie. You mustn't think that. Susan is deeply hurt, but if she's upset with anyone, it's herself." Gram set her cup down and picked up her fork. "I imagine she's wondering how she could have been such a poor judge of character."

"Do you think she really loved Frank?"

Gram shook her head. "Only she can tell you that. I'm just thankful we found out about him now and not several months or years later."

"Yeah." Jennie frowned and broke off another piece of scone. Several crumbs dropped onto her new pink jeans. She brushed them off. "Do you think Frank did it?"

"Are you referring to his wife or Courtney?"

"Both, I guess."

"Well, he was acquitted of his wife's murder. It's up to a jury to decide whether or not he assaulted Courtney."

"Yeah, but what do you think?"

"From what I hear, the district attorney has a strong case against Frank. Did you know about the blood and hair samples the police found in the trunk of one of his cars?"

Jennie straightened. "No. Courtney's?"

"It looks that way, but they're still waiting for the final results from the lab."

"Who told you all that?" She took a sip of chamomile tea and returned the gold-trimmed floral teacup to its matching saucer.

Gram smiled. "I have my sources."

"Then I guess that means he's guilty."

Gram raised an eyebrow. "I gather you have some doubts."

"I don't know what to think. At first I really thought Frank had done it. Now that he's been arrested . . ." Jennie leaned back in the chair and tipped her head back.

"What is it, Jennie?" Gram leaned forward and rested her arms on the table. "What's troubling you?"

Jennie hesitated, trying to gather her stray thoughts into a semblance of order. "Something isn't right. I can feel it here." She balled up her hand and pressed it to her stomach.

Gram nodded. "Perhaps the police have been too hasty. Frank was acquitted of his wife's murder. Apparently there wasn't enough evidence to convict him. As to the evidence linking him to Courtney's assault, even if the blood and hair samples are hers, it only proves she was in the trunk, not that he put her there."

"And something else, Gram." Jennie's sagging heart stirred. "I just figured out what's been bothering me so much about this. Courtney called me about half an hour after Frank left the house. So how could he have had time to go downtown, find Courtney, and beat her up?"

Gram poured a fresh cup of tea from a calico cat teapot. Clear brown liquid streamed out of the cat's mouth. "Good point. But are you certain the caller was Courtney?"

"Yes . . . no. Not really. She didn't sound like herself. Her voice was raspy, like she had a cold or something. Or . . ." Jennie paused and rubbed her forehead. "Gram, you don't think it was someone impersonating her—wanting me to think she was safe—maybe someone who wanted to get me into the park to . . . to kill me?"

"Let's hope that's not the case. It's possible that someone wanted you to think Courtney was safe at that time—perhaps to establish an alibi."

"Mr. Evans? You mean like he could have had her hidden all the time?" Jennie blew out a long breath. "Wow. He could have staged the whole thing—made everyone believe Courtney was missing and then put on this grieving father act."

"I suppose that's possible, Jennie. But why would he want to bring attention to himself by copycatting the first murder?"

"What do you mean?"

Gram cleared her throat. "This isn't the best conversation to be having over tea," she said. "Perhaps we should wait until later."

Jennie set her empty plate aside. "I'm done. Tell me now."

Gram glanced around her and lowered her voice. "Frank

Evans' wife was beaten to death. Her body was found in a dumpster."

Gram was right about it not being a pleasant tea topic. Jennie took a deep breath to calm her queasy stomach.

"It just seems to me," Gram continued, her voice back to its normal volume, "that he wouldn't want to draw that kind of attention to himself."

"So you think someone's framing him? Maybe Frank has some enemies in the wrong places. Maybe some drug dealers were blackmailing him back in Boston and followed him out here."

"Hmmm." Gram brought the teacup to her lips, then lowered it. "That's an interesting scenario. I think I'll have another chat with my friends in the department. They may want to investigate the case more thoroughly. This sounds like the sort of thing the FBI and the DEA might want to know about."

Jennie had several other ideas but didn't voice them aloud. She wanted to talk to Tina again, and Gavin, Cassie, Joel, and Lisa, along with some of the other kids. If Frank hadn't assaulted Courtney, who had? And why?

"I see those wheels turning, Jennie. You're not thinking of doing anything foolish, are you? Your mother is very worried about you." Gram hesitated. "In fact, she asked if I'd have a chat with you about involving yourself in this case."

Jennie grimaced and heaved an exasperated sigh. "Not you too. Why does everyone feel it's their honor-bound duty to lecture me? I'm not stupid."

"That, my dear, is part of the problem. You are extremely intelligent. Being your grandmother I may be just a tad biased, but . . ." Gram smiled and lifted her hands and shoulders in a shrug.

Jennie rested her elbows on the table and her chin on her hands. "So what's the problem now? I said I was sorry about going out alone the other night. I know I should have let Mom know."

"I think that's as much my fault as it is yours." Gram hesitated as a waitress in a black shirtwaist dress and white ruffled apron set the check on the table.

"I do hope you enjoyed your time with us," she peeped in a distinct British accent. "Do come again."

"Thank you, Bridgette," Gram said as if she'd known the woman all her life instead of the hour they'd been there. "We will."

Gram tabled their conversation until after she had paid the bill and she and Jennie had gotten into the Mustang. "Now then," she said, buckling herself in. "Where were we?"

Jennie grinned at her. "You were telling me how brilliant I am. And you were about to lecture me for taking after you."

Gram brushed a hand through her salt-and-pepper hair. A look of sadness crossed her features. "You're right about that. I was a wild one. Losing my parents during the war didn't help. I must have driven my grandmother crazy with worry over whether or not I'd survive." Gram cleared her throat. "But enough of that. We were talking about you."

"Gram, please. I promise I won't do anything dangerous. I won't ever go downtown at night unless I have someone with me. And I'll tell Mom where I'm going. Okay?"

"One more thing." Gram placed her hand on Jennie's shoulder. "I know you want to investigate this matter with Courtney, and I'm not saying you can't ask questions. But if you find anything—promise you'll tell me, or your mother, or the police."

Jennie promised.

That night, after a quick dinner, Jennie scrambled into her car again, this time heading across town to Sunnyside.

"Hi, I wondered when you'd show up." Lisa tugged a

brush through her long wet tresses and frowned. "Gram told me you were coming. How's Courtney?"

"Not good. She's still in a coma. They don't know if she'll make it."

Lisa looked ten times better—still too thin, of course, but her skin had lost that gray look and the dark circles under her eyes were almost gone.

"Mom told me about Frank being arrested. That is just so awful." Lisa shuddered. A moment later, she set her brush down, scooted to the edge of the bed, and dangled her legs over the side.

"Did Courtney ever say anything to you about her dad hitting her?" Jennie asked.

Lisa shook her head. "I noticed a couple of bruises the last time I saw her. When I asked her about them, she brushed it off. Said she'd bumped her arm against a door."

"She told Cassie and Joel that her dad had hit her." Jennie retrieved a lone chair resting against the far wall, pulled it closer to Lisa's bed and dropped into it. "They think that's why she ran away."

"I don't blame her. I'd run away too."

"Yeah. If that's what happened."

"What do you mean? You think Courtney lied?"

Jennie shrugged. "I talked to Gram this afternoon and we . . . well, Mr. Evans might have been framed. I thought I'd ask a few questions. See if I can come up with some other suspects. Do you know if Courtney had any enemies? Anyone who'd want to beat her up?"

Lisa had grown strangely silent. Her eyes held a kind of wary look. She knew something.

"Lisa?"

"No." Her cousin scooted back into her bed and drew the covers over her. "I don't know anyone who would do something like that." She sighed. "I'm sorry, Jennie, but I'm afraid I'm not very good company yet. I'm really tired." She closed her eyes and turned her face to the wall away from Jennie. A lone tear trailed down her cousin's cheek and dripped onto the pale pink pajama top, creating a dime-sized splotch of rose.

Lisa was protecting someone. But who? And why?

14

"Why are you doing this?" Jennie asked, her voice unsteady and tinged with anger.

Lisa didn't respond.

"Talk to me, Lisa! Who are you trying to protect? Is it Brad? Joel?"

"No!" Lisa turned back to face Jennie. "Why can't you just leave it alone?"

"I can't. Courtney ... . if you could see her you'd understand. The police think her father did it and I thought so too at first, only now I'm not so sure. Please, tell me what you know."

Lisa stared at the white bedspread. "It's Courtney, okay? She's the one I wanted to protect—and me. I didn't want her to get into trouble. She . . . she gave me some diet pills. I promised I wouldn't tell."

"So she was dealing drugs."

"No. Not like that. I mean, not the bad stuff."

Not the bad stuff? Jennie struggled between blowing up at Lisa and not saying anything at all. She chose the latter, stuffed her hands in her jean pockets, spun around, and stalked out of the room.

Her stomach hurt. Her head hurt. She felt like she had lost her best friend. In a way she had. Sure, Lisa would always be her cousin, but she seemed to be drifting farther and farther away. First secretly starving herself, then this—this drug thing.

Jennie needed to talk to someone who was objective. And she needed to go back downtown to pay another visit to Tina. Even though she didn't consider six-thirty all that late, Jennie figured she'd better not go alone.

She stopped at a pay phone and called Gavin. He seemed anxious to talk to her as well and gave her directions to his house.

Twenty minutes later, Jennie pulled into a winding drive lined with trees. In less than a tenth of a mile the trees thinned, giving way to fenced pasture on both sides of the road. Two llamas peered at her for a moment, then went back to whatever they were eating. A big white barn sat near a two-story farmhouse atop a gently rolling hill. The white picket fence surrounding the house reminded Jennie of Tom Sawyer and Huck Finn.

Gavin stood in the driveway with a stream of water directed at a pair of black rubber boots that reached his knees. He waved as she drove in.

"Hi. I'll be with you in a minute. Had to milk Samantha and Erin." He nodded his head toward two goats penned up near the barn. "You can wait out here if you want, or come inside." He brushed the hair out of his eyes and grinned at her.

"I'll stay out here. I didn't know you lived on a farm."

"I wouldn't call it a farm exactly. It's more like my mom's hobby." Gavin wound the hose and dropped it on a hook beside the barn door. "I need to change. Be right back."

He jogged to the house, set his boots beside the front door, and disappeared inside. Jennie eyed the goats warily and walked toward them. They, being equally curious, approached the fence and bleated as though looking for a handout. "Sorry, kids, I don't have anything for you."

"Here." A woman appeared beside her and handed her

some carrots. "They love these."

Jennie took them. "Thanks. You must be Gavin's mom." The woman was about her own mother's age, maybe older. A leather clasp held most of her long dark brown hair in a tail at the back of her neck. The rest hung in wispy curls framing her face. With her ankle-length multicolored skirt and gauzy overblouse adorned with gold chains, she reminded Jennie of a gypsy.

"I'm Maddie, short for Madeline." She broke off the tops of the carrots she still held and waved them in front of the goats. "You're Jennie, right?"

Jennie nodded.

"From what I've read, you're a very brave young lady. I can see why Gavin admires you so much."

Jennie could feel her cheeks heat up. Not knowing what to say, she broke a carrot in half and handed a piece to each goat, then pulled her hand back when the animals nibbled at her fingers.

"I saw on the news that the police have arrested Frank Evans," Maddie went on. "Next thing you know he'll be getting out on bail. If you can afford to hire a lawyer you can get away with anything these days. The justice system makes no sense. I mean, what if he's guilty?"

Maddie looked at Jennie and laughed. "Oh, I'm sorry. I didn't mean to go on like that. It's a throwback to my political activist days. I see injustice and I go ballistic—at least that's what Gavin tells me. I used to carry protest signs and stage sit-ins during the Vietnam war. Then I married Steven. He's so straight he makes an arrow look warped. These days I write. Somehow it just isn't the same."

What if he is guilty? What if he does get out on bail? Mrs. Winslow's words seared Jennie's brain.

"Oh dear," Maddie said. "I'm boring you. I forget that kids today aren't all that interested in politics."

"What? Oh no, I'm sorry, I was just thinking about what

you said about Mr. Evans." Jennie shoved the information about Evans aside and tried to concentrate on what Gavin's mom was saying. "You're a writer?"

"Have been for quite some time. I write young adult novels. Mysteries."

"I love mysteries—read them all the time." Jennie frowned. "I don't remember seeing your name."

"I use a pseudonym. M.J. Curtis."

Jennie wished she could have said, *Oh wow, I've read all your books*, but couldn't. Truth is, she'd never heard of M.J. Curtis and had no idea what she'd written.

Maddie moved away from the fence, her warm smile still in place. "It's okay, Jennie. I'm not exactly on the bestseller list. Tell you what. I'll give you a copy of my newest release. You can read it and tell me what you think."

Maddie disappeared inside and an instant later Gavin appeared. He'd exchanged his denim overalls for a pair of black jeans and a white dress shirt, unbuttoned at the collar, shirtsleeves rolled up showing lean but muscular, suntanned arms. "Ready to go?"

"Yeah. Your mom's getting me a book."

Gavin rolled his eyes and gave her the old parents-can-be-so-embarrassing look.

Maddie emerged and glided toward them, presenting Jennie with an autographed copy of *Nice Day for a Murder*.

"Thanks."

"Um . . . Jennie, I'm not sure how to ask, so . . . well, I guess I just will. From all the things I've read about you, I think you'd make a wonderful character for a book and screenplay I'd like to do."

"Mo-om," Gavin groaned.

"No, really. I know you wanted to ask her yourself, but she's here and . . ." Maddie shrugged. "Anyway, Jennie. Think about it. Read my book, see if you like the style, and if you're interested, we'll do an interview."

Jennie was flattered. Who wouldn't be? "Why didn't you tell me?" Jennie asked Gavin as she backed the car around and headed down the drive.

"Didn't want to get your hopes up. Mom's not exactly famous, and to be honest I don't know if she can pull it off. I just didn't want you to go through all that for nothing."

"Hey, it's okay. Anyway, it doesn't really matter. What matters right now is finding out who might have beaten up Courtney. Have you seen her?"

Gavin nodded, his face grim. "I can't imagine anyone doing something like that." He glanced at Jennie and frowned. "Why are you still looking? The police arrested Evans."

Jennie explained her concerns about whether or not Frank was guilty.

"So you don't think he did it?"

"I don't know. It's all very confusing. Something tells me there's more to the case than what we're seeing. Which is why I want to talk to Tina again."

"Well, if Frank didn't do it, about the only thing that makes sense to me is that maybe a drug deal went sour or she got mixed up with some gang members." He slapped his knee. "This is crazy Jennie. I don't care what the police found on Courtney. She didn't do drugs."

"She might not have been taking drugs herself, but that doesn't mean she wasn't a supplier." Jennie considered telling him about Lisa and the diet pills but decided not to. "She had access to all kinds of things at the pharmacy." Jennie made a left on the main road and headed back toward the freeway.

"It's also possible," Jennie continued, "that someone was using Courtney to get to the drugs. Remember when we were looking for Courtney the night after she disappeared? Randy, the guy at the restaurant, and Tina both said Courtney was waiting for someone. I'd love to know who that person was."

"You think that might be the guy who assaulted Court-ney?"

"Who knows. I'd just like to come up with a list of likely suspects."

Gavin slid his hand back and forth across the shoulder strap of his seat belt. "You asked me if Courtney had any en-emies. I could only come up with one person who might hate her enough to want her dead. And that's Tracy Parouski."

"You can't be serious. Just because Courtney was chosen over her for rally squad? Gavin, you don't kill people for something like that."

"You wouldn't. It's not that important to you. But some kids would do anything to win."

Like Lisa, Jennie reminded herself. *Abusing her body so she could lose enough weight.*

Gavin shifted in his seat so that he faced Jennie more fully. "Remember that incident a few years ago in Texas where a girl's mother hired someone to kill a classmate so her daughter could become cheerleader?"

"Yes, but it was the girl's mother and she was crazy. . . ."

"Tracy really wants to be on the rally squad. Not only did she lose out to Courtney there, but—and this is where the plot thickens. . . ."

"Joel used to date Tracy," Jennie finished. "After you wrote the article on Courtney, Joel left Tracy in the dust. I see what you mean. I guess. Only from what I know of Joel, Tracy's the one who came out ahead on that one."

"What do you mean?"

Jennie told Gavin about Joel's making a pass at her that night on the bus. "He's some piece of work. Courtney's been missing for a few hours and he's already looking for someone else?"

"Maybe that's what makes him appealing."

Jennie grimaced. "Yeah, right."

They parked in a multi-level garage above the *Real Mother*

Goose Art Gallery downtown and headed east, past Nordstrom and into Pioneer Square. An hour and what felt like ten miles later, they headed into The Eatery to wait. Randy, still trying to keep his narrow swatch of pale yellow hair out of his eyes, took their orders and their money.

"If you're still looking for Tina, I wouldn't hold my breath. Folks around here are not too likely to talk to you. Not after what happened to Courtney."

"We had nothing to do with that," Jennie said. "In fact, that's why we're here. We're trying to find out who Courtney was meeting that night."

He set two large glasses of kiwi-strawberry juice and a thick crust pepperoni pizza on the counter. "I can tell you that."

Jennie's head jerked up. "You can?"

"Yeah. Maybe." Randy tipped his head forward and back, flinging his tail temporarily out of the way. "After Tina and Courtney left that night, a big guy came in—about six foot, two hundred and fifty pounds. He looked around and left."

A picture of Joel flashed through her mind. "Why didn't you tell us before?"

"I didn't make the connection before."

"And you didn't tell the police?"

"You kidding?" He wiped the counter with a rag and tossed it into a basin. "I don't talk to the cops unless I have to. Besides, they arrested her old man so I figure it doesn't matter."

"This guy," Gavin said, "do you remember anything else about him, other than he was big? Hair color, eyes?"

Randy scrunched up his face, then shook his head. "Like I said, he just came in and out. I wouldn't have even connected him with her except, you know, when something bad happens you start to remember things."

"Do you remember anything else?"

"I'll let you know."

They thanked him for the information and found an empty table near the entrance so they'd be able to see Tina if she came in or walked by.

"You thinking what I'm thinking?" Gavin peeled the paper from his straw and dropped it into his drink.

"That it might have been Joel?"

Gavin nodded. "Only that doesn't make a lot of sense. If he wanted to talk to Courtney, why didn't he do it when he took her home? They'd gone out that night."

"Yeah, unless he was helping her run away. Maybe he dropped her off and came back."

"Or maybe it was someone else." Gavin pulled in half the drink in two gulps. "In case you hadn't noticed, there are a lot of guys built like trees in this town. Could be someone from the college."

"It could be anyone."

The restaurant door swung open and Tina backed in. Gavin jumped up to hold it for her.

"I got it," she said. "Thanks anyway."

She was still wearing the leather jacket, but instead of the yellow tank top and jeans, she wore a red denim miniskirt and red shirt that tied in the front. She turned to face Jennie and crutch-walked toward her. "I hear you wanted to see me."

Jennie smiled and pulled out the chair beside her. "I am so glad you decided to come. We're trying to piece together what happened to Courtney."

"First, you gotta know—she wasn't on no drugs. I don't care what the cops found."

"I agree," Gavin said. "If Courtney had drugs, somebody planted them on her."

"You got that right." A tray appeared in front of Tina and she tore away at the wrapping and bit into the burger.

"When we talked before, you said Courtney took care of you. What did you mean?" Jennie asked.

Tina stopped chewing and swallowed. Her ebony gaze

shifted from Jennie to Gavin and back again. "I guess it won't hurt to tell you now, but it probably don't have nothin' to do with what happened to her."

Tina set her hamburger down and took a deep breath. "I got diabetes. Courtney says that's why I got this sore on my foot. She kep' saying, 'Tina, you got to see a doctor.' Humph—ain't no way I'd do that—they ask too many questions. Anyway, she started bringing me stuff—bandages, antibiotics—stuff to keep me from gettin' gan'grene. She brought me syringes and insulin. Now I don't know what I'm gonna do."

Not the bad stuff. Lisa had said. "How many other kids had Courtney helped?" Jennie wondered aloud.

Tina shrugged, picking a piece of lettuce out of a salad Randy had given her. "She never told me, an' I never asked."

"What about the guy she was supposed to meet?" Gavin adjusted his glasses. "Randy said he thought it might have been the guy he saw come in the night before we talked to you. Big guy."

Tina nodded. "Yeah. I know who he means. When you guys came in that night after Courtney disappeared, you wanted to know who he was. I didn't want to tell you. He and his friends was handin' out the same flyer on Courtney as you. I thought maybe you were workin' together. Courtney was scared of him. She told me she couldn't give him what he wanted."

Joel. The name burned in Jennie's mind. "Did he have dark hair and brown eyes?"

Tina frowned and shook her head. "Nope. This guy had light hair. Name started with a 'B'."

Jennie sucked in her breath. No, it couldn't be. Not . . . She must have said his name out loud because Tina plunked her glass on the table.

"Brad. Yeah. That's it, girl. His name was Brad."

15

"Are you sure?" A slow burn started in the pit of Jennie's stomach and spread outward. She stared at her hands in disbelief. Why? Why would Brad meet Courtney after her date with Joel? Why would he meet her at all?

"Do you have a picture of him?" Tina asked. "I'd know him if I saw him."

Jennie rummaged through her bag. She did have some snapshots in her wallet but couldn't remember if Brad was in any of them. Jennie flipped through the plastic-cased photos. Lisa and her in a photo booth. Kurt and Nick sticking out their tongues at the camera. Mom and Michael. Dad. There. Lisa and Brad in another photo booth. She freed the picture from its plastic protector and handed it to Tina.

It took the girl all of two seconds to make a positive ID.

A few minutes later, Jennie murmured a thank you to Tina as she and Gavin left the restaurant.

"Whew," Gavin whistled once they were out on the sidewalk. "I never expected that. Do you think Brad and Courtney were seeing each other on the side?"

"All I know is that Brad Lewis has a lot of explaining to do."

Jennie dropped Gavin back at his house then headed home. The clock on the dash read 9:05. When she reached the freeway, Jennie considered driving over to the hospital to see her cousin.

111

She needed to talk to Lisa about Brad.

Maybe you'd better not, McGrady, she mused. *Lisa's pretty fragile right now. If Brad had been secretly seeing Courtney, the news would break her heart and maybe set her back.*

The best course of action, Jennie decided, was to talk to Brad before saying anything to Lisa. After all, Brad may have had a perfectly good reason for meeting Courtney.

Nick, Hannah, and Bernie attacked her the moment she walked in the door. Mom asked her to bathe the kids and get them ready for bed so she could get some work done for a client. Almost glad for the distraction, Jennie set her talk with Brad on hold.

"So," Jennie grinned at her two charges. "You two need a bath, huh? Should I take you out in the backyard and hose you down?"

"Jennie," Mom warned. "Don't get them all riled up. They're supposed to be settling down for the night."

"Slave driver," Jennie teased. "Well, you guys heard her. Who's first?"

"Me! Me!" they yelled in unison. Jennie picked them both up around the waist and carried them like sacks of flour up the stairs and into the bathroom. An hour later, she quietly closed the bedroom door and went in search of Mom. Jennie found her in the study, still working on the computer.

"You planning on making this an all-nighter?" Jennie asked, planting a light kiss on Mom's cheek.

Mom glanced at her watch. "No, another hour or so should do it. Thanks for your help, sweetie."

"No problem." Jennie started to leave, then swung around. "Mom?"

"Hmmm."

"We haven't gotten a chance to talk about Frank's arrest. You were there when the police picked him up at the hospital, weren't you?"

"Yes." Mom closed her eyes for a moment. "But if you

don't mind, I'd rather not talk about it right now."

"I just wondered how you felt about it, that's all."

"Jennie," Mom peered at her as if trying to decide whether or not to answer. "It doesn't change anything. Frank had already told me about his wife's murder and the trial. The jury found him innocent."

Not exactly innocent. They acquitted him for insufficient evidence. There's a difference. Jennie thought about arguing the point, but decided against it.

"I guess I can understand why the police might suspect him, though," Mom went on.

"But you think he's innocent?"

"Innocent?" Mom bit her bottom lip as though weighing her words, then finally said, "Yes, I do."

Jennie nodded. "Hmmm."

"I hope you don't plan on trying to change my mind." Mom brushed her bangs aside. Her eyes looked tired.

"No. At least not right now. I just wondered." Jennie considered asking her if she still planned to date Frank, then decided not to. "I'll be in my bedroom."

Mom said good-night, blew Jennie a kiss, and turned back to the computer screen.

Once in her room, Jennie took a pad and pen from her desk drawer and tucked her long slender form into a window seat. After fluffing several cushions behind her she leaned back and let her mind drift over the people and events of the last few days.

A few minutes later, with the long side of the paper at the top, she wrote "Suspects in the Courtney Evans Case." She then drew a horizontal line and four vertical lines. Between each line she wrote Suspects/Enemies, Relationship, Motive, Means, and Opportunity.

Frank Evans' name topped the list. Even after her talk with Gram, Jennie still considered him a suspect. The evidence against him was too strong to discount. Under relationship, she wrote, "Father." Motive? "Caught Courtney stealing drugs from the pharmacy."

Means? "Fists, maybe a blunt instrument of some sort." Jennie shuddered at the thought of it. *Come on, McGrady. You're losing your objectivity.* Jennie took a deep breath and went on.

Opportunity? That was the hard one. Frank had left their house only half an hour before Courtney's call asking Jennie to meet her. He had opportunity only if he knew exactly where to find her. *Or,* Jennie reminded herself, *if he'd had her hidden and forced Courtney to make the call.* But why?

Remembering her conversation with Gram, she wrote, "To establish an alibi."

Jennie drew a line under the entry she'd just made, then wrote, "Tracy." Definitely an enemy. Motive? *Jealousy—on two counts—Joel and cheerleading.* Means? *Tracy couldn't have beaten Courtney like that—at least not alone.* Jennie tapped her pen against the paper. *But she could have hired someone.* Beside Tracy's name she wrote "Hit man" and followed it with a large question mark.

She listed Brad next. Jennie wondered again about his relationship to Courtney. Before talking to Tina she'd have guessed they were just friends.

Jennie had a hard time picturing him as a cold-blooded killer. And that's what they were dealing with. Courtney may have come out of that dumpster alive, but someone obviously wanted her dead.

Unable to answer the questions on Brad, Jennie decided to fill them in after she talked to him and Lisa.

She thought about listing Tina. Courtney's diabetic friend couldn't have done it and certainly didn't seem to have a motive. *But...*what if Tina's gang member friends had? What if Courtney had been supplying them with drugs, then cut them off? A definite possibility. Under names, Jennie wrote "Drug Users/ Dealers." She had no problem defining motive, means, and opportunity. They had plenty.

Jennie was about to set her chart aside for the night when another possibility came to her. Gavin Winslow. She frowned and shook her head, discounting it at first. *Think about it, McGrady*, she told herself. *He says he's Courtney's friend. She dumps him for Joel. He's hurt and angry.* "He's not all that strong," Jennie argued against her own logic. Could he have beat Courtney up and tossed her body into a dumpster? *Maybe.*

The phone rang before Jennie could pursue the thought any further.

"It's me, Lisa," a soft voice whispered. "I need to talk to you. Can you come over?"

"Now?"

"Tomorrow, as soon as you can get here."

"Can't you tell me over the phone?" Jennie asked.

Silence.

"Lisa? Are you still there?"

"I . . . I'm sorry I got so upset with you this morning. I was wrong to take those diet pills. I've been wrong about a lot of things lately."

She waited for Lisa to go on. When she didn't, Jennie asked, "Do you want me to come now?"

"Yes, but you can't. Mom would have a fit. She's upset because I went for a drive with Brad after dinner. I'm not even supposed to be calling you."

"Your mom? Brad? You're at home?"

"Didn't your mom tell you?"

"Apparently not." Jennie considered being upset with Mom then cancelled the thought. Some things just weren't worth fighting over. "So what's going on?"

"The doctor discharged me this afternoon. Said I could go if I promised to behave myself. I will. Believe me, I have no intention of landing back in the hospital."

Jennie wanted to ask her about Brad, but didn't. Lisa

needed her rest. Tomorrow would be soon enough.

———

The next morning Jennie packed up Nick, Hannah, and Bernie and headed for Lisa's. She hadn't wanted to bring them, but it was either that or baby-sit at the house while Mom worked.

When Jennie drove up, Kate was turning off the sprinklers in the front yard. "Hi," she called as they piled out of the car. Kate met them halfway up the walk and gave each a hug, then bent down to pet Bernie.

"Where's Kurt?" Nick asked.

"In the backyard, I think."

"C'mon Hannah. Let's go play." Nick grabbed Hannah's hand and ran through the wet grass and disappeared around the corner of the house.

Kate put an arm around Jennie's shoulder. "I have some good news for you—at least I think it will be. Kurt's been begging me to take him swimming all week so Gram and I thought this would be a good day for it."

Jennie couldn't help but smile at her aunt's enthusiasm. Sometimes Kate went on like a wind-up toy with a battery that keeps going . . . and going.

"We'll take the kids out to Blue Lake for a picnic," Kate went on. "You and Lisa can come if you want, but I think Lisa would just as soon spend some time with you alone. She's upstairs if you want to talk to her about it."

"Thanks." Jennie gave her aunt another hug. "Um, Aunt Kate? Is Lisa going to be okay?"

Concern shaded Kate's dark blue eyes. "I hope so. She seemed in good spirits yesterday afternoon, but after being with Brad last night she looked . . . I don't know. Kind of sullen." Kate frowned. "Maybe she was just tired. Anyway, she's excited about spending the day with you." Kate squeezed Jennie's shoulder. "You watch out for her, okay?

Make sure she doesn't overdo it."

"Sure—at least I'll try." Jennie glanced toward the house. "Where's Gram? I want to talk to her before you go."

"You just missed her. She went to run a few errands and pick up some groceries for our picnic. Said she'd meet me out at the park around noon. If it's really important I can have her call you from the lake."

"No, that's okay. I'll talk to her later." Jennie was disappointed. She'd hoped to tell Gram about her chart of suspects. Jennie also wanted Gram's input before broaching the subject of Brad and Courtney with Lisa.

"Talk to who?" Lisa asked as she came down the front steps to join them. Her cheeks had filled out and although she was still too thin, she'd lost that haunting, hungry look.

"Gram," Jennie answered, then changed the subject. "So what do you want to do today?"

Lisa, as Kate predicted, didn't want to go to the lake. "I'd like to stay here for a while. And maybe this afternoon we could go to the school and watch football practice." Lisa gave Jennie a please-go-along-with-me look.

"Staying here is fine, Lisa," Kate said. "Only I'm not sure I want you going over to the school. Your short date with Brad last night wore you out."

Lisa flinched. "I wasn't tired. We . . ." Lisa hesitated and sighed. "We had a minor disagreement, that's all. I feel great this morning and I promise . . . swear on a stack of Bibles, that I won't overdo it."

Kate wrapped her arms around Lisa. "It's not that I don't want you to have fun, honey. I just want you safe and healthy."

Lisa returned the hug. "I know, Mom. I want to get well too."

"All right." Kate drew back. "But remember what the doctor said. And don't forget to eat."

The moment everyone left, Lisa dragged Jennie through

the house and into the kitchen. After fixing two glasses of lemonade, they continued out to the backyard to an enormous wooden deck. Though the house was located in a residential area, their two-acre lot gave the appearance of a country setting. The landscaping Aunt Kate and Uncle Kevin had done afforded lots of privacy.

Lisa and Jennie settled onto padded redwood chairs under arbors of grape and wisteria and surrounded by containers overflowing with impatiens, begonias, lobelia, and just about every other flower known to humankind. It seemed like the kind of place to be discussing love and peace and happiness. Certainly not the near murder of a classmate.

Jennie sipped at her juice wondering how to start. A lot of questions came to mind, like, *How well do you know Brad Lewis? Did you know he met Courtney downtown the night she supposedly ran away? No, McGrady. You need to be more subtle.*

"Something's wrong with Brad," Lisa said.

Then again, maybe not. Jennie set her glass on the redwood table beside her. "What do you mean?"

"I noticed it after he got back from football camp. I'm worried, Jennie. He's acting different. I tried to talk to him about it last night and he got mad at me. I mean really mad."

"Lisa . . ." Jennie hesitated, not certain as to how to proceed. "Um . . . did he hit you?"

Lisa bit her lip and stared at her glass as tears filled her sea green eyes.

16

"He didn't mean to. He apologized right after." Lisa went into the house and came back a few seconds later, clutching a tissue in her hand.

Jennie swallowed hard to stem the rising anger. "You shouldn't be making excuses for him. Has he ever hit you before?"

"No, of course not. I'd have told you."

"What happened?"

"We'd gone for a drive and he wanted to go up to Council Crest to watch the lights and . . . you know."

Jennie nodded. "Let me guess. He wanted more than kisses and you said no. He got mad."

Lisa took a deep, shuddering breath. "I was scared, Jen. He's never acted like that before. I got out of the car and he came after me. He yelled at me and kept pushing me back. I fell down and started crying. I guess that shook him up, because he stopped and apologized. After that he was really nice."

"Did you break up with him?"

"No." Lisa frowned. "Not yet. I like him a lot—at least I did." Lisa tipped her head back against the chair and closed her eyes. "Oh, Jen, I don't know what to do."

"Do you think he might be doing drugs?" Jennie asked, remembering the meeting he'd had with Courtney.

Lisa looked up, startled. "No . . . I mean, he'd never do that. The coach would kick him off the team in a second. Besides, he's a total health nut. Why would you even ask? I mean . . . I know a lot of kids use—even some of the athletes, but not Brad."

Here's your chance, McGrady. Jennie inhaled a deep breath and blew it out her mouth, then told Lisa the entire story.

When Jennie finished, Lisa loosened her grip on the chair. "You think Brad beat her up?"

"I think we need to talk to him."

Lisa nodded and stared straight ahead. "I can see why you asked about the drugs. I guess it's either that or he was seeing her on the side. I'm not sure which hurts worse."

"I was going to call him this morning," Jennie said, "and arrange a meeting. You want to be there when I talk to him?"

"Definitely." Lisa glanced at her watch. "He's working right now. But he should be home for lunch in about twenty minutes, then he'll be at football practice for the rest of the afternoon. If we head over to his house now, maybe we can catch him before he leaves again."

Jennie and Lisa had been waiting at the curb in front of Brad's house for only a few minutes when a battered white pickup with a *Lewis Landscaping* logo pulled into the driveway. The girls got out of the car and started toward it.

Brad jumped out of the truck and smiled when he saw them. "Hi." His smile melted into a question. "What are you guys doing here? I mean, it's not that I'm not glad to see you or anything, but this isn't a very good time. I have to shower and eat and get to practice."

He pulled off a soiled sleeveless denim shirt and used it to wipe perspiration from his forehead. It left a streak of dirt an inch wide on his angular cheek.

"We'd like to ask you a few questions about Courtney,"

Lisa began. "It shouldn't take very long."

He tossed the shirt into the back of the truck. "Look, I don't know anything about Courtney or about what happened to her. And I don't have time to play detective. I'll talk to you later, okay?"

He started to walk away and Lisa stepped in front of him, her green eyes flashing. "No, it's really not okay. One of the homeless kids Jennie talked to said you met Courtney downtown the night she supposedly ran away. That was the same night you came to see me at the hospital with Courtney and Joel. What I want to know is why you were meeting her so late. If you had things to say to each other, why didn't you say them earlier?"

Brad shook his head and pushed past Lisa. "I don't know what you're talking about. Whoever told you that was wrong. I haven't seen Courtney since she and Joel dropped me off Wednesday night. As far as I know she ran away." He turned to Jennie. "You heard what Cassie said about Courtney's old man."

"Don't lie to me, Brad." Lisa balled her hands into fists and folded her arms.

Brad turned around. "I told you—"

"I haven't said anything to the police yet," Jennie interrupted. "I wanted to hear your side of the story first."

Brad hesitated, then came back toward them. Hostility glinted in his steel blue eyes. "Okay, I did talk to Courtney that night, but I didn't have anything to do with her getting beat up."

"Why did you meet her?" Jennie asked.

"She called me. She wanted to talk to me about Joel." Brad turned to Lisa. "You have to believe that, Lis. Courtney was goin' with Joel. Besides, she's not my type. And I didn't do anything to hurt her."

"You hit Lisa last night," Jennie said. "Why should we believe you didn't beat up Courtney?"

"You told her?" Brad glowered at Lisa. He clenched his fist and took a step toward her.

Lisa straightened to her full five feet, two inches. "Go ahead. Hit me. Make my day."

Jennie winced. Her cousin was definitely improving. "I'd think twice about doing anything like that, Brad. Unless you'd like to spend the afternoon at the police station."

Brad glanced nervously from Lisa to Jennie and lowered his arm. "I wasn't going to hit anybody."

"What did you and Courtney talk about?" Lisa asked.

"I told you. She wanted to talk to me about Joel."

"What about him?" Jennie pressed.

"Okay, I promised I wouldn't tell anyone, but . . . I guess after all that's happened it doesn't really matter. She and Joel hadn't been getting along too good and she wanted some advice. I told her that things had been kind of tough for all us guys lately. Coach Haskell's been coming down on us real hard." Brad shifted from one foot to the other. "Anyway, Lis, you don't have to worry. We're still goin' together—aren't we?"

Lisa took a deep breath and shook her head. "I don't know, Brad. I honestly don't know."

"Look, I swear, I didn't have anything to do with what happened to Courtney. I didn't beat her up. You . . . you're not going to tell the police about that meeting, are you?"

"If you're innocent, you don't have anything to worry about," Jennie answered.

As Jennie turned to head back to the car, Brad grabbed her arm and spun her around. "There's more to it than that. If Coach Haskell finds out, he'll kick me off the team."

"What do you want us to do, Brad, forget it?" Jennie pulled her arm out of his grasp.

"All I'm saying is that the police have already arrested Frank Evans. Telling them about my meeting with Courtney wouldn't make any difference to their case, and it could ruin me."

"I'll think about it," Jennie said, backing away from him. "In the meantime, you'd better hustle or you'll be late for practice."

"Are you going to tell the police about Brad?" Lisa asked as they pulled away from the curb.

"Yeah, but first I want to talk to Joel. According to Brad, Joel and Courtney weren't getting along. Do you think he's telling the truth?"

"I wish I could say yes, but I don't know. Courtney did seem preoccupied that night, but I didn't get the impression that she was mad at Joel or anything." Lisa leaned her head against the seat and frowned. "Do you think maybe Joel beat her up?"

Jennie shrugged.

"We've known Joel and Brad for a long time, Jen. They're Christians. I just can't imagine either of them hurting Courtney like that."

"I know. But somebody sure did, and I'd really like to find out who."

"Why are you so sure it isn't her dad?"

"I'm not. I just can't get over the feeling that something else is going on. Gram thinks so too. It may be nothing, but I feel like I have to keep digging."

Jennie and Lisa stopped for hamburgers before going to football practice. Lisa protested, but Jennie insisted she eat. By the time they got to the school, Coach Haskell had half the team charging dummies and the other half trying to dance through a bunch of old tires—to condition themselves and improve their footwork, she'd been told.

Several kids were sitting in the bleachers as Jennie and Lisa approached. Tracy and her best friend, Corky, sat at the top and ignored Lisa's greeting. "She makes me so mad," Lisa muttered. "DeeDee gave Tracy Courtney's spot on the rally squad and Allison says she's been a total snob ever since."

Jennie leaned toward her cousin and whispered, "I've got her on my suspect list."

"Really?" Lisa seemed pleased by the prospect.

"Gavin suggested it. Said she'd do anything to get on the rally squad. By hiring some thug to get rid of Courtney, a spot opens up and she gets revenge at the same time."

"I take it you plan on questioning her too."

"You got it."

Cassie Nielsen, who was sitting near Gavin, greeted them as they approached. Faded denim cutoffs and a white T-shirt and cap showed off a healthy-looking tan. "Brad told us you'd gotten out of the hospital, Lisa. How are you doing?"

"Good," Lisa said. "I'm getting stronger all the time."

"Super." Cassie smiled, then turned serious. Her brown eyes widened in concern. "Listen, when the doctor says you're ready, you'll have to come over to the house. My dad will help us get you on a fantastic fitness program. He has this computer software that creates a plan exactly right for your age and body type. You don't have to diet to be in great shape. It's all got to do with attitude. Like Dad says, 'Treat your body like a temple and it'll be a great place to live.' "

Lisa sat down next to Cassie, and Jennie went up a couple of rows to where Gavin was fiddling with the lens on his camera.

"I thought you might show up here." He lowered the camera and looked at her with a smile.

"Lisa and I stopped to talk to Brad," Jennie explained as she sat on the bleacher in front of him.

His eyebrows shot up. "Yeah? What did old Brad have to say for himself?"

Jennie repeated their conversation. "So," she said when she'd finished, "I guess the next step is to find out if Joel and Courtney were having some problems."

Cassie twisted around and lifted a tan muscular leg over to straddle the bench. "Why do you want to know about Joel and Courtney?"

Jennie told her about Tina seeing Brad with Courtney and reiterated their conversation with Brad.

"I don't know why Brad would say something like that." Cassie sighed. "I mean . . . Joel and Courtney were getting along great. Not like they were thinking of getting married or anything, but they're friends—good friends."

She sighed again and ran a hand through her short brown hair. "Wow. Brad was seeing Courtney? That surprises me." She switched her gaze from Jennie to Lisa. "You must be totally bummed out."

"I'm numb." Lisa straightened and tucked strands of auburn ringlets behind her ear.

"Yeah. I can understand that." Cassie shook her head, apparently still having trouble assimilating the information. She looked up suddenly, light dawning in her chocolate eyes. "Wait a minute." She pointed a finger at Jennie. "You think Brad or Joel had something to do with Courtney's getting beat up, don't you?"

"The thought had occurred to me."

"Well, you can forget that," Cassie erupted. "I know these guys. If they were into anything even remotely out of line, I'd know about it."

Cassie's anger fizzled. "There's something you should know before you go around making accusations. Joel and Brad wouldn't do anything to jeopardize the team. They live, breathe, eat, and sleep sports. In fact, now that I think about it, maybe Courtney did want to talk to Brad about Joel. Maybe she was upset about the amount of time Joel spends working out and stuff."

"You really think so?" Lisa asked.

"Yeah, I bet that's it," Cassie agreed. "Besides, Lisa, Brad's always talking about you. When you were in the hospital he about went crazy with worry." Obviously pleased with her conclusion, she continued, "Whatever happened to Courtney couldn't have had anything to do with Brad or Joel."

Jennie wound her long ponytail around her hand. "Cassie? I was just wondering. You seemed to know Courtney pretty well. Was she into drugs?"

Cassie glanced around, then whispered, "I'm not a narc, but since the police already found stuff on her, I guess I can tell you. When Joel first started dating her, I'm sure she was clean. Then she started having more and more trouble with her dad. I can't say for sure . . . I mean, she never took anything around me or Joel but I wasn't surprised when the cops found it. With her dad owning the pharmacy and everything, it would be pretty easy for her to get whatever she wanted."

Jennie agreed.

On the field, the guys finished their workouts and were starting their scrimmage. They'd separated into two groups.

"They're looking good," Gavin said. "Even bigger and stronger than last year."

Jennie winced as number 47 tackled number 23 and about a dozen others piled on top. Talk about overkill. Cassie had made another good observation, Jennie decided. Joel and Brad loved sports.

Jennie glanced back at Tracy. The girls were giggling and didn't seem particularly interested in what was happening on the field. A good time to ask a few questions. "Be back in a minute," Jennie said to whoever might have been listening.

By the time she'd come within twenty feet of them, Tracy and Corky had stopped talking. They watched her approach and Jennie tried to ignore their frosty glares.

"What do you want, McGrady?" Tracy asked.

"Bet she's trying to play detective again," Corky said.

"Not a bad guess, Corky—except for the playing part. Believe me, this is no game."

Tracy rolled her eyes in disgust. "Get real, Jennie. The cops have already solved the case, so why don't you go home?"

Keep your cool, McGrady, Jennie told herself. *Don't let them get to you.* "I'm surprised at your attitude, Tracy. Remember what the Bible says about loving your neighbor? I don't see a lot of love coming from you two." Jennie usually didn't resort to preaching. Probably because she hated being preached at. But if anyone needed a sermon on love, these two did.

Jennie stood next to Tracy. She thought about sitting down, but decided not to. She struck a much more commanding pose by standing. In an attempt to look relaxed, Jennie set one foot a rung higher than the other and rested her arm on her bent leg. "What if I told you the police have the wrong person and with more evidence coming in, they're looking at other possibilities?"

"Oh yeah," Tracy sneered. "And like you'd know."

"What I know, Tracy Parouski, is that you are a prime suspect." Jennie didn't bother telling Tracy that she had drawn up the suspect list, not the police.

Tracy stiffened. *Good going, McGrady. You have her attention.* "I happen to know," Jennie continued, "that you had a pretty strong motive for wanting Courtney out of the way."

"That—that's crazy."

"Is it?" Jennie raised her eyebrows. *So far so good.* "My sources tell me you hated Courtney for taking Joel away from you. To make matters even worse, she was chosen over you for rally squad. Sounds like motive to me." Jennie moved what she hoped was a steady gaze from Tracy to Corky. "Don't you think so, Corky?"

Corky stared at Tracy, her mouth open. "You didn't . . ."

Tracy made an indignant huffing sound. "Of course not."

"Give me one good reason why I should believe you. You're the only one around here who would benefit with

Courtney out of the picture. And you certainly don't seem to be shedding any tears."

"I feel bad about what happened to Courtney," Tracy admitted. "But hey, she was doing drugs—she got what she deserved. I'm not going to pretend I feel bad about replacing her on rally. I don't. In fact, I'm thrilled. And as far as Joel's concerned, she can have him."

Now it was Jennie's turn to be surprised. "Really? I was under the impression you liked him."

"I did, at first. Who wouldn't? He's cute and built like a rock." Tracy looked out on the field. "But he's mean. When things don't go his way, he . . ."

An idea began to form in Jennie's mind. Why hadn't she thought of it before? Jennie watched the players with renewed interest. What was it Gavin had said? *They're bigger and stronger than ever.* Brad and Joel were the biggest guys on the team. In less than a year, they'd gone from being mediocre players to being pro material. They were dedicated to sports all right. Maybe too dedicated.

Excitement pumped through Jennie's veins like a raging river. She was finally on to something.

17

"Steroids," she murmured under her breath. *Joel and Brad were using steroids.*

"What did you say?" Tracy asked, looking from Jennie to the field of players.

"Nothing." She straightened and turned to go. "Thanks, Tracy. You've been a great help."

Jennie hurried back to where Gavin, Cassie, and Lisa were sitting, anxious to break the news. *Wait a minute, McGrady,* she stopped. *You can't say anything—not yet. You have no proof. An accusation like that could ruin the team and it might not be true. Besides, hadn't Cassie insisted that if the guys were into drugs she'd know?* Maybe she did know.

No. Wait. You're jumping to conclusions. Jennie needed to get away—to think things through. Steroids. That could explain Brad's clandestine meeting with Courtney. Was she supplying them? Had she cut them off? Had her dad found out about it?

The questions filled her mind faster than she could process them. Jennie needed to talk to Frank Evans and . . . the note Courtney had written and slipped to Jennie. It had the name of a drug on it. *Dianabol.* Had that been a clue?

"Well," Gavin asked when she approached. "Did she do it?"

"What?"

"Tracy. You just talked to her. What did you find out?"

Jennie shrugged her shoulders. "Not much. I hate to break this up, guys, but I've got to go. Lisa? Are you ready?"

Jennie had expected an argument, but Lisa said, "Sure," and followed Jennie down the bleachers.

"Are you okay?" Jennie asked, waiting at the bottom of the risers for Lisa to catch up.

"Yeah, I'm kind of tired."

"Maybe we shouldn't have come out here. You're not going to pass out on me again, are you?"

"No, really. I'm fine. I just need to rest for a while."

———

Jennie dropped Lisa off at her house at a few minutes before two, fixed her a snack, then headed for the library. She had desperately wanted to talk to Lisa about her suspicions, but was afraid Lisa would want to go with her. Jennie had no intention of being responsible for another relapse.

Once inside, she headed for a pay phone and called her mother to report in. Mom seemed pleased with Jennie's location. She might have had another reaction had she known what Jennie had gone there for.

"Mom," Jennie said, suddenly remembering another piece of the bizarre puzzle. "When you first started doing Frank's books he said something about a discrepancy in them. Did you ever find out what that was?"

Mom hesitated. "I'm not sure. After the police found drugs on Courtney, Frank was afraid she might have taken some of the narcotics and sold them. We checked the inventory against the billings from the pharmaceutical companies and those drugs were all accounted for. Why are you asking?"

"You might want to try some of the other stuff—like insulin, diet pills, and—steroids."

"Now, how would you know . . . Jennie, you're not . . ."

"Relax, Mom. I'm not in any trouble—or danger. I was

130

just talking to some of the kids. One of the street kids said Courtney had been giving her insulin. I'm just guessing on the others."

Mom sighed. "You're sure you're at the library?"

That annoyed her. "Yes," she said a little more harshly than necessary. "Do you want me to have the librarian call you to verify it?"

"I'm sorry, Jennie. I believe you. It's just . . . well, after what happened to Courtney."

"I'm fine, mom. Don't be such a worry wart. You know what Jesus said about not being anxious." Jennie winced at her own words. Quoting scripture twice in one day. You'd think she was headed for seminary instead of law school.

"He didn't have a daughter like you."

"I'm sorry I'm such a disappointment. I gotta go. Bye." Jennie hung up before her mom could say anything more.

For the next hour Jennie used computers to hunt down articles, books, and drug resources that might help her strengthen her theory.

"Hi." A familiar leather bag appeared next to a pile of books she'd pulled from the shelves.

Jennie almost jumped off her chair. "Gavin. What are you doing here? Did you follow me?"

"On my bike? You kidding?" He slid onto the chair next to hers. "I called your house. Your mom told me where you were. She's not disappointed."

"What?"

"Your Mom . . . she said, 'Tell Jennie I'm not disappointed.' Said you'd know what she meant."

"Oh." The corners of her mouth lifted in a smile. "I knew that."

"Whatever." He gave her a look that questioned her sanity, then nodded at her research project. "In case you hadn't noticed, school doesn't start until September."

"This isn't about school." She frowned. "It's about Courtney."

"Why am I not surprised? I knew you had something cooking when you left the school in such a hurry. Frankly, I'm hurt you didn't tell me. What is it?" His gaze roamed over the papers and books scattered over the table's surface.

"Just a hunch."

Gavin let out a low whistle. "Steroids? Jennie, I'm impressed. I can see the headlines now. *Strong Team Performance Due to Steroids—Not Prayer.*

"Gavin, stop it. I don't know anything for sure."

"What clued you in?"

"Mostly the changes in Brad and Joel and your comment about how much better the team has been doing. And this . . ." Jennie pulled a small piece of paper from under her note pad, then opened one of the large reference books to a place she'd marked.

"This is the note Courtney wrote to me. I've been so tuned in to to what she'd written I didn't pay that much attention to what she'd written the note on. I just figured since her dad was a pharmacist they had a lot of these scratch pads lying around. Anyway, I got to thinking maybe she used this particular pad for a reason."

"To let you know she was not only in trouble, but the kind of trouble she was in."

"Right. Dianabol is an anabolic steroid."

"Accusing the guys of taking 'roids is heavy stuff, McGrady. You telling the cops?"

"Not yet. I want to talk to Coach Haskell first. I could still be wrong about this, and if word leaked out it could hurt a lot of people."

"You think Haskell might be involved?"

Jennie gazed into Gavin's hazel eyes. His concern matched hers. "I don't know. I hope I'm wrong about this."

"Yeah. I know what you mean. So when are you planning on talking to the coach?"

Jennie glanced at her watch. "How long do the guys practice?"

"Until about four." Gavin removed his glasses and cleaned them on his shirttail. "I think I should go with you." He grasped the wire frames and set them back on his face.

"You look worried."

"I am—about you."

"Me?"

"Think about it, Jennie. Someone beat up Courtney. We don't know why. We've speculated that she may have cut off someone's drug supply, but she could have been beaten for something else—maybe threatening to expose the steroid users. If the police found out about it, it would mean the end of Trinity's football team. It could even mean the end of the sports program. Brad and Joel's careers would be ruined. There are a lot of people who wouldn't want that to happen. Joel's dad and Coach Haskell for sure. I could name others."

"Which means my suspect list isn't nearly long enough."

"Which means if you go on asking questions or even hint that you suspect the guys are using steroids, you could be next."

Jennie gathered up her papers and stuffed them into her black leather backpack.

Walking out of the library was like walking into a sauna. The clear, comfortably warm day had turned into a slightly overcast steam bath. They left Gavin's bike locked in the bike rack and drove back to the school. The guys were still scrimmaging.

Cassie occupied the space she had earlier and waved when she saw them. "Where's Lisa?" she called. "She okay?"

"She's taking a nap." Jennie trudged up the bleachers for the second time that day and plopped down beside Cassie. The climb had drained her. "How can they play so long in this heat? The sweat's dripping off me and we just walked in from the parking lot." Jennie used her arm to wipe the moisture from her forehead.

"It was great until about half an hour ago. Clouds moved in." Cassie removed her cap and peered at the gray sky. "We'll probably have a thunderstorm tonight."

Jennie nodded. She didn't want to talk about the weather. "Cassie? Do you know anything about steroids?"

Gavin winced and gave her a didn't-you-hear-a-word-I-said? look.

Cassie stared straight ahead, her body rigid as a marble statue. "Yeah. Some. I know it's bad stuff." Cassie turned slightly to face Jennie. "Why do you want to know?"

Jennie swallowed hard, wondering how much to say. "I think Courtney may have been supplying it to some of the guys on the team."

"You mean like Brad?"

And Joel, Jennie thought but didn't say it. "Maybe. Brad did meet Courtney the night she disappeared." Jennie pulled the note Courtney had written from her pocket. "I got to wondering about this drug so I looked it up."

"Coach," one of the players on the field yelled. "You'd better get over here quick. We got a man down."

The three spectators jumped to their feet at the same time. Jennie stuffed the note into the front pocket of her jeans and tried to focus on the guy lying spread-eagle on the grass.

Cassie gasped. "It's Joel. Something's wrong with Joel." She was at the bottom of the bleachers by the time she got the last word out. Jennie and Gavin followed. Jennie sprinted ahead and reached the players first, breaking through the huddle to get to Joel.

Coach Haskell hunkered down beside him, apparently checking for a pulse. "What happened here? I didn't see him get hit."

"He didn't," Brad offered. "He was staggering around

134

like he couldn't get his breath. Then he grabbed his gut and went down."

"One of you guys better call 9–1–1. I'm not getting a pulse."

18

"Joel!" Cassie screamed. "Oh no, how could this happen?"

"Stay back." Jennie stepped in front of her to keep her from getting in Coach Haskell's way. "Brad, hold on to her."

Coach Haskell tipped Joel's head back to get an airway and blew into his mouth. Joel's chest rose and fell.

The rest of the team stood there staring open-mouthed as though they'd never seen anyone do CPR before. Jennie whacked Leif Hanson, the guy standing closest to her, on the back. "You heard the coach. Call 9–1–1. Move!"

Leif mumbled something and left.

To Gavin she said, "Maybe you'd better go with him. He looks pretty shook." Gavin nodded and sprinted after Leif.

"McGrady? That you?" the coach asked as he stopped the breathing and moved to Joel's chest to start compressions.

"Yeah." Jennie knelt beside Joel's still body, ready to give assistance.

"Good. Three—four. Stand by. I may need you to relieve me."

A few minutes later, Coach Haskell signaled Jennie to take over for him. Jennie kept up the lifesaving rhythm until the paramedics arrived.

As she watched the ambulance drive away with Joel and

his sister inside, Jennie's arms and legs turned to Jell-O.

Coach Haskell put a hand on her shoulder. "Thanks for your help, McGrady. I wish more kids had CPR training. If you hadn't been here, I'm not sure I could have kept going. I got arthritis in my wrist and shoulders. . . . By the way, why are you here? I know it isn't because you love football." The creases in his face shifted into a warm smile.

"I wanted to talk to you, but . . ." Jennie glanced behind the coach to the twenty or so guys still glued to the field.

Haskell followed her gaze and blew his whistle. "What are you guys standing around for?" he yelled. "Hit the showers." They scattered like mice at a cat convention.

"They're pretty upset. Can't say as I blame them." He lifted his Miami Dolphins cap and brushed his thinning hair back. "You said you wanted to talk."

Jennie quickly shared her suspicions with the coach. His dark bushy eyebrows nearly came together as he frowned. "These are serious allegations, Jennie. You said Brad denies using anything."

"Yes, but . . ."

"And you don't know for sure that Courtney was dispensing drugs."

"No, but . . ."

"Then we have to give him the benefit of the doubt."

"But the symptoms. Joel and Brad have gotten huge and more aggressive. And just now with Joel. The stuff I read said steroid use could cause a person to have a heart attack."

"Jennie, listen. If Joel had a heart attack, and I doubt that's the case, it sure wasn't from using steroids. They're good boys. I watch them real close—even do drug screening every now and then to make sure."

Jennie opened her mouth to argue her case, but Coach Haskell held up a hand to silence her. "I can understand why you'd be concerned. They are bigger and more aggressive, but that's from the special training programs Buck and I have been putting them through. If they're getting rough with their girlfriends, then I'll have a talk with them. My boys have been training hard. They're growing up. And something else too, Jennie. All these years I've been praying—asking God for a strong healthy team." He raised his hands and glanced upward. "And I thank the Lord, He's finally come through. Now if you really want to be helpful, you'll start praying for Joel's recovery instead of spreading gossip about this steroid business. The only hormone in these guys is testosterone—the kind that comes naturally at their age.

"Now," he added, dismissing her, "I need to get back to the locker room and calm my boys down. Then I'll head over to the hospital."

"I'm going to the hospital too," Jennie said. "I guess I'll see you there."

"Now, Jennie," he said, placing a hand on her shoulder, "I want you to forget this nonsense. Whatever you do, don't go making any trouble for Joel and his family—or Brad either. You haven't told the police, have you?"

"No, I wanted to verify it first."

"Good. That's good. Tell you what, McGrady. I appreciate your concern and I promise I'll keep an eye out. In fact, I haven't tested for drug use in a while. I'll do that."

She offered him a half smile. At least he hadn't totally discounted her.

———

Jennie dropped Gavin off at the library to get his bike, then hurried home to shower and change. She briefly filled her mother in on Joel's collapse before leaving for the hospital.

"They have no idea what's wrong?" Mom asked as she accompanied Jennie to the front porch.

Jennie had an idea, but didn't voice it. "I'll call as soon as I find out anything."

"Why do I get the feeling you're holding something back?"

"Maybe because I am." Jennie leaned against the porch railing and hoisted herself up. "I guess it would be okay to tell you." She paused again, hoping she was doing the right thing. "I think Courtney may have been supplying Joel and Brad and maybe some of the other guys with steroids. I was reading about steroid use today, and both Brad and Joel fit the description of someone who's been on them for a while. That's why I asked you about them earlier. I talked to Coach Haskell, but he denies it."

Mom rubbed her forehead and sighed. "You may be right. I went back over Frank's invoices and statements. There were several that didn't balance with what he showed on his inventory. Two different drug companies billed Frank for merchandise he apparently never received."

"Steroids?" Jennie asked.

Mom nodded. "In both cases the company had shipped Dianabol. It looks as though Courtney may have placed the orders, taken the merchandise without ever putting it into inventory, then destroyed the invoices so Frank wouldn't know what had been ordered. Since she did a lot of the bookkeeping, she just made out the checks for Frank to sign."

Jennie hopped off the railing. She had the evidence she needed. It was time to talk to the police. "Mom, do me a favor and call Rocky. Give him the information about Joel and tell him to meet me at the hospital. Better call Michael too—I have a feeling that family and Coach Haskell are going to need a lot of prayer."

———

Jennie walked into the waiting room just off the large double doors labeled emergency. Cassie was sitting alone in a pale blue chair near the receptionist's desk. She glanced up from the magazine she'd been reading when Jennie slumped into the chair across from her.

"The doctor thinks Joel's had a heart attack." Cassie's voice held no hint of the fear Jennie had seen in her earlier. Now she seemed as composed as ever. "Which is impossible," she went on. "Joel's heart is perfect. He's in better shape than he's ever been in."

It's one of the side effects of steroid use. Jennie didn't express her opinion aloud. It didn't seem appropriate to make those kind of allegations right now. She'd wait for Rocky and Michael.

"I wish Dad and Mom would get here. Maybe the doctor will listen to them. They'll insist on another opinion."

A youngish man in green surgical scrubs and eyes that matched came through the ER doors. "Miss Nielsen," he said. "Your parents haven't arrived yet, I see." He glanced at Jennie. "Are you family?"

"No, I'm . . ." Jennie started to say friend, but that wasn't exactly right either.

"Her name is Jennie McGrady. She's the one who helped Coach Haskell with the CPR."

"I'm Doctor Clark." He stretched his hand in Jennie's direction. "I've heard about you."

Jennie grasped it. "Is Joel going to be okay? Cassie said you thought he had a heart attack."

"Yes. It certainly looks that way." His lean build and the way he wore his ash blond hair reminded her of Ryan. He turned back to Cassie. "Has your brother ever had seizures?"

"No." Cassie's eyes widened with the same fear Jennie had seen in them earlier. "Why?"

"He had one a few minutes ago. He's stable now. We're waiting for some blood work. Did your parents give you any indication when they might arrive?"

Cassie shook her head. "They both work at Nike. They're probably stuck in traffic."

Dr. Clark examined his watch. "Let the receptionist know the minute they arrive. Miss McGrady," he went on, his gaze drifting to Jennie again. "I'm glad you're here. Would you mind coming with me for a moment? I'd like to ask you a few questions about Joel's condition before the ambulance arrived."

"Sure." Jennie followed him through the doors and into a small office. She wondered which of the closed curtains Joel was behind.

He pointed to a chair, then instead of sitting in the one behind the desk, pulled a rolling stool from the next room and sat on it. "Now then, what can you tell me?"

Jennie opened her mouth, then closed it again.

"It's okay. I don't expect a professional opinion. Just tell me what you saw."

"Not that much, really." Jennie went back over the scene and told him what Brad and some of the others had told her.

He jotted down some notes. "How long did you administer CPR?"

"About fifteen minutes. Coach Haskell took the first seven, then I relieved him. You don't think there'll be any brain damage, do you?"

"I don't know. He did have a seizure. We're trying to determine a cause."

Steroids. The word screamed into Jennie's mind. Jennie stared at her hands. "Dr. Clark. Umm, there's something you should know about Joel. I . . . I don't know for sure, but I think he might be taking Dianabol."

Dr. Clark raised an eyebrow, but didn't seem surprised. He glanced over Jennie's head and spoke to someone behind her. "Can I help you?"

"Dean Rockford," a familiar voice said. "Police."

Rocky.

"I believe this young lady has some information that might be of interest to both of us," he said. "Mind if I sit in?"

Without waiting for an invitation, Rocky hooked a chair and dragged it into the cubicle. They were seated perfectly for three-cornered catch and Jennie wondered what they'd do with the information she was about to pitch to them.

After a brief explanation of what Rocky was doing there, Jennie launched into her story. It should have gotten easier with the telling, but the heartbreak of kids killing themselves to win a game made the possibility more and more difficult to accept.

When she'd finished, she felt drained. Doctor Clark made a teepee with his hands and rested his chin on the tips of his fingers. She almost expected him to say "v-e-r-r-y interest-ing." But he didn't. After a moment, he got up, thanked her for her help, and walked across the wide hall to the nurses station.

Rocky looked at her and shook his head.

"You don't believe me? You think I'm making this up?"

"Oh, I believe you, Jennie. I'm just trying to figure out what you think you're doing. You've known about this home-less girl for how long? Why am I hearing about all this for the first time today?"

Dr. Clark appeared again and nodded at Rocky. "Could I talk to you privately?" To Jennie he said, "You might be more comfortable in the waiting room."

Rocky walked with the doctor across the hall where they conversed in tones too low for her to hear. Jennie chewed on her lower lip, stretched her long legs out in front of her and crossed them. *Maybe you shouldn't have said anything, McGrady. What if you're wrong?*

19

"I am right," she murmured under her breath.

Jennie decided to take Dr. Clark's advice and made her way back down the hall and through the double doors, nearly colliding with the receptionist.

Once in the waiting room, she almost turned around and went back. Joel's parents had arrived and looked up at her expectantly. Cassie glared at her for a moment, then looked away. *She knows, McGrady. She knows you told them about the steroids.* Coach Haskell took a step toward her, then stopped. He probably knew too.

Michael, who'd most likely been consoling them, smiled at her. Only it was a surface smile. Underneath she could feel his uneasiness—nearly as strongly as she felt her own.

Had she made the wrong choice in revealing her suspicions? Using steroids was illegal—and dangerous. No. She'd done the right thing. So why did she feel so rotten?

"You must be Jennie." Mr. Nielsen, a tall angular man with narrow hips and wide shoulders, rose and walked toward her. His eyes were the same brown color as Joel and Cassie's. "Cassie was just telling us how you and Coach Haskell saved Joel's life. We're very grateful. Did they . . . did the doctor tell you anything?"

Jennie shook her head. "No, he just had some questions."

Dr. Clark emerged from the ER, his face somber. "Mr.

and Mrs. Nielsen. Good, you're here. Would you mind coming with me for a few minutes? I need you to sign some papers and . . ."

"The papers can wait," Nielsen growled. "How's my son? What's all this nonsense about a heart attack?"

"That's what I'd like to discuss." The doctor took a step back, obviously intimidated by Nielsen's size and fierceness. Like father, like son.

"Well, discuss it then," Nielsen shot back. "Whatever you have to say, you can say right here. I'd prefer having some witnesses around to confirm your misdiagnosis."

Dr. Clark glanced around and shrugged. "I know it's difficult to believe, but Joel did suffer a heart attack. And shortly after he arrived here he had a seizure."

"But he's so young!" Mrs. Nielsen spoke this time. "How could something like this happen?"

"There are a number of reasons." The doctor drew in a deep breath. "Mr. and Mrs. Nielsen, were you aware that your son was using steroids?"

Mr. Nielsen exploded. Mrs. Nielsen cried. Cassie glared at Jennie as though the entire incident had been her fault. Coach Haskell tossed Jennie a look of disbelief, then sank into a chair and stared at a muted brown, blue, and green weaving that hung on the far wall.

"You'll be hearing from my lawyer," Nielsen threatened when he ran out of expletives. Or maybe he just remembered that Michael was in the room.

"Buck, please." His wife stepped between the two men. "Dr. Clark. I don't understand any of this."

"Heart attacks in young men are rare. That along with his muscle mass led me to run a blood test to determine whether or not he'd been using steroids. The test came out positive."

Jennie had been right. But the knowledge didn't cheer her. Feeling more like a traitor than a hero, she left Joel's family and Coach Haskell in Michael's capable hands and wandered out into the hospital corridor.

Since the ambulance had taken Joel to the same hospital Courtney was in, Jennie decided to see how she was doing. First, though, she needed something to eat. In the cafeteria, she indulged herself with a Coke and a rich, gooey chocolate brownie. Probably the farthest you could get from health food. Which was fine with Jennie. She'd had it with the body beautiful crowd.

After tossing her trash in the garbage can, Jennie climbed the stairs to the fourth floor. The expected grip of panic didn't come. Instead she felt an overwhelming sense of sadness. For Joel and Brad—for the school and for far too many people to name. Each set of stairs brought a name to her lips and a prayer to her heart.

Jennie checked in at the nurses station before going to Courtney's room.

"She's a little better," the nurse told her. "We've upgraded her condition from critical to serious."

"She's still not out of the coma?"

"No, she's not. But we're hopeful."

Jennie thanked her and moved away from the desk. The sign on the door still forbade visitors. As she'd done before, Jennie stood outside the room and watched Courtney through the large window. She looked the same—pale and lifeless.

She heard voices down the hall and turned toward them. Gavin was there, probably getting the same report she had. He walked toward her.

Jennie wondered for a moment if Gavin might have been on steroids as well. He'd have been a likely candidate. She remembered their conversation about jocks getting the girls and Gavin's bitterness toward Courtney for dropping him. He hadn't developed any muscle that she could see. *You're getting paranoid, McGrady. Totally paranoid.*

She thought about mentioning the possibility to Rocky. Only she didn't want to. If the police wanted to know who else was involved in Courtney's drug dealings they could find out on their own.

"Think she's gonna make it?" Gavin said as he joined Jennie at the window.

"How would I know?" The words sounded harsher than she'd intended. She looked at their nearly identical shapes reflected in the window. The sight did not please her.

He frowned as he glanced at her, probably wondering what he'd done to deserve her anger.

"I'm sorry," Jennie said. "I shouldn't be taking it out on you."

Gavin shrugged and to her reflection said, "I can understand why you'd be upset. I stopped by the emergency room on my way up here. Nielsen is furious. He's threatening to sue the hospital, the school, the coach, and Mr. Evans. And you."

"Me?"

"Cassie told him you instigated the investigation."

"That's stupid. The doctor didn't need my input. He already knew."

"Well, don't feel bad. He'll probably sue me too when he reads the morning paper."

Jennie turned from their reflections to look at the real Gavin. "You've already done an article?"

"Yeah. All I need is your side of it." Gavin met her eyes for a moment, then looked away. "I'm not going to apologize, Jennie. If I'm going to make it as a reporter I have to be tough."

"When did you have time? I just left the ER twenty minutes ago."

"After you dropped me off at the house, I went to see Brad. I told him we knew about the steroids. At first he argued with me, but when I told him some of the side effects, and that Joel had had a heart attack, he buckled. Got real scared. Told me he and Joel started using the stuff about the same time Joel started dating Courtney."

"Did he say why?"

Gavin shrugged. "Only that Joel talked him into using it."

Jennie's heart felt like a lead weight. "They must have known how dangerous steroids can be."

"They knew it was bad stuff, but figured taking them for a year or two wouldn't be a big deal. They were only going to do it until they graduated."

"Did he confess to beating up Courtney?"

"No. He only admits to meeting her. She told him she didn't know how much longer she could supply the stuff. Her dad was getting suspicious. That's all he claims to know. Says he's glad things are out in the open."

Jennie turned around and leaned back against the window. "All we've managed to do is determine that Courtney was guilty of supplying drugs. We still don't know who wanted her dead."

Gavin moved up beside her, rested his knuckles on the windowsill, and let his forehead touch the glass. Jennie followed his gaze to the slender figure lying bruised and battered on the bed. "You're right about that," he said in a voice so quiet she could barely hear him. He pushed away from the wall again. "I'm a pretty good judge of character and I think Brad was telling the truth."

"Hmmm. I think he is too. I mean . . . since Courtney was their supplier, it makes no sense that he'd try to kill her."

Jennie felt like a player in a board game. She'd nearly completed the course then had gotten a card telling her to go back to square one.

"Why worry about it?" Gavin said. "I talked to your friend Rocky while I was upstairs. He says the D.A.'s got a solid case against Frank Evans."

"They did before."

"Yeah, well, my mom's been keeping really close tabs on the case. She says the blood and hair samples they found in the trunk of Evans' car definitely match Courtney's."

Jennie uncrossed her ankles and pushed herself away from the wall. "So I guess I was wrong in thinking it may have been someone else."

"I guess so." Gavin clasped her shoulder. "Hey, we can't be right all the time. Besides, you gotta let the police solve a case once in a while or they'd feel bad."

That brought a smile to Jennie's face. "Very funny."

"Listen, I gotta go finish my article." He started to leave then turned around again. "Um . . . how about doing me a favor? I'm heading over to *The Oregonian*—be there for a couple of hours. Could you pick me up later and take me out to the farm?"

"Sure—if you do me a favor."

He grinned. "Why do I get the feeling I'm being manipulated? Okay, I'll bite. What?"

"Don't say anything about me in your article. You really don't have to. The doctor's the one who found steroids in Joel's bloodstream. The police were already looking into the drug thing. Even if I hadn't done anything, the truth would have come out—eventually."

"You don't give yourself enough credit, Jen." Gavin smiled and left without giving her an answer.

Jennie watched him go. They were a lot alike, not just in physical stature, but mentally too. They both had an investigative bent and a desire to find the truth.

The truth. Jennie looked at Courtney again. Would they ever know what really happened to the girl with the rainbow hair?

Had her own father beat her up and left her for dead? Could this seemingly kind man, a man her mother was working for and dating, be a murderer? Jennie shivered. "Oh, Courtney," she whispered. "Please wake up. You're the only one who can tell us what really happened."

One of the monitors at the nurses' station switched from a rhythmic beep to a long dull tone. Jennie knew the sound. It meant someone on the unit may have gone into cardiac arrest.

"Excuse us, miss." Two nurses hurried into Courtney's room. They stood on either side of her bed, apparently checking her vital signs.

As Jennie watched, dread crept in and through her like maggots on a dead possum. *Don't die, Courtney. Please don't die.*

20

Jennie slowly opened her eyes.

The nurses hovered over Courtney, but they weren't acting like they had an emergency on their hands. One of the nurses flipped a switch on the panel at the head of the bed.

The respirator stopped pumping air into Courtney's lungs. Jennie stared at the still figure on the bed until tears blurred her vision.

Moments later she felt a hand on her shoulder. "Is something wrong?" It was the nurse who'd pulled the plug.

"Is she dead?" Jennie asked.

"Oh, goodness no. You mean because we disconnected the respirator? No. She's fine. We've been weaning her off and she's breathing on her own now."

"But the monitor . . ."

The nurse smiled. "You're very observant. Actually, one of the lines connected to the heart monitor came loose. We reattached it."

"So Courtney's getting better?"

"In some ways, yes. She's still in a coma and we have no way of knowing how long that will last. But, if she continues to make this kind of progress we'll be moving her out of intensive care as early as tomorrow."

Before heading home, Jennie decided to check on Joel. He'd been transferred to the coronary care unit on the second floor. Before going up, she stopped at a row of pay phones near the hospital entrance and called her mom again. The answering machine picked up. Jennie left a message letting Mom know where she was and hung up.

The Nielsens seemed much more subdued than when she'd seen them earlier. Maybe Michael had calmed them down. He was good at that. "I just came by to see how Joel was doing," she said, trying to sound cheerful, but not too much so.

"That was very sweet of you, dear," Mrs. Nielsen said. "Joel had another seizure."

Michael rose and walked toward Jennie. He placed an arm around her shoulders. "You look exhausted."

"I'm fine. Just a little tired. It seems like everyone I know is ending up in the hospital. Lisa. Courtney. Joel. It's scary." Jennie smiled up at him. "I have some good news, though."

"Oh yeah? And what might that be?"

"Courtney's off the respirator. She's definitely getting better."

"Really?" Cassie said, acknowledging Jennie's presence for the first time. "That's great." She glanced at the floor, then back up at Jennie. "I'm glad you came back. There's something I wanted to tell you. Um . . . do you want to go have a Coke or something?"

Jennie wanted to go home and have dinner. The sugar from the gooey chocolate bar had long since disappeared from her bloodstream. She also wanted to hear what Cassie had to say.

"Cassie. Wait a second," Mr. Nielsen said, digging into the hip pocket of his dark gray slacks and extracting his billfold. "Why don't you take Jennie down to the cafeteria and get some dinner. I think it's the least we can do." He handed a twenty to Cassie and she stuffed it in the front pocket of her powder blue cutoffs.

Jennie started to object, but when her stomach growled in protest, she acquiesced. Sometimes you just had to follow a higher calling.

"I owe you an apology," Cassie said while they waited for the elevator. I wasn't very nice to you earlier. I guess I felt like I had to blame somebody and you . . ."

"It's okay, really. You must have been really scared, seeing Joel go down like that."

"I was. To be honest, Jennie, when we were sitting in the stands and you asked if I knew anything about steroids I about panicked."

The elevator doors swooshed open. They waited for an orderly to push out an empty wheelchair, then stepped inside. Cassie pushed the "G" button and waited until the doors closed before she continued.

"I didn't know they were using 'roids until after Courtney disappeared. Then I overheard Brad and Joel talking. They were trying to figure out a way to get more when their supply ran out. I was so mad."

The elevator released them on the ground floor. Jennie and Cassie both passed on the cafeteria special—cheese enchiladas that looked like they'd already been through someone's digestive system. Instead they opted for the salad bar.

They found an unoccupied table along the far wall and sat down. Cassie speared a plump red strawberry and popped it into her mouth. Jennie started in on her garden salad, deciding to save the fruit for dessert.

"I know what you're thinking," Cassie said. "You're wondering why I didn't tell anyone. I guess for the same reason no one else did. I didn't want to ruin Joel's chances for a football career—Brad's either, but Joel was my main concern." She broke off a piece of bread and began buttering it. "See, it wasn't just Joel. I knew if my dad found out, it would destroy him. Well, you saw him. Dad's dream has been for Joel to get picked up by a major team. Dad's been grooming him since he was born."

"What's going to happen now?"

"I don't know. Once this gets out, Joel will be finished in sports. Dad might lose his endorsements. Mom says it will all work out and the most important thing now is for Joel to get well. I hope she's right." Cassie set her knife on the tray. The sadness in her deep brown eyes almost made Jennie cry.

Her sigh seemed to come from her toes. "Oh, Jennie. If I'd known where all this would lead, I'd have told Mom and Dad when I first suspected." A fat tear dripped down her tan cheek. She brushed it away with the back of her hand. "I'd have found some way to make them stop."

Jennie didn't know what to say or how to console her. The saddest part about their tragedy was that it could have been prevented.

Then something Cassie had said popped to the surface of Jennie's brain like a huge zit. "You said 'for the same reason no one else did.' You mean someone else knew? Like the coach?"

"No. Coach Haskell didn't suspect a thing. He did routine urine tests on the players. Joel and Brad had worked out this scam with a couple of the other guys. They switched containers."

"Why would anyone go along with them?"

"For the good of the team." Cassie heaved an exasperated sigh. "You just don't get it, do you, McGrady? Brad and Joel are the biggest guys on the team. Without them Trinity doesn't have a chance."

"So they justified breaking the law. You're right, Cassie, I don't get it. I know sports is important to a lot of people. I love swimming and going to games. When my dad was home, I used to hang out with him on weekends and watch the bowl games and the Olympics. But . . . I don't know. I might put my life on the line to save someone if I had to, but I'd never risk my life to win a game."

They ate in silence for a few minutes before Cassie spoke again. "You said Courtney's getting better . . . I'm glad. I mean, Courtney shouldn't have been supplying drugs but she didn't deserve to get beat up like that. Is she still in a coma?"

"Yes." Jennie sighed, glad for the change in subject. "The nurse told me she could wake up any time—or she might not wake up for years."

"Isn't there any way they can tell?"

"I guess not. We'll just have to wait and see."

Jennie left the hospital in a much better mood. Courtney was going to be okay. Even though the nurse had warned her against being overly optimistic, Jennie refused to think anything but positive thoughts about Courtney's condition.

She felt better about Joel too—though she hadn't been able to see him, his condition had been upgraded to serious by the time she and Cassie got back from dinner.

And poor Cassie. What a dilemma she'd been in. Jennie could understand why Cassie hadn't told anyone about the steroids. There had been so much at stake.

Jennie wished she hadn't agreed to meet Gavin. She felt like she'd been on a forty-eight-hour marathon and all she really wanted to do was sleep. The case was closed. Police had a suspect in Courtney's assault and Jennie had uncovered the steroid scandal.

But she couldn't go home just yet; she'd made a promise. When she pulled up in front of *The Oregonian* offices, Gavin was waiting outside. They secured his bike in her trunk and headed for the country. On the way, Jennie filled him in on Courtney's condition and her own encounter with the Nielsens.

When Jennie asked about the article, he pulled a folder

out of his pack and read it to her. When he'd finished he asked, "Well, what do you think?"

"You didn't mention me."

"You asked me not to."

"I know." Jennie flashed him a grin. "I just didn't think you'd do it. Thanks."

"You're welcome. So, how was it?"

"Good. Really good. I like the way you make your points without sounding judgmental. And that part about Courtney—a soft heart that went too far."

"She was wrong to give people drugs," Gavin admitted. "But I think in her own way she wanted to help. Like giving Tina the insulin. I keep wondering what I would have done. I mean . . . do you walk away and let someone die because they refuse to go to a doctor?"

"That would be such a hard decision."

"The part I have the hardest time with is the steroids." Gavin frowned. "How could she have agreed to supply Brad and Joel with that stuff?"

"How could she have picked him over me?" Gavin hadn't asked the question out loud but his expression left little doubt in Jennie's mind what he was thinking. Gavin's anger filled the car with an almost tangible aura. He stared straight ahead as sullen and still as the moments before a storm.

Tension knotted itself around her. She wanted to console him—to reassure him, but didn't know how.

By the time Jennie pulled into his driveway, Gavin had pulled himself together and was telling her about his plans for college.

Once Jennie got to the farm, she didn't want to leave—at least not right away. She loved being out in the open, away from buildings and the smog of the city. "I have relatives that own a ranch in Montana," Jennie said as the thought came to her. "Being out here reminded me. I wonder how they're doing?"

155

Gavin gave her a strange look. "You don't know?"

"Not really. Maggie—that's my mom's older sister—doesn't correspond much. About the only time we hear from them is Christmas. Last Christmas we got this picture of her family in front of some llamas. She didn't say much except that they were starting a new life in the Bitterroot Valley in Montana."

"Hmmm." Gavin stared into the field.

"Where's your mother?" Jennie asked, changing the subject.

"At class. She teaches writing at Portland State. Ummm—I have some chores to do before it gets dark. Want to help?"

"Sure." Jennie pulled on a pair of Maddie's rubber boots and slogged through the pasture and barn behind Gavin, feeding the llamas and goats. At nine-fifteen, Jennie firmly announced that she had to get home.

She'd tried calling her mother a couple times but no one had answered. Now she was getting worried. She'd just opened her car door when Maddie pulled in.

"Jennie, I'm glad you're here." If smiles were light bulbs, Maddie's would have lit up the entire yard.

"Hi, Mrs. Winslow." Jennie closed the door of her Mustang to turn off the door-open ding.

"Have you thought about the book?" Maddie asked. "I have wonderful news. I talked to my agent yesterday and she's thrilled. All we need is an okay from you and she'll start pursuing contracts for the book and a movie."

"Movie?" Jennie's heart did a triple flip. "Are you serious?"

"Absolutely. Oh, I know you'll need to talk to your mother, but I really hope this works out. It could be my big break—and yours too, Jennie."

"I wouldn't get my hopes up," Gavin interjected. "I mean

. . . your story would make a great novel, but Mom tends to overreact."

"Gavin." Maddie tossed him a disgruntled look. "Don't pay any attention to him, Jennie—he's picked up his father's practical bent. He's right, of course, there's a possibility it won't sell, but like I always tell my students, failure isn't determined by how often you fail. You only fail when you stop trying."

Maddie's enthusiasm spread over Jennie like infectious laughter. How could she say no? "I'll talk to my mom about it. I have to warn you, though, she's extremely practical."

"Would you like me to come by? It might help if your mother and I got better acquainted. I know if it were Gavin, I'd want to know all the details and be in on the plans."

"That'd be great. I'll call you. In the meantime, I'd better hustle. If I don't get home before eleven, Mom's liable to make good on her threat to lock me up until I'm twenty-one."

Maddie gave her a knowing wink. "I think your mother and I are going to get along just fine." Her face clouded over. "Speaking of your mother . . . have you heard the news at all today?"

"No, why?" Her stomach tightened as if preparing itself to expect the worst.

"Remember the other day when you were here and I was going on about how inadequate our judicial system is?"

Jennie nodded.

"Well, they did it up big this time. With all the evidence against him, they let him go. Frank Evans is out on bail."

21

"What are they thinking?" Maddie rolled her eyes. "We have more criminals out on the street these days than in prison."

"But what about the evidence against him?" Gavin asked, echoing Jennie's thoughts.

"Apparently, they feel aggravated assault isn't a serious enough charge." She threw up her hands. "I don't know why I let things like this get to me. I should be used to it by now. Even if he does go to trial and is found guilty, he probably won't get more than a slap on the wrist."

Maddie took a deep breath and let it out slowly. "I'm sorry, kids. I really shouldn't go on like that. It's just that sometimes it seems like our judicial system does little more than protect the criminal. I just hope the police think to post a guard outside Courtney's room. If he's guilty, he may try again."

"I'm sure they will, Mrs. Winslow." Jennie grasped the door handle of her Mustang. "I . . . I really have to go. It's getting late."

Jennie left feeling a bit overwhelmed and helpless. Some things were just too big to fight. *They let Frank Evans out on bail. What if he's guilty?* The thought exploded in her brain again and again. She had to get home. Courtney's safety concerned her, but someone else's safety occupied her thoughts even more. Mom. Did Mom know he was out? Did she still believe in his innocence?

"Please, God, keep her safe." Jennie repeated the prayer a dozen times on her way home.

The moment she turned from Elm onto Magnolia and saw the dark house, Jennie knew something was wrong. *What if he's guilty?* Her blood pounded the question out in rhythm through her veins. Until the courts proved otherwise, Frank Evans was a threat, whether Mom believed it or not.

She took several deep breaths and let them out slowly to calm her frayed nerves. Once parked and out of the car, Jennie raced up the walk and onto the porch. The door was locked. She let herself in.

"Mom?" Jennie yelled. The silence penetrated her heart like a knife.

What if he's guilty? A dim light from the kitchen drew her toward it. Mom had left the stove light on and a note on the table.

> *Jennie,*
> *Nick and Hannah are spending the night at Kevin and Kate's. I've gone with Frank to the pharmacy to help him sort out the inventory problem we talked about. The way it looks, I'll be there until at least midnight. Call me when you get home.*
> *Love you, Mom*

Jennie didn't like it. She grabbed the phone and punched in the numbers Mom had jotted down on the note. The clock on the microwave read ten-fifteen. After six rings, Frank finally picked up. "Hello."

"Hi, can I . . ."

". . . this is Evans' Pharmacy. I'm sorry we missed your call. Our hours are . . ."

The answering machine. Jennie slammed down the receiver. Maybe Mom was on her way home. *What if he's guilty?*

Jennie tried to push the unwanted thought away, but it clung to her like a wet T-shirt. Though the night was a balmy seventy degrees, goose bumps raised the hair on her arms and sent shivers through her body. She took several deep breaths. *Steady, McGrady. Mom's fine. She could be on her way home. Or maybe they went out for a snack or coffee.*

Okay, now what? She could call the police and have them check things out. Only that might upset Mom. Apparently she still believed in Frank's innocence or she'd never have agreed to go with him.

Jennie swallowed hard to settle the panic rising in her chest. She picked up the receiver and dialed 9-1-1. Okay. Maybe she was overreacting, but she couldn't ignore the gut feeling that Mom was in trouble.

After reporting her concerns to the 9-1-1 operator, Jennie sat down to wait. That lasted about two seconds. On her feet again, she paced back and forth a few dozen times, then wandered out of the kitchen, through the dining room, and into the living room. She plopped down on the couch, picked up the remote control, turned the television on, then off again. The last thing she needed was more bad news. She popped back up again. "I'm going down there," she announced to the blank television screen.

Jennie dug the keys out of her jeans pocket and headed out the door. On the ten-minute drive to the pharmacy, she turned on the radio and cranked the volume up to drown out the negative thoughts that kept forming in her mind. When that didn't work she just kept telling herself, *Mom's okay. She is. God, please—let her be okay.*

Jennie parked in front of the store. A *closed* sign hung in the metal-framed glass door. Black wrought-iron security bars protected the door and display windows from potential thieves. *But not from the pharmacist himself,* she mused. Jennie glanced around. No sign of a police car. Maybe they'd already checked the place.

Everything looked peaceful, but Jennie still couldn't get over the feeling that something was wrong. Suddenly, the store lit up. Light poured out of the windows and onto the sidewalk. Jennie heaved a sigh of relief. Maybe she'd guessed right. They'd gone out for coffee and were just now coming back. They must have used a back entrance.

She stepped out of the car and pounded on the door. "Mom! Frank! It's me, Jennie. I . . ."

The door moved beneath the pressure of her hand. Jennie pushed harder and it opened. It should have been locked. She released the breath she'd been holding and entered the store.

The lights, she realized, weren't the daytime kind, but the subdued type used at night to allow the police to see inside the stores when they patrolled a neighborhood. It allowed her to see, but not all that well.

Somewhere in the distance she heard a motor roar to life and the screeching of tires. Her mind raced as fast as her heart as it tried to take in her surroundings. All kinds of miscellaneous products and medical supplies lined the well-stocked shelves. Everything neatly labeled and in its place. A few steps more and Jennie's heart stopped. The area behind the counter, where pharmacists shelved prescription drugs, had been ransacked.

Quiet. It was too quiet.

"Mom!" she called, breaking the deadly silence with the sound of her own voice. "Frank?" Jennie felt as though someone had wrapped a tourniquet around her stomach and twisted it tight.

She heard a shuffling sound off to her right. Someone groaned. Jennie wouldn't have thought it possible, but her stomach tightened even more. She was beginning to feel lightheaded as she moved toward the sound. It had come from a room in the back of the store—probably the office.

Sucking in several deep breaths to steady herself, Jennie

moved into the darkened hallway. Her foot slipped in something wet. She reached out to catch herself. Her hand brushed against the wall as she dropped to her knees. The dark liquid oozed into her jeans. Blood?

Jennie swallowed hard. No. Not blood. A broken bottle of some kind of syrup lay on the floor a couple feet away.

Using the doorframe to steady herself, she stood up. That's when she saw the arm. A woman's hand and forearm lay on the floor, bathed in soft light. The rest of her body was obliterated by shadows.

No. McGrady, don't even think it. She reached inside the room and felt along the wall for a light switch. She found it. The white fluorescent light blinded her, but not enough. The woman lay on her stomach. A freckled arm disappeared into a creamy silk blouse splayed with strands of beautiful auburn hair.

22

"Mom . . . Oh no—no." Jennie knew the whimpering cries were coming from her own throat, but they seemed too far away to be real. Tears clouded the sight of her mother's body and bloody wound on the side of her head. Panic tore at her insides. She wanted to scream and run, but couldn't move. From somewhere deep inside the recesses of her memory, Jennie heard the calming voice of her CPR instructor: *No matter how terrible the trauma, put the victims needs above your own. Stay calm, McGrady. You know what to do. Check for a pulse.*

Jennie drew in a shuddering breath and obeyed. Her fingers felt numb and awkward against her mother's neck. One . . . two . . . three. The rhythm of her pulse was strong and steady. And she was still breathing. Jennie slowed her own breathing down again. She had to get help. And stop the bleeding.

After calling 9–1–1, Jennie knelt and turned her mother's limp body over so that she lay on her back, her head cradled in Jennie's arms. The silk cream blouse was splattered with blood. So far the only injury she could see was the open gash on her left temple. As near as Jennie could tell, the bleeding had already stopped.

"Hmmm." Mom groaned and lifted her arm.

Jennie grabbed her hand and squeezed it. "It's okay. I'm

here. The ambulance is on the way." Sirens she'd heard in the backgroud grew louder and louder and finally stopped. Red, blue, and white lights flashed on the wall in the hallway.

Mom's eyelids flickered open, her green eyes fearful and filling with tears. "Frank. . . ." She tried to sit up.

"Mom, please, lie still." Mom collapsed back against Jennie's lap.

Had Frank done this to her? Jennie wanted to ask, but didn't get the chance. Police swarmed in, then the paramedics. Once Jennie had supplied the information, she stepped aside and watched them transfer Mom to a stretcher.

"You did a fine job, Miss McGrady," an officer in a tan and brown uniform said. He placed an arm across her shoulders and led her out of the room. She tried to read his name tag but tears blurred her vision again.

Jennie sniffed, trying to hold back the torrent of emotions that threatened to wash her away.

"I'm Deputy Mosier," he said. "Any idea what happened here?"

Jennie's head was spinning. Her knees buckled. Mosier's strong hands grasped her under the arms and lowered her to the floor. He pressed her head down between her knees. "Take some deep breaths," Mosier instructed. "That's good."

Another officer's shiny black shoes and pressed brown slacks joined Mosier's. "She able to tell you anything?" he asked.

"Not yet. Poor kid. Coming in and finding her mother like that."

Mosier hunkered down beside her. "I know this is tough for you, but we need to ask you a few more questions. Are you up to it?"

"I think so." Jennie straightened. "My mom left a note saying she'd be here. She does the books. I called and no one answered and I got scared."

"So you came to check things out? You really should have called us, you know."

"I did. About ten-fifteen. I got here about twenty minutes later and I waited. No one came. I figured maybe someone already checked it out and left again."

"I doubt it. We've had a busy night. Big tanker jack-knifed up on the freeway. So what made you decide to go in?"

"The lights came on in the store and I thought Mom and Frank had gone for coffee or something and were just coming back." *Frank.* "He's responsible for this. He was released on bail and . . ."

"Whoa. Hold on, there." Mosier stopped writing. "Who's Frank?"

Jennie told him.

"Ain't it the way? Spend half our time dealing with guys that never should have been released. But what do you do?"

Jennie had no idea. Her head was beginning to clear. She needed to get away. To be with her mother. To think. "I'd like to go now."

Mosier gave her an understanding nod. "I'll come by the hospital—talk to you there. Hopefully your mother will have some answers for us. Did you want to go in the ambulance with her?"

"Yes . . . no. I have my car here."

"You sure you can drive? I can have someone—"

"No, I'll be okay."

A few minutes later she left the flashing lights behind and headed for the hospital.

By the time the receptionist had cleared Jennie to go into the emergency room, her mother had fully regained consciousness. A hospital gown had replaced the silk blouse. The gash in her forehead had been sutured shut, and a woman in scrubs and surgical gloves was lifting a rectangular piece of white gauze from a cloth-covered tray. "Hi. I'm Doctor Martin. You must be this lady's missing daughter."

"Jennie, honey." Mom held out a bloodstained hand. Jennie gripped it, surprised at her mother's strength. "I was getting worried."

"You were worried about me?" Jennie shook her head. "In case you hadn't noticed, you're the one getting stitches. Parents." She gave the doctor an exasperated look. "Can't leave them alone for a minute."

"Gives you a lot of trouble, does she?" Dr. Martin smiled.

Jennie and her mother both answered in the affirmative.

"That's it." Dr. Martin applied the last piece of tape across the bandage.

"Am I ready to go?" Mom asked.

"Not quite. I'd like to keep you a bit longer, just to be sure. You've got a nasty bump."

Mom sighed. "I'm fine, really."

"Then you won't mind answering some questions." Deputy Mosier stepped around the curtains and introduced himself.

Mom looked down at her unflattering attire and shrugged. "Why not. I'm not sure I'll be of any help."

"Just tell me what happened."

Mom closed her eyes. "I went with Frank to the pharmacy to verify some discrepancies I'd found in his books. We got there about eight. At around ten, Frank wanted to take a break. I wasn't at a place where I could stop, so I sent him out to get coffee and donuts."

"When did he get back?"

"He didn't." She glanced up at Jennie. Deep furrows lined her forehead. "You don't think he did this?"

"Who else would have?" Jennie asked. "Frank was out on bail. He . . ."

"No. It wasn't him." Mom raked her fingers through her hair. "I thought I heard him come in, but when I called out to him, no one answered. Then the lights went out. I got up. Someone came into the room and . . ." She touched her forehead. "Whoever it was shoved me down. I must have hit my head on the desk.

"But it wasn't Frank. The person who pushed me was smaller. Tall, but slender—younger." Mom's eyes widened. "Frank. He must be frantic. We need to find him."

"We've already done that, ma'am. He came in a few minutes after you left." Mosier's eyes narrowed. "He's been taken downtown for questioning. Says he got stuck in traffic—which may be true. Accident up on I–205 had traffic blocked for a couple of hours."

"Oh, that poor man. After all he's been through and then to have his store burglarized."

"That poor man?" Jennie was losing it. She couldn't understand how her mother could so adamantly defend a man everyone else thought was guilty. "Did you ever stop to think that all of this stuff might be happening because he's guilty?"

"Jennie, please. Lower your voice."

Jennie clamped her teeth together. She folded her arms and sank into a chair near the wall. How could Mom be so blind?

Jennie tuned out Mom and Mosier and thought back to the scene she'd encountered at the pharmacy. She'd been quick to name Frank as the suspect. Now that she thought about it, several questions surfaced. First, why would he burglarize his own store? And why take Mom to the store if he was going to hurt her? That didn't make much sense.

She glanced over at her mom who was still adamantly defending Evans. *Okay, McGrady, admit it. You jumped the gun. You let yourself get so worked up when you heard Frank was out on bail that you put your brain in neutral.*

Jennie unclenched her jaw, unfolded her arms, and went back to her mom's side. "I'm sorry I got mad."

Mom took hold of her hand and squeezed it.

"I . . . I think I'll go up and see how Courtney is doing," Jennie said. "I'll be back in half an hour or so."

"That sounds like a wonderful idea. Hopefully they'll be ready to let me go by then."

Jennie's spirits lifted some when the nurse told her Courtney was doing better. The rainbow girl was still in a coma, but they'd moved her out of intensive care. "She's been breathing well on her own since we removed the respirator. Would you like to see her?"

Jennie nodded.

"She's in room 435, just down the hall, first door on the left."

The door was closed. Jennie pushed it open and stepped inside. It took a moment for her eyes to adjust to the darkness. She wondered why the lights were out. It seemed to Jennie that the nurses would want as much light as possible.

She felt along the wall for a switch, but didn't find it. Oh well, she didn't need a light anyway. She'd come up to see Courtney, but more than that, Jennie needed time to think and a quiet place to do it.

She left the door open to afford some light and moved deeper into the darkness. The first bed was empty.

Courtney's slender body occupied the one next to the window. The room was quiet except for the sound of Courtney's breathing—and hers. Jennie heard a faint scraping sound off to her right. The curtain moved, then parted. A dark, menacing shadow lunged at her.

23

Jennie raised her arm to ward off the blow. Whatever had been meant for her head hit her forearm. She staggered then fell to her knees as the figure pushed her aside and raced for the door.

Jennie hurt too much to scream. She hurt too much to do anything but lie there and moan. A moment later the overhead lights came on.

"What's going on?" The voice belonged to Brenda Stone, the nurse Jennie had talked to at the desk.

"I don't know," someone answered. "I was just coming out of 436 and saw some guy go out the stairs exit."

"You'd better call security." Brenda knelt beside Jennie. "Looks like this one's been hurt. Get a doctor up here stat."

"Courtney," Jennie gasped, trying to sit up. "I think someone was trying to . . ." Jennie moaned when the nurse touched her arm. Or maybe it was a scream. Her brain seemed oblivious to everything but the searing pain.

"I think her arm's broken. Otherwise she looks okay. She's moving on her own. Ken, help me get her on a gurney. If she's stable, have someone take her down to ER."

A strong pair of arms lifted her off the floor and deposited her on a narrow bed. "There you go. You'll be more comfortable here." Jennie winced as Ken placed a pillow under her arm.

"Angie," Brenda hollered. "Call a code. Get a crash cart in here quick."

The rails on both sides of Jennie snapped up into place. Ken wheeled her into the hallway. "Sorry about this," he said. "We'll have somebody here to take care of you in a minute. You just try to relax."

Relax? Someone had attacked her and run, which made Jennie fairly certain the culprit hadn't been paying Courtney a friendly visit. Had Courtney's attempted murderer come back? Had he succeeded this time?

One thing Jennie knew for certain—the person who hit her hadn't been Frank. The intruder had been smaller. Besides, the police had Frank in custody. Then who and why? The same one that had broken into the pharmacy? Jennie tried to tune out the throbbing pain in her arm and the scurrying hospital staff to concentrate on the attacker. She couldn't.

At least a dozen hospital personnel streamed into Courtney's room. All apparently responding to the official voice that droned over the intercom. "Code 99. Code 99. All available staff report to room 435 stat." The message was repeated three times, with no more emotion than a person would use to announce the items in a breakfast menu.

After what seemed an hour rather than five minutes, one of the nurses stopped to check on Jennie. "I'm sorry you have to wait. Are you in very much pain? I'll get you an ice pack."

The pain had settled to a dull agonizing ache between her wrist and her elbow. "That'd be great. Thanks. How is Courtney?"

"I really can't tell you that right now. But I'll try to let you know." The nurse left and came back with a towel-covered ice pack, which she placed on Jennie's arm.

The arm, Jennie noticed, had turned an angry shade of red and had swollen to about twice its original size. It looked like one of Popeye's, only crooked.

She pulled her knees up to take some of the pressure off her back and closed her eyes. As she began to relax the noise in the background dimmed. Like a bad dream, the scene in Courtney's room replayed itself in her head. As the intruder appeared, she felt something brush against her. She jumped, sending spasms of pain through her arm again.

"I'm sorry, I didn't mean to startle you." A young man in a white uniform gazed down at her. "I'm Adam Janzen, and if you're Jennie McGrady, I'm here to take you down to the emergency room."

"I can't leave now," she whined. As much as her arm hurt, Jennie didn't want to leave until she found out what had happened to Courtney. "I think someone tried to kill her. I need to know if she's going to be okay."

"I'll see if I can find anything out for you." Adam poked his head into room 435. A few seconds later he popped back out again. "You must have a weird imagination. According to one of the aids in there, your friend was having an insulin reaction."

Insulin reaction? "But . . ." Jennie stammered. "Courtney's not a diabetic—is she?"

"I wouldn't know." Adam maneuvered the stretcher down the hall and into the elevator. "All I know is they're talking medication error."

The next couple of hours went by in a blur of exams, X-rays, cast application, and what-am-I-going-to-do-with-you looks from Mom. While a technician applied a cast, a police officer took her statement of what had happened earlier in Courtney's room. Mom and Michael hung around with somber faces, trying to decide what to do with Mom's accident-prone daughter. They finally left after Jennie was safely tucked into a bed on the orthopedic ward with a guard posted outside her door.

The pain medication dulled her senses and sent her adrift in a state between wakefulness and sleep. For that reason,

Jennie couldn't be sure if what she'd seen had been for real or only a dream. Mom and Michael had been standing next to her, their arms around each other. He'd asked her to marry him, saying between the two of them they should be able to handle one slightly damaged teenager with a penchant for trouble. Jennie couldn't remember Mom's response.

———

The first face Jennie saw when she woke up the next morning was Rocky's. His blue gaze was fastened on some papers. She smiled—or tried to. Her mouth felt like it had been sitting in a food dehydrator all night. "Hey, Rockford, we gotta stop meeting like this."

Rocky glanced up. He was obviously not amused. She braced herself for a lecture. It didn't come. "How's the arm?" he asked, setting his papers aside.

"Hurts," Jennie said. "What about Courtney? She okay?"

"She's stable. They moved her back into ICU. In fact, she's starting to come out of the coma. Doc says it's too soon to question her."

"The orderly told me she'd had an insulin reaction from a medication error. Is that what happened?"

His icy glare made her feel like a bug under a microscope. "I'll ask the questions, if you don't mind. You're going to have to stop trying to solve cases for us. Despite popular opinion, we do know what we're doing."

"Like I told the officer last night, I just went up to see Courtney. Only somebody else was already there."

"So I heard. We found a syringe on the floor with some of the insulin still in it. You apparently interrupted a murder. If you hadn't been there she may have died."

Jennie looked down at the cast on her arm and shrugged. "Glad I could help."

"Any idea who it might have been?" Rocky asked.

"I thought you didn't want me trying to solve crimes anymore."

"I don't. But you're a witness."

"I didn't see much. It was dark."

"But you did see something. Hair color? Height? Body type? Race? Clothing?"

"About my height and build. It happened so fast. That's about all I can think of."

"Did you know him?" Rocky's question caught her off guard. She hesitated a little too long. "You do, don't you?"

Jennie chewed on her lower lip. "I don't know who it is. All I can tell you is that he seemed familiar. I think it might be someone I know or have met."

"Was it your cousin's boyfriend?"

"No. Brad's much bigger than this guy." Jennie remembered something else. The insulin. Tina. Of course Tina hadn't been in the room, but it could have been one of her friends. No, Jennie reasoned. She'd been down that road before and it led to a dead end. Tina would have no reason to want Courtney dead. Jennie took a deep breath, wishing some of the puzzle pieces floating around in her brain cells would assemble themselves into some kind of order.

Rocky stood. "If your memory improves, give me a call."

"I will."

The doctor discharged Jennie that morning. Mom came to pick her up. They were halfway home before Jennie asked Mom about Michael. "Are you two back together?"

Mom's lips curled in a reluctant smile. "It looks that way. I've been doing some serious soul-searching over the last few days and realize I do love him. You were right."

"About what?"

"Remember what you said to me after we did that news conference—about you and I having to make adjustments and working things out?"

Jennie nodded.

"Well, don't let it go to your head, my darling daughter, but that was very wise counsel."

"Yeah?" Jennie grinned.

"So, yes, Michael and I are back together."

Jennie half smiled. It was good news—sort of. On the one hand she was happy for Michael and for Mom—on the other, she couldn't help wondering about Dad. And wishing the light in Mom's eyes could have been for him.

For two hours Nick and Hannah played doctor, with Jennie as their patient. For a while Jennie thought they were cute, sticking make-believe needles in her arm, poking Popsicle sticks in her mouth to take her temperature, and bringing real ice packs. When Nick asked Mom for a knife so he could do brain surgery, the game ended.

Michael came by around one and offered to take Nick and Hannah to the park. Jennie insisted Mom go along, which she finally did when Lisa showed up to keep Jennie company.

Once Mom, Michael, and kids were gone, Jennie sent Lisa into the kitchen to fix them some lemonade. Jennie went to her room to retrieve her suspect chart. Broken arm or not, she had to figure out who had attempted to kill Courtney for the second time.

Lisa, nearly back to her bubbly, exuberant self, had appointed herself Jennie's assistant.

With chilled, sweating glasses on the white wicker table and pillows to prop Jennie's arm up, she and Lisa sat on the porch swing and went to work.

"Now," Jennie began, "it stands to reason that whoever tried to kill Courtney last night at the hospital is the same one who beat her up."

"That makes sense. They didn't succeed the first time, so last night they tried again. But why didn't they try sooner?"

"Maybe they didn't see her as a threat before."

"Oh," Lisa's eyes brightened in understanding. "Because she's getting better."

"And because she was moved out of intensive care. In ICU, no one could get to her." Jennie handed Lisa the chart and asked her to hold it and make notes. "Having my right arm in a cast is definitely going to be a drag."

"Don't worry. I'll be your right arm for as long as you need me." Lisa grinned and struck a secretarial pose with pen and pad at the ready. "Where do we start?"

"Okay, I'm looking for suspects that could have been at both places and who fit the description of the person I surprised last night. It's someone who knew Courtney was a diabetic and who knew she was better. Which means we can cross Frank and Brad off the list."

Lisa drew a double wavy line through both names. "I know you're going to think I'm crazy, but I decided to give Brad another chance."

"Lisa. . . ."

Lisa held a hand up to silence her. "I know you think I should dump him, but I've made up my mind."

Jennie lifted her shoulders and let them fall. "Just be careful, okay?"

"I will." Lisa moved the pen down the list. "What about Tracy?"

Jennie closed her eyes and tried to visualize the figure in the dark room. "Tracy's too short, and I don't think she's strong enough to have done this." Jennie lifted her arm about two inches from the pillow and set it down again.

"On your chart you said she could have hired someone to beat Courtney up. If she did it once, she could do it again."

"True. The only thing is, if Tracy hired someone, why go back and finish up the job? She's already on rally squad. And she doesn't want Joel." Jennie sighed. "Leave her on for now." She wiggled her fingers, something the nurses had told her to do every once in a while.

"How come you don't have Joel on the list?"

"I didn't have time to finish it. But we'd have to cross him off now anyway. He has an airtight alibi for last night. He was still hooked up to a heart monitor in the coronary care unit."

"Who else did I write down?" Jennie asked, leaning over for a closer look.

"Gavin Winslow." Lisa looked up. "You can't be serious."

Gavin. As Jennie replayed the arm-breaking incident in her mind again, another memory imposed itself on the scene—the one of her standing next to Gavin at the window of Courtney's room.

No. Jennie refused to accept the possibility of Gavin's guilt. True, she'd penciled his name in on her suspect chart, but . . . Gavin was a friend. He cared for Courtney—Jennie had seen it in his eyes that day at the hospital and in the sensitive story he'd written about the rainbow girl—his rainbow girl. *Maybe he cared too much*, Jennie reminded herself. Courtney had dumped him for Joel. Hurts like that went pretty deep.

Suddenly it all fit. He knew Courtney was getting better. And in a brilliant move that would undoubtedly make her a laughingstock among amature sleuths, Jennie had filled him in on all the details, including the fact that the nurses would be moving Courtney out of ICU.

"Jennie? What's wrong?"

"Nothing. I . . ."

The phone rang, interrupting their conversation. Just as well. Jennie needed more time to process this new information before she could share it with anyone.

Lisa hurried in to answer the phone and came out less than a minute later. "It's Gavin. Says he needs to talk to you right away."

Jennie stood up and took a deep breath. On legs rubbery as gumbo, she went in to have a chat with the would-be murderer.

24

"No. Absolutely not," Rocky growled. "May I remind you, this is not a script for 'Murder, She Wrote.' And you are not Jessica Fletcher."

Jennie thought she'd handled the conversation with Gavin rather well. Her acting skills couldn't have been better. Her plan to catch the creep seemed impeccable. Unfortunately Rocky was demanding she change one of the scenes. Her idea had been to meet Gavin at his place. Gavin had told her he wanted to go to the hospital to see Courtney, but his bike tire was flat so he wanted her to pick him up.

Jennie saw through his story immediately. How could he think she'd be that naive? It upset her even more that she hadn't seen through his guise before. She agreed to meet him. Once there, she'd confront him with the evidence, he'd confess, then try to kill her. Of course, Rocky would be waiting off scene, rush in and save her.

Case closed. Rocky, spoilsport that he could be at times, had insisted she let the police handle it alone. After threatening to break her other arm if she tried anything foolish, Rocky hung up. So much for having a friend on the police force.

"Okay, maybe I did get carried away," she said, complaining to Lisa and getting no sympathy. "I just wanted to see the look on Gavin's face when I confronted him."

"Jennie McGrady, you're just mad because he conned you. You want to get even."

"I guess you're right," Jennie sighed. "I hate being wrong about people."

"You weren't totally wrong about him. You did have his name on the suspect list. Maybe that was your subconscious telling you he was guilty."

"Hmmph."

Jennie spent the next few hours resting and wondering what had happened with Gavin. Not that she expected the police to keep her informed of their every move. Still, she had hoped Rocky would let her know something. She'd begun to feel guilty about bringing the police in instead of meeting Gavin herself. Second, third, and fourth doubts surfaced and Jennie just wanted to be reassured that she'd done the right thing. *Of course you did, McGrady*, she told herself. *Gavin was definitely the guy in that hospital room. Definitely. Unless . . . stop it, McGrady. Just stop it.*

But the niggling memory of the person who'd been in Courtney's room lingered, and though the size and shape fit Gavin, something didn't. *The baseball cap.* Of course she wasn't certain that's what she'd seen, but Jennie's memory had brought forward the image of her attacker from a side view and she was almost certain he'd been wearing a cap. On the other hand, Jennie decided at last, Gavin could have worn a hat to throw suspicion off himself. Or not.

Lisa stayed for dinner and made plans to spend the night. After eating, Jennie and Lisa went up to her room. "How about brushing my hair, I'm having a hard time doing anything left-handed."

"Sure—I'll do a French braid. Your hair is perfect for that."

Lisa concentrated on Jennie's hair for the next few minutes. "How would you feel about going to the hospital to see Joel and Courtney tonight?" She sighed. "I haven't been to see either one of them. Guess I just couldn't stand being in the hospital again. Too many memories. I don't like being reminded of the stupid stunt I pulled."

It wasn't stupid, Jennie started to say, then didn't. Nearly killing herself to make the rally squad had been the dumbest move her cousin had ever made. "Sure," Jennie said. "But you'll have to drive."

Lisa and Jennie were about to leave for the hospital when the phone rang.

Lisa grabbed the receiver and handed it to Jennie.

"I need to talk to you, girl." Tina's voice faded in and out with a background of what sounded like cars on a busy street. She sounded out of breath—or frightened.

"What about?"

"Can't say. Jus' meet me at the park."

"Tina, are you all right?"

"No. Look, ya'll quit askin' questions and get on down here."

"Okay. Where are you?"

"Park Blocks."

"Yes, but where?"

"South end—by the college."

"Hang on, Tina, I'll be there as soon as I can." Jennie hung up. "Come on, Cuz. We're going for a ride. I'll explain on the way."

Jennie filled Lisa in on the runaway's strange phone call while Lisa drove.

"Why would she call you?"

"I'm not sure. Maybe she trusts me. All I know is that Tina's in trouble. She sounded scared and I can't help wondering if she's low on insulin."

"I wish I could park closer," Lisa said as she pulled up to the curb.

"This is fine."

"It's getting dark." Lisa stared into the trees and shadows that separated them from the area where Tina was supposed to be waiting. "I don't think we should go in there."

"We have to."

Jennie stepped out of the car, closed the door, and leaned in the window. "Stay here and wait for me. I'll take a quick look around. If I find her I'll bring her back to the car to talk. If I don't come back in the next five minutes, call the police."

"No." Lisa got out of the car. "I'll go with you."

They found Tina lying at the base of a tree. Only Tina wasn't saying anything. "I was afraid of this. I don't know that much about diabetes, but I do know they can die if they don't get insulin." Jennie tried to arouse her, but couldn't.

"Is she—"

"I don't know." Jennie felt for a pulse and found one. "Her pulse is weak. We passed a pay phone about a block west of here. Go call for help. I'll stay with her."

"Come on, Tina." Jennie lifted Tina into a sitting position after Lisa took off at a run. "Hang in there. We'll get you some help."

A figure stepped between Jennie and the setting sun. Jennie had the sinking feeling the person wasn't there to help. The menacing stance tipped her off, but the partly hidden gun solidified her notion.

"I don't think so, Jennie. She'll be dead before anyone can get to her. And so will you."

Jennie forced herself to stay calm. She raised her gaze from the gun barrel to the denim shirt to the baseball cap.

The scene from the night before slammed into her brain. This was the person she'd seen in Courtney's room. Tall and slender, like Jennie, only more muscular. *How could you have been so stupid, McGrady? The baseball cap. That should have clued you in immediately.* The family probably had dozens of them. Jennie doubted Gavin even owned one.

180

"You seem surprised. And here I thought you were such a good detective."

"I'd have figured it out soon enough."

"Yeah. That's what had me worried."

"How did you . . ." Jennie glanced down at Tina. "You had her call me? What did you do to her?" Jennie stood, ready to fight.

"I wouldn't try anything if I were you. I didn't hurt her. She did it all to herself—it's pretty stupid not to go to a doctor when you're out of insulin." She waved the gun. "Come on, let's go."

"I'm not leaving Tina."

Cassie shoved the cold steel into Jennie's ribs. "You'll go. Unless you want me to bring your cousin too."

That did it. Jennie allowed herself to be led back in the direction she and Lisa had come. "I don't get it," she said. "Why would you want to kill Courtney?"

"I didn't want to." Cassie opened a car door on the driver's side and pushed Jennie inside. "Don't get any ideas about running. I'm a good shot." Cassie hurried around to the passenger side and climbed in. She jammed the key in the ignition. "Start the car."

Jennie held up her casted arm. "I can't."

"Do it."

Jennie grasped the key and turned, gritting her teeth as a spasm of pain traveled up her arm. "I can't."

Cassie gave her a look of disgust and twisted the key. The engine started. Cassie shoved the automatic transmission into drive. "Let's go."

"Where?" Beads of perspiration formed on Jennie's forehead. Some from pain—most from fear.

Jennie used her left hand to maneuver the wheel and guided the car onto the one-way street. The traffic was light.

"Where are we going?"

"Just drive. I'll tell you when to turn."

"Since you're so intent on killing me, don't you think you could at least tell me why you're doing this?"

"You're the detective. You figure it out."

"It won't take long for the police to discover that Gavin didn't do it. Since you and I are about the same size too, I'd have eventually come around to you. But I don't get it. You said a few minutes ago you didn't want to beat up Courtney. . . ."

"I didn't."

The truth hit Jennie with the impact of a cement truck. "It was Joel. I should have guessed it. The way you protected him when you found out about the steroids. What happened?"

"Take a left on Lovejoy." The fact that Cassie didn't deny it told Jennie she'd guessed right.

Jennie angled off on Lovejoy, then onto Cornell Road and through the tunnels. A dozen scenarios of how she might escape marched through her brain. She dismissed all of them.

"Joel didn't mean to hurt her," Cassie said at last. "It was an accident. They got in an argument."

"And he beat her up."

"It was the steroids. They call it a 'roid rage. He thought he'd killed her. That night, after she talked to Brad, she went home. Brad called Joel and told him Courtney wouldn't be able to get them any more 'roids. Joel went to her house and . . ." She paused. "He was scared and didn't know what to do so he put her in the trunk of her car and called me. I told him to move his car a block or so away and come get me in her car."

"So it was your idea to throw her into a dumpster." Jennie shook her head. "But you didn't do that right away, did you? First, you had to plant the seed that she'd run away."

"It was the only way. I knew about Courtney's mom and the trial. With the blood in the trunk of her car, I figured they'd blame her dad."

"And you made sure by telling everyone Frank had abused her."

"Drive into the park," Cassie said.

"Why would you want to kill me? It won't help. Sooner or later Courtney's going to wake up and . . ."

"No. No she won't. And this time, you're not going to be around to stop me."

"Cassie, please. If you turn yourself in now, you'll be facing burglary and attempted murder charges. If you kill Courtney—and me, you'll . . ."

"Just shut up." She lifted the gun from her lap and pointed it at Jennie's head. "They're not going to find out."

"Why are you still trying to protect Joel? Everyone knows about the steroids."

"You just don't get it, do you? A lot of athletes use 'roids. They just manage to get away with it. Joel didn't. So, he'll get clean and maybe still be able to play pro ball in a couple of years. If word got out that Joel beat up Courtney it would be the end of our family. Joel would go to prison. My dad would lose his endorsements. He'd lose his job—we'd lose everything."

Jennie glanced at Cassie. She'd somehow convinced herself that she had to keep Joel's secret no matter what the cost. Reasoning with her wouldn't work. Jennie doubted she could take Cassie down. Even though they were close to the same height, Cassie was much stronger.

Your only chance is to outrun her, McGrady. Right. You may be fast, but only Superman and God can outrun a speeding bullet.

"Park over there." Cassie pointed to a parking area that led to a trail. No one would be walking it at night. If Cassie killed her it could be days before anyone found her body.

Jennie parked the car and left the keys in the ignition. She got out as Cassie instructed, then walked ahead of her. Jennie had outwitted a killer before, on a trail much like this one.

Jennie walked along in silence, waiting for the right moment. An owl hooted. Jennie stopped. Cassie closed the distance between them. Jennie slammed her left elbow into Cassie's stomach. She immediately swung around and brought her fist down on Cassie's wrist. The gun flew out of her hand and landed in the bushes. Jennie didn't wait around to find out if Cassie found it again. She raced back toward the parking lot. She climbed into the car and locked the doors, then twisted the key with her left hand.

She switched on the headlights and backed the car out of the parking space. Cassie emerged from the woods. She'd recovered the gun and raised it. Jennie ducked. The bullet ripped through the glass. She turned the wheel sharply to the left and hit the gas pedal. Raising her head just enough to see the road, Jennie tore out of the lot and up the road. She could barely see through the web of cracks that spread from the bullet hole across half the windshield.

Minutes later, Jennie drove into a gas station. On legs of rubber, she stumbled out of the car into a phone booth. She gave the police Cassie's description and location as well as her own, then hung up.

Instead of getting back into the car, Jennie leaned against the glass and metal booth and sank to the ground. She drew her knees to her chest and rested her throbbing casted arm on them and waited.

25

"I love happy endings," Lisa said as she balanced her food tray and gazed over the lunch crowd at Clackamas Town Center. "Courtney's awake and Tina's going to have a place to live. That really blew me away."

"You mean Mr. Evans agreeing to take her in?"

Lisa nodded. "I guess I shouldn't be so surprised. He was so glad to get Courtney back, he'd have promised her anything."

"What surprises me is that Tina agreed to live with them."

Lisa chuckled. "Poor Mr. Evans—can you imagine having Courtney and Tina in the same house?"

"One thing's for sure, it won't be dull."

Jennie spotted Gavin sitting alone at a small round table overlooking the ice rink. She nodded toward him and started walking his way.

"Hey," he said as Jennie and Lisa slid into the chairs opposite him. "I sure appreciate your agreeing to let my mom write about you. She's really excited." Gavin moved the Coke he'd just finished to the center of the table.

Jennie sat down and began nibbling on a French fry. "It's the least I could do. I still feel really bad about getting you arrested. Besides, she's a good writer. I loved her book."

"You don't need to feel bad about my being arrested. I

was pretty scared at first, but after a while I just told myself to calm down and take in all I could. Now I have the firsthand experience of being arrested. If I ever want to write about it, I know exactly how it feels."

"Well, I'm glad we can still be friends." Jennie smiled, grateful for his quick ability to forgive. She liked that about him. In fact, she liked a lot of things about Gavin. If she didn't care so much for Ryan, and if Gavin wasn't still crazy about his rainbow girl, she might even consider him boyfriend material. "I made a lot of enemies trying to solve this case."

Lisa shifted her green gaze from the turkey sandwich she was trying to eat, to Jennie. "You really shouldn't be so hard on yourself, Jen. You saved Courtney's life, and Tina's. And in the end, you solved the mystery."

"I guess." Jennie stuck a fry in a dab of ketchup. "Only it still feels all wrong. Cassie and Joel are just kids. Not that they're innocent. I mean, Joel did beat up Courtney and Cassie tried to cover it up."

"Cover it up?" Lisa grimaced. "That's putting it mildly. She tried to kill Courtney twice, broke into Evans' Pharmacy, knocked out your mom, and tried to kill you and Tina."

Jennie sighed. "I know. I'm not discounting her guilt—she'll have to serve time for what she did. It just seems to me the real crime in all of this is the adults like Coach Haskell and Mr. Nielsen who push kids to out-perform everyone else in sports."

"I'm with you, McGrady," Gavin said. "Joel and Cassie were pawns in a much bigger game. If anyone is ultimately to blame it's Joel's dad. Mr. Nielsen was disappointed in Joel's size and in his game. When Joel turned to steroids he got his dad's attention."

"Of course, some of the blame has to fall on Courtney," Jennie added. "She did supply the steroids."

"Under duress." Gavin leaned back in his chair and stretched his long legs out in front of him. "Courtney told me she never wanted to do it, but Joel and Brad convinced her it was okay. They even showed her an article where this German coach made his star athletes take steroids. She went along with it because she didn't want to let Joel down." Gavin closed his eyes and sighed. His Adam's apple bobbed up and down and Jennie wondered if he was going to cry.

"Have you heard any more about the charges against her?" Lisa asked.

"No." Gavin shifted forward, in control again. "The important thing is that she's awake and normal. She's been released into her dad's custody. She'll probably have to do community service time, but it looks like she's learned her lesson about supplying drugs—no matter how much a person might need it."

Lisa winced and stared at her unfinished fruit drink. "I didn't help matters. I wish now that I could go back and undo the damage I did."

"Seems to me," Gavin said as he pushed his glasses against his nose, "we'd all like to do things a little differently. Only we can't go back."

"But we can go forward." Jennie scrunched up her napkin and resolved to set the unpleasant case behind her. "Which reminds me, I'd better scoot. I promised Mom I'd be packed and ready to go tonight. We're flying out early tomorrow morning."

"Flying out?" Gavin raised his eyebrows. "Where are you going?"

"She gets to go to a dude ranch in Montana." Lisa pouted, stood, and tossed her empty cup in the trash. "I have to stay here. Mom thinks the trip would be too strenuous for me."

They set their trays on top of the food court's trash bins,

wove their way around the tables, and out into the main part of the mall.

"Maybe your parents will change their minds," Jennie said as they walked toward the exit. "I'll call them and tell them how healthy it is out there. All that fresh air and good food . . ."

Gavin glanced from one to another. "What—is this a vacation or something?"

"Not exactly. Mom got a letter from her sister, Maggie," Jennie began. "Her husband, Jeff White Cloud, is in the hospital. They had some kind of explosion that killed the foreman and badly injured Jeff. Anyway, they're at the height of the tourist season and Aunt Maggie needs help running the ranch."

"Where is it? I mean, Montana is a big state."

"The ranch is in western Montana near the Bitterroot Mountains," Lisa explained. "They call it *Dancing Waters*— isn't that a great name?" She sighed, her eyes huge and sad. "I'm so jealous. I love horses—and cowboys."

Jennie chuckled and draped an arm over Lisa's shoulders. "I'll check them out and let you know if it's worth the trip. Actually, I'm looking forward to seeing the llamas, *and* my cousins, of course."

"So, are you gonna solve the mystery?" Gavin asked.

"What mystery?"

"The bombing. I'm betting it's a terrorist act—those militia groups are big out there. Or maybe someone wants to cause your uncle a lot of trouble so he'll sell. Maybe he caught someone rustling cattle. Or, there could be silver or copper on the property. . . ."

"Whoa." Jennie tossed Gavin an incredulous look. "There's no mystery. I'm just going to help run the ranch until Uncle Jeff gets out of the hospital."

"Sure you are." Gavin winked at Lisa and gave her a knowing grin.

"Okay. I admit, I'm a little curious. Aunt Maggie did say the sheriff was investigating. And that some unusual things had been happening lately, but I'm not going out there to solve a mystery."

After saying goodbye, Jennie climbed into her Mustang and headed home. Excitement mounted with each mile. What would Montana really hold?

Betrayed

Patricia H. Rushford

Jennie McGrady Mystery Series

9601

Betrayed

Patricia H. Rushford

BETHANY HOUSE PUBLISHERS
MINNEAPOLIS, MINNESOTA 55438

Published by Bethany House Publishers
A Ministry of Bethany Fellowship, Inc.
11300 Hampshire Avenue South
Minneapolis, Minnesota 55438

Printed in the United States of America.

Library of Congress Cataloging-in-Publication Data

Rushford, Patricia H.
    Betrayed / Patricia Rushford
        p. cm. — (The Jennie McGrady mystery series ; 7)
    Summary: Jennie begins detective work when she arrives at the ranch owned by her uncle, a full-blooded American Indian, and learns that an explosion has killed one man and severely injured another.

    [1. Ranch life—Fiction. 2. Nez Percé Indians—Fiction. 3. Indians of North America—Fiction. 4. Mystery and detective stories.] I. Title. II. Series: Rushford, Patricia H. Jennie McGrady mystery series ; 7.
PZ7.R8972Be   1996
[Fic]—dc20   95–43935
ISBN 1–55661–560–4   CIP
                                     AC

Dedicated to Jan Bono
and her sixth-grade class
at Hilltop Elementary
in Illwaco, Washington.

PATRICIA RUSHFORD is an award-winning writer, speaker, and teacher who has published numerous articles and over twenty books, including *What Kids Need Most in a Mom, The Humpty Dumpty Syndrome: Putting Yourself Back Together Again*, and her first young adult novel, *Kristen's Choice*. She is a registered nurse and has a master's degree in counseling from Western Evangelical Seminary. She and her husband, Ron, live in Washington State and have two grown children, six grandchildren, and lots of nephews and nieces.

Pat has been reading mysteries for as long as she can remember and is delighted to be writing a series of her own. She is a member of Mystery Writers of America, Sisters in Crime, Society of Children's Book Writers and Illustrators, and several other writing organizations. She is also co-director of Writer's Weekend at the Beach.

1

"We've begun our final descent to Missoula." The pilot thanked them for flying with Horizon and added, "Looks like clear skies and eighty degrees."

Jennie twisted her long dark braid and peered at the rugged wilderness below. Butterflies soared through her stomach again as she thought of her aunt and uncle and the trouble they'd been having at the Dancing Waters Dude Ranch.

Take it easy, McGrady, Jennie told herself for the umpteenth time since leaving Portland. *You're getting worked up over nothing.* Aunt Maggie had called the explosion an accident. But what if she was wrong?

Since she'd often been accused of having an overactive imagination, Jennie blotted out the questions and focused instead on the snow-capped peaks and forest below.

"Ever been to Montana before?" the young man sitting beside Jennie asked.

"No." Jennie turned from the window to look at him. Until now her seatmate hadn't been in a talkative mood. He'd placed his black cowboy hat in the overhead bin, folded his muscular frame into the seat, and fallen asleep. His jeans, cowboy boots, and white western-style shirt suggested he might be a rancher—or a would-be cowboy.

"Then you're in for a real treat." His grin revealed a perfect set of white teeth. "By the way, I'm Marty Danielson."

7

Jennie returned the smile. "Jennie McGrady."

He tipped his head to one side and fixed his gaze on hers. "You sure got pretty eyes, Jennie McGrady. Deepest blue I've ever seen."

"Thanks." Jennie looked away, feeling a flush rise to her cheeks. "It's . . . um . . . a family trait. My dad and brother . . ." She let her voice trail off. Wanting to change the subject she asked, "Do you live around here?"

"Yep, I'm a freshman at the University of Montana, but I haven't been home in a month. Been on the rodeo circuit. My folks have a little spread south of town." He stretched his long legs, which wasn't easy when you were stuffed into a space that barely fit a ten-year-old. Being fairly tall herself, Jennie could empathize since she'd been sitting in the cramped window seat for the last two hours. She'd worn baggy cotton shorts and a matching shirt, but still felt uncomfortable. Of course, having her right arm in a cast didn't help.

As her gaze drifted to the bright blue fiberglass cast, so did Marty's. "What did you do to your arm?"

Jennie shrugged and gave what had become her standard answer. "Broke it in a fight." In part, her explanation was true. Her arm had taken a blow meant for her head.

When he raised an eyebrow, she grinned and said, "You should see the other guy." Jennie supposed she should be more specific, but how could she tell people she'd been an intended murder victim without spending ages explaining? The cast served as a grim reminder of Jennie's vulnerability, and she didn't like talking about it.

He threw her a look of disbelief, then said, "Must be pretty uncomfortable with your elbow locked like that."

"It's not bad. I'd much rather have it casted bent than straight."

"Broke my arm a couple years ago. A steer threw me, then spun around and stomped on me. Thought I was a goner."

"Sounds dangerous."

His smile faded. "Yep. Life is dangerous." He glanced away briefly then turned back to her, smiling again. "Say . . ." Marty's blue-gray eyes widened. "If you're gonna be in town for a while, maybe you could come by my place for a visit. I'll show you around. Teach you how to rope and ride."

Jennie was flattered, but not all that interested. "I'll be working—I think. My aunt and uncle own a ranch here."

"Yeah? Who are they? I know most of the ranchers in the area."

"Jeff and Maggie White Cloud. Aunt Maggie is my mom's sister. . . ."

Marty's eyes turned cold. "You seem like a nice girl, Jennie, so I'm gonna give you a little advice. When we land, you go to the ticket agent and tell them you want the next flight out of here."

"I don't understand. Why. . . ?"

"Jeff White Cloud and his family's been nothin' but trouble since they showed up out at Dancing Waters less than a year ago. You hang around out there and you're liable to get hurt."

His *advice* surprised her, and she wasn't sure how to respond. "Is that a threat?"

"Nothin' personal. Just that some folks round here aren't too friendly toward Indian lovers."

Jennie ignored the racist remark, hoping he'd answer some of her questions. "Do you know anything about the explosion at their ranch?"

Marty frowned. "Nope. I told you, I've been gone."

"The explosion killed the ranch foreman and injured my uncle—he's still in the hospital."

"Rick Jenkins?" He whistled. "That's too bad. Can't say I'm too surprised though. What does surprise me is that your uncle is still alive." Marty slumped in his seat and stared

9

straight ahead, a frown etching deep lines in his brow. Jennie thought he seemed more shaken by the news than he'd admitted.

As they landed, the prop plane, a thirty-seven-passenger Dornier, bounced a couple of times, then shuddered to a slow roll as the pilot brought it in. Right on time. Twelve-thirty.

Marty retrieved his carry-on, slapped the hat over his ash brown hair, then walked in front of her until they were inside the airport. He was tall—over six feet and the hat and boots gave him even more height. He spun around to face her. The coldness in his eyes had turned to concern. "I meant what I said, Jennie. Jeff White Cloud's got more enemies in the Bitterroot Valley than a killer mountain lion. If you're smart, you'll go back to Portland and forget about helping him."

Marty's warning hadn't exactly scared her, but he had stirred up her interest. Maybe her intuition was onto something after all. She'd suspected foul play from the moment she heard about the so-called accident. Marty could be holding the key to a murder, and Jennie didn't intend to walk away. "Guess I'm not too smart."

Marty gazed at her for a moment, then sighed. "Sorry to hear that." He spun around and walked off.

Jennie watched him go. Excitement shivered through her. At the same time, a band of fear tightened around her throat. *You're not here to solve a mystery, McGrady,* she reminded herself. *You're here to work. And there is nothing to be afraid of—at least not yet.*

Jennie glanced around the terminal, looking for the face she'd memorized from the photo Aunt Maggie had sent. *"Heather will be at the airport to pick you up,"* Maggie had assured her on the phone last night. *"I'll send her in plenty of time to meet your plane."*

Jennie scanned the crowd, but saw no one even resembling the girl in the picture. Heather White Cloud was half

Irish and half Nez Perce Indian. With her coal black hair and wide dark eyes, she looked like a model.

Fifteen minutes later, Jennie slipped on her black leather backpack and scooped up her duffle bag, then headed toward the baggage claim area. Maybe her cousin would be waiting there.

She wasn't.

Jennie retrieved her bags off the conveyer belt, set them on a luggage cart, then settled into a chair near the door where she could watch for Heather. A few minutes later she jumped up and paced, angry one minute and worried the next. Though she fought against it, the conversation she'd had with Marty niggled its way into her guarded thoughts. Jeff White Cloud had enemies. The explosion had killed one man and sent her uncle to the hospital. Could something have happened to Heather, too?

Jennie had Heather paged. No one responded. Another half hour passed and Jennie decided she'd better call the ranch. She groped inside the backpack for her wallet and pulled out Aunt Maggie's letter. She'd located a pay phone and was about to dial the number when she caught a glimpse of her cousin in the baggage claim area.

Jennie started to wave, then stopped. Heather apparently had more important things on her mind than picking up a relative.

She was even more gorgeous in person than in the photograph. Her straight black hair reached the small of her back. A barrette of feathers and a dream catcher adorned one side. Her tan skin contrasted with her gauzy white dress.

A guy in his late teens, maybe early twenties, wearing jeans and a baggy denim shirt stood beside her. Judging by the shoulder bag and camera hanging around his neck, Jennie thought he might be a professional photographer. Shifting his camera aside, he gathered Heather in his arms and kissed her.

Jennie glanced away, but curiosity about the guy and why Heather was with him instead of meeting her made her look back. A few minutes later they separated, and he left the terminal.

Jennie shifted her gaze to Heather. This time Heather spotted her, then smiled and waved. The seventeen-year-old walked toward her, reminding Jennie of a princess, which in a way she was. Her great-grandfather had been a tribal chief. Several people paused to admire her as she passed by. That kind of attention would have mortified Jennie. Heather seemed to enjoy it.

"Hi." Her mouth curved in a perfect smile. "I was afraid I wouldn't recognize you."

Heather's eyes were a deep shade of purple. Jennie could almost see herself in them. She could see something else too. Or maybe she just sensed it. Heather didn't look dangerous, but something about her spelled trouble with a capital T. Jennie thought about taking Marty's advice and flying back home. She wouldn't, of course. Jennie didn't back away from much of anything, especially a mystery.

"I'm sorry I'm late," Heather went on. "But I had a flat on the way in. Can you believe it?"

No. Come on, Heather, tell me the truth. Who was that guy, and why are you lying to me? Jennie wanted to confront her, but didn't. She answered with a polite, "Those things happen." Jennie had a lot of questions but decided to keep her mouth shut for now. After all, even though they were cousins, they had seen each other only once before, at Jennie's dad's funeral.

Fake funeral, Jennie reminded herself. Jason McGrady wasn't really dead, but no one knew that except Jennie, Gram, and a few government officials. He'd been working for the government on a drug case when his plane supposedly went down in the Puget Sound area near Seattle. The authorities never found the plane or his body.

12

A couple of months ago, Jennie discovered the truth. Her father had changed his identity and was working for the Drug Enforcement Agency. But that was another story. Something Jennie tried not to think about too much these days.

Heather nodded toward Jennie's cast. "What happened to your arm?"

"Broke it in a fight."

Heather grimaced. "How awful. You were fighting with someone?"

"Yeah. I didn't start it, but I got in the last lick."

"Oh." Heather stooped to pick up one of Jennie's bags.

Jennie shrugged. So much for making a good impression.

They collected Jennie's luggage and set it at the curb, where Jennie waited while Heather brought around a white Jeep Cherokee.

"Are you hungry?" Heather asked as they left the airport.

"Starved."

"We'll have lunch in town then. I promised Mom I'd run a few errands so we may be a while."

"Sounds good."

They pulled into the Watering Hole Restaurant. The waitress had just seated them when Marty Danielson approached their table.

He folded himself into the seat next to Heather. "Aren't you going to welcome me home?"

Heather ignored him.

The wistful look on Marty's face left no doubt that he didn't dislike all of the White Clouds. Marty switched his gaze to Jennie and flashed her a grin. "I'm sorry if I gave you the wrong impression back at the airport."

"You two know each other?" Heather's dark eyes sent Jennie an off-limits signal, which seemed pretty strange considering Heather's tryst with the photographer.

"Marty!" The harsh voice came from a grim-faced man in a tan shirt and camouflage pants who stood at the cash

13

register. He gave the girls a long disparaging look and motioned for Marty to join him.

"Um—I gotta go." Marty's Adam's apple shifted up and down. His self-assured attitude seemed to melt into the cracks of the rustic wood floor as he stood. "I'll see you."

After the men left, Heather repeated her question.

"He sat next to me on the plane." Jennie shrugged. "So, what's the deal between you two?"

"We dated a few times. Marty's okay, but his dad . . ." Heather dipped her head, but not fast enough to hide the tears pooling in her eyes. "Let's just say he doesn't like half-breeds."

"Marty seems to like you."

"Please don't get involved, Jennie. It doesn't matter anymore. I have other plans."

Plans that no doubt involve the photographer. Jennie picked at her salad, not knowing what to say or if she should say anything at all.

She missed Lisa, her cousin and best friend. They shared everything. Jennie doubted she and Heather would ever be that close. Still, a little comradarie would be nice. A few manners wouldn't hurt either.

Heather spoke little during the rest of their rabbit-food lunch. Jennie had dozens of questions about the ranch, about Aunt Maggie, Uncle Jeff, Heather's twin brother Hazen and their ten-year-old sister, Amber. Heather's mind seemed to be on other matters, so Jennie didn't ask.

A loud voice rose above the normal restaurant din. "No kidding, the buck had antlers on him as wide as this table." She glanced around and had no trouble locating the source. Several men wearing fatigues much like Marty's father occupied a large corner booth in the smoking section. Judging by the noise level and the comment she'd overheard, they were trading hunting stories.

In contrast to the rowdies, two men in business suits sat

in the booth behind Heather. They spoke in hushed voices, using terms like litigation, investments, and loans. When they got up to leave, one of them paused at the table and leveled a concerned gaze at Heather. "Hi, Heather. How's the family?"

Heather shrugged. "Okay, I guess."

"Is your dad home yet? I've been up to the hospital a couple times. I hope he's feeling better."

"He should be home in the next day or two."

"You tell him I asked about him, okay?"

"Sure."

The man nodded and smiled at Jennie, then left without an introduction. Heather turned her attention back to her salad.

Jennie watched out the window as the same two men climbed into a red convertible. They were about the same height but seemed as different as salt and pepper. The one who'd spoken to Heather was light skinned with sandy hair and a broad, friendly smile. The other was more serious looking with olive skin and dark hair.

"Who were those men?" Jennie asked when her curiosity begged for an answer.

Heather glanced out the window and shrugged. "A couple of Dad's friends. The one driving is Alex Dayton. The other one is Greg Bennett. He's Chad Elliot's lawyer."

"Who's Chad Elliot?"

Heather gave her a don't-you-know-anything look and took a sip of water. "He's the guy who's suing us to get his ranch back."

Oh, well, that explains everything. Jennie held back the sarcastic remark. She wanted to find out more, but Heather picked up the bill and slid out of the booth.

After paying the bill and using the rest room, they headed back to the Jeep. Someone had tucked a note under the windshield wiper. Heather ripped it off and threw it to the ground.

"Wait." Jennie retrieved it. "Don't you want to see what it says?"

"No. It won't be any different from the others." Heather climbed into the Jeep and jammed the key into the ignition. "Go ahead. Read it if you . . ." The roar of the engine obliterated the rest of her sentence.

Jennie walked around to the passenger side and unfolded the pale green paper. She closed her eyes and bit her lower lip. No wonder Heather hadn't wanted to read it. Jennie folded the note and stuffed it into the pocket of her shorts.

Even though she'd tucked the words out of sight, they burned in her mind like a searing brand on cowhide.

Tell your daddy next time he won't be so lucky.

2

"Do you know who left the note?" Jennie asked.

"Isn't that obvious? You're the hotshot detective, what do you think?" Heather's disposition had turned even more sour, but this time Jennie didn't blame her. Death threats could do that to a person.

Jennie shrugged. "Marty's dad was in the restaurant. He seemed pretty hostile."

"Him and about a dozen others I could name. It's no use, Jennie. Just forget you saw it."

"Shouldn't we show this note to the police or something?"

Heather sighed. "What's the point? They'd just hand the evidence over to Sheriff Mason, and he'd pretend to check it out."

"Pretend?" Jennie braced herself as Heather made a sharp right turn into the shopping mall parking lot.

"Just forget it. I don't want to talk about it—not now or ever. Do you want to come with me or stay in the car?"

Neither choice appealed to Jennie at the moment, but she opted to go along.

———

"Well, that's it," Heather announced an hour and three stores later as she and Jennie emptied the grocery cart. "We're out of here."

Jennie returned the cart while Heather started the Jeep, and a few minutes later they left the city behind and headed south on Highway 93.

"How far is Dancing Waters?" Jennie asked.

"About sixty-five miles. We're south of Darby, near an even smaller town called Cottonwood. There's a map and a brochure in the glove box if you want to check it out. I don't feel like playing tour guide right now."

Jennie retrieved both and hauled in a deep breath of country air. At least now she could understand her cousin's sullen mood. Getting threats like that had to be terrifying. Still, Jennie wished Heather had more courage. She should be fighting back, not giving up.

"Look," Jennie began. "I know we don't know each other very well, but maybe I can help."

"And just what do you think you could do? Oh, I heard all about how you rescued your little brother and . . . all those other cases. But you have a broken arm and . . . this is different. We're dealing with dangerous people who judge you by the color of your skin. There are too many of them to fight. Daddy should have listened—then maybe Rick wouldn't be dead and Dad wouldn't have lost his leg."

Jennie swallowed hard and closed her eyes. She hadn't known the extent of Jeff's injuries until now and didn't know what to say.

Jennie wished her grandmother could be with her. Gram was one of those people who seemed to know how to deal with everything. Having been a police officer, and now doing occasional jobs for the F.B.I., she had connections all over the country. Besides all that, she wrote articles for several major travel magazines.

Wait! That's it, McGrady. Gram could come to Dancing Waters undercover. She could pretend to be writing an article about the ranch, but in reality she'd be investigating the explosion and the threats.

18

With her arm still in a cast, Jennie didn't feel safe delving into the case alone, but the thought of Gram coming gave her a renewed sense of power. Jennie made a mental note to call Gram that night, then opened the map and brochure and worked on familiarizing herself with her new environment.

Ranches and companies that built log cabins lined the road. Mountains rose from the valley floor on both sides— the Saffire Mountains to the left and the Selway Bitterroot Wilderness on the right. According to the brochure, Dancing Waters, a working dude ranch, had everything. Guests could relax in natural hot springs, enjoy a massage, eat gourmet meals, or simply enjoy the view.

For the more rugged individual, Dancing Waters offered fishing, white water rafting, backpacking trips into the wilderness, packing with horses and llamas, or mountain climbing. They offered a month-long wilderness experience— where guests hiked into the mountains and lived off the land much as the Indians and the early settlers had.

Jennie leaned forward to place the papers back in the glove box. "Dancing Waters sounds fantastic. Do you guys really do all this stuff?"

"Hmmmph." Heather's enthusiasm was about as high as a gnat's elbow. "We work—the guests have fun—at least that's what they say they're having."

"Sounds as though you don't like it out here."

Heather sneered. "I'm from New York. I love the city. This place bores me. One way or another, I'm getting out."

Okay. Be that way. Jennie slumped back in her seat. So much for having a cousin to pal around with. For the rest of the trip, Jennie watched the scenery—the ranches, and the Bitterroot River as it curved and danced along beside them. *Dancing Waters.* Maybe that's how the ranch got its name. Jennie thought about asking Heather, but didn't—somehow she doubted Heather's answer would do the explanation justice.

At four-thirty Heather turned off the highway and pulled into a long, winding drive. They passed under a black wrought-iron arch with the words "Dancing Waters Dude Ranch" scrolled between double lines. Despite her companion's lack of enthusiasm, Jennie could hardly wait.

They bumped along for another half mile, finally stopping near a complex of at least a dozen buildings.

A little girl ran toward them screaming and ducked for cover behind the Jeep. An ostrich followed a few yards behind. Judging from the fiery look in its eyes, the bird was not a happy camper.

"Oh, great. The ostriches are loose. Poppy's getting away. We'd better head her off before she finds the road. Get in front of her and coax her back to the pen."

"Me?" Jennie sucked in a deep breath hoping a little courage would be mixed with the oxygen. Following Heather's lead, she climbed out of the Jeep and walked toward the huge bird.

"Take it easy, Poppy, you know you're not supposed to be out here," Heather cooed. "Come on, Jennie, hurry. Get over here now."

Jennie quickened her pace and placed herself between the ostrich and the road. The huge bird's long neck shifted up and down, then from one side to the other as if sizing Jennie up. She knew little about ostriches but remembered something about their being strong and powerful.

The girls stretched out their arms to create a human fence. As if sensing the weak link, the six-foot ostrich charged at Jennie.

3

Jennie screamed, then ducked and raised her right arm to protect her head. The ostrich, bent on escape, whacked Jennie's cast with her beak. Poppy sprang back, stunned. She stared vacantly, as though trying to focus her enormous eyes. After a few moments, Poppy turned around and trotted back toward a chain link fence.

"Wow." Heather grinned. "I'm impressed."

Jennie swallowed hard and stared at the shallow dent in her cast. "Me too." She followed Heather past the largest of the buildings into a courtyard. At the far end of the compound, three ostriches skittered back and forth, obviously trying to break free.

Dozens of people in a variety of shapes and sizes had gathered to watch the commotion. Several of the braver souls formed a semicircle around the loose ostriches, waving their hands and trying to herd the creatures back through the open gate. Three long-necked creatures loped along the perimeter of the human fence, scanning their captors, probably looking for an easy way out. Jennie joined the circle, but held her cast at the ready—just in case. One by one the birds gave up their quest and returned to the pen.

Before Jennie could recover, a woman with freckled skin and kinky auburn hair moved in close beside her. She wore a long denim skirt and vest, and a cream-colored cotton shirt with *Dancing Waters Dude Ranch* embroidered on the pocket. "Jennie, it's so good to have you here."

"I'm glad to be here—I think." Jennie wrapped her arms around her aunt, careful not to whack her with the cast. Maggie was seven years older than Mom, a couple inches taller, and thinner than Jennie remembered.

After a thorough hug, Aunt Maggie let her go. "What a welcome for you. Sorry about Poppy. She's usually not that aggressive." Maggie nodded toward the ostrich pen. "They may be worth a lot of money, but sometimes I wonder if they're worth the trouble."

She glanced down at Jennie's cast and frowned. "Good thing it was the cast and not your flesh. These guys may look harmless, but they can be mean. Some of them are ten feet tall and there's no stopping them once they decide to run. Fortunately, the girls in this pen are fairly docile."

"That's docile?"

Maggie examined Jennie's cast again. "Does your arm hurt?"

"Not anymore." Jennie glanced back at the pen. "Do the ostriches get out often?"

Maggie shook her head and sighed. "Someone must have left the gate unlatched. Probably Amber."

"I heard that, Mother, and you are wrong, wrong, wrong! I shut the gate tight and checked it." A lanky young girl with red-gold hair several shades lighter than Maggie's seemed on the verge of tears. "Someone else did it. Probably on purpose, like all the other stuff."

"We'll talk about it later, honey." Maggie gathered her close and stroked her curls. "We have a guest."

"Hi." She peered up at Jennie as she tucked her hands in the back pockets of her jeans. "Are you my cousin?"

"That depends. Are you Amber?"

Amber nodded and looked at her mother. "I thought you said there'd be three of them."

22

Maggie chuckled. "There will be. Eventually." To Jennie she said, "Your mom called earlier."

"When is she coming? Did she get the okay to bring Hannah?" The McGradys had been caring for Hannah, their four-year-old neighbor, in the weeks following her kidnapping. Unfortunately they'd hit a snag in taking her across state lines. Mom and Nick, Jennie's five-year-old brother, stayed behind to work things out with Children's Services. Since Maggie had been desperate for help, Mom insisted Jennie go on ahead.

"Um . . . They've run into some trouble, but you're not to worry. They should be here in three or four days."

"Three or four days!" Amber rolled her eyes. "I was planning on giving them a tour."

"Will I do?" Jennie asked. "I could use a guide. This place is huge."

"That's a wonderful idea, Amber," Maggie said, "but first we need to concentrate on dinner." To Jennie she said, "This is the height of the tourist season and I have a hundred guests looking forward to meal time. I still have to prepare the ostrich."

Jennie's mouth dropped open. "You eat them?"

"Occasionally. They're expensive, but . . ." Maggie closed her eyes in an expression of ecstasy. "Unbelievably good."

"Get used to it, Jennie," Amber advised. "This is the farm. We raise animals to eat." She took a deep breath. "That's what Daddy says. Actually, I'm thinking seriously about becoming a vegetarian."

Maggie's eyes sparkled with hidden laughter as she winked at Jennie. "I'll remember that next time we have a barbeque." She hugged Amber close, then released her. "Enough talk for now. We've got work to do. Amber, honey, get one of the hands to bring Jennie's things up to the house. Jennie, you can go on up to the house now if you want. Or if you'd rather you can just wander around here, maybe find a comfy place to rest. We'll have some time to chat later."

"I'm not much for sitting around—can I do something to help?"

Maggie glanced at the cast. "I certainly could use an extra hand in the dining room, but are you sure you can bus tables with that cast?"

"Sure. The doctor said I can do almost anything except straighten my arm." She held up her left hand. "Besides, I'm getting pretty good at being a lefty."

Maggie didn't look convinced. "Okay, if you're sure. But if you get tired or start hurting, I want you to stop."

Jennie agreed.

"Before you start working, why don't you take a few minutes to freshen up in one of the bathrooms here in the lodge?" Maggie sighed and hugged her again. "I know this isn't much of a welcome, but we'll catch up later. I promise."

Maggie escorted Jennie into an enormous log structure. Inside the lodge, rough-hewn timbers stretched across the rafters. A dozen or so guests sat in the plush leather couches and chairs in the lobby. A gray stone fireplace took up an entire wall, separating the lobby from a large dining hall. A few guests were already seated at round tables covered with white linen cloths. The dining room extended to a large outside deck overlooking a river. A small gift shop occupied one corner.

Maggie showed her the kitchen, then left her inside the rest room. Jennie would have loved a twenty-minute shower, but settled instead on washing her hands and face. She looked fairly good for someone who'd come five-hundred miles, been threatened by a cowboy, lied to by a cousin, and done battle with an ostrich.

Before heading back to the kitchen, she took a moment to call home. When no one answered, Jennie left a message on the machine and hung up. She tried calling Gram, but got the answering machine there as well. "God, please let everything go okay with Hannah," Jennie whispered as she glanced upward and walked through the milling guests toward the kitchen.

Helping with the meal turned out to be much more interesting than Jennie had imagined. She bussed tables, served food, talked to guests and, from time to time, paused to enjoy the view of the river as it passed—no, danced—beside the deck. *Dancing Waters*. That had to be how the ranch got its name.

At seven-thirty the last guest wandered out of the dining room. She'd heard nothing but praises about the food and could hardly wait for the meal Maggie had promised. Jennie picked up the dishes and silverware and carried the tray into the kitchen.

"Great job, Jennie." Maggie squeezed her shoulders. "Now it's our turn. Come on. We'll eat on the deck." Maggie led the way, and within minutes Jennie was drooling over the salad, steak, wild rice, and baby asparagus spears.

Maggie waited for Heather and Amber to join them, then said grace. Famished, Jennie cut into her steak and took a bite. "Mmmm." She raised her head only to discover three pairs of eyes trained on her.

"Um . . . did I do something wrong?"

"Not at all, Jennie." Maggie grinned. "Do you like the meat?"

"Yes. This is the best steak I've ever eaten." She sliced off another bite and lifted the fork to her mouth.

Amber giggled. "It's ostrich."

Jennie closed her mouth and set the fork back down. "No way. This is red meat—it's a steak. An ostrich is a bird. Wouldn't it taste more like chicken?"

"Nope. That's ostrich," Amber said. "We knew you wouldn't try it if we told you."

"You're right about that." Jennie took another bite. "This is so good."

"Wow, Jennie likes it. . . ." Heather speared a lettuce leaf. Her voice dripped with sarcasm and Jennie wondered what she'd done to make her cousin angry.

"Heather, please." Maggie placed a hand on her daughter's arm. "Not now."

"Jennie already knows how much I hate this place. Why pretend we're all one big happy family when we're not?"

"Couldn't you at least make an effort?"

"I am, Mother. You haven't given me much choice." Heather pushed her chair back and left the table.

After dinner Maggie, Amber, and Jennie walked up the hill to where the family lived. Unlike the rustic log cabins and lodge, the White Cloud home was as elegant as a Victorian mansion.

"You'll be sharing a room with Heather," Maggie said as they stepped into the tiled entry. "I hope that will be okay for you. Heather isn't usually this . . . ah . . . negative."

Amber rolled her eyes and took hold of Jennie's hand. "She has been since we moved out here. Come on, I'll show you where your room is. If my sister gets too weird, you can move in with me."

"I'll keep that in mind." Jennie wished some of Amber's charm would rub off on Heather.

She followed the ten-year-old up the winding staircase and down a long hall. "This one is Heather's." Amber pointed to the bedroom on the left. "And the bathroom." Amber pushed open the door to reveal a large room with a claw-foot tub. "The next one is the guest room. Your mom's gonna sleep there when she comes. Mom and Dad have the one at the end of the hall and my room is next to them." Amber skipped a door. It must have been her brother's. Jennie wondered why she didn't mention it.

Tour completed, they entered Heather's bedroom.

Heather wasn't there, and that suited Jennie fine. A large white bear, similar to one of hers, rested against a pink ruffled pillow. His whimsical black button eyes almost made her feel at home.

The room had two beds, and since her luggage had been set in front of the one on the left, Jennie assumed she'd be sleeping there.

"You can put your stuff in here," Amber said as she opened the door to a walk-in closet.

A poster of Heather and Hazen in native American costumes hung over a white chest of drawers. "Amber, where's your brother?"

Amber clasped her hands in front of her and gazed at the picture. Moisture pooled in her deep golden eyes. "Gone. He went away after my dad got hurt."

"Just like that? And you don't know where he is?"

"Nope. He just disappeared."

"Did someone kidnap him or. . . ?"

"I don't think so. He was with Daddy and Rick—that's the foreman that got killed. Hazen drove Daddy to the hospital, and we haven't seen him since."

Jennie shook her head. Maybe she had a misplaced sense of responsibility, but it seemed to her that Heather and Hazen should be helping their folks instead of feeling sorry for themselves. In her family if anyone got hurt, the others all pitched in to help. They didn't run away. *It isn't any of your business, McGrady. And don't be so judgmental—you've only been here a few hours. If Amber's story is right, Hazen may have saved his father's life.*

"Amber," Maggie called. "You need to get ready for bed."

Amber rolled her eyes. "I never get to stay up late." After saying good-night and giving Jennie a hug, Amber left.

Jennie began emptying her suitcase. Every time she passed the twin's poster she stopped to examine it. Something about it—about them—drew her like an invisible thread. She felt connected, yet distant. What a mystery they were. Beautiful, yet dangerous.

Dangerous? Oh, come on, McGrady. So Heather met a guy at the airport, then lied to you about it. And Hazen left home after the explosion. That doesn't make them dangerous. You're letting your imagination go wild again.

She continued to stare at the picture. Yet there was something. She'd seen it earlier in Heather. Now she saw the same expression on Hazen's handsome face—in those haunting dark eyes.

Jennie shook her head to dispel her foolish thoughts, then finished unpacking and hurried downstairs.

She found Maggie in the front room relaxing in a rocking chair. With her shoes off and her thick red hair cascading around her shoulders, she resembled Mom even more than before.

Jennie felt sad for her. She'd been through so much with her husband hurt and in the hospital. Why did Heather and Hazen have to be so selfish? Jennie closed out the angry thoughts and gave her aunt a hug.

"Did you get settled in?" Maggie asked.

"Yep. I love the room. And the house."

"I love it too. The original owners had it built in the early 1900s." She smiled. "Would you believe they ordered it out of a Sears & Roebuck catalog?"

Jennie sank into a couch next to Maggie's chair. "Really?"

"Really. In those days you could order anything. It's solid too. Better than most of the houses built today. All we had to do was resurface the flooring in a few of the rooms and paint."

Jennie wiggled deeper into the plush cushioned couch and closed her eyes.

She felt something on her arm and jumped. "Sorry if I startled you, Jennie." Maggie smiled down at her. "You look

28

like you're about to fall asleep."

At Maggie's suggestion, Jennie went upstairs and crawled into bed.

Some time later, a door clicked shut, pulling Jennie out of a sound sleep. Heather turned on a multicolored stained-glass lamp beside her bed, flooding the room in rainbows.

"I'm sorry," Heather said when Jennie sat up. "I didn't mean to wake you."

Jennie yawned. "What time is it?"

"Just nine-thirty."

Jennie had slept for only twenty minutes, but the short nap had revived her.

"Listen, Jennie. I've been acting like a brat, and I hope you'll forgive me. My only excuse is that so much has been happening around here lately. None of this is your fault and . . ."

"Hey, it's okay. I understand."

Heather smiled. "I'm glad. We kind of started off on the wrong foot, didn't we?"

Even though Heather's icy antagonism seemed to be melting, Jennie didn't trust her. "I'm willing to start over if you are."

"Great." Heather opened her closet door and stepped inside saying she needed to change. Jennie expected to see her in pajamas, but Heather emerged wearing a pair of black jeans and a loose white blouse under a black leather vest. A silver and turquoise necklace hung around her slender neck.

"You're going out?" Jennie asked.

"I have to meet someone." She shrugged on a black suede jacket. "I know it's asking a lot, but this is important to me."

"And you don't want me to tell your mom?" Jennie bit the inside of her cheek.

Heather winced. "I wouldn't ask, but Mom has so much on her mind with Dad being gone and Hazen running off. I don't want her to worry."

Jennie tossed her covers aside. "Are you doing something she'd be worried about?"

"No, of course not."

"Let me come with you."

"No! Stay out of this, Jennie. The less you know the better." Heather opened her bedroom window then disappeared in the foliage of a large maple tree. Jennie pulled her clothes on and stuffed her feet into her tennis shoes. By the time Jennie stepped onto the roof, Heather had reached the fence at the edge of the lawn. Jennie eyed the giant tree, then her casted arm, and took a deep breath. Using her left hand to grasp the limbs and her right arm for balance, she stepped onto an ample branch next to the roof and began her descent. Fortunately, the tree had been made for climbing and Jennie had no problem jumping from the lowest branch, which hung only three feet from the ground.

Once on the ground, Jennie glanced off in the direction she'd last seen her cousin. With the flashlight marking the way, Heather was heading into the woods.

A full moon illuminated the path. In the distance the beam from Heather's flashlight bounced through the trees. Jennie slowed and followed a safe distance behind.

"Who's there?" Heather stopped and spun around.

Jennie ducked behind a fir tree and waited for Heather to move on. Maintaining a greater distance between them, she trailed Heather for what seemed like forever, then stopped when the beam from the flashlight vanished. She strained to hear her cousin's footfall but heard only the sound of chattering leaves as a cool breeze swept through the forest.

Jennie hugged herself to ward off the chill. Was Heather playing games? "Okay, Heather, you win. I'm going back now."

No one answered. A twig snapped. She spun around in the direction of the sound. "Heather?"

Jennie cowered in the chilling silence. *This is ridiculous,*

McGrady. Go back to the house. She took a step in the direction she thought she'd come. The moon still provided a scant, filtered light, but nothing looked familiar.

A coyote howled. Then another. Jennie wrapped her jacket tightly around her. A cloud drifted across the moon, plunging the forest into total darkness.

4

"Okay," she whispered. "Just keep calm. There's a way out. You just have to find it." Jennie took several deep breaths and willed the fear to subside. She'd been in worse situations.

The oxygen revived her and cleared her mind. She sat on a stump and looked up at the sliver of light that lined the cloud. It seemed to promise hope and a way out. Jennie prayed for wisdom and courage. "And God," she added. "If you could spare a guardian angel, I could use one about now."

The leaves rustled again. For a moment she blamed it on the wind but felt no breeze against her skin. She swallowed hard. *There's no need to panic, McGrady. It could be anything. An owl, a squirrel, a racoon . . .* Jennie stopped her imagination from coming up with anything bigger.

The moon peeked out from behind the cloud. She tried to remember where it had been earlier, but couldn't. Jennie shivered and buttoned up her denim jacket, wishing she'd grabbed a sweatshirt.

She jumped up and marched in a circle, hoping the movement would warm her. Jennie thought about lying down and trying to sleep. Morning would bring the sun and she could use it as a guide. No, she did not want to spend the night in these woods. It was too cold and there were wild animals— mountain lions and bears. There had to be another option.

Heading northeast would take her to the east fork of the Bitterroot River. "The river!" Jennie stopped pacing. "It flows right through the ranch. If I can find it, I can follow it back." But how? She had no idea which direction she should go.

Leaves rustled again.

"Be still, my child." A deep masculine voice resonated through the forest. "Listen to the earth."

Jennie sucked in a wild breath and whipped around. "Who's there?" She saw no one and heard only the sounds of the trees. *There's got to be an explanation*, Jennie told herself. *Maybe it was God, or that angel you asked for. Or maybe it was just your imagination.*

Jennie pressed back against a tree and willed her racing heart to slow down. *Be still*, the voice had said. She remembered a story she'd heard in Sunday school about a prophet, Elijah. He'd been in the wilderness. God had told him to be still. Was God sending her the same message?

Listen to the earth. Jennie sat on the stump again and tried to clear her mind of everything except the sounds around her.

Being from the Northwest, Jennie knew the sound of water rushing over rocks. She'd even fallen over a waterfall once. If she could hear the river and follow the sound, maybe . . .

Somewhere in the distance an owl hooted. She concentrated harder and thought she could hear a steady shushing sound. Leaves in the wind? Or dancing waters? She couldn't be sure.

Listen to the earth. Of course. Jennie scrunched down on the forest floor. She'd seen movies where Indian guides would press their ears to the ground in order to hear the sound of horses' hooves. They could even tell what direction the riders were coming from.

Jennie put a hand over her left ear and pressed her right to the ground. "I can hear it," she said after a few minutes.

Excitement bubbled like a spring inside her. "I can really hear the water."

She walked in a widening circle, stopping to listen at intervals to determine which direction she should go. She paused where she heard the rushing sound the loudest, then set out to find the river she hoped would take her back to the ranch. Jennie prayed she was heading toward the right river and in the right direction.

As she walked, the sound of the water grew stronger. After about ten minutes, the forest gave way to a pasture and the distant lights told her she wasn't far from the highway. She stopped a moment at the edge of the forest and sat on a fallen log to rest. She could see the river now. Moonbeams turned the swirling waters from gray to silver, giving it a magical look. "Thank you," she called in case the owner of the voice was listening.

"You're welcome."

Jennie stopped and whipped around, half expecting to see an angel. But no one was there. Had she really heard the voice again? Had it been an angel? Or God—or merely the wind?

A cool breeze lifted the loosened tendrils of hair from Jennie's cheeks. With the moon still lighting her way, she broke into a run.

By the time Jennie reached the house, it had started to rain. She shuddered, partly from the cold and partly from the knowledge that if she hadn't listened to the voice, she'd still be wandering around out there.

Jennie climbed up the tree and onto the roof near Heather's bedroom window. She tried to push it up. When it wouldn't budge, she tapped on the glass. After several minutes Heather peered out, a confused expression on her face. Finally she unlatched the window and slid it open. "What are you doing out there?" she whispered.

"As if you didn't know. Why did you leave me alone in the woods?"

"I don't know what you're talking about. I didn't even know you went out." Heather straightened. "You followed me?"

"I . . . I was worried about you."

"You didn't need to be. I can take care of myself."

"So I see." Jennie had more questions for Heather, such as: Why did you lock the window? Didn't you think I'd make it back? Did you lose me out there on purpose? But Jennie didn't ask them. Instead she changed into her nightgown and crawled into bed.

Sleep didn't come easily. *Dangerous.* The word wove itself over, around, and through recent memories of being lost in the woods and being left at the airport. Marty and his dad. The photographer. The poster of Hazen and Heather. The explosion. Together they wove a dark and haunting tapestry. Did Heather know more than she was letting on? She wanted to go back to New York, but surely not badly enough to . . . No. Heather would never do anything to hurt her father—or would she?

————

The twangy sounds of country music drifted into Jennie's foggy brain, then stopped. She opened one eye expecting to see the large red numbers of her alarm announcing the time. It wasn't there. Neither was her nightstand. Then she remembered. She rubbed her eyes and sat up. A light went on in the walk-in closet. Outside, the sky glowed with the first blush of dawn. The neon green hands on Heather's clock radio read five-thirty. Was her cousin sneaking out again?

A few minutes later, Heather snapped off the closet light and emerged wearing a pink T-shirt imprinted with a Dancing Waters logo and black jeans. "Sorry if I woke you. I tried to be quiet."

"It's okay. What are you doing up so early?"

Heather flipped on the overhead light. "I ask myself that every morning. You'd better get used to it. We start work between six and six-thirty." Heather covered her shirt with a fringed black suede jacket, then pulled on her leather boots.

Jennie moaned. "So what kind of work do you do?"

"Different things. Today I'm taking a group of executives on a one-day trail ride." Heather ran a brush through her hair, separated it into three strands, and began braiding.

"Sounds like fun. Maybe I could go along sometime."

"Maybe." Heather secured the long braid with a band, then picked up a barrette and attached it in the back where the braid began. From it hung a white feather with a pink tip and a dream catcher.

Jennie had noticed about a dozen or so feathered clips in various colors hanging in the closet the night before. "You have a lot of those."

"Feel free to wear one if you want. I like them. Eric says they . . ." Heather's gaze met Jennie's in the mirror. "Don't ask." She said good-bye and left.

Jennie thought about going back to sleep, but her mind was already up and running, so she joined it. Wrapping her cast in plastic to keep it dry, she showered, then dressed, and hurriedly brushed through her hair. After making three attempts to pull her thick mane into a ponytail, she gave up. The cast made some things impossible. Maybe she could ask Maggie to put her hair up later. She tossed the brush on the dresser and headed downstairs.

Heather pushed her chair back just as Jennie sat down. "Don't worry, Mom. I can handle it. Besides, you know Papa will be out there. Sometimes I think he's more spirit than human the way he looks out for us. I'll be back around five."

More spirit than human? Jennie thought about the voice she'd heard the night before.

"Pass the syrup, please." Amber stuck her hand toward

36

Maggie and accepted the bottle.

"Did you sleep well, Jennie?" Maggie asked.

"I had a little trouble at first, but . . ." She glanced at Heather who shot her a don't-tell warning before heading out the door. "I did okay."

Jennie speared a slice of French toast and grabbed a couple pieces of bacon off the tray as Maggie passed it to her. "Who was Heather talking about?"

"Our grandfather, Joseph." Amber supplied the information. "Papa knows everything. But he isn't the spirit Heather was talking about. She thinks it is, but it's really White Cloud—our great-grandfather. He died in 1972 but his spirit . . ."

"Amber," Maggie rested a hand on Amber's arm. "What did I tell you about repeating those stories?" She winked at Jennie. "I don't know where she gets some of these ideas. She has such a vivid imagination. I can assure you, we have no ghosts, and Joseph is very human and very normal. You'll meet him soon."

Amber bounced up and down. "I'll take you to his house. Can I, Mom?"

"Not today. Maybe tomorrow. I need Jennie to work today." She gave Jennie an apologetic look. "That is, if you're up to it."

"Sure. Do you want me to help in the dining room again?"

Maggie picked up her coffee and scanned the clipboard lying beside her plate. "I've got a full crew in the kitchen. But I could use some help in maid service. Two of my girls called in sick. If it's okay with you, I'll rotate you around to different jobs. It will give you a chance to familiarize yourself with the ranch and to meet the staff."

"That sounds great." Even though Maggie hadn't said so, Jennie got the impression her aunt wanted her to keep an eye out for signs of trouble. Did she suspect disloyalty among staff members?

The back door opened and closed. Maggie glanced toward the kitchen. "That must be Bob." Turning to Jennie she explained, "Bob Lopez is the ranch manager—been here since Jeff was a little boy."

"Mornin', Maggie." Bob Lopez plucked off his beige cowboy hat and set it on the credenza, then sauntered toward them. He lowered his short, thick body onto the vacant chair between Amber and Maggie and ruffled Amber's hair with a large, calloused hand. "How's my little leprechaun?"

Amber giggled. "I'm not a leprechaun."

He reached for the carafe of coffee and poured himself a cup. "Then you must be my lucky charm." His dark brown eyes twinkled as he spoke, then clouded when he turned back to Maggie.

"Uh oh, I know that look," Maggie said. "More trouble?"

"'Fraid so." He took a tentative sip of the hot brew. "Danielson called this morning. Somebody cut the fencing again. Says there's about a dozen head of our buffalo in with his prize steers. He's afraid they'll contaminate his herd."

"Our buffalo are clean. Did you tell him that?"

"Yep. He's still threatening to sue."

Maggie slapped her cup down on the table. Coffee slopped out onto the bright floral tablecloth. She didn't bother mopping it up. "I'll bet anything he cut the wire himself." She looked at Jennie. "Another in a long string of irritations. They're all aimed at forcing us to sell."

"This your niece?" Lopez asked.

"Oh . . . ah . . . yes." Maggie paused for introductions, then added, "Jennie'll be helping out wherever we need her."

Lopez leaned back in the chair and winked at Jennie. "I could use another hand repairing that fence."

Maggie shook her head. "Not yet. I'm not sure Jennie's even ridden a horse."

"Only on the merry-go-round," Jennie admitted, "but I'd love to try. I've always wanted to ride." Along with mysteries, some of Jennie's favorite books were about horses. Lately she'd been reading a series by Lauraine Snelling. If imagination counted, she'd ridden at least a hundred times.

"I love your enthusiasm, Jennie, and we'll make sure you get your share of riding, but it's not safe right now. We've had some poachers and . . ." She hesitated and closed her eyes.

"Maggie's right. I wasn't thinking. We'll be working close to where the truck exploded."

"Bob, please. Jennie doesn't need to hear this." Maggie's hands shook as she grasped the table and pushed herself back. "Take a couple of the men out to help you. And be careful."

"Yes'm." Lopez took a gulp of his coffee and retrieved his hat.

"Oh, and, Bob—" Maggie stopped him on her way to put dishes in the sink. She'd lowered her voice, but Jennie overheard. "I know Jeff would disagree, but maybe you'd better start carrying your rifles out there—just in case."

5

"This is the last cabin, Jennie." Heidi Copeland, the maid service supervisor, adjusted the pillows on her side of the bed and waited for Jennie to do the same. "Are you ready to quit for the day?" She blew her wispy flaxen bangs off her forehead.

"I am definitely ready," Jennie said, "but I should check with Aunt Maggie. She might need me to help somewhere else."

"Such dedication for one so young." Deep dimples appeared on Heidi's flushed cheeks. "Maggie and Jeff are lucky to have you." She reached around to her back and tucked a loose end of her aqua Dancing Waters T-shirt into her jeans.

Nearly all the staff wore jeans and shirts with a Dancing Waters logo, and Jennie was no exception. It was a uniform of sorts, only they could choose whatever color they wanted. Jennie had picked a royal blue to match her cast.

"Thanks. I could say the same thing about you. You always seem so happy."

"I am happy, Jennie. Oh, sometimes I miss my family in Switzerland, but this is my home now."

"I'm curious, how did you end up in Montana?"

"I came to see the big sky and I fell in love with the land and its people."

One person especially, Jennie noted. Heidi's face took on

a special glow when she talked about John, her husband of three months. She and John had been working at Dancing Waters for a year—since Maggie and Jeff had opened it as a dude ranch.

Heidi supervised maid service. John worked as a ranch hand under Bob Lopez.

Jennie straightened and rubbed her back. It had been a grueling day. Since breakfast, Jennie had been introduced to more people than she could count. Okay, maybe she was exaggerating, but between guests and staff members she'd met at least fifty. She just hoped they wouldn't expect her to remember their names.

"Do you live here on the ranch?" Jennie asked as they left the cabin area and walked toward the main lodge.

"We did before we got married. The staff lodging is in the dorms behind the cabins. Jeff and Maggie offered to let us use one of the guest cabins, but they are much too small. We have a home in Cottonwood."

"Heidi," Jennie hesitated. She'd been wanting to ask the question all day, but the time hadn't seemed right. "I know there's been a lot of problems at the ranch, and I wondered if you had any ideas about it."

"Ideas? I don't understand."

"Do you know who might want them to leave?"

"No." The dimples vanished. Deep worry lines appeared on her forehead. "It would be best if you didn't ask such questions, Jennie. It is dangerous to know too much about these things."

"What about this Chad Elliot guy? Heather says he's suing."

Heidi shook her head. "I'm sorry, Jennie. I know nothing of Mr. Elliot—only rumors that he is an angry man."

They climbed the steps to the lodge. Instead of going in the main entrance, they followed the porch around to a side door marked "Office." Jennie collided with a young man backing out.

"I'm sorry," he said, turning around. "I should have been watching." He raked a hand through his walnut brown hair and smiled.

What are you doing here? Jennie started to ask, then caught herself. He was the guy she'd seen at the airport with Heather. And she wasn't supposed to know him.

Maggie joined them in the doorway. "Eric, this is my niece Jennie and this is Heidi. Heidi supervises our maid service. Ladies, meet Eric Summers. He's a photographer and has offered to do some promotional work for me. He'll also be helping Bob with maintenance around the ranch.

So this was Eric. Heather had let his name slip that morning. Jennie had a zillion questions.

"I was about to take Eric to the men's quarters. Did you two want to talk to me?"

"Yes," Heidi said, "but I can wait."

"Why don't I take him over, Aunt Maggie? It'll save you some time." *And give me a chance to check him out.*

"That'll be great." Maggie gave Jennie a knowing wink. "Eric, why don't you get settled? I'll have one of the men show you around after dinner and we'll talk in the morning. I should have a schedule ready for you by then."

"Sure thing, Mrs. White Cloud. And thanks." He turned to Heidi before leaving. "Nice meeting you." Eric's gaze lingered on the Swiss Miss a little longer than necessary.

"You can stop drooling, Eric," Jennie said when they were out of earshot. "She's married."

"Who?" He tossed her a questioning look.

Jennie shook her head. "You really are a piece of work. I don't know what Heather sees in you."

He stopped and grabbed her arm. "Heather . . . you know?"

"Of course I know." Jennie shook off his hand. She didn't

bother to tell him she knew very little, and hoped he wouldn't guess. "I'm her cousin. We share a room together. I was there when she snuck out of her room last night to meet you."

He frowned. "She said she wasn't going to tell anyone."

Bingo. She'd guessed right. "Well, don't blame her. I saw you two at the airport yesterday."

His tan cheeks turned a ruddy rose. "Um, look, Jennie. I'd appreciate it if you didn't say anything to Heather about . . ." He glanced back at the lodge. "I didn't mean anything by it."

"You mean Heidi?"

"Yeah. Heather and I go back a long way. We went to the same school."

"In New York."

He nodded. "We had a good thing going. She's a terrific model. I've already won some awards for my photography. I'd started putting together a portfolio and we had an agent ready to take us on."

"Hmm. You must have been really upset when her parents decided to move out west. She told me how much she hates it out here."

"You might find this hard to believe, but I love Heather. And one way or another we'll find a way to be together."

One way or another. While Jennie couldn't imagine Heather deliberately hurting her dad, she had no trouble adding Eric to her suspect list. His motive could be love, but Jennie suspected the stronger motive was money. If Heather made it in the modeling industry, she could be worth millions.

There's just one problem, McGrady. He wasn't here. He couldn't have had anything to do with the explosion—unless . . . "Is this your first trip to Montana?"

He nodded. "It's taken me a while to raise enough money."

They reached the bunk houses and Jennie stopped. End

43

of trail on both counts. Eric thanked her and said he'd see her later.

Jennie ambled back to the main lodge. Now what? She hated being stuck in the middle. So what had she done? Wedged herself in even deeper. Heather was headed for trouble, and Jennie didn't know what to do about it. Should she tell Maggie and risk alienating her cousin forever? Jennie rubbed her forehead. No, she'd confront Heather first and try to convince her to stop sneaking around and to tell her parents about Eric and her dreams to be a model. Maybe they could compromise.

Jennie knew what it was like to deal with a parent who didn't approve of her kid's career choice. Mom didn't want Jennie to go into law enforcement, but she was beginning to soften.

Amber hopped down the steps as Jennie approached. "There you are," she said in an accusing voice. "I've been waiting to show you around."

Jennie eyed the black, gold-trimmed Dodge Caravan that sat in the driveway. "Who's here?

Amber wrinkled her nose. "Mr. Bennett. He's talking to Mom."

Jennie took a step up, battling against the urge to sneak up to the door and eavesdrop. When the office door opened she jumped back.

"I hope when the litigation is all over you and Jeff will be able to overlook our differences. We should get together for dinner in town." Bennett extended a hand to Maggie and she shook it. "I hope so too, Greg. Tell Melissa I said hi."

"I surely will." He nodded at Jennie and Amber as he descended the stairs and stepped into his van. "I'll stop out again when Jeff is home. You have him call me, okay? There's still a chance we can settle out of court. I'm trying to talk my client into a compromise." He shrugged and offered an apologetic half smile.

Jennie wanted to sit down with her aunt and learn more about Bennett and his client, Chad Elliot, but Maggie had other plans.

"Oh good," she said, turning her attention from Bennett to Amber. "I see you've found her. Jennie, this would be a good time to take that tour with Amber. She wants to introduce you to some of our four-legged guests." The phone rang and Maggie excused herself, then hurried in to answer it.

Jennie thought about waiting around for a few minutes so she could ask Maggie some questions about the land deal. Like, if Bennett and Jeff were friends, why would he take Elliot's case? As she thought about it, Jennie realized it wasn't all that unusual. Lawyers often defended people they didn't necessarily agree with.

"Come on, Jen. What are you waiting for?"

"I'd like to talk to your mom for a minute."

"You might have a long wait." Amber sighed and pointed to the red convertible pulling up to the lodge.

Alex Dayton stepped out of the car and waved. He'd exchanged his Brooks Brothers' suit for khaki slacks and a brick-red shirt. "Hey Amber." He came along beside them and ruffled Amber's hair. "How's it going, Sunshine?"

"Fine."

"Your mother in the office?"

"Yep."

He reached into his shirt pocket and pulled out a Snicker's bar and handed it to Amber, gave Jennie a quick nod, then ran up the steps and disappeared into the office.

"See, I told you she was too busy." Amber yanked on Jennie's hand again, and this time she gave in and followed. Over the next hour, Amber introduced Jennie to two dogs, three cats, a shaggy new llama named Socks and his mother, Angel, named, Jennie suspected, for her tender disposition, her white coat, and her beautiful sky-blue eyes. Now it was time to meet Gabby.

"Gabby will be your horse while you're here." Amber led the way through the largest horse barn Jennie had ever seen. "He's a six-year-old gelding. He loves people and talks all the time. Come on, I'll show you." Amber approached a white horse and patted his nose. "Hi, Gabby." The horse snuffled a greeting and nodded. "I want you to meet my cousin Jennie."

"Nice to meet you, Jennie." A gravelly male voice said.

Jennie jumped back, thinking for a moment the horse had spoken. She laughed when she spotted the buckskin-colored hat. "You had me going there for a minute."

A short man in his late fifties unlatched the stable door and stepped out. He had the weathered look of a rancher who'd spent too many summers in the sun. His bright blue eyes twinkled as they caught Jennie's questioning gaze.

Amber took Jennie's hand and pulled her forward. "This is Dusty Coburn. He runs the stables."

"Howdy there, Jennie. Amber tells me you want to learn how to ride. Well, you've come to the right place." He lifted his hat and wiped perspiration from his brow with a red handkerchief he'd pulled from his back pocket. "You hang around awhile, get to know old Gabby here and we'll get 'im saddled up for ya."

Dusty limped away and disappeared into an office at the far end of the barn. "He's got arthritis," Amber said before Jennie could ask. "Dad says it's from all those falls he took when he was a jockey."

"Does he still ride?"

"Every day. Come on—you gotta meet the real Gabby."

Jennie reached up to stroke Gabby's white forelock, then yanked her hand back when the horse whinnied and shook his head. "I don't think he likes me."

"Oh, sure he does. Let's get him some grain and a few carrots and you'll be his friend for life."

Jennie spent the next half hour getting acquainted with

46

Gabby and several of the other horses including Cinnamon, Amber's mare. Amber worked with her on grooming skills until Dusty arrived to give Jennie her first riding lesson.

Following Dusty's instructions, Jennie led Gabby into the arena behind the stable. She watched as Dusty cupped his hands to give Amber a hand up onto Cinnamon's back.

Jennie raised her casted right arm up and rested it on the saddle. She slipped her foot into the stirrup, then grabbed the saddle horn with her left hand to steady herself, bounced up, and swung her right leg over the saddle.

"Hoowee," Dusty hooted. "You sure you've never been on a horse before, Jennie? You're a natural."

Jennie shrugged. "Not unless you count carousels."

He chuckled. "Who'd a thought it?"

"I just hope the cast won't be a problem."

Dusty shook his head. "Naw—you'll be holding the reins and guiding him with your left hand. You should do just fine."

For the next hour, Dusty taught her how to handle the reins to guide Gabby through the various courses he'd set up in the riding arena. They circled the arena dozens of times as she practiced turning and backing up, walking and trotting. Jennie loved it. Of course she'd always known she would.

That night, Jennie helped bus tables again and, after a late supper, dragged herself up to bed. A scraping sound woke her as Heather crawled in through the window. Jennie glanced at the clock. Midnight.

Jennie stretched and yawned. "Well, well, if it isn't Cinderella. Out with Prince Charming again?"

Heather closed the window and pulled down the blinds. "Eric told me about the little talk you had with him. That was sneaky, Jennie."

"Maybe it runs in the family. I just put two and two together. What I don't understand is why the big secret? Why don't you just tell your folks how you feel?"

"I've tried. Dad is totally against my being a model. If they knew about Eric and me, they'd . . . I don't know what they'd do. Please don't tell Mom. She'll tell Dad and . . ."

"So when do you plan on letting them know?"

"Soon. Eric has been doing photo shoots. He's got this fantastic layout. Oh, Jennie, he's a wonderful photographer. Wait until you see them. Once the photos start selling and I get some work, we'll have enough money to get married."

"Married?" Jennie snuggled back under the covers wishing she hadn't heard Heather's response. "Just for the record, I think you're making a big mistake." She sighed. "I won't say anything right now, but I'm not making any promises."

"You sound like my grandfather."

"He knows about Eric?"

"He knows I want to be a model and that I want to leave Dancing Waters." She sat on the bed and removed her boots. "He probably knows about Eric too."

"Why doesn't he tell your folks?"

"He says I am nearing womanhood and must make my own way." Heather closed her eyes, then brushed away the tears that had formed there. "Papa says I am at a fork in the road and I must be careful in the choosing."

"So you haven't made up your mind?"

She shook her head. "I love Eric. And I love modeling. But today—when I took those people into the wilderness, I felt . . . different. Riding through the woods felt so right."

Heather changed into a plaid flannel nightshirt that reached almost to her knees. After a trip to the bathroom, she crawled into bed and turned off the light. "Good night."

" 'Night."

"Jennie?"

"Hmm?"

"Thanks for understanding."

"Sure," Jennie murmured. She didn't like sharing secrets

like that, but she no longer felt as responsible. Heather's grandfather knew. She hadn't met Joseph White Cloud yet, but she already liked him.

———

After lunch in the lodge the following day, Maggie gave Jennie the afternoon off. "You've earned it. Besides, Amber thinks it's time you rode into the hills to visit Papa."

"He wants to meet you." Amber turned to her mom. "May I be excused, please? I need to pick up snacks and have Dusty get the horses ready."

"Yes, you may go." She watched Amber run out the door, and shook her head. "That girl. So much energy."

The gesture reminded Jennie of something her mother would do. "Oh no. I haven't called Mom back yet. I can't believe it."

"It's my fault. I should have reminded you last night before you went to bed." Maggie set her napkin on the table. "Why don't you call her now? You can use the phone in my office."

Jennie gulped down the rest of her milk and excused herself. Minutes later she was listening to the ring and waiting for Mom to pick up the phone.

"Hello." The break in the familiar voice told Jennie her mother was crying.

"Mom, what's wrong?"

"Oh, honey. It's so awful. I'm afraid we're going to lose Hannah!"

6

"What do you mean, lose Hannah?" An image of the little girl flooded Jennie's mind. Flaxen curls and heart-melting chocolate brown eyes. "Is she sick?"

"She's fine—physically. She cried when they took her."

"Took her?" Jennie shouted into the phone. "What do you mean? Who took her? Mom, what's going on?"

Mom sniffed and blew her nose. "Her case worker came this morning. Hannah's dad wants her back."

"No! They can't do that—can they?" The idea of Hannah going back to that terrible man repulsed Jennie. He didn't deserve to have his little girl back. He'd beaten his wife and . . . Jennie shoved the horrible images away. "You can't let him take her."

"We're doing what we can. Michael and I are seeing an attorney this afternoon."

Michael Rhodes was Mom's fiancé. The thought of him being involved brought some peace of mind. If anyone could stop them, he could. Being a youth director, he'd dealt with social workers before. He'd know what to do to get Hannah back.

"I don't think Children's Services will let Chuck take her," Mom went on, "but they're talking about sending her to Arizona to live with his parents."

"Maybe I should come home." Jennie hated being so far

away. Mom probably needed a hug. Nick would be devastated.

"There's nothing you could do here. Besides, Maggie needs help and—" Mom took a deep breath as if she was about to say something Jennie didn't want to hear. "Honey, we have to remember that Hannah doesn't belong to us. We basically have no claim to her."

"Sounds like you're giving up."

"I'm just facing reality. I want to keep her as much as you do—so does Michael."

"How does Gram feel about this? Is she going with you?"

"No." Mom hesitated. "Gram is out of town. I don't think she'll be back until next week."

"Oh, I was hoping she'd come here. It's a great resort. She could write an article about it."

"Jennie, are you homesick?"

"Of course not. I just thought Gram would enjoy it." No way was Jennie going to tell Mom what she really wanted Gram there for.

"I'll mention it if she calls."

They talked a few more minutes and hung up. Jennie grabbed some tissues out of the box on her aunt's desk and blew her nose.

"Jennie, what's wrong?" Maggie came in and closed the door.

Jennie explained as best she could. "It isn't fair. She's just a little girl."

Maggie put her arms around Jennie and held her. "I know. Life often isn't fair. Sometimes it's downright cruel."

Jennie felt suddenly ashamed. They hadn't even lost Hannah yet, but Maggie and Jeff had been through so much.

Amber pulled open the door. "I got the horses ready. . . . Hey, what's going on? Did you hurt yourself?"

"No." Jennie didn't feel like going through the story again. "Would you tell her?"

Maggie did and added, "Jennie's sad about Hannah and might not feel like going for a ride."

"But everything's ready. Besides, when I'm sad, riding makes me feel better."

Jennie hauled in a ton of air and blew it out again. "I'll go. It'll beat sitting around here feeling sorry for myself."

Within a few minutes, riding had put Jennie in a better mood. Her horse would have made a good psychiatrist. While she talked, Gabby listened and even made all the appropriate sounds. A nod here, a head shake there, and exactly the right amount of snorting and whinnying.

The news about Hannah still upset her, but after talking it over with Amber and Gabby, Jennie realized that Mom was right. Being at home wouldn't change matters. She just had to trust that God would work everything out right.

With Amber acting as trail guide, they headed toward the northwest corner of the White Cloud property where Joseph lived. They'd ridden about twenty minutes through the woods when they reached a fenced clearing. Several llamas grazing near the gate straightened and fixed curious gazes on them.

Amber twisted around in her saddle and waited for Jennie to catch up. "We have about a hundred head of llamas out here."

"Why do you separate them?" Jennie asked. "I noticed several by the stables."

"We keep several near the ranch for packing."

"Packing? You eat them too?"

Amber giggled. "I meant putting packs on them for wilderness treks. They're sure-footed and better than horses on some of the steeper trails."

"No offense, Cinni." Amber reached forward to pat the horse's neck, urging her forward. The name fit her. She glistened like warm cinnamon-and-sugar coating on a sticky bun.

They rode along the fence until they came to a gate that crossed a dirt road. They dismounted, led the horses through, secured the gate, then mounted and rode on.

"I can't believe how huge this place is," Jennie said, looking over the clearing and up into the foothills. "How much land do you own?"

"Twenty-thousand acres."

Jennie let out a long whistle. "That much land must be worth millions."

"The land belongs to Papa." Amber frowned. "Some of the people around here think Papa stole the land from the Elliots. They used to live here. Now that mean Chad Elliot is telling people that Dancing Waters belongs to him. He's lying though, 'cause Papa would never steal anything."

Enemies. Marty had said the White Clouds had a lot of them. "Do you think this Elliot guy could have . . ." Jennie stopped before mentioning the explosion. *This is not the conversation to be having with a ten-year-old,* Jennie reminded herself. Even though Amber sometimes sounded like an adult, she was still very much a child. "Never mind." Then hoping to cheer her cousin, Jennie said, "You probably don't need to worry. After all, your dad's a lawyer—I'll bet he's dealt with a lot of land disputes."

Amber sighed. "I hope so."

They rode along in silence for a while as Jennie tried to bring some kind of order to the bits and pieces of the clues she'd managed to glean so far. Chad Elliot was accusing the White Clouds of stealing his land. Could he have caused the explosion? Jennie definitely needed more information, but at least now she had some specific questions.

How did Joseph White Cloud, a Nez Perce Indian chief, come to own this much land? And who wanted that land bad enough to kill for it? Her pulse quickened, hoping Amber's grandfather would have some answers.

After a few minutes, they paused to admire a hillside

ablaze with Indian Paintbrush. Amber pointed out several other plants. "These are pretty, but you should see it in the spring. The pastures are covered with Bitterroot. That's how the valley got its name."

"The Montana state flower, right? I read about it on the map."

Amber nodded. "The Indians call it 'spetlum.' They used to eat the root. Papa told me an old Indian legend about how the flower came to be. Want to hear it?"

"Sure."

Amber's expressive eyes glistened with importance as she sat straighter in the saddle and cleared her throat. "In ancient times, an old woman slipped away one night, thinking that if she were gone, the family could have her share of the little food they had. After walking a long way, the woman stopped beside a brook and loosened her long silver hair. Soon she would sing her death song. The woman thought about her family and cried with deep sorrow."

Amber gracefully raised her hand to the sky. "The Great Spirit saw her unselfish act of courage and smiled. He honored her by sending a spirit bird whose breast was red as blood. The bird promised that she and her tribe would be saved. Food would come in the form of a flower with leaves the color of her silver hair and blossoms as red as the bird's breast. The roots would be bitter as the tears she had cried and filled with the strength she carried in her heart. Each spring the flowers came to give food to her hungry people. And they continue to bloom to this day."

"What a neat story, and you told it beautifully."

"Papa says I will become the family historian. He's teaching me to be a storyteller like him so I can pass our heritage on to our children and grandchildren."

"That's a great idea. . . ."

"Shh." Amber pulled Cinnamon up and signaled Jennie to be quiet, then pointed to a small clearing. Sun streaked through the branches of the giant fir trees, making it look like a holy place. A deer nibbled at a low shrub. She raised her head and looked straight at them. Jennie expected her to bolt. Instead she came toward Cinnamon and nuzzled Amber's saddlebags.

Amber slowly reached into the bag. The deer stretched out her neck and accepted the cookie Amber offered.

"She's beautiful." Jennie pulled a cookie out of her bag, too.

"Her name's Tasha. Papa found her when she was a fawn. A hunter killed her mother."

"Sounds like a Bambi story." Jennie leaned farther forward and extended her hand. "Here, Tasha." The doe ambled over and snatched the cookie Jennie offered.

Amber nodded. "Hunters aren't allowed here, but sometimes they come anyway. I worry about her."

"And well you should, Tiponi," a deep mellow voice said. "Tasha is young and has not yet learned to fear humans. If she is to live long enough to see her children grow, she must know this fear."

Startled by the voice, Jennie yanked on Gabby's reins. The horse sidestepped and reared, throwing her off balance. She grabbed for the saddlehorn with her casted right hand and missed. She yelped as she tumbled from the saddle and landed on her rear.

Tasha darted into the underbrush. Gabby turned and nuzzled Jennie as if to apologize.

A figure appeared in the haloed light and came toward her. "I frightened you. I'm sorry. Are you hurt?"

Still dazed, Jennie took the hand he offered and scrambled to her feet. Her fear melted the moment his steady gaze caught hers. "I—I don't think so." She brushed off the dirt and debris from the forest floor. Her leg and tailbone still hurt, but the pain was beginning to subside.

"It's my fault, Papa." Amber swung her legs to the side

and slid off Cinnamon's back. "I should have warned her about the way you sneak up on people."

He chuckled, then bent to embrace her. Amber kissed his brown furrowed cheek and hugged him. He wore a feather, Jennie noticed, a brown one with a white tip, tucked into the long gray braid that hung down his back. She'd expected him to be dressed like an Indian chief, in a feathered headdress and buckskin, but he wasn't. In his faded blue jeans and aqua chambray work shirt he looked like a typical rancher. Joseph gathered Gabby's and Cinnamon's reins in one hand and began walking. "Come, my children. I have been expecting you. I have made your favorite, Tiponi. Frybread. We will eat and share stories. I am eager to hear about Jennie and her family."

"And I want to hear about yours." Jennie took Amber's hand and fell into step in front of Joseph and the horses. "Why does he call you that strange name?" Jennie asked Amber.

"Tiponi? That's my Indian name." Her eyes widened and her lips parted in a wide smile. "It means 'child of importance.' "

"Tiponi. It's a beautiful name, and you know what? It fits."

"I know." Amber couldn't have beamed more if she'd have been a light bulb. "Maybe Papa will give you a name."

"Actually, Gram gave me one. Not a name exactly, but she says I'm like an eagle—steady and strong."

"It suits you," Joseph said. "Your grandmother sounds like a wise woman."

"She is."

As they walked, Jennie answered more questions about her family. Since he already knew about the Calhoun side— her mom and Uncle Kevin—she told him about the Mc-Gradys. Gram first, of course, and how she'd been married to Ian McGrady, a government agent who'd been killed nearly eleven years ago. Joseph seemed disappointed when Jennie told him Gram had recently married again.

When Joseph asked, she told him about her father, from whom she'd inherited her height, dark hair, and cobalt blue eyes.

"We're almost there," Amber announced, then ran ahead of them. Jennie dropped back and walked beside Joseph.

"Maggie tells me you are quite a detective," Joseph said. "This, I have seen for myself."

It took Jennie a moment to realize what he was referring to. "Oh, you mean the other night. You had me going there. I thought God had sent an angel."

His eyes twinkled. "Not an angel, but certainly an assistant. I was coming home from visiting a friend."

So the voice she'd heard in the woods had belonged to him. "Did you have to be so sneaky? Why didn't you just come out and tell me how to get back?"

Joseph had the smile of a man with many secrets. "If a child is always carried, he will never learn to walk."

"You mean if you had shown me the way, I wouldn't have learned to make it on my own. I wouldn't have learned how to listen to the earth."

"Or to your spirit." Their path ended at a rustic log cabin that looked as old as he did.

"Papa, Papa." Amber ran back to them, tears running down her cheeks.

"Hush, Tiponi." He knelt and pressed her head against his chest. "What has upset you?"

"They killed her," she sobbed and glanced toward the house. "They killed Tasha."

7

Jennie couldn't look. She closed her eyes, but still caught a glimpse of the white tail and rounded belly that lay on the ground near the far side of the cabin.

"How—how could . . ." Jennie stammered. "I—I didn't hear a shot."

"They must have used a silencer. Stay here with Tiponi while I check around." Joseph positioned Jennie and Amber beside a dark green Ford Ranger and ran into the house.

Glancing inside the vehicle, Jennie noticed a cellular phone. She could call for help if— Her thoughts dissipated as Joseph emerged from the house.

"Go inside and wait for me," he ordered. "Lock the door."

She and Amber sat at the kitchen table and waited. Only then did Jennie relax enough to notice her surroundings. A southwestern-style rug stretched from the sofa to a couple of matching leather chairs. Next to the fire stood an old wooden rocker with a worn cloth cushion. Tired of sitting, Jennie decided to explore.

The log cabin looked bigger from the inside. The main room served as a sitting room, kitchen, and eating area. A circular fire pit occupied the center of the room. Smoke from the fire escaped through a metal vent that looked like an upside-down funnel—narrow at the top where it met the ceiling. At one end of the room were three open doors leading to two bedrooms and a bath.

The furnishings were old, and Jennie took her time examining them. In one bedroom, a framed picture of Christ knocking at a door hung beside an embroidery of the Twenty-third Psalm. An antique Bible sat on a stand below the picture.

Thirty minutes passed before they saw Joseph again. His hands were covered with dirt and blood. "It was not Tasha," he said going to the kitchen sink. "This one was older. One of the poachers must have wounded it, then lost the trail."

Amber sighed. "I'm glad it wasn't her. Are you going to call the sheriff?"

"You must not concern yourself with these matters."

Jennie might have believed Joseph's explanation about the poacher except for two things. He hadn't looked into her eyes, and he had a piece of pale green paper in his shirt pocket that hadn't been there earlier. The paper had a frayed edge just like the one left on Heather's Jeep. When he turned around after washing his hands, the paper was gone.

Joseph excused himself to shower and change clothes, then went into his bedroom.

Jennie wondered what he'd done with the note. Maybe he'd show it to her later. Or maybe he'd already thrown it away.

Jennie looked over at the sink where Joseph had been standing, then pushed her chair back and casually sauntered into the kitchen. She opened the cupboard and checked the trash. Bingo. Her hunch had been right. She pulled out the crinkled bloodstained note and read it.

This could be you. Jennie folded the note and jammed it into the pocket of her jeans. Later she'd compare the handwriting. She wondered how many threatening notes the White Clouds had gotten and how many they'd handed over to the sheriff.

She headed to the leather sofa and sank into it. Amber, who'd been curled up in the armchair, got up, took a piece of firewood from a box beside the pit, and placed it in the ashes. "I hate it when deer get killed. I wish people couldn't hunt anymore. And I wish I was the sheriff. I'd round up all the hunters and put them in jail."

Jennie glanced at the mounted moose head with antlers nearly as wide as the room. "Your grandfather hunts. Would you put him in jail too?"

"That's different. Papa says the Creator gives us plants and animals for food and clothing. Some of the hunters are like Papa, but most of the poachers do it for fun. They use high-powered rifles and automatic weapons. . . ."

Joseph came out of his bedroom. "Tiponi," he scolded, "how do you know these things? Did your father tell you this?"

Amber shrugged. "I hear things, Papa. And I know."

Joseph pinched his lips together. His obsidian eyes clouded with concern, but he said no more about it. Instead he turned and walked into the kitchen area and pulled a piece of white cloth from a large lump of dough.

Joseph dropped pieces of the dough out on a floured cutting board and patted them until they were flat and round. One by one he formed them, slid them into a black iron skillet with hot oil to fry, then set them aside to drain.

Within a few minutes they were feasting on warm frybread, spread with butter and dripping with brilliant red strawberry jam.

Jennie, too warm to stay near the fire, chose a seat next to the large window in the living room. She gazed at the trees and a meadow dotted with colorful wild flowers. Like Jeff and Maggie's home, Joseph's had a great view. Here, though, you didn't just look at the mountains, you were in them.

"This is a wonderful place. It looks old."

"My father built it in 1901 when he married my mother.

Except for the wood floor and the fire pit I put in for Chenoa in 1948, it is the same."

"Chenoa? Your wife?" Jennie asked. She loved the sound of the Indian names.

Joseph nodded. His black eyes drifted closed in an almost reverent gesture.

"Papa and Daddy were both born in that bedroom back there." Amber pointed to an open door on the right. A worn, multicolor handmade quilt covered the bed.

"The quilt—did Chenoa make it?"

Joseph opened his eyes and looked toward the room. "A wedding gift from Nadi—my mother."

Jennie wanted to explore every inch of the cabin—to pick up each item and learn its history. It was like being in a museum.

"Come," Joseph said. "You have many questions. Too many for an old man to answer. But I will begin with the story of my people."

Joseph led them away from the cabin to a cleared grassy knoll overlooking the valley. A cemetery, Jennie realized as they drew closer. They stopped near five marble tombstones. Joseph sat on a rough-hewn log bench, looked briefly at each marker, then let his gaze move over the valley and down to the river.

Jennie read the writing on each stone. *Gray Wolf 1846–77*; *Dancing Waters 1849–1877*; *White Cloud 1872–1972*; *Nadi 1901–1971*; *Chenoa 1927–1988*. She pointed to Dancing Waters' tomb. "Who was this?"

"The ranch was named for her." Amber tucked several stray tendrils behind her ear, crossed her legs at the ankle, and dropped down next to her grandfather. "She was Gray Wolf's sister."

"You know of the Nez Perce, Jennie?" Joseph asked.

"Yes—some. I studied about Chief Joseph in school."

"Ah." He nodded. "I am named for Chief Joseph and for his father, Old Joseph."

"Are you related to them?"

"Not by blood, but they are my brothers. My great-grandfather was Chief Gray Wolf. He and Chief Joseph were friends and sought to maintain peaceful relations with the settlers. Unfortunately that was not to be. The settlers and miners wanted more and more of our land, especially after gold was discovered on the reservation in 1860."

Jennie sighed. "I remember reading about that. The government drew up a new treaty reducing the reservation to a tenth its original size." Jennie shook her head. "It all seems so unfair."

"At the time, we were considered savages. As Chief Joseph said, 'we were few, they were many. We were like deer. They were like grizzly bears. . . . We were content to let things remain as the Great Spirit Chief made them. They were not; and would change the rivers and mountains if they did not suit them.' "

"Tell her about the war, Papa." Amber leaned toward him.

"Patience, Tiponi." He chuckled and pulled her closer. "Perhaps Jennie already knows about the war."

"She doesn't know about our part," Amber protested.

"I do know about the Nez Perce War—the Battle at Big Hole in . . . um . . . 18—something."

"Yes. 1877. The battle was fought not far from here." Joseph pointed to a distant mountain range to the east.

"Papa's great-grandfather, Gray Wolf, was killed and so was Dancing Waters. Tell her, Papa."

"Since you are so eager, Tiponi, perhaps you should tell your cousin the story of our ancestors."

"Okay. But you tell me if I make a mistake."

"You won't," Jennie assured her as she shifted to find a more comfortable position. To Joseph she said, "You should have heard her tell me about the Bitterroot legend. You'd have been proud."

"Of Tiponi, I am always proud."

"Well," Amber straightened with the importance her name implied and began, "Gray Wolf was camped here in the valley with his sister, Dancing Waters, and his five-year-old son, White Cloud. White Cloud's mama died right after he was born. Gray Wolf and Dancing Waters became friends with Frank Elliot, the man who used to own this land.

"Mr. Elliot thought Dancing Waters was the most beautiful girl in the world and wanted to marry her." Amber sighed and shrugged her shoulders. "Dancing Waters loved him too, but she was already promised to . . . um . . . What was his name, Papa?"

"Red Fox."

"Oh, yeah. Anyway, several of the young warriors got mad because the settlers and miners kept taking their land. They killed some settlers and got all the Indians in trouble. The Nez Perce tried to avoid battle, but the soldiers kept coming after them.

"Lots of people died in the war at Big Hole." Amber glanced at Joseph. "How many, Papa?"

"Twenty-nine soldiers dead, forty wounded." Joseph paused. His sad gaze settled on the first two graves. "The Nez Perce won the battle, but lost as well. Eighty-two of our people died. Most of them were women, children, and old people."

"Dancing Waters died in the battle," Amber went on, "and Gray Wolf was wounded. Frank Elliot heard about the fighting and came the next day. He took Gray Wolf and little White Cloud, but Gray Wolf died the next day. Frank promised Gray Wolf that he would take care of White Cloud forever."

Jennie frowned, remembering what Amber had told her

earlier. "If Frank owned all of this land, how did you come to own it?"

"Does it surprise you?" Joseph asked.

"No—Well, I guess it does," Jennie admitted.

"Frank Elliot was a good man. He reared my father against the advice of many in the valley who thought Indians belonged on the reservation. Two years after the war, Frank married a young woman whose father had made a fortune in the mining industry.

"At first she accepted White Cloud and cared for him, but eventually she bore children of her own, and became jealous of the attention her husband paid to White Cloud. In an attempt to pacify his wife, and still keep his promise, Frank gave White Cloud five hundred acres.

"Frank's children, William and Tess, grew up spoiled and bitter." Joseph went on. "When Frank died, William took to alcohol and gambling. Heavy losses caused him to sell parcels of the land to my father and later to me. He asked us to keep the land deals a secret so that he could buy it back, but that day never came."

"And the family never knew?"

"Perhaps they never cared. Sale of the land brought in money. The money is gone now. William's grandson, Chad, has come back to claim the land he believes is his."

The old man sighed, looking weary and somehow older and more frail than when they'd first met. He stood and straightened slowly. "We have no more time for questions. I promised Maggie I'd send you home by four-thirty."

Reluctantly, Jennie and Amber headed for home. Late afternoon shadows stretched across the trail and dropped the temperature a good twenty degrees. They'd ridden about a mile and had just entered the llama pastures when a strange uneasiness settled in the pit of Jennie's stomach. The hair on the back of her neck bristled in warning.

"Amber, hold on a minute." She pulled back on the reins

and reached out to touch her cousin's arm, then scanned the area.

"What is it, Jennie?"

"I don't know. Something doesn't feel right. I know it sounds dumb, but I feel like we're being watched."

Amber grinned. "It's probably Papa. He sometimes follows me to make sure I get home okay."

Jennie relaxed some. "Maybe. Still, we should be careful." She sat high on Gabby's back and looked over the pasture again.

Just as Amber started forward Jennie saw him—a dark figure kneeling beside a large outcropping of rocks. His camouflage fatigues nearly hid him from view. He raised his rifle and looked through the scope.

"He's going to kill one of the llamas!" Amber cried. Before Jennie could stop her, Amber spurred Cinnamon forward. "Hey!" she yelled. "This is private property. What do you think you're doing?"

The man looked toward them. A black ski mask covered his face. He stood and swung the rifle around, then set his sights on Amber.

8

"No!" Jennie yelled as she urged Gabby forward. "Amber, wait!"

Amber didn't stop until she reached the rocks where they'd seen the gunman. "He's gone."

Jennie glanced around. "He hasn't had time to go far. We'd better get out of here."

"He was going to shoot the llamas. It's a good thing we came."

Jennie heard the roar of an engine. She dug her heels into Gabby's sides and raced toward the sound. By the time she reached the road leading out of the pasture, the truck, resembling an old army reject, rammed the gate and disappeared down the winding dirt road. She'd tried to read the license plate, but a billowing dust cloud obliterated her view.

"Let's follow him," Amber said as she caught up with Jennie. "See where he goes."

They rode as far as the gate when Jennie stopped her. "It's no use. We'll never catch him."

Amber jumped off Cinnamon and walked over to the broken gate. "We'd better fix this so the llamas don't get out."

The truck had splintered the two center posts and snapped the barbed wire. Amber picked up the broken gate and twisted the ends of the wires together. Jennie then helped her stretch the wires taut and hook a wire loop over a secure post.

"I wish we could have caught him," Amber said.

"Jennie stooped to pick up some pieces of glass and wood splinters.

"What are you doing?"

"Gathering evidence." She found a tissue in her jacket pocket and carefully wrapped the fragments, then inserted them in the pocket of her jean jacket. Judging from the amount of glass strewn about, he must have broken a headlight.

"We're lucky he didn't kill us." Jennie brushed the dirt from her hands. "Don't you know any better than to chase after guys with guns?"

Amber pursed her lips in a pout. "I didn't think about him hurting us. I was worried about the llamas."

Jennie hooked her left arm around Amber's neck and hugged her. "I know. You're a lot like me. Sometimes I act first and think later. Anyway, we'd better get going. We need to call the sheriff. I got a pretty good look at the truck. The sheriff should be able to find it. How many people around here have trucks like that?"

Amber sniffed. "Lots. The sheriff won't find him. He probably won't even try."

"I don't understand," Jennie said as they mounted their horses.

"Um . . . There's like this Montana Militia. I don't know much about them except they don't like us. They look like army guys. Papa and Daddy have been trying to keep them off our property. They think they have a right to be here 'cause the Elliots' caretaker let them use the ranch for their war games."

"War games?" Jennie felt sick. She'd been hearing a lot about militia groups since the bombing in Oklahoma. *Bombing.* Uncle Jeff had been injured in an explosion, and she'd seen several men in army fatigues since she'd arrived in Montana.

Including Marty's father. Only that morning, Maggie had suspected Mr. Danielson of cutting the fence bordering his property. Could he have been the man they'd just seen?

"Amber, do you know the Danielsons very well?"

"A little. Before the explosion, Mr. Danielson was always coming over to talk to Dad—well, argue mostly. Marty was Heather's boyfriend when we first came here. I don't like him."

"Who, Marty?"

"No, his dad."

They reached the stable at five-fifteen and told Dusty what had happened. Dusty called the sheriff and hustled the girls over to the lodge office.

A few minutes later, they told the story to Maggie, who scolded, fed, and hugged them, then asked Heidi to take Amber to the house while she and Jennie waited. Forty-five minutes later, the sheriff pulled up in front of the lodge office where Maggie had suggested they meet.

The sheriff stuffed his ample body into an armchair, laced his fingers together, and rested them on his belly. "Well, now, little lady. Suppose you tell me about this gunman of yours and why you felt it was so all-fired important for me to drive all the way out here." His tone implied Jennie had dreamed the whole thing up. She could see why Heather questioned his competence.

Jennie repeated the story, emphasizing the mask and the gun. "It looked like an assault weapon."

"Is that everything?"

"No, it isn't." She struggled to keep the irritation out of her voice. "He got away in a camouflaged truck." Jennie described the vehicle.

"Well, now we're getting somewhere." He gave Maggie a snide grin, then shifted his gaze back to Jennie. "Have you any idea how many folks in this county drive camouflaged trucks?"

"No, but this one would have a broken headlight and probably wood splinters caught in the bumper from the fence. I picked up a couple of pieces when I was out there." She retrieved the wood and glass from her pocket and handed them to him. "It shouldn't be hard to check out some of the trucks around here. You could start with the Danielsons."

"Now, don't be telling me how to do my job, little lady." Sheriff Mason set down his coffee cup and stood. He hooked a finger on either side of his tan pants and hitched them up. The handle of his gun made a dent in his bulging stomach. "I've heard tell how you assisted the police in Oregon with a couple of cases, but you'd better not be gettin' any ideas about doin' that here."

Before Jennie could reply, he turned to Maggie. "I'm right sorry about all the trouble you folks been havin' out here. I know seeing a fella like that can be alarmin', but my hunch is, the girls just surprised a hunter."

Maggie's angry gaze flitted to Jennie then back to the sheriff. "That gunman was no hunter, Sam Mason, and you know it. He was on our land. He aimed a gun at our llamas and at our children. I expect you to investigate this. I want that lunatic caught."

"Now, Maggie." Sheriff Mason straightened and backed away. "Don't be getting your dander up. All I'm saying is, this guy's probably one of the militia boys that didn't get the message about Dancing Waters bein' off limits now that the Elliots are gone. I'll ask around, but don't expect an arrest." The sheriff huffed. "Like findin' a blasted needle in a haystack. I don't have the manpower for wild goose chases like this."

––––––––––

"He's not going to do anything, is he?" Jennie asked after the sheriff left.

"Of course he will. Sheriff Mason is up for election soon.

He can't afford to slack off too much."

"I hope you're right."

Maggie motioned for Jennie to join her on the porch. "Come on. Walk with me up to the house. I want to check on Amber."

As they trudged up the hill, they talked about family matters and how Maggie hadn't felt like part of the family for the first dozen or so years of her marriage to Jeff. Jennie asked why.

"You mean you never heard the story?"

"Not your version. All I heard was that you were a rebellious hippie teenager and you ran off with an Indian. Mom never talked about you much."

"My fault. I guess I didn't feel welcome. Basically, the story is true. Jeff and I fell in love and wanted to get married. My parents wanted me to finish college and marry some wealthy businessman. I wanted Jeff. So we eloped. We had such high ideals—thought we could save the world. The twins were born a year later, and caring for them pretty much ended our political activist days. Not that I'm complaining; I love being a mother.

"For the longest time I was too hurt and full of pride to come home. Then at your father's funeral . . ." Tears misted her eyes and Maggie reached up to brush them away. "Listen to me going on like that. The past isn't important. What counts now is that all is forgiven. The prodigal daughter has returned to the fold."

"I'm glad you made up with Grandma and Grandpa Calhoun—and Mom and Uncle Kevin. Mom really missed you."

"I'm glad too." She rested an arm on Jennie's shoulder. "And I can't wait until that sister of mine gets here. We have so much catching up to do."

The phone rang as they walked into the kitchen.

"Hello," Maggie grabbed it on the first ring. She frowned.

70

"Yes, she's here. Just a second." Maggie handed the phone to Jennie. "It's Marty."

"How's it going?" Marty asked after they exchanged greetings. "Heard you spooked some hunter this afternoon and almost got yourself shot at."

"Where'd you hear about that?" Jennie asked. Suspicions so crowded her brain she could hardly hear his answer.

"Sheriff Mason. He dropped by to ask if we'd seen anything."

"Have you?" Jennie asked, surprised the sheriff had been there.

"Nope."

Jennie had a dozen questions to shoot at Marty Danielson. *Where were you this afternoon? Where was your father? Hit any fences with your truck lately?* She couldn't very well ask those over the phone for fear he'd hang up, so she didn't say anything.

Marty finally broke the awkward silence. "I . . . um . . . I guess you're wondering why I called."

"Yeah, now that you mention it."

"I just got to thinking about you. I'm free this evening and was wondering if maybe we could get together. I can show you around our ranch, then we can head into town and see a movie or get a hamburger or something."

"Sure. That would be terrific. I'd love to see your place." *And*, she thought, *look over your vehicles.*

"Great. I'll pick you up at seven."

After she hung up, Jennie began to wonder about the wisdom of her decision. What if the gunman had been Marty or his dad? If the sheriff had told them about the cases she'd helped solve recently, they might want her out of the way. Okay, maybe she shouldn't have accepted the invitation, but going to the Danielsons' would give her an opportunity to snoop around. For tonight, Jennie would play the part of a city girl enjoying a night out on the town with a handsome cowboy. Considering everything, she could have thought of worse ways to spend an evening.

Besides, she doubted Marty was involved. When they'd talked on the plane, he'd seemed surprised and sad when she told him about the explosion. *You're taking a big risk here, McGrady. You'd better hope your intuition is riding on the right trail.*

9

"I take it you're going out."

Jennie spun around. She'd forgotten about Maggie. "Um . . . Aunt Maggie, it's not what you think. I met Marty on the plane." She winced. "I'm sorry, I should have asked you first. If you don't want me to go, I can call him back."

"No. It's okay." Maggie frowned. "Just be careful, okay?" She stopped and took a deep breath, then smiled. "With all that's happening around here I've become rather paranoid. You go on ahead and have a good time."

"Um, Aunt Maggie. I know Heather used to date Marty and . . . well, you don't think she'd mind, do you?"

"Oh, I doubt it, Jennie. They haven't gone out in a long while."

"Well, I guess I'd better shower. I look like I've been rolling in dirt and smell like horse sweat."

"I'll leave you to it, then." Maggie started to leave, then turned back around. "Oh, Jennie. I meant to tell you. I'll be bringing Jeff home tonight. The doctor said I'd better come get him before all the nurses quit. He'll be happier here anyway where he can monitor things."

"Tonight? Are you sure you don't want me to stay?"

Maggie shook her head. "No need. I'll be taking Amber with me and it'll be late when we get back. I just wanted to warn you."

"Warn me?" Jennie frowned.

"He may not be in the best frame of mind. You see, he didn't want me to ask you and Susan to come. He doesn't like asking for help. If he seems . . . well, angry, it isn't that he's upset with you. He's blaming himself for everything that's happened."

Jennie smiled. "Don't worry about me, Aunt Maggie." The desire to find the person or persons responsible for the explosion burned in her heart with renewed intensity.

Maggie hugged her again, then went into the kitchen while Jennie hurried upstairs to shower.

Not knowing what to wear on a date with a cowboy, Jennie decided to go for the casual look, with a white long-sleeved shirt and jeans. She transferred the threatening notes to her clean jeans and slipped on her jean jacket. *You should have given the notes to the sheriff,* she reminded herself. Then again, maybe that wasn't the best idea. Jennie didn't trust him any more than Heather did.

She lifted strands of her limp, wet hair, wondering what to do with it. Maybe Maggie would braid it. Grabbing her brush and an elastic band along with one of Heather's feather barrettes, Jennie headed downstairs in search for her aunt, or someone who had the use of two hands.

True to his word, Marty picked Jennie up at seven in a red Dodge truck. Wearing a cowboy hat, cream-colored shirt, denim jacket, Wrangler jeans, and boots, he looked as ruggedly handsome as he had on the plane. His broad smile chased away any lingering doubts about his involvement— almost.

A tour of Double D ranch provided no clues. Jennie saw four vehicles but none of them resembled the truck she'd seen in the llama pasture. Maybe she'd been too hasty in suspecting Marty's dad.

On the other hand, Marty had hurried her past one of the out-buildings. He'd called it a machine shed. "Just full of old

74

machinery parts and tools," he'd told her.

She'd thought about telling him she loved tools, then decided against it. No sense being too obvious. Maybe later she'd take Gabby out, sneak over and check out the shop herself.

The tour ended with the Danielsons' modest log home. "Where are your folks?" Jennie asked after she'd been through the house.

Marty shrugged and led her outside. "Probably in town. Mom wanted to go out for dinner."

Marty leaned against one of the support beams on the porch. "Seen enough?"

"I guess. I like your place—it's homey. Have you lived here long?"

"All my life. You sure ask a lot of questions, Jennie McGrady. What gives?"

Jennie flashed him what she hoped was an innocent smile. "Just curious. I've always asked a lot of questions. Mom says I drove her and Dad nuts when I was little. Anyway, I grew up in the city and all this country stuff fascinates me. I want to learn as much as I can."

Marty must have taken her remark as a compliment. His grin widened as he pushed away from the post and hung an arm around her neck. "Then ask away. Let's head into town—see what kind of trouble we can get into."

"Trouble?"

He chuckled. "Just kidding. Thought maybe we'd do a little line dancing—listen to the band down at Willie's."

Jennie stopped. "Um . . . Willie's? That's not some kind of tavern is it? I mean . . . I'm only sixteen. And I'm not much into dancing. I have absolutely no coordination. I'm sure it's because I'm so tall. Takes too long for messages to travel from my brain to my feet."

He grabbed her hand and pulled her toward the truck. "Not to worry. They don't serve anything stronger than Sarsaparilla. People who own it named it after Willie Nelson. Guess he was there once."

————————

For the next two hours, Marty showed Jennie around town and introduced her to at least a dozen friends.

Several of the guys at Willie's wore fatigues, similar to those Marty's dad had worn at the restaurant. Probably members of the militia group Amber had told her about, but Jennie wanted to hear Marty's explanation. "What's the deal with so many of the guys around here wearing military fatigues? Is there an army base around here?"

Marty glanced up at the men in question, his blue eyes registering disapproval. "They're in an army all right, but not Uncle Sam's." He shifted his gaze back to Jennie. "No more questions, okay? We came here to relax and have some fun." Without giving her a chance to answer, he grabbed her hand and pulled her across the room. "Come on, let's pick out a song on the jukebox. Who's your favorite country singer?"

"I don't really have a favorite," Jennie said, deciding to put her questions on hold. For the next hour or so, they ate, talked, laughed, listened to country music, and drank sodas. At ten, Jennie could barely keep her eyes open, and her entire body was protesting from the unaccustomed paces she'd put it through. "I'm sorry, Marty, but I'd better get back. I'm not used to getting up so early or working so hard."

He looked disappointed, but didn't argue. On the drive back to Dancing Waters and the Double D, Marty surprised her by asking about the gunman. "You must have been pretty scared."

"You've got that right. Any idea who it might have been?"

"I told you earlier that I didn't."

"The sheriff said he was probably a hunter." Jennie shifted in her seat so she could watch his reactions. "Why would he think that?"

Marty shrugged. "It's a logical assumption. Why else would he be out there?"

"Marty, the guy had an automatic weapon. He was aiming at the llamas, wearing army fatigues and a black ski mask. That doesn't sound like any hunter I've ever seen. Amber said something about a militia group and war games."

"I know where you're going with this, but I can tell you right now that none of the militia guys around here would have caused the explosion out at Dancing Waters. For one thing, the foreman was a good friend of Dad's. They served in Nam together." Marty's hand tightened on the steering wheel. "The militia guys are mighty upset about not being able to use the property for their weekend maneuvers, but they wouldn't resort to killing—especially one of their own guys."

"How do you know one of them wouldn't? I mean, the gunman I saw today was definitely . . ."

Marty's dark look stopped her. "What? Can you positively identify him as being one of the militia guys? Anyone could buy an outfit like that. You don't know he wasn't a hunter. You probably don't even know if it was a guy."

Jennie leaned her head back against the seat. "You're right about that. For all I know it could have been you." Jennie clamped her lips together wishing she could take back the accusation. She didn't really suspect that Marty had anything to do with the explosion, only that he might know who did.

Marty sighed and stared straight ahead.

"I'm sorry. I didn't mean that."

"I think you did. You suspect my dad even more, don't you?"

Jennie shrugged. She thought about saying no, but decided to level with him. Honesty on her part might make him more apt to talk to her. "I know your dad and Uncle Jeff haven't been on good terms."

Marty laughed. "That's putting it mildly. They hate each other's guts."

"Why?"

"It's a long story."

"So, condense it for me."

"Most of it's political. Dad and his troops are ultra-conservative and anti-government. They don't like the way the country's being run and are out to change it. White Cloud is more liberal in his views. They're at each other's throats, but not literally. Dad may not love his neighbor, but he sure wouldn't kill him."

"I'm still not convinced." Jennie told him about the death threats Heather and Joseph had gotten and explained where they'd come from. "You and your dad were at the restaurant."

Marty glanced at the notes when Jennie dug them out of her pocket and held them up. "I didn't know about those. But my dad couldn't have put the note on Heather's Jeep. I was with him, remember?"

"Yes, but were you watching him the entire time?"

Silence stretched between them. Marty stared straight ahead. Was he beginning to wonder about his dad's involvement?

He slowed and flipped on the blinker as they neared the Double D. "Tell you what, Jennie. To put your mind at ease once and for all, I'm gonna take you back to the Double D to meet my dad. Maybe then you'll see why I keep defending him."

Jennie agreed. Marty had just turned off the highway when they heard a siren and saw the flashing lights behind them.

"Must be the sheriff. Wonder what he wants?" Marty eased the car onto the gravel shoulder.

"Apparently not you," Jennie said as the sheriff's car sped past.

"Something's wrong at the house." Marty whipped the truck back onto the road and raced after the patrol car.

10

Jennie jammed her feet on the floorboard and clutched the dash as Marty careened around a corner. "Slow down!" she shrieked. "Do you want to get us killed?"

"I have to get to Dad. He's got a bad heart." He slammed on the brakes and hooked a right into the Double D.

A camouflaged truck with a dented front end and a broken headlamp was parked in front of the machine shed.

Jennie stepped out of the truck and followed Marty to the porch where the sheriff was talking to Jake Danielson.

"What's going on?" Marty demanded, his jaw tight with concern.

Danielson stared at the truck. He clenched his fists and turned toward Jennie. "What's she doing here?" Jennie took a step back. She could almost feel the heat of his anger.

"This is all your doing," he yelled, jabbing a finger at Jennie. "You and them blasted Indians. Nobody sets up Jake Danielson and gets away with it. Nobody!"

Sheriff Mason ran a hand along his square jaw. "All right, Jake. Just settle down. No one's accusing you of anything. Just following up on a tip is all."

Marty glanced from the truck to his dad, his eyes glazed over with worry.

"Now let's take a look at that vehicle over there." The sheriff started walking, apparently expecting them to follow.

"Some guy called not more'n ten minutes ago. Said the camouflaged truck I was looking for was parked in your yard."

Even though the double-wide mercury light atop a pole near the house illuminated the entire yard, Sheriff Mason unsnapped a flashlight from his belt and directed the light toward the battered pickup.

"This your truck, Jake?"

Danielson swore. "You know it is. License plate'll bear that out. But I sure as heck wasn't driving it today. Haven't set foot on White Cloud's property in more'n a week."

"Well, little lady, good thing you're here. Save me the trouble of having to call you. This the truck you think you saw this afternoon?"

Jennie opened her mouth then closed it again. She glanced from Marty to Mr. Danielson, then back at the sheriff. "I didn't *think* I saw it, Sheriff. I *did* see it."

"That's not what I asked. Is this the vehicle you saw?"

"It looks like it."

He turned back to Jake. "I'm sorry about this, old buddy, but I'm going to have to get some forensics people out."

"The truck was stolen, Sam. You know that. I called your office early this morning to report it."

While the men talked, Jennie examined the rear of the truck, then walked around to the front end and knelt down to check out the dents and scratches. Pieces of wood mixed with the glass from the broken headlight were caught in the space behind the bumper and inside the broken light. Two scratches about a foot apart marred the hood. Jennie suspected they'd been caused by the barbed wire. This had to be the truck she'd seen.

She pointed out the scratches and wood chips to the sheriff. "I'm sure if you run a few tests on the wood and glass I gave you this afternoon . . ."

"Miss McGrady," the sheriff said in a patronizing tone. "I am perfectly capable of running my investigations without your interference. For your information, I collected a few samples of my own. I have little doubt that this is the truck you saw. Just wanted you to verify it." To Marty he said, "Why don't you take Jennie here back to Dancin' Waters before I haul her in for tampering with the evidence?"

Marty grabbed her elbow. "Come on," he murmured. "Let's get out of here."

"I hope you're not thinking about arresting me." Though Jake had spoken to the sheriff, he glared at Jennie.

Jennie could have said a lot of things, but she refused to stoop to Danielson's level. She clamped her lips together, shrugged Marty's hand away, then spun around and headed for his truck.

"Not at the moment," she heard Sheriff Mason answer. "Reckon I'll need to get a statement, though."

Jennie looked back at the two men as she opened the passenger-side door.

"I know."

The sheriff slapped Jake Danielson's back in a friendly sort of way. "Now what's say we go in and explain all this to Betty."

Marty didn't say much on the short drive to Dancing Waters. He seemed sad and confused. Jennie wanted to console him, but what could she say?

When they pulled up to the house, Marty caught her hand before she could open the door. "He didn't do it, Jennie. I know it looks bad, but . . ." He tipped his head back and after a sharp intake of breath said, "I don't know why I keep defending him. I mean, it's not like he isn't capable of violence. Maybe he did do it. Maybe . . ."

"Marty, I'm sorry this has happened. I hope your dad's innocent. He did say the truck had been stolen. It's possible someone's trying to pin this on him."

Marty smiled. "You really are something, Jennie. Here

my dad treats you like garbage and you're trying to make me feel better."

Jennie shrugged and looked away. "I'd better go in now. Keep me posted, okay?"

Marty nodded. "Sure. I'll call you tomorrow."

"Um . . . Marty, if you need someone to talk to about things . . . I mean . . . well, you know."

He leaned over and brushed his lips against her cheek. "Thanks."

Before going inside, Jennie turned to wave at the headlights.

The house was dark and Jennie had only the light from the moon to guide her to the porch. Where was everyone? Then she remembered that Maggie and Amber had gone into Missoula to pick up Uncle Jeff. Maybe they hadn't returned yet. Glancing over to the garage, she realized that wasn't the case. The White Clouds' station wagon sat next to the Jeep in front of the garage. Were they all sleeping?

It must have been later than she'd thought. She lifted her left arm to check her watch, but it was too dark. Jennie climbed the porch steps and went inside. She removed her shoes at the door, then tiptoed toward the stairs.

"A little late for you to be sneaking in, isn't it?" A man's harsh voice rang out in the stillness.

"Who. . . ?" Jennie whipped around. Fear exploded through her like a lightning bolt. Her heart began to quiet as she saw the silhouette of a man in a wheelchair against the silvery, moonlit window. One pajama-clad leg dangled from the chair. He seemed to be staring at something outside. Jennie took a step toward him, then stopped. Though darkness partially hid his features, his anger, almost tangible in its intensity, engulfed her like smoke from a forest fire. "I—I'm sorry, Uncle Jeff. I wanted to get here sooner, but . . ."

The cloud of fury dissipated. Jeff spun his wheelchair around and cleared his throat. "I'm the one who should apologize. I thought you were Heather."

Jennie offered him a tentative smile, closing the distance between them. If he'd been Uncle Kevin, Mom and Maggie's brother, she'd have wrapped her arms around his neck and hugged him. But here, now, Jennie held back. She'd only met him once before, at her dad's funeral.

"You went out with Marty Danielson."

The comment caught her off guard and held a strong hint of accusation. She lowered herself onto the arm of the sofa.

"I met him on the plane, and since he's your neighbor I thought he might have some insight as to what's been going on around here."

Jennie had grown accustomed to the scant light and could more easily see his features. He was a handsome man, with a square face and wide forehead which wrinkled in a frown. He wore his long dark hair pulled back in a braid like Joseph's. His eyes reminded her of Joseph's too, dark and penetrating as if they could see into her soul.

"And did you learn anything of interest?" He lifted his shoulders and adjusted the lapels of his robe.

Jennie ignored the condescending tone in his voice. "As a matter of fact, I learned quite a lot."

She told him about the gunman in the llama pasture and seeing the truck at the Double D ranch.

"So, you've met Danielson." He pointed to the stump that used to be a leg and said, "Do you think he did this?"

Jennie sucked in a deep breath. "I—I don't know. Marty doesn't think so, but . . ."

He gripped the wheels of his chair and whirled it back around to face the window. "It's late. You'd better go to bed. We'll talk more tomorrow."

Jennie watched him for a few seconds. Tears gathered in her eyes and she didn't know why. One thing she did know. No matter what the odds, she had to find out who had maimed Jeff and taken Rick Jenkins' life. Sure, the truck she'd seen earlier in the day had been found, and the sheriff would question Danielson, but Jennie couldn't help but feel that she was seeing only a small piece of a much bigger and more complex puzzle.

Jennie and Heather reached the bedroom at the same time. One through the window, the other through the door. Jennie was beginning to wonder if Heather ever entered her room in the normal way.

"How's Eric?" Jennie asked.

Heather didn't answer.

"Your dad's downstairs waiting for you. He thought I was you when I first came in."

After closing the window, she turned to face Jennie. "Did you say anything about Eric?"

Jennie shook her head. "The subject didn't come up."

Heather sighed. "Guess I'd better go down and talk to him."

"What are you going to tell him?"

"The truth, I suppose. It's about time."

"Want me to come along?"

"No, but thanks for asking." Heather reached for the doorknob. "Wish me luck."

Jennie changed into a nightgown and went across the hall to the bathroom. She heard the murmur of voices downstairs and thought about sneaking over to the top of the stairs to eavesdrop, but didn't. Some conversations were meant to be private. Still, she couldn't help wonder how her uncle would react.

Ten minutes later Heather came in. Ignoring Jennie's questioning look, she entered the large walk-in closet, changed into her pajamas, then stood in front of the mirror and brushed out her shimmering black hair. After crawling under the covers, she turned out the light. "I didn't tell him."

Jennie rested her elbow on the pillow and propped her head up on her hand. "Why?"

"I just couldn't."

"So how did you explain your being out tonight?"

"I didn't," Heather murmured. "I said I was here all the time."

"And he believed you?"

"I don't know. He just sat there in the dark. He wouldn't even look at me. I let him down, Jen. Hazen and I . . ." Heather's voice broke into deep sobs.

Jennie got out of bed and retrieved a box of tissues from the dresser, handed a couple to Heather, then sat on the bed beside her. Heather blew her nose, then buried her face in the pillow.

Jennie placed what she hoped was a comforting hand on Heather's shoulder. After a few minutes, Heather's sobs quieted to an occasional shudder.

When it became apparent that Heather didn't want to talk anymore, Jennie climbed back into her own bed. She stared up into the darkness wishing she'd brought a tissue with her. Empathetic tears leaked out of the corners of her eyes and dripped into her hair and onto the pillow. She brushed them away with her hand. "Oh God," she whispered. "Why does life have to be so hard?" Jennie closed her eyes, squeezing out the last of her tears. She prayed for the fractured family, then for her own as her thoughts drifted back to home and Mom, Nick, Michael, and Hannah. She'd forgotten to call again. With the time difference they'd still be up. She thought about getting out of bed and going downstairs to the kitchen. No, Uncle Jeff might still be there. She didn't want to disturb him—or face him. Tomorrow. She'd call home tomorrow.

———

The next day when Jennie awoke, Heather had already gone to work. Jennie dressed as fast as her stiff muscles would allow and limped downstairs. Amber, Maggie, Jeff, and Bob

Lopez had already started to eat breakfast.

"Mornin', Jennie." Lopez speared a large piece of ham and plopped it onto his already full plate of pancakes and scrambled eggs.

"Good morning." Jennie pulled out the chair between him and Uncle Jeff's wheelchair and folded herself onto it. Her uncle offered her a brief nod, then turned back to his plate.

"Better eat hearty this mornin'," Lopez said. "You got a mighty big day ahead of you."

"Why's that?" Jennie reached for the eggs and gave Maggie a questioning look.

Maggie glanced at Jeff, then back at Jennie. "We thought you might enjoy working with Bob today. They'll be repairing the gate out in the llama pasture then checking out the herd." Her gaze fell to Jennie's cast. "Of course, you don't have to. I don't want you hurting that arm."

Jennie raised the arm in question. "Actually, it's not near as much problem as I thought it would be. I'm getting used to it. In fact, it's the only part of my body that doesn't hurt this morning. Anyway, I'd like to go."

"I'm going with," Amber said, sitting straighter in her chair.

"Not today." Jeff sipped at his coffee. "I'd like you to stick around here and keep your old dad company." His warm smile seemed like a contradiction to the man she'd met last night, but it made Jennie wish she could stay behind and get to know him better.

"If there's time," Jeff said, his gaze settling on Lopez, "I'd like you to ride on out to Dad's and check his stock. See if he needs anything."

Lopez nodded. "Heard they nailed Danielson last night."

"Yeah?" Jeff set his cup down, acting like he didn't know anything about it. Jennie wondered why.

"Seems his truck's the one what rammed our gate. Danielson swears up and down he wasn't driving it."

"He have any idea who was?"

"Claims not." Lopez shook his head. "Says his truck was stolen. Some story, huh? We all know how he feels about you and Joseph taking over the ranch."

"How'd you hear all this so quickly?" Jeff asked.

Lopez shrugged. "Danged if I know. Some of the boys was talking about it this morning—you know how word gets around."

Jennie set her fork down. Now she knew what her uncle was getting at. She hadn't told anyone but Jeff about the arrest. How would the ranch hands have found out so soon unless . . . Had one of them been there in the shadows, watching? If so, why? And who?

Or, her mind took another road, *maybe the person wasn't watching. Maybe they already knew because they'd stolen the pickup, returned it, and called the sheriff with the tip. That means the gunman and possibly the person who left the notes and killed the foreman could have been one of their own employees—or a member of the family.*

Jennie shivered at the possibility.

11

"I appreciate your taking me along, Mr. Lopez." Jennie eased Gabby up next to the ranch manager's horse as they rode out toward the llama pasture.

"Glad to have your company." Lopez shifted in his saddle and glanced at the brown truck lumbering up the hill behind them. It carried the supplies they'd need to build a new gate and mend the broken wire.

Jennie eyed the two men in the front seat—John Copeland and Eric Summers. She already had Eric on her list of suspects and wondered if she shouldn't include John, Heidi's husband. Heidi had been reluctant to talk about the problems at Dancing Waters.

Of course, she'd need to add Bob Lopez as well. She waited until he turned back around, then asked, "How long have you worked at the ranch?"

Lopez adjusted his hat and fixed his gaze on the brim. "Oh, reckon it's been 'bout twenty-five years or so. Started way back when your uncle Jeff was a young'n. Worked for the Elliots before that. When Dan Elliot moved the family to California, he let most of the hands go. Joseph asked me to stay on and work for him, and I've been here ever since."

"So you knew the Elliots. Joseph and Amber told me a little about them. Do you know Chad Elliot?"

"Seen him a couple of times. His daddy went west before

he was born. Met Chad when he showed up a few months back claiming his family had been swindled." He shook his head. "Crazy business, that."

"He didn't know his grandfather had sold off all the land to Joseph? I mean—that sounds so weird."

Lopez reached up and swatted at the fly buzzing around his head. "I wouldn't know about none of that. I just take care of the stock and the land. Leave the business to the bankers and the owners. Which reminds me—sure way to find out about the land deal would be to talk to Alex Dayton. He's president of the Bitterroot Valley Bank over in Cottonwood."

"Thanks. I might do that." She tucked the information away for future reference. "Do you think Joseph and Uncle Jeff cheated the Elliots out of their land?"

"Nope. Ain't nobody in Montana more honest than Joseph White Cloud. If he says the land is his, I believe him."

Jennie reached forward to stroke Gabby's neck. "Mr. Lopez, tell me about the explosion. Were you there? Do you think it was an accident?"

"You sure ask a lot of questions." Lopez pulled back on the reins to slow his mount until Jennie pulled up beside him. "You ain't planning on getting involved in the goings-on out here, are ya?"

"Well, I . . ."

"Now, I know you couldn't help what happened out here yesterday, but you want to be careful who yer askin' questions of."

"I am. I can trust you, can't I?"

A broad smile broke the solemn expression on his brown, furrowed face. "Reckon you can at that."

"So what about the explosion?"

He sighed, then as though indulging the whims of a child, "I wasn't out there that day. Had a touch of the flu. You know

I've felt real bad about it. Maybe if I'd been there I could have prevented it."

"Or you may have been the one who got killed." When he didn't respond, Jennie asked, "Do you think someone meant to murder the foreman?"

Lopez shook his head. "Reckon it must've been accidental. Can't think of a soul who'd want to kill Rick Jenkins. Poor guy had enough troubles. Trying to make ends meet—most folks just felt sorry for him. Wife had cancer—died not more'n two months before Rick was killed."

"Well, what if they weren't after him? What if they were after Uncle Jeff?"

Lopez shook his head. "Hmm, he's got plenty of enemies all right. Don't know anybody that hates him enough to want to kill him, though."

"Okay, then what if the explosion was just meant to scare the White Clouds into leaving? Maybe nobody was supposed to get hurt."

"I suppose that's a possibility."

Jennie knew she was pushing it, but had to ask one more question. "Do you think Jake Danielson did it?"

Lopez took a long time to answer. "I wouldn't put it past Danielson to come over and bag a deer or elk and maybe cut some wire, but setting off a bomb—that's not his style—leastwise it hasn't been. Course, having Joseph hand over half the land to the U.S. Forest Service has stirred up a mighty big hornet's nest. Lot of bad feeling over it, that's for sure."

"He's giving land to the government?"

Lopez gave her a long hard look. "No more questions now or I'll be tempted to tell your uncle what you're up to. I suspect he'll put an end to it right quick. We already got us a sheriff, Jennie. Might be better all around if you just let old Sam ask the questions. He'll be able to do something about the answers."

Lopez went on ahead, and when they reached the broken

fence, he reined up his quarter horse and dismounted. Jennie did too, or tried to. Her legs had stiffened again during the ride and when her feet hit the ground, her knees buckled. "Ouch." She grabbed at the saddle to straighten herself up.

Lopez chuckled. "A little sore, are ya?"

"A lot sore." Jennie winced as she shifted her weight from one foot to the other.

Lopez chuckled. "After all the riding you did yesterday, it's no wonder. You think yer bad off now, wait till tonight. We'd best get started. You hustle over to the truck and help the boys unload. With that arm, you might want to play gopher—just fetch and carry. Think you can handle that?"

"Sure. No problem." Some of the stiffness wore off as she worked. For the rest of the day, they mended fence in three different spots, checked on the llamas, the buffalo, and Joseph's Appaloosas. The white-and-brown horses had originally been bred and developed by the Nez Perce so they could easily identify members of their own tribe by the markings on their horses' rumps.

While working with the men, Jennie gleaned a little more information about Rick Jenkins. He'd not only been Danielson's buddy and a member of the militia, with his wife's medical bills, he'd been hurting for money. That information brought on a new pile of questions, but still left the big question unresolved. Had the explosion been intentional?

By the time Jennie arrived back at the ranch, had showered, and begun eating dinner, she could hardly lift the fork to her mouth. Even her brain hurt.

"Aren't you hungry?" Maggie asked.

Jennie gazed at the fried chicken, mashed potatoes and gravy, and string beans fresh out of the garden. "Starved. The stomach is willing, but my body just doesn't want to cooperate." With her left hand, she massaged the cramped muscles in her legs.

"We've been working you too hard."

"Wrong," Jeff teased as he lifted a piece of chicken to his mouth. "It's living in the city. She's not getting enough of the right kind of exercise. Another week around here, Jennie, and you'll be in great shape."

Jennie groaned. "If you don't kill me first."

"Poor baby," Heather cooed. "Mom, why don't I take her up to the Crystal Hot Springs after dinner? We can spend the night on Blue Ridge."

"Oh, Heather, how thoughtful." Maggie split open a hot buttermilk biscuit. "Jennie, you'll love it up there."

"Not a bad idea," Jeff said, "but first Maggie and I would like to talk to you in my study."

"Me?" Jennie glanced around the table.

Heather and Amber shrugged.

Maggie cleared her throat. "I . . . we . . . there's something we need to discuss with you."

For the rest of the meal Jennie's mind raced with possibilities. Was she in trouble? Had Lopez complained about her? Were they sending her home? Each question settled in her stomach like a rock.

"I'll pack and call Dusty to get the horses ready," Heather offered.

Something in her cousin's eyes raised the hair on Jennie's neck. Could she be planning something other than the trip? For a moment Jennie thought about telling her she'd do her own packing, but that would be rude. "Thanks," she said instead. "Be sure to put in a plastic bag to wrap my cast in so it doesn't get wet. I shouldn't be too long." *I hope.*

"Amber, honey . . ." Maggie picked up the leftover chicken and potatoes and carried them to the kitchen, "clear the table while Daddy and I talk to Jennie, okay? I'll be out to help you in a few minutes." Jennie tried not to stare at her uncle's legs as he backed away from the table. Before there'd been only one—now there were two.

"It's a prosthesis," he said, answering her question before she could ask it.

"Oh, I—um, I didn't mean to stare. I'm surprised, that's all. I didn't know they'd give you one so soon."

"They fitted me with it the day after surgery." Apparently not wanting to discuss his condition further, he propelled his wheelchair toward the office.

"Sit down, Jennie." Jeff wheeled the chair behind his desk.

Jennie sat in one of the two forest green armchairs and glanced over the two walls of books. It looked like an office you'd expect a lawyer to have.

Maggie stood behind her and rested her hands on Jennie's shoulders.

"Okay, I give. What did I do wrong?"

"Wrong?" Jeff frowned then looked up at Maggie.

Maggie squeezed Jennie's shoulders. "You haven't done anything wrong. It's just that your mother called earlier and we thought it would be better to talk privately."

"Mom? Oh no. It's Hannah, isn't it? They couldn't get her back. I knew it. I should have gone home. . . ."

"There was nothing they could do." Jeff placed his elbows on his desk, locked his fingers together, and rested his chin on his hands. "Nothing you could do, either. Hannah's grandparents have exercised their right to care for Hannah. The judge granted them custody."

"But Chuck Stewart is a . . ." Jennie groped for a word but couldn't think of anything bad enough to describe him.

"Apparently he's never abused Hannah," Jeff went on. "She won't be living with him—at least not right away. He will have visitation rights, and may eventually gain custody, but for now, Mr. and Mrs. Stewart will be responsible for her. The court feels it's in Hannah's best interest to be with her biological family."

Jennie bit her lower lip, not bothering to wipe away the

tears that had broken loose. "It's not fair. Isn't there anything they could have done?"

"I'm afraid not, honey." Maggie covered Jennie's hand with her own. "Jeff says they can appeal, but Susan—um, your mother thinks it may be less disruptive for Hannah to let her go."

"How can she. . . ?" Jennie brushed the moisture off her cheeks with her palms. "I'd better call her."

Jeff wheeled his chair around the desk and pulled up next to the door. "I wish you could call her. To tell you the truth, the last thing I need to deal with right now is another problem."

"Jeff . . ." Maggie began.

Her uncle grabbed the doorknob, then turned back and sighed. "I'm sorry. I had no right to take my frustrations out on you."

"It's okay, Uncle Jeff. Why can't I call Mom?"

"She's on her way to Arizona with Michael and Nick." Maggie squeezed Jennie's hand.

"Arizona? What are they doing in Arizona? They're supposed to be coming here."

"They'll be here in a few days. Susan wanted to ease the transition for Hannah and check out her grandparents."

The thought of never seeing Hannah again dug a crater in Jennie's heart. She pressed the heels of her hands against her eyes. "How could Mom and Michael give up so easily?"

"Oh, honey." Maggie drew Jennie into her arms. "I know it's hard. But Susan said to tell you that Hannah's grandparents seem very nice."

"Think of it this way, Jennie," Jeff said. "Suppose you were in Hannah's place. Would you rather live with your neighbors or with your grandparents?"

Jennie raised her head. "I—when you put it that way—but . . ." She released a long, shuddering sigh. "Do you think she's really better off?"

"Only time will tell. Hannah's grandparents want you and your family to stay in touch. You can write and even visit."

"Really?"

"Yes. Since you didn't get to say good-bye to Hannah, you can fly down later this summer."

The thought of seeing Hannah for herself took the edge off the pain.

Jeff wheeled back to his desk again and picked up a folder. Maggie hugged Jennie and excused herself to go help Amber in the kitchen.

Jennie started to follow, then stopped at the door. "Uncle Jeff?" A nagging question had re-inserted itself in her mind and she had to ask.

He looked up from his papers. "Yes?"

"Can you tell me about the explosion?"

12

"I mean . . . was the explosion an accident or. . . ?" Jennie hesitated. Maybe he didn't want to talk about it yet.

"Did someone blow up the truck on purpose?" Jeff finished. He stared at something on his desk for a long time, then closed his eyes. "I wish I knew. The truth is, I can't remember. I close my eyes and all I can see is the explosion and the flames. Nothing more."

Jennie walked over to her uncle's desk. "Did you know about the death threats Heather and Joseph got while you were gone?"

"My father told me of the message left on the deer." He raised an eyebrow. "And how you took the note from his garbage."

Jennie's cheeks flushed. "I . . . he threw it away and I thought it might be important. Monday—the day I arrived—Heather and I had stopped for lunch and when we came out of the restaurant there was a note on the Jeep. They were written by the same person." She pulled the papers from her pocket to show him.

"Why didn't you give them to the sheriff?"

"I probably should have last night when he was over at the Danielsons, but I forgot. Actually, that's not entirely true. Maybe I didn't really forget. Heather said she didn't trust him. I wasn't too impressed with him either."

97

"Might be just as well, in case we have to go to another law enforcement agency. He let Danielson go," Jeff said, his voice flat and without the anger she expected.

"On bail?"

"Sam didn't arrest him."

"I can't believe that. Look at the evidence."

"He did. His deputies weren't able to lift any fingerprints from the interior of the truck, which means it had been wiped clean. He figures Danielson would have no reason to do that. There's nothing to indicate who drove it. What's more, Sam would need absolute proof to arrest Jake. The man's his brother-in-law and practically owns him."

"So you're saying that even if Danielson is guilty, he won't be arrested?"

"Not without infallible evidence, with eyewitnesses to testify against him. I should amend that to honest witnesses."

Jennie stared at her uncle. She wasn't sure how to respond. She placed her left arm on Jeff's desk and leaned toward him. "I don't get it. How come you're telling me all this? How come you're not shoving me out to play and telling me to mind my own business?"

"I don't trust Sam Mason. He's too easily swayed by special interest groups. Though he won't admit it, he's sympathetic to the white supremacists and anti-government groups and as far as I'm concerned that's a dangerous place to be. If I could be out there solving this case I would."

He paused and glanced down at his leg. "But I can't—leastwise not yet. I'd planned to tell you tomorrow when you came back from Blue Ridge, but I guess now is as good a time as any." He paused and held her in a long steady gaze. "I need someone to investigate for me."

Stunned, Jennie moved over to the chair and dropped into it. "You want me to . . . investigate?"

Jeff smiled. "Trust me, Jennie. If it were solely up to me, you would not be my first choice. Not that you aren't competent. But you are my sister-in-law's kid. If Maggie or Susan find out I've encouraged you, I'd be . . . well let's just say I'd rather you didn't tell either of them we're having this discussion."

"I don't get it."

"I spoke with my father today. He believes God has sent you to help us. He says that you are going to investigate with or without our blessing and, considering this, feels we should assist you. At the moment I'm not so sure. But my father is a wise man. I'm willing to support his decision, but you'll need to report everything you learn to me. If I'm not here you must speak with my father."

"Are you serious? You actually want me to investigate?"

Jeff nodded. "I'm afraid so. There's one more thing. Be careful. Don't go off alone with Marty Danielson or any of the other men around here. Don't even trust the sheriff. Snooping around and digging up information is one thing. I doubt any of these men will be taking you seriously, which gives us the advantage. Joseph and I will be watching out for you as best we can. So will Bob."

"He knows?"

"He came in to talk to me before dinner. Said you were asking all kinds of questions." Jeff grinned. "Don't worry, you can trust him. Bob Lopez is like a second father to me."

"Thanks, Uncle Jeff." Jennie bounced out of her chair, walked around the desk, and threw her arms around his neck. When the cast connected with his head she mumbled an apology and backed away. "Sorry."

"No problem."

"I guess I'd better go."

As she reached the door, Jeff stopped her. "There's one more thing, Jennie. If you happen to find Hazen—" His eyes closed and he frowned. "Just tell him I don't hold him responsible for anything that happened out there."

"What makes you think I'll see him?"

Jeff shook his head. "Wishful thinking, I guess. That and your track record."

Still stunned, Jennie left. Except for Gram he'd been the only adult to take her seriously. Excitement bubbled up inside her, then ebbed. *What if you fail, McGrady? What if you let them down? And who are you to take on a case like this? You're dealing with a militia group, not the Boy Scouts.*

"Come on, Jennie. I've got everything all ready." Heather stuffed a swimsuit into Jennie's hand a pushed her out of Jeff's office and in the direction of the main floor bathroom. As instructed, Jennie put the swimsuit on under her clothes.

When Jennie emerged, Heather led her out to the front porch where she'd set their boots. "You're going to love the surprise I have planned for you."

"What surprise?" Jennie sat on the steps beside Heather and pulled on her boots. "You said you were taking me to some hot springs, then camping on Blue Ridge. Is there more?"

"Definitely, but I can't tell you." Heather flashed her an infectious smile.

"I can hardly wait." Jennie set aside the warning bells and decided her cousin had gone through an attitude change. After all, they had grown closer in the last couple of days. Maybe Heather had decided they could be friends. Maybe.

Heather scrambled to her feet and reached down to give Jennie a hand up. The fast movement set off a chain reaction in her sore muscles. "Whoa. Take it easy."

"Sorry."

Mounting Gabby should have been getting easier, but Jennie's legs and hips protested more loudly with each try. "Ouch. I may have to give up riding if this gets any worse."

"Another day or two and you'll be fine." Heather turned her honey-colored mare named Brandy and headed southwest down the same path she'd taken on the night Jennie had gotten lost. The thought didn't exactly fill Jennie with confidence.

The deeper into the woods they rode, the stronger Jennie's suspicions grew. Heather chatted about her last photo shoot with Eric. "I am so excited, Jennie. His agent has me scheduled to do a photo session with Andre."

"Who's Andre?" Jennie asked.

"Only the most popular photographer on the West Coast. His photos have been on the cover of every major magazine in the country this year. And nearly all of his models are doing films. This is a major break for me."

"So, when is all this supposed to happen?" Jennie asked.

"You sound like you don't believe me."

"Oh, I believe *you*. It's Eric I'm worried about."

"Eric loves me. He wouldn't lie about something this important. It's our dream."

"When are you going to tell your folks?"

"I'm not. Well, I did leave them a note, but . . ."

"What do you mean, you left them a note?" Jennie's loud response startled Gabby. The horse shied, nearly dumping her on the trail. She grasped the saddle horn and held on tight.

"Whoa, Gabby. It's okay. I'm sorry." She patted Gabby's neck and glared at Heather. "Well?"

Heather stared back, unflinching. "I have to do this. I may never get another opportunity. My parents won't understand."

"All right. Go ahead. Mess up your life. But don't expect me to help you. I'm going back to the ranch." Jennie winced. She was beginning to sound like her mother.

"You're not going to tell, are you?"

"Yes . . . I don't know. I should. You could be setting yourself up for . . . anything. I've heard some pretty gruesome stories about girls who run away from home wanting to be models or actresses. They leave home expecting a career and end up living on the street."

"That's not going to happen."

"I hope not. What you're doing is dangerous."

"I thought maybe you'd understand. You can go back to the ranch, but even if you tell Mom and Dad it won't do any good. I'm going." Heather spurred her horse forward.

Jennie debated. Should she go back or stay with Heather? If she stayed, maybe she'd be able to talk her out of leaving.

"Okay, I give. I'll come with you. I won't tell your parents—yet. Just explain one thing. If you were going to run away, why drag me into it?"

"I wasn't dragging you in. Actually, I'm not leaving until tomorrow. I just wanted to share my good news and spend some time with you before I leave." Heather smiled. "It's hard to know when we'll get together again and I'm starting to like you."

Jennie wanted to believe her, but her intuition cautioned her to tread carefully.

A few minutes later, they emerged from the trees and rode along a ridge.

"We'll be there soon. Can you hear the waterfall?"

The rushing sound of water eased Jennie's nerves. Maybe Heather was just taking her to the hot springs. They rode on in silence for several minutes, then entered the woods again and rode until they came to a wide meadow divided by a creek.

The creek gave rise to a steep rock formation where water dropped from a hundred-foot cliff. Beside the waterfall, steam rose from an almost circular pool.

"Oh . . . Oh, Heather," Jennie whispered. "It's beautiful."

"I told you. Wait until you get in."

The girls tied their horses to a nearby tree, stripped down to their swimming suits, and set their towels on the rocks. Heather climbed in while Jennie sat on the edge and wrapped her cast in plastic wrap. She eased her body into the pool, taking care to keep the cast out of the water. Her aching muscles soon began to relax as the warm water melted away her tension.

"I've been thinking about what you said." Heather tipped her head back and gazed at the colorful western sky.

"About what?" The water had relaxed her so much Jennie had let their discussion about Eric float away. Now it drifted back. "Oh, you mean about running away?"

"You might be right. I mean, I do trust Eric, but I don't know anything about the agent. I may not show it sometimes, but I love my family. I wouldn't want to hurt them." Heather shifted her gaze from the pink and lavender sky to Jennie. "Do you think Mom and Dad would let me go?"

Jennie shrugged. "I don't know. They might say no, but if your folks are anything like my mom, they'd have a good reason."

"I don't think I could bear it if they said no."

"I sort of understand where you're coming from. I want to go into law enforcement—maybe become a detective or a police officer. Mom thinks being a lawyer is okay, but says the other is too dangerous. I figure I'll just give her some time to get used to the idea, go to college, then decide for sure. The one thing I know is that whatever choice I make, Mom will be there for me."

"Hmm. Maybe I will talk to them."

"They might surprise you."

Heather slid beneath the water again, her jet black hair splayed out on the water as she ducked under. She popped up laughing and splashing.

"Hey, no fair. I can't get all the way in." Jennie reciprocated by kicking up a wall of water. Heather called a truce.

"Look," Heather said, pointing up at the dusky sky. "The first star. Do you ever wish on it?"

Jennie nodded. "I used to wish I'd find my father. I

103

haven't made a wish for a long time."

"Star light, star bright, first star I see tonight. I wish I may, I wish I might, have the wish I wish tonight." Heather squeezed her eyes tight.

Jennie did the same. She wished for Heather to make the right choice. And for Hazen to come home. And for Hannah to be safe and well. "I have too many things to wish for."

"Me too." Heather sighed.

When they climbed out of the hot springs, the darkening sky had turned the stars to diamonds. After removing their wet suits, they toweled dry and dragged on their clothes. Jennie was amazed at how clearly she could see with only the moon for a night-light.

As Jennie slipped on a sweatshirt the hairs on the back of her head sprang to attention. She glanced around. "Heather?"

No one answered. Jennie walked around the rocks to where they'd left the horses. They were gone.

Oh no, not again. "Come on, Heather, this isn't funny."

An eerie silence bred fear in her heart. "Heather?"

A coyote howled an answer in the distance. Jennie shivered as she scanned the moonlit hills. Shadows. Too many shadows.

A twig snapped. Jennie whirled around. Not more than fifteen feet in front of her—astride a huge silver-white horse—sat an Indian warrior. Long black hair shimmered in the moonlight and streamed behind him as the wind sliced through the canyon. He stared at her with eyes dark as the night.

Jennie backed up against a rock. This couldn't be real. She half expected a director to walk on stage and tell her she was playing the scene all wrong. "Who—who are you?"

The warrior didn't answer. His menacing gaze fastened on her. Jennie thought about running, but couldn't move. He lifted a hatchet from his belt, raised it high above his head, and hurled it toward her.

13

"Is she all right?" The voice belonged to Heather.

Jennie gritted her teeth. *You should have known, McGrady. You should have seen it coming.*

"You think the tomahawk was too much?" The second voice was male. If he hadn't frightened her out of her wits she might have recognized him.

Jennie got to her knees, ignoring Hazen's offer of help. Like Heather, he had coal black hair and wide, dark eyes. Glistening white teeth appeared as he grinned at her. "Hi, Jennie. Welcome to Dancing Waters."

Jennie brushed herself off. Fury wiped away any fear she'd felt earlier. "I can't believe you'd trick me like that."

"Why?" they answered in unison.

Jennie shook her head. "You nearly gave me a heart attack. You could have killed me."

"Not a chance." Hazen jumped up on the rock and retrieved his tomahawk from a tree stump. "I missed you by at least two feet."

"Don't be mad at us, Jennie. It's my fault. I knew you wanted to meet Hazen and I thought this would be fun."

Jennie huffed. "Getting a hatchet tossed at me is not my idea of fun."

"Well, you have to admit we had you going." Hazen chuckled as he snapped his tomahawk back onto his belt. He reached toward her head.

Jennie flinched. "What are you doing?"

"Hold still." He pulled a twig out of her hair. "You're a mess."

"Thanks," Jennie muttered as she brushed the dirt off her hands and clothes.

"Let's go back in the water for a while," Heather suggested. "You need to wash off the dirt."

Jennie didn't argue and was, in fact, the first one in. The warm water worked its magic and after a while she could almost laugh at the practical joke her cousins had played on her. They talked for another half hour, then headed back to their horses.

"I hope this means we're forgiven, Jennie." Hazen draped one arm around Jennie's shoulders and the other around his sister.

"Are we really staying out here tonight?" Jennie asked, "or are we heading back to the ranch?"

"That's up to you." Heather swung up onto Brandy's back. "I'm staying out here. I think Hazen is too, but, if you want, we can escort you to the house, then come back out."

"No, don't do that. I'll stay, but no more practical jokes."

It took all of five minutes to make the trek to the one-room cabin that sat alone on Blue Ridge. The stars and moon hung so near, Jennie could almost touch them. Hazen built a fire in a pit near the cabin to chase away the mountain chill while Heather and Jennie cut branches for roasting marshmallows. They feasted on s'mores, chocolate bars and smooshed hot marshmallows sandwiched between two Graham crackers.

Around midnight, they pulled sleeping bags from the cabin and placed them out under the big Montana sky. Jennie snuggled into her bag. She'd never seen so many stars or been able to make out so many constellations. After a while her eyes drifted closed. Then she remembered what her uncle Jeff had said. "Hazen?" she whispered.

"What?" He raised up on his elbow.

"Your dad sent a message for you."

Hazen lowered his head to the pillow. "Do I want to hear this?"

"He doesn't hold you responsible for what happened."

After a long silence, Jennie turned onto her side facing him. "Why did you run away?"

Hazen glanced over at Heather, then unzipped his bag and crawled out. "She's asleep. Let's talk over there."

Jennie scrambled out of her bag and followed him to the other side of the cabin. He sat on an outcropping of rock and waited for Jennie to join him.

"My father is wrong," Hazen said. "It was my fault. I knew Rick was planning something. I'd seen him talking to Danielson a couple of days before. I should have told Dad, but I thought I'd just keep an eye on him myself."

"You think Rick caused the explosion?"

"I know he did. My guess is he was working for Danielson. I saw him toss something into the fuel tank. He took off running. Tripped on a rock. Section of tailgate caught him in the back."

"Oh, Hazen. How awful."

"Dad was supposed to die. Rick had waited until he thought I was out of sight. Only I'd forgotten a wire cutter and was riding back."

"I don't understand why you'd blame yourself."

"I was scared. All that blood . . . and my dad's leg. I tried to stop the bleeding. Took Dad to the hospital, but I couldn't stay. If I'd warned him about Rick, he might have fired the guy." Hazen lowered his head to his knees.

"You don't know that." Jennie placed her hand on his arm. "It's not your fault. If the explosion hadn't injured your father, the militia—or whoever is responsible—would have tried again. Come back to the ranch with me tomorrow. Your folks really want to see you—Amber too."

Hazen nodded. "I'll think about it."

As shades of dawn crept over the hills, Jennie awoke to the sound of horses' hooves and voices. She snuggled deeper inside the bag. A few minutes later the silence, not voices, brought her more fully awake. She stretched and rubbed her eyes, then eased out of her sleeping bag. The two bags that had been laid out next to her were gone. "Not again." Jennie was growing weary of the twins' idea of fun. She rolled up her bag, set it on the cabin steps, and went in search of Gabby. They'd tied the horses to some trees nearby, but now Jennie saw no sign of them or of her companions.

"Wonderful. I suppose they expect me to walk back." Jennie picked up her sleeping bag and banged open the door to the cabin. She groped along the wall for a light switch, and when she found it, flipped it on. Jennie tossed the sleeping bag on one of the six bunks and paced the floor. Her fury increased with each step. She stopped abruptly. Pacing and getting mad wasn't going to solve the problem.

At least they hadn't left her without food. The night before they'd told her the cabin was always well stocked. Jennie rummaged through the small refrigerator and pantry and before long the scent of bacon and eggs permeated the air.

A horse whinnied only moments before the door swung open. Hazen offered her a wide smile as he stepped inside. "Smells good. Make enough for me?" He'd exchanged his warrior look for jeans, western boots, and a forest green Dancing Waters Sweatshirt.

"You can have this. I'll make some more." Jennie scooped up a forkful of bacon and set it on paper towels to drain, then dished up the eggs. "I thought you'd gone. I was going to eat breakfast, then try to find my way back to the ranch."

Hazen came up behind her and grabbed a slice of bacon. "You thought we'd leave you out here alone?"

"You tossed a hatchet at me."

"Not at you. At a tree stump."

"What happened to the horses?"

"I took them down to the creek."

"Where's Heather?" Jennie finished dishing up a plate and handed it to him.

He carried it to the rustic wooden table and straddled the bench. "Gone."

"She went with Eric? I thought maybe she'd changed her mind." Jennie broke two eggs into a bowl and whisked them a bit harder than necessary, then poured them into the hot frying pan.

"Me too. I tried to talk her out of it." He shoveled a forkful of eggs into his mouth. "Maybe she'll still change her mind."

Jennie watched the eggs set, turning them with the spatula. "Why did she even bring me out here? Never mind. I think I know. She wanted to make it look like she was out camping with me so your parents wouldn't suspect."

"Don't be too angry with her, Jennie."

"Why not? She's been using me ever since I got here. First she keeps me waiting for hours at the airport so she can play kissy face with her boyfriend, then she makes up with me so I won't tell on her when she sneaks out in the middle of the night." Jennie piled the eggs and bacon on her plate, took it to the table, and began eating.

"I'm sorry." Hazen watched her eat and Jennie watched the sky outside the window lighten to a pale blue.

"Why do you keep looking at me like that?"

"I am amazed at how much we look alike. Your hair and eyes are so dark, yet you have no Indian blood."

She let her gaze latch onto his and frowned. "Your hair is darker."

"Not much. Our eyes are the same."

Jennie leaned closer. She hadn't noticed it before, but his were different from Heather's—more navy than violet.

A grin split his handsome bronzed face. "We could be twins."

"Speaking of twins, shouldn't we try to stop yours?" Jennie asked, changing the subject. "I mean, they can't have gone too far."

"No. This modeling thing is important to Heather. It may not be the right decision, but she needs to be the one to make it."

"I'll tell you one thing, I'm not looking forward to breaking the news to your parents."

Hazen shook his head. "Me either. I'm afraid Heather and I have been a great disappointment to them. This past year has been hard for all of us."

After breakfast, Jennie and Hazen cleaned up the dishes, then rode back to the ranch. During the hour-long ride, Hazen shared his struggles over the last few years in trying to balance his two vastly different cultures.

"Why has it been so hard for you? I think it would be neat to be part Indian."

"I am learning to be proud of my heritage now. Joseph is helping me to understand my people. For a long time I have felt like a man trapped between two worlds. I thought I had to choose between the two."

"Why would you have to choose? I mean, couldn't you just be yourself?"

Hazen chuckled. "It seems simple enough now. Heather has always been able to do that—and Amber. But not me. Mom always accuses me of doing things the hard way."

As they broke through the trees and came within view of the ranch, Hazen reined in his horse, an Appaloosa named Thunder. He closed his eyes and took a deep breath as if to brace himself for the storm ahead. And there would be one. Even though neither of them could have stopped Heather from leaving, both would be blamed.

"Well, this is it." He dug his heels into Thunder's sides.

They didn't slow down until they reached the house. Amber, Maggie, and Jeff were still seated at the breakfast table when Jennie and Hazen walked in.

"Hazen!" Amber bounced out of the chair and ran into his arms.

He lifted her up and spun her around. "Hey, Short Stuff. Did you miss me?"

"You shouldn't have gone away," Amber scolded.

"I know." When Hazen tried to lower her to the floor, Amber buried her face in his neck and held on tight. He gave up and carried her to the table.

Maggie pushed her chair back and, for a moment, Jennie thought she'd rush over to embrace Hazen as well, but Uncle Jeff gave her a hard look that seemed to freeze her in place. He shifted that look to Hazen. Were they going to argue?

"Your grandfather's stock needs looking after," Jeff said. "He's got a mare ready to foal. Could use your help out there today."

Hazen nodded. Jennie could almost feel his tension drain out along with her own. He unhooked Amber's arms from his neck and set her on her chair next to his.

"Where's Heather?" Jeff asked.

Hazen's gaze met Jennie's. "She's . . ."

"Jeff! Maggie!" The back door swung open and Lopez strode into the dining room. "You'd better come down to the stables quick. One of the hands just came in with a gunshot wound."

Maggie jumped to her feet. "Oh no. Who is it? What happened?"

"Don't know how or why, but it's that new guy you hired, Eric Summers. Somebody shot him."

14

If Eric's been shot, what happened to Heather? Jennie jumped to her feet, ran out the door, and leaped onto Gabby's back. Hazen followed with Thunder as they raced down to the stables. In one fluid motion, Hazen dismounted and ran into the barn with Jennie at his heels. A siren split the air as they reached the couch in Dusty's office where Eric now lay.

"Heather's pony brought him in," Dusty shifted to one side as Hazen dropped to one knee beside Eric.

"The bleeding's pretty well stopped, but I can't seem to rouse him."

Jennie hunkered down beside Hazen and pressed her fingers against Eric's neck. His face was pasty white, his lips blue. He'd been shot in the shoulder. Blood soaked a quarter of his shirt, seeping into his shirt pocket.

"I can feel a pulse, but it's weak." She rose and backed away to make room for the paramedics.

Hazen scrambled to his feet, plowed past the two men from the rescue unit. Jennie followed him out of the office to where they'd left the horses. He vaulted onto Thunder's back and raced away.

"Hazen, wait!" Jennie yelled into the dust kicked up by the horse's hooves. She reached for Gabby, then looked back at her uncle and Lopez who were making their way toward her.

112

Jeff's eyes narrowed as he stared after his son. "Let him go. Boy's running away from everything these days."

"It's not what you think. He's not running away. I think he's gone to find Heather. Whoever shot Eric . . ." Jennie stopped and sighed. "It's a long story."

Twenty minutes later, when the ambulance was gone and they'd all gathered back in Dusty's office, Jennie told her story to Sheriff Mason, Jeff, Lopez, and Maggie. She began by explaining the relationship between Heather and Eric. "Heather had been sneaking out to meet him and they were planning to go to California. Hazen and I tried to talk her out of it, but she was gone when I woke up this morning."

"Where was she supposed to meet him?" Jeff asked.

"She didn't say."

The sheriff straightened and, with a look on his face that accused her of lying, said, "Well now, little lady, that was quite a story." He brought a plastic bag out of his jacket pocket containing a blood-stained piece of paper. "We found this note in the boy's pocket. I've bagged it—want to check for prints, though I doubt we'll find any. Apparently your little girl's been kidnapped."

"What?" they chorused.

"Let me see it." Jeff reached for the bagged note.

The sheriff handed it to him. "I'll need to keep it as evidence."

"What does it say?" Jennie asked.

Jeff handed the plastic-protected note to her. On a pale green shade of paper she'd seen too many times before, someone had scrawled, *You'll see your daughter as soon as you deed Dancing Waters back over to its rightful owner.*

Jeff shook his head. "I can't believe Elliot would do something so stupid."

"Does seem strange he'd draw attention to himself that way, but you never know." Mason took back the bag and pocketed it. "I'll go on into town and have a talk with him—

that is if he's still around. Any idea where he might be staying?"

Jeff rubbed his forehead. "No. Greg Bennett should know. You might want to call him anyway. He'll want to know what his client's been up to."

Lopez lifted the brim of his hat with a forefinger, then let it drop back onto his head. "I might know where to find Elliot. Saw him a couple of days ago heading into Marsha's Bed & Breakfast. Only I don't reckon he's the one you're lookin' for. Chad Elliot don't seem like the type of man . . ."

"You've talked to him?" Jeff snapped.

"He . . . ah . . . called me when he first got to town. I reckon I should have told you."

"I reckon so." Jeff's jaw had gone rigid and Jennie wondered if the ranch manager's rendezvous with the enemy would get him fired. "We'll talk about this later."

Lopez rubbed a hand across his face. "Like I was saying, Elliot didn't seem like the kind that'd resort to kidnapping. He thinks he's got a good case—no sense jeopardizing that. I reckon Danielson's behind this. He'll do anything to keep Dancin' Waters from being signed over to the Forestry Service. He glared at Sheriff Mason. "If you'd a put him in jail this wouldn't have happened."

Sheriff Mason shot Lopez a disgusted look. "Not that I owe you any explanations, but we didn't have enough evidence against Jake to arrest him. He wouldn't have done something like this anyway. He's got a kid of his own."

Jeff clasped his hands together on his lap. "Look, Mason, I know you and I are at opposite ends of the poles politically, but—"

"What kind of man do you think I am, White Cloud? You think I'd let political differences interfere with upholding the law?" He started to leave, then turned back around at the door. "I've already got deputies at work on this. We'll find her."

He left then, but the tension in the room increased as Bob Lopez and Jeff White Cloud eyed each other like two bull moose laying claim to their territory. Lopez's confession, if that's what it was, called his character into question. He'd spoken with Chad Elliot. Could he also be conspiring with him against the White Clouds? He'd originally worked for the Elliots. Had Chad Elliot bought him back? The look on Jeff's face told Jennie he was wondering the same thing.

"I'm going to get back to work." Maggie released her white-knuckled hold on Jeff's chair. "The ranch isn't going to run itself."

Jeff reached up and squeezed Maggie's hand. "I'd better call Dad. Then I suspect I'll have to call Alex to get the papers ready just in case."

Maggie bent to kiss him, then straightened. "Jennie, come with me please."

Jennie followed Maggie out of the office and occasionally glanced at her aunt as they walked. Maggie reminded her more of Mom every day. She wished she could tell Maggie everything would be all right, but Jennie had no idea how things would turn out. "Aunt Maggie, I—I'm sorry about Heather. Hazen and I both tried to talk her out of going with Eric. Now—"

"Don't blame yourself, Jennie. If someone wanted to kidnap Heather they'd have done it regardless of whether or not she planned to leave. I wish we'd taken this modeling business more seriously. I just hope it's not too late."

Jennie didn't know what to say, so she settled for a hug. When they reached the steps of the main lodge, Maggie leaned against one of the thick logs on either side of the wide steps. "I'd like you to watch Amber for me today. I don't want her to be alone."

Jennie nodded. "I'll be happy to watch her."

"Um—if she gets too rambunctious you can take her down to the stables and ride in the arena, and maybe go swimming in the guest pool, but stay on the grounds. While you're in the house be sure you keep the doors locked."

Jennie nodded again. "I will."

"She's with Heidi right now. I'll need to tell her about Heather."

"We'll tell her together," Jeff said as he and Lopez approached them.

Lopez pushed the wheelchair up the ramp next to the lodge steps. "I'd best be going. I'll check in with you every hour or so." The ranch mananger tipped his hat, and left. Apparently they'd resolved their differences—at least for the time being.

"I'll call the house and have Heidi bring Amber down." Jeff grabbed the wheels and propelled himself into the lodge office.

Amber didn't say much when Jeff and Maggie told her about Heather and Eric. After they'd talked about it and reassured her, Amber's intense gaze drilled into her parents. "You're not giving up the ranch, are you?"

Maggie and Jeff looked at each other, then back at Amber. "I don't know," Jeff answered. "Amber—honey—no matter what happens, we'll be together as a family."

———

After a light lunch, Jennie and Amber left the lodge. "You girls be careful." Maggie hugged Amber for the tenth time. She and Jeff watched from the porch as Jennie pulled Amber down the steps. Deep furrows lined their foreheads.

"Let's exercise the horses," Amber suggested, turning toward the stables.

"Sure." Jennie remembered what Amber had said about how riding made her feel better. "I could use another lesson."

Alex Dayton pulled into the driveway, spraying gravel as he ground to a stop. He jumped out and jogged toward them, his tie flapping against his expensive black suit. "Have you heard anything?" he panted.

"No. Just the note so far," Jeff answered.

"I am so sorry about Heather. If there's anything I can do . . ."

"Thanks, Alex. We appreciate that."

Dayton's sky-blue gaze drifted from Jeff to Jennie and Amber. He reached down and ruffled Amber's hair. "How's the little Sunshine?"

Amber pulled back and adjusted her curls. "I'm mad."

Maggie gave Amber a behave-yourself look.

He shifted his attention to Jennie. "I've seen you around a couple of times, but I don't believe we've officially met. I'm Alex Dayton."

"I'm sorry," Maggie said. "I should have introduced you yesterday. Alex and his dad own most of the banks around these parts. He's been about the only friend that's stuck by us since all this land business started."

"Hi," Jennie replied.

Alex Dayton gave her a warm smile and a nod. "The pleasure's mine." He turned back to the adults, climbed up the steps, and stopped in front of Jeff. "I brought the information you wanted. Wish I could talk you out of it, but I suppose this is the best way. Let's just hope Sheriff Mason is able to find Heather. I know I shouldn't be breaking confidences, but I talked to Greg. He's hopping mad. Says he's wondering if Elliot and Danielson are in on it together. He's about ready to drop Elliot's case."

Jeff reached for the thick envelope Dayton held.

Dayton ran well-manicured fingers through his thinning blond hair. "There must be some other way, Jeff. Giving in to the kidnapper's demands just doesn't seem right."

"If you think of one, let us know." Uncle Jeff spun the chair around. "Let's talk in the office."

Jennie felt sick. She couldn't believe they'd give up Dancing Waters. "Come on, Amber. Let's go."

"We gotta do something to stop them, Jennie." Amber's eyes had changed, misted. "We just have to."

Jennie squeezed her cousin's hand, groping for the right words. None came.

They'd worked the horses for twenty minutes when Amber announced she wanted to go swimming. Jennie agreed and followed Amber out of the arena into the stables. Without waiting for Amber, Jennie swung off Gabby and came around to pet his forehead. "You are such a good horse. I could ride you all day."

Gabby snorted and snuffled at her shoulder. "How are you doing, Amber? Ready to help me with the saddle?" Jennie might have been able to manage the saddle alone but didn't want to take the chance of dropping it.

When Amber didn't answer, Jennie glanced toward Cinnamon's stall across the way. Amber wasn't there. She heard the clip-clop of hooves at the far end of the stable, then caught a glimpse of a red-brown rump and black tail as Cinnamon disappeared out the door.

"Uh-oh." Jennie pulled Gabby away from his stall and got back into the saddle. "I don't know what she thinks she's doing, but I have a feeling it's not good." She snapped the reins and urged the gelding forward. The horse trotted out the door and across the pasture. Jennie spotted Amber as she and Cinnamon jumped the fence. She groaned. Dusty came around the corner. He'd seen Amber too and started running after her.

"I'll get her," Jennie yelled. *Or die trying.*

Jennie stopped breathing before they reached the fence. She looped the reins around her wrist and held tight to the saddle horn, leaving her right arm free and waving in the air to help maintain her balance. A lesson or two on jumping might have been nice. She closed her eyes as Gabby's front hooves left the ground. *Please make it. Please.*

Her eyes flew open as Gabby's hooves hit the ground. He'd apparently done this before. The gelding galloped on, following Amber and Cinnamon into the woods.

The gray overcast sky grew darker as it started to rain.

Jennie caught up to Amber at the llama pasture, where she'd stopped to open the gate. "I'm surprised you didn't try to jump this one too," Jennie snapped.

"She could slip in the mud and get cut on the barbed wire. 'Sides, I didn't think you'd catch up to me so fast." Amber led Cinnamon through the gate and waited for Jennie. Rain had plastered her red-gold hair against her head. "I'm going to see Papa and you can't stop me."

"I could, but I won't." Jennie rode Gabby through, not bothering to get down. If Amber wanted to run off on her own, she could deal with the gate herself. Besides, she wasn't about to let Amber out of her sight again. "Your folks are probably worried sick by now." She paused to button her denim jacket, then turned up the collar to keep the water from dripping down her neck.

Amber pouted. "I don't care. I have to talk to Papa. He'll know what to do."

Maybe he would. At least there they'd be safe and dry. "Since we're closer to his place, we'll go to your grandfather's and call your folks." What worried Jennie was getting to Joseph's house. It was still a long way. The rain had grown into a relentless downpour.

Jennie let out a long sigh of relief when they finally rode into Joseph's yard, past his Ford Ranger, and up to the porch. They dismounted, tied the horses to the railing, and ran for cover. Jennie grimaced as she pulled the soaked denim away from her legs.

"Papa!" Amber pounded on the door.

Joseph didn't answer.

"Maybe he's out looking for us. Your mom and dad would have called him."

"No," Amber insisted. "He would have met us along the way."

"In the rain?" Jennie knocked again.

Amber tried the knob. The door swung open.

Hold it, McGrady. The hairs on the back of her neck bristled. *Something is very wrong here.* "Wait." Jennie grabbed at her cousin's arm and missed.

Amber disappeared inside.

15

Jennie followed her cousin into the cabin. Lightning flashed, illuminating the storm-darkened sky. Thunder shook the ground with a crash so loud Jennie had to cover her ears.

"Jennie—" Amber screamed.

"It's okay. I'm—" Jennie gasped and pulled Amber back against her. Her gaze swept over the interior of the house. Someone had trashed it.

"Papa," Amber called. "Where are you?" She gripped Jennie's hand. "What if somebody hurt Papa too?"

"Stay here," Jennie instructed as she reached behind her to flip on the light. "I'll look in the other rooms." *Joseph could be in the house somewhere, lying wounded or* . . . Jennie wouldn't let herself complete the thought.

"I'm coming with." Rainwater dripped from Amber's hair and mingled with her tears.

"Okay. Just stay behind me and don't touch anything," Jennie said as she began picking her way across the littered floor.

In the guest bedroom, a pile of bedclothes lay in a jumbled mess. The top mattress had been shoved half off the box springs. The dresser drawers had been emptied, their contents strewn across the room. The door to Joseph's bedroom was partially closed. Jennie bit her lower lip as she tapped the door open with her foot.

It too had been ransacked. The lovely wedding quilt lay rumpled on the floor next to White Cloud's Bible and a number of other books.

"Papa's going to be so sad." Amber sighed and knelt beside the Bible. "How could anybody be so mean?"

"I don't know. They were probably looking for something." But what? Papers, a deed, a will? Apparently something small enough to fit between the pages of a book. Jennie stooped to pick up the Bible and tried to straighten and replace the fragile pages.

You shouldn't be tampering with the evidence, a part of her reminded. True, but somehow it didn't seem right to leave the hundred-year-old Bible on the floor. Jennie placed it on the nightstand.

"What's this?" Jennie reached for a triangle that peeked out from under the dresser. She withdrew a piece of crisp paper, yellowed with age. The paper's ragged edge suggested it had been ripped out of a book. A date written at the top read May 7, 1903. "It looks like a page from a diary."

Amber nodded. "The women kept a record of all the things that happened. We read them together sometimes."

"So this would be Nadi's." Jennie scanned the neatly written cursive.

Today we will surely die. White Cloud prepares to battle for the right to keep our land safe from enemy hands. Even our friend Frank Elliot and the Reverend Joshua Bennett stand against us. "You are hungry," they say—"times are hard. Sell the land and you will have more than enough to feed your family." What do they know of hard times? Why do they not understand that the Indian way is not to ravage the land, but to nurture it? The land is rich and fertile. Is it not enough to have food from the field and meat from the animals The Great Spirit sends our way? We have no need . . .

Jennie turned the page over.

. . . of earthly treasures. Perhaps it is wrong to resist, but we have

seen what the white man has done with his wealth. They have turned forests and streams into a vast wasteland in order to fill their pockets with gold and drink their whiskey. The message ended in a prayer that God would keep them safe and turn their adversaries away. Jennie wanted to read more.

"Where is the diary?" Jennie asked, glancing around the room. They found it lying in the folds of the quilt, but when Jennie turned to the place where the page had been torn out, at least two of the previous pages were missing.

Jennie replaced the torn page and set the diary beside the Bible. What treasures had Nadi written about? And more important, why would anyone destroy Joseph's house to steal them?

Jennie set the questions aside to deal with later. Right now she had to check the rest of the house.

She stepped around the debris and headed for Joseph's bathroom. The medicine cabinet door hung open, a can of shaving cream lay in the sink—a shaver beside it. The shower curtain had been ripped off several of its hooks. Jennie noticed a rust-colored smear on the white linoleum. Blood?

The sky lit up as the lightning streaked and flickered outside the bathroom window. Thunder rumbled overhead and crashed so hard it shook the house. The lights flickered and went out.

"Jennie, I'm scared."

"Me too. Come on. We'd better call your folks and have them send the sheriff out here."

With Amber still attached to her casted arm, Jennie hurried back to the kitchen. The phone line was dead. Had the wires been cut? Jennie flipped the light switch on and off. Nothing. "Looks like the storm knocked out the electricity."

"Wait. Papa's cellular phone—the one he keeps in the Ranger . . ."

Jennie raced out to the Ranger and yanked open the door. The phone was gone. She hurried back inside and locked the

door. "Sorry, looks like your grandfather took it with him."
Or it had been stolen. "We'll wait until the rain lets up, then
ride back to the ranch."

Jennie started a fire in the fireplace, then rummaged
through Joseph's closets for something dry and warm.
"These will be huge on you," Jennie said, holding up a shirt
and a pair of jeans, "but if we roll up the sleeves and pantlegs,
and use some of that cord I saw in the kitchen, we can make
them fit."

Jennie helped Amber into the oversized clothing, then
went into the bathroom to strip off her soggy T-shirt and
pants. She wanted a shower, but that would have to wait
without power and water. Jennie settled for a quick wash.
The cast smelled like two-day-old road kill and felt damp and
heavy. Rain had soaked the padding and left a mushy mess.
It would definitely have to be replaced. She just hoped her
arm wouldn't rot off in the meantime. They'd never make the
cover of *Vogue*, but at least they'd quit shivering.

When Jennie returned to the kitchen, Amber was standing near the open door intently examining something black
and round. "Look at this, Jennie. Do you know what it is?"

Jennie took the object. "Looks like a camera lens," she
said, turning it around. "I know of only one person around
here who'd have a lens like this," Jennie said, thinking aloud.
"Eric Summers. But what would his equipment be doing out
here?"

Amber shrugged. "Maybe he came to take pictures of
Papa."

Or maybe he came to take something else. Maggie had hired
him to help develop a new brochure. According to Heather,
Joseph knew about Eric. Maybe Heather had brought him
here. Still, it seemed strange that Eric would lose something
as important as a camera lens. Jennie thought about the
blood smear in the bathroom.

"What are you thinking about, Jennie?" Amber pulled at her arm.

"Just wondering about this lens."

"Maybe Eric dropped it when he got shot."

"Maybe." Jennie didn't want to think about that possibility. "Heather and Eric could have come here to say goodbye." Jennie took a deep breath, not knowing how much of what she was thinking she could reveal to Amber.

Whoever had shot Eric, and sent him home on Heather's horse, could have abducted Heather *and* Joseph. She debated whether to leave the lens at the house or bring it with her. She knew better than to disturb a crime scene, but Amber had already picked it up. She opted to bring the lens along and give it to Jeff.

When the rain let up, Jennie and Amber checked the stables but found no sign of Joseph. They did, however, find an Appaloosa wandering free. "It's Hazen's," Amber insisted.

"This couldn't be Hazen's," Jennie argued. "He took off this morning, when he . . ." Her argument died when she realized Thunder's halter was still on. Had they gotten Hazen too? Had Danielson's army moved in? Were he and Chad Elliot working together? Were she and Amber next?

No, McGrady, don't even think it. Concentrate on getting Amber out of here.

Before they left, Jennie fixed them each a sandwich and packed a few snacks and some emergency equipment—a first-aid kit, flashlight, matches, and rain gear—in saddlebags she borrowed from the barn. By two-thirty they were on their way back to the dude ranch.

Even with the sun leaking through scattered holes in the bullet gray sky, Jennie worried about getting back safely since they were returning a different way. Amber had insisted they take the higher trail for fear the one they'd come in on would be flooded.

The sunshine lasted all of ten minutes. The holes in the

sky closed up, heavy clouds rolled in and opened fire on them again with a mixture of hail and rain. The girls donned the rain capes they'd packed and rode on.

Fifteen minutes later Amber pulled Cinnamon up next to a creek. "The water's up, but we can still make it across."

Jennie could barely hear her over the water's roar. "Maybe we'd better go back."

"No, we can make it."

Jennie wasn't so sure. The stream was a floodwater brown—so churned up with mud, it was hard to tell its depth.

"Come on." Amber spurred Cinnamon forward, but the horse pulled back in protest. Finally at Amber's insistence the horse plunged into the water.

"Amber," Jennie warned, "this is not a good idea. Let's go back." Gabby, apparently not wanting to be left behind, shuddered, then moved ahead, as though forging swollen streams was too great an adventure to miss.

They had nearly reached the other side when Cinnamon stumbled and fell. "Jennie, help." Amber toppled off Cinnamon's back as her horse tried to right herself. Jennie grabbed for the child. The rain slick poncho slipped from her grasp. She watched in horror as Amber's red-gold curls disappeared into the murky, swirling water.

16

"Amber!" Jennie struggled to keep her own balance. Gabby slipped on the eroded bank, but managed to regain his footing to escape the swollen creek. Jennie sprang from the saddle and raced downstream to where Amber floated to the surface, sputtering and kicking, then Jennie plunged into the icy waters in another attempt to rescue her.

Despite the awkwardness of the heavy, water-soaked cast, Jennie managed to grab Amber and drag her out of the water. "Stop kicking," she yelled when Amber's boots connected with her shins. "I've got you."

Amber kept thrashing.

Jennie guessed the water to be about four feet deep where she was standing, but fighting the current and her cousin was like battling a tidal wave. It took all her strength to plant her feet against the rocks and propel them toward shore.

She pushed Amber onto the bank, then climbed out and pulled the now limp child to safety. After making sure Amber was okay, Jennie collapsed on the wet ground. She hauled in as much of the moist air as her heaving lungs could hold. A stream of muddy brown water trickled out of her cast.

A few minutes later, Amber crawled closer and lay her head on Jennie's chest. "Guess we shouldn't have tried to go across."

"Guess not." Jennie closed her eyes as the rain pelted her

face. She soothed Amber's saturated curls. "But we made it." She sighed and rose onto her elbows when Amber sat up. "We'd better get home."

"My leg hurts." Amber leaned forward and lifted the plastic cape. Her jeans were torn at the knee and rain-diluted blood streamed from an inch-long gash. Amber stared at the wound for several seconds, then let out a wail Jennie felt certain could be heard in the next county. Her little tomboy cousin wasn't quite so tough after all.

"Shh. It's okay, Amber. Take it easy. I've got a first-aid kit in one of the saddlebags." Jennie glanced around expecting to see Gabby and Cinnamon nearby. They were close all right—only about fifty feet away, but they may as well have been in Albuquerque. The horses were grazing contentedly on the other side of the swollen creek.

"What in the. . . ?" Jennie stifled a cry of alarm. With surprising calm, she said, "First of all, Amber, I need to stop the bleeding."

"No! Don't touch it." Amber flapped her legs up and down.

"It won't hurt, I promise. Just hold still." Jennie peeled off her wet neckerchief, wrung it out, tied it around Amber's knee, and kept a steady pressure for several minutes while she tried to assess their situation.

Jennie soon realized she'd gotten turned around while trying to rescue Amber. Dancing Waters still lay on the other side of the creek.

Amber's sobs turned to whimpers. "What are we gonna do about the horses? How are we going to get home?"

Jennie had no idea. She wasn't about to wade through the creek again, but they couldn't stay where they were either. If the rain didn't let up, the entire valley would soon be under water.

"Come on." Jennie stood and extended a hand to Amber. "Let's get out of here. We'll walk back to Joseph's cabin. We may not have electricity, but we can build a fire and get some dry clothes."

Amber got halfway up, then sank back to the ground. "Ow! I can't walk."

"I know it hurts, but you have to try. Here." Jennie removed their slick rain ponchos, then knelt down in front of her. "Put your arm around my neck. I'll give you a piggyback ride." Jennie hoisted Amber onto her back, then settled the plastic over both of them like a tent. She crossed the mushy ground and headed for the highest point. After a few yards Jennie began altering her plans.

"Where are we going, Jennie?" Amber tightened her hold. "This isn't the way to Papa's."

"I know. But I can't carry you that far." Jennie stopped to adjust her heavy load. "I'm hoping there's some kind of cave or overhang up there." She pointed to an odd-looking rock formation. "Maybe we can stay there until the storm passes—or until help comes."

"No. Wait. Let's go to Papa's secret place. It's closer."

Jennie sighed. "This isn't a game, Amber."

"I know. But this is a for-real cave and it's up there—behind those bushes. Come on. I'll show you."

Jennie walked in the direction Amber pointed. When Amber told her to stop, Jennie set her cousin down on a boulder, then lifted her own rain-soaked bangs from her forehead. "I don't see a cave. Are you sure this is the right spot?"

"You can't see it from here. That's why it's secret. You have to go behind those bushes. There's a rock—only it isn't a rock, it's a door. You push this lever and the rock moves. Papa says it's so no one would find the gold."

"A rock that's a door? Gold? Come on, Amber, be serious."

"I am." Amber scooted closer. "There's a lever in the rocks behind these bushes."

Jennie moved the thick brush aside. Sure enough, a metal

handle protruded from a crevice. Following Amber's instructions she pulled it to one side.

The mountain itself seemed to groan and squeak as the rock that was really a door shuddered, then moved along a narrow track. When it stopped, it left a gaping black hole. "I can't believe it." Amber had been right. Except for one thing. This was no cave. It was a mine. But why. . . ?

"See, I told you. Only you gotta promise not to tell anyone. Papa said if the wrong people found out, they would destroy the mountain." Amber set a rock under the lever and Jennie helped her inside.

"What's the rock for?" Jennie asked.

"To make sure the door stays open. Yuk." Amber covered her face with her arm to ward off the spider webs that had been woven across the opening.

Jennie waved her hand back and forth to clear the webs away, hoping she wouldn't encounter the spiders themselves. The mine smelled musty and metallic, like an old dirt cellar. Except for the mottled patches of daylight coming through the branches, the mine shaft was dark as tar.

Jennie didn't want to leave her cousin or the safety of the mine, but she needed to get back down to the creek and figure out a way to get to the horses. Without the horses they could be stuck in the wilderness until help came or until Amber could walk. That could be days. Besides that, the first-aid equipment and supplies were still in the saddlebags. Maybe they'd survive without the food and supplies she'd packed, but Jennie didn't want to take the chance.

She settled Amber inside the opening and out of the rain.

"Listen," Jennie said, uncertain how to begin. "I have to go back down—see if I can get to the horses. I don't want to leave you, but I have to. I'll come back as soon as I can. Will you be okay?"

"I—I think so. Just hurry."

Jennie scrambled over the rocks and soon raced along the

sodden ground. Gabby and Cinnamon still waited in the meadow, only now the creek had risen. It raged with even more fury than it had before. Jennie scanned the banks looking for a fallen log, a tree, anything that might help her get across. Nothing.

She followed the creek downstream, praying with each step for a miracle. Her mind was so intent on her thoughts that she almost missed it. About half a mile from the place they'd tried to cross before, the creek widened, then separated, leaving a four-foot wide island in the middle. Two streams to cross, but the creek's energy would be divided. At least she hoped that would be the case.

Jennie took a deep breath, then tested the water. One foot in. Water swirled around her ankle. Next step, the same. With the next she sank to her knees and nearly lost her footing. She waded several more feet to the island, heaving a sigh of relief as her foot connected with the rocks. Crossing the island, she tilted her face to the sky. "Amber needs me, God," Jennie whispered. "And I need those horses. Please help me get across."

Jennie forded the second part of the creek more easily than the first and ran back upstream to where the horses still waited. God must have heard her pleas. Even the rain had let up a little.

Since the horses could easily cross at the spot she had, Jennie grabbed both horses' reins. On unsteady legs, Jennie climbed onto the saddle and headed back downstream. A few minutes later, they stood on the island, ready to make the final leg of what had seemed an impossible journey.

Jennie took a deep breath and urged Gabby forward. At that moment a white-hot streak of lightning slammed into a nearby tree. Both horses panicked. "Oh no," she moaned, "not again." Heaven rumbled with a steady roll of thunder as it crescendoed, then crashed. The entire mountainside seemed to explode as the tree splintered and crashed to the ground.

Jennie held tight to the saddlehorn and waved her casted arm wildly to keep from falling. Her hands had grown stiff and numb from the cold. Too late, Jennie remembered she held both of the horses' reins. Cinnamon rose on her back legs and pawed at the air, yanking Jennie sideways. Jennie released the mare's reins, but not soon enough. As if in slow motion, gravity propelled her downward.

Jennie landed on her hip and shoulders on the rocky ground and rolled to the side to escape the horses' hooves. Gabby reared, throwing the saddlebags off his back and onto the ground. The terrified horses bolted and ran. Jennie rolled over on her stomach and cried.

It wasn't in her nature to give up, but then nature had never tried to beat her to death until now. She ignored the insistent voice in her head that told her to get up and keep going. She hurt too much to move.

She rested her head on her uncasted arm and cried. After a few minutes she tried giving herself a pep talk. *Come on, McGrady. Get up. Okay, so you lost the horses. At least you've got the saddlebags.* Still, she didn't move.

Rain dripped steadily on her back and mingled with her tears. Rocks dug into her stomach and thighs. Bone-chilling water seeped into her already wet clothing and inside her cast. But that didn't make sense. She'd fallen onto dry land.

Jennie raised her head. The raging creek had covered the tiny island. The saddlebags were already floating away and if she didn't get out of there fast she'd be the next to go.

17

"Come back here!" Jennie scrambled to her feet.

The current lifted and dragged the heavy saddlebags over the rocks. "After all I went through to get you, you're not going to just float away." Jennie lunged for them. Despite the pain that now wracked her body, she settled them over her left shoulder then stumbled across the ever widening creek.

"Come on, McGrady, just one more step—a little farther." Jennie muttered the words over again as she slogged through the ankle-deep water in the meadow, then crawled up the slippery hillside to where she had left Amber. She collapsed near the mine's entrance, shivering, exhausted, and near tears.

"Oh please, no more." In the last few hours she'd been through more adventures than Harrison Ford in *Raiders of the Lost Ark* and apparently the show wasn't over. Jennie stared at the shrubs covering the opening to the mine shaft. Someone had closed the entrance.

Don't panic, she told herself. *Maybe Amber closed it herself.* Jennie doubted that. No ten-year-old child would deliberately lock herself in a dark mine shaft.

Steeling herself against what she might find, Jennie pulled the lever. As before, the metal door moved across the track. She took the flashlight out of the damp saddlebags, switched it on, and stepped inside. "Amber?" She called tentatively at first, then increased the volume when no one answered. "Amber, are you in here?"

Jennie crept deeper into the darkness that hovered beyond the reaches of her small light, listening, waiting for a response. None came. She took another step and collided with another curtain of spider webs. She stifled a scream and brushed the dusty webs away. "Amber," Jennie called again.

Still no answer. Jennie wondered how far back the cave went and if there was another opening. And what besides spiders lived in there. *Bats, probably, and snakes . . .*

"Stop it, McGrady," she reprimanded herself. "You are not going to scare yourself. Amber's gone and in two seconds you'll be out of here." But then what? As if answering her question, the door clicked, then rumbled closed, devouring the last traces of light from the opening.

"No!" Jennie dropped the flashlight and raced toward the door. She clawed at the wet, slippery surface, willing it to stop. Her efforts had about as much effect as a mouse trying to stop a train. She pulled her fingers back as the door snapped shut.

Panic stalked her like a rattlesnake, and struck. Its venom seeped into her pores. Jennie leaned back against the door. Her knees collapsed beneath her.

Now she understood why Amber had positioned a rock under the lever to keep the door open. She should have paid more attention. She closed her eyes and wrapped her arms around herself to stop the shivering. The terror she'd felt a moment before began to drain away, leaving her numb and cold.

Jennie wondered how low her body temperature had dropped and how long she would last. She was well aware of the dangers of hypothermia. "Oh, God," she whimpered, "what am I going to do?"

Only the silence answered. Yet in the stillness Jennie began to feel a strange sense of peace. She took several deep breaths and, after a few moments, opened her eyes, more curious now than afraid. Jennie leaned forward and rescued the flashlight she'd dropped and directed the beam over the mine walls and the wood supports that framed it. She forced her brain to focus on the possibility of escape rather than on her cold, wet clothing, or the numbness in her hands and fingers.

Think, McGrady. There has to be a way out. Just stay calm and think. If Joseph had devised a mechanism for opening the door on the outside, wouldn't he also place one inside?

Not necessarily. It could have been designed as a trap. There may be bones of men or women who found the cave, but who had taken the secret with them to their graves. Jennie tried to still her imagination before it zoomed out of control, but it had already boarded a fast train. She thought of the darkness and wondered how far back the mine shaft went and how many old bones it held in its depths.

"I told you to stop it, McGrady." Jennie tried to ignore the frightening images screaming through her head and focused on the dirt walls and wooden supports. Two wires ran along the right side of the door, but Jennie found no lever that might trigger the mechanism from the inside.

Was this the end? Trapped in a cave—a tomb. The revelation didn't frighten her like it should have. Maybe the encroaching hypothermia had numbed her brain cells. Or maybe, knowing in her heart that her spirit would live forever, she wasn't that afraid of dying.

"Poor Joseph," Jennie said aloud. He'd be heartbroken to know a tool he devised to keep people from discovering his secret mine had been her demise and maybe Amber's.

Amber. Was she still in the cave? Perhaps she'd fallen asleep. Or maybe she'd been injured more seriously than Jennie had first thought. She illuminated the mine floor as far as the flashlight beam reached, then reluctantly stood and went in deeper. Jennie called again. Still no answer.

After the first few steps, Jennie paused to examine the

glimmering substance on the walls. She brushed her fingers over a large section of iridescent rock. The flashlight's meager beam didn't allow her to see much, but it did reflect off the walls enough for Jennie to see the sparkling veins of— what? Jennie picked up a chunk of the shiny metal from the ground. Gold? Silver? Silver had been mined in this area for over a hundred years. But this looked like gold—probably iron pyrite or what miners called fool's gold. It had to be, she rationalized. That much real gold would have been mined years ago.

Or would it? What had Nadi said in her diary? *The Indian way is not to ravage the land, but to nurture it. . . . We have no need of earthly treasures . . . we have seen what the white man has done with his wealth. They have turned forests and streams into a vast wasteland . . .*

Jennie gasped. "White Cloud was preparing to fight for their land." *The mine? Oh wow! If that's true, this could be real gold.* "And worth millions," she murmured aloud. "A definite motive for murder." Possibilities flooded her head. Did Danielson know about the mine? Chad Elliot probably did. Who else?

Jennie slipped the rock in her pocket and yawned. Despite the excitement of possibly finding gold, she was growing weary. Probably as a result of the cold. Or maybe she was just plain exhausted. Jennie lowered herself to the ground and wrapped the plastic poncho more tightly around her. Maybe her body would generate enough heat to warm her limbs and send her temperature back up to normal. She leaned back against the dirt wall, wrapped her arms around her knees, and rested her head on them.

Why? The question hung in her fading consciousness. Joseph had a mine that could be worth millions. Why was it mined in the first place? If Joseph and his father didn't believe in tearing up the land, why build the mine shaft?

"Maybe he didn't," Jennie answered her own question.

"Maybe Frank Elliot or his son did." In reading the history of the Nez Perce Indians, Jennie remembered how the settlers had gone onto the reservation and found gold. Since the Indians believed that one could not own the land, white miners often went into areas designated as Indian territory and if they found gold, claimed the land for themselves. As far as she knew, Dancing Waters had never been part of a reservation, but suppose Elliot had ignored White Cloud's ownership, found gold, then tried to mine it against White Cloud's wishes? According to Joseph, though, Frank Elliot was a good man who made certain White Cloud was cared for.

Greed has corrupted a lot of people, Jennie reasoned. *Besides, his son, William, might have known about the mine. He'd been desperate for money. But if he were sitting on a gold mine, why sell off all the property?*

Other questions surfaced. Where did Eric fit into it all? And Danielson? Did she care? Did she want to spend her last moments trying to solve a mystery? Yes, but what good would it do? She didn't have enough information. She needed to take in a sample of the gold to have it analyzed. And she'd have to go to the library or courthouse to check on land use. "If . . . when I get out of here—"

The flashlight tumbled out of her numb fingers and clunked as it hit the ground. She thought about retrieving it, but couldn't make her body move. Her thoughts drifted to another tomb, owned by another Joseph. Jesus had been buried there after His death on the cross. Three days later the stone had been rolled away, and an angel told His followers the good news. *"He is risen."*

Three days. Would someone come to the mine and discover her lifeless body? Or would she somehow be resurrected? Jennie didn't feel like thinking anymore—didn't want to move. It was as if her entire body was shutting down. Was this what it felt like to die? The question went unanswered as Jennie closed her eyes.

18

Jennie smelled fire.

Its dry heat permeated and relaxed her cold, tense muscles. It crackled and sizzled, consuming wood laced with pitch.

And she smelled frybread.

"Hmm," she moaned softly, wanting to open her eyes but afraid that her warm, wonderful dream would vanish, leaving her alone in the cold, dark mine.

"She's waking up, Papa." The voice so reminded Jennie of Nick, tears gathered behind her eyelids. Would she ever see her little brother again? Or Mom? Her tears escaped their boundaries and slid over her temples and into her hair.

"Oh, Papa, she's crying."

"Hush, Tiponi. You will wake her."

"But she's sad. Maybe she's hurt."

Jennie pressed her hands to her eyes, squeezing out the moisture. Her eyes drifted open. Amber smiled and leaned over her, their noses nearly touching.

"I told Papa you were awake but he didn't believe me." Her eyes clouded in concern. "You're okay, aren't you, Jennie? I told Papa to wait longer. We looked for you. He thought you went back to the ranch and . . ."

"Whoa. Slow down. What are you talking about?" Jennie was beginning to adjust to the possibility that she'd been rescued and that this wasn't a dream after all. Joseph brought in a tray, set it on the coffee table, and helped her sit up. She was in Joseph's cabin, lying on the supple leather couch. Her wet clothes had been exchanged for her own clean dry ones—the jeans and chambray shirt she'd left at the cabin earlier. It was dark outside, but inside, a dozen or so candles bathed the room in subdued light. "How did I get here?"

"I will answer your questions in a moment." Joseph propped pillows behind her. "First, you must eat." He placed a tray on her lap. A piece of frybread, buttered and sprinkled with cinnamon and sugar, lay on a plate next to a bowl of what Joseph called venison stew.

"Thank you," Jennie murmured as she lifted the warm frybread to her mouth. It tasted so good, Jennie didn't care where she was for the moment, or how she'd gotten there.

Amber sat cross-legged on the rug near Jennie's head and watched her. Joseph poked at the glowing chunks of wood in the fireplace.

"What happened to you out there, Amber?" Jennie asked after taking another spoonful of Joseph's stew.

"Papa found me."

Jennie frowned. "How did you know where she was?"

Amber answered. "He knew we had been here at his cabin and came after us. We didn't want to leave you, but we looked everywhere for you. Papa thought you went back to the ranch. Where were you?"

"After I left you at the mine, I went downstream to find a shallow spot where I could get across safely—you remember. I wanted to get the horses and the first-aid kit." Jennie explained her misadventures in retrieving the horses, losing them again, nearly drowning, and being locked in the mine. She shifted her gaze from Amber to Joseph. "How did you know to come back for me?"

"When we got back here, Daddy called on the cellular and told us that Gabby and Cinnamon had come back without you. They sent out a search party. I told Papa we should go back and check the mine."

"That she did. I knew you'd try to get back to Amber if you could."

"That door you rigged at the mine locked me in. You should put a release mechanism inside."

"There is one, but it is hidden behind a beam. I'm sorry you could not find it."

Jennie finished off the soup and frybread, then asked, "Are you sure this is for real and that I'm not still dreaming? I mean, how could I not remember coming here?"

"You were exhausted." Joseph took her tray.

Jennie snuggled back into the cushions. She was still tired. "What time is it?"

"Ten-thirty. You should rest now. The rain has finally stopped. Perhaps the waters will recede enough for us to get you and Amber back to Dancing Waters. You need to have that cast replaced." He set the tray down on the counter, then returned to the living room. "And you, Tiponi. Off to bed now. It's way past your bedtime, and we'll both be in trouble if your mother finds out I let you stay up so long."

Amber started to argue but must have caught the stern look in Joseph's eyes. "Okay, but can Jennie sleep with me?"

"If she wants." He glanced at Jennie.

"I might be in later." Although she didn't say so, Jennie needed to talk with Joseph privately.

Amber gave Jennie a good-night kiss and headed for the bathroom. "Will you tell me some stories, Papa?"

"Not tonight. It is much too late."

"Joseph?" Jennie didn't know where to start. "There's so much I need to talk to you about. Your house, the mine, and . . ." Jennie glanced around, realizing the mess had been cleaned up. "Did you call the sheriff about the break-in? I tried to when I was here this morning, but the phone was dead. We were so worried about you."

Joseph's lips parted in a half smile as he nodded. "It still is. And the power. I'm sorry you have carried this burden. I went hunting this morning. When I returned and saw that someone had broken in, I called the sheriff on my cellular phone. Like me, he suspects it was vandalism. As far as I can tell, there is nothing missing."

"The diary—there are some pages missing." Jennie told him about the connection she'd made with Nadi's entry and the mine. "Do you think whoever broke in was looking for information about the mine?"

Joseph's brows knitted in a frown. "It's possible. Though I—"

"Papa. I'm ready."

"I must say good-night to my granddaughter, then we will talk." While he tucked Amber in, Jennie tossed the blanket aside, used the bathroom, then padded to the kitchen to fix Joseph and herself some herb tea.

Having retrieved Nadi's diary, Joseph returned to the living room and sank wearily into the chair closest to Jennie. He opened the book to where Jennie had inserted the loose page.

Joseph read for a moment, then leaned back and closed his eyes. "You may be right. Nadi writes of the mine just before this page. It doesn't give the location—only the legend of how it came to be. Whoever broke in may have been searching for a map. In which case he would have been disappointed."

"You don't have a map?"

"To my knowledge there never was one."

"Tell me the legend about the mine. Is there gold in it?"

"It's late."

"Oh please. I'll never be able to sleep until I know. Besides, you need to drink your tea."

Joseph sighed and picked up his cup. "Yes, it is gold." He reached into his shirt pocket, then tucked something into her hand. It was the rock she'd picked up on the mine floor.

"There is no need to have it analyzed."

Jennie flushed. "How did you know I was going to?"

"I am beginning to know you."

"I'm sorry for taking it." He held up his hand when she tried to return it.

"You may keep this as a souvenir of your visit. I think it best, however, if you don't tell anyone where it came from just yet."

"I won't say anything. But you still haven't told me why all the secrecy. And if you didn't want the gold to be mined, why is there a mine shaft?" Jennie took a tentative sip of the hot tea.

"As I mentioned before, Frank Elliot deeded 500 acres of Dancing Waters land over to White Cloud—my father—in 1889. What neither of them knew was that an old Dutch miner named Henry VonHassen had found gold here in 1885."

"How could they not know?"

"Over the years, VonHassen developed quite a reputation in Cottonwood. He'd come into town every couple of months with a pouchful of the purest gold the assayers had ever seen. The old man kept pretty much to himself. Never staked a claim or told anyone where he'd been mining. He led everyone to believe he'd just picked up pebbles here and there in the mountain streams. And for good reason—the property wasn't his." Joseph rocked back and forth as if waiting for the rest of story to come to him.

"Did anyone ever follow him and see where the gold came from?"

"Many tried. VonHassen figured on folks doing just that. He'd lead them into the mountains, get them good and lost, then come back to the mine."

"And neither White Cloud nor Elliot knew?"

Joseph stilled the rocker and took another sip of tea. "Not until White Cloud found him in a ravine the winter of 1897.

He'd fallen from a cliff. White Cloud tried to save him." Joseph frowned. "The old miner only lasted a couple days, but he told my father about the mine. I suppose he wanted to make amends before he died."

"In the diary, Nadi said Frank Elliot and a Reverend Bennett were trying to get White Cloud to work the mine. How did they know about it?" Jennie leaned forward to place her cup on the table, then tucked her legs under her.

"White Cloud told Frank about the mine and offered to give him back the land. He refused it and promised to keep the mine a secret."

"So the Reverend leaked the information?" Jennie asked.

Joseph shook his head. "No, he was not the kind of man who betrayed a trust."

"Then how?"

"VonHassen was found on White Cloud's land and people assumed his mine was there. Folks started telling stories and pretty soon treasure hunters were swarming all over those hills looking for the old Dutchman's mine."

"But they never found it," Jennie added.

"VonHassen had hidden it well. Eventually, the excitement died down and people lost interest."

"Until now. Do you think the mine is behind all that's happened at Dancing Waters—I mean the explosion and Heather?" Jennie bolted upright. "Oh, Heather . . . and Eric. Did you know about Eric getting shot and Heather being kidnapped? I can't believe I'm just now telling you."

Joseph placed his hands on his knees for leverage, then stood. "You have had much to occupy your mind today. But, yes, my son told me what happened. You must rest now. We'll talk more in the morning."

Jennie ignored his attempt to leave and kept talking. "Have they found her?"

"No."

"What about the ranch? Did you know Jeff was making

plans to meet the kidnapper's demands and deed the ranch over to Chad Elliot? That's what Amber was so upset about."

"I have spoken to my son." Joseph stoked the fire and added another log. "We will do what must be done to obtain Heather's release."

"But . . ."

"Good night, Jennie."

"I found something else," Jennie persisted, not wanting to give up until she'd gotten more of her questions answered. "A camera lens. I thought it might belong to Eric and wondered if Heather had brought him here."

Joseph shook his head. "Where is the lens?"

"In the saddlebags. If it is Eric's, he must have dropped it when he was searching the house." Jennie frowned. "But how could he have known about the mine? Unless . . . Did Heather know?"

"It did not seem wise to share the secret with the twins. They are not yet ready."

"Do you think Chad Elliot knows about the mine and maybe that's why he's so adamant about getting Dancing Waters back?"

"It is possible. He may have found a reference to the mine among his father's belongings." Joseph blew out all the candles but one, which he handed to Jennie. "There's a toothbrush and towels in the bathroom. If you need anything else, let me know."

"Um . . . could I ask you one more question?"

Joseph hesitated. "And what might that be?"

"Uncle Jeff told me what you said about letting me investigate. I just wanted to thank you and ask why—I mean, most adults would just tell me to mind my own business."

"Your grandmother calls you an eagle. Do you know about eagles, Jennie?"

"Only that they're birds of prey. And I love to watch them fly."

"To capture an eagle is like roping the wind. They are not easily caught. When an eagle is trapped, it will literally beat itself to death trying to escape. It is in your nature to seek answers, just as it is in the eagle's nature to soar in the heavens."

"I'm not getting anywhere with this case. I don't know if I can do it. I don't want to disappoint you and Uncle Jeff."

"Do you know more than you did this morning?" Joseph asked.

"Yes, but—"

"That is good." His smile affirmed her even more than his words. "Good night, Brave Eagle. Sleep well. Tonight we will pray for wisdom and tomorrow we will seek truth."

Jennie washed by candlelight, ignoring the bedraggled-looking creature that stared back at her in the mirror. *Sheesh, McGrady. You look more like Ruffled Feather than Brave Eagle.* She quickly tugged the rats out of her hair and brushed her teeth, then slipped into the flannel nightshirt Joseph had set out for her.

She eased her aching body under the covers and blew out the candle. Outside the living room window the subdued light from the porch created an odd mixture of shadows.

One of those shadows took on human form and began to move. Or had it? The hair on the back of her neck stood on end. *For Pete's sake, McGrady. It's probably just the wind. Besides, you're safe here.* Only, Jennie didn't feel safe. She threw the covers aside. She wouldn't rest until she'd confronted her fear and taken a look outside.

A figure moved out of the shadows and crept to the window.

Jennie stifled a scream as she looked point-blank into the intruder's face.

19

The figure straightened and stepped toward the front porch. Though she hadn't clearly seen his face, she recognized him.

Jennie willed her heart and stomach back to their respective places. She let Hazen in and locked the door behind him.

"What are you doing here?" Jennie asked, keeping her voice low. "More to the point, why did you take off like that this morning?"

He limped over to the couch and dropped onto it, moaning as he made contact.

"Hazen?"

He pulled up his legs and held his stomach. "It's nothing. Just get me an ice bag, will you?"

Jennie fumbled for the matches and lit the candle. She gasped when she saw his face. Dried blood made a path from his nostril to his chin. His lower lip was swollen and split. "What happened?" Jennie asked as she hurried to the freezer. "Who did this to you?"

She found a package of blue ice in the freezer and wrapped it in a towel, then grabbed a clean washcloth and wet it. When she reached his side, she handed the ice pack to him. "I'm not sure where you want it."

"Me either." He placed it over his swollen lip and bruised left cheek.

"So, what happened?" She gingerly dabbed at the dried blood.

Hazen peered at her through the eye that wasn't swollen shut. "Why don't you ask your friend Marty?"

"Marty did this? I thought . . ."

"Just forget it, will you?" He batted her hand away. "It's not your concern."

"Hazen!" Joseph's voice was harsh yet at the same time held a touch of compassion.

Jennie jumped. As usual, she hadn't heard him come in.

Hazen swung his legs off the couch and grimaced. "Geez, Gramps, do you have to sneak up on people that way?"

Instead of answering, Joseph ordered him to lie back down so he could examine his wounds. After a few moments he straightened. "I see nothing broken, but I want you to see a doctor tomorrow."

"I don't need a doctor." Hazen winced when he tried to sit up again.

Joseph sat in his rocker and motioned for Jennie to sit as well. "Now, we shall hear how my grandson spent his day."

For what seemed an eternity, Hazen looked up at the moose head on the wall, then at Jennie, and finally at his grandfather. "I wanted to find Heather. Figured Danielson had her. Marty's been pretty steamed since she dumped him."

"So you went to confront Marty and he beat you up?" Jennie asked.

"Not exactly. I rode over to Danielson's and told Marty he'd better let my sister go or I'd bash his head in. He told me he didn't know where Heather was and said I should ask Eric," Hazen huffed. "Like he didn't know Eric had been shot. My guess is that Marty's the one who shot him. Anyway, he started to leave and I nailed him."

Joseph shook his head in apparent disapproval.

"And he nailed you back?" Jennie prodded, wishing he'd get to the point.

"No. I took off. Thought I'd go up to the Danielsons' hunting cabin and check that out in case he'd hidden her up there. Never got that far. I stopped here to get a g—" he glanced nervously at Joseph. "A gun. A couple of militia guys caught up with me out in the woods behind the barn and . . ." Hazen raised his arm and covered his eyes.

"Did you recognize them?" Jennie asked.

"Yeah. They work for Danielson."

"Are you sure Marty sent them?" Jennie asked.

"Either him or his dad. They kept swearing at me and calling me names. Said if I was going to act like a half-breed savage they'd treat me like one."

Jennie looked at Joseph. The break-in. She hadn't said it aloud but he responded as though she had. His nod encouraged her to pursue her thoughts. "Hazen, do you know what time you got here?"

"No. Probably about an hour after I left home, I guess." He lowered his arm and looked at her. "Why?"

Jennie told him about the break-in and asked if the men who beat him up had also ransacked the cabin.

"I don't know. Could be, I guess. All I know is I woke up long enough to crawl into the barn to get out of the rain. Been there ever since."

"That explains why your horse was here. You must have been out there when Amber and I came. We looked around, but didn't see anyone. I feel awful that you were out there all that time."

"You couldn't have known." Joseph sighed. "Jennie, perhaps you could heat up a bowl of stew for Hazen while I help him get cleaned up."

"Sure." Glad for something to do besides stare at her handsome cousin's disfigured face, Jennie put a kettle on for tea and heated some leftover venison stew. There was no frybread left, so she made toast and set it all on a placemat at the table.

After a few minutes, Joseph and Hazen returned. Hazen still looked like he'd been used as a punching bag. He devoured the stew and asked for seconds.

After he'd eaten, Hazen returned to the couch where Jennie had been sleeping. Jennie headed for the guest room where she would share the bed with Amber. Hazen and his grandfather were still talking when Jennie left.

"Ow," Hazen moaned, "I hurt all over."

Jennie hadn't intended to listen, but their voices flowed clearly through the inch-wide opening under the door.

"It serves you right for thinking you can fight battles with fists and guns."

"How else do we fight them? Words mean nothing to men like Danielson," Hazen said. "If I don't defend our honor, who will? You and Dad and this non-violence garbage don't cut it."

Joseph sighed audibly. "You do not defend our honor by fighting—you dishonor us. Honor is given to each of us by our Creator. No man or woman can strip it away—you can only do that to yourself. You, my son, dishonor yourself by being ashamed of your heritage."

"Spare me the lecture. Marty and his dad have Heather and I'll prove it. Tomorrow I'm riding up to their hunting lodge."

"Even if they are guilty, they would not be foolish enough to keep her there."

"I'm still going. You coming along?"

"No. I must take Amber and Jennie back to Dancing Waters. And I would like to have a word with the sheriff. Perhaps he has learned more about Heather and Eric."

"Why bother? We both know Jake and Marty did it. Danielson makes no secret of the fact that he wants your land for his military training."

"We may not believe in what Danielson does, my son, but he does not strike me as the kind of man who would kidnap a young girl."

"Why not? It's not like the sheriff is going to arrest him. Sheriff Mason is one of them."

"Enough. We will speak no more of this tonight. I'd like you to come with me tomorrow when I take the girls home. We will need to file a complaint against the men who beat you; and your father will want to see you."

A short time later, as she lay in the dark, quiet room, Jennie let Joseph's words wash over her again and again. *Honor is given by our Creator. No man can strip it away—you can only do that to yourself.* Joseph had said that Hazen dishonored himself by being ashamed of his Indian heritage. Along with her prayers for wisdom that night, Jennie prayed that Hazen would learn to honor and respect himself and that Heather would be found safe and alive.

When Jennie woke up the next morning, Hazen was gone. Joseph did not mention the fact, so Jennie didn't either. She hoped Hazen was wrong and that Marty and his father didn't have Heather hidden in their cabin. He'd be placing himself in danger again, and this time he might not be so lucky.

After breakfast, Amber and Jennie gathered their belongings and piled into Joseph's Ford Ranger. He'd reached the end of the driveway when Hazen galloped in as though he were being chased by a gang of marauders. He stopped beside the Ranger and handed Joseph a pink-and-white feathered barrette.

"It's Heather's. This proves she was there. They must have moved her yesterday after I talked to them."

"You are certain it was in the cabin?" Joseph stroked the feather, his brows knitted together.

"I found it on the floor. Don't you see? It's proof. I'm heading back home to tell Dad." He took the feather back, turned Thunder around, and raced away. "I'll meet you there," he yelled over his shoulder.

Jennie wished she could be as excited about Hazen's "proof" as he was. Unfortunately, it meant nothing. Heather could have gone to the cabin while she and Marty had been dating. Hazen could have planted it there. The worst part of it was that Hazen had tampered with the evidence. She doubted the sheriff would even believe him.

Back at the ranch, Maggie and Jeff welcomed Amber and Jennie home. Maggie promptly whisked Amber off to help her change and do all the things worried mothers do. Jennie followed Joseph and her uncle into Jeff's office.

Joseph brought his son up to date. Jennie then offered her version of the break-in, telling him about the diary's missing pages and the camera lens she'd found. She'd just finished when Hazen walked in. He tossed Heather's barrette on the desk.

Jeff listened as Hazen made vehement accusations against the Danielsons, then said, "I think it's time we pool our resources here and do a little brainstorming. I just got off the phone with Sheriff Mason, and he thinks he's got the case wrapped up. To be honest, I'm not convinced."

"You mean he actually arrested Marty and his dad?" Hazen asked.

"No. He's arrested Eric."

20

"What?" Hazen stared at his father as though he'd sided with the enemy.

"Apparently, Eric confessed to breaking into Dad's place. He also says he was the gunman Jennie and Amber saw in the llama pasture." Jeff fingered his daughter's barrette. "He hasn't confessed to Rick's murder or to kidnapping Heather, but Sam seems to think a full confession is forthcoming."

"That's crazy." Hazen exploded from his chair. "He's using Eric as a scapegoat because he can't—or won't—arrest Danielson. Eric didn't kill Rick. Rick killed himself. He—"

"Wait a minute," Jeff interrupted. "What are you saying?"

Joseph stood as if to intervene.

Hazen sank back into his chair, pale and shaking. "I—I saw him, Dad."

Joseph placed his hands on his grandson's shoulders. "Go on, son."

"I saw Rick throw something into the gas tank. He tried to run, but tripped. He meant to—to kill you." Hazen covered his eyes with his hand.

Jeff's dark eyes softened. "Why didn't you speak up before now?"

"I couldn't." He jerked his hand away from his face. "If I'd acted quicker, maybe I could have saved you. I didn't even

152

yell at you to get out of the way."

"So you blamed yourself. That's why you left?"

Hazen nodded. "I figured Rick was working for Danielson. I'd seen them together and knew he was a militia member. I thought maybe if I could prove who did it and bring the creep in—"

Jeff ran both hands through his thick, dark hair. He was wearing it loose, Jennie noticed, like his father and his son.

"All right. Um—look, Jennie. I want to get your views on all this, but right now I need to talk to Hazen. You understand."

"Sure." Jennie felt relieved to be going. "If it's okay with you, I'd like to borrow a car and drive into Cottonwood to get this cast changed. It's getting pretty rank." She met Jeff's gaze. "I—um—thought maybe I'd stop at the jail on the way and talk to Eric and run a couple of errands. That is if it's okay with you."

Jeff handed her the camera lens and barrette. "Maybe you could drop these off at the sheriff's office—tell him what you told me. I'll call and let him know you're coming. We wouldn't want to be cited for withholding evidence."

"Okay." Jennie took the items and started to leave.

Joseph stopped her at the door. "Would you like me to go with you?"

Jennie glanced back at Hazen and Jeff. "If you want, but I'll be fine. It looks like those two need you more than I do right now. Oh, should I tell the sheriff about the mine?" She stopped, remembering Hazen didn't know about the mine yet. "I mean, with Eric taking the pages out of the diary and all."

"I don't think we need to reveal its whereabouts just now. But tell him that Eric must have heard the old legend about the mine and was looking for a map. Only, to our knowledge, there is no map." Joseph patted her shoulder and gave her a knowing smile.

"Mine?" Hazen's confused gaze darted from Jennie to Joseph. "What mine?"

Jennie didn't stick around to hear the explanation.

After a shower, clean clothes, and a quick hair-braiding session with Maggie and Amber, Jennie borrowed the white Jeep she'd ridden in when she'd first arrived. Since Maggie had called in to make an appointment for Jennie with Doctor Clark, their family doctor, the cast replacement went off without a hitch. Well, almost. Jennie had to listen to a half-hour lecture about what to do and what not to do when wearing a cast.

At eleven-thirty Jennie escaped the clinic and walked a block and a half up main street to the municipal building. Sheriff Mason rose to greet her when she entered. The office was actually one big room that held four desks and a high counter that stretched all the way across the room, separating the officers and their staff from the visitors. A half door at the far end provided the only access. A deputy sat at one desk, and a clerk—a woman in her forties whose nameplate read Sandy Mason—occupied another. The sheriff's wife?

"Well, well, if it isn't our little celebrity detective. Jeff White Cloud tells me you have some information for me." Sheriff Mason walked to the counter and rested his elbows on it.

Jennie ignored his condescending smile and handed him the lens and Heather's feather barrette. As she offered explanations, she almost wished she could find indisputable evidence to prove him wrong about Eric. That might knock him off his arrogant throne.

Only she had nothing at this point and Eric had confessed to the break-in. So, she offered up a quick prayer that Mason lose the next election.

When she'd finished her version of the break-in and Hazen's discovery, the sheriff rubbed his chin and stared at something on the other side of the room. "So, Hazen found his sister's barrette out at Jake's hunting lodge."

"Yes. I know he should have left it out there, but . . ."

"Somebody's going through a lot of trouble to make Jake look bad. I'm beginning to wonder if your uncle is behind all this."

"That's ridiculous."

"Is it? Jeff White Cloud has a long history as a political activist. Some of these guys will stop at nothing to get what they want. Just recently we've seen where some environmentalists have falsified records to sway public opinion. What better way to destroy your strongest political opponent than by discrediting him in the public's eyes? Framing him for murder and kidnapping would do it, don't you think?"

Jennie opened her mouth to respond, but couldn't think of anything to say.

"You seem surprised. Well, little lady, maybe you're not such a sharp detective after all. Don't tell me you didn't know your uncle plans to run for the State Senate against Danielson next year."

"No, but that wouldn't—"

"Since you're intent on bein' involved in this investigation, maybe you ought to get some of your facts straight. Go on over to the bank and talk to Alex Dayton. He's your uncle's biggest backer. 'Course he'll probably pull out when he gets wind of my theory."

Jennie stared at him. "You actually think my uncle caused an explosion that cost him a leg or that he kidnapped his own daughter?"

"Wouldn't be the first time a criminal shot himself in the foot."

Jennie pressed her lips together, deciding it might be better to keep her angry thoughts to herself. "May I visit Eric before I go, please?"

"Why?" he demanded.

"He's my cousin's boyfriend. He worked for my aunt and

uncle. I'd like to ask him why he betrayed them like he did."

He eyed her a moment, then apparently dismissed her as harmless. Either that or he suspected she might get something out of Eric that he hadn't. "Well, I guess it wouldn't hurt."

After searching her and walking her through a metal detector to make certain she wasn't carrying a weapon or some sort of escape device, the deputy, a man in his mid-thirties whose name pin read Luke Nelson, led her into a small cubicle with a glass partition down the middle. She sat at a table and waited. Five minutes later, the sheriff hauled Eric in and shoved him into the chair.

Eric's face contorted with pain. Jennie thought the rough handling unnecessary—especially when Eric had suffered a gunshot wound only yesterday.

"You got ten minutes," Sheriff Mason said, then left the room. Deputy Nelson stood at the door, rigid and unsmiling.

"Hi." Jennie leaned toward Eric and spoke into the speaker vent in the glass partition.

Eric stared at the table. He bore little resemblance to the handsome young photographer she'd met only a few days before. His unshaven face and messy hair made him look like a criminal. *Maybe that's because he is one, McGrady.*

Jennie ignored her impressions, deciding she'd better get to the point. "I heard you confessed. Why did you break into Joseph's cabin?"

Eric focused his hard blue gaze on her. "Why do you care? I admitted to doing it, isn't that enough?"

"No. Heather has been kidnapped, but then you knew that, didn't you?"

His gaze softened. "Yeah, I heard. Sheriff keeps telling me I did it." He shook his head. "I'd never hurt Heather. I love her."

"But you did break into her grandfather's cabin."

"I said I did. I was looking for something."

156

"A map?"

"Yeah." He frowned. "How did you know about that?"

"It doesn't matter. What I want to know is why."

Eric glared at her, then broke eye contact. "Heather told me about the mine. She wanted to find the map. I don't know what she thought she'd do with it. Maybe take some of the gold with her to California. I told her I had mon—" His gaze darted back to Jennie.

He was lying. Heather didn't know about the mine. At least Joseph hadn't told her. And where would he have gotten the idea there was a map? "Where is Heather now?"

"I don't know."

"She was going to meet you yesterday morning."

Eric closed his eyes. "I . . . she changed her mind. Said we should wait."

"And you got mad. Where is she, Eric?"

"I don't know, honest. I was going to leave as soon as I got my money—" He paused as if he'd said too much, then added, ". . . my paycheck from Mrs. White Cloud. I was out at Joseph's when somebody snuck up on me. Hit me on the head—knocked me out. I don't remember a thing until I woke up in the hospital."

Jennie shook her head. "You're saying someone knocked you out then shot you? That doesn't make much sense to me."

"That's what happened."

"The sheriff said you were the gunman Amber and I surprised in the llama pasture, and that you stole Danielson's pickup then returned it later that evening. Is that true?"

"Yeah."

"Why?"

"I was mad at Heather's old man. Look, I wanted to get back at him for keeping Heather and me apart. Figured maybe he'd sell out if he had enough bad luck. Move back to New York."

"Where did you get the gun?"

"Enough with the questions. You're starting to sound like the sheriff."

Jennie winced. She wasn't sure what had gotten into her. She wasn't usually so aggressive. But pieces of the puzzle were finally starting to slip into place.

"I'd just like some answers. You may love Heather, but you're more in love with the money you stand to inherit if she marries you. But that wasn't enough. Someone hired you to finish the job Rick Jenkins botched—to get the White Clouds to sell their land. Who might that be? Chad Elliot? Jake Danielson?"

"You're way off base. That explosion happened before I got here. I'm not working for anybody."

"I say you are and I'm going to keep digging until I find out who that is. What I don't understand is your loyalty to this person. They've kidnapped Heather, for Pete's sake, and shot you. If I were you I wouldn't go to jail for someone else's crimes. I'll bet the prosecutor would be willing to cut a deal if you told them who's behind this operation." Jennie leaned back, rather pleased with her performance.

Eric shook his head. "Come off it. You've been watching too much television. The only people paying my wages are the White Clouds, so give it a rest." Eric stood and signaled the deputy.

Jennie felt sorry for Eric. Someone was using him. She could see it in his eyes. "*Always watch the eyes when you question people,*" Gram had told her. "*They say so much more than words.*" Eric had expressive eyes. In their brief meeting he'd revealed his love for Heather, his guilt and shame for the crimes he'd committed. And fear. Part of what he'd told her had been the truth and part of it a lie. She needed to sort it all out.

The deputy ushered Jennie down the hall and through the office area. A well-dressed man in his late twenties was standing at the counter talking to Sally Mason. "You tell the sheriff I want to see him as soon as possible. I'm still staying at Marsha's Bed & Breakfast."

"You just missed him, Mr. Elliot," Sally said. "I'll let him know as soon as he comes in—unless it's urgent—then I can get him on the cellular."

"No, it'll wait."

So this was the famous Chad Elliot. Funny, he didn't look nearly as sinister as she'd pictured him. "Hello, Mr. Elliot." Jennie walked through the half door to his side of the counter.

Elliot frowned. "Do I know you?"

"Jennie McGrady. I'm Maggie and Jeff White Cloud's niece."

"I remember hearing about you." He smiled and opened the door, waited for her to exit, then stepped outside. "How's your uncle doing? It's a shame about his leg."

"He's better." Jennie wished she could think of something intelligent and witty to say. *Where do you fit into all this?* she wanted to ask. "And what do you need to see the sheriff about?" The thought slipped out. Too late, Jennie snapped her mouth shut and must have turned a dozen shades of red.

"What did you say?"

"I was just curious about your wanting to see the sheriff, that's all."

"That's none of your business." His annoyance melted into concern. "Look, Miss McGrady—um Jennie. I know the White Clouds hold me responsible for the explosion and all that's happened out at Dancing Waters, and now this kidnapping thing. I've had nothing to do with any of it."

"How do you explain the ransom note in Eric's pocket asking that Dancing Waters be deeded back over to you?"

Chad shook his head. "Do you honestly think I'd send a ransom note with my name on it? I do want the ranch back, but I fight my battles in court."

And with hired hit men, Jennie thought. "Did you hire Eric Summers?"

"Who? Oh, you mean the man who was shot yesterday. Sorry. I've never met him. I know you think of me as an adversary, but I'm really a nice guy."

That's what they all say.

Elliot glanced at his watch. "Have you had lunch?"

"No. I was just going to grab a hamburger."

"Then let me buy you one. There's a place around the corner that serves buffalo burgers."

"Buffalo?"

"You've never had it?"

"No." Jennie winced. "And I'm not sure I want to. But I had ostrich the other day and loved it, so why not?" As they walked Jennie chided herself for accepting his offer. *This guy could be dangerous, McGrady.* She ignored the warning and excused her actions on the basis that Chad Elliot might have information pertinent to the investigation.

She just hoped he didn't have anything more sinister on his mind than feeding her buffalo.

21

Jennie folded herself onto the seat of a picnic table in front of the Burger Barn. "Thanks," she said as Elliot set a large burger, fries, and a Diet Coke in front of her. He sat opposite her with the identical fare. She tried not to look surprised when he bowed his head and said grace.

Jennie lifted the burger to her mouth. Elliot watched as she took the first bite. "Good, huh?"

She nodded. "Mmmm."

"This is one of the original eating places in Cottonwood. My great-grandfather, Frank Elliot, practically built this town."

"I know. Joseph told me a lot about him. Sounds like he was a wonderful person."

"It blows me away to think about it sometimes. Frank settled here back in 1861. These are my roots. Ever since I was a little kid I dreamed of coming home to Dancing Waters." He stopped to take another bite of his burger, then went on, "Do you know how Dancing Waters got its name?"

Jennie nodded while she finished a French fry. "Joseph told me. It's such a sad story."

"I wish I'd talked to him before all this happened. Now that I've been established as 'the enemy' I'll probably never hear the full story. My lawyer started proceedings before I knew much of anything about the history of the place."

"Why don't you talk to him anyway? Joseph is one of the nicest and wisest men I've ever met. I'm sure he'd be happy to tell you about your family."

"I'd like to, but Bennett, that's my lawyer, says I shouldn't." He sighed. "I never could understand why my father left. Our roots are here and I had to come back."

She'd been wrong about Chad Elliot, Jennie realized. She'd judged and convicted him without hearing his side. "It must have been a shock to discover the land had been sold."

"Shock? That's putting it mildly. I was angry and hurt when the lawyer contacted me, so I decided to fight for what was rightfully mine. I'm not after all that much, you know. Just enough land to raise horses and a few head of cattle. I want to get married someday and rear my children here. . . ."

"What if you lose? What if you find out that Dancing Waters really does belong to Joseph? What will you do?"

He gave her a look of surprise. "White Cloud owns the land free and clear. I'm not contesting that."

"I don't understand. If you're not disputing ownership, what are the lawsuit and criminal charges about?"

"When I first found out about the land deal, I thought Joseph had taken advantage of my grandfather's alcoholism and had swindled him. But that wasn't the case. My grandfather sold the land with the idea of being able to buy it back someday. He died before he had the opportunity. Daniel— my father—didn't care. I do. All I'm asking for is the right to buy back part of the land Joseph plans to deed over to the park service. I still don't understand what the problem is. The bank has offered to loan me a hundred percent of the purchase price. It'll be a big mortgage, but I'm sure I can handle it."

"You just want to buy some of the land back? Do Joseph and Jeff know that?" Jennie doubted it.

"I assumed so. My lawyer's been negotiating with the White Clouds for months." He looked at his watch again. "I must be going. Thanks for listening. You're the first person I've actually talked to about my agenda other than my lawyer."

"I still think you should talk to Jeff and Joseph yourself. I have a feeling your lawyer may not be representing your best interests."

He grinned. "Now I don't feel so bad. You're suspicious of everyone, aren't you? But don't worry. I had Greg Bennett checked out before I hired him. He's well thought of in the community. His great-grandfather was one of the founding fathers. I'll talk to him, though—make sure we're communicating on the same level." He gathered their trash, dumped it in a nearby container, then waved good-bye. "Give my regards to your family."

Jennie walked the block and a half from the Burger Barn to the Cottonwood Historical Society. Now she could narrow down her list of suspects by one. Unfortunately, she had to add another—Greg Bennett. Bennett. Hmm. She dug into her memory, knowing she'd heard his name in another context. Nadi's diary. The Reverend Joshua Bennett. Could the lawyer be a relative? Had the Reverend passed the secret of the mine down to his sons and grandsons?

Cottonwood's historical society was housed in the Dayton Mansion. Myrtle Dayton, a white-haired volunteer who had to be at least eighty, greeted Jennie at the door. "Oh, do come in. You're my first visitor today. What can I do for you?"

"I'd like some information on Cottonwood back in the late 1800s—like the people who lived here then and who still have relatives living here today. Some information about the—"

"Wait," Mrs. Dayton interrupted. "Let me show you around the house first. It has a fascinating history. I grew up here, and when my parents died I donated it to the citizens of Cottonwood. It has most of the original furniture and looks much like it did when my grandfather Alexander Dayton had it built in 1895."

"Are you related to Alex Dayton, at the bank?" Jennie asked.

"He's my nephew." She pointed to a little boy in a family portrait. "There. My brother's son. Such a sweet boy. I live with him and his family."

"Is that his sister standing next to him?" Jennie asked.

Myrtle nodded. "Melissa is a Bennett now. Both of the children married well. My how the time flies. It seems like only yesterday I was changing their diapers and now their children are almost grown."

"Melissa Bennett? Greg Bennett's wife?" Jennie asked.

"Why, yes. Fine family. His father and grandfather were both ministers."

"Was his grandfather the Reverend Joshua Bennett?"

Myrtle gave her a look of surprise. "As a matter of fact, he was."

Excitement shivered up her spine. Now she was getting somewhere. Greg Bennett must have found out about the mine from his grandfather. What was it Chad had said—that Bennett had contacted him? She could hardly wait to get back to the ranch and report her findings to Jeff and Joseph.

As they were walking through the kitchen, Jennie heard a scraping noise that seemed to be coming from the basement. "What's that?" Jennie asked.

"Oh, I'm so embarrassed. It appears we have squirrels or some such animal." She shuddered. "I've called the exterminator and he should be out this afternoon."

Obviously embarrassed, Myrtle hurried Jennie out of the kitchen into the gift shop, where she helped Jennie pick out several books, journals, and pamphlets about the area and the early settlers. She gave Jennie photocopies of family trees—Elliot, White Cloud, VonHassen, Danielson, Mason, Dayton, Bennett, and any other families with roots going back into the late 1800s. Myrtle even loaned her a set of tapes telling the history of the area, which Jennie planned to listen to on her way back to the ranch.

"There are so many stories, dear. It's wonderful that a girl your age would take an interest in the past. So many don't, you know. My grandchildren, for example, haven't the vaguest interest. Except for Carey—that's Melissa's little girl. I have a feeling she'll end up being a lawyer like her daddy." She sighed. "There I go, rambling on again."

When she finally left the Dayton Mansion, Jennie's brain felt as sluggish as an out-of-memory computer. Jennie had a hunch the past played an important role in the case and only by unraveling it would the crimes of the present make sense. She needed a clear view of how their lives had connected and intertwined then and now.

On her way back to the car her certainty of Greg Bennett's guilt began to waver. She thought again about her talk with Chad Elliot. Had Greg Bennett been misrepresenting him? The times she'd seen Bennett, he'd seemed abrupt and cool—except toward Maggie—when he'd been out at the ranch. The way he'd talked, Jennie had gotten the impression he and his wife and Jeff and Maggie were friends. A moment ago she'd been ready to close the case, now she wasn't so sure.

Jennie's thoughts were interrupted by protests of two men standing on the steps outside the sheriff's office.

"Luke, you have to stop him." Alex Dayton followed the deputy down the steps. "Surely there's been some mistake. Sam can't be serious."

" 'Fraid so. I'm supposed to meet him out at Dancing Waters. He's called for armed backup in case there's trouble." Luke ducked into a squad car and peeled out.

"What's going on?" Jennie asked breathlessly as she came alongside Dayton. "What's he talking about?"

Dayton looked at her with a dazed expression—as if she

were the last person he'd expected to see. After a moment's hesitation, he said, "Do you believe in God, Jennie?"

"Sure. Why?"

"Then you'd better start saying your prayers. If I know Sheriff Mason, he's got an army of deputies out there. Most of them are members of the militia group, and there isn't a one that wouldn't like to see Jeff White Cloud dead."

"The militia—can't we stop them?" Jennie gasped. A mass of knots settled in her stomach.

"I'm afraid not. We'll just have to hope Jeff gives up without a fight. Somehow I don't think that's gonna happen."

"The sheriff's gone to arrest him?"

"That's right."

"On what charge?" The sheriff had speculated about Jeff, but as far as she knew he didn't have any proof.

"I'm not sure. Conspiracy, fraud, maybe even murder. He thinks White Cloud is behind the whole thing. Even set up the explosion."

"But that's not possible."

"I didn't think so either, but sometimes people aren't what they seem. The sheriff mentioned the possibility of Jeff's involvement and told me I'd be wise to pull my financial support."

Jennie stared at the man. How could he be thinking of money at a time like this? "Excuse me, Mr. Dayton. I need to find a way to stop Sheriff Mason. I have a pretty good idea now of who's behind this, and it is not my uncle."

Jennie jogged to a pay phone about half a block away. She fumbled with the tattered phone book, hunting through the yellow pages for the number of the state patrol, the FBI, anything but the sheriff's department.

"Oh no," she mumbled. As was the case at most pay phones, half the pages had been torn out. She tore open her bag and retrieved some change.

"Excuse me, but you seem to be rather frazzled. Can I

help you with something?" Alex Dayton asked.

Jennie jumped. "Oh, I didn't see you."

"I'm sorry if I startled you. I was just on my way back to the bank."

"I need to call the state patrol or someone to let them know what the sheriff is doing."

"You said something a few minutes ago about knowing who's behind all this. Have you been investigating?"

"Yes. But I don't have time to talk about it. Do you have some change I could borrow?"

He reached in his pocket and pulled up a couple of dimes and a few pennies. "Sorry, but I do have a phone. The bank is just across the street, why don't you use one of the phones over there?"

Within a few minutes Jennie was sitting in Alex Dayton's executive chair, dialing the State Patrol. She explained her concerns to the operator, then again to a man she assumed was an officer.

"Thank you for calling, Miss McGrady," he said when she finished. "We'll take your complaint about the sheriff's department under consideration. I'll pass the information along and have an officer get back to you." Before Jennie could argue, the man hung up.

Jennie slammed the phone down.

"Having trouble?" Dayton came back into the office.

"Yes. They said they'd get back to me." She looked up another number and dialed Joseph's cabin.

"Who are you trying now?"

"Joseph. Maybe he went back home. He'll know what to do." Jennie wished the banker would leave, but couldn't very well ask him to mind his own business. It was his office. Besides, he seemed as concerned about the situation as she did.

"No problem. I've got to lock up—I'll be back in a few minutes." Dayton left, closing the door behind him.

Joseph didn't answer. Frustrated, Jennie hung up. She

placed her cast on the desk and in the process of standing, knocked off a pile of papers that had been precariously stacked near the edge.

"Clumsy," Jennie muttered as she stooped to pick them up. She gathered the papers and reached for an envelope that had sailed under the chair. The name "Eric Summers" was written on it. Jennie lifted the flap and peered inside. Her heart beat a path to her throat.

Inside was a check signed by Jeff White Cloud made out to Eric Summers in the amount of ten thousand dollars. According to the date it had been drawn that day. She couldn't be certain, but the signature resembled the handwriting on the two death threats. Her heart stopped. Could the sheriff have been right after all? Had Jeff paid Eric to kidnap Heather? One thing she knew for certain—Eric did not make that kind of money taking photos and doing odd jobs on the ranch.

Wait a minute, McGrady, back up. What's the check doing in Mr. Dayton's office? Could this be some of the paper work he'd brought by the ranch yesterday? If so, he had to be involved somehow. The entire affair was beginning to look like a massive conspiracy. Jennie knew she couldn't rule out any suspects yet, but she just couldn't imagine her uncle being involved in something so sinister.

Jennie rummaged through the desk. In the third drawer down, buried beneath a stack of Dayton's stationery, she found two yellowed pages from Nadi's diary. Jennie left the evidence in place and eased the drawer closed.

The doorknob clicked and turned. Jennie slipped the check to Eric back into the envelope and buried it in the pile of papers. She'd been fast, but not fast enough. Dayton looked from the papers on the desk to her face.

Jennie's stomach lurched, threatening to set her buffalo burger free. "Some papers fell on the floor," she explained in what she hoped was a calm voice. "I was just picking them up for you."

"Is that right?" Their gazes collided. His kind blue eyes had turned an iron gray.

"You couldn't leave well enough alone, could you?"

"What do you mean?" Jennie feigned innocence, hoping she'd read him wrong.

Alex Dayton's eyes showed a trace of regret. He reached inside his suit jacket as if going for a gun. Jennie flinched—he was going to kill her.

22

She released the breath she'd been holding when he pulled out a white handkerchief and dabbed at his forehead and upper lip.

"Too bad," he said. "Now I'm going to have to alter my plans. But don't worry, it shouldn't prove too difficult. An accidental death should do it."

He walked toward her, stopping at a large oak cabinet near his desk. Jennie backed up and hit the wall. The window was open. Jennie thought about jumping through it.

"I wouldn't do that if I were you." He withdrew an automatic rifle from the cabinet and snapped in a cartridge.

Jennie sucked in a shallow breath and stared at the collection of at least a dozen weapons in his private arsenal—shotguns, pistols, even a crossbow. *This guy is supposed to be funding Jeff White Cloud's political campaign against the militia? That'd be like terrorists lobbying for gun control.*

Training the gun on her, he pawed through the papers on his desk and retrieved Eric's check. He waved the gun toward the door. "Let's go."

Jennie's hope moved up several notches. He couldn't possibly get her out of the building without being seen. She'd scream for help and dive behind a desk or something. Good plan. Bad timing. The bank was empty. So that's what he'd meant by locking up. "Where is everyone?"

"I gave them the rest of the day off with pay. We don't take tragedies lightly in this town. And a siege at Dancing Waters qualifies, don't you think? After all, several of my employees have family working out there."

Dayton ushered Jennie out the back door and shoved her into a waiting van—black with gold trim. She'd seen it out at Dancing Waters before and as soon as she stepped inside, realized who it belonged to.

Chad Elliot's lawyer, Greg Bennett, sat behind the wheel. "Hurry up."

Dayton jumped in, closed the sliding door, then grabbed a rope from under the passenger seat. He yanked Jennie's arms behind her.

"Ow. Take it easy." Jennie imagined herself yanking her arm out of his grasp and slamming the cast into his smug face.

"What are you doing?" The highly recommended lawyer started the van.

"Tying her up. What else am I going to do with a rope, hang her?"

"Forget that. If the authorities find rope marks on her wrist they'll get suspicious. You'll just have to strap her in and keep an eye on her." He glanced at his watch. "Where is Summers? I thought you told him to meet us as soon as he got out."

"Don't worry. He'll be here. White Cloud posted bail nearly an hour ago. I've got his money. Which he won't get until he does this one last job for us."

Bennett laughed. "Don't you mean for White Cloud?"

"Of course. Everything leads back to White Cloud." Dayton handed the gun to his partner and climbed into the front seat. He swiveled around, took the gun back, and trained it on Jennie.

"Here he comes." Bennett lowered the power window a

couple of inches. "It's about time. Get in the back and keep an eye on our guest."

Bennett had the van rolling before Eric could sit down. He swung around and dropped into the seat beside her.

Surprise registered on his face, then anger. "What's she doing here? You hire her too?"

Jennie glared at him. "Not everyone has a price."

Eric caught her gaze, had the decency to look guilty, then glanced back at the two businessmen.

"Our snoopy young investigator here is about to be the victim of a few stray bullets," Bennett sneered. "Gunned down by one of the dozens of deputies combing the grounds."

"You're going to kill her?"

"No, you are."

"Why?"

"She knows too much." Dayton frowned. "When we get out to the ranch I'm going to turn you loose with this." He held up the weapon. "Pump about half a dozen bullets into her, then we're out of here. We'll take you up to the airport in Missoula."

Fear raced through her like a raging fire. *There has to be a way out, McGrady,* she told herself. *You've gotten out of tight spots before. Right, but he's got an automatic rifle and he's driving straight into a war zone.* Jennie could see the headlines now: "Teenager Accidentally Killed in Indian Massacre at Dancing Waters."

When she'd been trapped in the mine she'd experienced a strange and welcome peace. And earlier when she'd been lost in the woods, Joseph had reminded her to be still. God had been faithful to bring her this far. With the faith of her grandmother and Joseph, Jennie took a deep breath and swallowed back the rising terror. She leaned back against the seat. Somehow she'd find a way out of this.

"You got my money?" Eric asked.

Dayton patted his breast pocket. "And the deed to your new condominium in Fort Lauderdale. All courtesy of Jeff White Cloud."

Eric nodded and stared straight ahead, his mouth set in a hard line. He'd cleaned up before getting out of jail and looked like Heather's handsome young photographer friend again.

How ironic, Jennie thought. *On the outside, they look like the professionals they claim to be.* Success oozed out of every thread in their expensive clothes. But inside they were nothing but slime.

"Everyone has a dark side," Gram had told her. *"We are all capable of good and evil. The weakest of us are those who allow the evil to control them."*

The men's voices broke in on her thoughts.

"Did you ever find the map?" Bennett asked.

Dayton shook his head. "I was sure it would be in the old man's house. Even looked in his and Jeff's safety deposit boxes at the bank—nothing."

The mine. Jennie had an idea. It would mean revealing Joseph's secret and disclosing its whereabouts. She hesitated a moment. Should she? What would Joseph say? Since it seemed her only chance for escape, Jennie felt certain Joseph and Uncle Jeff would approve. "There is no map."

Bennett peered at her through the rearview mirror. "And just how would you know that?"

"Joseph told me."

"You're lying!" Eric snapped. "Back at the jail—"

"I mentioned the map because I wanted more information from you. I had a hunch that's what you were looking for because of the missing pages in Nadi's diary. I also knew you were lying when you said Heather told you about the mine. She didn't know about it."

Jennie turned her attention back to the two men in the front seat. "But then that's why you kidnapped her, isn't it?

173

Were you going to have her lead you to the mine? Did you offer to pay her off too? And when she refused you—"

Dayton silenced Jennie with a steel gray stare. "You ask too many questions."

"I know—it's a habit." Jennie struggled to maintain a sense of calm. She had to make them think she was tough. "Look, you're going to kill me anyway, so why not satisfy my curiosity. Where's Heather? Eric already told me she'd changed her mind about going with him."

When no one answered, Jennie leveled an accusing gaze on Eric. "Is that when you decided to kidnap her? Or had that been part of the plan? What I don't understand, Eric, is how you could still cover for these guys. I mean, they shot you and abducted Heather."

"I'll heal. They promised they wouldn't hurt her." Eric closed his eyes. "Besides, she doesn't know anything. Eventually she'll get my letter and find out that her dad hired me and that the kidnapping thing was all a ruse to discredit Elliot."

Jennie shook her head. "This is the craziest scheme I've ever heard. You can't possibly get away with it."

"I'm afraid we can," Dayton said. "You see, Jennie, we're the only ones above suspicion in this deal. Eric's letter to Heather and the fact that White Cloud paid his bail was all the proof Sheriff Mason needed. In the end, Danielson, White Cloud, and Elliot will all be dead. Dancing Waters will revert back to the bank, go up for auction, and be sold to the highest bidders. Which, of course, will be myself and Greg. We'll be buying it out of a deep sense of loss for our dearly departed friends."

Eric stiffened beside her. His eyes widened and his Adam's apple moved up and down as he swallowed. He had to know they wouldn't let him leave. He knew even more than she did about their plans.

Bennett made a right onto a gravel road. It was one that

she'd taken that morning with Joseph. It ran between the Danielsons' ranch and Dancing Waters. Jennie decided it was time to put her plan into action. "Maybe I was wrong about not having a price," Jennie said. "I know where the mine is. Maybe we can make a deal."

Bennett braked. The van spun out on the loose gravel and the lawyer almost lost control. He managed to right the vehicle, stopped it, and whipped around in his seat.

"What kind of deal?" both men asked at once.

"Well, I might be persuaded to take you there for, say, half a million dollars. I might even be persuaded to go home with a case of amnesia for say—another half mil."

Bennett and Dayton looked at each other. "We might be willing to work something out," Bennett said, "but only if the mine's as rich as my grandfather said it was."

"Oh, it's rich all right. There's a foot-wide vein of pure gold not more than fifteen feet from the entrance." Jennie dug into her pocket and handed the nugget to Dayton. "I picked this up off the mine floor. I was going to have it assayed, but Joseph assured me it was the real thing."

Dayton fingered the gold, weighed it in the palm of his hand, and bit into it. "She's right."

Jennie shuddered at the look in his eyes. Greed. She'd seen it before and knew it had the power to turn people into savages.

"Where is it?" Bennett asked.

"Just keep driving," Jennie said. "I'll tell you where to stop. We'll have to hike into the woods a ways."

"What do you think, Alex?" Bennett started the van and pulled back onto the road. "She being straight with us?"

"We'll know soon enough. It'll put us a little behind schedule, but that shouldn't matter now."

They drove on in silence. Dayton still faced toward the back, with his gun at the ready. Eric kept looking at her, his eyes sending repentant messages to let her know he wanted out.

It was a little late for that, but Eric would be a valuable witness against Dayton and Bennett. Maybe she should bring him with her when she made her escape. Maybe not. Eric may have been scared straight, but Jennie just plain didn't trust him.

"Pull off on the other side of the bridge," Jennie said.

"Are you sure?" Bennett asked, braking and coming to a stop at a wide spot in the road where the bridge ended.

"Yes. I haven't come in this way, but we'll follow the creek up. You'll need a flashlight for when we go into the mine."

She led the three men along the creek bank. The water had receded, leaving mud and debris in its path. "Those aren't the best shoes for hiking." Jennie suppressed a snicker as Dayton slipped down the bank into the creek. By the time they reached the meadow below the mine, both men looked like they'd been mud wrestling. She and Eric didn't look much better, but that didn't matter. Soon she'd be free.

On the hike in, Jennie replayed her escape scene over and over in her head—had it planned out to the second. She just hoped the men wouldn't kill her before she got them into the mine.

23

Jennie held her breath as she climbed up the familiar hill-side.

"There's nothing up here," Bennett said, panting heavily. He stopped about a fourth of the way up. "She's just trying to wear us out so she can get away."

Dayton, red-faced and looking as if he might have a heart attack at any moment, paused to catch his breath. "Let's go." He nudged Bennett, then started climbing again.

"It's just a little farther." Had Jennie known what poor physical condition they were in, she might have tried running, but they had a powerful gun and she doubted she could have outrun the bullets.

She reached the mine's entrance and stopped. Eric was right behind her, the others about thirty yards behind.

"What are you going to do?" Eric whispered.

"Show them the mine."

"You mean it's really up here?"

Jennie nodded.

"I know you're up to something. I want to help. Look, remember what you said earlier at the jail about getting a lighter sentence? Maybe—" Eric stopped as Dayton and Bennett caught up with them.

Bennett leaned against an outcropping of rock. "I told you she was lying. There's no mine."

"It's hidden." Jennie moved aside the brush and pushed the lever. As before, the door shuddered open. She ducked inside.

"Well I'll be." Still panting, Dayton pushed Eric in ahead of him. Bennett followed, switching on the flashlight as he entered.

"The vein I told you about is back here. I'll show you." Jennie rushed ahead of them. She stopped and pointed, then stepped out of the way.

Bennett shined the flashlight on the gold and both men gasped in greedy delight. "She was right."

"Woo-wee," Dayton whooped. "I've never seen anything like it."

While the gold enticed the men, Jennie backed out of the circle of light toward the entrance. Any second the door would close, trapping them inside. Near the entrance now, she listened for the click. When she heard it, she spun around and dove through the opening. She could hear bullets ping as they hit the inside of the metal door.

Jennie scrambled to her feet. That's when she discovered her escape hadn't gone quite as smoothly as she'd hoped. Eric winced as he sat up. He rubbed his arm just below the bullet wound, then reached up to pull some twigs from his hair. "Wow! That was some escape."

"How did you know what I was going to do?"

"I didn't. I just followed your lead." Favoring his injured arm, he stood and brushed the dirt from his jeans. "Look, Jennie. What I did was wrong. I should have gone to Jeff as soon as Dayton contacted me. I didn't do it just for the money. They threatened to hurt Heather. I shouldn't have listened. He and Bennett may have already killed her."

"You better hope not." Jennie picked up a rock and jammed it against the lever. Even if Bennett and Dayton discovered how to open it from the inside, they wouldn't be able to get out—she hoped.

"What now?" Eric asked.

Though Jennie still didn't fully trust him, she wasn't afraid of him either. If she could have managed it, she'd have handcuffed him to a tree and left him for the sheriff, but that wasn't an option. "I'm heading back to the ranch. I'd suggest you come along and turn yourself in." Without waiting for an answer, Jennie raced down the hill toward the creek. She had to stop the sheriff and his deputies. She just hoped it wasn't too late.

"Jennie, wait up," Eric panted as Jennie started to cross the creek. "Where are you going?"

"Back to the ranch. Are you coming or not?"

"Why don't we take the van?"

Jennie stopped and spun around. "It would be quicker, but the keys—" She paused as he held them up, grinning like he'd pulled off a major coup. "When did you. . . ?"

"While they were busy keeping an eye on you. Come on, let's go." He took off running toward the road where the van sat waiting.

When they arrived at the dude ranch twenty minutes later, an ambulance with sirens and lights engaged pulled away from the lodge. Jennie didn't want to think about who might be in it—or how many more there'd be.

The ambulance was the only sign of trouble. The ranch looked much as it had when Jennie had first arrived. Guests milled around and ostriches stared at her from the security of their pen. Sheriff Mason was standing on the porch outside the lodge office shaking Jeff's hand as though they'd just finished coffee.

Maggie, who'd been standing between Jeff and Chad Elliot, spotted her, ran down the steps, and threw her arms around Jennie's neck. "Thank God you're safe." She stepped back and frowned. "You're filthy. What happened? And what's Eric doing here?"

"It's a long story," Jennie said. "But . . . I'm confused. I thought the sheriff had come out here with Danielson's militia group to arrest Uncle Jeff. I expected the place to look like a war zone."

Chad Elliot came down the steps toward her. "I think I can help you out there, Jennie. After you and I talked, I got to thinking about what you said and decided to take your advice. Came out to talk to the White Clouds myself. And it's a good thing I did. I was here when the sheriff and his deputies arrived. You were right, Bennett has been misrepresenting me from the beginning. We've been having a long talk about who might be behind all this."

"I'd better head on into town." Sheriff Mason adjusted his hat. "I still can't believe Bennett's our guy. But I'll follow up on your suspicions."

"Believe it, Sheriff," Jennie said. "Bennett's guilty—so is his brother-in-law."

"Alex?" Jeff stared at her as though she'd just grown another head. "I can't believe he'd be involved in something like this. Are you sure?"

"Positive. They developed this incredible plan to take over Dancing Waters. Only you won't find them in town, Sheriff." She gave him a brief accounting of what had happened.

"Let me get this straight." Sheriff Mason looked skeptical. "You trapped Bennett and Dayton in a gold mine?" He shook his head and laughed. "Now I've heard everything."

Eric, who'd been silent to that point stepped between Jennie and the sheriff. "She's telling the truth. They hired me to stir up trouble between the Danielsons and White Clouds. They hired Rick Jenkins too, only he messed up. They were going to make me kill Jennie. I—I'm willing to testify against them if—well, Jennie said if I testified I could get a lighter sentence."

"Is that right?" Sheriff Mason glowered at her, but Jennie thought she noted a sliver of respect. "Last time I looked, I was wearing the badge around here." He fussed a little more about people taking the law into their own hands, then asked a deputy to take Eric into town. After promising to make a concerted effort to find Heather, Mason followed Joseph to the mine to pick up Bennett and Dayton.

"Who was in the ambulance?" Jennie asked Maggie and Jeff after they'd gone.

Maggie pinched her lips together and squeezed Jennie's shoulder.

"Oh no, not Hazen?"

"No, honey. Hazen went into town to look for you. When you didn't come back we got worried. He should be calling in any time, and we'll let him know you're here."

"Then, who?"

"Jake Danielson. The excitement was too much for him. He had a heart attack."

"Is he dead?"

"No, at least he wasn't when he left."

Jennie felt relieved and sad at the same time. "Poor Marty." Jennie sank onto the steps and rested her head against a post.

Maggie sat down beside her. "You must be exhausted. Why don't you head up to the house, take a shower and rest for a while?"

"Can't." She yawned and let her eyes drift closed. Just for a minute. "I need to find Heather."

"Jennie McGrady." Maggie heaved an exasperated sigh and wrapped an arm around Jennie's shoulders. "No wonder your mother worries about you. You don't know when to quit."

Jennie didn't, but apparently her body did. Though she desperately wanted to look for Heather, she followed Maggie's orders and let Lopez drive her up to the house. After a quick shower, she went to bed.

When Jennie awoke, it was dark. A narrow strip of light

seeped out from under the closet door. After a few minutes, the light went out and the door opened. A slender figure emerged.

Jennie threw back her covers. "Don't tell me you're sneaking out again?"

"Oh," Heather squealed. "You scared me. I thought you were sleeping."

"I was. Now I'm awake." Jennie rubbed her eyes. "Wait a minute. Is this a dream? What are you doing here?"

"Sheriff Mason brought me home." Heather reached for the stained-glass lamp and turned it on. Rainbows of light splintered the darkness.

"Really? He found you? When?"

"He didn't find me. Hazen and Mrs. Dayton did."

Jennie rubbed her forehead. "Mrs. Dayton? But how—wait, don't tell me. Mr. Dayton hid you in the mansion. You were making the noises we heard."

"I heard your voice and tried to get your attention."

Jennie knocked herself alongside the head. "I can't believe it. I was so focused on the research I was doing, it didn't even occur to me that it might be you."

"Don't be so hard on yourself," Heather said. "If it hadn't been for you . . . well, you uncovered Dayton and Bennet's plot and caught them. You saved our lives."

Jennie's face warmed with the compliment. "You said Hazen and Mrs. Dayton found you?"

"Actually he was in town looking for you. Someone said they'd seen you go into the mansion. When I heard him, I made as much noise as I could. And . . . I called to him in my mind." She shrugged. "I know it sounds weird, but being twins we can sometimes hear each other's thoughts. Anyway, Hazen decided to check out the noises—and there I was."

"Are you okay? They didn't hurt you?"

"I'm fine. My wrists are sore and my mouth still hurts from the gag."

Jennie swung her legs off the bed and sat up all the way. "I'm really glad you're home. I was afraid they'd killed you."

"Yeah." Heather stood and walked to the door. "I have to go. Marty's waiting for me downstairs. Mom said if you were awake I should have you come down for dinner."

"You're going out with Marty?"

"I promised I'd go to the hospital with him to see his dad."

Jennie nodded. "Tell him hi."

"I will." Heather opened the door.

"Heather?" Jennie closed the distance between them and gave Heather a hug. "I'm so glad you're back."

Tears gathered in her cousin's eyes. "Me too."

Jennie flipped on the overhead light and got dressed. She felt strange—sort of unfinished. Maybe it was because she'd missed connecting Heather to the Dayton Mansion. "You can't win them all, McGrady," she told her mirror image as she brushed through her long tresses. Jennie tipped her head to one side and clipped on one of Heather's feathered barrettes. She may not have solved the case single-handedly, but Jennie took comfort in knowing that even if she hadn't survived her abduction, Bennett and Dayton would have been caught. Their plan had begun to unravel in too many places.

Jennie glanced toward the ceiling. "Thank you," she whispered, then headed downstairs.

24

Two days later, after one of Maggie's gourmet dinners, Jennie stretched out on the carpeted living-room floor between Nick and Amber and watched her mother and Maggie erase the years that had separated them.

Mom and Nick had flown in the day before. Jennie had driven up to Missoula to get them. They'd spent the entire drive catching up. After hearing about Hannah's grandparents and their home in Arizona, Jennie felt better about the little girl being there. Nick didn't. But his bad mood began to dissipate the minute Amber introduced him to the animals—especially the horses.

Jennie felt as if she'd already had a full day. The mid-morning ceremony had gone off without so much as a protest sign. In the headdresses and beaded buckskin of their ancestors, Joseph, Jeff, Hazen, Heather, and Amber presented the U.S. Forestry Service with ten thousand acres of prime land to be preserved for future generations.

Now, as Jennie watched their faces and felt their anticipation, she knew there was more excitement to come.

"Can't tell you how glad I am I talked to you," Chad Elliot told Jennie for the umpteenth time since dinner. "I just feel so gullible to have been taken in by those creeps."

"You mustn't blame yourself, Chad." Maggie perched on the arm of the chair in which her husband sat.

"We were all taken in." Jeff had exchanged the wheelchair for a pair of crutches. In another week or two, he'd be walking on his own.

"There is no deeper wound than the betrayal of a friend. It will take time for these wounds to heal. But I have something that may help." Joseph excused himself and came back a few moments later with an envelope.

Hazen, Heather, Maggie, and Jeff all looked at one another as though they were sharing a private joke.

"Chad," Joseph said as he sat back down. "You told us earlier you wished to have the opportunity to purchase back a portion of the land."

"Yes." He sighed. "But I'm not sure that will be possible now. I don't think I can get a loan from anyone else. I should have been suspicious of Dayton's motives when he offered to loan me such a large amount with so little collateral."

Joseph handed him an envelope. "We had a meeting to discuss your request and have come up with a plan we think will be acceptable to you."

Chad opened the envelope and pulled out an official-looking letter. Tears gathered in his eyes as he read. "I can't believe this. After all that's happened. I don't know what to say."

Curiosity got the better of Jennie. "What is it?"

Joseph chuckled. "Patience, Brave Eagle. You will know soon enough."

"You were absolutely right about these people, Jennie," Elliot said. "They've just given me the deed to the five hundred acres my great-grandfather gave White Cloud. I can't accept this, Joseph, it's your home."

"But, Papa, where will you live?" Amber asked.

"I am old, Tiponi. I don't have many years left. I will move into one of the guest houses."

His news delighted Amber. "Then I can see you every day?"

185

"Every day."

"Still," Elliot argued, "this is too much."

"There are a few stipulations," Jeff said. "Now that the mine is no longer a secret, and we can enforce laws to preserve the environment, we thought it might be best to reopen it. We've decided to ask you to oversee the mining operation. You'll receive a salary along with a share of the profits."

"I don't know what to say." Elliot glanced around the room.

"We'll work out the details later." Joseph nodded to Jeff. "Now we must give Jennie her reward for bringing Dayton and Bennett to justice."

"We're setting up a trust fund for you, Jennie," Jeff said. "A percent of the profits from the mine will go into an account bearing your name. Law school costs a lot of money and I want you to have the best."

Jennie glanced at her mother, expecting an objection. Mom just smiled. As Jennie looked from one person to the next, their faces faded behind a veil of tears. Her thank-yous barely made it past the baseball-size lump that clogged her throat. She circled the room and hugged them all.

———

A week later, they stood in the shadow of the Bitterroot Mountains saying a final good-bye to Jake Danielson. On top of his coffin Marty placed a crate of his father's guns. He removed his hat and bowed his head. "I loved my father. We didn't always agree, but he did right by me. By burying his guns with him, I'm not saying that my father's involvement in the militia was right or wrong. All I'm saying is The Double D is mine now and I got plans that don't include the use of weapons or military training. This is a ranch, pure and simple." He glanced up at the man wearing a clerical collar. "That's all I got to say."

The Reverend Pierce, who served at the church where the

Danielsons were members, took charge. "Let us pray. Our Father . . ."

After the funeral they all went back to Dancing Waters where Aunt Maggie and Mom served a buffet lunch and consoled Mrs. Danielson and the other mourners.

Jennie, Hazen, Marty, and Heather changed clothes, packed up their camping gear, and headed into the woods toward Crystal Hot Springs. Since this was Jennie's last night, they'd decided to spend it camping under the stars on Blue Ridge. "I wish you could stay longer, Jennie," Hazen said.

"Me too. I'm going to miss this place." Jennie scooped up a pine cone and threw it at a tree. "The mountains and trees, the horses—"

"What about us?" Hazen teased. "I know we're weird, but won't you miss us a little?"

"A lot. But I have a hunch we'll see each other more often now that our mothers have gotten back together."

"Why don't you come back next year?" Heather turned around and walked backward. "Stay for the whole summer." Although Heather had no intention of giving up modeling, she'd agreed to finish college and stay at Dancing Waters— a decision which had Marty Danielson's full approval.

"I think you should," Marty looped an arm around Heather's neck and grinned. "These guys need somebody to keep them out of trouble and I'm not sure I can handle the job myself."

"I might, provided they don't lure me into the woods and throw tomahawks at me."

"Naw." Hazen grinned and raised his eyebrows. "But we might be able to come up with something else. Like dumping a few spiders into your sleeping bag."

"You wouldn't."

"On the other hand, I'll probably be too busy to get into trouble."

"Yeah?"

"Dad and Gramps have taken me on as a partner. I'll be heading the new trailblazing unit."

"Which is—"

"We'll be taking guests on wilderness treks in the mountains and teaching them to respect and nurture the land."

"Tell them your Indian name, Hazen," Heather said. "Papa decided Hazen was ready."

"*Yuma*. It means 'chief's son.' "

"Congratulations, Yuma." Jennie flashed him a wide smile. She glanced from Hazen to Heather and back again. The three of them had been almost inseparable the last few days. And now Jennie didn't just count them as cousins, but friends. She had only one wish—that Lisa could be there with them. Maybe next time.

The following day it rained. Their flight went on as scheduled.

Jennie's sadness over leaving Dancing Waters turned into joy as they arrived in Portland. Her best friend and cousin was waiting at the gate.

"I can't wait to hear about your trip," Lisa said. "But first I've got to tell you what happened. Someone broke into the school and . . ."

Jennie sighed. *Forget it, McGrady. Don't even think about getting involved. This is one case you are going to ignore.*

Uh-huh, her adventurous spirit contradicted, *wanna bet?*

In Too Deep

Patricia H. Rushford

Jennie McGrady
Mystery Series

9608

In Too Deep

Patricia H. Rushford

BETHANY HOUSE PUBLISHERS
MINNEAPOLIS, MINNESOTA 55438

In Too Deep
Copyright © 1996
Patricia Rushford

Cover illustration by Andrea Jorgenson

Published by Bethany House Publishers
A Ministry of Bethany Fellowship, Inc.
11300 Hampshire Avenue South
Minneapolis, Minnesota 55438

Printed in the United States of America.

Library of Congress Cataloging-in-Publication Data

Rushford, Patricia H.
    In Too Deep / Patricia H. Rushford.
        p.   cm. — (The Jennie McGrady mystery series ; 8)
    Summary: Jennie becomes involved when someone
breaks into the high school to steal chemicals and then the
chemistry teacher is found shot dead.
    ISBN 1-55661-561-2 (pbk.)
    [1. Mystery and detective stories. 2. Christian life—
Fiction. I. Title. II. Series. III. Series: Rushford,
Patricia H. Jennie McGrady mystery series ; 8.
PZ7.R8962In   1996
[Fic]—dc20   96-25285
                                                CIP
                                                  AC

To Mrs. Rockne's fourth-grade class
at Grand Forks Christian School

A special thank you to the Vancouver and Camas
Police Departments in Washington State—especially
to Officer Jane McNicholas and Officer Paul Pierce
for lending valuable insight and authenticity.

PATRICIA RUSHFORD is an award-winning writer, speaker, and teacher who has published numerous articles and more than twenty books, including *What Kids Need Most in a Mom, The Jack and Jill Syndrome: Healing for Broken Children*, and her first young adult novel, *Kristen's Choice*. She is a registered nurse and has a master's degree in counseling from Western Evangelical Seminary. She and her husband, Ron, live in Washington State and have two grown children, six grandchildren, and lots of nephews and nieces.

Pat has been reading mysteries for as long as she can remember and is delighted to be writing a series of her own. She is a member of Mystery Writers of America, Sisters in Crime, Society of Children's Book Writers and Illustrators, and several other writing organizations. She is also co-director of Writer's Weekend at the Beach.

1

"You're going to work on the case, aren't you?" Lisa Calhoun's green eyes sparkled with excitement as she followed Jennie into her bedroom and closed the door. "Come on, admit it."

Jennie McGrady shook her head. "No way." The *case* her cousin was talking about involved a burglary at Trinity High. Someone had broken into the chemistry lab and stolen chemicals and supplies. The police suspected whoever did it planned to set up a meth lab. "I'm going to talk to Mr. Mancini about my chemistry project. I told you that." Jennie yanked off her T-shirt and ducked into her closet to get a short-sleeved white cotton shirt. She loved wearing white in the summer—especially when she had a tan.

"I know, but I can't believe the chem project is the only reason you're going. School doesn't start for three weeks."

"I'm home-schooled, remember?" Being a single parent, Jennie's mom had created a part home-school, part private school situation so Jennie could be home afternoons to baby-sit her five-year-old brother, Nick. "Besides, I want to get a head start. I told you that too."

Though Jennie rarely missed an opportunity to solve a crime, she had no intention of trying to track down the thief—especially not after what her friend with the Portland police had told her. Rocky (a.k.a. Dean Rockwell) had lectured her for an hour about the toxic chemicals involved in the making of clandestine drug labs. He'd called them "kitchens of death." *"These labs are deathtraps, Jennie,"* he'd said. *"You don't want to have anything to do with this case."* With a pained look in his blue eyes and a catch in his voice he'd told her about a friend of his who'd accidentally triggered a booby trap in a meth lab. Just breathing in the chemical fumes for a few seconds had caused the officer's lungs to collapse. Rocky had other stories too—all of them tragic—and convincing.

Jennie pushed the disturbing thoughts aside. "Anyway," she continued, "it's too dangerous."

"That hasn't stopped you before." Lisa joined her in the small walk-in closet and wrinkled her nose. "We really need to take you shopping. You have absolutely nothing to wear for school this year."

Jennie pulled the white shirt off the hanger and slipped it on. Glancing around her closet, she had to agree. She and her mom had cleaned out everything she'd either worn to death or that no longer fit—which was just about everything she owned. "Maybe later." She tucked the shirttail into her faded jeans, kicked off her sneakers, and stuffed her feet into a pair of leather loafers. "Where'd I put my vest?"

"It's on the bed." Lisa retrieved the denim vest and held it while Jennie slipped her arms into it.

Jennie moved to her dresser, brushed her long dark hair, and pulled it into a ponytail. She picked up a small gold necklace, secured it around her neck, and opened the heart that dangled from the chain.

"What's that?"

"A locket—Hannah sent it to me. Says I should wear it all the time so I'll never forget her. Like that could happen." Hannah, Jennie's four-year-old neighbor girl and victim of a kidnapping, had stayed with them as a foster child for a couple of weeks before going to live with her grandparents in Arizona. Jennie had rescued the girl and wanted very much to make her part of the McGrady family, but it didn't happen.

"You still miss her, don't you?"

"Yeah." Jennie sighed, then glanced down at the adorable flaxen-haired child in the small photo. "But she seems happy—I guess that's what really matters. Her grandparents are nice—they wrote a letter to us saying how much they appreciated our taking care of her."

"I thought you were going to Arizona to visit them."

"I wanted to, but when have I had a chance?"

Lisa chuckled. "I guess you have been pretty busy. Maybe you still can before school starts."

"Maybe. Mom and I talked about my going down in a couple of months—maybe over Labor Day weekend." Jennie closed the locket, then let it drop against her chest. "But that's a ways off. Are you coming with me to the school?"

Lisa tipped her head to one side as her gaze met Jennie's. "Well, if you were going to investigate the theft, I might, but if you're really only going to talk about chemistry, I'll pass."

"What, and miss the chance to hear about the molecular structure of acetylsalicylic acid?"

"Yeah—like that really excites me. Honestly, Jen, sometimes I think you're weird."

Jennie chuckled. "Different strokes." Actually, Jennie wasn't all that excited about chemistry. She mainly wanted a high grade-point average for college, where she planned to study law.

"I know. I know. It isn't that I hate chemistry—not really," Lisa said as she headed for the door, her copper-colored curls swaying as she walked. "It's just that I don't think Mr. Mancini likes me, and the feeling is mutual."

"Why?"

"Let's just say he doesn't have much patience for students with less than a four-point average." Without turning around Lisa added, "Allison and B.J. invited us to go swimming.

9

Why don't you meet me there after you talk to Mr. Mancini?"

"Sounds great as long as Mom doesn't need me to baby-sit Nick."

"She doesn't. I already asked."

After Lisa left, Jennie grabbed her leather backpack and followed the giggling sounds to the kitchen to say goodbye to her mom and brother. Five-year-old Nick greeted her with a chocolate grin. "Mom's makin' brownies and she's lettin' me lick the bowl."

"Can I have some?"

"Nope."

"Nick." The warning in Susan McGrady's voice changed his mind.

"Okay. Long as you don't be a pig." Nick released his hold on the glass bowl and slid it toward his sister.

"Do I look like a pig?" Jennie snuffled and snorted and blew a raspberry against the side of his neck. Nick wiggled and squealed, arms and legs flying.

"Whoa." She caught him just as he slipped off the tall wicker stool. The spatula slapped a wide streak of chocolate across her cheek.

"Jennie, quit teasing him. You'll end up with brownie mix all over yourself." Mom grabbed a washcloth from a drawer, wet it, and tossed it to Jennie. "You'd better hustle or you'll be late for your appointment."

"I'm going." She washed her face, then scooped up a mass of the silky chocolate mixture with her finger and stuck it in her mouth. When she'd licked her finger clean, she washed her hands in the sink and grabbed her keys from the hook by the kitchen door. "Do you mind if I go over to the Beaumonts' to swim this afternoon?"

"Not a problem as long as you're home by five. Michael's coming over for dinner. We have something we'd like to talk to you about."

"Sure." Jennie's good mood faded as she rummaged

through a clean laundry basket for her swimsuit and a towel. She stuffed them in a canvas beach bag, kissed Mom and Nick goodbye, and left.

"Jennie! Wait!" Nick caught up to her on the porch. "I gotta ax you somethin'."

"Can't it wait till tonight? I have to go."

His bony little shoulders rose and fell in an exaggerated sigh. "I guess so."

"Okay," Jennie lowered herself onto the top step. "I suppose I can spare a couple of minutes."

Nick hunkered down with his elbows resting on his knees. "If Mommy marries Michael and my real daddy comes back, will I have two daddies?"

The question took Jennie by surprise. Nick rarely talked about Dad since Mom brought Michael home. "Not exactly." Jennie pulled Nick onto her lap and hugged him. "Michael would be your stepdad."

"Oh . . . but what if my real dad comes home and finds out that Michael is my other dad? Won't he be sad?"

"Um—I don't think Dad will come back. But I know he'd want you to have a stepdad like Michael. Anyway, I thought you loved Michael?"

"I do—him and me is buddies."

"How come you're asking all these questions about Dad?"

" 'Cause you and Mama never show me his pictures anymore, and I think that would make him sad."

Before Michael came along, she, Nick, and Mom would go through the photo album and talk about Dad's coming back someday. Then Mom decided to get on with her life. End of story. "Tell you what. I miss seeing Dad's pictures too. Maybe tonight we can look at them before you go to bed. But right now, I gotta go."

Nick wrapped his wiry arms around her neck, gave her

one of his super-duper bear hugs, and deposited a chocolate kiss on her mouth.

By the time she reached her Mustang, Jennie felt downright depressed. There were no clouds in the late summer sky; they were all in her head.

It didn't take a genius to figure out what Mom and her fiancé wanted to discuss. They had been engaged on and off for several months, and Jennie suspected tonight's dinner plans included setting a wedding date. At first, Jennie had been furious that her mom would even think of getting married. Now she didn't know what to think.

"Come off it, McGrady," Jennie muttered to herself as she twisted the key in the ignition. "Michael's a great guy."

But he's not Dad. Jennie frowned and tried to put the entire mess out of her mind. Her parents had made their decisions, and there wasn't much she could do about it. Or was there? Maybe if she told Mom that Dad was still alive it would make a difference. *Don't even think it, McGrady. You promised Dad and the government you would keep his secret.*

"It just isn't fair," she said aloud.

"Life isn't fair," her father had responded when she'd said those same words to him.

"Oh, Dad," Jennie murmured, "please come home. Sometimes I wish I hadn't tried to find you. In some ways it was better not knowing."

Dad worked for the DEA, the Drug Enforcement Agency, as an undercover agent and supposedly died five years ago in a plane crash. Besides Jennie, only a few key government officials knew he was still alive. Coming home would pose a danger to him and his family. He'd changed his identity several times. Still, Jennie had this dream that he and Mom would someday get back together. Fat chance of that happening now.

Jennie pulled to a stop at a red light, wishing she could control her emotions as easily as she could her car. Even if

Mom knew Dad was alive, she probably wouldn't change her mind. Her parents were officially divorced—Mom had done that after meeting Michael so she wouldn't have to wait the full seven years it took to have someone declared legally dead.

As Jennie approached Trinity Center, she took a deep breath and shoved her memories and her feelings into the bottom drawer of her mind. The sun glinted off the blue metal roof, giving the multilevel complex the appearance of a peacock's tail. The building housed a private school as well as a church and day-care center. The church sat in the center with the school fanning out on either side—the grade school on one side and the high school on the other. Jennie drove down the steep, winding drive to the far parking lot, pulled into a space near the school office, and jogged inside.

"Hi, Jennie. What brings you here?" Mrs. Talbot's round face dimpled when she smiled. "I don't have your schedule done yet."

"I know. I'm here to see Mr. Mancini." Jennie adjusted the strap of her leather backpack, shifting it more securely over her left shoulder.

"Oh yes. You must be the student he was expecting. Said to send you on back." Mrs. Talbot turned her attention back to her computer and began typing.

"Thanks." Ignoring the butterflies that had mysteriously appeared in her stomach, Jennie hurried down the empty hall. Sunlight poured in through the windows that lined the hall on one side, turning the area into an oven. The air-conditioner did little to curb the powerful effect of solar heat.

The chemistry department was located at the end of the hallway. Jennie paused at the door and took a deep breath. An odd sensation crept up her spine—the kind you get when you know someone's watching you. She looked around, half expecting to see the secretary, or one of the other students.

13

The hall remained empty. Her only companion was her own elongated shadow on the wall.

Jennie shivered. *Stop it, McGrady. You're letting your imagination run wild again.* She was probably just nervous about meeting Mr. Mancini. The chemistry teacher was fairly new to Trinity. He'd come in during the last two weeks of school as a substitute for Dr. Adams, who'd had a stroke. Since Jennie had completed her studies early, she hadn't met him—which was fine with her. From what Lisa had said, he had the personality of a warthog.

Pushing the door to the chemistry lab open, Jennie stepped inside. The lights were out, giving the room the feel of an overcast day. Unlike most of the rooms, this one had only a bank of narrow windows near the roof. One of them had been left open. She paused to switch on the overhead fluorescent lights. "Mr. Mancini? It's me—Jennie McGrady."

The room felt cold next to the overheated hallway. She stepped farther into the room, letting the door close behind her. A pungent odor hung on the air. Cleaning solution maybe, and something else—like a match that had just been lit and blown out. The black counters glistened as though they'd recently been washed. Jennie set her bag on the floor and skimmed her hand across the shiny surface. Still damp.

A shuffling sound from the office at the back of the lab caught her attention. She hurried toward it and knocked. "Mr. Mancini?" she called again. When no one answered, Jennie tried the knob. The door opened easily, but the large, two-desk office was empty. Another door leading to a faculty parking lot stood ajar.

Jennie stepped outside to investigate. A steel gray car sat in a nearby parking space, but there was no sign of a teacher or anyone else. Whoever had been in the office was gone. The small sign on the building identified the space as Mancini's.

"This is too weird," Jennie said aloud. It was almost as if

14

someone had heard her come in and run away when she called. She doubted that person was Mancini. Unless she'd gotten the time wrong. Jennie glanced at her watch. One o'clock. That's when he'd said to meet him.

Jennie shrugged and stepped back into the office. Her curious gaze scanned the room. The smaller desk looked like it hadn't been used in a while. When school started it would be assigned to Mr. Mancini's lab assistant—usually a senior. The computer on Mr. Mancini's desk was on, and Jennie hit the space bar to eliminate the tropical fish screen saver. The screen was a jumble of figures and odd shapes—pentagons, hexagons, and circles. It looked like some sort of formula. She recognized a few of the symbols: NaOH—sodium hydroxide—and Br_2, which was bromine, and HCL or hydrochloric acid. It had been written by someone with a great deal more knowledge about chemistry than she had. Probably her teacher. She hoped it wasn't the makings of a pop quiz.

Mancini had to be around somewhere. An open briefcase sat near the computer. Papers were strewn all over the desk and some had fallen on the floor. Jennie stooped to pick them up and placed them on top of the pile. Maybe that had been the sound she'd heard. Papers falling.

Her teacher could have gone to the rest room or something. But through the back entrance? And why would he leave the door open?

The burglary. Jennie's heart lurched. Of course. What if the thief had come back? Maybe she'd interrupted him.

Wait a minute. Calm down. Don't jump to conclusions. She sank into the teacher's squeaky wooden chair and picked up the phone to call the police. An instant later she set it down. Maybe it wasn't a burglary. "It could have been the janitor," she said aloud, remembering the still-damp counters. "Everything looks spotless in the lab. And Mr. Olsen is hard of hearing."

Jennie took a deep breath and released it. *Okay,* she rationalized. *Mancini's car is in the parking lot, so he has to be around somewhere.* Best to find out before calling the police. Jennie retraced her steps through the lab and out the door. Halfway down the hall she remembered her backpack, thought about going back to retrieve it, and decided she could pick it up later.

"My, that was quick." Mrs. Talbot pushed away from her desk as Jennie approached.

"I haven't seen him yet."

"Oh?"

"Yeah. Kind of strange, really. I heard something in the office, but when I went to check, he wasn't there and the door to the faculty parking lot was open. His car is still there, but I got worried—I mean, he could have just gone out for a few minutes, but I got to thinking about the burglary and everything. Maybe we should call the police."

"Oh, dear, I hate to do that—in case it's a false alarm. Still, it does seem rather strange. When was your meeting?"

"At one." They both looked at the white-faced clock on the wall. It was now one-ten.

Mrs. Talbot frowned. "It's certainly not like Mr. Mancini to be late. He's the most punctual man I've ever met." She grabbed the phone and punched out a three-digit extension. "He isn't answering. Could be he had to step over to the church office for something." She punched out three more numbers. Into the phone she said, "Sarah—is Mr. Mancini over there?"

The church secretary's answer must have been no because Mrs. Talbot's frown lines deepened. "Um . . . we may have a problem. Could I speak with Pastor Dave or Michael?"

Mrs. Talbot focused a concerned gaze on Jennie and started to say something, then spoke into the phone instead. "Yes, Michael. Jennie's here to see Tom. His car is here, but

16

he doesn't seem to be anywhere around. I wondered if you could check the rest room . . . he does have a heart condition, you know, and—yes. Thanks."

"He'll be right over." Miss Talbot hung up.

Jennie felt sick. She hadn't considered the possibility of a heart attack or injury. She hurried out to the hall and reached the men's rest room just as Michael did. He swung open the door and disappeared inside. Seconds later he emerged shaking his head. "He's not there."

Without waiting for a response he jogged past Jennie and Mrs. Talbot and headed for the chemistry department. Jennie raced after him.

"Don't come in," Michael yelled when Jennie pushed open the door a few seconds later.

"Is he hurt?" She glanced around, but saw no sign of Michael or Tom Mancini. "I can do CPR, Michael. If he's had a heart attack—"

"No!" Michael rose from between the two long counters, then came around to her join her. "That won't be necessary, Jennie." He placed an arm around her shoulders and guided her toward the door. "Mr. Mancini is dead."

2

"Dead?" Jennie tried to turn back. "But how do you—I mean, shouldn't we call 9-1-1? Shouldn't we do CPR?"

Michael tightened his hold on her shoulder and escorted her into the hall. "There's nothing either of us can do for him now."

After leading her back to the office and ordering her to stay put, he whispered something to Mrs. Talbot, ducked into the principal's office, and closed the door. She watched him through the open blinds as he picked up the phone. Michael sat on the edge of the desk and rubbed his forehead. Jennie strained to hear his side of the conversation, but the room didn't lend itself to eavesdropping—especially with Mrs. Talbot gasping and moaning in the background.

Michael glanced up and caught Jennie watching him and for a moment neither looked away. Michael was keeping something from her. She could read it in his stunned expression just before he broke eye contact and hung up. Running a hand through his wavy brown hair, he picked up the phone again. A few seconds later he opened the door. "All we can do now is wait." He looked at Jennie and sighed. "I think we'd better talk."

His look made Jennie feel guilty. Like she'd somehow been responsible. Maybe she had in a way. If she'd thought to look behind the counter, maybe . . . "D-did he have a heart attack?" She dropped into one of the chairs nearest the office door.

Michael folded his hands and closed his eyes as if saying a prayer. He looked up a moment later. "It's—there's no easy way to say this."

"Michael, what's going on?"

"It wasn't a heart attack. Mr. Mancini's been shot."

"Shot?" She couldn't have heard right. "Are you sure?"

Michael nodded. "I've called the police. They should be here any minute."

Jennie stared at the window behind him still trying to take it in. "But that means—" She couldn't quite finish the sentence. If Michael was right, Jennie may have been a breath away from witnessing a murder.

———

Within minutes the entire complex had been invaded by swarms of police officers. At least a dozen official cars were parked at odd angles in front of the high school. They'd be securing the crime scene with their yellow tape, taking pictures of everything in the lab, dusting for fingerprints. And they'd be asking questions.

Fingerprints. Jennie's heart slammed into her throat and began beating so hard she could hardly breathe. Her fingerprints. Her backpack.

She wanted to run, even looked for an escape route. She hadn't done anything wrong, but the police might think otherwise. *Oh, come on, McGrady. Don't go jumping to conclusions. They're not going to think you did it.*

"Jennie?"

"Wha—" Her thoughts exploded as she caught sight of the blue uniform and the holstered gun.

Michael was standing beside a wiry young woman with short, dishwater blond hair. "This is Jennie McGrady—the student I was telling you about," he explained to the officer, then turned to Jennie. "Jennie, this is Officer Phelps. She'd like to ask you a few questions. Are you okay with that?"

"Yeah." Jennie's voice sounded hollow, like she was in a tunnel. She stared at her folded hands, wondering how they got that way.

The officer continued to stand. She wrote something in her notebook, then said, "I understand you had a meeting with Mr. Mancini at one this afternoon."

Jennie swallowed hard. Her mouth felt dry. She wanted to look the officer in the eyes and say yes, but the word wouldn't come out and her eyes refused to travel up past the name badge. She could only nod in response. *What is wrong with you, McGrady?*

"Can you tell me what happened?"

She nodded again. "Um—would you mind if I got a drink of water first?"

Officer Phelps scrutinized Jennie and, after a few torturous seconds, said, "Sure. Go ahead."

Jennie stood up on legs about as sturdy as a block of Jell-O and made her way out of the office. After a short walk to the fountain and back, she felt almost normal. *Just tell them the truth, McGrady,* she reminded herself. *They're not going to blame you.*

"I'm sorry," she said as she returned to the office. "My mouth was so dry I could hardly talk." Jennie's gaze shifted from Officer Phelps to the young man standing next to her. The concerned look in his blue eyes melted her fears. "Rocky." She even managed a half-smile.

"You two know each other?" Phelps folded her arms across her chest, her dark brown gaze shifting from one to the other.

"Jennie and I go way back." Rocky rubbed his chin. "I heard she was here and thought I'd better check it out. Jennie has a habit of playing junior detective."

"I was about to question her," Phelps said. "Want to stick around?"

Oh, please stay, Jennie pleaded silently. *Please*. Somehow having Rocky there made her feel more at ease and in control.

"Sure. I've got a few questions of my own. Like what were you doing here? I thought I told you not to get involved in the burglary investigation."

Jennie shook her head. "I wasn't. Honest. After you told me about the meth labs, I decided to take your advice. I was just here to talk to Mr. Mancini about my chemistry project."

"I know you, Jennie. I know how your mind works."

Rocky didn't believe her. Jennie felt the panic rising again. Okay, so maybe she wasn't being entirely honest with him or herself. She hadn't intended to investigate the theft, but if the subject had come up she might have asked a few questions. "I came to the school to talk to Mr. Mancini about chemistry. Only, when I got here I couldn't find him." Jennie went on to tell them about the noise she'd heard, trying to retrace her steps and give them every detail she could remember.

"You were in the lab, but you didn't find the body?" Phelps paused in her note taking, suspicion evident in her serious features.

"N-no—I never dreamed he'd be dead. I just thought he'd forgotten our appointment or had to make a quick trip to the rest room or maybe he got held up talking to someone."

"Mrs. Talbot told us you were concerned about a second burglary."

"Yes. Um—I wasn't sure what to think with the back door standing open. I started to call you guys but decided I'd better talk to Mrs. Talbot first. That's why I went back to the office."

"Okay." Phelps flipped back through her notes, then asked for and wrote down Jennie's address and phone number. "I think that'll do it for now." She glanced up at Rocky. "I'm heading back over to the lab. You coming?"

"In a minute."

Phelps hesitated as though she wanted to say something, then turned abruptly and left. Rocky watched her go, then settled his gaze on Jennie. "You going to be okay?"

"I—I think so. I feel terrible about not finding Mr. Mancini's body when I was in the lab. If I'd gotten to him I might have been able to—"

"Don't. It's better you didn't see it. Of course, it is possible the shooting took place after you'd came back here to talk to Mrs. Talbot."

"I don't think so. There was this funny smell in the lab—disinfectant and something else—like sulfur. I didn't think much about it at the time, but it could have been from a gun being shot. I mean—I didn't hear a shot, but the killer could have used a silencer."

"I know I've said this before, Jennie, but you've got to stop getting involved in these criminal cases. You've been lucky so far, but sooner or later—"

"I wasn't getting involved. I told you—"

"Look," Rocky interrupted, "maybe you did go to see Mancini about schoolwork, or maybe you went to question him about the theft. It doesn't really matter. The thing is, you could have been killed in there. And from what you've told us, the danger isn't over. If the guy was still in the office when you walked in, and if you announced your arrival like you said, he knows who you are."

"But I didn't see anything."

"Maybe not, but he doesn't know that."

"Can I go now?"

"Not yet. Lieutenant Rastovski will probably want to talk to you after he finishes up in the lab."

"Well, can I at least get my book bag? I left it in the lab."

"That was yours?" He shook his head. "I don't think

22

you'll be seeing it for a while. It'll be processed as part of the evidence."

"Oh no. You can't—it's got my notebook and my keys—and my driver's license."

"Sorry, Jennie, you know the routine. I'm sure someone around here can give you a ride home."

"Am I a suspect?"

"Everyone is. You, Michael, even Mrs. Talbot."

"That's ridiculous."

Rocky shifted from one foot to the other. "A man's been found dead. We have to pursue every possible lead."

"I know. It's just that—"

The radio hooked to his collar made a scratchy sound and he ducked his head to talk into it. "David 4—on my way." More static.

Jennie wondered how they ever managed to understand each other.

"Ten-four." Rocky spoke into his lapel mike again, then squeezed her shoulder. "I gotta get back to work. You hang in there. Um—if you need to talk about what happened—well, just let me know."

"Sure."

After promising to call her later, Rocky mumbled something unintelligible and left.

She was alone in the office now. Both Mrs. Talbot and Michael had disappeared. Probably being questioned some more. At the far end of the hall, several police officers milled around outside the lab. She thought about heading down that way to ask a few questions of her own but decided it wouldn't do any good.

Unable to sit still, Jennie paced from the office door to the main entrance, then wandered down to the drinking fountain. She sipped at the cool water, then wiped the drips off her chin with the back of her hand. A few minutes later she went back to the office again, then dropped into the principal's leather chair and swung it around so she could look outside. The window faced a wooded park, and Jennie focused on a bed of flowers that circled one of the trees.

Although she tried not to think about what had happened, Jennie's curious nature kept asking questions. Who killed Mr. Mancini and why? Could the burglars have struck again? Had Mr. Mancini witnessed it? What if she had walked in a few minutes earlier—what would she have seen?

Her thoughts raced with possibilities. In one scenario the gunman turned on her as she opened the door. It gave her teacher the break he needed. He tackled the gunman. The gun went off and instead of the bullet striking Mr. Mancini it went straight into Jennie's heart.

"No." She shoved the disturbing scene aside. "It wouldn't have happened like that."

"Like what?"

Jennie whirled around in the chair, her heart hammering. "I—I didn't hear anyone come in. I was just thinking."

"Apparently." The man standing in front of the desk was tall and angular. His skin had the bronzed color of someone who spent a lot of time in the sun. He cleared his throat. "You must be Jennie McGrady. Officer Phelps told me I'd find you here."

She nodded. Her gaze drifted from his gray-streaked black hair and mustache to his nearly black eyes. He looked to be about Gram's age—maybe younger.

"I'm Lieutenant Rastovski." He raised his arm and set her book bag on the desk. "I believe this is yours."

Jennie smiled. "Yeah. Thanks. Rocky—um, Officer Rockwell—said I might not get it back for a while. Does this mean I'm in the clear?"

"Looks that way. From what we can determine so far, it looks like a suicide."

3

"Suicide? But that doesn't make sense. Why would he make an appointment with me, then kill himself?" Jennie tipped her head back against the chair.

The lieutenant shook his head. "Who knows? People do crazy things. Maybe he forgot he had an appointment."

Jennie doubted that. "Are you sure it was suicide? I mean, how can you tell?"

"He left a note, for one thing. The position of the body— and his gun. I won't go into details, but so far the evidence is consistent with a suicide."

"What about the noise I heard in the office?"

"Noise?"

"I told Officer Phelps about it. I was in the lab and heard something. I called out, but no one answered. Then I went to check. The outer door was open about six inches, but no one was there or in the parking lot."

The lieutenant frowned and tugged at the corner of his mustache. "Could have been the wind."

"Maybe. There were some papers scattered on the floor. I picked them up," Jennie winced, then added, "but that was before I knew about the body. I do know better than to tamper with evidence."

"I see. Hopefully it won't matter in this case. The medical examiner's looking at suicide as well. Once she's done the autopsy we'll know for sure. Wish they were all this easy."

Call it a hunch, call it intuition, but something didn't feel right about labeling Mr. Mancini's death a suicide. She thought about enlightening the lieutenant, but doubted the guy would listen. And what did she know anyway? So she'd heard a noise. Jennie stared at Rastovski's striped tie. *The wind? Maybe*. A gust of wind could have scattered the papers on the floor. *Give it up, McGrady. Let the police do their job*.

"Can I go now?" Jennie glanced up to meet his eyes. He reminded her of someone—her cousin, Hazen White Cloud. She wondered if he might be of Indian or Spanish descent. Hazen was half Irish and half Nez Perce Indian. Lieutenant Rastovski looked like an older version and might even have been as handsome at one time. Now, though, his face had more of a rugged, lived-in look.

"We'll need to get prints so we can cross-check them with others we find at the crime scene, then you can go." The scar that ran along his jaw moved as he spoke.

Jennie found herself wondering how it happened. Law enforcement could be a dangerous business. For a moment her mind flickered back to her father. Was he still alive? Would anyone notify her if he'd been wounded? Jennie shook the macabre thoughts aside and focused back on what Rastovski had told her—something about fingerprints.

"You already have my prints on file."

His forehead creased in a disapproving frown. "Really."

"I've never been arrested, if that's what you're thinking. A few weeks ago my brother was kidnapped. The police fingerprinted all of us for comparison prints."

The lieutenant looked as if he meant to start questioning her all over again but only nodded. "Then you're free to go." He retrieved a business card from his shirt pocket and handed it to her. "Just in case you remember something or want to talk to me. I'll be in touch."

Jennie had almost made it to her car when a familiar bespectacled guy with a camera jogged toward her. "I might have known you'd be out here." She opened the door to the Mustang and tossed her bag in the backseat.

"I could say the same about you." Gavin Winslow—a skinny version of Clark Kent—grinned and raised his camera. "You must be the unidentified student the police were talking about."

"If I am, I'd just as soon stay that way." Jennie stuck her hand over the lens. "Come on, Gavin, give it a rest." Gavin worked as a part-time reporter at *The Oregonian*, Portland's primary newspaper. He was also a student at Trinity High and during the school year wrote and published the school paper.

"Sorry. Um, listen, I've got about all the dirt they're going to give me. I was hoping I could catch a ride back into town. Left my bike at the office." Gavin brushed a hand through his straight dark hair, drawing it off his forehead. His face was flushed and sweaty.

"How'd you get out here?"

"Hitched a ride with one of the other reporters." He shrugged. "The jerk left without me." Jennie sighed and looked at her watch. Two-thirty. She didn't want to drive back to Portland, especially with Gavin. He'd spend the entire time drilling her. What she really wanted to do was relax, swim a few laps, and laze in the sun. "I wasn't going home. I'm meeting Lisa over at Allison and B.J.'s. If you're not in a hurry you could come swimming with us and I could run you home after." She'd made the invitation knowing he wouldn't accept. Guilt slipped in and twisted at one of the knots still coiled in her stomach.

"I wish I could, but I gotta get back to the office." Gavin took a step back, looking like he'd been the last one picked for a baseball team. "Um—you go ahead. I'll see if I can find someone—"

"Okay, okay. I'll take you."

"Are you sure?" Without waiting for a response, he ran around to the passenger side of the car, yanked open the door, set his battered tan camera bag in the back, and folded his lanky form into the front seat. "I wouldn't want you to go out of your way."

"Yeah, right." Jennie winced as she came in contact with the hot black vinyl. "It's hot enough to bake bread in here."

Gavin wasn't listening. He read through the notes he'd taken on a steno pad, then wrote some more. Within a couple of minutes the air-conditioner had kicked in. Jennie ignored her passenger and concentrated on maneuvering around the empty police car that nearly blocked the driveway.

Once they were out on the main road, Gavin jotted the name Curtis Bolton off to the side of his notes and underlined it, then snapped the notebook closed. It was only then that Jennie realized he probably knew more about Mr. Mancini's death than she did.

"Did you get your story?" she asked.

"What?" he glanced at her, then back outside. "Oh yeah. I guess."

"Did you know him? Mr. Mancini, I mean."

Gavin nodded. "Some. Finished up the last couple weeks of chemistry with him. I questioned him last week about the break-in."

"And—"

"Nothing." He chewed on his bottom lip.

Jennie had a dozen questions but didn't ask them. Gavin didn't seem very talkative. She remembered something her grandmother had told her about getting people to open up. *"Let the silence work for you,"* Gram had said. *"Just listen and eventually they'll start talking."*

Gram was one of the wisest people Jennie knew. She'd retired from the police department a few years ago to become a travel writer. Gram did other things too, like occasionally working as a secret agent. Jennie made a mental note to call her later. She wanted to get Gram's views on the chemistry teacher's death. She also wanted to talk to Gram about Mom and Michael.

"They tell you it was a suicide?"

Gavin's question scattered her thoughts. She nodded.

"Hard to believe. I didn't know him all that well." Gavin tapped his pen against his note pad. "When we first got the call he'd been shot, I thought maybe it was related to that burglary."

"It still could be. They're not saying anything for sure yet." Jennie checked behind her for traffic, then eased onto the eastbound lanes of the Sunset Highway.

"True." He eyed her for a long moment. "So, what were you doing there, anyway?"

"I was supposed to have a meeting with Mr. Mancini to decide what I wanted to do for my project this quarter. I also wanted to set up a schedule. I had things pretty well worked out with Dr. Adams, but Mr. Mancini was having a hard time with my part-time status."

"I'm not surprised. The guy was totally inflexible. Did you ever meet him?"

"Just over the phone. He came in after I'd already finished my chemistry module. I left school a couple weeks early so I could go with Gram to Florida."

"Lucky you."

"Sounds as though you don't like him."

"We got along okay—but then, I like chemistry. Bolton and I are about the only two who did."

"Curtis Bolton? I noticed you wrote his name down in your notebook."

"He knew Mancini as well as anyone—thought I'd talk to him—see if he can shed any light on what happened." Gavin reached forward and turned the fan down a couple of notches. "Hope you don't mind. It's getting a little cool."

"No, we can shut it off and open the windows if you

want." He did. Jennie switched the lever to vent and cranked down her window.

The wind felt good whipping through her hair. If it hadn't been for Mr. Mancini she'd have rated the day a perfect ten. Sunshine, about 72 degrees, a slight breeze. The dark clouds of death had plunged it down to a two. She didn't want to think about Mr. Mancini, or why he'd killed himself, or why someone might have killed him.

Glancing over at her passenger, Jennie smiled. "Sure you don't want to go swimming?"

"I'd like to, but I have to finish up my story." He frowned, rubbed his forehead, and left his hand over his eyes. "I don't know if I can write this one, Jen. I'm a reporter, right? And I'm supposed to be objective—you know, detached. But I can't help thinking about him and wondering how he could have done something like that."

"Yeah, me too." Jennie hoped Gavin wasn't going to cry. She'd probably end up blubbering as well.

"Do you want to help me investigate?" Gavin asked.

"What?"

"I gotta know why he killed himself. What motivated him. Guys like Mancini don't commit suicide without a reason. And to use a gun. It's so messy. Besides, I still think there might be a connection to the burglary."

Jennie shook her head. "I'm sure the police will come up with an explanation."

"Yeah, right." Gavin turned to look out the window.

"I understand he left a note. Did they tell you what it said?"

"No."

"How come you're being so secretive?"

"How come you're asking so many questions? I thought you weren't interested."

"I'm curious. I want to know what's going on too."

He grinned. "I knew you couldn't resist. Maybe we can

get together after dinner and I'll show you what I've got so far."

"Call me first. Michael's coming over for dinner."

"You got it."

A few minutes later Jennie dropped Gavin off at *The Oregonian* and headed back out to the Lake Oswego area and the Beaumont Mansion. Not wanting to mull over the chemistry teacher's demise, she cranked the radio up and sang along with half a dozen contemporary artists. The songs didn't help. Maybe swimming would.

The Beaumont house sat back from the road, on a hill—like an elegant dollhouse on an expanse of plush green carpet. Driving up the long driveway Jennie waved at Manuel and his son, Rafael, who were weeding one of numerous rose gardens. The grounds keeper waved back. "*Hola*, Jennie," he called when she parked the car and got out. "The girls have been waiting for you. I have orders to tell you to go straight back to the pool."

"Thanks." Jennie paused on the way in to stick her nose into one of the fragrant salmon-colored blossoms that lined the walk.

When she looked up, Rafael glowered at her, and Jennie wondered what she'd done to deserve his anger. She didn't know him all that well. He and his mom and dad and four brothers and sisters had come from Mexico just a few weeks before. The Beaumonts were sponsoring them and had provided jobs and a home—the guest cottage behind the main house. Jennie thought about confronting him about his sullen attitude, then decided against it. Maybe he was just in a bad mood. Maybe he was jealous and would rather be swimming than pulling weeds. She could understand that.

Jennie grabbed her beach bag, let herself in, and hurried into the bathroom off the kitchen to change. The bathroom had two doors, the second of which led to the patio and pool area. Jennie pulled on her blue knit suit, hung her clothes on

31

one of the many wooden hooks, and stepped outside.

"It's about time you got here." Lisa scrambled to her feet and hurried toward Jennie. "We heard about Mr. Mancini."

"I can't believe you were actually there." Allison stayed in her chair under the umbrella and, like the princess she was, waited for Jennie to reach her. Her sky-blue gaze traveled up to Jennie's face. "Are you okay?"

Jennie nodded. "I guess. How'd you hear about it so fast?"

"Michael called Dad." Allison tipped her head to one side to escape the sun, sending her straight, silky blond pageboy into motion. "Mom and Dad went to be with Mrs. Mancini and Alexis."

B.J., who'd been lying facedown on a chaise lounge, turned around and sat up, brushing damp curls out of her face. "So what gives, McGrady? You go in to question the new teach about the theft and he ends up dead."

Jennie sighed. "First of all, I didn't go in to question him. Secondly, I have no idea what gives." She eased into one of the white wrought-iron patio chairs, reached for the pitcher of pink lemonade, and snatched an empty glass from the tray. "I got there after it happened—at least I think so." After guzzling down half the lemonade and waiting for Lisa to sit, Jennie told the story the same way she'd told it to Officer Phelps and Lieutenant Rastovski.

"Any idea who might have killed him?" B.J. flipped a chair around and straddled it, draping her tan arms across the chairback.

"The police think he committed suicide."

"No kidding." B.J. whistled. "You just never know."

Lisa hugged herself. "I'm glad I didn't go with you."

Allison leaned forward, arms on the table. "It's just awful. I don't understand how someone could do that. I mean, think about his poor wife and Alex. They must be devastated."

"I doubt it." The sarcastic tone in B.J.'s voice brought Jennie up short.

"B.J., that's a terrible thing to say." Allison shot her younger sister a mind-your-manners look.

"Well, it's true. Which is why the suicide bit surprises me. Now, if you'd told me Mancini had been murdered, I wouldn't have any trouble believing it. And I can tell you, I'd put Alex and her mother right at the top of the suspect list." She dismounted the chair in much the same way one would get off a horse, walked over to the pool, and dove in.

4

"Honestly, Jennie, I don't know why B.J. would say something like that." Allison scowled at her sister's surfacing form. "Alex and Mrs. Mancini are both really nice people."

"Sounds like you know them pretty well."

"You could say that. Mrs. Mancini and our stepmom met at the Trinity women's retreat in June and really hit it off. They meet at the mall for lunch all the time, so Alex, B.J., and I hang out together—when we can get B.J. to come. You know how she hates to shop."

"Yeah, I know." Jennie glanced at Lisa and grinned. Lisa could relate all too well. Jennie wasn't crazy about the shopping thing either. Why shop when you didn't have money to buy anything? Of course these days B.J. had plenty of money. So did Jennie for that matter—not as much, but enough to put herself through college and law school. She'd been paid well for a couple of her crime-solving efforts. Still, old habits were hard to break. Besides, why spend money on stuff you didn't really need?

"Did you meet them, Lis?" Jennie asked.

Lisa shrugged. "At church. They seemed okay. Alex is a total snob, but other than that—"

"Lisa!" Allison swung around to object.

"Well, she is. She acts different to different people. She's nice to us—but I've seen the way she snubs some of the kids

34

at the mall—like she's too good to be seen with them."

Jennie sighed, then turning back to Allison, said, "Maybe B.J. saw some things you didn't. Anyway, we can talk about that later. I'm going for a swim."

Tossing her towel and watch on the nearest chaise lounge, Jennie walked to the edge of the Olympic-sized pool and watched her friend swim. Did B.J. actually know something about the situation, or was she just trying to goad them? Jennie had a hunch B.J.'s and Lisa's assessments were closer to the truth than Allison's. Not that Allison would lie—she just tended to overlook the darker side of life. Probably because, unlike B.J., she'd never seen much of it.

The sisters were about as different as siblings could get. Part of that was personality, but a lot had to do with how they were raised. They were victims of divorce. The first Mrs. Beaumont had run off when Allison was a year old. What she never bothered to tell Allison's dad was that she was pregnant. B.J. never knew about her dad and sister until her mom died and a social worker found a birth certificate. B.J. had spent most of her fifteen years trying to survive, sometimes even living on the streets and going hungry. Allison had always had everything she needed and more. Jennie tended to trust B.J.'s instincts—especially since they often mirrored her own.

Jennie climbed on the diving board, reached the end in two strides, and dove in. For a few heavenly moments, the cool, clear water washed away the awful sense of being held prisoner. By what, Jennie didn't know. She hadn't even been able to put a name to the oppressive feelings until now. She surfaced, hauled in air, swam ten lengths of the pool, then stopped at the shallow end to catch her breath. *You're out of shape, McGrady.*

"You going to be on the swim team again this year?" B.J. splashed up to Jennie and hoisted herself out of the pool, then sat on the edge, dangling her feet in the water.

"Probably."

"So am I."

Jennie grinned. "Really? Coach Dayton got to you, huh?"

"No, I just decided you needed a little competition."

Jennie backed away from the side and sent a wall of water flying in B.J.'s direction. She hit her target and then some. Lisa shrieked as the cool water hit her sun-warmed back. "I'll get you for that." Lisa hit the tile running and cannonballed into the pool.

Their horseplay took on a serious note when B.J. suggested volleyball. They strung a net across the pool and paired off, Jennie and Lisa against Allison and B.J.

Some time later, Jennie climbed out of the pool to check the time. "Oh, wow, it's five-thirty," she moaned. "Mom's going to kill me. I was supposed to be home by five."

"I'd better go too." Lisa slipped a matching skirt over her swimsuit. The neon tropical fish on her skirt came to life as she towel dried her hair.

Jennie pulled an oversized T-shirt on over her suit, slipped on sandals, and scurried into the bathroom to get her clothes. After giving Mom a call to say she was on her way home, Jennie and her cousin said their goodbyes and walked out to their cars.

"What are you going to do now?" Lisa asked.

"Go home."

"No, I mean about Mr. Mancini."

"Nothing." Jennie opened the door of her Mustang and turned to face Lisa. "I know that seems strange coming from me, but I don't want to know what happened to Mr. Mancini. I don't want to think about it."

"Really got to you, didn't it?"

Jennie swallowed back an unexpected flow of tears. "Yeah, I guess it did."

"I'm sorry I brought it up."

"It's okay. Um—we'll talk later, okay? I gotta get home

before Mom decides to ground me for the next six months."

"Okay, I'll see you later." Lisa's green gaze drifted from Jennie's face back toward the house. She smiled, her already flushed cheeks glowing brighter.

Jennie turned to see what or who she was looking at. "Rafael?" The gardener leaned on the hoe and watched them. His mood apparently hadn't improved.

"Isn't he a hunk? I thought Brad was cute, but Rafael is—I don't know. So mysterious and—" She sighed and had that dreamy look in her eyes Jennie recognized all too well.

"I thought you were giving Brad another chance." Brad had been Lisa's boyfriend most of the summer.

Lisa wrinkled her freckled nose. "We broke up—it was mutual."

"So, have you and Rafael gone out?"

"Not yet. I keep hoping he'll ask. I think he wants to, but for some reason . . ."

"Maybe he's embarrassed. I mean, he's a gardener and you're the boss's daughter's friend. That could be intimidating."

"That shouldn't matter. I think he's just shy."

"So go talk to him."

Lisa grinned. "You sound just like B.J. Maybe I will." Instead of getting into the car, Lisa started back toward the garden. "Wish me luck."

"As if you need it," Jennie murmured. Lisa had no trouble getting guys. She was cute and bubbly and sweet and altogether a very nice person.

Jennie put the towel over the black vinyl, tossed in her beach bag, folded herself into the car, and drove off. Normally it took twenty minutes to make the drive from the Lake Oswego area where the Beaumonts and Lisa lived to the Crystal Lake area on the east side of the Willamette River. Normally. Rush-hour traffic slowed her to a crawl, and the commute took over an hour.

By the time she finally got home, Mom and Michael were clearing off the dinner dishes. After the grueling drive, the last thing Jennie needed was a lecture on the importance of being on time, but that's what she got. Thanks to Michael, it was a shortened version.

"Being late was bad enough, Jennie," Mom said as she neared the end of her speech. "What really upsets me is that you didn't call me."

"I did—from Allison's."

"I'm talking about the incident at the school. My daughter and fiancé find a . . ." She glanced down at Nick and spelled b-o-d-y. ". . . and I have to hear about it on the news."

"Honey, I told you I was sorry. I should have called." Michael slipped an arm around Mom's shoulders. "It's just that with all the meetings and arrangements . . ."

Mom folded her arms and stepped away from him. "I don't want to hear any excuses from either of you." She grabbed a platter of leftover salmon from the table and headed for the kitchen. "Jennie, I'll leave the food out. Fix yourself a plate. When you've finished eating you can do the dishes."

Michael and Jennie looked at each other. He had a kind of what-do-I-do-now look on his face and Jennie felt sorry for him. But not sorry enough to reassure him. For a moment Jennie found herself hoping maybe he'd change his mind about marrying Mom. "What can I say? Mom's got a terrible temper."

"I know." He smiled. "But she's beautiful when she's mad."

Jennie rolled her eyes and headed for the kitchen. People in love were hopeless.

Having worked up an appetite swimming, Jennie piled her plate with grilled salmon, wild rice, and green beans, covered it, and set it in the microwave to heat. While she waited, she finished off the remaining Caesar salad and set the bowl on the counter next to the sink. She ate dinner alone. Well, not quite. She could hear Michael reading to Nick in the other room. Bernie, Nick's St. Bernard puppy, looked bored as he ambled into the kitchen. He sat quietly beside her stool and watched her eat, his sad brown eyes filled with longing.

"Don't look at me like that," she said. "I can't feed you. Dogs aren't supposed to have fish—too many bones."

He whimpered.

"Hey, I'm sorry. I don't make the rules."

"Woof." He wagged his tail and lifted his left paw, then tapped Jennie's foot.

"You don't make it easy, do you?" She broke off a piece of salmon and, after checking it carefully for bones, surrendered the delicate pink morsel. Bernie gently licked it off her hand, then sat back down.

Six bites later Jennie held up her empty hands. "That's it. All gone." With Bernie still looking for a handout, she gathered her dishes and took them to the sink.

She'd almost finished the dishes when the phone rang. "I'll get it." Jennie half expected it to be Lisa calling to say she was going out with Rafael. Maybe that's why she didn't recognize the voice at first.

"Jennie, this is Maddie Winslow, Gavin's mom."

"Oh, hi, Mrs. Winslow. How's it going?"

"All right. Is Gavin there? He hasn't come home and I'm getting worried."

"No. I haven't seen him since this afternoon. I dropped him off at *The Oregonian* around three." Jennie tucked the phone between her chin and shoulder and began washing off the counter.

"His boss said he left there at four-thirty. I don't know where else to call."

"Did you try Courtney's?" Courtney Evans was Gavin's girlfriend.

"She's working and hasn't seen him all day. I sent his dad out to check the roads. I hate having him ride his bike in all that traffic."

It was a long way from downtown Portland to the Winslows' farm in east county. "I'm sure he's okay, Mrs. Winslow. He may still be working on the story about Mr. Mancini."

"Oh yes. Wasn't that awful? I don't know what the world's coming to. Well, I won't keep you. If you hear from Gavin, tell him to call me."

Jennie promised she would and hung up.

After finishing her kitchen chores, Jennie headed into the living room. Apparently Mom and Michael had made up. They were snuggled together watching television. Nick had fallen asleep on Michael's lap.

"Who was on the phone, honey?" Mom had apparently forgiven her too.

"Maddie Winslow. She was looking for Gavin."

Mom twisted around to look at her. "Oh, he called earlier. Around six. I'm sorry, with dinner and everything, I forgot."

"Where is he? What did he want?"

"Just wanted you to call him. Something about a major breakthrough."

"Did he leave a number?"

"It's on the pad by the phone."

Back in the kitchen, Jennie tore the number off the scratch pad, then raced upstairs to her private phone. She punched out the numbers thinking they seemed familiar. After a couple of rings an answering machine came on. "You have reached the offices of Trinity High School. Our office hours are—"

Jennie hung up. Her stomach tied itself in at least a dozen knots. She set the scrap of paper beside the phone and sank onto her bed. Why had Gavin called from the school at that time of night? How could he have gotten in?

She didn't want to think the worst, but what could she do? Her mind kept digging up bits and pieces that seemed to form a dark and frightening picture. The theft at the school, Rocky's warning about clandestine labs, Gavin's snoopy nature, and Mr. Mancini's death.

Gavin Winslow was in trouble.

5

Okay, McGrady. Just calm down. If Gavin was at the school office he couldn't have been alone. Maybe Mrs. Talbot had stayed late. Jennie pulled out the school directory and called Mrs. Talbot. No answer. After leaving a message on the machine, she ran back downstairs to talk to Michael and nearly collided with him on the stairs. He and Mom were bringing Nick up to bed.

Nick, head on Michael's shoulder, yawned and reached for Jennie. "You were s'posed to show me the pictures."

Jennie brushed a lock of dark hair from his forehead and kissed him on the nose. "Too late tonight, Buddy. We'll look at them tomorrow."

Surprisingly, he didn't argue.

"Michael, I need to talk to you," she whispered and followed them to Nick's room.

After settling Nick onto the bed, Mom stayed to get Nick into his pajamas. Michael came back into the hall. "What's going on? You look worried."

"I am—about Gavin." She explained the phone message and added, "I thought maybe you'd seen him."

Michael shook his head. "He shouldn't have been in the school. Mrs. Talbot left at four-thirty. Unless someone with a key was with him he couldn't have gotten in without setting off the alarm."

42

"Could he have gotten a key?"

"Not likely. I'd better make some calls. He may have met someone there."

Jennie nodded. "While you're doing that I'll call his mom."

Back in her room, Jennie looked up Gavin's number. As it rang, she closed her eyes. *Oh, please God, let him be home. Please.*

"Hello!"

Jennie could tell by the worried note in Mrs. Winslow's voice that Gavin hadn't come back. She took a deep breath and told her about Gavin's phone call.

"I don't understand why he'd give you the number at the school. How could he have gotten in? I'm sure Mrs. Talbot leaves around four."

"Actually, she went home at four-thirty. I talked to Michael and he's calling some of the other staff members. I thought you should know."

"Thank you. Um—could you let me know if Michael finds anything? Maybe I'll call Mrs. Talbot at home. She could have gone back—"

"I already did. There's no answer." An image of the secretary and Gavin lying dead in the school office slammed into her mind. Jennie willed it to go away. *Stop it, McGrady. You've been reading too many mysteries. It didn't happen.* But it could have.

"I suppose it's too soon to call the police."

Jennie didn't know what to tell her. "Um—maybe we should wait and see what Michael finds out."

"Yes. I'll do that. Thank you."

After hanging up, Jennie went back downstairs. She found Michael in the living room, phone in hand. "I see. Okay, thanks. Yeah, I'll let you know."

"Did you find out anything?" Jennie asked when he hung up.

43

"No one's seen him, and all the keys are accounted for except Mrs. Talbot's and Tom Mancini's. The police should have Mr. Mancini's."

"What about Mrs. Talbot? Any idea where she might be?"

"No. She was still pretty shaken over Mancini's death when she left. Might have gone to a friend's."

"Or she might be at the school." The horrible images of Mrs. Talbot and Gavin hovered again in the periphery of her mind. "I think we should drive over there and take a look around."

"Might not be a bad idea."

"Drive over where?" Mom's gaze darted from Michael to Jennie. "What's going on?"

"Gavin Winslow hasn't been home this evening and Mrs. Talbot isn't home," Michael answered. "That number he gave you was for the school."

"Have you thought about calling the police to check things out?"

Michael ran a hand through his hair. "Yes. But I hate to involve them unnecessarily."

"Unnecessarily?" Mom heaved a deep sigh. "Let me get this straight. You've had burglary—and a suicide—and now Gavin is missing? What are you waiting for?"

Michael frowned. "Susan, please try to understand. We've been getting a lot of bad press lately. Our attendance is down. We just can't afford to have the papers running more negative stories about the school. I'm just going to run over and see if everything is okay."

"All right, fine. Do what you have to do."

"Thanks, Mom. We won't be too long."

"Hold it!" Mom grabbed Jennie's arm. "You're not going anywhere."

"But Gavin—"

"No."

"Your mother's right, Jennie."

44

"But you said—"

"I said it was a good idea. For me—not for you." He grabbed his keys off the dining room table. "I'll call."

"Michael." Mom stopped him at the door. "Be careful."

Michael nodded, then folded her into his arms and kissed her. Jennie plodded into the living room and flopped into the recliner.

A few seconds later she heard the front door close. Mom walked into the living room, picked up the cups they'd left on the coffee table, and went into the kitchen.

Jennie waited for her mother to join her and deliver another lecture. Seven minutes passed and Mom still hadn't come back. Curious, Jennie unfolded her arms and headed into the dining room. She stopped when she reached the entry to the kitchen.

Mom was sitting at the table reading. Beside her Bible and devotional book sat a large chocolate brownie with whipped topping and a cup of tea. A second brownie and teacup sat in front of an empty chair. Jennie's annoyance faded into a smile. She should have known.

"I was about to start without you." Mom closed her Bible, set it to the side, and pulled the cream-topped brownie toward her.

"Yeah, right. I'll bet you already had one." Jennie drew out the chair next to Mom and sat down.

Mom smiled. "I did—after dinner."

"What kind of tea did you make?" Jennie lifted the cosy off the teapot and poured the greenish liquid into her cup.

"Your favorite."

Jennie held the cup to her lips and sipped. As the delicate peppermint scent drifted into her nostrils, she felt herself relax. Of all the traditions Gram had passed down to her family, this was the best. *Tea quiets the soul*, Gram would tell them. And it did. Over the years they'd solved a lot of problems over tea.

"You've had a rough day." Mom picked up her fork and scooped up a dollop of whipped topping.

Jennie sighed. "Yeah." She speared a piece of the moist brownie and popped it into her mouth, then ate several more bites before speaking again.

"Mom—"

"Jennie—" They both spoke at once and laughed at each other.

"You go first," Mom said.

"I just wanted to tell you I'm sorry about not getting home on time and for not calling you about Mr. Mancini. What were you going to say?"

"Just that I'm sorry too. I should have been more understanding. I didn't know about your teacher until I watched the five-o'clock news and couldn't believe it. And to have you both involved—I'm not sure who I was more angry with, you or Michael. Then when you didn't come home . . ."

"I don't know why I didn't call you. I guess I kind of thought Michael had. When it first happened he called the police, then Beaumonts'. I thought he called you too. Guess I should have asked."

"Hmm." Mom finished a mouthful of brownie, then asked, "Do you feel like talking about it?"

"What?"

"Mr. Mancini. It must have been terrible for you. Michael said you felt guilty you didn't find him first and that you were thinking you might have been able to help."

"I did. I still do." Jennie set her fork down.

"Oh, sweetheart." Mom reached for Jennie's hand. "From what Michael told me, Mr. Mancini had to have died instantly."

Jennie brought the cup to her lips and let the soothing tea warm her insides. "I can't stop thinking about it. It's like this voice inside me keeps telling me to—"

"To what, Jennie?"

46

To keep looking. To find out what really happened. Jennie kept the thought to herself. Mom wouldn't understand. "I just can't let it go."

Mom nodded. "Give it time, honey. You've had a traumatic experience. Might even want to see Gloria."

Jennie didn't answer. Gloria was one of the counselors at Trinity Center. She'd helped Jennie deal with Mom's decision to get a divorce and date Michael. She doubted the counselor could help much in this case. What Jennie needed most at the moment were a few answers—and to know Gavin was safe.

"Would you like me to make an appointment?"

"Uh—no. I'll be fine."

"Okay, but if you change your mind . . ."

Jennie glanced at the digital green numbers of the microwave. Ten o'clock. Michael should have been there by now. She chewed on her bottom lip wondering what he'd find there. Needing to change the subject, she asked Mom about the wedding. "So, have you two set a date? I sort of thought that was what tonight's dinner was about."

"It was. Only we didn't get a chance to discuss it." She pressed her fork down on the plate to gather the crumbs. "After I blew up at him today, he'll probably call the whole thing off."

"I doubt it. He thinks you're beautiful when you're angry."

Mom's green eyes brightened. "He said that? How sweet."

Oh, Mom, Jennie longed to say. *Don't marry Michael. He loves you, but so does Dad. Dad is alive, Mom, and someday maybe he'll be able to come home. It's too dangerous right now, but . . .* It just wasn't right. The government should have told Mom the truth. Dad should find a way to let her know.

The phone rang. Jennie shot out of her chair and grabbed it before it could ring a second time. "Michael?"

"Um, no, this is Rocky."

"Oh, hi." The race for the phone had left her breathless.

"I hope I'm not calling too late. I just got off work and wanted to see how you were holding up."

"Okay. Did you find out anything more about Mr. Mancini's death?"

"It's looking more and more like a suicide. There was gunpowder residue on his hands. And it looks like he may have been taking crank."

"What?"

"The story'll be in the paper tomorrow morning. The medical examiner says he was using some kind of methamphetamine. Found a syringe in the office waste basket under a bunch of papers. We figure he might have been the one who stole the supplies from the lab."

"That's awful. Are you sure?"

"It's not my call. Just talked to Lieutenant Rastovski. He's hoping to close the case soon."

"So it was suicide. I wonder if that's why Gavin called."

"You kids aren't playing private detective again are you?"

"No. Not exactly. I mean—Gavin might have been investigating the theft." Jennie briefly filled him in on the conversation she'd had earlier with Gavin.

"Gavin is missing and no one bothered to call us?"

"Michael wanted to see if he could find him first."

"I'm on my way home. I'll drive around out by the school, see what I can find out. Give me Winslow's address, and I'll ask someone to check around out there as well. Normally it would be too soon for his parents to file a missing-persons report, but considering the circumstances I feel like we should investigate."

Jennie thanked him and had just hung up when the phone rang again. This time it was Michael calling from the school. "We didn't find him. I called Maddie and she still hasn't seen him."

48

"I just talked to Rocky, he should be there in a few minutes. Could you tell if Gavin had been there?"

When Michael hesitated, Jennie's stomach tightened. "You found something."

"His bike. Found it parked in the faculty parking lot next to Mancini's car."

6

"It's my fault." Jennie sat at the kitchen table, her head buried in her arms. "If I'd been paying attention to the time, I wouldn't have been late. I wouldn't have gotten stuck in traffic." She paused to blow her nose. "I should have been here when he called. . . ."

"Sweetheart, you couldn't have known." Mom laid her hand on Jennie's arm. "Right now I'm glad you *were* late. If you'd gone to meet him, you might be missing as well."

"But I could have talked to him—found out what he was doing at the school. At least I'd have some names. I'd know what he wanted to tell me."

Jennie took a deep, shuddering breath. *Crying isn't doing you any good at all, McGrady. Just stop whining and do something.* A police officer would be coming to question her any minute. She had to pull herself together.

After washing her face, she felt better. Jennie hated crying and avoided it whenever possible. Tears left her face all splotchy, but she couldn't help it. Hearing about Gavin had triggered a landslide of the stuff that had been building all day.

The doorbell rang. Jennie pressed a cool washcloth to her eyes one more time, then dried her hands and face before making her way downstairs.

Officer Phelps stood in the entry talking to Mom. "Sorry

to bother you this late, ma'am, but I'll need to ask you and your daughter some questions about the Winslow boy."

"Of course, but I'm not sure we'll be much help, though. Come in." Mom led the way into the living room. "Would you like to sit down?"

"Thank you, but that won't be necessary." The officer pulled a black notebook out of her back pocket and flipped it open. She was as officious as she had been at the school.

"Can I get you coffee or anything?" Mom offered.

"I'm fine, thank you. I understand Gavin called here around six." Phelps didn't look fine. Jennie noted the lines under her eyes. Apparently it had been a long day for her as well.

Mom gave her the information. "That's all I can tell you, I'm afraid."

Phelps leveled a cool gaze on Jennie. "When did you last see him?"

"Um—this afternoon—after I left the school. He needed a ride downtown so I dropped him off." Jennie had a distinct feeling the officer didn't like her, but she couldn't imagine why.

"Did he give you any indication he'd be going back out to the school?"

"No. He just asked me if I wanted to help him investigate."

"Investigate what?"

Jennie frowned. "The burglary and Mr. Mancini's death. He thought they might be related."

"And what did you tell him?"

Jennie squirmed under the officer's condemning gaze. "I really wasn't planning to get involved in the case—especially after Rocky told me about the drug labs."

"By Rocky, I assume you mean Officer Rockwell?" Phelps glanced up from her note taking.

Jennie nodded.

51

"Is this Winslow kid your boyfriend?"

"No. Just a friend. My boyfriend is in Alaska—fishing. But then, you don't need to know that, do you?"

"Not unless he's missing too."

Though she hadn't heard from Ryan in a while, Jennie didn't think he was and told Officer Phelps as much.

A tiny grin escaped the stern officer's lips until she pressed them together.

The questioning over, Officer Phelps left. Mom straightened the throw pillows on the couch and slipped an arm around Jennie's waist. "We'd better get some rest."

Jennie, being nearly a head taller, rested her cheek on Mom's hair. "I'll never be able to sleep."

"Then just close your eyes." They walked arm in arm through the dining room and up the stairs.

"Is Michael coming back tonight?"

"No. He called while you were upstairs. He's going out to the Winslows' to lend some moral support."

"That's good. Maddie must be frantic by now."

"I imagine so." Mom passed by Jennie's room and stopped at Nick's door. "I'd better check on him—he's been rather troubled for the last few days." She frowned. "Jennie, have you been talking to Nick about your father possibly coming home again?"

"No. How could I? He asked me about Dad this morning, though. Seems to be worried about having two dads."

"Yes. He mentioned that to me as well. I haven't told him, you know. About Jason being dead. I'm not sure I want to yet. I thought I'd wait another year. On the other hand I don't want to encourage him either. Tonight he wanted to go to sleep with his real dad's picture instead of Coco bear and his blanket."

Jennie shrugged. "Nick isn't stupid, Mom. He knows Michael isn't his real dad. Maybe he feels like he's betraying Dad by loving Michael. Today I told him Dad would understand and that since he couldn't be with us he'd want Nick to have a stepdad like Michael."

"Did you?" Mom smiled. "That was very nice of you."

"Thanks. Good night, Mom. I love you." Jennie ducked into her room before she said something she shouldn't—couldn't—say.

As she often did when she was anxious or nervous, Jennie paced. Pausing at her desk, she picked up a multicolor glass paperweight. She stared into the swirling shades of crimson and blue. Random patterns. Gram and J.B. had brought it back from Europe several weeks before. Austrian crystal. Jennie set the paperweight down and tried calling her grandmother. As was so often the case lately, no one was home. Not even the answering machine picked up.

She dialed Lisa's number, but the line was busy.

Jennie changed into her pajamas—a cotton T-shirt tie-dyed in shades of blue and matching shorts. For the next hour or so, she wrote in her diary, which consisted mainly of letters to her father. She hadn't written a letter to him in a long time—not since she discovered he was still alive.

Dear Dad,

I'm feeling pretty rotten right now. My friend Gavin is missing—not officially, of course, but at least the cops are taking it seriously. I'm worried that it might have something to do with Mr. Mancini's death. Police think he committed suicide. I'm having trouble with that. Gavin did too. Maybe that's why he's missing.

There may be drugs involved. That's a scary thought. I wish you could be here to handle it. That's your specialty, right? Do you ever think about working in the States? I suppose it's not as exciting as being in the tropics, but wouldn't you be safer? By the way, Mom and Michael are back together again and talking marriage—like really soon. . . .

Jennie continued to write, telling him about Montana and getting to know Mom's sister Maggie and her twin cousins, Heather and Hazen, and their little sister, Amber. Thinking about them spurred her to write a letter to them too. At least she could mail that one. Maybe she'd write a letter to Hannah as well, to thank her for the locket.

It was midnight before Jennie finally crawled into bed. Trying to keep her mind from dwelling on all the terrible things that could have happened to Gavin, she started reading a new mystery. Unfortunately, she couldn't concentrate on the story. At twelve-thirty she set the book aside, closed her eyes, and said a prayer for Gavin and his family, and for the Mancinis.

As she drifted into sleep, Jennie felt herself falling. Something or someone was pulling her into a deep, dark, frightening place. She fought against it, but the force was too great and she finally let go.

————

Birds chirping outside her window and the sun peeking through the blinds urged Jennie awake. She stretched and yawned as bits and pieces of the day before settled into place. The anxious feeling that had gone to bed for the night crept back into her stomach. Jennie tossed the covers aside and padded across the plush carpet to the window seat. Moving a couple of her stuffed bears to one side, she sat on the wide cushioned bench and raised the blinds, then leaned back and let the sun melt away the chill she felt inside.

Was Gavin still missing? Part of her wanted to run downstairs to find out. Another part didn't want to know. Finally, unable to stand not knowing, Jennie left her cozy perch. She found her mother at the kitchen table, drinking coffee and reading the paper.

Jennie kissed Mom's cheek. "Where's Nick?"

"Still sleeping."

"Have you heard anything about Gavin?"

Mom shook her head and set her mug on the table. "Michael called a few minutes ago. Other than the bike and helmet, they haven't found any sign of him."

No news is good news, Jennie reminded herself while she fixed a bowl of granola and blueberry yogurt and sat down at the table. She hoped the adage held true.

"The police haven't declared him officially missing yet," Mom went on. "It hasn't been twenty-four hours."

"How's Mrs. Winslow doing?"

"Worried, of course. I'm going out there as soon as Nick gets up—do you want to come along?"

"Um—no. I think I'll hang around here—maybe clean my room and head over to Lisa's later. I tried calling Gram last night. Are she and J.B. still in town?"

"I think so. They said something about going back to the coast today, though."

"So soon? I hardly ever get to see her since she married J.B." Gram had been busy before, but being married to an FBI agent tended to complicate things even more. "I miss her."

"I know you do. Maybe you can go down to the coast and stay for a week or so before school starts."

"I'd love that!" Despite the seriousness of the situation with Gavin and Mr. Mancini, Jennie's spirits took an upward turn. Ryan would be home soon, and since he was Gram's next-door neighbor, she'd be able to spend some time with him as well.

"I'm going to shower and get Nick up. Could you take care of Bernie?"

"Sure."

Mom dumped the remains of her coffee in the sink, rinsed the cup, and left. Jennie finished her cereal, downed a glass of juice, then went out to the back porch.

"Hi, big guy," Jennie cooed as she hunkered down to pet

Bernie. "You don't like being out here away from all of us, do you?"

Bernie whined and stretched up to lick Jennie's face. When they'd first gotten the St. Bernard he'd been allowed to sleep and eat in the house. Now Mom said he was too big. So, Michael and Nick built a doghouse and moved him out to the back porch.

After giving him fresh water and a mountain of dog food, Jennie hurried upstairs to shower and dress.

At ten o'clock Mom and Nick waved goodbye, leaving Jennie with requests to do the breakfast dishes and vacuum. Lisa drove in as they were leaving.

Lisa looked anything but pleased as she climbed out of the maroon Ford Taurus and joined Jennie on the front porch. "I can't believe you didn't call me when you found out about Gavin."

"I tried, but your line was busy."

"Oh." Her freckled cheeks flushed bright pink. "I was talking to Rafael. Mom says I shouldn't be calling him. She thinks I should wait until he makes the first move. But that's dumb. I mean, it's okay for girls to call guys." She shrugged her shoulders. "Anyway, it didn't do much good. He still didn't ask me out. I may have to ask him. Do you think I'm being too pushy?"

"You're asking me? You're the expert on guys. Anyway, I wouldn't worry about it. He'll come around." Jennie followed her cousin inside and closed the door. "So how did you find out about Gavin?"

"Mom told me this morning. I guess Mrs. Winslow called her late last night to see if we'd seen him. They must have called everyone they could think of. That is so scary. I hope they find him soon."

"Me too." Jennie opened the hall closet and pulled out the upright vacuum cleaner. "I have to do some housework. Want to help?"

"No, but I will."

Jennie sent Lisa into the kitchen while she straightened the living room, dusted, and vacuumed. She wanted to be out looking for Gavin but had no idea where to begin. Maybe she'd call Rocky and the Winslows later and get an official update.

Lisa wandered in from the kitchen just as Jennie was putting the vacuum cleaner away. She was munching on an apple and reading a section of newspaper.

"Did you see this?"

"What?" Jennie closed the hall closet door and looked over her cousin's shoulder.

"This article about Mr. Mancini." Lisa handed her the paper and shuddered. "It is just so gruesome. If I were going to kill myself, which I'd never do, I wouldn't use a gun—especially if I had drugs around. I mean, wouldn't it have been more efficient, not to mention less messy, to take an overdose?"

"Good question. Be quiet for a minute and let me read it." The headline declared the teacher's death a suicide. Jennie didn't recognize the name under the title and wondered what had happened to Gavin's story. There were no surprises in the first few paragraphs. As Rocky had told her the night before, the police suspected drug use had contributed to the teacher's decision to end his life in such a violent way.

The article went on to tell how Mr. Mancini's body had been discovered by an unidentified student and the youth pastor at the adjoining church. The reporter had interviewed Mrs. Mancini, Michael, Mrs. Talbot, and several others including Mr. Mancini's current lab assistant, Curtis Bolton. They all shared the same kind of shock and disbelief.

As she read, she began thinking in terms of talking to these people herself, especially Mrs. Mancini and Curtis Bolton. Of course she'd never met Mrs. Mancini, but she vaguely knew Curtis and wasn't surprised at his being the new lab assistant. He tended to be a loner—quiet and shy—a four-point student who'd end up being a college professor, an inventor, or a rocket scientist someday. He was kind of cute in a studious sort of way, straw-colored hair, gangly arms and legs that didn't go with the rest of his body.

"Lisa, what do you know about Curtis Bolton? It says here he's Mr. Mancini's lab assistant."

"He's super intelligent and comes from a very wealthy family. I think they live out in east county—near the Winslows." Lisa pinched her eyes closed as if that might help her memory. "He has a brother—Ray—and a married sister who lives in California."

"How do you remember all that?"

"They were at church a couple of weeks ago and Pastor Dave congratulated Ray on graduating from Oregon State. After church I talked to him and his brother."

"And . . ."

"Nothing. I invited Curtis to come to our youth meetings when they start up in the fall, and he said he'd think about it."

Jennie scanned the rest of the article, then went back and reread the part about the suicide note.

"This is strange."

"What's that?" Lisa grabbed hold of the paper and pulled it toward her.

"This article says Mr. Mancini had left a suicide note on his computer, but he couldn't have. I was in his office. The only thing I saw on his computer was some kind of chemical equation or formula. Definitely not a suicide note."

"Maybe the paper made a mistake or someone gave them the wrong information."

"I need to find out for sure."

"Does it matter all that much?"

"Of course it does. Don't you see? If the police found a suicide note on the computer it had to have been written after

58

I left the office. That means Mr. Mancini didn't write it."
Jennie frowned. "Unless I was wrong about his being dead
before I got there."

"What did the note say?" Lisa asked.

"I thought you read it."

"Not completely."

Jennie began reading. *"For Sandra and Alex and my good
friends at Trinity, when you find this note I'll be gone. I can no
longer live with the shame of what I have done. Please forgive me.
You and the school will be better off without me. Tom Mancini."*

"Wait a minute." Lisa grabbed hold of the paper. "Read
that again."

"Why, what's wrong?"

Lisa pointed to the first line. "It says, 'for Alex.' "

"That's his daughter, right?"

"Jennie, you're right. Mr. Mancini didn't write this note."

"How can you tell?"

"The only people who call her Alex are her friends. She
told me Mr. Mancini hated that name. He made it a point to
always call her Alexis."

7

"I need to talk to Lieutenant Rastovski." Jennie set the paper on the table, then went in search of her book bag. After several minutes of pawing through miscellaneous scraps of paper in her wallet, she found the card he'd given her.

The operator transferred the call to the lieutenant, whose voice mail told her he wasn't available and to leave a message. Jennie did, then called again and this time asked for Rocky.

"Officer Rockford is on patrol," the woman answering the phone told her. "If this is an emergency you'll need to call 9–1–1."

"No, it isn't, but I need to talk to him or Lieutenant Rastovski as soon as possible—I have some information about the Mancini case."

"I see. Lieutenant Rastovski is tied up in a meeting this morning. But I'll see that he gets your message."

"When will he be free?"

"By noon, I expect."

Jennie gave her name and number and hung up. Frustrated, she stuffed the card in the pocket of her jeans and turned back to Lisa. "No one's ever around when you need them. Looks like Rastovski won't be in for another hour."

Lisa retrieved a Diet Coke from the refrigerator. "Want one?"

"I guess."

She pulled out another one along with a tray of ice from the freezer and set them on the counter. "Want yours in a glass?"

"Yep." Jennie leaned against the counter and watched her. Lisa's resemblance to Mom always amazed Jennie. Jennie had the McGrady genes—dark hair and eyes. She took after Gram, Dad, and Lisa's mother, Kate, who was Dad's twin sister. Lisa, on the other hand, took after the Calhoun side of the family, with their red hair and freckles. Mom was Lisa's dad's sister, so she was a Calhoun too. It was all very complicated and it really didn't matter all that much. They were all one big happy family—most of the time. Which explained why Lisa was as much at home in the McGrady kitchen as Jennie.

"Thanks," Jennie said when Lisa handed her a glass. "Want to wait out on the porch? It should be shady by now."

"I guess."

Jennie carried their drinks out to the front porch and set them on the white wicker table. The screen door squeaked and banged shut.

She stretched out on the porch swing, left leg dangling, and watched a squirrel scurry up a nearby tree. A patrol car cruised up to the curb and stopped. *Rocky.* Jennie scrambled to her feet and met him halfway up the walk. "Hi. I didn't think you'd get my message so quickly."

"What message? I came by to see if you'd heard from your friend."

"Unfortunately no, but I left a call for you." Jennie explained how she and Lisa had found the discrepancies in the suicide note.

"Hmm. Interesting observation, but I didn't see the note. You need to talk to Lieutenant Rastovski. He'll be able to answer your questions better than I can."

"Do you think he'll listen? I mean he seemed pretty sure it was suicide."

"Makes it a whole lot easier for the department if it is. Rastovski's got a case load like you wouldn't believe."

Rocky's radio emitted static along with a series of words and numbers that apparently meant something to him. He mumbled into the transmitter, told Jennie he'd talk to her later, then left.

After Jennie and Lisa had drained their drinks, Jennie had had it with waiting around. "I'm going down there."

"To the police department?"

"It could be hours before Rastovski calls me back. I want to try to catch him when he gets out of his meeting."

Lisa glanced at her watch. "I have to go. Allison and B.J. and I might go to the mall. Besides, if I hurry I can get to their house in time to watch Rafael clean the pool."

"Clean the—Lisa, that is so tacky." Jennie picked up their glasses and Lisa's plate.

"No it isn't." Lisa held open the door and followed Jennie inside. "We have it all planned. We'll swim for a while, and then Allison and B.J. will go inside. I'll say I want to get in a couple more laps. I am supposed to be exercising, you know, and I'll just happen to be in the pool when he comes to clean it. We'll talk for a few minutes and—" She shrugged. "Who knows."

Jennie shook her head. She had long ago given up trying to understand how she and Lisa could be so different when it came to guys. Lisa was so outgoing and flirtatious, while Jennie tended to be more cautious. She didn't date much, not because she didn't get asked—this summer she'd met more guys than she had in her entire life. It was just that the guys she really liked were either too old—like Rocky—or weren't around—like Ryan.

"Wish me luck," Lisa yelled as she started to leave. "Oh, and call me if you hear anything about Gavin." She suddenly turned serious. "I wish there was more we could do."

"Me too. I might go out to his house after I talk to Lieutenant Rastovski. Thought I'd get a list of Gavin's friends—people he's talked to lately. Maybe his mom will let me look around his room."

"Um—do you want me to go with you, Jen?" Lisa chewed on her bottom lip. "I can watch Rafael and go to the mall anytime."

Jennie smiled. "No, but there is something you can do."

"What?"

"Remember yesterday at the Beaumonts when we were talking about Mrs. Mancini and Alex?"

"You want to meet them, right?"

"Uh-huh. I think it's time. Why don't you bring Alexis to the mall—I'll meet you there . . . say around one-thirty."

Half an hour later, Jennie parked her car, plugged the meter, and walked the two blocks to the police station. Lieutenant Rastovski was coming down the steps while she was still a block away. She hollered at him, but he either didn't hear her or didn't want to. He took off in the opposite direction. Not about to let him get away, Jennie broke into a run.

"Excuse me," she panted as she caught up to him at the intersection. "Lieutenant Rastovski? I left a message for you."

"I know. You had information about the Mancini case." Rastovski had one of those go-away-kid-you-bother-me looks.

Jennie ignored it. "See, I happen to know Mr. Mancini didn't write that suicide note."

"Is that right?"

The light changed and Jennie crossed the street with him. "Which means he was murdered."

Rastovski sighed. "Look, Miss McGrady. This is all very interesting, but I'm going to lunch now. If you want to talk to me, go back to the station and wait until I get back."

"But this is important."

"So's my stomach."

Jennie tagged after him, growling under her breath. She stopped at the next intersection when the light flashed *Don't Walk*. The lieutenant kept going. Jennie hurried after him and almost got hit by a driver making a right turn.

"You need to be more careful crossing the street," he muttered when she caught up to him again.

"Why can't you just take a minute and listen to me?"

He stopped. "All right. I'm listening."

"Mr. Mancini never would have called his daughter Alex. And the note wasn't on the computer screen when I was in the office."

He started walking again. "Suicide is still a possibility. The guy was using his position as a chemistry teacher to manufacture drugs. He steals the equipment, sets up shop, then his conscience starts bothering him. Crank tends to make people delusional and paranoid. We see a lot of violent acts."

Jennie heaved an exasperated sigh, continuing to tag along behind him, barely able to keep up with his long strides. How was she going to make him listen? She'd sensed from the beginning that Mr. Mancini had been murdered, and her hunches were usually right. Maybe if she told him that—*Yeah, right, McGrady. Tell him you have a gut feeling. He'll get a big laugh out of that.*

Lieutenant Rastovski stopped in front of Lacy's Deli. "It's been nice visiting with you, Miss McGrady, but this is where we part company."

"I can't believe you won't listen to me. All I'm asking is that we sit down together and go back over some of the evidence. If you found a suicide note on the computer, then someone put it there after I was in the office."

"Jennie—" If it was possible, he sounded even more irritated than he had before. "I know you want to help, but I can't discuss this case with you."

"I'm not asking you to discuss it. I want to tell you what

64

I saw and you can decide if there's a problem."

"Why is this so important to you?" He was melting.

"Because—if I'm right and Mr. Mancini really didn't commit suicide, you're letting someone get away with murder. And my friend Gavin Winslow may be the next victim."

He frowned. "Who's this Winslow character and what does he have to do with the case?"

Jennie started to tell him about Gavin, but the door to the deli opened and they had to move aside. Luscious smells wafted out and set Jennie's stomach to growling.

"Um . . . hold on." He glanced at the deli door that was slowly closing, then back at Jennie. "Tell you what. I'm starving and the smells coming out of this place are about to drive me nuts. Come on. I'll buy you lunch and you can tell me all about your friend and this murder theory of yours."

Yes! Jennie felt like punching the air and cheering. Instead, she thanked the lieutenant and walked inside when he opened the door. A waiter wearing a Jewish skull cap ushered them to the only empty booth. Jennie had the feeling her escort had been there many times before. She slid into the tan vinyl booth and tucked her bag against the wall.

"The usual, sir?" the waiter asked as he set a couple of beat-up and badly stained menus on the Formica table.

"Yep—and whatever the young lady wants."

Jennie glanced at the menu. "A roast turkey sandwich and a bottle of mineral water."

"You got it."

As soon as the waiter left, Jennie filled the lieutenant in on the conversation she'd had with Gavin the afternoon before he'd disappeared. "I can't believe you didn't know he was missing."

Rastovski scowled. "I can't either. If it's related to the Mancini case, someone should have told me. Though I'm not sure when they'd have had the time. So tell me more about this kid. He was taking it upon himself to investigate Mancini's death?"

"He's a reporter and wanted me to help him. He called me around six last night and wanted to talk to me about a big breakthrough. I wasn't home so Mom took the message, only she didn't tell me until later. Anyway, he never went home last night."

"Here you go." The waiter set their orders down. "Condiments are behind you. Whistle if you need anything else."

Rastovski assured him they would. His "usual" turned out to be a bowl of soup and a six-inch-tall Reuben sandwich. By the time Jennie had pulled the fancy toothpicks out of her sandwich, Rastovski had downed half of his Reuben.

"Sorry to start ahead of you. I haven't had a chance to eat since two this morning."

"You were up all night?"

"Had three homicides last night." He stuffed a portion of sandwich in his mouth and wiped a drip of mustard off his chin.

Wow. No wonder he hadn't felt like talking about Mr. Mancini. Their conversation dwindled down to an occasional comment on the quality and portions of food while they finished eating. While Lieutenant Rastovski finished off his meal with coffee and a piece of deep-dish berry pie a la mode, Jennie dropped half of her meal into a doggy bag for Bernie.

She watched Rastovski eat for a moment. "If you ate like that in front of my mom, she'd have a fit."

"Why's that?"

"You're eating too fast."

"You're right. It comes with the job. Always eating on the run." He set his fork down and reached for his coffee. "I appreciate you telling me about your friend, but I wouldn't worry too much about him. He'll probably turn up in the next day or so. Every day we get dozens of calls from frantic parents saying their teenager's missing. Some of them run away. Some get busy smoking joints and just don't bother to go home."

Rastovski, you are a first-class jerk. She wanted to say it— almost did, but she couldn't quite bring herself to it.

"Gavin isn't like that. He'd never—"

"Right. How many times have I heard that? Tell you what, Jennie. I should have reports from the crime lab and the medical examiner's office by now. I'll go over all the reports along with your statement. If you're right and we are dealing with a homicide—you'll be the first to know. But I wouldn't hold my breath if I were you. I don't think we're going to come up with anything other than suicide on this one."

8

On the way back to the station, Rastovski chewed on a toothpick and ignored Jennie for the first block. "Tell me something," he said when they stopped at an intersection. "I understand this isn't the first case you've shown an interest in. Officer Rockwell tells me you've developed quite a reputation for solving crimes. You just nosy, or what?"

Jennie glanced down at her scruffy tennis shoes, then met his gaze head on. "I'd like to go into law enforcement. My grandmother used to be a police officer here in Portland—and my father is—*was* a DEA agent." *Way to go, McGrady.* She hoped he hadn't noticed the slip.

"Yeah? Locally?"

"No, um—he was on a case when his plane went down in the Puget Sound area five years ago. They never found it."

"Must be tough."

Jennie shrugged. "Sometimes."

"You trying to fill his shoes? Happens sometimes. Kids lose a parent and kind of take over that parent's role."

"I'm not sure what you mean."

"Your father may have been a DEA agent, but you aren't. You need to stop trying to be your dad. Stop trying to prove Mancini was murdered."

He paused in front of the station. "I got enough to do without dealing with some kid who fancies herself another

68

Nancy Drew. I appreciate your concerns about whether or not this was a suicide, and I thank you for sharing your views. Now that you've done your duty, I want you to go home and forget about it. Go hang out with your friends or whatever kids your age do these days. And no more playing cops and robbers."

"But you said you were going to—"

"I will check into it, but you won't. Goodbye, Jennie. I'll be in touch."

Jerk. Jennie had a hard time understanding Rastovski's attitude. *I am not pretending to be my dad. I'm me.* Okay, so maybe this guy was overworked and had too many crimes to solve. That was no reason to treat her like she didn't have the intelligence God gave a goose.

At least she'd gotten him to agree to look over the evidence again. She'd liked to have followed the man into the station and told him off but remembered she'd parked in a half-hour zone over an hour ago. Jennie broke into a run and reached the ticketed car just as the meter maid, in her little white cart, putt-putted around the corner.

Rats. She kicked the Mustang's wheel. When the pain subsided, Jennie grabbed the ticket from under the windshield wiper, unlocked her car, and slid inside. "Why me?" she grumbled. "I should send the stupid ticket to Rastovski. It's his fault I'm late. If he'd—"

She threw the ticket on the seat, jammed the key in the ignition, and took a deep breath. She was not going to let him get to her. The lieutenant had suggested she go hang out with friends, and that's exactly what she planned to do.

Clackamas Town Center was packed with kids and parents taking advantage of the early back-to-school sales, and Jennie had to park in what felt like the next county. She wove through the crowds to the food court located just above the skating rink.

It took her fifteen minutes and two times around the court to spot Lisa, Allison, and B.J. Of course, part of that time had been spent on the phone to Mrs. Winslow. They still hadn't heard from Gavin.

"I wish there was something I could do," Jennie had told her.

"I know," Maddie said. "I appreciate that. Just keep praying. At least the police are more involved now. Your friend Rocky has been wonderful. He talked his superiors into launching a full investigation. We also got some news coverage, so we're hoping someone may have seen him."

Jennie hoped that was the case. *Keep praying*, Maddie had said. Jennie offered up a prayer as she made her way toward her friends.

"Hi!" Lisa waved her over. "We were about to give up on you."

Jennie folded herself into one of the four chairs attached to the table. "Sorry I'm late. It took me longer than I thought."

"Did you get to talk to the lieutenant?"

"Yeah, but he didn't seem too interested."

"What did he say?" Lisa stirred her drink with a straw.

Jennie outlined the main points. "Personally, I think he's more concerned about me minding my own business than learning the truth about Mr. Mancini."

"Well, you can't give up now. Alex should be here any minute. She had to go with her mom to make funeral arrangements."

"There they are." Allison stood up and waved to a tall, thin, dark-haired woman about Mom's age and a girl with short magenta-and-black-striped hair. They waved back. Mrs. Mancini opened her bag and extracted some money and handed it to Alex. The woman was wearing a pink linen-type

70

suit and a matching hat and seemed out of place among the casually dressed shoppers, but then so did her daughter. Okay, so maybe Alex's appearance wasn't all that unusual. A lot of kids experimented with hair dyes and weird, off-the-wall clothes. But not at Trinity High. True, school hadn't started yet, but Alex Mancini had a lot of work to do if she planned to comply with the school's strict dress code.

Mrs. Mancini said something to Alex, then turned to go in the opposite direction. Jennie's gaze swung back to Alex. She was about Lisa's height, but weighed about twenty pounds more—of course some of that may have been the baggy overalls she was wearing. Her nearly white skin, blood red lipstick, and matching nail polish made her look like Dracula's sister.

"Excuse me while I go barf." B.J. picked up a tray and after depositing the garbage in the trash, set it on top of about a dozen other trays.

"B.J., be nice." Allison rolled her eyes and gave Jennie and Lisa a you'll-have-to-forgive-her-she's-nuts look.

"I am. It's the vampire you need to worry about." B.J. stopped behind Jennie and whispered, "Watch her fangs, McGrady. I'll call you later."

"Her what?" Jennie had heard her but was having a hard time understanding why B.J., of all people, was coming down so hard on the girl.

"Never mind. I'll let you figure it out for yourself."

"B.J., where will I find you?" Allison asked.

"Don't worry. I'll be back. Just don't leave without me."

"It would serve her right if I did." Allison sat back down. "It's nice having a sister at times, but she can be such a brat."

"Allison, Lisa, hi." Alex grinned, revealing a full set of braces. She plopped a huge canvas bag on B.J.'s chair, then reached inside to pull out a twenty. "I am so glad you called. Being around my family right now is not fun. They're constantly talking about death."

71

Not unusual when someone has just died, Jennie started to reply, but didn't.

"You must be Jennie. I have heard so much about you." She reached up and touched what looked like a diamond stud in her pierced left nostril. The red circle of skin around it made it look like a huge, glowing zit.

"I've heard a lot about you too." Jennie shifted her gaze from the nose to the eyes. Alex had turquoise eyes—the color of a chlorinated pool. Contacts, most likely. Jennie found it hard not to stare.

"Good stuff, I hope." Alex blinked and looked away.

You could tell a lot about people by their eyes. Alex was nervous about something—or afraid. Jennie had seen the look before in the eyes of a woman who was being abused by her husband. She couldn't help wondering about the girl in front of her.

"I—um—I'm sorry about your dad," Jennie said.

"Stepdad." She glanced at Allison and Lisa. "I'm starved. You guys want anything?"

Allison and Lisa both declined.

"A Diet Coke," Jennie said, digging into her wallet for money and pulling out a dollar bill and some change. "If you don't mind."

"Not at all." She waved Jennie's hand away. "My treat."

"Well," Jennie mused when she was out of earshot, "B.J. was right about one thing. She doesn't seem too broken up over her stepfather's death."

"I didn't know Mr. Mancini was her stepfather." Allison frowned. "Maybe she didn't like him."

Jennie stretched her long legs, leaned back, and folded her arms. "Did she ever talk about him?"

"I don't think so." Allison thought for a moment. "I did ask her once how it felt having a teacher for a parent. Can't remember what she said, but I don't think it was very complimentary."

"What are you thinking, Jennie?" Lisa placed her hand on Jennie's arm. "Oh, wait. You think he might have been abusing her?"

"The thought crossed my mind. Did she ever say anything—?"

"No." Both girls shook their heads.

Jennie had a lot of questions for Alex Mancini. Unfortunately, Lisa, Allison, and Alex went into a shopping mode and Jennie could do little more than tag along and pick up snatches of conversation.

"Oh, look, this will be perfect for your trip abroad." Allison held up a white and navy dress.

"What trip?" Jennie jerked to attention.

Alex draped the dress over her arm along with about five other outfits she'd picked out. "My mom and I are going to Europe."

"Really? Before school?"

"Yes, actually during school. We'll be living in England for six months."

"Wow. Sounds like fun."

"Oh, it will be, especially without—" Her lips clamped shut. "It's going to be a blast."

"Do you have relatives there or something?" Lisa asked.

"No. Mom says we'll stay in bed-and-breakfasts for a while, then she's going to try to find a place to rent."

"Sounds expensive." Jennie wandered to the next rack, pretending to be less interested than she really was.

"We can afford it. Tom left Mom and me a lot of money, and Mom has always wanted to go to Europe."

"So, when are you leaving?" Jennie picked a dress from the rack and held it up.

"In two weeks."

"You must have been planning this for a long time."

"Actually, no." Alex grabbed another dress and headed

for the dressing room. "Mom made the arrangements this morning."

"Did you hear that?" Jennie put the dress back and joined Lisa and Allison at a sales rack.

"You mean about the trip to Europe? Isn't that great?" Allison grinned. "We went last summer."

"I'd love to go to Europe," Lisa said. "Maybe Gram will take us sometime, Jennie. Wouldn't that be neat?"

"Don't you guys get it? That trip has got to cost a fortune."

"Well sure, but—"

"I could be wrong, but what kind of person would plan a six-month trip to Europe the same day she makes arrangements to bury her husband?"

Two hours and a dozen department stores later, Jennie dropped into one of the chairs in the shoe department in Nordstrom. After sitting for a few more minutes, watching Lisa and Allison give their opinion while Alex tried on shoes, Jennie announced she was leaving.

"Oh no, Jennie." Lisa sidestepped half a dozen boxes and crossed the aisle to where Jennie was sitting. "You can't go yet—we haven't done any shopping for you."

Jennie shook her head. "Not today. You know how I feel about shopping. It's fun for a while, but I'm bored out of my skull." She lowered her voice. "Besides, the main reason I came was to talk to Alex, and I think I've gotten about all I'm going to."

Lisa sighed. "Okay. Are you going out to Gavin's?"

"I don't think so. I'll probably call before I leave here, though."

"I sure hope he's turned up."

"Me too." Jennie backed away. "Call me later. Oh, and try to find out what Mr. Mancini was like at home."

After taking the escalator upstairs, Jennie made her way back to customer service and plugged a quarter in the pay phone. Mrs. Winslow picked up on the third ring.

"It's me, Jennie. Any word on Gavin?"

"No, but I'm glad you called. There was an inspector here looking for you—Ratski or something like that."

"Rastovski?"

"Right. He was here with a DEA agent and said he needed to ask you some questions. Apparently Michael told them you might be here. He wanted me to have you call him."

Jennie thanked her and hung up. DEA? Her heart did a triple flip. For a moment she let herself fantasize that the agent was her father, but only for a moment. *Forget it, McGrady. It isn't going to happen.*

9

Jennie retrieved Lieutenant Rastovski's card and plunked another quarter into the pay phone. He wasn't in. "No, he can't call me back. Just tell him I'll be home in twenty minutes. I'll try again from there."

Rastovski and the DEA agent were waiting in her driveway when she got home. He wasn't her father—at least she didn't think so. This guy had more hair—a sandy gray color. He looked like any other guy, really. A brown tweed sports jacket and tan slacks. He was leaning against a deep green Honda Accord. An unmarked police car, she realized as she pulled up beside it. He had an unlit cigarette dangling from his mouth that he tucked into his shirt pocket.

"Jennie," Rastovski greeted when she stepped out of her Mustang. "This is an old friend of mine with the DEA, Steve Douglas."

"Hi, Jennie." He reached out a hand and Jennie shook it. His blue gaze met hers head on. "The lieutenant's been telling me about the Mancini case and your interest in it."

They were definitely not Dad's eyes. Jennie let her gaze travel back to Rastovski.

He answered her question before she could ask it. "The DEA has an interest in the case, and Steve here wants to ask you a few questions. After reading over the reports on Mancini's death, I have a couple more questions of my own."

They were taking her seriously. She couldn't believe it. "Sure. Um—do you want to come inside?"

"Actually, we'd like you to come to the high school," Rastovski said. "Show us exactly what you did and saw."

"This may sound stupid, but why didn't you have me do that before?"

"Mr. Rhodes thought it would be too traumatic for you."

"Michael should mind his own business," Jennie muttered. "I could have handled it."

The two men looked at each other, then back at Jennie.

Okay, so maybe seeing a dead body would have given her nightmares for the next ten years, she admitted to herself. Maybe Michael had been right, but he shouldn't have made the decision for her. He was not her father. Changing the subject she asked, "Do you want me to drive my car or come with you?"

"You'd better meet us out there." Douglas's keys jangled as he pulled them out of his pocket.

Jennie nodded. "I need to leave Mom a note." She glanced at her watch. Nearly five. Mom and Nick would be home soon. "I'll meet you there in about half an hour—unless the traffic is really bad. Um, Lieutenant Rastovski," she called him back, "does this mean you've decided to call Mancini's death a homicide?"

"Beginning to look that way."

Jennie could feel the makings of a smile curl her lips. She loved being right.

When the men left, Jennie let herself into the house. A note tacked on the refrigerator told her Mom had already been there and gone. *Having dinner at Kevin and Kate's tonight with Gram and J.B. See you there. Love, Mom.*

Jennie called Aunt Kate's. Gram answered.

"Sweetheart, I'm so glad you called. You will be here tonight, won't you? I've missed you terribly."

"I've missed you too." It felt good hearing Gram's voice

again. "I'll be there, but I have to meet Lieutenant Rastovski and a DEA agent out at Trinity High so I might be late. What time's dinner?"

"Probably around seven. We'll wait for you."

"Did you hear about Mr. Mancini?"

"I've been reading about it in the papers, and your mother's been filling us in on the details. I'm sorry you had to be there when it happened."

"Actually, I'm glad I was there. Otherwise the police might have dismissed it as a suicide."

"You don't think it was?"

"No, but I'll talk to you about that later. I gotta run."

Traffic wasn't bad until she reached Highway 26. Her half-hour guess had been a good one. In exactly thirty-two minutes she pulled into the Trinity parking lot. There were two cars already parked in the main lot in front of the complex—Michael's BMW and Douglas's Honda. Both were empty.

Jennie took a deep breath to settle the butterflies in her stomach. She didn't know why she felt nervous. She just did. The butterflies were still dive-bombing when Jennie walked down the hall with Rastovski and Douglas. They'd wanted to question her and Michael separately.

"Okay." Jennie paused at the door to the chemistry lab. Her face was hot and sweaty enough to dampen her bangs. "It was about one o'clock when I opened the door. I went in. The first thing I noticed was the dark—and this antiseptic smell—like someone had just cleaned it. I smelled something else too—like sulphur. I didn't think much of it at first, because chemistry labs usually smell strange. I figured Mr. Mancini had been experimenting. It wasn't until I found out that Mr. Mancini had been shot that I realized the sulphur smell might have been from the gun."

Douglas raised an eyebrow. "And that's a scent you're familiar with?"

"My grandmother's taken me to the shooting range where she practices a few times. It's been a while, but—" Jennie shrugged.

"Her grandmother is an ex-cop," Rastovski supplied the explanation as he glanced around the room. "Jennie, I'd like you to retrace your steps for us."

She nodded. "I set my bag down and turned on the light. That's when I noticed the counters were damp—like they'd just been cleaned. Oh—" She glanced up toward the row of windows. They were all closed. "One of those windows was open—the second one over."

Rastovski and Douglas both paused to look up, then jotted the information down on their pads.

"This open window," Douglas mused. "Was it finger-printed?"

"Yep," Rastovski said. "Only prints we found were the janitor's and Mancini's."

"As I recall, the window had been open after the burglary as well, right?" Douglas walked to the window to examine it more closely.

"That's right, but I don't think the killer came in and out that way. There were pry marks around the window, but no scuff marks on the sill or wall to indicate that anyone had climbed in or out. I have a hunch the window was left open to lead us to believe someone had broken in."

"Hmm." Douglas frowned as he ran his hand along the wall. Both men went back to where Jennie was standing, and Rastovski asked her to continue.

"I called to Mr. Mancini. He didn't answer, but I heard a sound in the office and went to look."

Jennie led them into the room and explained about the open door and the papers on the floor.

"What did you do with the papers?" Rastovski frowned.

"I picked the ones up that were on the floor and set them on top of the desk."

"Are you sure?"

"Yeah, why?"

"The desk was like this when I got here. Neat and tidy."

"Someone cleaned it up after I left then." Jennie stepped around the desk. The computer displayed the same screen saver she'd seen before. "The newspaper said the suicide note was on the screen, but that's not what I saw."

"So you say. According to Phelps, you thought it was a formula or equation of some sort." Standing beside her, Rastovski tapped the space bar. "The suicide note is still here. This is what was on the computer when we got here. The attending officer's report confirms it."

"Can you remember anything about the formula you saw, Jennie?" Douglas came up behind her and looked at the screen.

"Not really. I mean, I wasn't paying that much attention. If I'd known about"—her gaze darted into the other room— "about Mr. Mancini. If I'd known it was evidence I'd have written it down. I might be able to remember parts of it." Jennie picked up a piece of scratch paper from beside the phone and began drawing figures as she remembered them.

Douglas eased in front of her and pulled out the chair, then sat down. "Let's see what kind of files your teacher had on this thing. Maybe I can find something that looks like what you saw."

For the next few minutes the DEA agent's fingers clicked across the keyboard. Jennie paused in her drawing to watch as he called up a number of documents under the heading "corres," like Trinity, general, Dawson, and several others Jennie didn't recognize. Under Trinity there were several files named Michael—then a number and a letter. The same for Pastor Dave and another grouping for the school's principal. Easy enough to figure out.

Douglas called up the latest memo to Michael, dated the day before Mr. Mancini's death. Looking over Douglas's shoulder, Jennie scanned the text. It was short and to the point.

I understand your desire to assist the young man we spoke about yesterday. After going over his files, however, I've decided to deny your request. Sincerely, Tom Mancini

Jennie wondered who the young man was and why Mancini hadn't mentioned a name.

Douglas zipped through several other files and menus. All easily assessable. Except the one named Dawson. "Looks like he didn't want anyone to see it—which means we'll have to find a way to access it. I want to know what's in there."

Rastovski rubbed a hand across his chin and gave Jennie a cursory glance. "I appreciate your help on this, Jennie. You can go on home now. We'll take it from here."

Jennie's stomach contracted. She hated being dismissed like that. Still, she supposed she should go. Kate was waiting dinner for her. While she watched the two investigators, an idea took form.

She cleared her throat and swallowed the grapefruit-sized lump in her throat. "I—I think I know of a way to catch the killer."

Douglas whirled around in the chair and Rastovski turned and looked at her as if she'd grown two heads.

They didn't ask, but she told them anyway. "I must have scared away Mr. Mancini's killer. It would have been easy for him—or her—to hide close by. The woods are only a few feet away. Anyway, when I left, they must have come back inside, straightened Mr. Mancini's desk, and written the note. The point is, whoever killed him knows I was there. I even said my name. Since you've been calling it a suicide, the killer has nothing to worry about. But now that we know it was a murder—I mean, I really don't know much, but what if we tell the press I saw the person running away and could make a positive identification."

"No." Rastovski's dark eyebrows almost met when he

frowned. "It's too dangerous."

"He's right, Jennie." Douglas swung back around to the computer. "Better leave this to the police."

"You could wire me and have someone watching."

Neither man answered. "Wait a second." Rastovski pointed to the screen. "Looks like Mancini's lab assistant has logged in a lot of hours this summer."

"You talk to him?" Douglas asked

"Not yet." Rastovski eyed the screen, then jotted something down in his notebook. Jennie eased up behind them and read the name on the screen. Curtis Bolton.

"Gavin knew about him," Jennie murmured, remembering the name Gavin had written in his notebook just before he closed it.

"The kid who's missing?" Douglas asked. "How well do you know this Curtis guy?"

"Not well. I remember seeing him around, but we never really talked. He's a senior. Quiet. Studious."

"Any friends?"

Jennie shook her head. "I don't know. I never saw him hanging out with anyone from school. And he didn't come to our youth group at church."

Douglas thanked her and stayed with the computer. Rastovski walked her back through the lab. "Appreciate your help, Jennie. We may need to talk to you again, but you can go on home now."

She was being dismissed again. Maybe they figured it was the only way to get rid of her. Jennie wanted to hang out with them—learn as much as she could. "Don't know why they couldn't have taken my suggestion," she muttered. "I don't mind being bait."

"Going fishing?" Michael asked.

She jumped. "What—?" Jennie had been looking at the mottled shadows on the floor and hadn't seen him approach.

"You said something about bait."

82

"Oh. No. Um—just talking to myself. You going down to talk to Rastovski and Douglas?"

"Yes. Though I don't know what more I can tell them. I'll be glad when this is over."

"Michael, there was a letter on Mr. Mancini's computer about a student you and he were talking about. He decided not to honor your request."

Michael shook his head. "I'm afraid that's privileged information, Jennie."

She glanced back at the lab. "They're going to ask you about it."

"They'll get the same answer I've given you."

"Can't you tell me anything? Not even what it was about?"

He shrugged. "This was all being handled in confidence. Just someone who wanted another chance. Mancini was being a—never mind. I'd better get going."

"Are you coming to dinner tonight at Aunt Kate's?"

"No. I have some paper work I have to catch up on. Say hello to everyone for me."

"Sure." She went a few feet, then stopped and spun around. "Michael?"

He paused and turned, hands in his pockets.

"What's going on with Gavin? Any word?"

"I wish I knew. He seems to have vanished."

She wanted to ask him more, but this wasn't the time. Later, maybe tomorrow, she'd ask him about Curtis. Or more to the point, how well did Gavin know Curtis? Could the lab assistant be mixed up in this? And where was he?

Jennie watched Michael until he entered the lab, then jogged past the office and out the main entrance, pawing through her bag for her keys as she went. When she got home she'd draw a chart and plug in names of possible suspects like she'd done on other cases. She stopped herself in mid-thought. *What are you doing, McGrady? Now that the police*

83

know it's a murder they'll handle it.

Jennie looked at her reflection in the car window. She knew herself pretty well, and the face looking back at her was one of determination. She hadn't meant to get involved. Probably should just let it go. But she was in too deep and knew she wouldn't be able to rest until Mancini's killer had been brought to justice.

Jennie stuck her key in the lock, then realized she'd forgotten to lock it. She slid onto the seat and checked the rearview mirror. Just as the engine roared to life, she heard a noise behing her.

Jennie's heart leapt into her throat. She gripped the steering wheel. *You should have checked, McGrady. Always look in and around the car before you get in.* Too late she remembered number three in the list of safety rules Gram had given her. The hairs on her neck stood erect.

She heard the sound again.

Someone was in the backseat.

10

Jennie squeezed her eyes closed, half expecting to feel a gun at the back of her head—or a knife at her throat.

Little by little the panic subsided. Nothing happened. Had she imagined the sounds? No, there it was again. Jennie glanced in the rearview mirror. No sinister face looked back. Taking a deep breath, she ventured a look into the backseat.

"Gavin!"

Jennie's screech brought a grimace to his haggard features. He covered his eyes and moved his lips, but nothing came out. He looked rumpled and confused.

"What are you doing here? Where have you been?" The questions poured out of Jennie's mouth, but she may as well have been talking to a mannequin. Adrenalin still pumping through her veins, she shot out of the car and pushed the seat forward.

"Gavin, for Pete's sake, what's going on? Are you hurt?"

He groaned and peered at her through glazed eyes.

Other than several facial bruises and some scratches on his arm, Jennie couldn't see any injuries, but she wasn't about to take a chance on moving him.

"Stay here. I'm going for help."

"No," he gasped. "Wait." He reached out a hand to stop her, but it fell back against his chest.

"I'll be right back. The police are in the chemistry lab with Michael. They'll help."

Ignoring his protests, Jennie raced into the building and down the hall. Her shouts brought Michael, Rastovski, and Douglas running.

"It's Gavin. He's in the backseat of my car. I was afraid to move him. He might be hurt. I can't be sure, but from the way he was acting, I think he may have been drugged."

The two officers charged ahead. By the time Michael and Jennie joined them, which couldn't have been more than a few seconds, Douglas was on the radio.

"What is this, a joke?" Rastovski had his hand on top of the Mustang's open door.

"What do you mean?" Jennie approached the car. The backseat was empty. "He was here. I swear."

"You're sure?"

"Of course. Not even my imagination could come up with something like that. He can't have gotten far. He looked really sick. We have to find him."

"All right, I'll take your word for it."

Douglas called for backup. Rastovski shouted orders. "Rhodes, check inside the school. Steve and I will head into the woods."

"What about me?" Jennie pushed in front of Michael.

"Stay here." Rastovski raked his fingers through his hair.

"But—"

"In case he comes back."

"Do it, Jennie," Michael warned, then ran back inside the building.

Jennie was tempted to ignore their orders but instead slammed the car door shut and leaned against it. "What is going on here, Gavin?" she muttered.

Gavin must have crawled into her car, but where had he been all this time? Had someone kidnapped him and drugged him, then let him go? But why? What had he stumbled into?

Jennie shoved the questions aside. Gavin had a lot of explaining to do when—if—they were able to find him again.

They would, she was certain of that. Like she'd told the lieutenant, Gavin couldn't have gone far. Unless he'd been faking. Jennie doubted that. In his condition, Gavin would barely have been able to get out of the car, let alone run away.

Wait a minute, McGrady. Maybe he didn't even try to run. Maybe he's closer than anyone imagined. Jennie pushed away from the car and walked toward the school.

The landscaping on either side of the entrance consisted of a dozen or so rhododendrons of various sizes pressed against the brick facing. In front of them was about a three-foot band of azaleas. Then came the lower shrubs and flowering plants. Jennie stepped over the curb and crossed the narrow expanse of lawn to the flower garden to the left side of the steps, nearest her car.

There were no clear footprints. A thick layer of bark dust covered the ground. Jennie hunkered down to examine the area more closely. Most of the bark had faded, but beside a clump of purple-blue lobelia, Jennie spotted a small patch of darker wood chips that had been turned over. As if someone had stepped wrong and churned it up. A short distance beyond that was another.

Jennie inched deeper into the plants, taking care not to step on them. When she reached the large rhodies in the back, she paused, then eased the branches aside.

"Don't come any closer or I'll shoot." Gavin's voice was hoarse. He sat cross-legged on the ground leaning against the building. His matted hair stood up at odd angles.

Jennie scrunched down and crawled toward him, pushing his weapon—a foot-long stick—to the side. "Put that thing away before you poke someone's eyes out."

"I mean it, get away from me." Staring wild-eyed, he jabbed it at her.

She jumped back. "What is *wrong* with you?"

"Leave me alone. Got to find—my—my . . ." He looked like he was about to cry.

"Gavin, put that thing down and let me help you."

"No—I can't. Go away before I shoot—"

She didn't hear the rest. Someone grabbed her around the waist and yanked her backward.

"What do you think you're doing?" she screamed at Rastovski.

The lieutenant didn't stop until they reached the Mustang. "Stay down," he growled, his arm pinning her in place.

The next few seconds cut into slow motion, and Jennie felt like she'd been thrown on to a television production of *Homicide*.

"Police! Come out with your hands above your head. Now!" Douglas crouched beside the stairs, about twenty feet away, his gun trained at the big rhododendron that still hid Gavin. Michael hunkered down behind him.

Lieutenant Rastovski moved away from her. Using the car as a shield, he drew his weapon.

"Don't shoot him!" Jennie grabbed at Rastovski's jacket and pulled him back.

The bushes parted. Gavin came out, but his hands weren't up. He yelled something Jennie couldn't understand and charged straight at Douglas.

"No!" Michael slammed his fist down on Douglas's arm just as the agent fired.

It seemed forever before anyone spoke. Douglas called for an ambulance.

Stunned, Jennie stared at Gavin writhing on the grass, turning patches of it crimson with blood. She broke away from Rastovski and ran to help her friend. Blood pumped out of a gaping wound in his thigh, saturating his jeans.

Stop the bleeding. She could almost hear her CPR instructor's voice going back over the procedures. Mechanically, Jennie pressed her hand against the wound, pinning his leg to the ground.

"Don't touch me!" Gavin struggled against her.

"Hold still," she yelled when he tried to kick her away.

Rastovski knelt beside her and opened up a first-aid kit he'd gotten from Douglas's trunk. "The way that sucker is pumping, I must have hit an artery." Douglas came up on the other side. He and Michael held Gavin down. Rastovski and Jennie applied a tourniquet and wrapped the wound.

A fire truck barreled in a few minutes later. Two EMTs jumped out, grabbed their supplies, and jogged toward them.

Ten minutes later Jennie's hands shook as she pressed the soap dispenser in the girls' rest room and washed Gavin's blood from her hands and arms. She couldn't be sure what shook her up the most—the shooting or Rastovski's rage.

The moment the ambulance left, he turned on her. "Don't you ever do anything like that again."

The lieutenant didn't have to explain what she'd done wrong. Jennie knew. She and Michael could both face charges for interfering with an officer. "He didn't have a gun," Jennie had argued. "You might have killed him."

"What if he'd *had* a gun, Jennie? What if he'd come out of those bushes waving an automatic rifle? We'd all be dead."

"But he didn't. You shouldn't have gone after him like that. I was doing just fine."

"He was threatening you."

"With a stick. I don't think he even knew what he was saying. You sound like you're sorry he wasn't hurt worse— or killed."

Rastovski drew a hand down his face, over his mustache, and was probably counting to ten. "Look, we'll talk about this later. I want you down at the station tomorrow morning." He looked over at Michael. "That goes for you too."

Douglas and Rastovski left a few minutes later to follow up with Gavin. Michael had sent her into the rest room to clean up with the promise he'd be waiting for her when she finished.

Jennie caught sight of her reflection in the mirror. A rust

streak ran across one cheek where she'd used her blood-streaked hand to brush the tears from her face. She hadn't meant to cry. It shouldn't have mattered what Rastovski and Douglas thought of her. But it did. In their minds, she'd messed up royally.

You did the right thing, she reminded herself. *So did Michael. If you hadn't intervened, Gavin might be dead.*

"You okay?" Michael asked when she got back to the office.

She nodded. "I guess." She glanced at her watch. Five after seven. "Looks like I'm late again. I'd better call and tell them I won't be there for dinner."

"I'm sure they'll wait for you, Jennie." He squeezed her shoulder.

"I know that. It's just—I have to go to the hospital. Make sure Gavin's okay."

"Let me do that. From the condition he was in, I don't think he'll be able to have visitors for some time."

"But I need to find out what happened to him. It's obvious he was high on something."

"Hmm. Sad, isn't it? You think you know someone and—"

"You don't think Gavin took drugs on his own, do you?"

"Do you have a better explanation?"

"Yeah, I do. Somebody killed Mr. Mancini. Gavin knew that, and I think he may have been getting too close. Maybe the killer abducted Gavin and drugged him to get him out of the way."

"That doesn't make sense, Jennie. Why wouldn't Mancini's murderer just kill Gavin as well?"

"Maybe he was going to—and Gavin escaped." Jennie tucked an annoying strand of hair behind an ear.

"There's really no point second guessing, is there? Hopefully tomorrow he'll be able to tell us what this disappearance thing was all about."

Jennie didn't know if she could wait that long. Okay, so she'd have dinner with her family. *Then* she'd drive to the hospital.

Before leaving the school, Jennie called Aunt Kate to explain what had happened. "I'll be there in about ten minutes."

"No problem. I'll put the spaghetti on."

Despite all that had happened, Jennie's stomach warmed at the thought of eating Aunt Kate's spaghetti. The rich meat sauce would have simmered all day in her industrial-sized crock pot. They'd have salad and warm, toasty garlic bread.

When Jennie pulled up to the curb, Bernie, Nick, Lisa, and Kurt, Lisa's little brother, ran out to meet her.

" 'Bout time you got here. We're starving." Kurt's freckled cheeks were flushed and hot. His chestnut curls hung limp on his brow.

"Sorry about that, but I had an emergency." Jennie stroked Bernie's silky fur.

He welcomed her with a bark and a slurpy kiss on her hand.

"How come you've got blood all over you?" Lisa asked.

"Oh, gross." Jennie glanced down at the rust-colored splatters on her lavender knit shirt and blue jeans. "I should have gone home to change."

"Don't worry about it. You can wear something of mine," Lisa said.

Nick wrapped his skinny arms around his sister's leg and hung there while she started up the driveway. "Where was you?"

"Where *were* you?" Jennie corrected.

Nick giggled. "I been here. Where was you?"

She rumpled his hair and pulled him up into her arms. "Oh, man, you are getting to be one heavy dude."

"I'm forty-one pounds."

"Mom said you found Gavin." Lisa came up beside her.

"Yep." Jennie gave her an I'll-tell-you-later look.

"Did the police believe you about the m-u-r-d-e-r?" She spelled out the last word.

"Uh-huh. At least I think so." She deposited Nick on the steps.

He shot into the house behind Kurt, yelling, "She's here! She's here. Now can we eat?"

"It's almost ready," Aunt Kate hollered back.

"We've still got a few minutes before dinner. Let's go up to my room so you can change. Mom," Lisa called, "we'll be in my room. Call us when dinner's ready."

"Will do. Hi, Jennie."

"Hi!" Through the sliding glass doors that led out onto the patio, Jennie could see Mom, Gram, J.B., and Uncle Kevin talking. They looked up when they heard Lisa and waved. Jennie waved back, then dutifully followed her cousin to her bedroom.

Lisa pulled a denim skirt and sleeveless blouse out of her closet and tossed them at Jennie. "These should fit you—they're a little too big for me right now."

"Wish I had time for a shower," Jennie shrugged out of her blood-stained shirt and slipped on the fresh one. She snagged a brush from the dresser, plopped onto Lisa's bed, and began loosening her braid.

"Hand me the brush. Let me do it. You talk." Lisa climbed onto the bed behind Jennie.

"What did your Mom tell you?"

"Just that you found Gavin and he's in the hospital. I have a feeling she left out a lot."

"She did." Jennie leaned back as Lisa brushed through her hair. "You should have seen him. I don't know what he was on, but it made him crazy. He threatened to kill me with a stick." Jennie gave Lisa the highlights.

Lisa remained silent as Jennie spoke. And no wonder. As

the scene replayed itself in Jennie's head, it seemed unreal—
like it hadn't really happened.

Lisa finished Jennie's braid and gave it a tug. "All done."

After setting the brush on the dresser, Lisa settled back
on the bed. "How could they have shot him, Jennie? I mean,
he didn't have a gun—and how much harm could he do with
a stick?"

"It was a mistake. Rastovski and Douglas heard him
threaten me. They couldn't see him and thought he was
armed. They were trying to protect me."

"Poor Gavin. I'd like to go with you to the hospital after
dinner."

"Sure."

"Um—" Lisa glanced down at her hands and splayed her
fingers. She'd painted the nails a pale pink to match the
shorts outfit she wore. "I found out something today—about
Alex."

"Yeah?"

"First, she hated her stepfather. When I asked if he
abused her, she said not in the way I was thinking. The main
reason Alex was mad at him was because of the way he'd
treated her boyfriend."

"Girls!" Aunt Kate knocked on the door. "Dinner's on.
We're eating on the patio. Just dish up your plates and join
us."

"Be right there," Lisa answered, then turned back to Jennie.

"Who's her boyfriend?"

"Brian Stone."

"You're kidding." Somehow Jennie had trouble picturing
the eccentric Alexis Mancini with the tall, blond jock. Brian
was a total sports nut. He'd asked Jennie out a couple of
times, but she'd refused. Not that he wasn't cute. The guy
looked like a blond Tom Cruise. He just happened to be a
few sandwiches short of a picnic in the brains department.

"No, I'm not, but get this. Mancini flunked Brian last year. Brian tried to get reinstated and said he'd do a summer class. Mancini wouldn't take him back."

"Which means no football this fall." Jennie followed Lisa into the kitchen and grabbed a plate. Jennie wondered if Brian had been the student Mancini had written to Michael about.

"Exactly. The thing is, with Mancini out of the way, Brian gets another chance."

"So you're thinking he might have killed Mancini?" She piled spaghetti on her plate and stirred the thick, savory meat sauce.

"Or maybe Alex and Brian did it together."

11

"I hope you don't mind my accompanying you to visit your friend. Lisa seemed rather relieved when I offered to go in her place." Gram slid in behind the wheel of her cherry red 1955 classic Thunderbird convertible.

"Not at all. I love being with you—and riding in your car."

Lisa had begged off after getting a phone call from Rafael and inviting him over. The way she'd bounced around, you'd have thought she'd been nominated for an Academy Award. Jennie didn't think any guy was worth that much excitement. Except maybe Ryan. She was getting butterflies just thinking about his finally coming home.

"Good. I've been wanting to talk with you." Gram started the engine and adjusted the rearview mirror.

"Me too—I mean, to talk to you." Jennie buckled her seat belt—Gram had had them installed in the antique car several years ago when Oregon passed a mandatory seat belt law. Other than the belts, and an occasional part, Gram tried to stay true to the car's original design.

"Um—did Mom say anything about my coming down to the beach and staying with you for a week or two before school starts?"

"As a matter a fact, she did." Looking behind her, Gram backed out of the driveway and onto the street.

"And?"

"I think it's a wonderful idea. So does J.B. Do you want to come with us tomorrow?"

"Um—no—I mean, I'd like to, but I can't leave right now."

Gram smiled in understanding. "Of course, your friend Gavin."

"I wouldn't feel right about leaving until I know if he's going to be all right."

"Have you any ideas regarding the Mancini case? I've been following the story in the news. Do the police still think he committed suicide? He didn't, you know."

"I know—I spent half the day trying to tell Lieutenant Rastovski that. But how did you know? Did Lisa tell you?"

"We talked about it. But I'd already questioned the idea from what I'd gleaned from the papers and television."

"Why?"

"I found it rather odd that a man who took such pride in his work and who had just cleaned his own chemistry lab would then mess it up by shooting himself."

"That's exactly what Gavin told me." Jennie tipped her head back and smiled. She didn't know what felt best— knowing Gram shared her views, or feeling the warm summer wind whipping around her as she snuggled against the leather seats. "What does J.B. think about it?"

"The case is out of his jurisdiction, of course, but he agrees. Now tell me how you managed to get involved in all of this."

Jennie spent most of the drive to the hospital filling Gram in on the events of the past two days.

"A baffling case," Gram said, turning into the hospital parking lot. "Even more baffling is the man himself."

"What do you mean?"

"I did some checking of my own, and it seems your Mr. Mancini has a rather interesting past—some of which may have swayed Lieutenant Rastovski to so stubbornly hold on to the idea of suicide."

"Really?" Jennie smoothed back the hair that had escaped her braid to ride the wind.

Gram finger-combed her own windblown salt-and-pepper hair. Like magic, it settled into place. "Come on," she said, opening the car door. "I'll tell you on the way in."

When Jennie joined her behind the car, Gram gave her a one-armed hug. "Have I told you lately how proud I am of you?"

"Yeah, but you can tell me again." Changing the subject, Jennie said, "By the way, I like your new haircut."

They began walking toward the hospital's main entrance. "So do I. It is so much easier to take care of than the shoulder-length style I'd been wearing."

"Gram?"

"Yes, darling?"

"You were going to tell me about Mr. Mancini."

"Yes, I guess I was." She frowned. "Jennie, by telling you this, I don't mean to encourage you to carry out your own investigation in this case. In fact, I've been commissioned by your mother to find out exactly what it is you're up to and put a stop to it."

Jennie chewed her lower lip and after a few seconds said, "I'm not investigating—I mean—not really."

Gram gave her a skeptical look.

"I'm just asking a few questions. You know how I am. I don't mean to go against Mom. But, Gram, telling me to stop thinking about it is like telling me not to breathe."

"Which is what makes it so hard for me to have to discourage you. You are far too much like me in that regard. But we are dealing with a murder here. It's one thing for you to speculate about it with me, but quite another to get physically involved."

"I've already had enough lectures from Rocky and Lieutenant Rastovski. All I can promise is that if I find out anything relating to the case, I'll tell the police."

Gram nodded. "I guess that will have to do." The automatic doors swished open as they approached.

"I don't understand why everybody has to be so paranoid. I've solved seven cases in the last three months. Not by myself, of course, but I helped."

"Yes, and unfortunately you've given all of us cause for concern. Jennie, if your mother seems overprotective at times it's because she loves you. She doesn't want to see you get hurt—none of us do."

"I won't get hurt."

"My dear girl, may I remind you that this summer alone you've been kidnapped, held at gunpoint, narrowly escaped a fire, been shot at, and had your arm broken."

"It was just a small break." Jennie held up her right arm. "See, they even took the cast off early."

"I know you plan on going into law enforcement, and I think that's wonderful. But don't ever minimize the danger."

Jennie didn't want to argue with Gram—or anybody for that matter. She didn't mean to be disagreeable, but why couldn't they understand? "Nancy Drew never had problems like this," Jennie muttered. "People practically knocked her door down trying to get her to investigate crimes."

Gram smiled. "Nancy Drew is a fictional character. You are real and very much alive, and we'd like to keep you that way."

Despite her annoyance, Jennie chuckled. "Okay, just tell Mom I won't do anything you wouldn't do."

"Oh, that's very funny. I'm sure that will make her feel much better."

"Well, it should. Especially since she doesn't know about your undercover work."

"Shh. You're not supposed to know either."

They stopped at the front desk and got Gavin's room number.

"We'd better table this discussion for now." Gram led the way down the hall and into the gift shop. "Would you like to pick up a gift for Gavin? Flowers? Balloons?"

After making a mental note to remind Gram to tell her what she'd learned about Mr. Mancini, Jennie said, "Balloons."

They bought one nylon balloon with a duck on it proclaiming, "Get well soon" and two bright blue latex balloons to accompany it. After picking out a get-well card and signing it, they headed for the elevator.

Gavin was lying in a bed rigged with some kind of traction device. His right leg had been raised off the bed and rested in a sling. A trapeze-like bar hung over his head. He reached to grab it when he saw her, his face contorting with pain.

Maddie Winslow was sitting beside the bed, typing on a laptop computer—probably working on her latest book. She wrote mysteries for young adults and was hoping to break into movies with one of the cases Jennie had helped solve this summer.

"Hi." Jennie stepped into the room, careful not to snag the balloons in the doorway.

"Jennie." Maddie looked up from her screen. "Your mother said you'd be by." Her gaze drifted to Gram. "Helen, how nice to see you again."

Gram returned the greeting and asked Gavin how he was doing.

"Wonderful." He sounded hoarse. "I've always wanted to know what it felt like to get shot—now I know."

"At least you haven't lost your sense of humor."

"Nope, only blood." He licked his lips. Maddie picked up a glass of water and placed the straw in his mouth. After a couple of swallows he pushed it away.

"They're giving him two units of packed cells," Maddie

said, nodding toward the IV stand and bags hanging there. One was blood, the other some sort of saline solution. "The bullet fractured his femur."

The strange effects of whatever drug or drugs he'd been on seemed to be gone. His eyes no longer had that wild look. He just looked like any normal person would in his condition.

"Um—" Jennie held the balloon bouquet toward him. "These are for you."

"Thanks."

"They're lovely." Maddie took them and secured the strings to Gavin's tray table.

Jennie opened her mouth to ask Gavin where he had disappeared to and how he'd ended up in her car, but he'd closed his eyes. She asked his mom instead. Maddie motioned them outside the room and closed the door. "We should let him rest."

"I'm sorry. I guess I shouldn't be asking questions."

"It's all right, Jennie. The police told us what happened and—I'm just so grateful you and Michael were there."

"Did you find out what kind of drug he was on?"

She shook her head. "The doctor said it may have been a methamphetamine, or possibly LSD, but we don't know yet."

"Gavin didn't say?"

"Gavin says he can't remember anything. The police tried to question him but finally gave up. I guess we'll have to wait until tomorrow. Maybe he'll be more coherent. I certainly hope so." Maddie started to cry.

Gram placed an arm around Maddie's shoulders in an effort to comfort her.

"What are we going to do? Gavin's never done anything like this before. He's always been so dependable."

"You don't think he took drugs himself, do you?" Jennie asked.

Maddie shook her head and blew her nose with the tissue

Gram handed her. "No, of course not. It's just that the police keep telling me he did. When I stand up for Gavin, they act like I'm lying."

They talked a few minutes longer, then at nine-fifteen Jennie and Gram left.

"I hate this." Jennie followed Gram into the elevator and hit the button for the first floor.

"What's that, dear?"

"Not knowing what's going on with Gavin. I wish I could say for sure he wasn't taking drugs. Thing is, I don't know him well enough to say that."

"Hmm. What do your instincts tell you?"

The elevator doors opened and they stepped out. Jennie thought for a moment before she answered. Instincts. Gram had always told her to trust them—that often it was the Holy Spirit whispering truth. "I guess if I had to choose based on what I know about Gavin, I'd side with Maddie. I don't think Gavin took the drugs on his own."

"Then that's what you need to hold on to. Now if that's your premise, what's your deduction?"

"It's not just because he isn't the type—theoretically, anyone could become a user. Gavin was on to something. He felt there was a connection between Mancini's murder and the burglary. A few hours later he calls to tell me he's had this major breakthrough—then he disappears. The next day he shows up stoned out of his mind. He may have stumbled onto something important—or was about to. I have a hunch that if he knew too much, he'd be dead. Looks more like he was getting too close and someone wanted him out of the way."

"So they discredit him by making him look like a drug user." Gram pulled her keys out of her handbag.

"Something like that."

Gram nodded. "It's plausible. In a way I wish J.B. and I weren't going back to the coast, but I do need to get home.

I have an article due for Northwest Magazine in a couple of days."

When they reached the car, Jennie remembered the interrupted conversation they'd had coming in. "You started to tell me something about Mr. Mancini earlier."

"Oh yes." Gram got into the car but didn't start it. "It's rather curious, really. Your *Mr.* Mancini is actually *Doctor* Mancini. He graduated with honors from Harvard and went on to become a chemistry professor there, then later moved to Berkeley. Seems he got a grant from a pharmaceutical company to create a new drug."

"Wow. That's impressive, but if that's the case, what was he doing at Trinity High? Why would he go from a prestigious university like Harvard to a small private school?"

"That, my dear, is precisely the question I had."

"Well, did you find out?"

"As a matter of fact, I did. It seems Dr. Mancini was asked to resign after several students reported that he had been making, selling, and using designer drugs."

12

Talk about bombshells. Jennie felt the impact of Gram's revelation clear down to her toes. "That sure changes things," she said above the roar of the car's engine. "Maybe Mr.—um *Doctor*—Mancini stole the supplies from the chemistry lab at Trinity and started doing the drug thing again."

"That's a possibility, but you also need to know that Dr. Mancini was never convicted. In fact, the case never went to trial."

"Why not?"

"Not enough evidence."

Jennie pondered the news. Even if Dr. Mancini had been responsible for the burglary at Trinity High, that left another big question. Who had killed him? After mulling the question over and not getting anywhere, Jennie placed it in the back of her mind with the other information she'd gleaned. She'd bring it all out and write it down, then go back over it again when she wasn't so tired. Besides, there was one more very important issue she needed to talk with Gram about.

"Gram?" Jennie began, not certain what approach to take. "I need to ask you something really important."

"Hmm—I think I know that look. Trouble at home?"

Jennie sighed. "Sort of. It's about Mom marrying Michael. I mean—I like Michael—it's just that every time I think about them getting married, I get this sick feeling in the pit of my stomach."

"Let me guess. This has something to do with your father."

"Yes. I can't stand knowing he's alive and not being able to tell Mom." Jennie glanced at her grandmother. "It isn't fair that we can't tell her. She should know before she gets married again."

"She did get a divorce."

"I know it would be legal, but that's not the problem. It just feels so wrong. Dad shouldn't be deceiving her like that. And something else—I can't help but think she might not marry Michael if she knew Dad was still alive. Maybe it's wishful thinking—but . . ."

Gram reached over and squeezed Jennie's hand. "I've given the situation a lot of thought myself. And I've talked to J.B."

"You have?"

"We both feel your father was wrong in making some of the choices he did. And to be honest, sometimes I think the government tends to be a bit more clandestine than necessary. Jason should never have put the responsibility of keeping his secret on your shoulders nor on mine. He should have found a way to tell Susan."

Even though Jennie agreed and had brought the subject up, she felt a sudden urge to defend Dad's actions. "But he was doing what he had to do to protect us. And we wouldn't have found out if I hadn't been so determined to find him. My trying to find him proved how dangerous being around him could be."

"True. I believe he did what he felt he had to do. Perhaps it's still too dangerous for him to come home, but you're absolutely right—your mother deserves to know the truth."

"So, can we tell her?"

"That's not a decision we can make on our own, and I don't think you or I should be the ones to break the news. But I have asked J.B. to talk to your father's superiors. There may be a way we can resolve the problem."

Excitement bounded through Jennie's veins as she thought of the possibilities. "Do you think I could see him again—talk to him?" *Oh, please say yes . . . please.*

"I don't know. Personally, I'd like nothing more than to see Jason come back to us—even if it is under a different persona. I do think it would be a mistake, though, for you to get your hopes up. Even if your mother is told the truth about Jason, I doubt she'd change her mind about marrying Michael. And I doubt Jason would be willing to change careers to please your mother."

"You're probably right. Mom hated his being an agent. But she's changed, Gram. She and Michael split up because he was so involved with his work. Michael is still involved, but Mom went back to him anyway." Of course, being a pastor wasn't as dangerous as being in law enforcement, but Jennie didn't want to think about that.

After a few minutes Jennie asked, "How soon will you know?"

"That's a difficult question to answer. I'll talk to J.B. again tonight."

Jennie leaned back against the seat and closed her eyes. She imagined Dad coming home and telling Mom he was still alive. Mom would be upset, of course, but she'd soon come to understand the sacrifice Dad had made. He wouldn't look like himself, either. He'd be blond, Jennie decided, with a wonderful tan from having worked in the tropics. And he'd be wearing glasses. Or maybe contacts.

Jennie thought again about Douglas. Could contacts make eyes a lighter shade of blue? Douglas had a tan. She'd look at him more closely next time she saw him. On the other hand, wouldn't he find a way to let her know if he was her father? Not necessarily.

Don't get your hopes up, McGrady, she reminded herself again. Not an easy task. No matter how hard she tried to block the images out, they came again and again. Dad showing up on the doorstep and pulling Mom into his arms. Mom telling Michael she couldn't marry him. Mom and Jennie introducing Nick to his real daddy. And Mom and Dad, not Mom and Michael, walking down the aisle. Jennie wondered if a person could annul a divorce the same way they annulled a marriage. That would be easier—but not as romantic.

Though she'd tried to stay awake, Jennie drifted off, coming to when Gram pulled into Aunt Kate's driveway and cut the engine. "We're back, dear."

Opening the car door, Jennie unfolded herself from the less than spacious front seat and stretched, rubbing the kink out of her neck at the same time.

"Are you coming in?" Gram came around the car and joined her in the driveway.

"I guess." She glanced around. The only cars parked in the driveway besides her own were Gram's T-Bird and the Calhouns' Taurus. "Looks like Mom and Nick have gone home. Wonder how Lisa's evening with Rafael went."

"I don't think you'll have to wait long to find out. From the way Lisa is grinning, I'd say the evening was a complete success."

Lisa ran down the stairs toward them. "It's about time you got here. We were getting worried. Actually, I was hoping you'd be back before Rafael had to leave. He is so wonderful—even our moms thought so. I can't wait for you to meet him, Gram."

Lisa spent the next five minutes filling them in on the details. How Rafael didn't speak very good English and that's why he hadn't called her sooner. How he planned to become a U.S. citizen, liked the same things Lisa did, had a married sister still living in Mexico, and about a hundred or so other vital statistics.

"Hi, you two." Aunt Kate rescued them from Lisa's litany. "You're just in time for some tea. I put the kettle on just before I tucked the boys in."

"Nick's staying over?" Jennie followed her aunt and grandmother into the kitchen.

"Sure is. You're welcome to as well, Jennie. Just call your mom and let her know either way."

"I'll stay." Being with Mom and not telling her about Dad had been growing harder by the day. Now, after talking with Gram, keeping the secret would be even more difficult. Jennie picked up the phone and punched in her home phone number. It rang twice before the answering machine came on. She waited for the beep, then said, "Hi, Mom, it's me. Just wanted to tell you I'm staying over at Lisa's. I'll talk to you tomorrow."

"I take it she wasn't home," Gram said when Jennie hung up.

"Nope." Jennie glanced at her watch. "When did she leave here?"

"Shortly after you and Gram did. But don't worry. She said she was meeting someone."

"Michael?" Jennie dropped into the chair between Lisa and Gram and rested her elbows on the table.

Kate shrugged. "Probably."

"Maybe I'd better go home—make sure she's okay."

Kate came up from behind and hugged her. "You worry too much. Your mother is just fine. She was being a bit secretive—I have a hunch she and Michael wanted to spend some romantic time alone."

Thanks, I really wanted to hear that. Jennie's stomach was starting to hurt again. The tea helped, as did listening to Kate talk about her latest decorating job. Unfortunately the talk turned to Gavin, and Jennie felt herself getting edgy again as she and Gram brought Lisa and Kate up to date. Tomorrow she'd go back to the hospital and talk to Gavin again. Hopefully he'd have some answers.

13

The following morning after breakfast, Jennie packed up her little brother and Bernie and headed home. When she pulled into the empty driveway she felt a moment's panic. That subsided when Mom opened the door. Mom had parked the Oldsmobile in the garage.

Nick paused to get kissed and hugged, then broke away. "Come on, Bernie—let's find you some food."

"Clean out his dishes first," Mom yelled after him.

After a quick hug, Jennie followed her mother inside and asked how her evening with Michael had gone.

"Michael?" Mom looked confused. "Where did you get the idea I was with Michael?"

"Kate said you were meeting someone—I mean—who else would you meet?"

"Any number of people, actually." She closed the door and headed for the kitchen.

"So who was it?"

"I'd rather not talk about that just now. I'm in the middle of a project." She headed for the office. "Shouldn't take me too long—another hour."

"Mom," Jennie whined. "I hate it when you do that. Tell me. Did you find another boyfriend or something?"

"Don't take that tone with me, young lady. You're in enough trouble already."

"I'm sorry. I didn't mean to be snotty, I'm just curious."

She hauled in a deep what-am-I-going-to-do-with-you sigh. "Yes, and that curiosity is precisely what Lieutenant Rastovski and I were talking about last evening."

"You were out with Rastovski? Mom, how could you? Michael is—"

"Michael is my fiancé. And no, I'm not dating the lieutenant—nor do I intend to. We do, however, have a mutual interest in you."

Jennie plunked herself down on the chair Mom kept in her office for clients. "You were right, I don't want to know."

"He called me yesterday and asked if we could meet to discuss you—or rather your interference in the Mancini case."

Jennie winced. "I was only trying to help. He thought Mancini committed suicide—"

"And you decided to straighten him out."

"He was wrong—" Anger seeped in to replace her confusion. "Rastovski had no business talking to you about me."

"I beg your pardon." Mom's cheeks were nearly as red as her hair. "The last time I looked, you were still underage. That makes me responsible for you. And as a responsible parent I intend to keep you out of trouble."

Jennie folded her arms and clamped her jaws together. It was going to be a long day.

"Jennie, despite what you often read in mysteries or have seen on *Murder, She Wrote*," Mom went on, "police officers are not bungling idiots who'll do anything to keep from solving murder cases."

"I know that, but—"

"You also committed a crime," Mom interrupted.

"Yeah, well, so did Michael. For your information, we saved Gavin's life."

"Lieutenant Rastovski is thinking seriously about arresting both of you for obstruction of justice. He's hoping maybe that will cure you of this crazy idea you have about being a detective."

"Fine, let them arrest me. I'll call Uncle Jeff." Jeff White Cloud was Mom's brother-in-law and a lawyer.

Mom raised her hands in mock surrender, tossed Jennie a why-me look, then scooped up a folder. "You're grounded. For the next week, or until the police solve this case, you are not leaving this house."

"That's not fair! I haven't done anything wrong. Just because Rastovski says so—this was his idea, wasn't it? He wants me out of the way so he talked you into grounding me!"

"It was a mutual decision. And it isn't because he wants you out of the way. We're afraid you'll end up hurt. However, if you'd rather, I suppose I could call him and tell him you'd rather spend the time in jail."

Jennie jumped out of the chair and stalked out.

"And don't bother calling Gram. It won't do any good."

"I'll be in my room." Jennie stomped up the stairs into her room, slammed the door shut, and threw herself on the bed. After beating the bejeebers out of her pillow, she got up and paced.

A few minutes later she yanked open her desk drawer. "Oh no." Jennie watched as paper clips, pens, papers, and staples rolled and skidded over every inch of the floor. She covered her eyes and clenched her teeth. *Chill out, McGrady*, she told herself. *Take a deep breath and count to ten.* Jennie fell back onto her bed and closed her eyes. In between numbers, she had a few words with God.

One "I think you should know, I am not happy about this. But then I guess you can see that, can't you?"

Two "Why are you letting them get away with this? I mean, it's not like I've done anything all that bad. What was I supposed to do, let them kill Gavin?"

Three "Are you trying to tell me something here? Gram

says I should find good in everything. That isn't easy."

Four "I can't just forget about Mancini's murder—or Gavin."

Five "I suppose I could use the time by myself to make a chart. And I do have the telephone. I can make some phone calls."

Jennie skipped the remaining five numbers and hurriedly picked the stuff up from the floor and put it away. After a much-needed shower and a change of clothes, she picked up a blue spiral notebook and pen, climbed into the window seat, and began jotting down notes to herself. She began with a journal entry in which she wrote every detail she could remember, from her first contact with Mancini to the present.

Then, turning a fresh piece of paper sideways, she started her chart, making five columns, and labeling them Suspect, Motive, Means, Opportunity, and Clues. To the far left she wrote *1) Alexis Mancini*. Under Motive—*money and freedom*, but as she remembered what Lisa had said about Brian Stone, Alex's boyfriend, she added *revenge*. Jennie left the Opportunity column blank. She'd have to find out later whether or not Alex had an alibi. Under Clues, Jennie listed the trip to Europe and how Alex seemed almost glad that her stepfather was dead.

She listed Mrs. Mancini next and placed a star beside the name. Jennie wanted to have a nice little chat with her too. Under Clues she wrote: *Dr. Mancini's wife—planned his funeral and a trip to Europe on the same day*.

Brian Stone came next, then Curtis Bolton. She still hadn't had a chance to talk to Curtis or Brian either, but Jennie hoped to remedy that soon. Maybe she'd call them.

After thumbing through the phone directory, Jennie dialed Brian Stone's number. His mother answered. No, Brian wasn't there, but he'd be home after six. "Can I take a message?"

"This is Jennie McGrady—could you have him call me? My number is—"

"What's this in regard to?" Mrs. Stone's voice turned razor sharp.

"Um—" What could she say? She didn't want to lie. On the other hand, she couldn't tell her what she really wanted.

"Never mind. I think I know what you're up to. You want to ask him about Mr. Mancini's death. For your information, Jennie McGrady, Brian had nothing to do with it. He was working that day. It's bad enough that the police have been hammering away at him, but to have his schoolmates—wait a minute. Did the police put you up to this?"

"No, I—I was at the school when Michael found the body. I heard about Brian's trouble with Dr. Mancini and—"

"That information was strictly confidential." Her voice went up another octave and Jennie flinched. "My son is not a murderer. Like I told the police, the incident is in the past. Brian will be going to another school next year where they have a more flexible teaching staff."

After mumbling an apology for bothering her, Jennie hung up and scribbled out Brian's name on her suspect list. "This is stupid." Jennie tossed the notebook to the floor and let the pen drop beside it. "You don't know what you're doing, McGrady. For all you know, the murderer could be some drug pusher who didn't like the deal Mancini was cutting him." If the accusations against Dr. Mancini were true, that certainly was a possibility.

From what Rocky had told her about the manufacturing of illegal drugs, the idea made a lot of sense. Which, of course, meant the suspect list would be endless. So why was she even bothering?

Jennie's gaze drifted outside and down the quiet street they lived on. A patrol car came to a stop at the end of the street, then turned onto Magnolia. She wondered if it might be Rocky. The car pulled up to the curb in front of Jennie's house. Officer Phelps got out. A few seconds later, another car came up behind her. An officer Jennie didn't recognize joined Phelps on the street then started walking up the driveway.

Normally, Jennie wasn't afraid of the police. Yet at the moment, her stomach churned, then tied itself into one huge knot. Maybe it was what Rastovski had said about arresting her. No, he was just trying to scare her. Wasn't he?

When she heard the doorbell ring, Jennie took a deep breath and let it out slowly. *For Pete's sake, McGrady, relax. They probably just want to ask some more questions.*

"Jennie," Mom called. "There's someone here to see you."

"Coming." Jennie descended the stairs, trying to act as nonchalant about the officers' visit as possible.

"Hi." Jennie gripped the railing, willing herself to stay calm.

They waited until she reached the main floor before speaking. "Sorry to bother you, Mrs. McGrady," Officer Phelps said. "This is Officer Kelly." Phelps glanced at Mom, then back to Jennie. "But we got a tip that your daughter has been dealing drugs."

"What? You're kidding, right?" Jennie's knees threatened to buckle.

"I'm afraid not," Officer Kelly said. "Would you mind if we looked around?"

"Yes, as a matter of fact I do." Mom gripped the door.

"It's okay, Mom. I don't have anything to hide."

"In that case, you won't mind if we take a look at your car." Phelps spoke this time.

Jennie felt like a mouse being stalked by two hungry cats as she retrieved her keys from the hook in the kitchen and led the officers out to the Mustang. She unlocked the car door and stepped back while Kelly methodically searched the car.

"I don't understand this." Jennie brushed damp bangs

from her forehead. "Why would anyone—"

"Looks like we hit pay dirt." Kelly emerged from the backseat holding up a quart-sized plastic bag.

Jennie gasped and shook her head. "I—I didn't."

Phelps reached behind her and pulled out a pair of handcuffs. In the next second, Phelps spun Jennie around and pressed her against the trunk of the Mustang. She slapped the cuffs on her wrists. "You are under arrest for possession of narcotics—"

14

"—whatever you say can and will be held against you in a court of law."

"Wait a minute." Mom tried to grab the arresting officer's arm. Kelly held her back. "You can't just come into our home and—"

"Mrs. McGrady," Phelps said. "I know this must come as a shock to you, but it happens all the time."

"This is insane. Jennie would never—"

Officer Phelps leveled a steady gaze on Mom. "We just found a stash of methamphetamine in your daughter's car. Right where the Winslow boy said it would be."

"Gavin?" Jennie looked from one officer to the other. "That's impossible."

"Let's go. You'll have a chance to tell your story later." Phelps grasped Jennie's arm.

"No." Jennie jerked away. "You can't arrest me. Mom—" She looked back as the officers led her down the driveway. "Don't let them do this. You know I don't do drugs. Tell them."

"It's all right, Jennie." Mom seemed to have regained control while Jennie was quickly losing hers. "I'll get someone to watch Nick and be right down. Don't say anything until we get a lawyer."

"Does Rocky know about this?" Jennie asked as she let

Phelps guide her to the squad car.

"If you mean Officer Rockwell, I doubt it. He's working swing today."

"Well, call him. Tell him what's going on. He knows I wouldn't—"

"Get into the car." Officer Phelps opened the back door.

Ducking her head, Jennie folded herself inside and cringed when the door shut. Her breath came in short gasps that turned to sobs.

Don't you dare cry, McGrady. Jennie fought to keep her tears at bay. *You are not going to fall apart. You're not!*

On the way to the station, Phelps glanced frequently into the rearview mirror but didn't speak. For some reason Phelps didn't like her, and Jennie couldn't imagine why. She wondered briefly if the officer had planted the evidence but quickly shrugged off the notion—what possible reason could she have?

Jennie hauled in a shuddering sigh, then forced herself to take deep breaths. *Calm down, McGrady. You'll get through this. You've been in worse scrapes.* Still, she offered up a silent prayer, wishing there was something she could say or do to turn things around. But what could she say? She was being set up. If the police really had found drugs in her car, someone had planted them. But Gavin? Was that what he'd been doing in her car when she found him? Why? The questions haunted her all the way downtown.

Rocky was at the station when Phelps brought her in. His eyes narrowed when he saw her. "Devon, what's going on?" His gaze shifted from Jennie to Phelps.

"What are you doing here? Thought you said you were off today." Officer Phelps deposited Jennie in a chair.

"I am. Her mother called me."

Phelps harrumphed. "And you hot-foot it down here to be with her in her hour of need. How touching." In the look that passed between Rocky and Phelps, Jennie finally figured out what was going on. Devon Phelps was jealous. Somehow she'd gotten the idea that Jennie and Rocky were an item. How funny. Not that Jennie hadn't had her moments. Sometimes she still wished Rocky were younger—or that she was a little older—but mostly, she was just glad to have him as a friend.

"It isn't what you think—" Rocky ran a hand through his sandy hair. "Look, we'll talk about that later. In the meantime, I suggest you lighten up." He nodded toward Jennie. "What have you got on her?"

"Your little would-be cop seems to think she's above the law. Found a bag of ice stashed under the seat of her car."

"Tell her I'm innocent, Rocky." Jennie's pleading dark eyes searched for some kind of empathy from him. "You know I wouldn't do anything like that. Besides, I'm not stupid. Do you really think that if I were into drugs I'd leave the stuff in my car?"

"What tipped you off?" Rocky ignored Jennie's pleas.

"The Winslow kid confessed this morning. Told us she might have been the one who drugged him. Says someone knocked him out. Doesn't remember much after that."

"He's lying. I'd never do anything like that. Rocky, tell her." She may as well have been invisible for all the attention Rocky and Devon Phelps were paying to her. They moved a few feet away from her and lowered their voices so she couldn't hear.

Jennie tipped her head back in exasperation and whacked the wall. "Ouch." Great, now she had a headache to go along with everything else. How could Gavin have implicated her like that? Why would he lie?

"Fine," Phelps said in a voice loud enough for Jennie to hear. "You can talk to her while I'm doing my report. Rastovski and Douglas want to question her too, so you can call them in when you're finished."

"You heading back out?" Rocky asked.

"Yeah—we got a shooting down on the waterfront. It's a mess down there." Officer Phelps paused beside Jennie long enough to remove the handcuffs, then left.

"Let's go someplace where we can talk." Rocky grabbed her by the elbow and pulled her up.

Jennie dutifully followed Rocky down a long hall and into a small room that was sparsely furnished with a scarred wooden library table and four mismatched chairs. An interrogation room, Jennie decided. "Is someone watching from the other room?"

Rocky glanced up at the mirror and shrugged. "I doubt it. I'm not acting in an official capacity at the moment. What you say to me you say as a friend." He pulled out a chair away from a long rectangular table. "Have a seat. Want something to drink? Water, Coke?"

Jennie shook her head. "Maybe later. Um—am I supposed to be fingerprinted or something?"

"Yeah—but I'd like to hear what happened first."

Some of the knots in Jennie's stomach had come undone, and she was beginning to relax. Mom would be there soon with a lawyer and she'd be released. And when she was, she planned to have a long talk with Gavin Winslow.

Rocky sat on the edge of the table.

"You believe me, don't you? I've never used drugs. And I never would."

"There's a lot of money in the drug business. Not all dealers are users."

Jennie's jaw dropped. "You can't be serious. I'm on your side, remember?"

His blue gaze caught hers. "I know, Jennie. You got any ideas on how and when the meth got in your car?"

Jennie rubbed her forehead trying to remember. "Yesterday at the school. I forgot to lock my car. Gavin crawled into the backseat." Jennie broke eye contact and stared at a jagged *A* someone had carved into the table. "Gavin must have planted the drugs there, but I can't understand why. He doesn't do drugs either. At least I don't think so."

"Look, Jennie, I don't know if you realize it, but you're in a lot of trouble here."

"I didn't *do* anything. Why can't you believe me?"

"What I believe doesn't matter. What counts here is the evidence. Unfortunately, this drug thing is only the tip of the iceberg. You're also a suspect in Mancini's murder."

"B-but that's crazy!" Jennie sputtered. "I'm the one who convinced Rastovski the case wasn't a suicide."

Rocky's blue gaze settled on her again. "I told you all your snooping around would get you into trouble one of these days. Rastovski thinks you know too much to be an innocent bystander. And now, with the Winslow kid fingering you as one of his assailants . . ."

"Couldn't you talk to him?"

"I have. Rastovski is fairly new to the department. He's a good cop—at least that's what we've been told. The guy's got a reputation for being a bulldog. Right now he's sniffing around, looking for suspects, possible connections. He'll circle around until he's sure he's got a case before he makes an arrest."

Jennie leaned her elbows on the table and buried her face in her hands. "What am I going to do? How can I convince him I'm innocent?"

"Tell him everything you know. If it makes you feel any better, I think he's leaning more toward Michael than you. Did you know your future stepfather and Mancini almost came to blows—about an hour before the shooting? Any idea what they might have been arguing about?"

Jennie straightened. Though she suspected Michael had been protecting Brian Stone, she didn't know for certain. "I—I can't imagine Michael fighting with anyone. Why are you asking me—I mean, why not just ask Michael?"

Rocky sighed. "He's not talking. Says the object of his

discussion with Mancini has nothing to do with the case and he won't break a confidence."

"Maybe I could talk to him."

Jennie never did hear Rocky's reply. The door opened and Rastovski and Douglas walked in, followed by Mom and a guy Jennie recognized as one of Trinity's board members.

Mom leaned over to hug Jennie. "I got here as quickly as I could, sweetheart." Her glance darted from her daughter to the man who now had his briefcase open on the table. "You remember Mr. Collins? He's an attorney."

"Hi, Jennie." He smiled and stretched a hand toward Jennie. After a quick handshake, he dropped his gaze to the briefcase, pulled out a yellow legal pad and pen, and sat down.

For the next few minutes, Jennie felt like she may as well have been on another planet. They spoke in a jargon she barely understood and acted as though she didn't exist. Which was okay with her as long as the charges were dropped and she could leave.

Unfortunately, that didn't happen. Rastovski turned away from the lawyer, slammed a fist on the table, and walked out. "Book her."

Jennie nearly bit through her lower lip. This couldn't be happening. She took a deep breath and turned to the lawyer.

"Why are they booking me? What did you say to him to make him mad?"

Mr. Collins glanced up from his note taking and met her tearful gaze head on. "I just told him that questioning you would be pointless."

"But won't that make me look guilty? Call him back. I'll tell him everything I know." Jennie stood and aimed for the door. "I don't want to go to jail."

"You won't. Since this is your first offense, they'll process you and with any luck we'll have you back home by dinner."

"My first offense? What do you mean? You don't think I'm guilty, do you?"

"They do have some compelling evidence, Jennie. But, like I said, in all probability you won't even have to stand trial. I think we can plea bargain and get you off with community service."

"Community—wait a minute. Why would I have to do anything? I'm innocent."

He sighed. "That may be. It's a rather complicated situation, but our chances are much better if the case doesn't go to trial."

"Honey, please." Mom grasped Jennie's shoulder. "For once, just do as you're told. Mr. Collins knows what he's doing."

Jennie glanced at Rocky, who was still leaning against the wall next to Douglas. His eyes were narrow slits devoid of compassion. Another officer stepped into the room and escorted Jennie away.

Feeling about as helpless as a piece of toilet paper, Jennie finally gave up and let the authorities flush her through their bureaucratic system.

Hours later, Jennie walked out of the station and ducked into her mom's Oldsmobile. They didn't speak for the first few minutes. Jennie stole several quick glances to determine Mom's mood. She wasn't mad, Jennie decided, but she wasn't too happy either.

"Well," Jennie said after another few minutes of silence, "aren't you going to lecture me?"

Mom frowned, taking her eyes off the road for a moment. "What for? You said you didn't do it, and I believe you."

"Oh." Jennie sank back against the seat. She supposed she should have said thanks, or some such thing. But at the moment Jennie didn't trust herself to say anything for fear the lump in her throat would dislodge and reduce her to tears.

"What we're going to have to find out," Mom continued, "is why Gavin Winslow would lie about your involvement. I've talked to Maddie and she's very upset."

Jennie leaned forward wondering if she'd heard right. "With me or Gavin?"

"Gavin, of course. She believes you too."

"So are we going to the hospital?"

"Yes. Maddie's meeting us there."

―――――――

"Susan, Jennie . . ." Maddie hugged each of them when they stepped off the elevator. "Thanks so much for coming."

Maddie led them to a small waiting room. Jennie paused at the door and looked down the empty hallway. Gavin's room was several doors down. She wanted nothing more than to march into Gavin's room and confront him. The only thing that stopped her was a slight pressure against her arm where Maddie had placed her hand.

"You can go in to see him in a few minutes," she whispered, "but I need to talk to you first."

After pouring herself and Mom coffee from a large pot on the counter at the far end of the room, Maddie sat on the edge of a maroon chair. She took a sip and grimaced. "It's hard to know where to begin. I suppose I should start with an apology. Jennie, I'm so sorry Gavin involved you in all of this."

"Me too." Jennie stared at a wrinkle on her white cotton shorts. "Any idea why he did?"

Maddie shook her head. "He's terribly confused."

"That's for sure. It's almost like he's been programmed or something."

Maddie's head snapped up. "Programmed. Jennie, you may be right. I wrote a book a couple of years ago based on a true story about a sixteen-year-old girl who left home and joined this bizarre religious sect. A private detective agency finally found her, but all they could do was let the parents know she was safe. Her twin, who is a lot like you, Jennie, went undercover and joined the group to get her sister out. The thing is, this girl had been programmed to believe in all kinds of terrible things. They called themselves The True Believers and claimed to be Christians, but nearly everything they did opposed the Christian faith. They executed hate crimes against people of other races. They all shaved their heads and acted much like some of the extreme groups we see today—only they were into sacrifices—let's just say they didn't always stop with animals."

Mom shook her head. "I get so tired of that sort of thing. These extremists get all the press and give anyone who believes in God a bad rap."

"Tell me about it." Maddie took another sip of coffee. "It's almost embarrassing to call myself a Christian anymore. There are so many radicals out there doing horrible things in God's name."

"Well, there really isn't much we can do about it except show people that Christ's message is love, not hate."

Uh-oh. The two things you never wanted to get Mom discussing were politics and religion. She could go on for hours debating issues. Jennie had a hunch if she didn't stop them, they'd be there all day. "Um, Maddie," Jennie interrupted, trying to get the conversation back on track. "Is there any way to tell if Gavin was programmed?"

"What—oh, I don't know. I'll talk to a psychologist friend of mine and find out."

Mom looked at the dark liquid in her cup, then at Jennie. "I think it's obvious that Gavin was either programmed or coerced into naming Jennie as a drug dealer. The question I have is why."

"I've been asking myself the same thing." Maddie set her half-empty cup on a coffee table. "The only possible answer is that someone wants both Jennie and Gavin out of the way."

"And if that's the case, we need to ask ourselves who."

Jennie shuddered. Even though she'd been asking the same questions herself, it seemed more frightening to hear it out loud. *I think the who is obvious.* Jennie thought the response but didn't say it. *The only person Gavin and I are a threat to is the person who tried to make Mancini's murder look like a suicide.*

Jennie's gaze drifted from her mother to Maddie. The two were now talking in hushed voices and acting as if Jennie had faded into the woodwork. She thought about reminding them she was still there but didn't. It seemed strange to see them—especially Mom—talking about the case as if they planned to get involved.

Not so unusual, maybe. Mom could be pretty intense at times—especially when her children were in jeopardy. On occasion the mild-mannered bookkeeper would shed her cautious and inhibited lifestyle and slip into what Jennie called her "wonder woman" role. A smile tugged at the corner of Jennie's mouth. In some ways Mom and Dad had more in common than Mom cared to admit.

Jennie cleared her throat and stood up. "I'm going to see Gavin now."

Maddie and Mom looked up at her then at each other. "Oh, I'm sorry, Jennie," Maddie said. "We didn't mean to exclude you. By all means, go see Gavin. He had a couple of friends with him. Ray left about fifteen minutes ago—Curtis may be gone as well."

"Ray—Curtis?" The names went through her like an electric impulse, jerking the hairs on the back of her neck to attention.

"Yes." Maddie smiled. "Curtis Bolton and his brother Ray."

Jennie's feet seemed to have glued themselves to the floor. "I didn't know they were friends."

"Oh my, yes. Curtis and Gavin have been close friends

since kindergarten. The Boltons live about half a mile from us. The poor boy is devastated about what's happened. He was Mr. Mancini's lab assistant, you know. And then to have his best friend shot." Maddie paused for a moment. "Actually, Jennie, I just had a thought. You might want to talk to Curtis. Maybe you can cheer him up."

"I'll—um—I'll see what I can do." Jennie managed to get her feet moving again and practically ran out the door. She couldn't believe it. Why hadn't Gavin mentioned that Curtis was his friend? She wanted to talk to him all right, but cheering him up wasn't on her agenda.

15

Curtis was just coming out of Gavin's room when Jennie started down the hall. He smiled when he saw her. He'd grown since she'd last seen him. Last year they were the same height—now she had to look up to meet his gaze. He'd filled out some—lost that awkward, gangly adolescent look. In fact, with his long blond hair and baby blues, he looked like a model for those steamy novels Mom wouldn't let her read. Not that she wanted to. Lisa had sneaked one once and assured Jennie it hadn't been worth the bother. One thing for sure, Curtis Bolton had turned into a total babe. Especially when he smiled. No wonder Lisa had remembered him so easily.

"Hi, Jennie." He stopped in front of her. "I was hoping I'd run in to you. In fact, I planned to call you tonight." Curtis stuffed his hands in the pockets of his cutoffs. "I—um—heard about what happened—to you, I mean—getting arrested and all."

"How'd you hear about it so quickly? I was just released about an hour ago and I know it didn't make the news."

"Maddie told me. Funny, I never figured you or Gavin for getting involved in drugs."

"I am not involved in anything." Jennie had so much to talk to Curtis about, she didn't know where to begin. She glanced toward Gavin's room. "How is he?"

"Sleeping right now. Poor guy's really been through it."

"Haven't we all? Did he tell you anything?"

Curtis shook his head. "Nothing coherent."

"Actually, I've been wanting to talk to you too. Maybe you could come by the house later—after dinner."

"Tonight?" Curtis's gaze darted to the floor and back up to her face. From his surprised expression you'd have thought she'd suggested meeting him on the moon.

"It doesn't have to be tonight—if you're busy—"

"Um—no. I was going to do something with my brother, but—" His grin slipped back into place. "Tonight's fine."

"Are you sure?"

He nodded and took a step back. "Seven okay?"

"Fine." Jennie watched as he turned around and headed back in the same direction he'd come. A second or two later, he stopped and headed back toward her. "Wrong way." He laughed at his mistake and hurried past, then ducked into the waiting room, probably to say goodbye to Maddie. *Curious,* Jennie mused. *Wonder what he was so flustered about?*

Jennie slipped into Gavin's room and sat in a chair that had been pulled over to the bed. She'd been furious with him all day, but now, watching him sleep, she felt sorry for him. His forehead wrinkled and he arched his back as if he were in pain or having a bad dream.

His eyes flew open and collided with hers.

Jennie grasped the bed rail and pulled herself up. "I'm sorry I frightened you. I—"

"No," he gasped. "Stay away from me. They'll kill you."

"What?" She backed off a bit and lifted her hands to show him they were empty. "You're not making any sense. Just settle down. I'm not going to hurt you."

Gavin grabbed the trapeze above his head, his face contorted with pain. "Just go away. Please. I can't talk to you."

"Gavin, it's okay. I'm here." Maddie stepped in front of

Jennie. "Shh. It's all right, sweetheart. Jennie just came by to say hi. She's your friend."

"No," he whimpered like a small child. "Keep her away from me."

"Okay—just settle down. She's leaving now." Maddie glanced apologetically at Jennie.

"I-I'm sorry," Jennie stammered as she backed out of the room.

"Oh, man, it hurts so bad."

"I'll have the nurse bring you something for pain." Maddie pressed the button on the call light.

Outside the room, Jennie leaned against the wall and closed her eyes. Her heart hammered against her chest. Tears gathered behind her eyelids.

"Honey—" Mom's arms went around Jennie in an attempt to comfort her.

"Don't." Jennie pulled away and headed down the hall. "Let's just go home, okay?"

"Do you want to talk about it?" Mom joined Jennie in the car ten minutes later.

"No." Jennie folded her arms across her chest.

"Maddie told me what he said to you. You have to understand, Jennie, Gavin doesn't know what he's doing." She started the car and put it in reverse.

"Doesn't he?" Jennie glanced at Mom, then turned to look out the side window. "What if he does? What if he's in on it and is just trying to throw the police off the track by blaming me and acting crazy?"

"Jennie . . ."

"Well, it's possible."

"Maddie and I believe both you and Gavin are innocent of any wrongdoing—except maybe being a little too nosy for your own good."

"How can you know for sure? A lot of parents say they

can't believe their kids could do drugs. Lots of times they're wrong."

"Ever hear of intuition?"

"Of course."

"Well, my intuition is usually right on where you're concerned. Unfortunately, I don't always pay close enough attention. When you're in trouble, I can feel it. I know when you are being honest with me and when you're not. And Jennie, trust me on this. If you were to ever experiment with drugs, which I doubt you would, I'd know. Deep inside, I'd know."

Do you know about Dad too? Jennie wanted to ask. *Do you know I'm keeping a secret from you?* "So, it's like you can read my mind?"

"Not exactly. I just know when something is bothering you. Like with your father."

Jennie snapped to attention.

"What about him?"

Mom shook her head. "I'm not sure. I keep hoping someday you'll talk about it and let me know how you really feel. You're putting up a good front. I can tell you're hesitant about my marrying Michael. There's just an unsettled feeling about it. I can sense it in you—and in myself for that matter."

"Does that mean you're having second thoughts?" *Oh, Mom, say yes—please say yes.*

"Sometimes I hear this voice in my head saying not to marry him—other times I feel like it's the right thing to do." Her shoulders rose and fell. She glanced at Jennie for a second, setting her shimmering red hair in motion. Her somber expression gave way to a smile. "I wonder if one can ever feel sure about decisions like this."

"Maybe you should wait awhile, then."

"Hmm. Michael and I talked this afternoon. I'd called to tell him what happened. He thinks we should postpone the wedding at least until this business with the murder is over.

I guess maybe that's why I'm having second thoughts again. He's been impossible lately."

"Like how?"

"Jumpy, irritable. He's protecting someone, and that concerns me."

"Rocky said something about that. Did you know Michael is a suspect?"

Mom nodded. "Lieutenant Rastovski told me. He and that DEA agent questioned me for about an hour this afternoon while you were being processed."

"Did they tell you I was a suspect in the murder case too?"

"Yes, but I think I convinced them you had nothing to do with the murder."

"And the drugs?"

Mom bit her lip. "I'm not sure about that."

Jennie forced her thoughts back to Gavin. "It was really weird, Mom—what Gavin said, I mean."

"I should say so. Whatever happened to him must have been terrifying to have him react to you the way he did."

"What he said didn't make sense. At first I thought maybe he was afraid of me. While I was waiting for you in the car, I wrote down what he said—word for word. Listen to this." Jennie reached into the backseat for the pad and read, "First he looks at me like he is seeing a ghost, then he says, *No—Stay away from me. They'll kill you.* I tried to calm him down, but he wouldn't listen. Then he says, *Just go away. Please. I can't talk to you.* Doesn't that sound strange to you? Like, if he was really scared of me, why wouldn't he say something like, 'Don't kill me'? And it seems like he would have said 'I don't *want* to talk to you,' instead of *'I can't.'* "

"I admit it does seem a bit odd, but Maddie did say he was confused. He's still on pain medication."

"I know, but I got this feeling." Jennie tossed her mother a grin. "Intuition. Anyway, I got to wondering if maybe

Gavin isn't as confused as everybody thinks. Maybe he wasn't scared *of* me, but *for* me."

"I don't follow."

"Okay." Jennie twisted sideways and loosened the seat belt. "Gavin disappears. The next day he shows up stoned out of his mind. Let's say our intuition is right and he doesn't do drugs. That means someone abducted him and drugged him. Why would they do that? Because he knows too much? Because he's a threat?"

"Why didn't they just kill him?" Mom frowned. "Did you hear what I just said? I can't believe I would have such a cold-blooded thought."

"That, my dear mother, is an excellent point. Maybe the murderer isn't a cold-blooded killer. Maybe he—or she—didn't mean to kill Dr. Mancini. Mancini may have interrupted a second burglary and the thief got scared. Thing is, this person might not want to kill again but has to do something to keep from being caught."

"All right, go on."

Jennie hesitated. It seemed strange to be having this kind of discussion with Mom. "I will, but first I gotta ask you a question."

"Sure."

"Why are you letting me talk about this? You grounded me this morning for getting involved."

Mom pulled into their driveway and turned off the car. Silence stretched between them. Mom finally broke it. "That's a difficult question. Let's talk about it over an iced tea."

A few minutes later, Jennie tapped her foot against the floor, sending the front porch swing into motion.

Mom pressed the frosty glass to her flushed cheeks. "Bet we'll have a thunderstorm tonight. Hot and muggy afternoons like this usually bring them on."

Jennie peered at the hazy blue sky and pushed her damp

bangs off her forehead. "Am I still grounded?"

"No." Mom stared at the amber liquid in her glass. "I overreacted, Jennie, and I apologize. Lieutenant Rastovski frightened me. Keeping you locked up isn't going to solve anything. While I was waiting for you at the police station this afternoon, I got to thinking back to a conversation I had with Joseph White Cloud."

Joseph was Uncle Jeff's father—a Nez Perce Indian and just about the wisest man Jennie had ever met. There'd been a murder at the dude ranch the White Clouds owned—and a major land dispute. Joseph had actually supported her efforts to solve the crime.

"Joseph reminded me that it was in your nature to solve puzzles," Mom went on. "He said you had a wonderful mind and that I should cherish your gifts rather than keep you from using them. He said I should trust you more and be thankful that strong will of yours seeks to do good and not evil."

Jennie lifted the glass to her mouth, not trusting herself to speak. She could almost hear the old man's voice in her mother's words and see his wrinkled face as he must have looked when he'd spoken them.

"Don't get the wrong idea, though, Jennie. I'm not giving you *carte blanche.*"

Jennie frowned. "What's that?"

"A blank check—in other words, you can't do anything you want to. All I'm saying is that I'll try to be more understanding and maybe work with you instead of against you."

For the next few minutes they drank their tea in the quiet of the late afternoon. With Nick and Bernie staying overnight with Kurt again, the place was almost too quiet.

"So," Mom said, setting her glass on the white wicker table, "tell me more about this theory of yours on Gavin's abduction."

"It isn't much of a theory so far, just a clue—like a piece of the puzzle. See, the way a mystery works, Mom, is you look for clues, ask questions, and gather information from as many sources as possible. Pretty soon you have a lot of pieces. Some fit, others don't. You just keep working at it and hope that it will eventually come together."

"You said Gavin might have been afraid *for* you rather than *of* you. If you're right, that means whoever went after Gavin could come after you next."

"Or they may have used Gavin to get me out of the way."

"How so?"

"They have Gavin plant drugs in my car and somehow get him to name me as a drug dealer. Maybe they figure I'll be so busy getting myself out of trouble I won't have time to think about the murder. It accomplished something else too. Having the police thinking I'm involved in drugs pretty much shoots my credibility—and Gavin's too."

"Hmm. Yours maybe, but not mine or Maddie's."

"What are you saying? You can't—"

"Get involved? Honey, we already are. We have children who, for some reason, have been accused of crimes they didn't commit. The police aren't the least bit interested in clearing your names, but we are. Can't have you two applying to Harvard or Yale with a criminal record, now, can we?"

"But it's too—"

"Dangerous? I don't think so. Maddie and I will be very discreet." Mom's green eyes sparked with determination.

The telephone rang and Mom hurried to answer it. Jennie managed to get her gaping mouth closed and followed her inside. *This is all a sick joke, McGrady,* Jennie told herself. *Mom is just playing some kind of mind game. Reverse psychology. She probably just wants you to know how it feels when you pull stuff like that on her.* But what if it wasn't? What if Mom and Maddie really did plan to get involved? Mom didn't know the first thing about solving crimes, and Jennie doubted that Maddie did either. She had to find a way to stop them before they got hurt.

16

"Sure, I guess that would be okay. We're just having a salad and bread, but . . ." After a few seconds Mom hung up the phone and turned around and headed for the refrigerator. A frown creased her forehead.

"Who was that?"

"Lieutenant Rastovski. He just invited himself to dinner."

Jennie grimaced. "He wants to question me, I'll bet. Without the lawyer."

"I don't think so." Mom opened the refrigerator door and closed it again.

"You don't think he's coming to arrest me, do you?"

"No. I don't know why, but I have this awful feeling it has something to do with Michael."

A short time later, Lieutenant Rastovski, frowning and intense, sat at the dining room table shoveling Mom's Chinese chicken salad into his mouth like he hadn't eaten in a week.

"I—ah—I'm sorry I don't have anything more substantial to offer you," Mom said. "I had planned on having trout, but—"

"This is fine, thanks. I appreciate getting a chance to eat. All I've had today is coffee. Not good, Mrs. McGrady. This case has been driving me crazy."

"Oh?" Mom speared a piece of lettuce and lifted it to her mouth.

"I keep goin' around in circles. Got too many suspects and not enough solid evidence." He guzzled down half a glass of milk and reached for another slice of sourdough bread. "One of those suspects is your fiancé."

"Which is nonsense. I told you yesterday that Michael had nothing to do with that teacher's murder."

"We ran a background check on Rhodes—came up clean—no priors."

"He's one of the good guys," Jennie remembered her father saying shortly after she'd found him. They were in a speed boat cruising back to Cozumel. *"Michael will make a good husband for your mother and a good father to you and Nick. Be nice to him, Jennie. He's one of the good guys."* She'd wanted so much to have Dad tell her he was coming home. But he couldn't give her false hope. Dad had another mission. He always had another mission.

"How long have you known him, Mrs. McGrady?"

"Um—seven, eight months now. We met at a Christmas party at church last year."

"Love at first sight?" The sharp tone in his voice brought Jennie out of her daydream.

Jennie glanced up at him and groaned inwardly. *Oh no, not another one.* Rastovski was jealous. Mom was becoming far too popular.

"No." Mom pushed a piece of chicken around on her plate. "We were attracted to each other, but—" Mom took a deep breath. "Lieutenant, is this really necessary?"

"I need to know as much as possible about Michael Rhodes, Mrs. McGrady. We have some compelling evidence connecting him to his co-worker's murder." Rastovski's expression softened. "I know this is difficult for you, but necessary."

Jennie's heart did a double flip. *Oh no.* Jennie backed out of the thought the moment it hit her. Like a dead-end street it would lead to nowhere.

"I—um—I'll take care of the dishes," Jennie stammered, eager to get away and get a grip.

Neither of them seemed to notice as she gathered the plates and headed for the kitchen. After setting the plates on the counter, Jennie stood in the kitchen for a few minutes, willing the wild fantasy of Mom and Lieutenant Rastovski getting married out of her head. Mom was in love with Michael. She shouldn't really be interested in either man—in case Dad ever came back.

"That's stupid," Jennie muttered. She felt like marching right back into the dining room and announcing to her mother that she had no business being so pretty and—Jennie shook her head. That was even dumber. *What's the matter with you, McGrady?* Maybe being arrested had damaged her brain. She sure was having trouble thinking clearly.

Jennie squared her shoulders and went back into the dining room. Mom and Lieutenant Rastovski were heading out to the porch. Jennie watched them through the bay window, hoping he'd leave. No such luck. They settled into the porch swing—both of them—together—their shoulders almost touching. Rastovski had dropped the Mrs. and was calling her Susan.

Jennie couldn't name the jumble of emotions clamoring around inside her. She had no idea what to do or say. With robotic movements, Jennie finished clearing off the table, listening to bits and pieces of Mom's and Rastovski's conversation as the sounds drifted into the open window and screen door. She washed and dried the table and replaced the tablecloth and colorful dahlia centerpiece.

Mom was talking about Dad now, and Jennie wondered how and why they'd made the transition from Michael.

"Jason was a good man," Mom said. "But I think his priorities were misplaced. I suppose I shouldn't judge him so harshly, but I never could understand why he felt so strongly about staying in a field that took him away from his family so much."

Not wanting to hear any more negative garbage about Dad, Jennie wandered into the kitchen and made a pitcher of lemonade. Curtis would be there in less than half an hour. The thought did nothing to settle her churning stomach. Jennie considered him a suspect and had a hunch the police did as well.

She poured lemonade into two tall glasses, dropped in straws, and carried them out to Mom and the lieutenant. Rastovski was gone.

"When did he leave?" Jennie asked. "I didn't hear his car."

"About five minutes ago." She took the drink Jennie handed her. "Thanks. He had to respond to a call."

"He likes you."

"I know." Mom ducked her head. A fat tear dripped down and landed on Mom's hand.

"What's wrong?"

"I wish I knew. Jennie, I feel so foolish and confused."

Jennie eased onto the empty spot on the swing, wishing she could think of something appropriate to say.

"I like him too. It's the strangest thing." Mom ran a hand through her thick mop of natural curls, made even more curly by the humidity. "This can't be happening," she groaned. "I'm an engaged woman. I'm not supposed to be attracted to other men. What am I going to tell Michael?"

"M-maybe you shouldn't tell him anything. At least not yet. Remember how you thought you liked Mr. Evans and you and Michael broke up? After a while, you realized you didn't love Frank. Maybe it'll be the same with Lieutenant Rastovski."

"You make me sound like—never mind. I was going to say adolescent, but you're an adolescent and at the moment you seem to be much more rational than I am. Maybe I'm going through a midlife crisis."

You sure are going through something. "Mom?"

"What?"

"I forgot to tell you earlier, but there's a guy from school coming over in a few minutes. A friend of Gavin's."

"The one that was visiting Gavin while we were at the hospital?"

"Yeah. Curtis Bolton."

"And you'd like me to get lost, right?"

"Well, I do want to ask him some questions, and he's more likely to talk to me if my mother isn't hanging around."

"He seemed like a very nice young man—and very handsome. Maddie and I were both wishing we were a few years younger."

"Mo-ther!"

"I'm just kidding, sweetheart." Mom stood up just as a guy on a motorcycle cornered Elm and Magnolia, going at least ten miles over the posted twenty-five miles per hour. His tires screeched as he turned into the driveway. "Oh, dear," Mom muttered under her breath. "Tell me that isn't him."

"Sorry, Mom."

Curtis pulled off his helmet, shaking loose a mass of gold curls. Settling the helmet on his Harley, he waved at Jennie and started toward the house. He was still wearing his cutoffs and the open denim shirt.

"Be still my heart." Mom patted her chest and sighed, then winked at Jennie. "All right, I'm going. I promise I won't embarrass you. Just make sure blondie there keeps his distance."

Jennie rolled her eyes. "He's not my type," she muttered out of the corner of her mouth.

"Hi." Curtis trudged up the steps and sank into one of the padded wicker chairs. "Nice house."

"Thanks. Would you like a lemonade or something?"

"Yeah. Could I get a glass of water first, though, and maybe wash up and clean some of the bugs off my body? My windshield is being fixed, and I managed to pick up half the bugs in the county."

Though she tried not to look, her gaze drifted down to his bug-splattered chest. "I see what you mean." Trying not to laugh, Jennie led him to the bathroom. "You're welcome to take a shower." She handed him a towel and a bar of soap, then closed the door and barely made it to the kitchen before collapsing in a fit of giggles.

"What's so funny?" Mom set a couple glasses in the dishwasher and dried her hands.

Jennie held her stomach and gasped out the explanation.

Mom chuckled. "This is awful. We shouldn't be laughing at him."

"I know—but all those bugs . . ." She doubled over in another attack of laughter. By the time Curtis emerged from the bathroom, Jennie had managed to compose herself.

"Hey, thanks for the use of the shower." Curtis stood in the doorway of the kitchen and leaned against the doorjamb. His damp hair hung in ringlets and dripped water onto his broad shoulders.

"I hate to bother you, but I really could use a drink of water."

"Sure." Jennie handed him a glass, carried his lemonade out to the porch, and set the tray on the wicker table.

Jennie took the swing and Curtis lowered himself onto the chaise lounge and stretched his long, muscular legs out in front of him. After downing his ice water, he set the glass aside and tossed Jennie a lazy grin. "Did you get to see Gavin?"

"Yeah—only he didn't want to see me."

"I sort of figured that."

"Why? Did he tell you something about me?" Jennie set

the swing in motion and tucked one of her legs underneath her.

"Just off-the-wall stuff. He says you shot him."

"What?" Jennie bounced to her feet. "That ungrateful creep—I saved his life."

"Hey." Curtis raised his hands as if he expected her to hit him. "I didn't say I believed him."

"How could he say something like that?" Jennie backed up until the back of her knees hit the swing and fell back against the cushions. "I could understand when he was stoned out of his mind, but you'd think whatever he was on would have worn off by now."

"Some drugs are hallucinogenic. The effects can last for several days."

"Like LSD."

"Right. For the record, Jennie, I know you didn't do any of the stuff he's saying you did. That's why I wanted to talk to you. I might know who killed Dr. Mancini. But I need your help to prove it."

Jennie stilled the swing. "How did you know he was a doctor?"

Curtis shrugged. "He told me."

"Why come to me?" Jennie asked. "If you have information, you should be talking to the police."

"I told them, but they aren't interested. They're sure whoever killed Dr. Mancini was close to him—a friend or family member. Hey, they're even looking at Alex and Mrs. Mancini." He paused to take a drink.

"And you?"

"At first. Fortunately I have an alibi. I was working. My brother has this Harley dealership."

"What makes you think the police aren't interested in what you have to say? Did you talk to Lieutenant Rastovski?"

"Yeah. He thought my theory—and unfortunately that's all it is right now—sounded like a plot for a medical thriller.

Said they had enough viable suspects without chasing some fantasy."

Jennie leaned forward. "I like medical thrillers myself."

Curtis grinned. "I was hoping you'd say that. See, I think we should pool our resources. Maybe between the two of us, we can come up with enough evidence to convince the police they're on the wrong trail. There's just one problem, Jennie. We have to keep our investigation totally confidential. I mean you can't tell anybody what we're doing."

Jennie eyed him suspiciously. "Why?"

Curtis glanced around, then shifted over to the swing and lowered his voice. "The people involved in this project are extremely powerful. If they think for one minute we're on to them, they'll kill us."

"Sounds like you're talking about a drug cartel or the mob."

"They're worse, Jennie." His sky-blue eyes grayed with a mixture of concern and fear. "A lot worse."

17

Jennie could see why Lieutenant Rastovski might be skeptical—especially if Curtis had been as melodramatic with the police as he had been with her. If he hadn't seemed so sincere, she might have laughed at the idea herself. But Jennie figured it was just crazy enough to have some validity. And that frightened her.

Jennie shook her head to emphasize the point. "No way am I getting involved in anything that dangerous."

"It'll only be dangerous if the wrong people find out."

"Curtis—"

"Wait. Don't make up your mind yet. At least wait until I tell you what Dr. Mancini was working on."

Jennie pulled her long, thick braid from behind her back and wound it around her hand. "Okay. I'm listening, but do you think you could move back to the other chair?" For some strange reason, having Curtis sitting so close was stirring up the butterflies in her stomach.

He frowned. "Sure. Um—do I have bad breath or something?"

"No, nothing like that."

"So sitting close to me bothers you?" Curtis caught her gaze and held it. A knowing smile lifted the corners of his mouth. "Cool."

"Go." She shoved his shoulder when he scooted closer.

Still grinning, he plopped himself down on the chair closest to the swing. "I'm sorry, Jen. That was crude. Um—you're a really nice girl and—"

"Forget it. Just tell me about Mancini."

Suddenly serious again, Curtis raked both hands through his drying hair and pulled it back away from his face. "I'm not sure where to start."

"The beginning's always good. Like when did you meet him? And what's he like?"

"Right. Mancini came in as a sub right after Mr. Adams got sick. I knew right off there was something special about him."

"I heard a lot of kids didn't like him."

"That's putting it mildly. He expected a lot out of his students—too much. In fact, if it hadn't been for Michael, he'd probably have flunked half the class."

"What did Michael do?"

"Do you know Brian Stone? What am I saying? Everybody knows Brian. Anyway, Mancini failed Brian. Brian and his dad went in to talk to Michael and complained. It's a long story, but the school board had a little talk with Mancini, telling him to lower his standards and use a curve to grade the kids or risk losing his job.

"Mancini grumbled about it but complied. He passed everyone except Brian. Brian might have squeaked through too if he hadn't cheated on the final. When Mancini found out about it he banned Brian from the class—permanently."

"Do you think Brian killed Dr. Mancini? I know the sports business is big, but—"

"No—at least I'm pretty sure he didn't. I'm only telling you this to make a point. Mancini didn't act like a high school teacher, so I checked up on him."

"And you found out he's really a professor and that he lost his job at Berkeley because he was using and selling drugs."

"Who told you that?"

Jennie started to tell him but decided not to. "It doesn't matter."

He shrugged. "It isn't true. When Dr. Mancini was interviewing me for lab assistant, I asked him why he'd taken a job at Trinity. He told me there'd been a big misunderstanding at the university. Someone started the rumor about him making and selling designer drugs, and he was asked to resign. Well, he *was* working on drugs—a drug—to be exact, but it was for Dawson's—a big pharmaceutical company in the Midwest. Dr. Mancini had a grant to develop a medication that would counter addictive behavior."

Dawson—Jennie remembered having seen the name on the computer when Douglas and Rastovski were looking through his files. It was the one Douglas couldn't access. "Addictive behavior? Like drugs and alcohol?"

"And tobacco and food—everything."

"Oh, come on." Jennie stopped the swing.

"I know it sounds too good to be true. Maybe that's why the police didn't believe me. But this drug is for real, Jennie. I've been working with Dr. Mancini all summer. He was getting ready to do the final tests on it. Now he's dead. I know there's a connection."

"I'm sorry, Curtis, but I don't follow you. This *medication*—if there is such a thing—would be wonderful. Why would anyone want to stop it from coming out?"

"Think about what might happen if a drug like that hit the market, Jennie."

"I imagine it would sell like crazy, making Dr. Mancini and the Dawson Pharmaceuticals very wealthy." Jennie frowned. "Are you saying someone stole the formula?"

"Someone did steal the formula. It was on a disk he kept locked up in his desk. He also had a copy on his hard drive—they're both gone."

"And you told the police all this?"

"That's part of the reason they don't believe me. They asked me to show them the notes and stuff, but there was nothing in the computer to back me up. Everything is gone."

"Do you think the pharmaceutical company took the formula to avoid having to pay Mancini a share?"

"No. I think it was someone who stood to lose a lot of money if the drug ever became available to the general public. The person who murdered Dr. Mancini and took the formula wanted to make sure it never got out."

"You mean like the alcohol and tobacco industries, or drug dealers."

"That's exactly what I mean."

Strange as it seemed, Curtis's medical thriller fantasy was beginning to make perfect sense. "If that's the case, how could you ever pin down the killer? A drug like that could cost alcohol and tobacco industries billions, and the drug business—both legal and illegal. We're talking about thousands of suspects here. There's no way we could track down the killer. Maybe the local police aren't interested in your story, but I'll bet my—" Jennie caught herself. She'd almost said Dad. "Um—my grandfather is an FBI agent. And there's a DEA agent—Douglas—who's working on the case with Lieutenant Rastovski. Did you talk to him?"

Curtis propped his elbows on his knees and rested his head on his hands for a long moment, then looked up. "Yeah. Douglas seemed kind of interested at first, but when I couldn't substantiate my story, he wrote me off too."

Jennie didn't know how to respond. She had no answers. If Curtis was right, finding Mancini's killer would be like trying to catch a guppy in the ocean. She told Curtis as much.

"I know it sounds impossible and maybe I'm crazy for even trying—I was just hoping we could work together. At least tell me what you have. I know you've been investigating on your own."

Jennie laughed. "I'd hardly call it that. All I've done so

far is convince the police that Mancini didn't commit suicide. I've drawn up a partial list of suspects, but that's about it."

"How did you know it wasn't suicide?"

Jennie explained about the suicide note and how it had been written after she'd been in the lab. "What I saw was a—" She glanced up at Curtis.

"What?"

"Maybe that's what it was—Dr. Mancini's formula."

"Can you remember any of it? A title, words?"

"Some. I wrote it down on a piece of paper."

"Where is it? Can I see?"

"I can't remember. I had it in Dr. Mancini's office." She closed her eyes trying to remember what she'd done with her notes. "Sorry, I probably gave it to the lieutenant or Douglas."

"Can you remember what you saw?"

Jennie described what she'd seen. "It's not much, I know, but who knows? I may remember more later."

"Not that it will do much good. The formula is gone."

"You said you'd worked with Dr. Mancini. Don't you remember it?"

"Bits and pieces. He never let me see the entire work. Told me I was better off not knowing. Maybe he was right."

Curtis glanced up at the sky. The hazy blue had turned to battleship gray. Thunder rumbled in the distance. "I should go. I want to stop and see Gavin before I head home."

Jennie stood up when he did and walked him to the porch steps. "I'd have you tell him hi from me, but he'd probably freak out."

"He'll come out of it eventually. At least I hope so." The worried look in his eyes didn't offer much hope.

After he left, Jennie stuck a pillow against the arm of the swing and leaned against it, settling her legs on the seat. The darkening crimson sky began to deliver on its promise of rain. *Angel's teardrops*, Dad had told her once. Jennie smiled at the distant memory. If that was the case, all the angels in heaven were terribly sad at the moment.

Curtis would be drenched by the time he reached the hospital—but at least he wouldn't be covered with bugs. She chuckled softly. Though she found Curtis attractive—who wouldn't—she'd never date him. She could see it now. He'd put his arm around her, they'd close their eyes, and he'd lower his head and press his lips against hers. Then she'd remember the bugs and shatter the romantic mood by laughing herself into hysterics.

Besides, she reminded herself, *you aren't really interested in Curtis Bolton—you have Ryan Johnson. And in a few days you'll be able to see him.*

Still, she found Curtis a definite curiosity. He'd changed physically, but there were other changes too. Like the motorcycle, and maybe even his personality. She hadn't known Curtis that well but remembered him as being more of a nerd—studious, withdrawn, and shy. Now he seemed more self-assured—a little on the wild side. Jennie shrugged. Maybe he was just going through a phase—trying to find himself. At least that's what Mom would say.

She shifted her attention from Curtis to the professor. So, Dr. Mancini had been working for a pharmaceutical company—just like Gram had said. Interesting. Maybe that's where Mrs. Mancini and Alex got the money for their trip to Europe. If that was the case, it didn't seem likely they'd have killed him for a life insurance policy. He'd have been worth much more alive and stood to make millions if the drug was ever approved by the FDA.

Mancini had been forced to leave Berkeley after a rumor of drug use. Jennie found that especially believable since someone was trying to set her up as well. Coincidence? She doubted it. Had someone followed him to Portland—which brought up another question. How had he ended up at Trinity? It seemed an odd transition. Maybe she'd ask Michael about it tomorrow—after Dr. Mancini's funeral. She'd have another talk with Rastovski too and maybe Douglas. It seemed strange that they'd ignore Curtis's theory altogether. Maybe they hadn't. Jennie had a feeling Rastovski was one of those guys who didn't miss a beat.

The light drizzle turned into a deluge, and Jennie set her questions and plans on hold. For the moment, she wanted to close out anything to do with the murder and concentrate on the spectacular summer storm.

Jennie breathed deeply, relishing the musty sweet smell of wet earth and grass. She closed her eyes and listened as the rain pattered against the roof above her and rattled through the downspout on the side of the house.

The door opened and a board creaked as Mom came out to join her. "Hi. Thought you might be getting cold." Mom covered her with a patchwork quilt of purple, pink, and teal.

Jennie sat up and snuggled under it, just now aware of the goose bumps on her arms and legs. "Thanks. Want to watch the storm with me?"

"Wouldn't miss it."

Jennie shifted around so her mother could share the quilt.

The downpour continued for about ten minutes, then let up as the light show began in earnest. Thunder rolled and crashed with the fury of waves against the rocks at high tide. The streetlights sputtered and died. For brief spine-chilling moments, lightning turned the night to day. Their excitement grew as the storm moved over them. Between clashes of thunder Jennie thought she could hear the sound of a motorcycle and wondered briefly if Curtis had decided to come back.

A clap of thunder shook the house, and the sky around them flashed white. Mother and daughter ducked in unison. The action tipped them out of the swing and dumped them on the porch.

Jennie started to get up. Another sharp crack, then another, made her duck again. Something whizzed past her head and slammed into the wood above their heads. *Thunk. Thunk.*

"What in the world—?" Mom raised up on her knees to look at the splintered wood.

"Stay down." Jennie reached for her mother and sprawled behind the porch railing. "Stay down," she gasped again. "Someone's shooting at us!"

18

Thunder exploded around them again, nearly obliterating the screech of tires and the distinctive sound of a motorcycle speeding away.

Silence stretched for an eternity. Jennie's heart slammed against her chest so hard she felt certain she was putting dents in the floor beneath her.

"I think he's gone," Mom whispered.

"I hope so." Jennie lifted her head and peered between the posts on the railing. The streetlights flickered on, then off, then on again.

"I'll crawl into the house and call the police." Mom began moving toward the door.

"Wait." Jennie grabbed an ankle. "It might be safer if we go around back."

They crawled along the side porch. When they reached the rear of the house, they sprinted over the grass and in the back door.

Mom dove for the phone and called 9–1–1.

Jennie huddled under the quilt she'd dragged in with her from the porch. She hadn't realized she'd brought it until that moment. A shiver ran through her and she pulled the quilt tighter. Jennie thought about turning on the light, then decided against it. They hadn't drawn the shades, and the light would make them clear targets if the gunman was still around. The streetlamp provided enough light for the moment.

When her knees threatened to give way, Jennie shuffled to the kitchen table and dropped into a chair.

Mom hung up the phone after talking to the 9–1–1 operator. "Someone will be out in a few minutes. I suppose I should turn on the porch light." Instead of going to the front door Mom grasped Jennie's shoulders and began massaging them.

That's how Lieutenant Rastovski found them. He hadn't bothered to knock—just barged in. He snapped on the kitchen light and stared from Mom to Jennie, then back to Mom again. Maybe he thought they'd been killed or something, because he sure looked relieved when he saw them.

Mom's fingers dug into Jennie's shoulders.

"I was on my way home when the call came in." He cleared his throat.

The tension between them was like a magnetic force so strong Jennie felt certain that any second now they'd end up in each other's arms.

Rastovski looked away. "I take it I'm the first officer to arrive?"

"I only called a few minutes ago." Mom released Jennie's shoulders, walked over to the cupboard, and retrieved two cups. "Would you like some coffee?"

Mom was in shock, Jennie realized. Maybe they all were.

The lieutenant shook his head. "Just tell me what happened."

"Jennie and I were sitting on the porch watching the thunderstorm when someone shot at us."

"Did you see anything?"

"No," Jennie answered this time. "It was too dark. But I heard something, a motorcycle." She told him about Curtis Bolton's visit. "He said he was going to the hospital, but he may have decided to come back and shoot me instead."

"Why would he do that? You two have an argument?"

"No." Jennie wished she'd kept her mouth shut. "It probably wasn't him—it's just that I thought I heard a motorcycle and wondered if he'd come back. After the shooting, I heard the motorcycle take off again."

"Show me where it happened."

Mom led the way to the porch and Jennie followed. They were pointing out the bullet holes and wood splinters when a squad car pulled up to the curb—lights flashing. Another car screeched in behind, then another.

"Stay here," Rastovski ordered, then descended the steps to meet the officers. "What took you so long?"

"Got here as fast as we could. A lot going down tonight." The officer hitched up his belt. "What have we got?"

"Looks like a drive-by. Not sure about motive. No injuries. We're looking for a biker. Check on the whereabouts of a Curtis Bolton. Young kid, long blond hair. He was supposed to be visiting a friend—Gavin Winslow over at Sunnyside. See if he made it. If not, find him."

They talked for a few minutes, then two officers went to their cars while a third retrieved a roll of yellow tape from his trunk and began taping off their porch.

Rastovski returned to where Jennie and Mom were standing and herded them back into the house. "We'll have a team of officers out here for a while, gathering evidence," he told them. "Appreciate it if you could stay inside."

"Lieutenant?" Jennie stopped in the entry and turned around. "Can you match a bike's tires to the skid marks on the pavement?"

"Sometimes. Why?"

"Well, when Curtis came, he squealed around the corner." She pointed toward Magnolia and Elm. "Whoever shot at us burned rubber when he accelerated. He was heading back around the same corner."

"Thanks, Jennie. We'll check it out." His dark gaze

caught hers in an affirming gesture.

Maybe Rastovski wasn't such a bad guy after all.

"Isn't there something I could do to help?" Mom asked. "I feel so restless and—it's not every day one gets shot at."

"Maybe you could bake something."

Mom tipped her head and gave him an odd look. "Brownies?"

"Sounds good to me." Rastovski looked like he was about to pull Mom into his arms and kiss her.

He's a cop, Mom, Jennie wanted to shout in warning. *You don't like cops, remember?* "I'll be in my room," she announced instead, then trounced up the stairs and didn't look back.

Shutting her bedroom door did nothing to close out the vision of Rastovski and Mom. The more Jennie saw the two of them together, the more puzzled she became. Mom was falling for this guy, hard and fast, which wasn't like Mom at all. After Dad had disappeared, she waited almost five years before even starting to date again. With Michael, things had progressed slowly. Mom had seemed sure for a while, then backed off. She'd seen Rastovski two, maybe three times, and she was acting more in love than she ever had with Michael.

Jennie wandered over to her dresser and picked up Dad's picture. His dark blue eyes smiled up at her. "Oh, Dad. What are we going to do? Please come home before it's too late. The way she looks at Lieutenant Rastovski would break your heart." Tears gathered in her eyes and dripped onto the glass. She gathered the photo to her chest and hugged it, then curled up in her window seat.

After a while, the sobbing stopped. It did no good at all to cry. Life was getting too complicated, but that didn't mean she had to give up. She set Dad's photo back and padded to the phone. After dialing, she fell back onto the bed.

"Hello?"

Just hearing Gram's voice settled Jennie's frazzled nerves. "Hi, Gram. It's me."

"Jennie! I'm so glad you called. J.B. and I were watching the news. They reported a drive-by shooting in your area but didn't released any names. We were worried."

"It was here. They were shooting at Mom and me."

"Oh, my goodness! Are you all right?"

"We're fine. The police are here." Jennie went on to explain what had happened.

"Was Nick there too? That poor darling—"

"No. He's staying over at Kate's tonight."

"How is your mother taking it? I imagine she's terrified."

"Actually, she's doing pretty well. She's baking brownies for Lieutenant Rastovski."

"Really?"

"Gram, she just made a batch on Monday. I think she's losing it." Jennie filled her in on that complication as well and ended by telling about having been arrested that morning.

"My, you have had a busy day. Hold on a moment, darling. I need to talk to J.B."

Jennie could hear Gram giving J.B. the condensed version of what had been going on. "We'll be there around ten tomorrow morning, Jennie. Has your mother called Kate?"

"No."

"I'll call her. We need to let her know before she hears it on the news. I don't understand why Susan didn't call."

"She's pretty upset—and with Rastovski hanging around—I don't know, Gram. You need to have a talk with her."

"It can't be that bad."

"It is. I'm afraid she's falling for this guy and—we need to tell her about Dad before she gets too involved. Um—did you find out any more?"

"I'm afraid not, dear. J.B. says your father's superiors have taken the matter under consideration, but they're not divulging any information."

"Not even to you and J.B.?"

"No. J.B. thinks they may have him hooked into a big case, so it may be a while. At any rate, I don't think you need to worry. Your mother is one of the most level-headed women I know. She's not going to rush in to anything—especially a wedding."

"I hope not."

"Jennie, one more thing. I don't feel comfortable having you and your mother in the house alone tonight. You should go over to Kate's."

Jennie agreed and after hanging up released a long, low whistle. Gram and J.B. were coming back. Feeling ten times better, Jennie headed downstairs to check on Mom and to let her know they had company coming.

Jennie followed the decadent scent of dark fudge brownies into the kitchen. They were cooling on a rack near the stove. Jennie licked her lips and retrieved a knife. After cutting out a one-inch square she popped it into her mouth. "Hmm."

Susan McGrady gave her daughter a cursory glance, then went back to unloading the dishwasher. "He's quite something, isn't he?" Mom said before Jennie had a chance to give her the good news.

"Who?"

"The lieutenant."

Jennie shrugged. "Something as in bossy and arrogant—"

Mom closed the dishwasher. "He reminds me of your father in some ways—only he's more attentive—more considerate."

"Oh, please. He's nothing like Dad. He's mean-tempered, and he actually thinks I might be a murderer. Dad would never think that."

"Hmm," Mom went on as if Jennie hadn't said a word. "He even has some of the same mannerisms." Mom pulled the teakettle from the burner when it began whistling. "Would you like some tea?"

Jennie stared at her. "If Rastovski reminds you of Dad, why do you like him so much?"

Now it was Mom's turn to stare. "I loved your father, Jennie. We didn't agree on a lot of things, but . . ." She shook her head as if coming out of a trance, then poured water into two cups, dunking a tea bag in one, then the other.

"I called Gram," Jennie announced. "She and J.B. are coming back tomorrow. Did you call Aunt Kate?"

"No—I—" Mom brushed her hand across her forehead and frowned. "I suppose I should"—she glanced at her watch—"they're probably still up."

"Don't worry about it. Gram's calling her."

Mom sighed and brought the steaming cups to the table. "I don't know what's gotten into me lately. I hope Gram isn't upset with me."

"Mom, it's okay. I took care of it."

Mom pulled out a chair and lowered herself into it. "You said they'd be down tomorrow?"

"Uh-huh. Gram said we should go over to Kate's tonight. We'll be safer there."

Mom shook her head. "It's too late. I don't think that's necessary."

The doorbell rang. Jennie jumped up. "I'll get it. Just drink your tea." Mom looked pale and shaky—and tired.

Rastovski walked in before Jennie could get to the door. "Where's your mother?" He headed toward the kitchen without waiting for an answer.

"Did you find out anything?" Jennie followed him down the hall into the kitchen.

He didn't respond. Instead he stopped next to the table and tugged at his tie. "I want you two out of the house tonight. You got someplace you can stay? If not, I'll put you up in a hotel."

Mom shook her head. "I'm not leaving. I absolutely refuse to be chased out of my own home by some hoodlum."

"Susan—"

"No. Jennie can go stay with Kate—my sister-in-law. In fact, that's probably not a bad idea, but I'm staying."

"Mom, he's right. We should go—Gram even said so."

Mom shook her head.

"Are you always this stubborn?"

"Only when it matters."

"And this matters."

"Yes—yes it does."

"Fine," Rastovski pulled out a chair and sat down. "You stay, then I'll stay. I can sleep on the couch."

"There's no need—"

"Yes, there is. This wasn't a random drive-by. I had an officer check out the lead Jennie gave us on the Bolton kid. She was right. He never showed up at the hospital."

19

Rastovski must have read the shock on Jennie's face. "Why are you so surprised—you're the one who put us on to him."

"I just didn't think—I mean—I only mentioned him because of the motorcycle. I didn't really believe he'd try to shoot me."

"We don't know for sure, of course, but we put out an APB on him. If he's out there, we'll find him. In the meantime, I want you two in a safe place."

"You think he'll come back?" Mom asked.

"My guess is he was after Jennie. He either wanted to scare her or kill her. If it's the first, we probably don't have to worry about him showing up again. If it's the latter, he missed and will probably try again. The police chief isn't willing to put out the money for an officer to stand guard all night, so that leaves two options. Either you and Jennie go somewhere safe, or I stay here."

When Mom stood up, Rastovski straightened and eyed her wearily.

"Would you like some coffee to go with your brownies?" She turned away from him and headed for the counter.

"Please." He fastened a dark, wistful gaze on Mom before turning to Jennie. "Tell me everything you know about this Bolton kid."

"That wouldn't be much. I've known him from school since sixth grade, but we were never friends. He and Gavin hung out together. I didn't know that until today."

"Why was he here? You two have a date or something?"

"No. He was at the hospital when Mom and I went to see Gavin. He said he wanted to talk to me. Told me about an anti-addiction drug Dr. Mancini was working on."

Rastovski leaned back when Mom returned with his brownie and a cup of coffee. "Anything else?"

"He seemed to think someone had framed Dr. Mancini at Berkeley in order to keep the drug from being manufactured and that someone may have killed him and stolen the formula." She reiterated Curtis's theory.

"He told us the same story, but why would he tell you?"

"Because you didn't believe him and he thought maybe I could help him solve the case."

"Then he comes back and tries to gun you down? I don't think so." He picked up his fork and cut off a sizeable chunk of the rich dessert, then dipped it into the whipped topping Mom had placed on top. "He didn't want your help in solving the case, Jennie. He wanted information. What did you tell him?"

"Just that I saw something on the computer screen that might have been Dr. Mancini's formula. I told him what I remembered about it. Which reminds me. Did you take the paper I wrote part of the formula on when we were in Dr. Mancini's office?"

"Agent Douglas is checking it out."

Mom placed two more desserts on the table, then sat down. "Lieutenant, doesn't it seem rather strange to you that we now have three kids—probably three of the top students at Trinity High—who have suddenly turned criminal?"

Rastovski chased his bite with a swig of coffee. "I'm not sure I follow you."

"Well, first Gavin Winslow turns up missing. He's obviously been given drugs and somehow brainwashed to believe Jennie was involved in abducting him and dealing drugs. Then someone, possibly Gavin, plants drugs in Jennie's car and turns her in. She's arrested, taking her out of circulation. Since that apparently didn't stop her, they try to gun her—or us—down. Now Curtis is being sought in a drive-by shooting."

"Your point?" Rastovski's annoyed tone didn't match the twinkle in his eyes. He seemed amused and disgruntled at the same time. It was almost as though he liked the idea that Mom would have an opinion on the case.

"These kids have several things in common," Mom continued. "They are all top students, they all go to Trinity High, and they have all been trying to make sense of their teacher's murder."

When Mom paused to eat a bite of her brownie, Jennie took up the slack. "Mom has a good point. Someone has been trying to discredit—or maybe even get rid of—Gavin and me, just like they did Dr. Mancini at Berkeley. Maybe Curtis is being set up too."

"So you're thinking Bolton's conspiracy theory has merit?" Rastovski directed his question at Mom.

"It makes perfect sense to me. Gavin called Jennie just before he disappeared saying he had a major breakthrough in the case. Jennie interrupted the killer and saw something on that computer screen that could have been an important piece of evidence. And Curtis? If what he told Jennie about working with Dr. Mancini on this miracle drug is true, he may be able to reproduce it."

Jennie glanced at Rastovski, who seemed to be seriously considering Mom's ideas. "So, if Bolton is right in thinking someone wants to keep the drug off the market, that would make him a threat too."

"Exactly."

Rastovski popped the last piece of brownie in his mouth,

looking thoughtful as he chewed. "We got a lot of *if*s here. I agree, there may be some merit to Bolton's story, but I'm not sure I buy this idea of Mancini developing a drug that's going to make addictions a thing of the past. Too far fetched. Still, the DEA is working that angle. Douglas is more inclined to think Mancini was using the lab at Trinity to produce designer drugs. Either Bolton was working with him, or the professor was stringing him along with the story about the anti-addiction pill."

"Designer drugs?" Mom stroked the rim of her cup. "I've heard that term before, but I'm not sure what it means."

"It's a term we give certain look-alike drugs. They contain over-the-counter ingredients and resemble various prescription or illegal dugs." For the next ten minutes Rastovski lectured them about the availability of drugs and how the DEA and other law-enforcement agencies barely made a dent in the street availability of narcotics.

Despite her fascination with Rastovski's explanations, Jennie's eyes kept closing and her brain seemed bent on shutting down for the night. She folded her arms on the table and rested her head. *Just for a minute*, she told herself. *I'll just close my eyes for a minute.*

"Jennie? Come on, sweetheart, wake up. Better get to bed." Mom squeezed Jennie's shoulders. "I'll be up as soon as I clear the table."

Jennie obeyed the voice and didn't resist the strong, masculine arms that helped her to her feet and half carried her out of the kitchen and up the stairs.

"Come on, princess," a tender baritone voice whispered in her ear. "Just a few more steps."

Still more than half asleep, Jennie stumbled into her room and turned on the lamp beside her bed. After saying goodnight to the closing door, she tossed aside the decorative pillows and turned down the covers. She thought briefly of getting up and changing into her pajamas, but that would require a hundred times more energy than she had at the moment. She barely had the strength to reach up and turn off the light.

Stretching out on the bed, Jennie glanced at the red numbers on her digital clock. Twelve-thirty. Why wasn't she falling asleep? Something important scratched at the back of her mind like a dog wanting to be let in. She closed her eyes tight, but the harder she tried to sleep, the more restless she became.

The room was too light. She'd forgotten to close the blinds. The storm had passed and the moon beamed in almost enough light to read by. Jennie groaned and got up. After closing the blinds, she padded to her closet and flipped on the light.

Then it hit her. Rastovski had burst into the house only minutes after the shooting and hit the light switch in the kitchen like he was familiar with the place. He'd called her princess.

Jennie gasped for air, her closet suddenly too small and cramped for the emotions exploding around and through her. She ran to her dresser, grabbed Dad's picture, and turned on the bedside lamp. Dropping onto the bed, she studied the familiar face in the photo.

It couldn't be him. He looked so different, yet there were similarities as well. When she'd first met Rastovski he'd looked familiar to her. She thought he reminded her of her cousin, Hazen, with his dark hair and eyes. The McGradys had dark features as well.

You are so dense, McGrady. You should have seen it right away. Of course, the last time she'd seen Dad, he'd lightened his hair—and had a receding hairline. She hadn't recognized him right away then either. His eyes had finally given him away. Rastovski's eyes were the color of dark chocolate. And the scar on his face—a recent injury? His voice was different too—harsher, raspier—except for when he'd called her princess.

She examined the photo again and tried to superimpose the features of the man. It couldn't be. Yet—maybe it could. Rastovski was new to the area—Rocky had told her that.

"What happened, Dad? Are you Nate Rastovski? If so, why are you here? Have you told Mom?" Jennie didn't think so. Mom would have said something. Wouldn't she?

Jennie set the photo down and headed for the door. What was the point in asking herself all those questions when her father was downstairs?

No way would she be able to sleep now. She tiptoed into the dark hallway. Two doors down a light leaked out of Mom's bedroom onto the taupe carpet. Good, Mom was probably in bed.

Jennie crept downstairs and paused before going into the living room—partly to let her eyes adjust to the darkness and partly to muster up enough courage to confront Rastovski. *What if you're wrong, McGrady? Dad is a DEA agent, not a homicide investigator.*

Yes, but Rastovski knows an awful lot about drugs. Maybe he changed jobs.

He'd never do that, Jennie argued against her own logic. *And Dad would never have discussed a case with her and Mom like Rastovski had.*

But he had called her princess. She had to know.

"Thought you were asleep." Rastovski's husky voice shattered the silence and her thoughts. He adjusted the pillows on the couch and sat down.

"I was—almost—only now I can't sleep." Jennie sank down beside him.

"Join the club."

"Why didn't you tell me?"

The momentary silence as he removed his shoes gave her the assurance she needed. This man was definitely her father.

163

"Tell you what?"

"Who you really are."

He hesitated again.

"You called me princess." Jennie's eyes had adjusted to the semidarkness, but she still couldn't make out his features.

He sighed. "I was hoping you hadn't noticed. I should have known better."

"You knew where the light switch was in the kitchen—and you still like brownies."

"Your mother had me going for a while with that. I thought maybe she'd figured it out."

"You haven't told her?"

"Not yet. To be honest, I hadn't expected our paths to cross quite so soon. I was hoping to get settled in my job and get some loose ends tied up. I will tell her, though. I just haven't found the right time. Guess I wanted to see if there was a possibility of us getting together."

"Of course there is. She likes you a lot."

"You really think so?"

"Yeah." Jennie glanced at him—part of her wanted to throw her arms around his neck—part of her wanted to strangle him. "Are you staying?"

"If I can. If your mother will take me back."

"What about your job with the DEA?"

"I haven't worked for the DEA in weeks. After you met me in the Caribbean, I went on to Jamaica. Major cartel there. We set up a sting operation, but someone set us up. Five of us walked into a trap—three agents were killed. Douglas and I made it out, but we both ended up in a hospital in Florida. He took a bullet in the shoulder. I was there for about three weeks, getting myself sewn back together." He reached up and touched the scar on his face.

"Why didn't you let me know? I could have come to see you."

"I couldn't at that time."

"Too dangerous?"

"That and other things. Anyway, being laid up gave me a lot of time to think about my life—about what really mattered. Got to talking to God a lot and praying. I realized I made a big mistake years ago by placing my career so far ahead of my family. Thought I was making the big sacrifice. Noble as my goals were, I made some choices I deeply regret. I just hope you and Susan and Nick can forgive me. There's nothing I can do about the past. But I *can* do something about the present. Things have changed, princess. I've changed. I want to come home. Be with my wife and kids. I just hope it isn't too late."

"Oh, Dad." Jennie touched his arm. "It's never too late. But promise me you'll tell Mom right away. It's been awful trying to keep secrets from her. I prayed every night that you'd come back before she married Michael. Now you're here."

"She's going to be furious when she learns how the government—how we lied to her—letting her believe I was dead."

"She'll get over it." *I hope.* "Besides, you did it to protect us. She'll understand."

Dad slipped an arm around her shoulder. "It feels so good to be home—I'm glad you figured it out."

"I'm glad you finally got here." Jennie sighed. "There's just one problem."

"What's that?"

"Why did you have to come back as Nate Rastovski? The guy's a total jerk."

Jennie bounced off the sofa before he could swat her. She came around behind him and wrapped her arms around his neck. "Good night, Dad."

"Good night, Jennie."

Jennie paused when she got to the stairs, then spun around and joined her father on the couch. "I know it's late, but there's something I gotta know."

"What's that?"

"Are you for real working with the Portland police on this Mancini case?"

"Yeah, and a number of others."

"How come you were so ready to call it a suicide? Did you really think it was?"

"It would have been so much easier if it had been." He smiled. "But no. As soon as I read the crime scene analysis and autopsy report I knew."

Jennie lifted her hair into a tail and pulled it foward. "So you really didn't need me to tell you."

"I think I'd have eventually figured it out, yes. But I really did appreciate your insight."

"What was it like? Seeing a dead body, I mean. I keep imagining what it must have looked like—pretty messy, huh?"

"No, not really." Rastovski stretched his long legs out in front of him and crossed them at the ankle. "That's one of the things that threw us at first. It looked as though Mancini had wrapped a towel around his head before he shot himself. One way of keeping his lab clean—it was consistent with his penchant for neatness. It also made it more difficult for us to determine exactly what happened. Most of the time we can pretty much look at the blood spatters and determine what went down."

"So how did the medical examiner figure out it wasn't a suicide?"

"Two things. There was a bump and cut on the back of his head. At first we figured he must have bumped it when he fell after the shooting. Only that wasn't consistent with what we found. The medical examiner says he had to have hit his head on the counter before wrapping his head in a towel and shooting himself, only that couldn't have happened because the first head wound killed him."

"Wow. So he was already dead when someone shot him."
Jennie was getting more excited by the second—imagine, discussing a murder with her own father.

"Right."

"You said there were two things that tipped you off. What was the other?"

"The crank he was supposed to have taken was injected after he'd already died."

Jennie bit her lower lip. She had a feeling she knew what he'd say, but had to ask anyway. "I still think you should use me as bait to flush out the killer."

"Absolutely not. I wouldn't let any kid do that, Jennie, especially not my daughter. Like I said before, Douglas and I will take care of it. We have a number of leads."

"Speaking of which—did you really consider me a suspect?"

"Of course not."

"Then why did you have me arrested?"

"I had to treat you like I would anyone else under those circumstances."

"I suppose I shouldn't ask you to fix a ticket for me then."

He chuckled. "What do you think?"

Jennie shrugged her shoulders. "Yes?"

"Go to bed, Jennie. We'll have lots of time to talk later, but right now we both need some rest."

Jennie moaned. "Maybe I could stay down here with you. I could sleep on the floor—"

"I don't think so, Jennie."

"Okay, okay. I'm going." She hugged him again, then one more time for good measure and reluctantly climbed back up the stairs.

As pumped as she was, Jennie had no trouble falling asleep. Staying that way proved more difficult. She'd heard a car door slam at five-thirty. The phone rang at six. Jennie cuddled the receiver to her ear. "H'lo."

"Jennie—this is Gavin. Get over here right away."

"Where are you?"

"At the hospital—I have to talk to you."

"But I thought—"

"Look, I'm sorry, okay?"

"No, it's not okay—you caused me a lot of trouble—"

"Just get here as soon as you can. We don't have much time."

20

Jennie hung up and pulled the covers over her head. "I'm not going," she muttered into her pillow.

Come on, McGrady, get up. You have to go.

The phone rang again. She thought about ignoring it but reached for the receiver anyway.

"I'm sorry I hung up on you."

"What do you want, Gavin?"

"Please come. I am so scared. They got Curtis and we're going to be next."

"What are you talking about?"

"Curtis was supposed to come by the hospital last night—only he didn't. The cops came instead. They think he shot at you, but he didn't—someone is setting him up."

"This isn't making any sense."

"Look, Jen—it's a long story. I—I can't talk now." He hung up again.

Jennie heaved an exasperated sigh and climbed out of bed. Raising the blinds, she noticed Rastovski's—Dad's—car was still parked in the driveway. Douglas's green Honda stood behind it. He was probably downstairs going over the details of the case with Dad. *Dad.* Wow, the thought of having her father home sent her spirits flying.

The sun was just coming up, promising a clear day. The scent of bacon wafted up through the floor vents and made her stomach growl.

Jennie showered and dressed quickly in her jeans and a T-shirt—the royal blue one with a Dancing Waters Dude Ranch logo on the pocket. Wearing it again made her long for the mountains and the cousins, aunt, and uncle she'd left behind. She had to remember to write them another letter— as soon as this nightmare with Mancini and her own arrest were over. She had no doubt it would be over soon with Dad working on the case. Maybe he'd even fix her parking ticket.

Downstairs in the kitchen, Mom, Rastovski, and Douglas were talking in hushed tones over bacon, eggs, hashbrowns, toast, and grapefruit halves. And of course, coffee.

They stopped talking when she came in. "My, you're up early," Mom said. "Hope we didn't wake you."

"No." Jennie kissed her mother on the cheek and moved toward Dad, then froze when she realized what she'd almost done. She was going to have to be extremely careful—at least until Dad let Mom know the truth. "Hi, guys," she patted her father's shoulder. "Catch the creep who shot at us yet?"

"No." Douglas scowled. "But we will."

Mom started to get up, but Jennie stopped her. "I'll get my own." She popped a slice of sourdough bread in the toaster and dished up a couple of eggs. While she waited for the toast, she poured a glass of milk. "Um—Mom, do you mind if I go to the hospital this morning to see how Gavin is doing?"

"Are you sure you want to? After yesterday—"

"He called me this morning and wants to see me. I think whatever he was on must have worn off, 'cause he sounded more like his old self."

"That is good news." She glanced at her watch. "I guess it would be okay. You could stop at Kate and Kevin's and pick up Nick and Bernie for me on your way home—save me a trip. I have got to get some filing done today. My office is starting to look like a storage room."

"I don't like it." Dad's scowl matched his friend's. These

guys were obviously in a foul mood. "You shouldn't be going out by yourself."

The toast popped up, and Jennie's heart jumped with it. He wasn't going to let her go.

"I could take her," Douglas said. "I need to question the Winslow kid again anyway."

"That's great. Thanks." Jennie set her breakfast on the table and returned to the counter to get her milk. "After we see Gavin, you could drop me off at Kate's, and Lisa could bring Nick and me home later." She glanced at Mom. "That way you'd have more time to work."

Dad seemed pleased with the arrangement and excused himself, saying he had to get to work. "I'd like to come by later," he told Mom. "See how things are going. Be sure to keep the doors locked. I'll alert the officers assigned to this area to keep an eye on the house."

"I appreciate your concern, Lieutenant, but I'm sure I'll be fine." Mom gathered up empty plates and took them to the sink.

"Hate to break up the party, Mrs. McGrady, but I need to make a few phone calls." Douglas stood up and picked up the cell phone lying on the table. "Thanks for breakfast. I'll be out in my car when you're ready, Jennie."

Dad waited until Douglas was gone, then pushed his chair back. "I'd better be going too."

Mom tossed the dishcloth in the sink. "I'll walk you to the door."

Jennie wished she could tag along—be a fly on the wall and watch her parents say goodbye. Would he kiss her? Would he choose that moment to tell her? No, probably not—he needed a romantic dinner with candlelight and roses for that. Maybe she'd arrange something for that evening.

Before tackling her meal, Jennie asked a blessing. *Oh, and God, thanks for bringing Dad back. Open Mom's heart. Please don't let her be mad when she finds out.* She opened her eyes and picked up her fork.

"It'll work out," she murmured, trying to erase the uneasy feeling in the pit of her stomach. "It just has to."

Ten minutes later, Jennie grabbed her leather bag, kissed her mom goodbye, and ran out to the car. Douglas straightened, took a last drag of his cigarette, dropped it on the concrete, then ground it out with his shoe.

Jennie bristled but didn't say anything. Some people who smoked had the most disgusting habits—like blowing smoke in people's faces and tossing the butts on the ground. She was beginning to have second thoughts about riding with Douglas if she had to breathe in his secondhand smoke. But she did need to get to the hospital.

His car smelled of stale tobacco and, from the looks of the Burger King bag stuffed between the seats, yesterday's lunch.

Besides that, Jennie wasn't sure how things would work out with Douglas going with her to the hospital. Would he give her time alone with Gavin?

"Thanks for taking me." Jennie buckled her seat belt and tossed Douglas a smile she hoped looked sincere.

"No problem."

Douglas called in to the dispatch operator and told her he was on his way to Sunnyside, then tucked the receiver back on the radio. He wasn't much of a talker, and after several minutes of listening to the garbled message on the radio, Jennie felt like an overinflated balloon.

"S-so," she said, letting the word hiss through her teeth. "How long have you worked for the DEA?"

"About ten years." He glanced behind him and pulled into the right-hand lane.

"Bet you've cracked a lot of drug cases."

"Yep. Your dad and I have been through a lot together."

"How—?"

"He told me this morning. You're a clever girl, Jennie. Jason didn't think anyone would recognize him after his surgery."

"I guess there are some things a person can't erase."

"I suppose that's true."

"Have you changed your identity too? Do you have a family?"

"No on both counts."

"Um—Dad said you thought Dr. Mancini was making drugs in the lab at Trinity. Is that possible? I've heard about drug labs, but I thought they smelled really bad. Someone would have noticed."

"Not necessarily. Depends on what drugs are being manufactured and how they're processed. You're probably thinking of meth labs. Those will often have a strong odor—similar to cat urine."

"Curtis says Dr. Mancini was developing an anti-addiction drug."

He snorted. "So I hear."

"It should be pretty easy to find out—I mean, all you'd have to do is contact Dawson Pharmaceuticals."

"And you think we haven't done that?"

Jennie pinched her lips together. Great, now she'd offended him. Maybe she should just keep her mouth shut. "I'm sorry. I didn't mean to imply you weren't doing your job. I'm just curious—that's all."

"Don't worry. We're on top of it." Douglas exited the freeway and made a left on Sunnyside Road. He dropped her off in front of the hospital and said he'd meet her later in Gavin's room. Good, she'd have a chance to talk to Gavin alone—at least for as long as it took him to find a place to park. From the looks of the full parking lot, that could take a while.

"It's about time you got here," Gavin growled as she entered the room.

"You're lucky I got here at all. Now, what's so important

you had to get me out of bed at six in the morning?"

"Your life, for one thing." He glanced toward the open door.

Jennie pushed it shut, then picked up a chair on her way back to the bed. "Okay, what's up? You can start by telling me why you told the police I was a drug dealer." She dropped into the chair and propped one foot on the bed rail.

"I had no choice. They threatened to kill you and my parents if I didn't."

Jennie straightened and leaned forward. "Who're they?"

"I don't know."

"I'm not buying it, Gavin. Why didn't you just tell the police about the threats?"

"Oh, yeah, right. You know what they'd do. Nothing. I figured you'd be safer in jail. I knew you'd get off eventually."

"Thanks." Jennie folded her arms and leaned back. "Where does Curtis figure into all of this?"

"I'm not sure. All I know is he didn't shoot at you. And he doesn't do drugs."

"Are you sure about that? He's changed."

"Not really." Gavin used his trapeze to scoot up in bed.

"He showed up at my house on a motorcycle."

"His older brother has a dealership and gave Curtis a Harley for his birthday a few months ago."

"That's what Curtis told me. Whoever shot at me was riding a bike."

"Well, it couldn't have been Curtis."

"How can you be so sure?"

"Curtis would never get involved in anything like that. I know this guy, Jen."

Jennie sighed. "Okay, let's say he didn't shoot at me and he isn't into drugs. You said his brother sells bikes—could he be involved?"

"Hardly. Ray is the executive type."

"With a Harley dealership?"

"Yeah—he also owns a couple other companies."

"What about Brian Stone? Does he ride a motorcycle?"

"Brian? I have no idea. What does he have to do with anything?"

"Never mind. Just tell me what happened to you and we'll go from there."

"I'll try. All I know is that I got a call at the paper that day after you dropped me off—right after Mancini was killed. Curtis wanted me to meet him at Trinity. When I got there, he used his key to let us in the office."

"His key or Mancini's?"

"I don't know—he's the lab assistant, so I figured he'd have a key."

"But it was taped off—you weren't supposed to—"

"I know. It's just that Curtis was so torn up about the whole thing. He went on and on about how Mancini was such a nice guy and didn't deserve to die that way. He told me about the drug Mancini had developed and that now they'd be after him because he knew too much." Gavin recanted the same story Curtis had told her.

"I think he was on to something, Jennie. We were there for close to an hour trying to find Mancini's notes."

"Is that when you called me?"

"Yeah. I wanted you to be there."

"I'm glad I wasn't."

Gavin shot her a menacing look. "Just shut up and listen. Anyway, at around seven I told him I was leaving and stepped outside and closed the door. That's the last thing I remember until I woke up in some kind of meth lab—I know that's what it was because it had that strange smell."

"Where was Curtis while all this was going on?"

"He didn't hear a thing and thought I'd just gone home. He felt pretty awful. Told me it should have been him instead of me."

"Do you think whoever abducted you made a mistake?"

"Maybe." Gavin closed his eyes then opened them again. "I wondered about it, but I think they might have just wanted me out of the way. See, before Mancini's murder I'd been snooping around, asking questions. Maybe I just got too close. I just wish I could remember more. Like I told the police, they kept me drugged, and when they let me go they blindfolded me."

"You didn't see their faces?"

"No. I just know there were a lot of them. I heard vehicles coming and going all the time."

"Motorcycles?"

"Some, but there were cars and trucks too. I think I even heard a helicopter once." Jennie followed Gavin's gaze to the door.

"Excuse me." A woman in a white lab coat stepped into the room carrying a tray. "I'm afraid I'll have to ask you to step out for a moment, miss. I need to draw some blood."

Douglas followed her in. "Bad timing, I see."

"This will only take a minute." The woman whipped the curtains around Gavin's bed and disappeared behind them. Jennie followed Douglas out of the room.

"I hate to cut your visit short, but I need to leave. I'll have to come back and talk to him later. Would you mind if I dropped you off at your aunt's place now?"

"No, that's okay. Just let me say goodbye."

He nodded. "I'll meet you at the entrance in about five minutes."

Jennie waited until the nurse left, then went back in. "I have to go."

"I wish you could stay. Jennie, I really feel bad about this. I should have been straight with you from the start."

"Me too, but I understand why you did it. I just wish you hadn't planted the crank in my car. Evidence like that is hard to refute."

Gavin frowned. "What are you talking about? I didn't plant anything in your car."

"Gavin, how would you know? You were stoned out of your mind."

"I would have remembered that—I think. I remember crawling into your car. Thought I'd be safe there, but you went for help. I couldn't let the police see me like that. I was doing crazy stuff and . . . I guess I must have been acting pretty weird. Maybe you're right—maybe I did plant the stuff, but I don't remember. But if I did, I didn't do it on purpose."

"It's okay. Hopefully we'll be able to find out who's responsible for all this. I'm glad you finally decided to confide in me. Which reminds me, why did you?"

"When the police told me you'd been shot at, I realized it wouldn't make a difference whether I did what they said or not. I think they're planning to kill us both."

"I think you're right. I'll tell Agent Douglas and Lieutenant Rastovski what you said. Maybe they'll be able to solve the case before—well, before it's too late."

"Be careful," Gavin warned as Jennie turned to go.

On her way out, the impact of Gavin's words and the shooting of the night before took on an ominous reality. The fact that someone was out to kill her hadn't fully registered. "Oh, God," she prayed in the confines of the elevator. "I don't want to die. And I don't want Gavin to die either."

The elevator doors opened and Jennie stepped out, nearly colliding with a heavyset man wearing a black T-shirt and black jeans. Her face came within two inches of his scraggly gray beard. She gasped and stepped back inside.

"Sorry, ma'am." He smiled, revealing a couple of gold fillings. His long hair had been pulled back into a ponytail.

"It's okay." Jennie ducked out, trying not to stare at the hairy, tattooed arm that reached out to hold the door open. The man stepped into the elevator and nodded to her again as the doors slid shut. Jennie released the breath she'd been holding and chastised herself for being so jumpy. It hadn't helped that the tattoo had been a skull with two roses crossed beneath it. Strange.

She hurried to meet Douglas, all the while telling herself that she and Gavin would be fine. Dad and Douglas would make certain nothing happened to them.

Jennie hauled in a lungful of air and swallowed back her fears. With her shoulders straight and her head high, she exited the building and headed for Douglas's car. Her hand on the door handle, Jennie paused. The hair raised on the back of her neck and an odd chill ran through her veins like ice water. Was the shooter out there?

Glancing around behind her, she yanked the car door open and slipped inside. At least there she'd be safe.

Jennie slammed the door and scanned the hospital entry. "I could be wrong," she said, "but I think someone was following—"

Her thoughts froze as she turned toward the driver. Jennie stared at the cold, steel blue eyes, then dropped her gaze to the gun in the driver's hand.

21

Jennie pressed back against the door and groped for the handle. He was already moving, but maybe she could make a jump for it.

"Don't even think about it." He raised the gun for emphasis. "Just turn around and put your seat belt on. We're going to take a nice little ride."

Jennie did as she'd been told. She had to stay calm. *Look for a means of escape. But not yet. Play along. Wait for the right moment.* She just hoped that moment would come.

"That's a good girl. Now fold your hands and put them on your lap where I can see them." He chuckled and snapped a pair of handcuffs over her wrists.

"Who . . . who are you? Where's Douglas?"

The man sneered. "Let's just say he got a little testy about my wanting to borrow his car. Had to get a little forceful."

She glanced back. Douglas was lying on the seat, unconscious, blood caked on his nose and cheek. "Is he . . . dead?"

"Naw, not yet. Couldn't very well shoot him in the parking lot, could I? Besides, I got a much better means of getting rid of both of you."

Jennie willed her heart to slow down. At the rate it was pounding it would beat itself to death on her rib cage. "Who are you?" She forced herself to examine the driver closely. If she ever did make it out alive, she wanted to be able to identify her assailant. He looked vaguely familiar, but Jennie couldn't place him.

"You don't know me, Jennie McGrady, but I know you. My little brother seems to think you're worth saving, which is about the only thing that's kept me from blowing you away before now."

"You—you're the one who shot at me last night?" She could see the family resemblance now—Ray Bolton, Curtis's brother. Only he didn't look at all like the executive type— even though he was wearing an expensive-looking suit. Amazing how a gun could alter one's appearance.

The gun clunked against the steering wheel as he rolled down the window. Wind whipped loose strands of sun-bleached kinky hair into his face. "You've got it all wrong, Jennie. I'd never indulge in that kind of thing—especially not when there are so many guys out there who could use the work."

"You paid someone to kill me? Why?"

"You're a witness. You know too much. I'd have had someone blow you away sooner, but Curtis didn't think you'd be a problem." He set the gun on the seat beside him. "You got lucky last night, but I don't intend to let that happen again."

Jennie pretended not to notice, keeping her eyes focused on his face. Maybe he'd get distracted and she could grab the gun.

He pulled a pack of cigarettes out of his shirt pocket and tapped it against his hand, then pulled one free with his lips. "Want one?" He handed the pack over to her.

Jennie shrank back and shook her head. "I don't smoke."

"That's good. These things'll kill you." He chuckled and lit his cigarette, drew in deeply, and blew a thick stream of smoke in her face. "'Course, there are other things even more dangerous. Like sticking your nose in where it doesn't belong."

Jennie coughed. Using the driver's side controls, Ray lowered her window.

"Where are you taking me?"

Leaving the hospital parking lot, he turned right on Sunnyside Road and was heading out into the country—toward the Winslows' farm. Curtis lived out there as well. "You'll see soon enough." Smoke escaped in puffs as he spoke.

Jennie watched the houses whiz by. Soon the housing developments would give way to farmland. There was a corn field, Jennie remembered, on the right-hand side of the road, where you turn to go to Gavin's. If he turned there, maybe she could jump out of the car. Maybe she could use the field for cover. With any luck she might be able to outrun him.

Ray slowed down when he reached Delemeter Road and flipped on the indicator. Good, he was turning right. She glanced out at the field. Her spirits plummeted. The corn was there all right, about ten feet inside a high barbed wire fence. She'd never be able to vault the fence and make it to the corn in time. Jennie took some slow, deep breaths to settle herself down and prayed for another opportunity.

Ray picked up speed again and bounced along the potholed road. Jennie could see the Winslow place ahead. All kinds of scenarios drifted through Jennie's head as she frantically looked for escape routes. Both of the Winslows' cars were gone, which meant there'd be no one to help. Even if she managed to get to the house, she couldn't get in.

As if sensing her escape plans, Ray picked up the gun and trained it on her. "If you're thinking of running, I wouldn't."

Okay, Jennie bit her lip and tried to think rationally. *It won't do any good to panic. Douglas is still alive. He has to wake up soon.* And when he did, they could work together.

Jennie's fists tightened in determination. She'd always been a fighter and no way would she give up now. "Since you're planning to kill me anyway, why don't you tell me what's going on?"

"You're too much. Why don't you just shut up? You'll find out soon enough."

About half a mile past the Winslows', the road curved to the east, then south again and dead-ended at a huge new house that sat on a knoll. Ray passed the circular driveway, cut through a short stretch of field, then turned onto a narrow, windy dirt road. After a few minutes, he jammed on the brakes in front of a fence. "Stay put." Ray waved the gun at her, then jumped out.

In the few seconds it took for him to undo the latch and swing the gate inward, Jennie reached for the car radio. She pressed down on the button to send. With so many things to say, she wasn't sure where to begin. "This is an emergency. Agent Douglas has been injured. We're just south of Bo—"

The sentence ended in a scream as Ray reached in though the passenger-side window, grabbed a handful of hair, and yanked her back against the seat.

She raised her arms to ward off his fist.

Ray gritted his teeth and swore, then ran around to the driver's side. Reaching inside, he yanked the radio wires loose, cutting off the dispatcher in midsentence.

Jennie whimpered and closed her eyes. Her arm throbbed where he'd smashed his fist into it. She cowered against the door.

"Don't try anything like that again," he snapped. "You mess me up and I'll make sure that cute little brother of yours doesn't make it to his next birthday."

No. Not Nick. She sniffed, not daring to say anything in case she'd make him more angry.

"I see that got your attention." He drove through the opening but didn't bother to get out to fasten the gate again.

Pull yourself together, McGrady. Jennie tried giving herself another pep talk. It wasn't doing much good. She hadn't

182

been able to give much information to the dispatch operator. Jennie prayed it would be enough. She'd always been taught to think positively. But there weren't many positives left. Even if the police figured out what she'd been trying to say, she doubted it would do any good. The Boltons' house was over a mile away. By the time the police found this place, if they ever found it, she and Douglas would be dead.

Ray pulled up in front of an older white two-story house. Half a dozen motorcycles and a large late model motor home cluttered the overgrown front yard. A couple of stripped-down rusty car skeletons sat half buried in the tall dry grass beside the house. A bed of pink and white impatiens grew in the shade beside some rickety wooden steps.

Two men wearing leathers and chains stepped onto the small, cluttered porch carrying the biggest flask Jennie had ever seen.

It didn't take a genius to figure out what they'd been doing. This must have been the meth lab Gavin had mentioned.

" 'Bout time you got here, Ray," the man facing them said. "Beginnin' to think ya'd run out on us."

"Not likely. Just had some last-minute details to take care of." He glared at Jennie, then turned back to the men. "You guys almost done here? We don't have much time."

"Got most of it. Couple more trips."

"Good. Remember to leave enough supplies in the kitchen to make it look like a small operation."

"Right. We left most of what we took from that school your brother goes to." They carried the flask to the motor home and set it inside, then headed back to the house.

From what she'd learned about clandestine labs from Rocky, this was a typical setup. Take over a vacant house, set up a lab for a few weeks, then move on. These guys looked like they'd done this sort of thing before.

Looked like Douglas and Rastovski—Dad—had been wrong about one thing. Curtis and Mancini hadn't been using Trinity's lab. A wave of grief crashed through her when she thought of Dad. All these years of wishing and praying and hoping he'd come home, and now that he finally had she wasn't going to be around long enough to enjoy it.

Jennie shook off the dismal thought. She wondered what Dad would do in her place—or Gram or J.B. *They wouldn't give up,* a voice inside her seemed to say. *And neither will you.*

"Looks like you're getting ready to leave." Jennie's voice came out surprisingly strong.

"How very astute."

"Ray." Curtis appeared in the doorway. "What took you so—" His startled gaze swept to Jennie. "What's she doing here? I told you—"

"Let's get something straight, little brother." Ray grabbed hold of Jennie's arm and dragged her toward the steps. "From now on, you don't tell me anything. I'm running things around here, and don't you forget it."

"But—"

"Forget her. And the Winslow kid. If you want to work for me, you can't afford to get personally involved."

The look on Curtis's face told Jennie he didn't want to work for Ray. Only Ray was the type of person who didn't take no for an answer.

"Did you get that last batch set up?"

Curtis nodded. "I still don't understand why you're leaving all this stuff. Between the equipment and the latest batch of crank, you're looking at close to thirty grand."

"More like forty, but like I told you before, that's part of the expense of doing business. Keeps the cops off our tails. We go in, set up shop, make a few bucks, then close things down. After we're gone the cops get an anonymous tip, come out, and find a two-bit operation run by local high school kids."

"You're not going to get away with this," Jennie said. "Do

you honestly think the police will believe I'm running a meth lab?"

"Why not? They arrested you for possession. The way I see it, you and the Winslow kid had a profitable business going here. Unfortunately, you got scared. You went to see your friend, Winslow, and slipped him a lethal dose of heroin."

Jennie jerked away. "You killed Gavin? What kind of an animal are you?"

He laughed, adding fuel to the rage welling up inside her.

"You are not going to get away with this."

"Watch me." Ray raised his pistol. "I had planned on letting you take an overdose of the drug you've been cooking up, but I can just as well shoot you. See, Agent Douglas was on to you. He followed you out here, and when you tried to escape he shot you. Then he goes into the house to investigate and trips our little booby trap. Poor guy can't make it out of the house in time."

"You tell a great story, Ray, but the police aren't going to buy it."

"Jennie, shut up. You're just making things worse." Curtis jumped down from the steps and stepped between his brother and Jennie. "Ray, please. Leave her alone."

"Get out of my way." Ray pushed Curtis aside, but Curtis outweighed Ray by about thirty pounds.

"No, you'll have to shoot me first."

"The boy's right, Ray." Douglas walked toward them. "Shooting Jennie would be a big mistake. But not as big as jumping me and stealing my car." He stretched his hand toward Ray. "Give me my gun."

Ray shook his head. "You're a bigger fool that I thought."

Douglas dove at Ray, knocking him to the ground. The gun went off. Jennie dropped to her knees and crawled to the steps. Hunkering down beside them, she tried to stay out of the line of fire as the two men fought for possession of the gun.

Curtis crouched down behind her. "I'm so sorry you had to get involved in this, Jennie. I never meant—"

The gun went off again. The two men lay in a motionless heap in the bed of flowers. Douglas lay on the bottom. A crimson stain began to spread across Ray Bolton's back. Douglas pushed the injured Ray aside and got to his feet.

Curtis yelped like a wounded dog and ran to his brother's side.

Jennie shuddered and looked away, relieved yet horrified. Now what? Douglas had taken out one man, but there were others. As if to prove her point, five men all looking like members of a notorious motorcycle gang moved out from behind vehicles and stepped outside the motor home and house where they'd apparently taken cover. They stood their ground, as if daring Douglas to make a move. All of them, Jennie noticed, wore the same tattoo on their forearms as the man she'd seen at the hospital—the one who had probably been sent to kill Gavin.

Not knowing what to do or what to expect, Jennie pressed herself against the foundation, wishing she could disappear into the rotting wood.

"Put him in the backseat of my car and get Curtis into the house." Douglas barked the order, and to Jennie's surprise two of the men looked as if they were going to obey him.

As he holstered his gun, terror streaked through her like a lightning bolt. DEA Agent Steve Douglas was one of them.

22

"Get in the house." Douglas walked toward her. His rumpled suit and bloodstained shirt made him look like a villain in a monster movie. Dried blood still clung to his face where Ray had hit him. For a brief moment Jennie wondered if maybe the bikers were with the DEA, but only for a moment.

Jennie straightened and started up the steps, then turned back to face him. "Why?"

His eyebrow arched. "Money. What else? Do you have any idea what it's like to watch these thugs get wealthier by the day? I worked my tail off trying to fight the President's war on drugs, and what do I have to show for it?—squat. I can pull in more in a day manufacturing drugs than I can in a year working for the government."

"You betrayed the other agents—my father. Dad trusted you. You were the informer that nearly got him killed, weren't you?" Douglas had probably been leaking information to the drug dealers all along. No wonder Dad's enemies could so easily track him down. It had been too dangerous for him to come home—now she knew why.

"It's war, Jennie." She thought she might have seen a flicker of regret pass through his eyes, but if she did, it quickly disappeared. "Now move."

She took another step and stopped again. "W-what are you going to do with me?"

"Not a thing. You see, that's the beauty of it. My hands are clean."

No, they aren't, Jennie wanted to say. *They're covered with blood. Not just Ray's, but the DEA agents' who trusted you.*

Douglas nodded toward his car. "In a little over an hour, I'll be heading back into town with Ray Bolton's body. I'll be credited with breaking up yet another drug operation. And with finding Dr. Mancini's killer.

"Thing is, I'll have some bad news. You see, Jennie, in raiding this meth lab, my good friend, Lieutenant Rastovski, gets caught in a deadly booby trap set, of course, by Ray Bolton and his little band of honor students. He goes into the house to rescue you and Curtis while I go after Ray, but by the time I manage to take Ray down everyone in the house is dead. It'll make a great story, don't you think?"

The bitterness in his tone dripped like acid on Jennie's heart, eating away at any hope she had left of getting out alive. "Why? You don't have to bring my father into it."

"Save the tears, kid. Sooner or later he'd figure out who's behind the leaks. He's already asking questions. I can't take that chance. Now get inside."

"No one will believe you. The police will find us tied up— they'll know we're innocent."

"You won't be tied up when they find you. And as for believing me." He shook his head. "Jennie, Jennie. I'm a DEA agent. You and the Winslow kid have been caught with drugs—"

"You planted the crank in my car?"

He didn't need to answer. Jennie could see the admission written all over his face.

"Joey," he yelled over his shoulder at one of the bikers. "Tell Buck to get the motor home ready. We'd better move now if we want to hit Spokane by nightfall. We'll go ahead with the plan we had before—just a few alterations."

"You got it." A big burly guy with a scraggly beard and

black eyes signaled one of the other bikers.

"I said get inside." Douglas gave her a push. Jennie tripped on the threshold and went sprawling across the entry. He pulled her up and released one end of the handcuffs still circling Jennie's wrist, then hauled her to the staircase. "Sit down."

Jennie sniffed and dragged her hand across her eyes. The room reaked like a litter box that hadn't been cleaned in months. *This is it, McGrady. You're going to die.* The whole world would think she was a drug dealer. Except Mom and Gram.

Douglas wrapped the chain around the newel post at the bottom of the stairs, then snapped the cuff back on her wrist. "That ought to hold you." He went outside and came back a few minutes later wearing a clean suit. He'd washed the blood off his hands and face. Clean. How ironic that people who looked cleanest on the outside were often the blackest on the inside.

Jennie heard the motor home start up and drive away. A few minutes later Joey came in with Curtis. "What do you want me to do with the kid?"

"Tie him to the stairs beside Jennie. They can comfort each other."

Joey did as he'd been told, then joined Douglas in the kitchen. "So, what's the plan?"

Jennie could no longer see them. Unfortunately, she could hear them all too well. She inched closer to the railing, away from Curtis, and rested her head against the post.

"The cops are going to find two kids in here instead of one. With Ray dead, there's no reason to take Curtis with us. I don't trust him to keep his mouth shut. Unfortunately, the kid's got a conscience."

"He's one of the best cooks we've ever had."

"We'll find another one. Every town has its share of chemists."

"What about the formula? The only reason Ray wanted the kid along was because of the pill Dr. Mancini developed. We can't afford to let a drug like that hit the market."

Jennie's head jerked up. She glanced at Curtis. So Mancini really had been working on an anti-addiction pill. The conspiracy theory hadn't been all that far-fetched after all. Who more than these drug manufacturers would want to prevent a medication like that from being available to the public?

"We don't have to worry about that," Douglas added. "Mrs. Mancini was all too happy to hand her husband's computer disks over to me. Wanted to make sure her husband's lifelong work didn't get into the wrong hands. Right now they're in the evidence locker down at the station."

"But—"

Douglas chuckled. "I phonied them up. Erased his research data and replaced it with a couple recipes for designer drugs. My report will reflect the latter. Sad, isn't it? You can't trust anybody these days. Seems as though Dawson Pharmaceuticals payed Mancini for research he never did."

Joey chuckled. "I gotta hand it to you, boss. You don't miss a trick."

Douglas came out of the kitchen carrying a tin pie plate, which he set on the floor near the door. Joey followed with another dish and a coil of twine.

"Ever see an acid trap, Jennie?" Douglas took the container from Joey and held it up. "It's really very simple—but effective. We rig this up so the unlucky stiff who opens the door inadvertently pulls the acid container over. The acid spills into the sodium cyanide crystals." He pointed to the pie tin on the floor. "When mixed, these two ingredients create a deadly gas. "This one's especially potent. One whiff can kill you."

"You're not going to get away with this," Jennie said

again. Maybe if she said it often enough and believed hard enough it would be true.

"Of course I am, Jennie. I'm one of the best DEA agents in the business. Your dad will vouch for that."

"He won't come out here alone. He'll bring half a dozen units with him."

Douglas nodded. "That's what I'm counting on. I'll call in my location and meet them at the end of the road. We'll head out in different directions looking for Ray Bolton. See, after Bolton jumped me and abducted you, I managed to escape. I'm not sure where he went—only that it's down in this general area. We'll split up in pairs. My long-time partner and I will come back here. Like I said before, he'll be intent on rescuing you. Now, Jennie, if you'll excuse me, I need to get these guys on the road and make a phone call."

"I'll scream. I'll warn him and he won't come in."

"Sorry, Jennie. If you do that, I'll be forced to shoot him in the back. Or rather Ray will shoot him—and I'll be forced to kill Ray. Any way you play it, I can't lose."

Douglas turned to the biker. "Joey, there's some duct tape on the counter in the kitchen. You know what to do with it. Be sure to secure the doors when you leave."

Joey ripped off a strip of gray tape and pressed it over Jennie's mouth and repeated the procedure with Curtis. He tossed the tape aside and, after setting the booby trap, stepped outside.

A few minutes later Jennie heard the rev of engines as the motorcycles departed in tandem. They were all gone now, except for Douglas. He was out on the porch calling his old friend Jason McGrady, alias Nate Rastovski, for backup.

Jennie ducked her face to her hands and peeled off the tape. Joey wasn't too bright. He should have put their hands behind their backs, not left them in front. Not that being able to talk did much good. If she tried to warn Dad, Douglas would shoot him. Jennie had to find a way to disarm the booby trap or at least get out of there before Douglas and her father came back. Things looked pretty bleak, but Jennie held tight to God's promise that all things are possible to those who believe. There had to be a way out.

She wrapped her hands around the four-inch-thick carved post Douglas had handcuffed her to, trying to pull it free or break it.

"It's no use, Jennie," Curtis murmured after he'd removed the tape from his mouth. "The only thing that will bust these posts is an axe."

Jennie glared at him. "Don't talk to me, you creep."

"I—" Curtis heaved a shuddering sigh. "I'm sorry. I didn't want to have anything to do with this. They forced me to cook for them. They stole equipment from the lab at school and threatened to blame it on me. Later they threatened to kill Gavin—and you. I should have told the police the truth when I had a chance, but I couldn't. Ray's my brother."

Jennie shook her head. "And that's supposed to make things okay?"

"No, it's just . . ."

"You know what really burns me? You come over to my house with this 'You gotta help me find Mr. Mancini's killer' garbage, and all the while you were one of them. Which reminds me, why did you tell the police and me about Dr. Mancini's anti-addiction drug?"

"Ray told me to. Said it would take the heat off us. Look, Jennie, I didn't want to get involved in this—you gotta believe that. Besides, what I said was true. Ray wanted me to destroy Dr. Mancini's formula. Said some guy offered to pay him five hundred grand to make sure the anti-addiction pills never hit the market."

"Douglas?"

Curtis nodded. "I didn't know Douglas was involved until last night when Ray told me it was time to get rid of his boss and strike out on his own." He chewed on his lower lip. "I guess his plans kind of backfired."

"Is that what you were trying to do the day Mancini was killed? What happened, did he interrupt your plans?"

Curtis glanced over at her. "Yeah. Ray forced me to go with him to the school that afternoon. I didn't know Dr. Mancini would be there—or you. He was working in the lab and must have heard us talking in his office. He threatened to call the police. Ray pulled a gun on him and he ran back into the lab. I went after him and tried to talk to him, but . . ."

The pained expression in his eyes told Jennie more than she wanted to know. "You killed him?"

"I didn't mean to. He came at me and I pushed him back. He fell against the counter in the lab and hit his head. I couldn't believe he was dead. I wanted to call the police, but Ray—Ray put the gun in Dr. Mancini's hand."

" . . . and set things up to look like a suicide," Jennie finished.

Curtis nodded. "Things went downhill from there. You showed up, and I thought he was going to kill you. We hid behind the counter. I kept praying you wouldn't see us or Mancini. I knew if you had, Ray would have killed you too."

Tears stung her eyes. "The noise I heard came from the office."

"We'd left the door ajar—the wind must have opened it more and blown some of Mancini's notes off the desk."

"And when I left, you took them."

"They were notes and correspondence pertaining to the anti-addiction drug. When you left, I grabbed the papers and erased the formula from the disk. Ray made me type a suicide note."

"But you used Alex instead of Alexis. You, of all people, must have known how Dr. Mancini felt about his stepdaughter's name."

"I did. I guess I wanted the police to know it wasn't a

suicide. I told Ray I didn't want any more to do with him and his thugs. That's when he threatened to kill you and Gavin if I didn't cooperate."

In the distance Jennie could hear the wail of sirens. She sucked in a long, slow breath to stem the panic rising inside her, then wished she hadn't. The putrid smell of the methamphetamine still cooking in the kitchen gagged her. She wretched, then coughed.

"Breathe through your mouth and it's not so bad."

Jennie nodded. "Douglas will be back with Lieutenant Rastovski any minute. You got any ideas?"

"Maybe, if I can just reach the sodium cyanide with my foot and kick it away. When the door opens the acid would still tip over, but at least it won't be toxic. It's our only chance."

"Try it. Just be careful." The way the mechanism worked, if Curtis accidentally snagged his foot on the chair holding the acid, it would be over for both of them. "Better take off your shoes or you'll never get your foot under the chair."

Curtis removed his shoes, then stretched out on the floor and eased his foot under the chair. His toe was still at least six inches from the pie tin—it may as well have been a mile. "It's no use."

"Let me try it." Jennie wasn't quite as tall, but she had been handcuffed to the side closest to the trap. She slipped off her sneakers, rolled over on her side, and extended one leg.

"Look out, the chair."

Jennie pulled her foot back. Holding her breath, Jennie eased her foot under the rung of the scarred wooden chair. She pressed the top of her foot against the pie tin and inched it forward. "I'm getting it." When her foot touched the front chair leg, she stopped.

"It's not far enough," she breathed. "When the acid comes down it's still going to hit the bowl."

"Okay. What you're going to have to do is kick it as hard as you can across the floor. With any luck the tin will slide on the linoleum."

"But I'll hit the chair."

"I know, and the acid will go flying, but if you can shove the plate far enough away and if the acid doesn't spill. . . . Just make sure you pull your foot back fast."

Jennie didn't have to ask why. If the acid landed on her foot, she'd probably lose it. Jennie closed her eyes and said a prayer. She went through the motions in her mind, planning each detail. *Do it, McGrady*, she coached herself. *Do it now*.

She heard muffled voices outside. Douglas was back. Any minute now, Dad would be coming through the front door. Jennie laid her foot alongside the tin.

Footsteps sounded on the steps outside. *Please don't spill. Please . . . please . . . please*. Jennie swallowed hard. And kicked. She jerked back and screamed as the acid crashed to the floor.

23

"You did it." Curtis leaned toward her. "The acid—did you?"

"No. I don't think I got any on me." Jennie grabbed the post at the base of the stairs and pulled herself back onto the step.

The front door flew open and slammed against the wall.

Lieutenant Rastovski stared at the mess barring his way. "What the—" His gaze traveled across the entry and landed on Jennie. He shoved the chair aside and stepped across the pool of acid now eating through the cheap linoleum. "Thank God you're all right."

"Douglas is behind all this. He's going to kill you."

"What are you talking about?"

The porch steps creaked and a shadow filled the doorway. "You must live a charmed life, McGrady. Or you have until now." Douglas raised his revolver and clicked back the hammer. He fired. Jennie screamed.

The force of the bullet knocked Rastovski back. He leapt forward and slammed into the man who had called himself a friend. Douglas grunted and flew backward, landing on the porch steps. Rastovski dove on top of him.

Though only seconds passed, it seemed like forever before her father moved away from Douglas's still form. The detective clutched at his chest and staggered back inside.

Again careful to overt the acid, he dropped down on the stairs beside Jennie, a key to the handcuffs in his hand. He managed to release her before collapsing on the entry floor.

"Dad—" Had he been shot? Jennie couldn't see an injury and felt a moment of relief when she saw he was wearing a bulletproof vest.

He moaned and grimaced. "Think I broke a rib—" His breaths were shallow and ragged, and Jennie suspected the injury was much more serious than that. Possibly a punctured lung.

"Don't try to talk. I'll go for help."

"Wait," he gasped. "Take my gun. Signal for help. Three shots."

"Three shots. Got it."

Once outside again, she aimed upward, gripped the handle of the gun, and fired. The recoil nearly knocked her to the ground. She steadied herself and fired two more shots, set the gun on the planter, then took off running. With any luck she'd find Dad's car phone to call an ambulance. As she rounded the first bend Jennie spotted a squad car. She waved for the officer to stop. Officer Phelps paused long enough to hear Jennie's explanation, then called for backup. "Get in." She was on the move before Jennie could get the door closed.

"You'd better have someone check on Gavin Winslow." Jennie braced herself against the dash for the rough ride back to the farmhouse.

Phelps tossed her a questioning look.

"I'll explain later. I just hope we're not too late."

She picked up the radio and asked the dispatch operator to send someone over to Sunnyside, then scrambled out of the car. A second squad car, then a third, pulled into the driveway behind them.

———

After riding to the hospital in the ambulance with her father, Jennie spent most of the next two hours answering questions and explaining what had happened and who had done what. She told the police everything except the fact that Nate Rastovski was actually her father. She couldn't remember if Curtis had heard her call him dad. Not that it mattered. At the moment, Curtis was too busy confessing his involvement in Mancini's murder and the drug operation and giving the police a rundown on one of the most sophisticated drug rings in the country. The state patrol would soon be picking up the bikers and the motor home heading for Spokane.

"I think that's about it, Jennie." Officer Phelps tucked her notebook into her back pocket. "We'll probably have more questions later. I . . . um—what you did in disarming that booby trap—you saved Lieutenant Rastovski's life. I can see now why Officer Rockwell thinks so highly of you. You managed to stay cool under extreme circumstances. You're going to make a good cop someday."

"Thanks. Uh—have you heard anything about Gavin?"

"Sure did. You were right. Ray had one of his crew visit Gavin right after you left. A nurse walked in and caught him getting ready to inject your friend with a hefty dose of heroin. When she tried to stop him, he took off. A couple of security guards caught up with him and called the police before he could leave the hospital. Your friend lucked out. If that nurse hadn't come along when she did, he'd never have made it."

"More than luck. I prayed a lot."

Devon nodded and pressed her lips together. "I'd better get back to the station—this is going to be one heck of a report to fill out. Can I drop you off or anything?"

"No, I want to be here when Lieutenant Rastovski gets out of surgery."

Jennie paced the waiting room floor in the surgical unit. Dad had broken a rib all right and punctured a lung. They were putting in a chest tube to suck the air out of the chest cavity so his lung could reinflate. The surgeon had assured her he'd be fine in a few days.

Twice Jennie started to call Mom to let her know. But what could she say? *"Mom. Your new boyfriend's been hurt. But he's not really Nate Rastovski, Mom, he's your husband. And guess what, Mom, I was abducted and almost died."* Not something you could tell your mom over the phone.

She stopped at the pay phone, inserted a quarter, and dialed home again, this time waiting for Mom to answer.

"Hello?"

Her grandmother's warm greeting sent a flurry of relief through Jennie. "Oh, Gram, I'm so glad you're there. I have to talk to you. Dad's in surgery and Mom still doesn't know he's back."

"Whoa . . . slow down, darling—what are you talking about?"

Jennie blurted out the morning's disastrous events, her visit to Gavin, the abduction, the DEA agent and his double life as a drug lord, and the fact that Lieutenant Nate Rastovski was actually her father.

"Jennie, you're certain of that? Only this morning we learned that Jason had left the DEA and would be surfacing under a different name, but we didn't expect it would be so soon."

"I don't think he meant it to be, but with me being involved in the Mancini murder case, it just happened. We have to tell Mom."

"She isn't here, Jennie. I'm not sure where she's gone." Gram paused. "We—J.B. and I thought it might be best if she knew Jason was still alive before he actually contacted her. We felt she should be prepared. Now I'm not certain that was such a good idea."

"What did she say?"

"Not much, I'm afraid. She's very upset."

After promising to get to the hospital right away, Gram hung up.

Jennie paced. How could one family get so messed up? And talk about confusion. Now Mom knew Dad was alive, but she didn't know Dad was Nate Rastovski. Jennie shuddered to think of how Mom would react when she found that out. Dad should have told her right away. What frightened Jennie most though was the uncertainty surrounding her father. Would he stay in Portland like he'd said? Douglas was no longer a threat, but how many others like him were out there? Jennie didn't want to think about that. She had to get hold of Mom.

Leaning against the wall next to the phone, Jennie tried to imagine where Mom would go.

Michael. Maybe she went to see Michael.

Jennie called the church. Michael wasn't in. He'd gone to lunch with Mom. "Would you like to leave a message?" Sarah asked.

"Yes. Tell my mom that Lieutenant Rastovski's been shot."

"Oh, my goodness. Isn't he the man working on Mr. Mancini's murder?"

"Yeah. Um—he's in surgery right now." Jennie told her where.

"I'll be sure to tell her. Would you like me to put Mr. Rastovski on our prayer chain?"

"I think that would be a good idea. Thanks."

Prayer—she could use some herself. Nothing short of divine intervention could help them now. Jennie made her way to the small chapel on the first floor. She slipped into the backseat and bowed her head. Light streamed through the stained-glass window of Jesus holding the lost sheep. *God, I just wanted to thank you for bringing Dad home. Now I need another favor. Please, please let him be okay.* Bathed in rainbows from the sun streaming through the colored glass, Jennie felt almost as though she'd been visited by an angel. Smiling, she remembered a television program about angels visiting the earth and helping people through difficult times.

"I wish you'd send me an angel, God," Jennie murmured. "And one to Mom. Make her see that Dad loves her and needs her. Tell her to break up with Michael." The lights blurred as tears gathered in her eyes and dripped down her cheeks.

"God doesn't work that way, darling." Gram slipped into the pew next to Jennie. "You know that. He won't *make* your mother break her engagement to Michael or remarry your father. She has to make those decisions on her own."

Jennie took the tissue Gram handed her and dabbed at her eyes. "But God is supposed to answer our prayers."

"God does answer prayer—but sometimes His answers aren't always what we'd like them to be."

Jennie sighed. "I want us all back together as a family. But I want Mom and Dad to be happy—not like they were before."

"Do you think that's possible?"

"Anything is possible, but it's not likely, is it?"

Gram gave her a hug and suggested they go see how her father was doing. They walked arm in arm back to the surgical unit. Jennie's heart felt heavier than a truckload of rocks. She tried to lighten the load by concentrating on the positives. Dr. Mancini's murderer and a ruthless drug ring had been captured. Gavin was safe. She, Dad, and Curtis had survived what might have been a deathtrap. All in all, a good day. And there was still a chance Mom would be happy when she learned that Nate Rastovski was really her husband—ex-husband. Still a chance that she'd dump Michael, remarry Dad, and live happily ever after. Okay, a *remote* possibility.

24

"Come on, Jennie, everyone's waiting." Lisa pulled at her cousin's arm.

Jennie stood in front of the mirror in Lisa's bedroom wishing the world would suddenly come to an end. Weddings were supposed to be joyous affairs, but Jennie felt anything but. "You go ahead. I'll be down in a minute."

"All right, but hurry. They're going to start the processional in five minutes." Lisa turned to go, her pink satin bridesmaid's dress swirled around her ankles, showing off the matching satin pumps.

She looked gorgeous—they all did. Even Jennie felt pretty. Her hair piled on her head, then cascading down in dozens of ringlets. Jennie's dress, a duplicate of Lisa's, showed off her slender figure.

She padded to the window and stared down into Kate's and Kevin's backyard. Thirty white wooden folding chairs had been set in five rows of six, separated down the middle by a four-foot band of lawn. The bridal party would walk out of the house, across the deck, and through an arched trellis. Decorated in ribbons and all types of colorful flowers, it looked like the perfect place for a romantic wedding. With only two days' notice, Aunt Kate had done a fantastic job. Only a few of the chairs toward the back were empty.

"I'm sorry, Dad," Jennie whispered. "I tried so hard to

talk her into marrying you instead of Michael. But you know Mom. Once she makes up her mind there isn't much anyone can say. I just wish you hadn't gone away again. That might have helped. Mom says you're unreliable. Maybe she has a point."

After spending three days in the hospital, Dad had gone to stay with Gram and J.B. at the coast. He'd only been there a couple of days when he went back to work. There were a lot of details to clear up, he'd said. Mom hadn't believed him—or hadn't wanted to. Now Jennie was beginning to wonder if he'd come back at all, or if he'd changed his name again and reenlisted in the war against drugs.

Mom still hadn't forgiven him for lying to her. She'd refused his phone calls and his flowers and told him she never wanted to see him again. Then in a move so totally unlike Mom, she decided to marry Michael—immediately. Jennie wondered what would have happened if Dad had stayed in Portland—or even stayed with Gram. Now she'd never know.

"There is one good thing in all of this," Jennie murmured. "Michael will make a great dad for Nick."

She hauled in a deep breath and squared her shoulders, then hurried downstairs to the family room to join the others. Kate, Mom's matron of honor, gathered everyone together. Clucking like a mother hen, she set them in their respective places for walking down the aisle. Kate hadn't said much when she'd learned that her twin brother was still alive. Maybe it hadn't sunk in yet. Or maybe she was angry with him too.

Either way, she'd supported Mom's decision to marry Michael. So had Gram, for that matter. Jennie couldn't understand how they could all be so gracious.

Kate had hired a guitarist from church to provide the music, and when she gave him the signal he started playing "The Wedding Song." The haunting refrain drifted through the yard, filling Jennie's heart with a bittersweet pain.

Michael, Pastor Dave, Uncle Kevin, and Kurt stood near a white wooden podium framed in large arrangements of pink and white gladiolus.

Nick started the procession. He looked adorable in his little tuxedo, carrying a pair of gold rings on a heart-shaped satin pillow. Bernie followed close at his heels, looking almost as important as his master.

Lisa stepped outside next, ducked through the trellis, and walked gracefully up to the front. Jennie was next. Just before stepping outside, she turned back to where Mom stood waiting. Their gazes met.

Don't make trouble, Mom's green eyes warned. She adjusted the lace-trimmed ivory gown.

Jennie's sent back a final plea. *Please, Mom, don't do this. You know you still love Dad.*

Mom broke eye contact, but not before Jennie saw a glimmer of uncertainty.

"Jennie, go." Kate gave her a little push and Jennie moved ahead, ducking through the vine-covered trellis. Step right—slide. Step left—slide. She kept her eyes focused on the podium. Reaching the front, she turned left, then stopped next to Lisa. Once Kate had taken her place, the music stopped. Everyone stood and waited for Mom to appear.

There wouldn't be a wedding march—Mom hadn't wanted that. She'd chosen a love song.

The guitarist strummed. Mom didn't come. After a few minutes, Gram, who'd been sitting with J.B. in the front row, excused herself and went back into the house.

Another five minutes went by. Jennie was getting worried. "I'm going in to see what's going on."

"Michael," Gram called from the patio. "I think you'd better come inside. You too, Pastor."

"Something's wrong with Mom." Jennie hurried inside as Kate began making excuses to the guests.

Mom was sitting on the floor in the middle of the dining

room, a ragged tissue balled up in her hand.

"Susan," Michael's voice was strained. "What happened?"

"Oh, Michael, I'm so sorry," Mom sobbed. "I thought I could go through with it. I wanted so much to love you, but I—"

Michael hunkered down beside her. "I don't understand. You seemed so sure."

"I know. I didn't want to hurt you. I thought if I could just make up my mind everything would be all right."

"You need more time. Is that it?" Michael cupped her elbow in his hand. "Listen—it's okay. We'll postpone the wedding for a few weeks or even a year."

Mom shook her head. "No, I can't. I've been lying to myself and you. The truth is, I'm still in love with Jason."

Michael straightened, his gray eyes misting like a storm on the ocean. His gaze traveled from Jennie to Gram, then settled on Pastor Dave. "I guess that's it, then. Maybe you could tell Kate and the others. . . . I'll be at the church."

One by one the guests offered their embarrassed goodbyes and left. Kate and Gram were doing their best to cheer Mom up. Lisa had gone up to her room to change. Jennie had changed earlier and was seriously thinking of going home.

"Hey!" Nick burst into the room and came to an abrupt halt in front of his mother. "Mama, why are you crying? Did you hurt yourself?"

"In a way, I guess I did."

He pulled at her hand. "Well, get over it. You have to come and see who I found. My dad's here."

"Don't be silly, Nick. Your father is . . ." She frowned at Jennie. "Did you tell him?"

"No, of course not." No one had told Nick about Dad— they'd all agreed it would be too traumatic and confusing for him—especially since Mom had decided to marry Michael.

"Slow down, Nick." Jennie snagged him as he flew past her. "What's going on?"

"It's my dad. He's here."

"Where?"

"Outside. He just got out of his car and is coming up the walk. Now Mom doesn't hafta marry Michael. We can have our real dad."

Mom blew her nose. "Jennie McGrady, if you've been filling this child's head with nonsense again, I'll—"

The front doorbell rang, and Jennie didn't wait for Mom to finish her accusation. She ran through the formal living room, into the entry, and yanked open the door.

"Dad—it *is* you." The dark brown contacts and mustache were gone. So were the silver streaks in his hair. Except for the scar, he looked like his picture.

"See, I told you." Nick scooted around her and took Dad's hand. "We been waiting a long time for you."

Jason McGrady grinned, scooped Nick into his arms, and stepped inside.

Once in the family room, Nick squirmed out of his dad's arms and ran down the hallway. "You stay here. I gotta go find Kurt. Boy, will he be surprised."

"Jason!" Gram opened her arms when he approached. "I'm so glad you decided to come back. I was beginning to wonder."

"I told you I would." He hugged Gram, then Kate. "What's going on here? Looks like a wedding." He frowned and let his cobalt gaze settle on Mom. "Susan, you didn't—"

"No, thanks to you, Nate Rastovski, or whoever you are these days."

He flinched. "I think you'll all be happy to know that I've decided to drop the charades. From now on I'm back to being Jason McGrady. Only I no longer work for the DEA. I did, however, decide to keep the job in Portland as an inspector in the homicide division."

"Really?" Mom eyed him warily.

"Won't that be dangerous?" Jennie asked. "What about the guys who were after you?"

"With Douglas out of the picture, we should be okay. I plan to keep a low profile—just hanging out with my family. It's going to take some getting used to, but if Susan's willing to give me another chance—" His gaze swept to Mom. "I know you said you didn't want to see me again, but I couldn't give up that easily. When we met for coffee that day, I suspected you still felt something for me. And I have never stopped loving you."

"Oh, Jason." Mom shook her head. "I don't know what to say."

Dad dropped down on his knees in front of her. "Don't say anything right now. Just think about it. In the meantime, how about having dinner with me?"

Mom nodded, then smiled. "All right, but we'd better take the kids. I think it's time they spent a little time with their father."

The heavy weight Jennie had been carrying around for a week finally fell away from her heart. It looked like her parents' love story might have a happy ending after all.

Teen Series From
Bethany House Publishers

Early Teen Fiction (11–14)

HIGH HURDLES by Lauraine Snelling
Show jumper DJ Randall strives to defy the odds and achieve her dream of winning Olympic Gold.

SUMMERHILL SECRETS by Beverly Lewis
Fun-loving Merry Hanson encounters mystery and excitement in Pennsylvania's Amish country.

THE TIME NAVIGATORS by Gilbert Morris
Travel back in time with Danny and Dixie as they explore unforgettable moments in history.

Young Adult Fiction (12 and up)

CEDAR RIVER DAYDREAMS by Judy Baer
Experience the challenges and excitement of high school life with Lexi Leighton and her friends—over one million books sold!

GOLDEN FILLY SERIES by Lauraine Snelling
Readers are in for an exhilarating ride as Tricia Evanston races to become the first female jockey to win the sought-after Triple Crown.

JENNIE MCGRADY MYSTERIES by Patricia Rushford
A contemporary Nancy Drew, Jennie McGrady's sleuthing talents promise to keep readers on the edge of their seats.

LIVE! FROM BRENTWOOD HIGH by Judy Baer
When eight teenagers invade the newsroom, the result is an action-packed teen-run news show exploring the love, laughter, and tears of high school life.

THE SPECTRUM CHRONICLES by Thomas Locke
Adventure and romance await readers in this fantasy series set in another place and time.

SPRINGSONG BOOKS by various authors
Compelling love stories and contemporary themes promise to capture the hearts of readers.

WHITE DOVE ROMANCES by Yvonne Lehman
Romance, suspense, and fast-paced action for teens committed to finding pure love.

Over the Edge

Patricia H. Rushford

Jennie McGrady
Mystery Series

Helen Bradley
Mystery Series

Over the Edge

Patricia H. Rushford

BETHANY HOUSE PUBLISHERS
MINNEAPOLIS, MINNESOTA 55438

Over the Edge
Copyright © 1997
Patricia Rushford

Cover illustration by Sergio Giovine

Published by Bethany House Publishers
A Ministry of Bethany Fellowship, Inc.
11300 Hampshire Avenue South
Minneapolis, Minnesota 55438

Printed in the United States of America.

Library of Congress Cataloging-in-Publication Data

Rushford, Patricia H.
    Over the edge / by Patricia H. Rushford.
        p. — . —(Jennie McGrady mysteries ; 9)
    Summary: When his best friend is arrested for murder,
Ryan teams up with his girlfriend Jennie to find the real
killer.
    ISBN 1–55661–562–0 (pbk.)
    [1. Murder—Fiction. 2. Mystery and detective
stories.] I. Title. II. Series: Rushford, Patricia H. Jennie
McGrady mystery series ; 9.
PZ7.R8962Ov   997
[Fic]—dc21   97–4713
                                     CIP
                                     AC

Dedicated to five faithful fans:
Sarah Stark,
Amanda Wilkins,
Jill Taylor,
Tiffany Naiman,
Tyler Doupe

A special thanks to my "promise ring girls"
and to my experts:
Jan Bono,
Michael Curtis,
Margo Power,
and my husband, Ron

PATRICIA RUSHFORD is an award-winning writer, speaker, and teacher who has published numerous articles and over twenty books, including *What Kids Need Most in a Mom, The Jack and Jill Syndrome: Healing for Broken Children, Have You Hugged your Tennager Today?*, and her first young adult novel, *Kristen's Choice*. She is a registered nurse and has a master's degree in counseling from Western Evangelical Seminary. She and her husband, Ron, live in Washington State and have two grown children, six grandchildren, and lots of nephews and nieces.

Pat has been reading mysteries for as long as she can remember and is delighted to be writing a series of her own. She is a member of Mystery Writers of America, Sisters in Crime, and several other writing organizations. She is also co-director of Writer's Weekend at the Beach.

1

"Hang on, Bernie." Jennie McGrady smiled at the St. Bernard pup who climbed into the front passenger seat. Up until then he'd been curled up on the floor in the back keeping an eye on his young master—Jennie's five-year-old brother, Nick.

"We're almost there." She slowed when she approached the gravel road leading into the quiet neighborhood north of Bay Village. Gram's house stood near the end of the street, perched on a cliff overlooking the Oregon Coast. The cool ocean air she'd hit coming over the coastal range thirty minutes before tugged at the dark strands of hair escaping her braid.

Jennie's heart tripped over itself with the prospect of spending the next two weeks here. But most of her joy—and the reason her heart had careened into overdrive—was due to the fact that she'd finally be able to hang out with Ryan Johnson. Ryan was Gram's next-door neighbor, and they had been friends for years, but early in the summer their friendship had taken on a new dimension. She'd hoped to see more of him this summer, but he'd gone fishing in Alaska. Well, he was back, and Jennie had a great vacation planned.

The subject of her dreams was at this moment walking toward her. Or maybe he was walking toward his mailbox. It didn't matter. She pulled into Gram's driveway and nearly fell flat on her face trying to get out of the car. But part of that was Bernie's fault. The dog seemed almost as excited to see Ryan as Jennie was.

7

Ryan closed the mailbox and waved at her, then bent to give Bernie a pat on the head. "You're early. Gram said you weren't coming until this afternoon."

Jennie's heart skidded to a stop. *Okay, Johnson, what's the deal? What kind of welcome is that? Aren't you even going to kiss me? Is it over between us? Have you found someone else?* She didn't ask any of those questions, of course, but they all tumbled around in her head when she saw the sad look in Ryan's sky-blue eyes.

His greeting didn't please Bernie either. The pup whimpered and rubbed his head against Ryan's leg.

"I'm glad you're here." His lips turned up in a half smile, then flat-lined again. He made no move to hug her as he had the last time they'd been together.

"You . . . um . . . you don't *look* glad. If I didn't know any better, I'd say you were disappointed."

Ryan shook his head, and a lock of sandy blond hair drooped onto his forehead. He brushed it back. "It's not you. I . . . I'm sorry, but something's happened and—" His Adam's apple shifted up and down as he swallowed.

He was breaking up with her—no, worse than that. Maybe something had happened to—Jennie grabbed his arm, suddenly aware of the empty driveway and the fact that Gram hadn't come out to greet them. "What? Is it Gram? J.B.?"

"No. They're fine." Ryan closed his eyes and gathered her close. "They went shopping—should be back in an hour or so."

Jennie wrapped her arms around him, resting her forehead against his chin. "Then what?" Reluctant to step out of the halfhearted embrace, Jennie tilted her head back so she could see his face. "Not your folks?"

"It's a friend of mine—Todd Kopelund." Ryan frowned and dropped his arms to his side. "He's a suspect in a murder investigation. They think he killed his girlfriend."

"Oh no. Ryan, I'm so sorry." Todd was one of Ryan's *best* friends. Lisa, Jennie's cousin and best friend, had had a crush

8

on Todd one summer a couple of years back. And no wonder. Todd had a linebacker build, eyes the color of dark chocolate, and hair that couldn't decide if it was blond or brown. "Who's—I mean, who was his girlfriend?" Jennie asked. "Do I know her?"

"Maybe. Her name was Jessica Ames. She went to a private school in Portland and was home for the summer."

"The mayor's daughter?" She did remember Jessica—talented, beautiful, and spoiled. Jennie had met her at a fundraiser of some sort that Gram had dragged her to.

"Yeah, and her folks are out for blood."

"Why was she dating Todd?" He was not only younger but definitely not on the same social level.

"He'd liked her for a long time. I never did understand what he saw in her—she was nice enough but . . ." Ryan's words trailed off. His gaze drifted back to Jennie. "He didn't do it. I know Todd, and I can't believe he'd kill anyone—especially Jessica. He loved her."

Jennie pinched her lips together partly because she didn't know what to say and partly to keep from telling him that people weren't always as they seemed. "Have you talked to Gram and J.B.?" With her grandfather being an FBI agent and Gram an ex-police officer, Jennie figured they'd have some insight on the case and might even be working on it. Gram had a thing for solving mysteries—for that matter, so did Jennie.

"Not yet. I'm not sure they even know. It happened last week while they were gone, and I haven't had much chance to talk to them."

Jennie was about to ask him for details when Mrs. Johnson opened the back door. "Ryan, telephone—it's Todd." She waved. "Hi, Jennie—welcome back. Helen called a few minutes ago—said if you got here before they did to make yourself at home. Door's unlocked."

"I'll talk to you later," Ryan called over his shoulder and jogged across the yard to his house.

Apparently feeling as rejected as Jennie did, Bernie moved up beside her and licked her hand. She absently stroked his silky coat. "I have a feeling this is going to be a long two weeks, Bern. And here I thought this vacation was going to be fun. Silly me."

When the door to the Johnson home closed, Jennie shuffled back to her Mustang and glanced into the backseat. Nick was still asleep. He'd managed to stay awake for an hour on their drive down from Portland and would probably be out for a while.

Not wanting to wake him, she pulled the key out of the ignition, gently closed the door, and opened the trunk. Might as well haul their stuff in and get settled.

Ten minutes later, while filling Bernie's water dish, Jennie heard a car door slam. She leaned over the sink to look out the kitchen window. Ryan backed his car out of the garage, whipped around, and headed down the drive, spraying gravel and raising a cloud of dust.

Her stomach knotted. Where was he going in such a hurry, and why hadn't he asked her to go with him? Not that she could have with Nick still asleep, but at least he could have asked. She had a strong hunch it had something to do with Todd.

Jennie sighed and moved away from the window, then set the dish on the back porch where Bernie waited. *Forget it, McGrady*, she told herself. *Ryan still likes you. He's just worried about his friend.* She vowed to be understanding, left the pup lapping, then went to check on Nick again.

"Hey, little buddy." Jennie pulled the seat forward and helped Nick out.

Nick scowled the way he usually did after a nap. Like a four-armed octopus, he wrapped his skinny arms and legs around her neck and waist. She carried him into the house and she settled into the rocker, nuzzling his neck. "You gonna sleep all day?"

He murmured something unintelligible against her shoulder.

Jennie smiled and kissed the top of his head. The thick black hair tickled her nose. "Bernie's waiting to play ball with you."

"Where's Gram and Papa?" Nick raised his head and let his hands drop onto his thighs.

"Shopping—bet they'll be bringing home something special for us."

Nick's navy blue eyes widened. "Like Gummi worms?"

Jennie chuckled. "Maybe. I was thinking more like crab and shrimp."

He yawned. "I'd rather have worms."

Gravel crunched as a car pulled into the driveway. Nick scampered off Jennie's lap and hit the floor running. "They're here!"

Jennie hurried after him, and the two watched Gram maneuver her classic 1955 Thunderbird convertible into the space beside Jennie's Mustang.

"Well, if it isn't two of my favorite grandchildren." J.B.'s Irish blue eyes twinkled as he stepped out of the car and spread his arms to welcome them. The way he scooped Nick up and hugged him made it seem as if he'd been a grandfather all his life instead of only a couple of months.

Jennie got her hug from J.B. and hurried around to greet Gram.

Gram wrapped her slender arms around Jennie. "It's so good to see you." Her warmth almost made up for Ryan's coolness.

"You too." Jennie gave her grandmother an extra squeeze before letting her go.

"Did your mom and dad get off all right?" Gram finger-combed her mussed-up salt-and-pepper hair.

"Yep. Which is why I'm early. Had to take them to the airport at six this morning." Jennie could almost feel her eyes brighten when she spoke. Susan and Jason McGrady were heading to Hawaii to celebrate their second marriage—to each other.

"I'm so glad they were able to resolve their differences. Did they seem happy?"

"Sickeningly so." Jennie grinned at the memory of her parents mooning over each other like newlyweds.

Gram chuckled. "Let's put these groceries away, then we'll have a nice long visit and some tea on the patio."

J.B. draped an arm around Gram's shoulder. "Why don't you two lovely ladies go on inside? The lad and I will fetch the groceries in."

"Yeah, me and Papa will do it." Nick bounced up and down waiting for J.B. to open the trunk.

Jennie followed Gram into the house. She couldn't wait to find out what, if anything, Gram knew about Jessica and Todd. Only after the groceries had been brought in and piled on the counter and the "guys" had taken Bernie for a run on the beach did Jennie have a chance to talk with Gram alone.

"How about putting these in my big fruit bowl." Gram handed Jennie a bag of various fruits and a hand-thrown bowl decorated with colorful salmon. "You'll need to wash them first."

"Sure." Jennie pulled out a large cluster of grapes, set them in a colander, and rinsed them with cold water.

"Have you seen Ryan yet?" Gram asked.

"For a minute. He left after he got a phone call from his friend Todd Kopelund. I guess the police think Todd killed Jessica Ames. Did you hear about that?"

"Yes, just a few minutes ago. We saw Annie Costello in the post office." Gram paused to stash a package of salmon in the refrigerator. "You remember her, don't you? Todd's cousin?"

Jennie frowned, trying to put a face with the name.

"She's the caterer we had when I hosted an art benefit last year."

"Oh yeah." A picture of a short, curly-headed strawberry blonde came to mind. "So what did she say?"

"She told me about Jessica, of course." Gram opened the pantry and stacked cans of tomato sauce in a tidy row next to the green beans. "Such a tragedy."

"What happened to her?" Jennie asked. "Ryan said someone killed her, but—"

"You're not planning to get involved in this, are you?" Gram interrupted.

"No. Just curious." Though Jennie was being totally honest, an opposing voice in her head practically accused her of lying.

Gram took several long seconds to respond. "Her body was found on the rocks below the Ameses' home."

Jennie shivered. Like Gram, the Ames family lived high on a cliff overlooking the ocean. It would have been about a twenty-five-foot drop. "What makes the sheriff think Todd did it?"

"I'm not sure. The authorities have been trying to ascertain whether it was an accident or if someone pushed her. Apparently Todd was the last person to see her alive."

Jennie and Gram had just finished putting away the groceries and settled into lounge chairs on the patio when the doorbell rang. Jennie, being closest, offered to get it.

"Thank goodness you're here," Mrs. Johnson sobbed once Jennie opened the door. "I need one of you to drive me into town—to the hospital."

Jennie's heart constricted remembering Ryan's hasty departure. "What's wrong?"

"Ryan's been in an accident."

2

"Are you sure you're not too upset to drive, Jennie?" Gram asked. "I'll be happy to take her. Or I can leave a note for J.B. and Nick and we could both go."

"No, I want to drive." Jennie blinked back an onslaught of tears. "But I'd like it if you came along."

Gram left a note on the table and hurried out to the car.

"I'm sorry to bother you about this," Mrs. Johnson said as she slid into the front seat. "It's just that with my husband out of town there's only one car, and according to the sheriff it's not exactly drivable at the moment."

"It's no bother," Gram said from the back.

Mrs. Johnson must have read the worried look on Jennie's face. "The sheriff assures me he's all right, Jennie. Just a few cuts and bruises."

Jennie swallowed back the lump in her throat and nodded. She concentrated on sticking the key into the ignition . . . backing the car around . . . and driving to the main road. During the trip to Lincoln City and the nearest hospital, Jennie half listened to the two women talk. Mostly, though, her mind was on Ryan and the accident. Maybe she was reading more into it than was actually there, but her suspicions rose like the sea at high tide and created patterns of doubt in her head. *Why now?* Mrs. Johnson told them that Ryan had gone to see Todd. Had Ryan's involvement in the case caused

14

concern for the real killer? Was Ryan's life in danger?

Why couldn't you stay out of it? Jennie told the image of Ryan that invaded her brain. *Why can't you just let the police take care of things? If he's innocent, they'll let him go.*

Even as the thoughts formed, Jennie knew they weren't entirely true. Too often she had heard about cases where the wrong man or woman was arrested and sentenced and the real killer got off. When it came right down to it, she would probably do whatever it took to prove a person innocent if she believed them to be—especially a friend. Jennie sighed. She and Ryan needed to talk.

The emergency room bustled with activity—green-clad figures scurrying here and there—but Jennie's gaze focused only on the cubicle in front of her. Her stomach rebelled at the sight of blood smeared into Ryan's hair and staining parts of his blue denim shirt a dark purple. The bright lights faded Ryan's summer tan. The emergency room staff and equipment settled into a distant hum. The doctor looked up from his stitching and smiled at Mrs. Johnson when she introduced herself and Jennie.

"He's going to be fine," the doctor said. "I'll be done sewing him up in a minute."

"Should we wait outside?" Mrs. Johnson's chalky complexion suggested she'd be better off in the waiting room with Gram. Jennie grabbed a vacant chair and rolled it up behind Mrs. Johnson, suggesting she sit down. Lucky thing. Mrs. Johnson's knees buckled, and she almost ended up on the floor.

"Bless you, Jennie." She fixed her gaze on something on the other side of the room.

"Can he talk?" Jennie asked the doctor.

"Why are you asking him?" Ryan murmured. "Like he told you, I'm fine."

"You don't look fine." Jennie bit her lower lip, wishing she

15

could take back the remark and the harsh tone of her voice when she said it.

"Why are you here?"

"Because your mom asked me to drive her." *And I was afraid you'd been hurt.* Jennie decided not to say too much. Accident or not, she was beginning to resent his nasty disposition. Besides, she didn't want to let him know she still loved him in case the feeling was no longer mutual.

"Now, now, kids." The doctor straightened and winked at Jennie. "Keep that up and I may have to alter my original assessment."

"What do you mean?" Ryan asked.

"You must have hit your head harder than I thought. No guy in his right mind would pick a fight with an attractive young lady like Jennie here. Unless she's your sister. . . ."

"She's not my sister." Ryan glanced in Jennie's direction.

Jennie's face and neck warmed with a flush of embarrassment. "We're friends," she responded before he could. "At least we used to be."

"Ah . . . a disagreement. I can see we need to get you out of here, Ryan. Looks like you two need to sort things out." The doctor stood and turned to the nurse. "Put a dressing on that and clean him up, would you?"

Jennie, feeling about as useless and unwanted as a mouse, mumbled something about meeting him in the waiting area and scurried out of the room.

On the way home from the hospital, Ryan remained sullen. Even though his mother had insisted he ride in front with Jennie, he didn't say much. As she drove, Jennie reminded herself again and again that they were still friends and eventually Ryan would get over his bad mood. She vowed not to feel sorry for herself and was determined not to let anything spoil her vacation at the beach. Still, it seemed strange that Ryan would shut her out like that.

Once home they piled out of the car. Ryan managed to

mumble what sounded like an insincere thank-you and came up with a semienthusiastic "I'll see you later."

———

Later came and went. After eating a late dinner and reading bedtime stories to Nick, Jennie made the excuse that she was tired and went up to what would be her room for the next two weeks. Of the three guest rooms in Gram's house, Jennie had always liked this one best. It was small and cozy with a daybed and a big window that faced the ocean. Jennie unpacked her bags, then flopped onto the bed to read one of the new mysteries Mom had given her for the trip.

Thinking about Mom and Dad honeymooning in Hawaii almost made her forget her disappointment over Ryan. That Mom and Dad had decided to try again had been nothing short of a miracle. Dad's homecoming had been a miracle too. Jennie couldn't remember being happier than when her parents had announced their plans to remarry.

Funny how life went. She remembered a friend once saying, *"Life is a ball, but it sometimes rolls over you."* That's how she felt now. Rolled over. Like road kill on a lonesome highway. Jennie groaned at her macabre thoughts and sat up. She didn't feel much like reading. What she wanted more than anything was to go over and drag Ryan down to the rocks where they used to spend hours talking and watching the sun go down. Only she couldn't do that. What if he said no? Besides, he'd just been in an accident.

"Okay, McGrady," she said aloud, "go by yourself. You don't need Ryan along to enjoy the sunset."

Jennie grabbed a gray sweat shirt and went downstairs. She paused to let Gram and J.B. know where she was going, then made her way down the familiar path and out onto the rocks. Someone was already sitting there. Jennie thought about leaving.

"Don't go." Ryan turned toward her. "I was hoping you'd come."

Why, so you could break up with me face-to-face? That's what she felt like saying. What she actually said was, "You were?"

"Yeah. I need to ask you a favor."

Jennie teetered on the narrow rock ledge, then picked her way around the chasm that separated them. When she reached his side, he grabbed her hand and pulled her down beside him.

"So what's the favor?" Jennie looked at the hand that still held hers. She didn't want to look at his face or into his eyes, didn't want to think about what might be written there.

"In a minute. First, I want to tell you I'm sorry about the way I acted today. I know there's no excuse, but . . ." He shook his head. "Let's just say it's been a rotten day all around. It started with Todd telling me he was leaving town."

"That doesn't sound like a very smart move." She looked at him then, watching his profile as he spoke into the wind.

"I told him that." Ryan glanced at her, then turned back toward the ocean.

"Did he leave?" Jennie tried to concentrate on their conversation and not on the emotions churning around inside her like the boiling water in the deep crevices below.

"Not exactly. He got as far as Whale Cove when the sheriff arrested him."

"That must mean they have a case against him."

Ryan nodded. "So they say. I haven't been able to find out anything." He shifted his gaze back to Jennie. This time he didn't turn away.

Jennie's heart stopped, and she couldn't breathe.

Ryan reached out to cup her chin. "I've missed you."

"I . . ." The words melted as Ryan's lips connected with hers.

It was a short kiss, but definitely a kiss, and Jennie rated it a ten. Her heart started again, racing faster than a sand-piper in the surf. She wanted a repeat performance, but Ryan had turned away and was watching the lavender and pink sky.

"I'd like to borrow your car."

Jennie pulled her hand free of his grasp. "You really are a piece of work, Johnson. You act like I don't exist, then all of a sudden you're apologizing and . . ." She scrambled to her feet.

"Wait a minute." Ryan jumped up and blocked her path. "What did I do?"

"As if you didn't know." She gave him a shove. Ryan slipped on the rock and started to fall backward, waving his arms in the air.

Jennie grabbed his hand and yanked him toward her. She landed on her rear and slid down the incline, grabbing at the craggy rock face. Her foot caught in a crevice, jerking her to a stop.

"What were you trying to do, kill me?" Ryan caught him-self and reached for her hand, hauling her up and into his arms.

"I'm sorry," Jennie gasped. Beneath her ear, his chest seemed to be beating as wildly as hers. "I thought you were using me and . . ."

Ryan leaned back. "What are you talking about?"

Okay, McGrady, think for once before you speak. Maybe you're wrong about Ryan making up with you just so he can bor-row your car. She had to know.

"Ryan, do you still like me?"

"Of course I do. Why would you ask a stupid question like that?"

"Maybe I'm reading you wrong here, but the way you were acting when I arrived this morning and again at the hos-pital, I had the distinct impression you were planning on breaking up with me."

His shoulders slumped. He let go of her and dropped

down to the rock. "It's not you, Jennie. I still feel the same way about you as I did before. I thought you knew that. It's this whole thing with Todd. I've been so wrapped up in that, I haven't been able to think straight. Which is why I ended up ramming the car into the back of a truck."

Jennie felt like a jerk. She'd been so caught up in her own feelings she hadn't taken the time to really think about what Ryan must be going through. "Ryan, I'm so sorry." She laced her fingers through his. "About the car. I can't let you drive it. The insurance only covers Mom and me right now. Not that I don't trust you, it's just that Mom would probably ground me for the rest of my life if I let anyone else drive it."

"It's okay. I can probably find someone else—"

Jennie thumped his arm. "I wasn't finished. I was going to say that I can't let you drive the car, but I'll drive you wherever you need to go."

Ryan draped an arm around her shoulder. "Thanks, Jennie, but I can't let you do that."

"Why? Are you planning on going places you shouldn't?"

"No . . . it's just that—"

"You want to find out what really happened to Jessica, right?"

He nodded. "I guess maybe I do. I know it sounds stupid. Like what can I do?"

"*We*. I'm not sure we can do anything. But I'm getting pretty good at this sort of thing."

"I know, but this is different. Somebody killed a girl our age. I wouldn't want anything to happen to you."

"I don't want anything to happen to you, either, but if we work together we can protect each other. I don't know the details, but if you really believe Todd is innocent, then I'll do whatever I can to help you prove it."

Ryan squeezed her hand and pulled her closer. "You make it sound so easy. Maybe I should have more faith. I try, it's just that when the sheriff actually arrested Todd today, I got this hopeless feeling. Like it was all over."

Jennie didn't answer. She knew the feeling all too well. She squeezed his hand and leaned against him. Shoulder to shoulder they sat and watched the brilliant red sun sink into the sea. While they waited for the moon, they talked about family and fishing, and Jennie brought Ryan up-to-date on her dad's homecoming.

Ryan had been in Alaska most of the summer working on a commercial fishing boat. He was excited to be home but depressed at the thought of having to go back to school soon. Now with the murder and his best friend in jail, he felt at odds.

"I hate to say it, Jennie, but we'd better go back." Ryan stood and gave Jennie a hand up.

"I'm glad I came out here tonight."

"Me too."

They scrambled over the familiar rocks and headed into the woods. Neither had remembered a flashlight, but they didn't need one—they'd walked the same path a hundred times before. When they reached Gram's yard, Ryan stopped. "We should talk about tomorrow."

"Sure. What about it?"

"I need you to drive me to the courthouse in the morning. Todd's being arraigned at nine-thirty. I want to talk to Greg and Annie about getting enough money together for bail."

"Who's Greg?"

"Todd's brother."

"Did I miss something? Why would you talk to his cousin and his brother about bail—what about his parents?"

"They're dead. His mom died of cancer when he was little. He lost his dad in a logging accident several years back. Greg sort of took over raising Todd."

"That's so sad."

"Yeah. They've had a rough time. Anyway, none of them

21

make much money. I thought if we went together maybe we could come up with enough."

"Do you really think they'll let him out?" Jennie doubted it—not on a murder charge.

"Maybe. He's never been in trouble before—at least not that I know of."

"I need to talk to Gram and make sure she can take care of Nick."

"There's one more thing I want to do. It won't be very pleasant, but maybe we'll find something." Ryan chewed on his lower lip.

"What's that?"

"Visit the scene of the crime."

3

Jennie woke from a fitful sleep the next morning. She kept imagining Jessica Ames falling to her death on the jagged rocks below her home. Sometimes the victim's face was Jessica's—sometimes it was Jennie's. Try as she might, she couldn't stop the images from hurling themselves into her mind.

She kept remembering how she'd pushed Ryan and almost lost him. What if Ryan had fallen into the fierce, pounding surf? Would she be facing murder charges?

At eight-fifteen, Jennie gave up the notion of sleep and crawled out of bed. A shower revived her, and at eight-forty-five she headed downstairs.

"Ryan called while you were in the shower. Wanted to make sure you were up." Gram set half a grapefruit and a bowl of oatmeal on the table.

"Where are J.B. and Nick?" Jennie settled into a chair, then poured a glass of orange juice.

Gram chuckled. "Off doing guy stuff. J.B. took him down to the dock to watch the fishing boats. He said something about teaching the 'lad' how to fish."

"That's neat." Jennie had told Gram and J.B. of her plans to meet with Ryan the night before, and they'd agreed to watch Nick. "J.B.'s really good at being a grandfather. Nick sure loves him."

"The feeling's mutual. J.B.'s never been around children much, so he's having the time of his life." Gram poured a cup of hot water from the teapot and sat down beside Jennie. "I'm glad to see you and Ryan are speaking again."

Jennie shrugged. "Guess he has a hard time focusing on more than one thing at once. I thought he didn't like me, but he's just too worried about Todd to notice much else."

"And now?"

"He says nothing has changed between us." Jennie sighed. "He's hoping I'll help him find evidence to prove Todd didn't kill Jessica."

"You'll be seeing Todd today, is that right?"

"Uh-huh."

"I'll be anxious to hear what you think after you talk to him."

Jennie set her spoon down. "Is there something you're not telling me?" Gram had that knowing look in her eyes.

"No, it's just a feeling I have—and this." Gram handed her a folded newspaper and pointed to the headline. *Suspect Arrested in Ames Murder.* Jennie scanned the article, her heart sinking. It didn't look good for Todd. According to an interview with Mayor Ames, Todd had been the last person to see Jessica alive. Todd claimed he was innocent and that he had dropped Jessica off around ten and gone home. But Mrs. Ames says she saw them sitting by the stone wall much later than that. And Mayor Ames claims he saw Todd drive away just as he was coming home at midnight. Jennie almost cried when she read the quote from the mayor: *"I went to her room to say good-night. Her light was on, but she wasn't there, so I asked Mari if she'd seen her. Mari said to look outside. Jessica loved to sit in the gazebo or on the wall at night. That's when I found her."*

Jennie set the paper on the table, her breath swishing out. "You think Todd's guilty, don't you?"

Gram took a sip of her tea before answering. "At this

point I don't know enough to speculate."

Jennie twisted her braid around her hand. "I have a question for you. Mayor Ames found Jessica late at night, right?"

"According to the reports, yes."

"Hmm."

"What are you thinking?" Gram set her cup down and leaned forward.

"That the mayor might have killed her."

"Really. How do you come up with that?"

Jennie chewed on her lower lip. "Why would he have looked over the edge? It seems strange to me. You'd think he'd search the house and grounds first. It was like he knew where to look."

Gram nodded. "Perhaps, but he may have paused to look at the ocean and happened to see her."

"Yeah—but it was dark. How could he have seen anything twenty some feet below him?"

"Flood lights, Jennie. They light up the area at night. I would imagine he turned them on before he went to look for her."

"Oh." Embarrassed, Jennie picked up the paper again.

"It was valid question," Gram said, encouraging her like always. "And I'm sure the investigating officers asked the same thing."

Jennie glanced over the incriminating article. "It looks bad for Todd, doesn't it?"

"Yes, it does. Forrest and Mari Ames are reputable people. I doubt they'd lie about something like this."

"Looks like Ryan and I have our work cut out for us." Jennie shifted her gaze to Gram, expecting the usual word of caution—wishing in a way Gram would tell her to forget about it. "Aren't you going to warn me to be careful?"

"Do I need to?"

"No. I won't take any unnecessary chances, and I'll let you know what I'm doing and call you or the sheriff if I find anything that might be important to the case."

"Well, then you'd better get a move on." She glanced at her watch. "Ryan should be here any minute."

"After we talk to Todd, Ryan wants to go over to where Jessica's body was found. Do you think that's a good idea?"

"Sounds as if you're not very excited about it." Gram spread a dab of cream cheese on a cinnamon-raisin bagel.

"It seems kind of gruesome. Anyway, the sheriff will have taken away any evidence, so we won't be able to see anything."

"Sometimes being there helps to put yourself in the victim's place."

Jennie shuddered. "I've been doing that all night."

"Are you feeling all right, dear? You don't seem your usual perky self."

Jennie pushed her empty dish toward the center of the table. She wasn't feeling all that great. Maybe it was the dream. All morning she'd had an uneasy feeling and couldn't seem to shake it. As much as she wanted to learn about the case, she found herself growing more and more reluctant. The article hadn't helped matters. "I'm okay, I guess. I'm just not sure I'm ready to go to this hearing. What I really want to do is find a secluded beach and read a novel." She scrunched up her nose. "I know this sounds weird coming from me, but I'm not sure I want to get involved."

"Why don't you call Ryan and tell him you can't go? You can lie around and read—take a nice warm bubble bath and a nap—"

The doorbell rang, and Ryan let himself in.

"Sounds good, Gram," Jennie said, "but Ryan needs my car. Besides, I promised."

"Promised what?" Ryan sauntered in, whipped a chair around, and straddled it, resting his arms on the chair back.

"That I'd make sure you stayed out of trouble." Jennie

picked up her dishes and set them in the sink and began rinsing them.

"Leave those, Jennie. You two run along."

After a hasty good-bye, Jennie and Ryan headed for the courthouse.

"I appreciate you driving me." Ryan clasped his hands in front of him, resting them on his knees. "I hate being without wheels. The mechanic says it'll be another week before I can get the car back."

"No problem. I'll be around."

Ryan heaved a sigh, flashed her a nervous grin, then fixed his gaze on the car in front of them.

Jennie wanted to say something intelligent or encouraging, but the right words evaded her. She couldn't very well tell Ryan everything would be okay when she had no idea whether it would or not. "So, how's your head?"

He gave her a blank look. "My head?"

"Yeah, you were in an accident yesterday, remember?"

He touched the white square dressing on his forehead. "Oh, um—fine. It hardly hurts at all." Ryan was spaced-out again, no doubt thinking of Todd.

Fortunately the ride to the courthouse lasted only a few minutes. The gravel crunched as Jennie pulled into the unpaved lot and parked beside a dark green Lexus.

"The mayor's here." Ryan thumped the roof of her car. "I was afraid he'd show up."

Ryan's uneasiness filtered through to her. "I take it that's not good."

"If Ames has his way, Todd will be put away for life." Ryan headed for the courthouse, and Jennie hurried to catch up with him.

According to the date etched into a beige stone rock above the entry, the courthouse had been built in 1910. Their footsteps echoed on the marble floor as they entered.

"Ryan!" Annie hurried toward them. "I'm glad you

came. Todd needs all the support he can get." She glanced at Jennie and smiled. "I should know you—don't tell me." Her green eyes brightened in recognition. "You're Helen's granddaughter, Jennie."

"Right." Jennie slid her hand along the thin strap of her small handbag.

"I'm Todd's cousin, Annie. It's good to see you again."

"You too," Jennie replied.

"Did you get my message?" Ryan asked. "About going together on the bail?"

Annie nodded. "Greg told me. I have no idea what it will be. A lot, I expect—if the judge will even let him out. He's getting a lot of pressure from the mayor and the press. Greg isn't sure he wants to put up bail even if the judge sets it."

"Why not? We can't just leave Todd in jail. He didn't do it."

"Money's tight for him, Ryan—for me too." She pinched her lips together, letting her gaze drop to the floor. "Besides, we really don't know for sure that he's innocent."

"That's crazy." Ryan shoved his hands into his pockets and frowned. "You know Todd would never hurt anyone—especially Jessica."

Annie glanced at the oversized watch on her thin wrist. "We should go inside," she said, then added, "Greg's late—he should have been here by now."

Before Ryan could respond, the object of their discussion walked in. Wearing faded jeans and a plaid flannel shirt, Greg looked like he'd just come off his boat—which he probably had. Greg Kopelund was about Ryan's height and nearly twice as broad across the chest and shoulders. His short ash brown hair, mussed by the wind, settled neatly into place when he ran a hand through it. From the stern look on his face, the courthouse was the last place Greg wanted to be. He paused to greet Ryan and Jennie, then followed Annie into the courtroom.

At least twenty people were already seated on the scarred old benches. Half a dozen spectators, probably reporters, judging by the steno pads, sat in the back row. Annie and Greg went to the front and eased into the second row behind the defense table. Mayor Ames and his wife, Mari, sat opposite them on the side of the prosecution. Jennie's heart lurched when she saw them. How awful for them to have lost a daughter, then face the person thought to have done it. Mari Ames turned and caught Jennie watching her. For a moment neither looked away.

Jennie broke eye contact when she felt the pressure of Ryan's hand on her back, guiding her into a bench seat three rows behind Annie and Greg. For some inexplicable reason, Jennie felt like a traitor. She should be sitting on the other side—with Jessica's parents. Mari Ames' haunting look made Jennie's heart ache all the more.

"Todd's got a court-appointed lawyer," Ryan whispered. "I hope she's good." He nodded toward the woman seated at a table in front of the railing. The attorney pulled a file folder out of her open briefcase, then glanced over at the prosecuting attorney. Her smile told Jennie they may be on opposite sides in the courtroom, but not on the outside.

"I wonder who appointed her," Ryan added when he saw the interchange between the two. A door to the right near the judge's desk opened, and a deputy ushered Todd in. Todd looked smaller than his six feet, probably because of the slump of his shoulders and the way his head drooped. His chocolate brown gaze settled on Ryan, then shifted briefly to Jennie. He turned around and sat down beside his attorney. Gram had often said you could read a person's heart by looking into their eyes. In Todd's she'd read neither guilt nor innocence. One thing was for sure, though. Todd Kopelund was one frightened and unhappy young man. She just wished she could share Ryan's conviction.

"All rise," a bailiff ordered in preparation for the judge's entrance.

A man Jennie recognized as Charlie Crookston hurried in, his robe billowing around his small frame. In addition to being a judge, Charlie ran an ice cream parlor on main street. Jennie and Gram had spent many afternoons there sipping lattés and eating pistachio ice cream cones. In his shop, Charlie would always stop to chat with her and Gram. Today, however, he was all business. Grim faced, he mounted the stairs behind the bench and gave Todd a glare that could melt steel at fifty paces. Charlie had a reputation for being tough on crime. From where Jennie sat, things did not look good for Ryan's friend.

"Lincoln County Court is now in session, the honorable Charles Crookston presiding."

The judge slammed the gavel on the desk to make it legal.

Thirty minutes later it was over. Todd pleaded innocent and was bound over for trial. The court date had been set for two weeks from the day, and Todd would be held without bail. The prosecuting attorney had presented a strong case against setting bail, citing the fact that Todd had tried to flee the day before. Todd's court-appointed attorney had argued in Todd's defense, citing that the evidence collected so far was circumstantial and that Todd had never had so much as a traffic citation. The judge disagreed.

Jennie didn't say so, but had she been the judge, she'd have made the same decision. Something she didn't dare tell Ryan.

"Can you believe those guys?" Ryan squeezed into the passenger seat of her Mustang and slammed the door. "I mean, it's like they've got him tried and convicted already." He shook his head. "And that lawyer—bet anything the mayor paid her to go along with the prosecution."

Jennie cleared her throat. "I doubt that, Ryan. You have

to admit Todd brought it on himself. He shouldn't have tried to leave town."

"He was scared."

Wanting to change the subject, Jennie asked, "Are you hungry?"

"Not really, but I guess we'd better eat. Let's get something at the Burger Hut and take it to the beach. We have to plan our next move."

Jennie had no idea what the next move would be. All she could think about was the condemning newspaper article she'd read that morning and the pain-filled faces of the murdered girl's parents at the arraignment. But the most vivid in her mind was the mayor's outburst when Todd was leaving the courtroom. Mayor Ames had stood up and pointed an accusing finger at Todd and yelled, "He killed her! That animal killed my little girl!"

4

"I never thought I'd say this, Gram, but I'm so glad Ryan decided to go home and rest. I can hardly stand to be around him." Jennie dropped onto the couch and tipped her head back against the cushions. After lunch Ryan had complained of a headache and opted to take a nap before heading over to the jail to see Todd and then visiting the crime scene.

Gram looked up from her computer. After retiring from police work, Gram had turned to writing. "Sounds serious. What's the trouble?"

"He's too intense, for one thing. He's too close to Todd to be objective," Jennie groaned. "I'm afraid to say anything because I might upset him. He's totally freaked out that Judge Crookston wouldn't let Todd out on bail."

"I take it the hearing didn't go well then."

"You could say that."

Gram rolled her chair back from the desk and picked up her mug. "Why don't you come into the kitchen? We can talk over tea."

Tea was Gram's answer to just about everything. Jennie dutifully followed her grandmother into the brightly lit room, selecting a chair bathed in sunshine. Gram placed two cups in the microwave, then set cranberry scones and butter on the table and waited for the water to heat.

When the water was ready, Gram dunked a tea bag in her

cup. "Now tell me what happened at the hearing."

Jennie related the essentials. "I guess the defense has enough evidence to bring the case to trial and to keep Todd in jail." Jennie sipped at her peppermint tea. The quiet scent calmed her jangled nerves. "Ryan won't accept the fact that Todd might have done it."

"Do you think he did?"

Jennie set her cup on the table. "To be honest, I don't know what to think. Mr. and Mrs. Ames were so devastated. I felt like . . . like a traitor."

"I'm not sure I understand."

"Me either. I felt like I was rooting for the wrong guy just by sitting on the same side of the room as Todd. What if he did it, like the mayor says? I'm not sure I want to be on Todd's side—but I don't want Ryan to be mad at me either."

"Why do you have to be on anyone's side? If it bothers you so much, don't get involved."

"It's not that easy. I can't stop thinking about Jessica, and I want to know for sure who killed her."

"That's a tall order." Gram rubbed her finger over the ridges of her cup. "What do you plan to do?"

"Nothing right now." After a few seconds Jennie stood up. "I'm going down to the rocks to read—unless you need me to help you with something."

"No, you go ahead. I have to get back to work. I'm hoping to finish my article before J.B. and Nick get back."

"They're still fishing?"

Gram smiled. "Not exactly. They've gone to the aquarium in Newport to see the whale."

"Keiko? I should have gone with them. I haven't seen him yet." The famous whale from the *Free Willy* movie had been brought to Oregon from Mexico, and Jennie had planned to ask Ryan if he'd go to the aquarium with her. Another disappointment. Until this business with Todd and Jessica was over, she doubted Ryan would want to do anything.

"Perhaps you and I will go. I'm certain J.B. and Nick would love to visit Keiko again."

Jennie headed to her room to retrieve a book, then slipped out the front door and took the familiar path to the rocks. Once there she settled into a crevice resembling a reclining chair and started reading. Two pages later Jennie had no idea what she'd read. Her mind kept drifting back to Jessica.

Jennie was sitting only about half a mile from where it happened. She could climb over the rocks and get to the Ameses' place within ten minutes. Almost of their own volition, her hands pressed against the rocks and her knees bent. She jumped to her feet, stuffed her book in her back pocket, and scrambled over the rough rock formations created by some ancient volcano. Only hours ago, she'd been squeamish about visiting the scene of the crime—now she couldn't wait to get there.

It took longer than she expected, but that was because of the tricky places where she had to wait for water to recede before moving on. It wasn't until she reached the estate—or rather the rocks in front of the estate—that she began to question the wisdom of her venture.

High above her, at the top of a sheer cliff, stood a gray stone wall. Not far below lay the surging and powerful Pacific Ocean. Jessica had fallen over the cliff and landed somewhere near where she was standing. Jennie swallowed back the catch in her throat. It seemed odd being there. Like she was trespassing or something. Not that Jennie was superstitious or even believed in ghosts, but she simply couldn't get over the feeling that she needed to somehow be where Jessica had been and see the people Jessica had seen before her death. Following the footsteps of a dead girl might prove difficult—maybe even deadly.

Definitely eerie. Maybe coming here had been a mistake. "You should have thought of that sooner," she muttered to herself. Jennie shivered, wishing she'd thought to bring a jacket or sweat shirt. The wind had picked up and now blew through her thin cotton T-shirt. Clouds were gathering to the west. She'd have to head back soon.

Despite the cold, she sat on the outcropping of rocks and gazed out over the ocean. After a few minutes of not moving except to tip her head to watch the screeching sea gulls, an odd sensation crept up her spine. Was she being watched? She twisted around, her gaze traveling the length of the stone wall, but saw no one. When she turned back, she caught sight of something shiny tucked into one of the many crevices on the rock face just beneath her. A piece of jewelry? Chances are it was just one of those aluminum rings from a pop can, but she had to find out.

Jennie scooted forward but couldn't reach it without falling headfirst into the water. Maybe if she got on her stomach she could hook her toes over a ridge and stretch out. She did and managed to snare the object. It was a ring all right, but not aluminum. The letters inscribed in the dainty gold band read *True Love Waits*. Jennie had seen rings like it before. Several girls in her youth group at church had gotten them as a symbol of their vow to remain sexually pure until marriage. Had it been Jessica's? If so, why wasn't it on Jessica's hand rather than on the rocks?

Jennie placed the ring on her finger for safe keeping and glanced up at the gray wall, wishing God would give her some answers. Water crashed against the rocks and splashed into the crevice where she'd found the ring. Panic clawed at Jennie's stomach.

The tide.

How could she have been so stupid? She hadn't bothered to check the tide schedule, and now it was too late. The way she'd come and the only way out was now a swollen, churning chasm of ocean and seaweed. As she searched the cliff for possible footholds, another wave hit, swirling around her feet and drenching her shoes and ankles.

"Help!" she screamed. With any luck someone might be in the Ameses' yard and could toss her a rope. What started out as a second cry for help ended in a scream as another wave hit. It crashed onto the rock, sending a wall of water over her. Jennie fell to her knees and clawed at the rock as her body slid downward.

5

The wave dissipated, leaving Jennie's legs dangling over the edge of the precipice. She crawled arm over arm back to where she'd been standing. Another wave like that and she'd end up as fish food. The chilling salt water clung to her clothes and dripped from her hair into her eyes.

"Come on, McGrady, move," Jennie grunted as she pulled herself up another few inches, nearly cheering when her knee finally connected with the ledge.

"Hey! What are you doing down there?"

Jennie was almost afraid to look up—afraid the voice calling down to her was only a figment of her overactive imagination.

"Hey, you! Do you need some help?"

Jennie brushed aside her dripping bangs and tipped her head back. A young boy about fourteen peered over the wall.

Jennie waved and yelled, "I'm trapped down here. Can you get a rope?"

"Hang on—be right back!"

"Hurry!" Jennie glanced back at the ocean and scrambled to her feet, grasping the finger-thin branch of a shrub that jutted out from the rock just inches above her head. Another wave smashed against her, this time reaching to her waist. When she looked up, the boy was gone.

Minutes later he returned with a yellow nylon rope and a

friend. Issuing orders for her to slip her foot into the loop at the end, they lowered it. Jennie grabbed on and swung away from the sheer rock face, using her free foot to keep from slamming into the cliff.

"Okay, hold on and we'll pull you up."

Jennie did, praying the rope wouldn't fray as it strained against the rock and concrete.

Inch by inch they hauled her up. When she reached the top of the stone wall, she hooked an arm over it and anchored herself. Moments later she sat looking back at where she'd been. The rocks below disappeared under another crashing wave. Jennie turned away and gasped out a thank-you to her rescuers.

"No problem."

"I was afraid no one would hear me," Jennie said breathlessly.

"Are you kidding?" The boy brushed back his straight brown hair and slapped on a silver-and-blue baseball cap with a logo that read *Dallas Cowboys*. "Me and Don could hear you clear from my room." He pointed toward the three-story house. "Who are you, anyway?"

"Jennie McGrady." Jennie wrapped her arms around herself and bit her lip. The wind off the ocean was quickly turning her into an ice cube.

"Oh yeah, I remember seeing you around. You're Ryan Johnson's girlfriend."

"Used to be. These days I'm not so sure. You must be Jessica's brother."

"Yep. I'm Micky."

"How'd you get down there?" the other boy asked.

"I was exploring. My grandmother lives around on the other side of the inlet. Ah . . ." She turned to Micky. "Do you think I could borrow a dry shirt or something? I'm freezing."

"Sure." Micky grinned. "Come up to the house. You could probably fit into my sister's clothes. She was about your size." His eyes clouded, and he glanced away.

Jennie followed the boys through the back entrance and large kitchen, then up a flight of stairs.

"My sister's room is in there." Micky stopped at a closed door in the middle of the long hallway and glanced up at her. "There's lots of clothes and stuff in her closet."

"Dork." Don elbowed his friend. "She probably wants a hot shower first." He raised his eyebrows and looked at her, not quite meeting her eyes, then stuffed his hands in the pockets of his baggy shorts. "You'll have to excuse Micky— he's not used to rescuing pretty girls."

Micky scowled. "Yeah, like *you* are." He turned to Jennie and said, "There's a bathroom back there." Micky pointed to the left side of the room. "It's got towels and everything."

"Thanks. Um, listen, guys. You were great back there . . . you saved my life. I wish there were something—"

"Hey, no problem." Don grinned. The boys started to go, looking like a set of twins from behind. Don turned back around. "We'll be in the kitchen making some hot chocolate. That'll warm you up."

Micky whacked him in the arm. "Get real, toad-head."

"What?"

Jennie closed the door and tried to ignore the odd sensation creeping up her spine. She hurried into the bathroom and stripped out of the still-dripping shorts and T-shirt, discarding her now saturated mystery novel. After waiting for the water to warm, she ducked under the shower head and didn't emerge for fifteen minutes.

Feeling ten times better, Jennie stepped into Jessica's bedroom. The large, bright room had windows overlooking the beach. The walls and carpet were all off-white. The only color came from pastel peach, mint green, and soft pink pillows and large watercolor paintings of seashells and beach scenes in the same colors. Flouncy sheer curtains hung on the windows. Jessica's full-size bed had an antique brass frame. The bed, covered with an ivory down comforter, faced the windows and offered a spectacular view—a view of the very place where her body had been found.

Jennie shivered, wrapped her arms around herself, and moved away from the window.

A historical novel lay on the nightstand. Jennie reached for it, then snatched her hand back. *You shouldn't be snooping, McGrady.* Pulling the towel more tightly around her, she entered the walk-in closet and grabbed an oversized pink shirt and a pair of denim shorts from the nearest shelf. When she did, a book dropped to the floor. Jennie stooped to pick it up. It was a small booklet on overcoming addictions to gambling. Strange. She turned to the page marked by a brochure from the Soaring Eagle Casino at Siletz Bay. On the page were ten questions on how to tell if you're addicted to gambling.

"Whoa," Jennie mumbled aloud. "Whoever took this test definitely has a problem." Jessica? Or maybe she was taking the test for someone else—like Todd or one of her parents? Jennie set the book on the shelf and tucked the information away. Later she'd ask Ryan if either Todd or Jessica or someone else she'd known had a gambling problem.

After finding the appropriate underclothes, Jennie got dressed. Micky had been right; Jessica and she were close to the same size. The shorts, a size eight, fit perfectly. Jennie gathered up her damp clothes, wrapped them in a towel, and headed for the door—then stopped. *What are you thinking? You're in Jessica's room. What better way to find out more about her?* She argued with herself for a moment, then decided maybe it wouldn't hurt to look around.

Jennie set her bundle of clothes, towels, and shoes in a white wicker chair and moved back into the center of the room. She stood there awhile—listening, waiting—getting a feel for Jessica's personal space. She again had the oddest sensation of being watched. Yet there was no one in the room or at the windows. Jennie's heart skittered into high gear.

Unsettled and frightened as she felt, Jennie forced herself to walk over to a dresser to look at the various photos. One of Jessica and Todd standing in front of a boat. Another, a family portrait of the Ames family with a background of trees. A candid snapshot of Micky and his friend making faces at the camera.

Still another showed Jessica and a second girl in front of a tall and elaborate sand castle. Jennie remembered seeing her before as well, but couldn't think where. She turned the photo over, and a brief note read, *Camilla and me at Cannon Beach*. Jennie studied the girl's features—a small, pixielike face framed by straw-colored short hair.

Jennie picked up an eight-by-ten portrait of Jessica and focused on the flawless face smiling back at her. "I wish I'd known you better. Did you love Todd? Was it your ring I found? How did the ring end up on the rocks? How did you end up on the rocks?"

Jennie heard a noise behind her and spun around. The door to Jessica's room opened.

Mrs. Ames stepped in and fastened her startled gaze on Jennie. She dropped the vase and flowers she'd been holding and screamed. Then fainted.

6

Half an hour later, Jennie, the boys, and Mrs. Ames sat in the family room off the kitchen. Jennie took a sip of hot chocolate while she listened to Micky explain why she had been in Jessica's room.

"I understand that, Micky. Saving Jennie's life was admirable—an act of heroism." Mrs. Ames folded and refolded the wet washcloth Jennie had placed on her forehead after she'd fainted. "But why couldn't you have told me she was here?" She heaved a shuddering sigh. "Jennie, I do hope you'll forgive me. I . . . when I saw you standing there I thought . . . well . . . with you wearing Jessica's clothing and all, I thought you were her."

"I'm sorry, Mrs. Ames," Jennie said for the umpteenth time. "I didn't mean to frighten you." Jennie hadn't meant to stay so long either. Gram would be worried. And Ryan would be—what? Worried? Angry? She'd told him she'd pick him up fifteen minutes ago. "Do you think I could use your phone? I need to call my grandmother."

Mrs. Ames nodded and directed Jennie to the ivory phone on the wall near the pantry in the kitchen.

Gram thanked God that Jennie had survived, then scolded her for not being more careful of the tide. "Do you need me to come pick you up?" she asked.

"Would you?" Jennie glanced down at her clothes. "And

maybe you could bring me clean jeans and a shirt and underwear. I'm wearing Jessica's stuff right now."

Micky and Don left to go skateboarding right after Jennie hung up. Saying good-bye, she thanked them again. While she waited for Gram, Jennie sat on the sofa, wishing she could think of something comforting to say to Mrs. Ames.

All Jennie could think of was to offer another apology.

Mrs. Ames patted Jennie's hand. "It's all right. Please don't give it another thought. It's just that when someone you love dies . . . I guess everything reminds you of them."

Jennie nodded. "Mrs. Ames, can I ask you something?"

"About Jessica?"

"Yeah—but if it will upset you too much . . ."

Mrs. Ames closed her eyes and opened them as if bracing herself for a painful procedure. "What would you like to know?"

"When I got the clothes out of her closet I found a book—about gambling addiction."

"Gambling? I don't understand. Why would she have a book like that?"

"I was hoping you could tell me."

"I have no idea."

"Was Jessica into gambling?" Jennie persisted.

"Absolutely not." Mrs. Ames fumbled with her damp tissue, picking off little pieces and rolling them into balls. "She was too young, of course, but even if she'd been of age, Jessica was against gambling. We all are. She and her father and I have lobbied against all the casinos in Oregon. The only reason she'd have a book like that would be if she were studying the subject or trying to help someone else. Jessica was like that—always helping others."

"That thought crossed my mind. Any idea who she might have wanted to help?"

"Todd maybe. Or Todd's brother. Greg has been known to frequent the casinos and the bars."

Jennie wondered if the gambling thing was somehow connected to Jessica's death. A definite possibility and one she intended to pursue. First, though, she needed to ask about the ring. Jennie pulled it from her pocket and showed it to Mrs. Ames. "Do you recognize this?"

Mari Ames' already pale skin turned even whiter. "It's Jessica's. Todd gave it to her on her birthday not quite a year ago. She never took it off. How. . . ?"

"I found it down on the rocks."

Jennie had other questions but decided not to ask them. Mrs. Ames seemed to be preoccupied with something. Her eyes had glazed over, and she stared out at the green expanse of lawn.

Jennie's gaze took the same path—the one trailing through the grass to the white gazebo and hanging baskets of ferns and flowers. A perfect spot to bring friends and talk—Jessica would have done that. Somehow Jennie knew without asking that Todd had sat on the bench there with Jessica, laughing, holding hands. It might have been where he gave her the ring.

A huge question draped itself across Jennie's mind. Why had Jessica taken the ring off? Had she been about to break up with Todd?

The doorbell rang, bringing them both back to the present. Jennie absently slipped the ring back on her finger. "I'll get it," she offered. "It's probably Gram."

It was. Jennie changed clothes in the large main bathroom. It felt good to be in her own clothing. Thinking about Jessica had left her tired and frustrated. When she'd finished dressing and brushing her hair back into a ponytail, she made her way down the wide hall to the high-ceiling living room where Gram and Mrs. Ames were deep in conversation. The room looked like an art gallery featuring dozens of paintings and sculptures.

Mrs. Ames held a fresh tissue in her hand. "I do hope you'll be there, Helen. I've invited three of my favorite local artists. We'll be showing their work and selling some pieces in our silent auction." She seemed animated now—almost excited.

"Dana Coons and Nicole Hemingway will be there. Dana does those lovely paintings of children." Mrs. Ames waved a hand toward the large portrait of two small children playing in the sand. "I commissioned her to do that one from an old photograph of Jessica and Micky."

"It's beautiful." Gram studied the painting, then glanced over at Mrs. Ames, who'd moved over to an ornate teapot in blacks, browns, and an iridescent copper and green. "And this is one of Nicole's raku works." Without waiting for a response, she went to the sea-green sculpture of a mermaid swimming in a spiral—her hair flowing behind. Mrs. Ames slid her hand down the mermaid's smooth back and tail.

"Eric Meyers," Gram said. "I'd love to have one of his pieces. As for coming to the benefit, I'll have to check with J.B."

"Your new husband. I'd love to meet him."

"If we don't come Wednesday night, I'll be sure to bring him over sometime soon."

Jennie entered the room, and for a moment neither woman spoke.

"There you are, darling," Gram said. "Are you ready to go?"

Mrs. Ames looked Jennie's way. "Of course you must bring Jennie as well."

More than ready. Jennie tossed the silent message to Gram, then asked, "Bring me to what?"

"The benefit," Mrs. Ames responded. "Each year we feature a different artist's work at an auction to raise money for the Coastal Arts Association. Actually, this year we're turning it into a fund-raiser to earn money to keep gambling out of Bay Village. You really should come. All three artists said they were doing something special to honor Jessica."

"Jessica knew them?" Jennie asked.

"Oh yes. She studied art this summer and spent a couple weeks working under each of them."

45

Jennie made up her mind to go but didn't say so. She'd have to clear it with Gram. They thanked Mrs. Ames and within a few minutes were on their way.

"She seems nice," Jennie said. "But strange."

"In what way?" Gram snapped her seat belt in place and started the car.

Jennie shrugged. "Earlier when we were talking about Jessica, she looked ready to cry—and just now, it was like nothing happened. How could she switch like that?"

"Oh, I have a feeling all of this art business is her way of coping. She's doing what a lot of people do after they lose a loved one—trying to stay busy and concentrate on other things."

"Hmm." Jennie paused to wave at Micky and Don as they arranged a ramp in the driveway to practice jumps with their skateboards. Glancing back at Gram she asked, "Did you do that when Grandpa Ian died?" Gram's first husband had been a government agent assigned to a special task force in the Middle East when the building he'd been working in was bombed.

"I sure did—for a while. I worked a little too hard. Then I sort of checked out for a while."

"I don't remember that."

Gram smiled. "No one knew. Except maybe Kate and your father. I went on a cruise and started writing. It took a long time to get to where I could function normally again."

"So you think Mrs. Ames is acting normal?"

"For someone who's lost a child there is no normal."

"What was she like before?"

"I don't know her that well." Gram turned left onto the main highway. "She entertains quite a bit—seems I'm always getting invitations to social functions. Most of them are political. The mayor likes to entertain too."

"You sound like you don't especially like him."

"He's nice enough. I just don't happen to agree with him on certain political issues."

46

"Like?"

"Abortion for one. I'm an advocate for children—even those who haven't been born. He's pro-choice. He's also a member of the National Rifle Association, and while he's willing to look at some reforms regarding gun control, he doesn't go far enough in my opinion. We do agree on some things—like environmental issues and gambling. He's against the initiative to bring a Vegas-style casino to Bay Village."

Jennie told her about the book she'd found in Jessica's room and Mrs. Ames' response to it. "About the only people Mrs. Ames could think of that Jessica might be helping were Todd or his brother."

"Interesting. Of course Todd is underage, but looks old-enough—it's possible. More likely, though, it would be Greg. I didn't realize he had a problem in that area, but then I don't know the family all that well. Annie Costello is a cousin, so all I know about the boys is what she tells me from time to time."

Jennie turned in her seat and rested the back of her head against the window. "What did she tell you?"

"The boys lost their father about ten years ago. Tragic accident in the woods. Mr. Kopelund was a logger. His brother—Annie's father—worked with him and lost the use of both legs. Annie, bless her heart, not only had to care for her invalid father but took the boys in as well. Greg was only fifteen at the time, and though they received a small pension, it wasn't enough for them to live on. He quit school and went to work on a fishing boat."

"Oh, Gram, that's so sad. Do you think losing his dad messed him up?"

"Hmm. I do get the feeling Greg resents his lot in life—which is a tragedy in itself. Eventually, Annie was able to leave her father with a caregiver part time and develop her catering business. And Greg worked very hard to build his business. He and Todd moved into a place of their own three or four years ago. He does quite well for himself."

"What does he do?"

"Takes tourists out on fishing and whale-watching excursions. He has three boats now, and Todd works with him. That's about all I can tell you. Maybe Ryan can give you more information."

Jennie groaned. "Ryan . . . he's probably furious with me by now."

"Relax, darling. I told him what happened before I came to pick you up. He wants you to call him when you get in."

Gram pulled into Orcas Lane. Bernie bounded out to meet them, followed by Nick and Ryan.

"Hey, guys, did you miss me?" Jennie asked.

"Yay! Jennie's here." Nick leapt into Jennie's arms, and Bernie nearly knocked her down. Ryan stood back a few feet, his jaw set, his arms crossed.

When Nick and Bernie turned their attention to Gram, Jennie walked over to him. "Sorry I'm late."

"I thought we were going over to the Ameses' together."

"I . . . um . . . I didn't mean to go there." She sighed. "I'll explain later. Did you still want to go?"

"No. Let's go see Todd."

"Sure. Hang on while I get my keys."

After telling Gram where she was going and making sure it was okay to leave Nick, they set off in Jennie's Mustang. When they reached the main road, Ryan asked, "Did you find anything?"

Jennie quickly filled him in on her adventure—finding the ring, the book, and her conversation with Jessica's mom.

"So Mrs. Ames thinks Todd is into gambling. I can't believe she'd tell you that. It's not true."

"What about Greg?"

Ryan hesitated a moment too long. "He goes to the casino once in a while. But Todd's never said anything about it being a problem or anything."

"Could Jessica have been trying to talk to Todd about his

48

brother's problem?" Jennie's gaze drifted to Ryan, then back to the road.

"Maybe, but what would that have to do with Jessica's murder?"

"I'm not sure it does. Jessica and Todd could have gotten into an argument over it and—"

Ryan's angry gaze collided with hers. "You think Todd killed Jessica because Greg gambles a little?"

"I didn't say that." Jennie turned into the parking lot of the municipal building.

"No, but you were thinking it."

"How do you know what I'm thinking?"

"I can see it in your eyes and the expression you get when we talk about it. You think Todd killed her."

"Ryan . . ." Jennie brought her volume down a few notches.

Ryan didn't. "Save the explanations. I thought I could count on you to help me clear Todd, but I was wrong."

Jennie pulled into a parking space and braked a little harder than necessary. "That's not fair. I'm just trying to be objective. I don't know if Todd killed her or not."

"He didn't!" Ryan released his seat belt and climbed out of the car. Slamming the door shut, he leaned through the open window. "Maybe it would be better if you didn't come in with me to see Todd right now. Thanks for the ride. I'll find my own way home."

Stunned, Jennie stared at Ryan's back as he walked away. Part of her felt like running after him and trying to explain. Another part wanted to punch him. *There's no point going after him*, she told herself. Ryan seemed totally convinced of Todd's innocence. While Jennie wished she could side with him, she couldn't—not yet. Maybe not ever.

7

"Back so soon?" Gram looked up, then turned her attention back to the baking dish and the big salmon filet inside it.

"Ryan hates me." Jennie slumped into one of the kitchen chairs and watched Gram peel a clove of garlic. "I didn't say a thing, and he's convinced I think Todd is guilty. He won't listen to me."

"Hmm, a rather strong reaction coming from Ryan. I wonder if maybe he's having some doubts about his friend."

"Are you kidding? He's absolutely, positively, one-hundred-percent certain that Todd is innocent."

"So he says. My hunch is that he may not be so sure, and his uncertainty is making him angry with himself."

"Then why is he mad at me?"

Gram squeezed fresh lemon over the fish, then sprinkled on a bunch of diced garlic. "Human behavior can be rather complicated where emotions are concerned. And of course I can't say for certain, but Ryan may be aiming his anger at you because you're willing to accept something he can't."

"That makes no sense to me. All I know is he's being a jerk." Jennie unfolded herself from the chair. "Do you want me to help with dinner?"

Gram handed her an onion. "You could slice this for me. We'll put about half of it on the fish."

The tears came as Jennie sliced. Onions always made her cry, but she was glad for the cover. Her anger with Ryan was turning into a huge weight in her chest.

"Oh, Gram," Jennie sobbed. "What am I gonna do? I can't tell Ryan I agree with him about Todd. I'd be lying. There's a lot of evidence against him. And I may have found more." Jennie paused to mop up her tears, then blubbered on about the ring and her suspicion that Jessica may have been trying to break up with him. "Maybe she was handing the ring back, and they argued . . . then he pushed her."

"Or she could have lost the ring days before she died. Did Mrs. Ames say how Jessica felt about Todd?"

"Only that Jessica never took her ring off—which reminds me, I forgot to give it back to Mrs. Ames. Oh well, I should turn it over to the authorities anyway." Jennie grabbed a couple tissues to deal with the rest of her tears, then went to the sink to wash her hands. "I'm going to talk to some other people Jessica knew." Remembering the picture on Jessica's dresser, Jennie asked, "Do you know a girl named Camilla? I think she might be a friend of Jessica's."

"Camilla." Gram stared at the ceiling as if she might find the answer there, then shifted her gaze back to Jennie. "Matt and Nancy Daniels have a daughter named Camilla—yes, she's probably about the right age."

"Where do they live?"

"I'm not sure—in Lincoln City, I think. They run the Whale and Dolphin Gift Shop & Bakery in downtown Bay Village. In fact, Camilla may work for them."

"She does." Jennie's memory of where she'd seen the girl in the picture snapped into place. "Thanks, Gram. I knew I'd seen her somewhere." Jennie dried her hands and glanced at her watch. She couldn't catch Camilla today. The stores in Bay Village closed at five, and it was now ten after. She considered calling first but decided a drop-in visit might be better.

Jennie's tears had dried up from the onions and from her disappointment with Ryan. While the salmon baked, Jennie made the salad and set the table.

The baked salmon—one of Jennie's favorites—turned out perfect, but then it always did when Gram made it. J.B. and Nick arrived in time for dinner. The good food and companionable conversation with Gram, her new grandfather, and Nick made Jennie almost forget about her argument with Ryan. In fact, she might have done just fine if Ryan hadn't come over at seven-thirty to see her.

Feelings of frustration and anger mingled with excitement bubbled up all over again when he rang the doorbell. She thought seriously of having Gram tell him she didn't want to talk to him, but she didn't. Truth was, she did want to see him—very much. Jennie swallowed back her injured pride and met him at the door.

"Hi." Ryan's blue eyes met hers. He leaned against the door jamb, acting like nothing had happened. "Um . . . I wondered if you wanted to go down on the rocks and watch the sunset."

Jennie couldn't quite bring herself to say no, but she didn't want to seem too eager either. "I guess." She slipped back inside to get her jacket, then, stuffing her hands in her pockets, joined him on the porch. They walked most of the way to the rocks without speaking.

"Supposed to be warm tomorrow," Ryan said.

Jennie didn't answer.

"Would you like to go to Newport with me? We could go to the aquarium and maybe walk on the beach."

Normally Jennie would have been thrilled with the invitation, but their relationship had slipped too far, and Jennie wasn't sure she wanted to spend the day with him—at least not unless he was willing to apologize. "I thought you were mad at me."

"I am—about Todd. But we shouldn't let a difference of

opinion keep us from being friends."

Jennie stopped. Ryan took four steps before he realized she wasn't beside him, then turned around and came back. "What's wrong?"

"I'm not sure what you're trying to say, Ryan. A friend doesn't act like you did today. You wouldn't even listen to me."

Ryan tipped back on his heels and sighed. "I . . . I know. And I'm sorry about that. It's making me crazy. I wish there were something I could do. If we could find one shred of evidence that would clear him. I was hoping you could help, but . . . so far all you've done is make things look worse for him."

"Not on purpose. I'm not going out to deliberately prove Todd killed Jessica. I just want to know the truth. Don't you?"

Jennie started walking again, and Ryan fell into step beside her. "I guess, but what if all the evidence points to Todd? I know he didn't do it."

"See, that's the problem. What if he's lying to you?"

"I don't think he is."

Jennie shrugged. "Okay, say he's telling the truth. Then the real killer must be planting evidence to pin the crime on Todd. What we need to find out is who. Who would want Jessica dead? And why?"

"I can't think of anyone. I guess that's what's so frustrating to me. I keep looking for a reason. Everyone liked Jessica. Well, maybe not everyone. Todd sometimes thought she should mind her own business—she was kind of an activist. Got involved in political issues."

"Like?"

"Environmental stuff. She and her mom put on a couple of big benefits to bring Keiko up to Oregon. And she tied herself to a tree once. But I can't think of anyone who'd be upset with her for that."

"What about this gambling thing? If she's against it—"

"I doubt Jessica's influence is broad enough to make a difference." Ryan took her hand to help her over a wide crack in the rocks. "I'm against the gambling, too, my entire family is—in fact, most of the people in my church are. The only really influential people opposed to the gambling are Mayor Ames, Senator Baker, and Judge Crookston, but you don't see anyone going after them."

"Unless—" Jennie stopped herself. The idea was too far-fetched. Bay Village was much too small. Still, it was something to consider. What if someone wanted gambling in Bay Village badly enough to kill? What if Jessica was murdered because she was the mayor's daughter?

"What were you going to say?" Ryan slipped an arm around her shoulders.

"Never mind." Jennie set the bizarre thought aside and changed the subject. "Gram says maybe you got mad at me because you're having doubts about Todd."

His eyebrows almost met when he frowned. "She might be right. I want to believe Todd, and I do, but . . . I don't know. You really threw me with that business about the ring and the gambling. I asked Todd about it. He said he doesn't gamble and swears he never talked to Jessica about Greg. He also told me Jessica was wearing the ring the last time he saw her."

"How can you be sure he's telling the truth?"

"I trust him, Jen—he's my friend. Anyway, let's not talk about Jessica or Todd right now." Ryan turned to face her and pulled her close.

"What do you want to talk about?" Her voice sounded strange and breathless.

"At the moment, nothing."

One light kiss on the lips and she almost managed to put the case out of her mind. Another and it faded to a distant memory.

The next morning, Jennie woke up daydreaming abut Ryan. They'd watched the sunset together and talked about the future—school, mostly, and what they hoped to do after graduation and college. True to his word, Ryan hadn't mentioned Jessica or Todd. Jennie had enjoyed their time together, but something had changed. As much as she wanted to deny it, she could still feel the tension between them. Ryan seemed farther away than ever.

The door creaked open. Jennie flopped onto her stomach and pulled the covers over her head.

"C'mon, Jennie." Nick ran in and climbed up on the bed and onto her back.

"Ouch, Nick," Jennie groaned. "I don't feel like playing horsey this morning. Go away."

"Gram said I'm s'posed to wake you up for breakfast." He kept bouncing.

How anyone could have that much energy at seven in the morning was completely beyond Jennie's comprehension. She managed to turn onto her back between bounces and reel him in. "Hold still for a minute. I want to ask you something."

"What?" Nick snuggled up against her and looked at her nose-to-nose, his big navy blue eyes only inches away.

Jennie chuckled as they rubbed noses. "How come you're so rambunctious this morning?"

"I'm not ra-bun-chus, I'm adorable—Gram said so." He climbed off the bed. "Gram said I should tell you she made blueberry pancakes. I gotta go get some."

"I'll be down in a minute. Don't forget to feed Bernie."

"Papa and me already did."

After taking a quick shower, Jennie pulled on jeans and a navy sweat shirt sporting a picture of whales and the words *Oregon Coast*.

55

She and Ryan would be heading to Newport at nine-thirty. That gave her exactly two hours to eat and go into town to talk to Camilla.

———

At eight, Jennie pulled up in front of the Whale and Dolphin Gift Shop & Bakery. The wind blew a cold rain against her windshield. Jennie took a deep breath and raced for the covered wooden porch of the old Victorian house turned gift shop. Mrs. Daniels opened the door with a cheery good-morning.

Jennie introduced herself. "Is Camilla here?"

"Not yet." Mrs. Daniels turned her closed sign around to read open. "She'll be here in about fifteen minutes. You're welcome to wait."

Jennie glanced around trying to decide whether to hang around or come back. She decided to stay. She'd already eaten breakfast but ordered a cranberry scone and a cup of herbal tea anyway, then settled into a chair near the window.

At eight-fifteen, Jennie watched Camilla pull up in a white Toyota. The wind whipped through her short, curly blond hair as she climbed out of the car.

The door to the shop flew open when she grasped the handle, and Camilla released a bird-like squeal, then pushed the door against the wind.

"Looks like it's getting nasty out there." Mrs. Daniels looked over the counter.

"Typical." Camilla pulled off her Windbreaker and headed for a room behind the counter. She emerged seconds later wearing a white apron over her pale yellow shirt and faded blue jeans.

"Mom, would you mind if I leave early today? I'm going out with this really great guy tonight."

"Really? You sound excited."

"I am. I've been waiting two years for him to notice me."

"Do I know him?"

"I think so." Camilla hugged herself and twirled around. "It's Ryan Johnson."

8

Jennie gasped, sucked a piece of scone down her windpipe, and went into a coughing fit. When she could finally talk, Camilla and Mrs. Daniels were hovering over her. Not that she cared. At the moment she wished they'd go away and let her suffer in peace. Ryan and Camilla—if she weren't so frantically trying to clear her trachea, she'd be racing to her car. And the tears in her eyes would be for Ryan instead of a result of the choking.

"Are you all right?" Mrs. Daniels patted her on the back. "Camilla, get her some water."

Camilla hurried off and came back a few moments later. Jennie drank several swallows and tried to clear her throat for the umpteenth time.

"What happened?" Camilla asked.

Jennie shook her head. "Swallowed wrong. I'm okay." She wasn't, of course. Camilla's announcement about her date with Ryan hurt far more than the crumbs in her throat. She couldn't decide whether to cry or throw a fit. Jennie did neither. She had to concentrate on why she'd come.

"You're sure you're okay?" Mrs. Daniels hunkered down in front of her. "Maybe some more hot tea will help. Can I get you a refill?"

"Yes, please." Jennie wanted nothing more than to escape, but she'd come to talk to Camilla and wasn't about to leave without some answers. The tea would help soothe her throat and hopefully settle the chaos churning inside.

"I'll get it." Camilla started to get up, but Mrs. Daniels stopped her. "Stay. Jennie's been waiting to talk with you."

Camilla's questioning blue-green gaze drifted to Jennie. "You have?"

Jennie nodded, then cleared her throat. After introducing herself, she added, "I wanted to ask you some questions about Jessica."

Camilla slid into the chair across from Jennie, her features shifting from concern to sadness. "Why?"

Jennie could hardly mention that Ryan had asked her to investigate Jessica's murder. "It's hard to explain. I saw your picture in Jessica's room, and I knew you worked here." She paused when the bell tinkled and a couple walked in. They wandered over to the pastry window and drooled over the selections.

Mrs. Daniels brought a fresh pot of water and a tea bag and set it down in front of Jennie, then went to wait on her customers.

"Why do you want to know?" Camilla folded her arms and leaned over the table.

"A friend of mine thinks the police have the wrong person in jail and . . ."

"Oh, I do too. Poor Todd. It's all so terrible and unnecessary. I don't believe Todd killed Jessica—I don't think anyone did."

"Then what. . . ?"

Camilla leaned closer. "I think she killed herself."

"Suicide?" Jennie had wondered about that possibility herself. "What do the police say?"

Camilla looked at a car pulling into the parking lot and sighed. "They thought so at first, but the coroner ruled out suicide because of the position of the body, some scratches, and because she was holding a shirt in her hand."

"Todd's shirt?"

"Yes." Her gaze shifted back to Jennie. "But that doesn't mean anything. He could have loaned it to her. She liked wearing guy's shirts over her tank tops. Anyway, Jessica was really depressed the day she died, and it wasn't about Todd."

"You saw her that day?" Jennie swirled her peppermint tea bag in the water and lifted it, watching the green-tinged liquid drip back into the cup. Normally she would have made eye contact. Unfortunately, whenever she looked into Camilla's eyes she thought of Ryan looking into them. He had a lot of explaining to do.

"A couple of times. She came into the shop in the morning to get some bakery stuff for her mom and some artist friends they were having over for coffee. I stopped by after work for a few minutes. She was upset about something but wouldn't tell me. It couldn't have been about Todd because she'd have talked to me about that—I mean, like if she were breaking up with him. She always told me about Todd."

Jennie pulled the ring off her finger and held it out to Camilla. "Have you ever seen this before?"

"Where did you get that?"

"On the rocks by where Jessica's body was found. It had lodged in a crack. Mrs. Ames says Todd gave it to Jessica."

"He did. It's a promise ring. They loved each other and wanted to get married someday, and the ring was a promise to each other that they'd stay pure—you know—abstain from sex."

"Was she wearing it the last time you saw her alive?"

"Yes." Camilla frowned. "I'm sure she was. She had this little habit of twisting it around on her finger. That's how I knew she was really nervous. She kept turning it and pulling it on and off."

"But she didn't say anything about giving it back to Todd?"

"No." Camilla pinched her lips together. Tears gathered

in her eyes. She grabbed a napkin and dabbed at them.

The bell above the door jingled. Two women came in and headed for the counter. Camilla excused herself to go wait on them.

Jennie thought about staying and asking her about Ryan. *What good would that do?* she asked herself. *The one you need to talk to is Ryan.*

She tucked Jessica's ring in her pocket, mumbled a hasty thank-you and good-bye, then left.

———

Jennie pulled into Gram's driveway at nine-forty-five—half an hour later than when she'd planned to be back. The trip from town to Gram's normally took five minutes. Jennie had spent the other twenty-five sitting in her car overlooking the ocean. She'd watched the rain slam against her windshield, blurring her view. She'd practiced over and over what to say to Ryan. Without crying.

Ryan jogged across the yard toward her, pulled open the passenger side door, then folded himself into the seat. "I was getting worried about you. I thought we were leaving at nine-thirty."

Jennie glanced at him, then back at the sky. She focused on the small swatch of blue between the clouds, but it was far too close to the color of Ryan's eyes. "I'm not going."

"Why? What's the matter? Are you sick or something?"

"I guess you could say that."

"What's wrong?"

Jennie took a deep breath and steeled herself to meet his gaze. "I went to see Camilla Daniels this morning."

"Why didn't you tell me? I'd have gone with you." His blue eyes showed no sign of guilt. "What did she say?"

Jennie gripped the steering wheel. "About you or Todd?"

"Todd, of course. Why would she say anything about me?" As if remembering something important Ryan closed

61

his eyes and tipped his head back against the seat. "Oh man." He drew both hands down his face. "She told you we were having dinner?"

"Not exactly." Jennie glanced at Ryan, taking small comfort in his embarrassment. "She didn't say where you were going or what you were doing. Only that she'd been waiting for two years for you to notice her."

"Jennie, Camilla is a friend. The only reason I'm seeing her is to ask her about Jessica. I was going to ask you to come along."

Remembering the excitement in Camilla's voice, Jennie doubted it. "Yeah, right. You need me to drive."

"I swear, Jennie—"

"Save it. I saw the look in her eyes when she came into the store this morning. You might think of her as a friend, but she doesn't think of you that way." Jennie looked away from him again, remembering back to her own friendship with Ryan. Maybe that's all she was to him too. He'd said he loved her once, but that had been months ago. He'd kissed her the night before—twice, but he'd said nothing about love.

Ryan reached for the door handle. "What do you want me to do, cancel? I'll do that if it will make you happy."

Jennie cringed at the hard edge in his voice. *Yes, call her, tell her you changed your mind. Tell her you're going out with me instead.* She wanted to say the words but couldn't. "The only thing that will make me happy right now is for you to get out of my car and leave me alone."

"Fine." He jerked open the door and climbed out. "I'm not going to argue with you. I'm sorry you won't believe me."

"I believe what I see."

He leaned over and caught her faltering gaze. Rain pelted his face and dripped from his eyelashes onto his cheeks. "If you want to come with me to talk to Camilla, be at my house by six-thirty. Otherwise I'm going without you." He slammed the door and stalked down the driveway to his house.

Jennie placed her arms across the steering wheel and rested her head against her forearms. The fact that Ryan still planned to see Camilla was proof enough that he was interested in her. And who wouldn't be? Camilla was cute, and she believed in Todd's innocence. They had at least that in common. Ryan didn't have to take Camilla to dinner to get information. He could have just gone to see her, like Jennie had. Or he could have asked Jennie what she'd found out.

You're better off without him, she told herself. *Anyway, it isn't like you're engaged. You never agreed not to go out with other people*. Ryan's words from the day before marched through her brain like tiny soldiers standing at attention. *"I don't want this thing with Todd to ruin our friendship."* Friendship. Not relationship. He'd been clear enough about that. Yet he'd kissed her like he cared. *Just forget it*. Jennie jerked open the car door and stormed into the house. She stomped on the rug, as much to deal with her anger as to shake off the rain.

The house was empty. A note on the kitchen table told Jennie that Gram and J.B. had taken Nick to Lincoln City for the day. They'd be staying in town for dinner. Jennie went to the refrigerator and stared unseeing at its contents. She retrieved a can of Diet Coke and a handful of peeled baby carrots. Popping the top of the can, she went into the living room and flopped onto the couch.

Great. Just what she needed—an entire day to herself. Jennie vacillated between feeling sorry for herself and being grateful for the time alone. Once she'd drained her drink and crunched the carrots, she had a better perspective on things. She tucked her argument with Ryan aside. Time would tell if he was telling the truth. Maybe he did think of Camilla as just a friend. Maybe not. Jennie thought about taking Ryan up on his offer to go along with him when he met Camilla. She wouldn't, she decided. It would be too uncomfortable for all of them—especially for Camilla.

In the meantime, she'd use her unexpected gift of time to

concentrate on Jessica Ames' death. There were a lot of other people to talk to and no time like now to make plans. On a fresh sheet of paper, Jennie began listing the names. Mayor Ames, Annie, Greg, the three artists, and Jessica's brother, Micky. And of course, Todd. She looked the list over again, then folded it and tucked it into the back pocket of her jeans. Too many people—so little time.

Jennie took her can to the kitchen and dumped it in the recycling bin, then grabbed the phone book. She ran her finger down the Lincoln County listings and picked up the phone.

"Municipal building," the crisp male voice answered.

"Hi." Jennie swallowed back the anxiety rising like a flock of frightened swallows from the pit of her stomach. "Could you tell me when visiting hours are? I'd like to come to the jail to see Todd Kopelund."

9

Todd was wearing the same scared look he'd had in the courtroom. Jennie sat at a table opposite him. He rested his handcuffed wrists on the scarred wooden table and leaned toward her. "I sure didn't expect to see you," he said, his deep brown eyes assessing her.

"Why?" Jennie lifted a pad of paper out of her backpack.

"I don't know—just didn't. Why are you here?"

"I'm curious. Ryan thinks I should hear your side of the story."

"Funny—he didn't think you were interested. What if I don't feel like telling you?"

"Then don't." She pushed her chair back.

"Wait." His broad shoulders sagged as his gaze dropped to his hands. "I'm sorry. It's just that things are looking pretty hopeless. The evidence is stacked against me, but I didn't do it. I loved Jessica. I wouldn't do anything to hurt her. I wish people could believe that."

"Was she breaking up with you?"

"No." He glanced up at Jennie, then looked away.

Watching his expression, Jennie pulled the ring out of her pocket and explained where she'd found it. "Any idea how it got down on the rocks?"

"No."

Jennie didn't believe him. She had a hard time seeing him

as a killer, but she didn't trust him either.

"Why was she holding your shirt?"

"I have no idea—look, she said she was cold, okay? I loaned it to her and said she could give it back later."

"Lying isn't going to help your case, Todd. Maybe if you'd tell the truth—"

"Truth?" His nostrils flared. "These people don't care about the truth. Jessica's father is out for blood—mine. He's the one who's lying."

Jennie arched an eyebrow in disbelief. "Why would Mayor Ames lie?"

Todd leaned closer, glanced at the guard by the door, then whispered, "Maybe he's been paid to protect the real killer. Or maybe someone is threatening to kill him or another member of the family. I wouldn't be surprised is he isn't paying off the sheriff and the D.A. to make sure I take the blame. He's made some powerful enemies coming out against the gambling bill."

Chewing on the inside of her cheek, Jennie held back her skeptical response. Not that she intended to write off his comments—she didn't. In fact, the idea intrigued her, and she'd make it a point to find out as much about the mayor as possible. Todd's accusations were in line with what she had been thinking earlier—that maybe someone had gotten to the mayor through his daughter.

"You really believe Jessica's death has something to do with the gambling issue?" Jennie asked.

"I told you I did."

"Mrs. Ames said you might have talked to Jessica about Greg's gambling problem. Is it possible she might have confronted him and—"

"What are you saying? You think my brother killed her?" Todd's handcuffs clunked against the table when he stood. The guard moved closer, resting his hand on his weapon.

Todd's hot gaze shifted back and forth between the guard and Jennie.

Todd retreated back to his chair, his anger dissipating like fire in water. The guard moved a discreet distance away.

Jennie rose from the table and hooked her backpack over her shoulder. Maybe coming to see Todd hadn't been a such a wise decision. "I'd better go."

"My brother didn't do anything wrong." Todd heaved a deep sigh. "He gambles sometimes, but not that much. Anyway, even if Jessica did talk to him, he'd have no reason to kill her."

"How does he feel about bringing gambling into Bay Village?"

"He's for the initiative, but—" Todd frowned. "Look, Jennie, Greg doesn't care if Bay Village gets a casino. He can always drive up to the Soaring Eagle or into Lincoln City. If you really want to find out who killed Jessica, talk to the people who stand to lose the most if the bill is defeated."

"Any idea who that might be?" Jennie pushed the chair in and remained standing.

"The guys who want to build it. The developers. Whoever put up the money for the campaign."

"Can you give me any names?"

"No. But Greg might be able to."

Jennie adjusted the strap on her bag. "Thanks. I'll talk to him. Do you know where I might find him?"

"He's probably out fishing right now. He'll be down on the docks later—around four. Look for the *Linda Sue*. He'll either be there or on one of the two boats in the slips beside her."

Jennie nodded. "Todd . . ."

"What?"

Jennie waited until his gaze met hers before speaking. "About the ring."

Todd closed his eyes. "I took Jessica home around ten

67

that night. She was wearing the ring then."

"The paper said Mayor Ames saw you pull out of the driveway around midnight."

"I don't know who he saw, but it wasn't me."

On her way out, Jennie stopped by the office to ask where she might find the sheriff. The deputy grinned up at her. "You're in luck, young lady. Sheriff Adams just walked in."

"Adams? As in Joe?" Jennie turned toward the door and the sound of footsteps in the marble entry.

"Jennie!" Joe Adams flashed her a wide grin. "It's great to see you." He turned to the man at the desk and made the introductions. "Jennie is Helen Bradley's granddaughter."

"That so?" The clerk nodded in approval, then turned back to answer the ringing phone.

"Did you want to see me about something?" Joe asked, motioning toward one of two offices to their right.

"Yeah." Jennie went in ahead of him and sat down. Something about Joe always flustered her. Maybe it was his movie-star face—or the way his dark eyes captured hers as if he were trying to read something written on her soul.

She waited until he was seated, then asked, "So how's the arm?" The last time she'd seen Joe he'd been shot. Jennie had been credited with saving his life.

"Great. I'm still doing therapy, but I was able to come back to work the first of the month."

"That's good."

"You didn't come in just to ask about my health."

"Um . . . no." She fished the ring out of her pocket and handed it to him. "This was Jessica's—I found it on the rocks by where she fell."

He scrutinized the ring, then set it on the desk blotter in front of him. "How do you know it's Jessica's?"

"Her mom and best friend *and* Todd identified it."

"Hmm. I appreciate your bringing it in, but in the future you might want to turn over evidence right away and let us do the investigating. Is there anything else I should know?"

"Maybe." Joe's steady gaze kept Jennie talking until she'd told him everything she'd said and done in the last few days, including her argument with Ryan.

When she finished, Joe leaned back in his chair and clasped his hands behind his neck.

Jennie cleared her throat, feeling pinned like a specimen under a microscope. She looked away, then back again. "Why don't you say something?"

He straightened and tapped his fingers on the desk. "Any idea how the ring ended up on the rocks?"

"The only thing I can think of is that Jessica broke up with him—maybe they argued and she threw the ring away."

"Do you think Todd is guilty?"

"Huh?"

"You heard me."

"Yeah . . . I just didn't expect—" Jennie sighed. "I don't know. Ryan doesn't think so. I'm not so sure."

"I'm not either. We've got the evidence and a couple of eyewitnesses that put him at the scene at the appropriate time, but something about this isn't ringing true."

Jennie didn't know how to respond. She'd expected to be yelled at and warned away, but she certainly hadn't expected Joe to take her into his confidence. "What's that?"

"Motive. As it stands now, we really don't have one—unless Jessica did break up with him. You're not the only one with that theory, by the way. The mayor suspects that as well. If your suspicions are true, that still leaves us with a big question—did he kill her?"

"They could have fought, and he could have pushed her," Jennie surmised.

"It's possible. He's got a history of getting hot-headed, but according to Annie and Greg and some of his friends, he's never come to blows with anyone." He shook his head. "It's a real puzzle."

"It could have been an accident." Jennie recounted her near disaster with Ryan on the rocks.

"Could be, but why would Todd lie about it? What would you have done if Ryan had fallen?"

"I'd have tried to save him."

"Exactly. I think if Todd had been there he'd have called for help and gone down to try to save her. I can't see him leaving her like that."

"What about the possibility of suicide?"

"We've pretty much ruled that out. She'd definitely struggled with someone before she fell." He picked up the ring and studied it again, then set it down.

His dark brows drew together. "Jessica may have been killed by someone wanting to silence her—or her father. If my hunch is right, and someone other than Todd killed Jessica, I'd just as soon not have you or Ryan snooping around."

Without waiting for a response, Joe rose and came around to the front of his desk and leaned against it. "I could get hard-nosed at this point and order you to stay out of the investigation. I'm not going to do that, but I am going to ask for your cooperation."

If his plan had been to intimidate her, it was working. "Sure. How can I help?"

"As far as the press and anyone else is concerned, we've got our killer. No one, outside of yourself and a few law enforcement people I'm working with, knows I'm not convinced of Todd's guilt. I'd just as soon keep it that way for a while."

"So the real killer won't feel threatened?"

"Among other things. I don't want you kids out there asking questions and stirring things up. The last thing I need is another murder."

Jennie swallowed back the rising concern that she or Ryan had already asked too many questions. "That's okay with me.

I think you'd better have a talk with Ryan, though. He's determined to prove Todd didn't do it."

Joe sighed and glanced heavenward. "I used to think amateur detectives only made life miserable for cops in books and on television."

Jennie's lips shifted to form a smile. "At least you don't have to worry about Gram. She's too busy writing to get involved in this one."

"Actually, I think of your grandmother as one of us. She's helped the department solve a number of cases. The thing is, Jennie—and I can't stress this enough—we're not playing games here. You can rest assured the investigation is in good hands. Besides the local authorities, we've got the FBI involved. I'll talk to Ryan, but in the meantime I need your promise that you'll leave Jessica's murder investigation to me."

"The FBI? Why would they be involved?"

Joe folded his arms across his chest. "There's a possibility we're dealing with organized crime. They're looking into Vegas connections. Like I said, Jennie, it's best if you stay out of it."

Jennie agreed and felt a rush of relief at the thought of not being involved anymore. Now maybe she could relax and enjoy the rest of her vacation—even if she did have to spend it without Ryan. She loved being with her family, and she should be spending more time with Nick anyway.

Jennie wished Joe luck and left the office, then maneuvered her Mustang out of the gravel parking lot onto the highway.

Back at Gram's, Jennie started a fire in the fireplace and was just settling down on the couch to read when the doorbell rang. Grumbling, she hurried to answer it. No one was there. Only her Mustang sat in the driveway. Whoever had been there must have been on foot. Ryan?

She leaned out and looked toward his house. Rustling

leaves and a movement of bushes to the right brought hairs on Jennie's neck to attention. She slammed the door shut and slid the deadbolt lock into place.

Jennie had one terrifying thought. The sheriff's warning to mind her own business may have come too late. What if some hit man had been sent to kill her? Her heart thundering, Jennie ran to the other entry to make certain that door was locked as well. Not that locking it would help. If someone wanted to get in, all they had to do was break the glass.

Jennie methodically checked the windows, closed the blinds, and retreated to the couch. After a few minutes, she began to feel foolish. The noise may have been an animal or a bird. Determined not to be scared out of her wits, Jennie took a deep breath and ventured outside.

10

"All right, guys." Jennie scooped up a skateboard and parted the wet bushes. "Come on out." It hadn't taken long to figure out the source of the noise.

"I told ya we shouldn't have hid." Micky Ames crept out on all fours, followed by his friend Don. "It was his fault. He wanted to talk to you and then chickened out."

"I did not—I mean, he's the one that chickened out." Don's cheeks had turned a vibrant rose, and it wasn't entirely from the cold.

Jennie handed Don his skateboard. "Do you two want to come inside?"

They hesitated until Jennie offered hot chocolate. She hung their dripping jackets in the entry, then led the way to the kitchen. Once they were seated around the table, steaming cups in hand, Jennie asked the obvious question. "What did you want to talk to me about?"

Micky licked the chocolate mustache from his upper lip and glanced at his friend. "Don likes you. He wanted to see if you'd come to the party with him."

Don rolled his eyes. "Don't listen to him, Jennie. He's being a dork. He's the one that wanted you to come to the party. We just thought we could get you in easier if I brought you."

"What party?"

"The benefit my mom and dad are having," Micky replied.

"Um—guys, I'm flattered, really, but I think I'm a little too old—"

"It's not like a date," Micky said. "We just want you to come 'cause maybe you can help us find out who killed Jessica."

Jennie wagged her head back and forth. "Whoa. You've got the wrong girl. I'm not—"

"But you have to." Micky set his cup down as if to emphasize his point. "See, we know Todd didn't hurt Jessica, and we don't think it's fair that he's in jail."

"Do you have proof?"

"No, but you could help us find it."

This was getting downright weird. Why did everyone think she could prove anything? "I don't think so. The person you really need to be talking to is the sheriff."

"Give her the book," Don said.

Jennie looked from one to the other.

Micky got up and withdrew a small, cloth-covered book from the pocket of his baggy pants. He set it on the table and slid it toward Jennie.

"What's this?"

"Jessica's diary. There are pages missing, but Don and me figured out some of it."

Jennie stared at the book. "You should take it to Sheriff Adams."

The floral design seemed to draw her hand forward. She didn't mean to open it, but she couldn't stop herself. The entries started at the beginning of summer. She noted Todd's name often and Camilla's. Nothing out of the ordinary until she came to where the writing stopped. Her last entry ended with *Todd and I went out again tonight and*

The next two pages had been ripped out.

Micky came around behind her and pointed to the rough edges in the book's crease. "We could see that something had been written there so we used a pencil and scribbled over it.

74

You can see part of what she wrote."

The pencil shading had revealed what may have been Jessica's final message to the world.

I can't believe he'd do something like this. I'm going to talk to him tonight. It's late—almost midnight, but I need to know the truth. . . . I hear a car . . . he's back.

Micky went back to his chair. "We know she wasn't talking about Todd because she always wrote in her diary at night after he dropped her off."

"And we know he dropped her off at ten," Don added.

"So he says. He could have come back." Jennie stared at the words, committing them to memory.

"Naw, he wouldn't have done that."

"You seem sure."

"I am," Micky said, picking up his drink again. "I was watching TV in my room, and when I went to the bathroom around ten-thirty, I saw Jessica go into her room. I went in to ask her if she wanted to watch a show with me, and she said, 'Not tonight. I have something important to do.'

" 'How's Todd?' I asked, and she said, 'Todd's fine.'

"Then I said, 'You're home kind of early.' She told me Todd had to go to work at five in the morning 'cause he had a charter. She seemed kind of spacy—like something was wrong. Then she told me to go away 'cause she wanted to write." Micky chewed on his lip and glanced toward the window.

With an empathetic look at his friend, Don added, "That was the last time he saw her."

Jennie set the diary back on the table and reached for her cocoa. "Why didn't the sheriff take this earlier? It's evidence."

"Probably because they didn't find it. See, at first I thought they did take it 'cause it wasn't in the place she usually kept it."

"You knew where?"

Micky flushed. "Yeah. Only it wasn't there—I mean, when I went in her room this morning, the diary was lying on her nightstand."

"So you're saying someone took the diary before the police could find it, ripped out the pages, and held on to it until today?"

"Yeah—I guess. M-maybe whoever killed her."

"Why would they put it back?"

Micky shrugged.

"I got an idea." Don wiped his sleeve across his mouth. "What if Jessica's ghost got it from the killer and put it there to help us?"

Jennie gave him a you've-got-to-be-kidding look. "I don't think so. We need to get this to Joe. Micky, did you tell anyone when you saw Jessica come in?"

"Yeah, a couple of deputies, but they didn't believe me 'cause Dad told them Todd was just leaving when he came home. I guess that was around midnight."

"Are you saying your father lied?"

"No! He wouldn't do that. It was dark—maybe he just thought he saw Todd's car."

"Or maybe Todd came back." Jennie picked up the diary—more carefully this time. Any prints that had been there were probably gone by now. She stuck it in a plastic bag to protect it as much as possible, then insisted the boys accompany her to the sheriff's office to give Joe the diary.

───────

Joe listened to the story, then gave Micky and Don a stern lecture. By handling the diary, they may have destroyed crucial evidence. "And another thing—" Joe paused to make eye contact with all three of them. "I could arrest you for withholding evidence. No more playing cops and robbers. Is that clear?"

"Yes, sir," Micky and Don echoed.

"That goes for you, too, Jennie."

"I know. Which is why I thought you should know about the diary."

Joe flashed her one of his perfect grins and winked. "I'm glad you did. Now I'd appreciate it if you all went about your business. If you see or hear anything, you tell me. No more trying to figure it out on your own."

Jennie herded the boys to her car again with plans to drop them off. When they emerged from the municipal building, the sun greeted them so warmly that Micky and Don opted to skateboard home. That was fine with Jennie.

Deciding to take advantage of the sun herself, Jennie parked in downtown Bay Village near the seawall. Bay Village had a coastal flavor and was especially beautiful with the mountains to the east and a terrific view of the coastline to the north and south. It sat on a rocky bluff overlooking the ocean. Jennie stood looking at the water for a while. Out beyond the surf she could see four boats—probably loaded with tourists fishing or looking for whales. Speaking of which . . . out beyond the breakers, a whale rose out of the water and spouted. Its spray shot into the air and dissipated.

Jennie loved spotting the whales. She'd seen them from a boat once several years ago. It would be fun to do it again— maybe with Ryan. Jennie turned away and started walking. Maybe not.

Determined not to dwell on her disappointments where Ryan was concerned, Jennie spent the next half hour walking along the seawall, then ducking into the many shops and art galleries along the way. Though Jennie fully intended to leave the investigation of Jessica's death to the authorities, she couldn't turn off her mind. And she couldn't help but notice the political signs in the windows and on doors. *Vote no on gambling. No on Initiative 39.* Nearly every shopkeeper was against it. However, in an empty lot at the end of town, proponents of the bill had erected a huge billboard showing a fabulous multimillion-dollar high-rise. To the left of the bill-board was written:

The Bay Village Resort and Casino will bring

- 2,000 new jobs to Lincoln County
- Millions in increased revenue for Bay Village and Oregon schools
- Fun! Fun! Fun! for the entire family

Vote Yes on Initiative 39

In nearly all of the store windows she'd seen something else too—a flyer inviting people to come to the mayor's fund-raiser. She'd read something about how the casino actually hurt shopkeepers. The casinos brought in tons more people as advertised, but the traffic was so bad no one wanted to stop at the stores along the way. There were other reasons to oppose gambling, of course. Like the increase in people with gambling addictions.

Maybe she would go to the benefit if Gram didn't mind. She'd meet the artists and some of the other people Jessica hung around with.

Jennie watched a boat come in and wandered down to the docks. Several people disembarked carrying bags of fish they'd caught.

"Looks like you had a good day." Jennie directed her comment to the man still on board.

He had his back to her and was hosing out the fish box. "Had better." He turned around, and Jennie almost backed into the water.

"Oh. Hi. I didn't realize it was you."

Greg Kopelund's puzzled gaze met hers. "Do I know you?"

"Jennie McGrady. Ryan Johnson's friend."

"Oh, right—the junior detective who was going to figure

out how to get my brother out of jail." Greg coiled the hose and jumped onto the wharf.

"You don't need to be sarcastic."

"No, I suppose I don't." He paused and looked her up and down. "You here to ask me questions too? I've already talked to the cops half a dozen times. Guess once more won't hurt."

"No. I just came down to look at the fish. I didn't know it was you. . . ."

"Sure. So what did you want to ask? Do I think Todd is guilty? Of course not. He didn't kill Jessica."

"What time did he get home?"

Greg shrugged. "A little after ten."

"Did he go out again?"

"How should I know? I went to bed."

"Then he could have gone back."

"He says he didn't, and I believe him." Greg smiled, softening his stern features. "I thought you didn't come out here to ask questions."

"You offered to answer them."

"Let me tell you something, Jennie McGrady. My brother's not a killer. If he was, I'd expect the law to come down hard on him. In fact, I'd probably turn him in myself. People should pay for their mistakes. Don't you think?"

"Yes, but—"

"Sorry, Jennie, but I can't stick around. I have an appointment. Annie and I are trying to get some money together for a decent lawyer for Todd. That court-appointed broad couldn't care less. With the mayor pulling out all the stops, I figure we'd better do something."

He boarded the *Linda Sue* and disappeared below deck. Jennie let out a long breath and walked back to the main drag.

Feeling a bit peeved and in dire need of something to drink, Jennie made a sharp right into Charlie Crookston's ice cream parlor. After using the rest room facilities, she went back to the counter and looked over a neatly printed list of available coffee drinks and sodas. The judge must have been working alone, as no one came to wait on her. He sat at a cluttered desk in the back room talking to someone on the phone and slicing open an envelope with a black letter opener.

"I don't care what you have to do. We need to find out what happened to those funds." Charlie's angry look faded when he glanced up at Jennie and mouthed, *Be right there*. Back into the phone he said, "All right. See that you do. We'd better get to the bottom of this and fast. If we let 39 pass it'll be the end of Bay Village as we know it." He paused, then added, "You do that."

Charlie ambled out of the office. "Afternoon, Jennie. What can I get for you today?"

"An Italian soda with the white chocolate macadamia syrup."

"Coming up." After dispensing clear, bubbly soda into a tall glass, Charlie poured in a shot of syrup and another of cream and, after giving it a quick stir, set it on the counter. "Not quite as nosy as your old Gram, are you?"

"What do you mean?" Jennie pulled a five out of her pocket and handed it to him.

He chuckled and gave her back the change. "Helen would have been drilling me about the conversation I just had, and I'd be fixing myself a cup of coffee and telling her all about it."

Putting her change away, Jennie shrugged. "I'm curious, just not as brave."

"In that case, have yourself a seat. I'm busting to tell somebody, and seeing as you're Helen's granddaughter . . ." Charlie poured himself a cup of coffee and joined Jennie at one of the wrought-iron patio tables.

"You been keeping abreast of the big fight we got going on here over the gambling initiative?"

"Sort of." Jennie took a drink of the delicious concoction and would have moaned in ecstasy had someone other than Charlie been sitting there.

"It's an important one," he went on. "You probably heard me tell the sheriff about the missing funds."

Jennie nodded. "Someone stole money from the campaign?"

"Had to fire our campaign manager. Claims he doesn't know what happened." Charlie's face reddened as his voice rose. "Likely story. I'll bet anything he got paid by the enemy camp to siphon the funds over to them. Talk about dirty politics. Now we're left with no money and no one to run the office. Maybe I'll ask your grandmother. She's had experience—and I know we can trust her. Think she'd do it?"

"I don't know—she's pretty busy."

"Aren't we all. Speaking of which—how'd you like a job? I could use some extra help in the shop while I'm trying to straighten up this mess. My daughter usually helps out, but she quit to stay home with the baby." Charlie whipped out photos of his first grandchild.

Twenty minutes later Jennie stood behind the counter making her first latté for her first customer, trying to figure out how she'd let Charlie talk her into it.

"You'll do fine, Jennie." Charlie shrugged into his jacket and reached for the door. "If you have any trouble, call Mindy. Her number's on the yellow Post-it next to the phone."

With that he was gone—headed for the office to find a new campaign manager. Jennie turned back to her customer, Betty Stone, the owner of the used bookstore down the street. "Would you like cream?"

"I suppose I should say no." She patted her ample stomach. "But what the hey. You only live once."

Jennie dropped a spoonful of whipped cream on the hot caramel-colored latté and covered it with a plastic lid. After

Mrs. Stone left, the store was quiet for all of five minutes—long enough for Jennie to call Gram and leave a message on the machine and to read Charlie's personal invitation to the mayor's benefit. Looked like she wouldn't be going after all. One hundred dollars a plate was a little over budget for her.

While she was waiting on the next customer, the phone rang. Before Jennie could break free to answer it, the answering machine clicked on. "Charlie, I need to talk to you right away."

The caller, a woman, hadn't left a name, but Jennie had heard the voice before—Mari Ames. Jennie quickly jotted down the message on the telephone note pad. Another customer came in, then another. The sun was bringing out tourists in droves, and for the next two hours Jennie barely had time to breathe. At five, she pulled off her apron, stepped outside to haul in the two-sided wooden sign, turned the open sign around to read closed, and collapsed on the nearest chair.

She'd expected Charlie back an hour ago and was beginning to worry. Not knowing what to do with the money from the till, Jennie counted it, pulled out the $100 in change and small bills Charlie had told her to leave in the till for the next day, and made out a deposit slip. She put the money—$382.25—and the deposit slip in a bank bag she found lying on the judge's cluttered desk and returned the change to the till. When Charlie still hadn't shown up, Jennie called Mindy.

"Hi, Jennie. How's it going?"

Jennie filled her in, absently picking up the ornate black letter opener. It had a mother-of-pearl inlay—a bit large for a letter opener—and rather lethal-looking with its long and very sharp point. She set it back on the desk. "I guess I did okay, but what do I do with the money?"

"All that's left is to lock up and take the deposit to the bank," Mindy said. "I really appreciate your taking over. Sounds like you have everything under control."

Jennie thanked Mindy and hung up, relieved that she didn't have to wait around for Charlie to come back. She left him a note, collected her backpack, and grabbed her coat. Tucking the deposit bag under one arm, Jennie locked the door and started for her car. A black limousine drove up, blocking her path. The chauffeur, a tall, dark-haired man with a wide forehead and beaklike nose, stepped out and came toward her. Jennie clutched the money tighter, wishing she'd thought to put it out of sight in her backpack.

"Um—I'm sorry, we're closed," she managed to say.

"Where's Judge Crookston?"

"I don't know. He was supposed to—"

"What have you got there?" The man's dark, piercing gaze shifted from her face to the money bag.

"N-nothing," Jennie stammered. She looked wildly from the man to the street. No way was she going to let him get his hands on Charlie's money. Jennie took a step back, then turned and ran.

She made it about two steps.

A firm hand gripped her arm and spun her around. "Not so fast." The man drew a gun from under his jacket. "Get in the car."

11

"How many times do I have to tell you I wasn't stealing the money?" Jennie sat in back of the limousine next to the chauffeur with the gun and across from Mayor Ames.

"Then why did you run?" the mayor asked.

"Are you kidding? Have you taken a good look at your bodyguard lately?"

Mayor Ames rubbed his nearly bald head. He looked like a man with a lot of worries. Jennie could understand why. "Hawk, for heaven's sake, put the gun away. She's just a kid."

Hawk did as he was told. "Do you want me to call the sheriff?"

"Not yet. Let's try the judge again." When Hawk picked up the cellular phone, the mayor turned back to Jennie. "I find it hard to believe Judge Crookston would hand over his business to you. Especially since he told me he'd have to meet me here because he couldn't leave the store."

"Charlie hired me so he could take care of some other business. Someone stole the campaign money they'd collected to oppose Initiative 39. I happened to be in the store when he needed someone to take over, that's all."

Hawk set the phone back in its holder. "He isn't answering."

"Call Mindy—his daughter. I just talked to her. She told me to take the money to the bank. She'll verify my story."

Jennie handed him the keys and told them where to find the number. She watched the long-legged Hawk extricate himself from the car. The fear Jennie had felt a few minutes before now settled in an annoying ache in the pit of her stomach. Or maybe it was hunger.

Jennie couldn't remember if she'd eaten since breakfast. She took a deep breath. It would be over soon. They'd hear the truth and let her go. She'd make the deposit at the bank and go back to Gram's. Then she'd call the judge and tell him what he could do with his job.

When she glanced at Mayor Ames, a feeling of sadness mingled with her anger. She opened her mouth to tell him she was sorry about Jessica when Hawk swung open the car door.

"You'd better come inside." Hawk scowled. "I found Charlie."

The dark look on his face told Jennie the news wasn't good. Hawk gripped her arm and pulled her out. Jennie's heart slammed against her chest wall like a sledgehammer.

"What's wrong?" Mayor Ames climbed out of the car behind her, then hurried to catch up.

Hawk was lean, but he had the strength of a weight lifter. He hauled Jennie into the store and pushed her toward the office.

"Take it easy." Jennie plunged in, grabbing the desk to keep from falling flat on her face. Further protests lodged in her throat when she saw the cause of Hawk's fury. Judge Crookston was lying face down on the floor just inside the back door.

"What the . . ." Mayor Ames shoved past her and knelt down at Charlie's side. He turned him over, revealing a bloodstained white shirt.

Ames stood and turned his horror-glazed face toward her. "What have you done?"

"N-nothing, I didn't—" Jennie clutched at the desk's

edge, willing her knees not to buckle. *Stay calm*, she heard a distant voice inside her head say. *Don't panic.* Jennie closed her eyes for an instant, hoping that when she opened them, Judge Crookston's body wouldn't be there and she'd be alone, counting the money, getting ready to close up the shop—or better yet, she'd be drinking her soda, minding her own business. She'd realize the entire afternoon had been a nightmare.

When she opened her eyes, Charlie was still lying on the floor. Hawk had dialed 9–1–1, and Mayor Ames' complexion had turned nearly as chalky white as Charlie's. It was then her brain kicked back in. "I know CPR." Jennie moved away from the desk and forced her legs to make the trek to the motionless man a few feet away. Reaching his side, she dropped to her knees and checked Charlie's airway. She expelled her own breath the moment she felt his against her face and heard his heart beating faintly in her ear. "He's still alive."

"Are you sure?" The mayor hunkered down beside her. "He looks so—"

Jennie cut him off and asked Hawk to hand her a towel from a shelf of linens behind him. She could hear the welcome sound of sirens as she unbuttoned the judge's shirt. He had been stabbed. The small stab wound was no longer bleeding, but Jennie pressed the cloth to it anyway, then backed away when the EMTs from the nearby fire station charged in and took over. Joe Adams and a deputy arrived seconds later to assist, and within five minutes Charlie Crookston was on his way to the hospital.

"Care to explain what happened here?" Joe took a note pad and pen out of his breast pocket.

Jennie, Hawk, and the mayor all started talking at once.

"Whoa. Hold on." Joe held up his hand to silence them. "One at a time. Jennie, suppose you start."

Jennie explained how she'd gone for a walk and ended up with a job and being detained by the mayor and Hawk. "All

I know is that Judge Crookston wasn't here when I left. He must have come in the back after I locked up. Or someone brought him in." She looked up and cringed at the hard, beady-eyed gaze Hawk leveled at her. It was a good nickname for him. At any moment she expected him to swoop down on her. His long, bony fingers gripped the back of the judge's wooden chair like talons. It seemed odd the mayor would hang around with a man like that.

"What do you mean—someone brought him in?" Joe asked, dragging Jennie's mind back to Charlie.

Jennie nodded toward the back door. "There's not much blood on the floor—at least not that I could see. 'Course, the wound isn't very big. And I don't see a weapon either. Whoever stabbed the judge must have done it somewhere else. Maybe outside or—"

Almost as if on cue, the deputy came out of the office where he'd been going over the room looking for evidence. "Found the weapon." He held up a clear plastic baggy.

Jennie sucked in a wild breath. The officer was holding the ornate ebony and mother-of-pearl letter opener she'd played with not more than a half hour ago.

"It's about the right size," Joe said. "I'll lay odds Charlie's blood is all over it. Did you dust it for prints?"

The deputy nodded. "Got a couple real clear ones—small—possibly a woman's."

"I . . . they might be mine." Jennie hardly recognized her strained, high-pitched voice. She cleared her throat and tried again. "It was on his desk earlier. I picked it up when I was on the phone."

Joe didn't seem surprised or angry. He simply nodded, made a notation on his pad, and moved back to the questions he'd been asking before. It didn't take long to verify that Jennie had indeed been working for the judge and that Mayor Ames and Hawk had been operating under a false assumption. Joe let Jennie go, promising to let her know as soon as he learned anything about Charlie's condition.

"You'll be in town for a while, won't you, Jennie?"

"Sure—till the end of next week."

Jennie's hands were shaking when she inserted the key into the door to unlock her car. Glancing around to make sure she wasn't being followed, she checked the backseat, then climbed in. For good measure she locked herself in and headed for the bank. It had closed at six, so Jennie pulled in close to the drive-through and dropped the bag in the night deposit slot.

"Relax," she told herself. "There's no one following you." Jennie started to pull out of the bank parking lot, then stopped when she noticed a white Toyota whiz by. Camilla's car. And Ryan was driving. Ryan either hadn't seen her or had chosen not to acknowledge her. Jennie suspected the latter. Fine.

Ignoring the lump in her throat and the even bigger one in her stomach, Jennie turned in the opposite direction and headed back to Gram's. At least there everything would be normal.

Jennie pulled into Orcas Drive just as J.B., Gram, and Nick were pulling out. She moved over to the side and rolled down the window. "Where are you headed?"

"To dinner. We came back from town earlier than we expected and hoped you'd be here," Gram said. "Thought we'd stop at Charlie's to see if we could find you."

"Why don't you park your car, lass, and come join us?" J.B. suggested. "We'll be going to your gram's favorite restaurant to catch the sunset."

"Sounds great. Would you mind waiting while I change? I feel pretty grungy." They agreed and a half hour later they piled into J.B.'s Cadillac. Nick scooted close and snuggled against her.

"We got a postcard from Mom and Dad!" he announced. "They shoulda took us with them."

Jennie hugged him and buckled herself, then him in. "I don't think so. Kids don't usually go along on honeymoons."

"They could. Mama said she wished we were there and next time they'll bring us along."

Jennie wrapped an arm around him and laughed. "I wish they would have taken us too." She didn't add that at the moment she'd rather be anywhere else but in the same state as Ryan Johnson.

Listening to Nick and J.B. talk about their outing, Jennie began to relax. She needed to tell Gram and J.B. about Charlie, but that could wait until later—when Nick had gone to bed.

The evening promised to be a good one. Jennie snuggled back against the plush leather seat and switched between making faces at Nick and talking with Gram and J.B. about Hawaii. They'd both been there. She hadn't. But she had been in the Caribbean and could imagine the tropical breezes and palm trees.

She wondered how Mom and Dad were getting along. Jennie told herself not to worry. They loved each other and had vowed to work things out. Still, the old concerns about their differences and arguments crept through the back of her mind.

The sun, still a glowing red ball, hung in the western sky when they pulled into the parking lot at The Tidal Waves. Jennie climbed out of the car and waited for Nick to join her. He raced to the door and strained to open it. J.B. chuckled and gave him a hand.

Jennie shut the car door and straightened. Her heart dropped like a runaway elevator and hit bottom. They'd pulled in right next to Camilla's car.

"Darling, are you all right?" Gram asked.

Jennie nodded. "Ryan's here with Camilla."

"Oh, dear." Gram wrapped an arm around Jennie's

shoulders. "Do you want to leave? We can go somewhere else."

"No," Jennie answered quickly. "It's okay." It wasn't, of course, but Jennie refused to run away. Sooner or later she'd have to face him—might as well be now. The town was too small to dodge him and Camilla forever.

Jennie straightened and walked into the restaurant with her head high.

They waited a few minutes for the busboy to clear a table by the window, then followed the hostess down the steps. The restaurant was small, built on two levels, and offered an unobstructed view of Depoe Bay and the ocean beyond. For a few wonderful moments, Jennie thought perhaps she'd been mistaken about Camilla's car. It wasn't until she sat down that she caught sight of Ryan and his date. They were seated on the upper level at the opposite end of the restaurant. Camilla leaned forward and apparently said something funny. Ryan laughed. Jennie tried to ignore the jealousy gnawing at her stomach, choosing instead to call it hunger.

"I'm starved," she said aloud, lifting the menu high enough to cover her view of the happy couple.

She ordered halibut fish and chips with a shrimp salad, doubting she'd be able to eat a bite, then focused on the sunset as it turned the bay into a magical array of color. The next time she looked up, Camilla and Ryan were gone. Jennie doubted Ryan had even seen them. Or if he had, he'd chosen to ignore her.

Relief poured out in a long sigh. Seeing them together had been hurtful but not impossible. When her meal came, Jennie downed her food, then finished off with half of Nick's decadent brownie a la mode.

J.B. paid the bill, and they left. The day was nearly over, and Jennie could hardly wait until bedtime. In fact, as they turned off the main road, heading for home, she seriously considered going to her room and hiding out with a good book. She might have, too, if Ryan hadn't come over the minute they pulled into the driveway.

"What does he want?" she muttered under her breath.

"Don't you like Ryan anymore?" Nick asked.

Jennie didn't know how to answer. Of course she liked him. She told Nick as much. "I'm kind of upset with him right now because he likes someone else."

"But you're still friends, right? My teacher says that when friends get other friends then that's good 'cause you can have more friends 'cause maybe their friends can be yours."

Some friend. "It's hard to explain, Nick." Jennie climbed out of the car, eager to escape.

After greeting Gram, J.B., and Nick, Ryan pulled Jennie aside. "We have to talk."

Jennie stuffed her hands in her jacket pockets and waited until the others had gone inside. "I'm not sure we have anything to talk about."

"Come on, McGrady. Knock it off. I took Camilla to dinner to talk to her about Todd and Jessica—that's all. You could have come."

"I did, but you were having so much fun I didn't want to disturb you." Jennie cringed at the ugly sarcasm in her voice.

"You were at the restaurant?"

"Yes, and I saw the way you were *talking* to her."

"What's that supposed to mean?"

"Nothing."

"You're jealous." Ryan smiled when he said it.

"I'm not." Jennie turned her face away from him. "I couldn't care less."

"Well, if you're not jealous and you don't care, then there's no problem." Ryan extended his hand to her, palm up. "Let's go for a walk."

Jennie hesitated. She'd always had trouble resisting those eyes. Now was no exception. She took his hand and walked with him down Orcas Lane.

Ryan didn't speak again until they reached the main road and cut back down a side road that would eventually lead them around a loop through one of Bay Village's wealthier neighborhoods and past the Ames house.

Jennie liked the silence. Her thoughts drifted between calling herself names for being so forgiving and thinking how perfect her hand fit into Ryan's and how right it felt to be walking beside him.

"I heard you went to see Todd today." Ryan held firm to her hand when she started to withdraw it.

"So?"

"So, what did you talk about?"

"Basically he told me he didn't do it."

"And you called him a liar." Ryan's hair turned the color of spun gold as they passed under a streetlight.

"He tell you that?"

"Yeah. He told me something else too, Jennie. You were right, Jennie. Todd lied—to me and to all of us. It looks like he may have killed Jessica after all."

12

"Oh no . . ." Jennie started to tell him about the political overtones of the case and the possibility that Todd had been set up, but Ryan didn't give her the opportunity.

"Joe questioned him about the ring, and he started crying. He admitted that Jessica really had broken up with him. She tried to give him back the ring, but he wouldn't take it so she set it on the wall and went inside. He claims he doesn't know how it got down on the rocks."

"What made him decide to tell the truth—that is, if he's telling the truth?"

"You . . . the ring." Ryan stopped and drew her into the circle of his arms.

Jennie leaned back. "Did he confess to pushing her over the cliff?"

"You seem surprised." He dropped his arms to his side. "Isn't that what you were thinking all along?"

"No—I mean, yes, but—" Jennie shook her head. After what had happened with Charlie, Jennie felt certain Todd must be innocent, but maybe the two cases were unrelated. Maybe Jessica's death had nothing to do with the attack on Charlie. Still, they hung together in Jennie's mind like matching socks, both with holes big enough to poke a fist through. And after what Joe had said about organized crime . . . "Did Todd tell you he killed Jessica?" she asked again.

"Not exactly. I left after he told me about the argument."

"So you're just assuming he did it."

"Who else would have done it, Jennie?" He raked a hand through his hair. "I don't get it. All this time I'm saying Todd's innocent, and you don't think so. Now I'm agreeing that I think he's probably guilty, and you sound like you think he isn't. What gives?"

"I wish I knew." Jennie told him about her run-in with the mayor and Hawk—and about Charlie. "I could be way wrong, but I have a strong hunch Jessica's murder, the attack on Charlie, and the stolen money are all related."

"Seems to me Joe is right. We're better off staying as far away from the case as possible. What you just described sounds like one of those old gangster movies. You know, where some big lug gets word from his boss to knock off somebody's relative to make sure they follow the *rules*." Ryan emphasized the last word.

"I was thinking the same thing. Hawk could be cast in the movie. He's scary. I guess that's a good thing to have in a bodyguard." Jennie paused for a moment, letting her new thoughts jell. "Ryan, this Hawk guy, I don't think I've ever seen him around before. Come to think of it, I don't remember the mayor riding around in a limo before either. And why would he need a bodyguard . . . unless someone was threatening him?"

"I suppose that's a possibility. I can understand him wanting a bodyguard, coming out against the gambling initiative like he has. As for the limo—the mayor likes to use one when he's going to some big party or fund-raiser, so that's not unusual. I guess some people are impressed by it. My folks say it's a waste of taxpayers' money."

"Hmm. A lot to think about." Jennie tipped her head back, letting the wind and mist off the ocean hit her full in the face.

As they walked past Jessica's place, Jennie's thoughts

switched from the mayor to his daughter. The house was dark except for a large yard light and another light over the porch. The porch led directly into the kitchen. Like so many houses, Gram's included, the back of the house faced the street. The front faced the ocean to take advantage of the view. Jennie had the strongest urge to turn into the driveway. Her mind drifted back to Jessica's diary and the missing pages. If she could get inside . . . maybe—

"Where are you going?" Ryan pulled her back beside him.

"I—" Jennie stopped. Without realizing it, she'd turned into the driveway. "Um—I don't know." She shivered. "Never mind, it's just too weird."

Jennie glanced back at the house. A light went on in one of the rooms upstairs. Whatever had compelled her was gone now. She hooked her arm around Ryan's elbow and started toward home.

"Jennie," Ryan began after they'd gone a few steps. "You were right about Camilla."

"What do you mean?"

"You said she thought of me as more than a friend."

"I'm not sure I want to hear this." Jennie held her breath.

"I think you need to. See, I should have listened to you. By going out to dinner with her I hurt you both. I didn't mean to." He squeezed Jennie's hand. "I got too focused on trying to prove Todd innocent. Anyway, I straightened Camilla out. Told her I didn't see her as anything more than a friend."

Jennie swallowed. "So now you have to straighten me out too, huh?"

"Yep—that's my plan." He stopped under a streetlamp and turned to face her. He clasped both hands behind her head, trapping her and forcing her to meet his eyes. "I told Camilla I already had a girlfriend—someone I care a lot about."

"Oh." Jennie released a puff of breath that turned white

95

when it hit the cold air. Butterflies flittered in chaotic movements when Ryan kissed her.

When he raised his head an instant later, Jennie smiled. "I take it that means we're more than friends."

He chuckled and slung an arm over her shoulder. "You could say that."

———

The next morning during a French toast and sausage breakfast, Joe came by.

Gram insisted he stay for breakfast and poured him a cup of coffee. "How's poor Charlie this morning?"

"Better." Joe pulled out the empty chair next to Jennie and sat down. "He's a lucky man. That letter opener missed his heart by about a quarter of an inch." Joe took a sip of coffee and let his dark brown gaze settle on Jennie. "I know it was a nuisance for you, Jennie, having the mayor and Hawk think you were stealing that money, but it was a blessing in disguise. If you hadn't gone back into the office, old Charlie would have died."

"Glad I could help."

Joe gave her a crooked grin. "Looks like he'll be going home in a day or two."

"Any idea who might have wanted to do him in?" J.B. asked.

"Not yet. The only good prints we found on the weapon are Jennie's." He buttered his French toast and reached for the syrup.

"You don't think Jennie—" J.B. scowled.

"Not at all." Joe sliced off a square of French toast and popped it into his mouth. After an expectant moment, he added, "Charlie can't identify his assailant but says he got him from behind. All he remembers is getting a thump on the head and seeing stars. He was at the campaign office going through some files at the time. For whatever reason, the attacker took him back to the office and stuck him with his own letter opener."

"Maybe he wanted to make it look like a break-in," Gram said.

"Looks that way. They apparently waited until Jennie left, then went in the back door, dumped the body, and took off."

"Any suspects?" J.B. asked, finishing off his sausage.

"Trevor Smith. He's the campaign manager Charlie fired. Claims he had nothing to do with the missing money or the attack on the judge." Joe shifted his gaze to Gram, then Jennie, then back to J.B. "It's looking more and more like the pro-gambling constituents have taken to playing dirty. Then again, it might not have anything to do with the campaign— being a judge, he's stepped on a lot of toes."

After finishing his breakfast and coffee, Joe started to leave. Jennie followed him out, wanting to ask about Mayor Ames and his bodyguard. The more she thought about it, the more puzzled she became. Who was Hawk, and why was he driving the mayor around in a limo? Jennie asked but didn't get the response she'd hoped for.

"Why the questions, Jennie?" Joe asked. "I thought I told you to stay out of the investigation."

"Just curious. I think I have a right to know who he is. He did hold me at gunpoint."

"Well, you can put your suspicions aside. Hawk's not nearly as fierce as he looks. His uncle runs the casino in Siletz Bay."

"How come I've never seen him around before?"

Joe shrugged and opened his car door. "He hasn't worked for the mayor all that long."

Jennie waited until he'd gotten into his car and rolled down the window, then asked, "You said his uncle runs the casino. Does that mean he wants the gambling bill to pass?"

"Not necessarily. Why do you ask?"

"If he's for it, don't you find it strange that he'd be working for the mayor?"

Joe shook his head and picked up his radio receiver in response to a call. "On my way." He started the engine and shifted into reverse. "I'm not sure where you're going with this, Jennie, but I suggest you find something else to occupy your time. In the meantime, I'd better go. The mayor's carrying out his campaign promise to be tough on crime. Problem is, he keeps passing the ball to me."

Jennie watched him drive away, then ran back into the house.

It wasn't much, but the oddity of the mayor's choice of chauffeur/bodyguard set off her sense of curiosity. So did the fact that the mayor and Hawk just happened to be in the area when Charlie was hurt, and Hawk just happened to find him. Okay, so Joe had told her not to get involved in Jessica's murder investigation, but he hadn't said anything about Charlie or the gambling initiative or the stolen money. Maybe she could do some digging—discreetly, of course. Joe had suggested she find something else to occupy her time.

"Jennie! Telephone," Gram called from the kitchen.

"Who is it?" Jennie hurried through the entry and took the phone from Gram's extended hand.

"It's Charlie."

"Hi, Jennie," Charlie greeted. "I heard about the trouble you had with the mayor and his driver. Sorry you had to go through all that."

"It was worth the trouble to have found you. How are you feeling?"

"Not bad, considering. Listen, I know it's a lot to ask, but I'd sure appreciate it if you could keep working at the shop until I can get out of here. Your gram's agreed to help with the campaign."

No way, she started to say but couldn't. "Sure. I guess."

"That's great. Somehow I knew I could count on you two. Do you still have the keys?"

"Yeah." Hawk had given them back to her the night before.

Jennie didn't share Charlie's enthusiasm. "Um, Judge Crookston, could I ask you something?"

"Fire away."

"You know the mayor pretty well, don't you?"

"Yep. Forrest and I go way back."

"Have you met his bodyguard—a guy named Hawk?"

"Hawk—" He hesitated. "Can't say as I have. Why do you ask?"

"Just curious. I guess he must be new."

After receiving some last-minute instructions about the shop, Charlie wished her luck and reminded her to call Mindy if she needed help. Jennie returned the phone to its base.

"What's wrong, darling?" Gram slid an arm around Jennie's shoulder. "If you're that upset about working at the shop, we can call Charlie back. I'm sure he can find someone. . . ."

"No, it isn't that. I think Judge Crookston just lied to me."

13

Gram raised an eyebrow. "Are you certain? I've known Charlie a long time, Jennie, and I've never known him to be dishonest."

"Charlie said he didn't know Hawk. But Hawk knew Charlie. At least well enough to recognize him yesterday. Hawk went into the office to call Mindy. Then he came out and said he found Charlie. It wasn't like 'I think I found him.' He knew."

"I'm not certain that means anything. I would imagine a lot of people know Charlie that he wouldn't recognize. But it is an interesting point. Perhaps I could stop by the hospital and have a little chat with him on my way to the campaign office today."

"That'd be great." Jennie glanced around. "What happened to Nick and J.B.?"

"They've taken Bernie for a walk."

"Oh." She was supposed be caring for Nick, but J.B. seemed to be doing everything. "Do you think it's a good idea if we both work? I mean—what about Nick?"

"J.B. said he'd be happy to take care of Nick while we're gone. In case you haven't noticed, those two are inseparable."

Jennie smiled. "I've noticed. Are you sure he can manage? I mean, he's not used to having kids around."

100

"Oh, I think they'll manage just fine."

———

At nine-thirty, Jennie inserted the key into the lock, pushed open the door to Charlie's ice cream shop, and turned on the lights. The first thing she did was close the door to the office so she wouldn't have to think about coming in and seeing Charlie there with a hole in his chest.

Maybe scooping ice cream, cream-cheesing bagels, and making lattés was a good thing. Relishing in the sunshine that streamed through the windows, Jennie made coffee and set out all the essential tools and the recipes for all the coffee drinks and various cream-cheese mixtures, then cleaned the tables with a special bleach solution as Charlie had instructed. Mindy had replenished the cream cheeses the day before so she wouldn't have to make up any new. At least not right away.

At nine-forty-five, she opened the door and accepted the load of bagels that, according to the driver, had been baked fresh in Lincoln City that morning.

At ten, she set out the advertising board, turned the sign from closed to open, and went behind the counter. The morning sped by as Jennie served one customer after another—a steady stream, but not unmanageable. Noontime, though, brought dozens, and Jennie worked harder at staying calm than at serving customers. When Ryan came in to see how she was doing, she put him to work taking orders and delivering them to the tables. He stayed until two, when business settled back down again.

"I nearly forgot what I came in to tell you." Ryan slipped on his jacket. "Gram said we should go with her to the benefit at the mayor's house."

"We're going? It's kind of spendy, isn't it?"

"Too rich for me, that's for sure, but since she's the new campaign manager, we all get to go free. It should be fun."

"Yeah. Um—what are we supposed to wear?" Jennie hoped it would be casual since she hadn't brought much other than jeans and tops.

He shrugged. "Something dressy. Gram said she'd get you something." A car pulled up in front of the store, and two women got out. Ryan left, probably to avoid being put back to work.

————

When Jennie closed up shop for the day, she had no black limo waiting for her, nor was she accosted making her run to the bank to deposit the money. The afternoon had been just busy enough to keep her from being bored or from thinking too much about Charlie—and Jessica.

Now, as she made her way home, Jennie's mind drifted back to the cliff in front of Forrest and Mari Ames' home and back to the girl who'd experienced a tragic death there. Jessica had broken up with Todd, and he'd lied about it. He denied killing her though, and after what had happened to Charlie, Jennie tended to believe him.

"What did Charlie and Jessica have in common?" she asked her reflection in the rear view mirror. The answer came back like it had before—the fight against gambling in Bay Village. Still, it seemed farfetched to think Jessica would be involved enough to warrant being murdered unless—Jennie went back to an old premise—Jessica knew something or was simply used as a means to get to the mayor.

Jennie had read books and seen movies where people who were into gambling would at times do terrible things to get their way. Despite Joe's reassurance that Hawk was not a threat, Jennie puzzled about him working for the mayor. Unless the mayor was up to something. Pulling into the drive, Jennie sighed. Things were getting more complicated by the minute. Maybe she'd learn something tonight at the benefit.

The house seemed empty when she first stepped inside. "Gram? Are you home?"

"Upstairs."

Jennie took the stairs two at a time. Gram had half the clothes out of her closet and lying on the bed.

"What are you doing?"

"Trying to find something suitable to wear tonight—for both of us."

"Is it formal?"

"Suit-and-tie. You'll need something other than jeans."

"I don't need to go."

"Of course you do. You'll enjoy it."

"Who'll take care of Nick?"

"J.B." Gram grinned. "Who else? He called a bit ago to tell me they'd gone back to the aquarium. Nick's quite taken by the whale. Claims Keiko smiles and waves at him."

"That wouldn't surprise me. Whales and dolphins do some pretty unique things." Jennie flopped on a clear spot of bed. "Did you find out about Hawk?"

"No, Jennie, I'm sorry. No one I talked with today knew much about him. Only that Forrest hired him after Jessica's death. Perhaps we can find out more at the benefit tonight."

"My thoughts exactly."

Gram reached into the back of her closet and pulled out a magenta dress with a V neck and a white jacket. "This one should fit you. I'm afraid I don't have many clothes in your size." Although Jennie and Gram were similar in height, Gram was a size or two larger.

It wasn't exactly a style Jennie would have chosen. Too matronly. But Jennie didn't really care. As long as it fit—which it did. She borrowed a pair of low-heeled shoes and nylons.

Gram chose a loose-fitting gauzy white dress with gold chains at the neck. She looked artistic and beautiful.

Jennie, Ryan, and Gram drove up to the door of the mayor's home at seven sharp. A valet took the keys from Gram when she stepped out. Ryan escorted both women inside. He looked gorgeous in his rented tux. For a moment Jennie wished she'd let Gram take her into Lincoln City to pick up a new dress. But logic prevailed. The last thing she needed was another fancy dress. The one she had gotten for her cruise was hanging in her closet next to a bridesmaid dress she'd probably never wear again.

Sucking in a determined breath, Jennie stepped inside. Clothes weren't that important to her—on the other hand, she didn't want to seem out of place. She needn't have worried. While most of the men wore tuxes, the women were dressed in a variety of suits and dresses from casual to sequined evening wear.

"Want something to drink?" Ryan eyed the tables at the far end of the formal dining room.

"Sure."

He wandered over to a table set up with punch and coffee and dipped a silver ladle into a large crystal bowl. There must have been a hundred food items set out on the lavishly decorated tables.

Annie, dressed in a white tunic and chef hat, brought in a bowl of something and set it on the table.

"Hi." Jennie approached Annie warily. It seemed strange to see Todd's cousin at an event put on by the mayor and his wife—especially with the mayor being so adamant about Todd's guilt.

When Jennie asked about it, Annie gave her a wry smile.

"I suspect it's because Mayor Ames is a fair man. He knows I'm not responsible for what Todd did—or may have done. Besides, he's crazy about my cooking."

"What about you? Doesn't it bother you to work for

someone who thinks Todd killed their daughter?"

Annie bit into her lower lip. "It's money."

Mayor Ames approached, then, bringing an end to Jennie's questions.

"You've done it again, Annie. Everything looks great." Mayor Ames lifted the lid on one of the hot items. Steam rose to his face. He sniffed deeply. "Mind if I sample?"

Annie laughed. "Not from this one. I fixed you a plate in the kitchen so you wouldn't be getting into my artwork before it's ready."

Mayor Ames followed Annie into the other room like a puppy begging for table scraps.

"What are you laughing at?" Ryan handed her a goblet of pink punch.

"The mayor. He went into the kitchen with Annie to sample the food."

"That's funny?"

"Never mind." Jennie's smile faded as she wondered what had happened to Hawk. If he really was a bodyguard, wouldn't he be hanging around? Anything could happen at a party like this. Jennie made a mental note to check later.

Ryan glanced around. "Hey, there's a guy with an hors d'oeuvres tray. You hungry?"

"Not yet. You go ahead. I want to look around."

"I'll catch up to you later." Ryan wandered off again.

Jennie felt almost relieved to be on her own. Like before, something about the house or its former occupant seemed to be nagging at her. She needed to think and had the feeling she ought to be taking notes.

Only a handful of people had come on time. Gram was talking to Mari Ames and some people Jennie didn't recognize. Jennie moved away from the entry into the living room, where the artists were showing their work. The artists who'd donated pieces to the show—and who'd worked with Jessica.

Several new bronze pieces sat on the living room floor.

One of them drew Jennie forward. Eric had created a thirty-six-inch bronze of Jessica in ballet slippers and a delicate swirling satin dress, lifting her kitten high above her head. Exquisite was the only word Jennie could come up with to describe it. The features of the face looked as though Jessica herself had somehow been miniaturized and dipped in the liquid metal.

"You like it." A man in his thirties ambled up beside her. "I can tell."

"It's beautiful." Jennie's gaze met his gray-green one. "You're the artist, aren't you?"

"Am I that obvious?" Before she could answer, he held out a hand. "Eric Meyers."

Jennie introduced herself and shook his hand before turning back to the bronze. "How do you make them so lifelike?"

"I've had a lot of practice. He glanced admiringly at the piece, then said, "I should tell you—this one isn't for sale. I made it as a gift to Mari and Forrest."

"Jessica took classes from you, didn't she?"

Eric studied her for a moment. His eyes grayed. "Yes. Unfortunately she died before she could finish her first project. She'd hoped to give this to her parents."

"Jessica did this?"

"Um—no, actually. She drew it but never quite got the hang of sculpting it."

"Did you know Jessica well?"

"Well enough. Mari is a good friend. Jessica came more to please her mother than herself. I don't think she was particularly interested in bronze work—seemed more suited to clay."

"Eric!" Gram came up to them. "Good to see you again. Eric is one of my favorite artists, Jennie. I've had my eye on his mermaids for a long time."

"Perhaps now would be a good time to purchase a piece," Eric said. "I brought one of my favorites. You can own your sculpture and help keep gambling out of Bay Village with only one check."

Gram laughed. "Such a bargain."

Jennie left them to work out the details of what could prove to be a profitable evening for Eric and a costly one for Gram. Needing to find a rest room, Jennie made her way down the hallway. The rest room was the first door to the left, but voices coming from the room to the right stopped her.

"I told you I had everything under control," a man's raspy voice said.

"Control!" The second, more menacing voice sounded in danger of losing it. "Crookston came *this* close to finding out. Need I remind you what that would do to our operation?"

"Not to mention *your* reputation." He paused. "Don't worry. Everything is set. I can assure you there won't be any slipups."

Jennie moved closer to the door and grasped the knob. If she could open it a crack, she might be able to see. The doorknob turned in her hand. Someone was coming out.

14

Jennie's heart skittered like a frightened rabbit. She slipped into the bathroom across the hall. Holding the door partway open, she peeked through the narrow slit, trying to see who the voices belonged to. Because of the angle, Jennie couldn't see them but suspected one of those voices must belong to the mayor. Or someone who knew his house. If Jennie remembered right from her previous visit—that room was Mayor Ames' office.

After using the facilities, Jennie paused at the room the two men had come out of and turned the knob—it was locked. She hurried back to the party. Maybe if she listened to the voices of some of the guests, she'd be able to tell whom she'd overheard. The information could lead to Charlie's attacker—and perhaps even to Jessica's killer.

Jennie spotted Mayor Ames walking toward the buffet table. She glanced around at the guests. There were about twenty or so now and more arriving every few minutes. Silver-haired and stately, Senator Baker stood near the entry beside his wife—a petite woman who barely came up to his shoulder. His eyes narrowed when he glanced in the mayor's direction.

Jennie sensed hostility in the way he crossed the room—like a lion stalking its prey. Mayor Ames greeted the senator with a smile, then motioned for him to follow. Which he did, down the hall and into the office.

Jennie waited until the door closed, then trailed after them—or she would have if someone hadn't grabbed her arm.

"Where do you think you're going?" Hawk's dark eyes peered down at her, holding her in place. "And don't tell me you're headed for the bathroom because you just came from there."

"I . . . I just wanted to look around."

"Don't you mean snoop? What the senator and Mayor Ames are discussing is no concern of yours. Now I suggest you run along. I understand the food is great, and I think there's a young man looking for you."

Hawk released her and blocked the hallway. Had he been the one in the mayor's office earlier? Maybe she'd been right about Hawk and the mayor being involved in Charlie's near-death experience.

Jennie found Ryan talking to Annie at the buffet table.

"I didn't realize you were such a good cook." Ryan popped a tiny meatball coated in some kind of sauce into his mouth.

"Been cooking for a long time. After my father's accident I had to learn to satisfy all the hungry men in my family. Todd and Greg still eat half their meals at my house."

"Well, anytime you need a guinea pig to sample new stuff, I'll volunteer."

"I just might take you up on that, but only if you'll take the job. I'm desperate for an assistant."

"Sorry, but I'm already taken. I'll be working for Greg for the next couple months."

"Too bad. If you change your mind, I have better benefits."

"When did you decide to work for Greg?" Jennie asked.

"Yesterday."

Annie lifted the lid from a huge stainless-steel pot and

dipped in a ladle, lifting up a tomato broth and a variety of shellfish.

"Is that cioppino?" The seafood soup was one of Jennie's favorites.

"Mmm—my second batch. Want a sample?" At Jennie's enthusiastic nod, Annie scooped some into a bowl and handed it to her.

"Thanks."

Ryan caught Jennie's gaze and grinned. "Want to walk out to the gazebo with me?"

Jennie hesitated. What she really wanted to do was ask questions of some of the guests. One glance back told her the predator was still watching. She picked up a plate, set the cioppino on it, gathered a few other delicacies, then followed Ryan outside.

"Where'd you disappear to anyway?" Ryan asked as he sat on the white bench inside the gazebo.

She told him about the discussion she'd overheard and how Hawk had stopped her from following Senator Baker and Mayor Ames. "They're up to something, Ryan. Whatever it is, Charlie got too close and posed a danger, so they tried to kill him."

"If you're suggesting Mayor Ames or Senator Baker had anything to do with the attack on Charlie, you can forget it. They're all close friends. On the other hand, maybe they're all being threatened."

Jennie speared a spiced prawn. "I don't suppose you saw who came out of the mayor's office a few minutes ago, did you?"

"I saw him with several people." Ryan scanned the crowd that had gathered on the lawn. "There, next to Mrs. Ames. He might be the one. I noticed him talking to the mayor earlier."

Jennie swung around to look. The man, obviously a Native American, had a wide, chiseled face and a long dark braid. Mrs. Ames looked as though she were about to cry, then abruptly walked away. The man shook his head and watched Mrs. Ames for a moment before turning back into the house.

"I'm going to talk to him." Jennie kept her gaze riveted on the stranger's broad back.

"You may want to wait."

Eric Meyers stepped on a platform and spoke into a microphone. "Everyone, I'd like your attention, please." His voice rose above the din, effectively stilling the numerous conversations. "As you know, Jessica Ames had a deep appreciation of the arts—as do her parents, Forrest and Mari Ames. She was also a strong advocate for keeping gambling out of Bay Village. For that reason, Mayor Ames and Mari have dedicated this benefit to her."

Jennie glanced back to where she'd last seen the Native American. He was gone. Making a mental note to catch him later, she and Ryan moved with the others closer to the podium.

Eric went on and on, making a big deal out of donating his gift to the Ameses, then introduced two other artists who'd also brought gifts. While each artist talked, Jennie wondered what kind of role they had played in Jessica's life and how well they knew her.

It seemed odd to Jennie that all three of the artists would have a work either made or begun by Jessica to present. It was a farfetched idea, but Jennie went with it nonetheless. Often in a murder case, the least likely suspect ended up being the killer. Could one of these artists have had anything to do with Jessica's death?

Naw. She shook her head. It didn't fit. What would their motives be? They all seemed genuinely saddened by Jessica's passing. Better to listen for clues into Jessica's character than get hung up with more suspicions.

Dana Coons had become famous for her portraits of

children and presented the Ameses with a portrait of Jessica. The painting was one of Jessica in a white gauzy dress, sitting on a rock with the water lapping at her feet.

Nicole Hemingway, the next artist to speak, was a potter. Nicole presented Jessica's parents with a clay figure Jessica herself had made only days before her death. The crude, hand-built piece had been raku fired. A shiny copper cape hung lifelessly on a figure with no head. The cape opened halfway down to reveal a child's face. Lack of glaze on the face made it a haunting shade of charcoal gray.

When they'd finished the presentations, Eric reminded them why they'd come. "On each piece you'll find an opening bid. As this is a silent auction, you'll want to write down the amount you're willing to pay. Someone may outbid you during the course of the evening. Remember, the one with the last bid will be the new owner."

The murmuring crowd dispersed. Many made their way into the house to look over the artwork and make their bids.

Mari Ames again thanked the artists, then moved toward her husband. "Forrest, I'm sorry—" She leaned against him and rubbed her head. "All this excitement has brought on another headache. I hope you don't mind taking over for me while I rest for a few minutes."

"Certainly, sweetheart—would you like me to walk you up?"

"No, stay with our guests."

Mrs. Ames went inside. After watching his wife for a long moment, the mayor turned back to the artists.

The gifts had been placed on a black velvet-covered table near the podium, and Jennie and Ryan wandered over to take a closer look. Only one had actually been done by Jessica alone. Jennie found the child's face eerie and wondered if the work might have some special meaning. Maybe it did. The piece was draped in shiny colors, while inside—

"Ryan, that's it," Jennie said. "What Jessica's saying is

that her life is glossy and warm on the outside, but it's drab— or colorless, cool—or maybe even dark on the inside. She wasn't what people thought. Or maybe the cape represents her father—or mother—an authority figure. The key is that the outside is a facade. She's insignificant, but she can see the world outside. She can see the truth."

Ryan looked at her as though she'd turned into a space alien while she continued. "I think it's her true self trying to come out. Of course, if you consider what happened to the clay—it's been through fire. Part came out beautiful—the rest charred and dull."

Jennie stared at the piece, hoping it might have an answer as to why someone wanted Jessica dead. Nothing more came. Working on her hunch that all was not as it seemed in the Ames family, Jennie announced to Ryan her plans to talk to the mayor, who had gone through the buffet again and was walking toward the stone wall. Jennie glanced around and, seeing no sign of Hawk, followed Mayor Ames across the lawn.

"Hello, Jennie," he said as she approached. "I hope you've recovered from our little misunderstanding yesterday."

"I'm glad it happened, otherwise Charlie might not have been found in time."

"Yes. That's a good way to look at it. Things happen for a reason." Mayor Ames' gaze drifted out to sea. He remained silent for several seconds, then said, "She fell to her death on these rocks. It's a miracle she wasn't washed away. I was the first to find her, you know."

"That must have been really hard for you."

"I've been trying to find a reason. Can't think of any. Every day I ask God why. Why did my baby girl have to die? Why couldn't it have been me?" He looked at Jennie. A film of tears covered his pale blue eyes.

Jennie swallowed back the lump of empathy in her throat. "I don't know."

"No, of course you don't. I wish I'd come back earlier that night—wish I'd never gone into town." He hauled in a deep breath and closed his eyes. Perspiration beaded his upper lip. His hand shook as he pulled a handkerchief out of his breast pocket and dabbed at his mouth, then his forehead.

"The tide was out, and the moon full and bright. I'll never forget seeing her in that white cotton dress—so still and—" The mayor's eyes went big and round—his face contorted in pain. He grabbed his stomach. The nearly full plate slithered to the ground, and Mayor Ames crumpled over on top of it.

15

One cry of help from Jennie brought Hawk and several others running.

"What happened?"

"I'm not sure. He may have choked on something." Jennie struggled to get the mayor into a sitting position. "He's too heavy for me."

Hawk took over and did a finger sweep of the mayor's mouth, then hoisted him up. Grabbing him around the chest from behind, he made a fist and pulled hard against him, easily executing the Heimlich maneuver Jennie had been attempting.

Hawk's efforts to revive the mayor failed. Jennie ran into the house and called 9-1-1. Thankfully, two of the guests were doctors, and within fifteen minutes the mayor was on his way to the hospital. Hawk and Mrs. Ames followed the ambulance in the limo after asking Gram to take over as host.

Speculations about the mayor's sudden illness ran from food poisoning to gall stones to a heart attack. Whatever had happened seemed to make people extra charitable. Every work of art sold, and people handed Gram checks for $500 to $50,000.

Gram figured the campaign fund against the gambling initiative had raised around half a million dollars. Enough to launch a respectable counterattack.

That was the good news. The bad news was that Mayor Ames would never see the fruits of his efforts. Most of the one hundred or so guests had gone home by the time Sheriff Joe Adams returned to tell them of the mayor's death.

With Ryan and Jennie's help, Annie had loaded up the leftover food and dishes. Now she sat on a white folding chair staring at the one remaining platter on the stained linen table cloth. "It couldn't have been my food. You know how careful I am."

"He was poisoned, Annie." Joe hunkered down in front of her. "Now, I'm sure you had nothing to do with it, but somebody put something in whatever he'd been eating or drinking."

Annie grabbed Joe's hand. "You have to find out who. Something like this could ruin my business. It's all I have."

"We'll do our best. Right now, though, I have to run samples of all the food over to the lab in Lincoln City for the medical examiner. And I need a list of everyone who helped set up and handled the food." He was talking to her as one would a wounded child. Gentle and reassuring. Jennie wondered if maybe they had feelings for each other. Joe let go of Annie's hand and stood.

Annie sighed. "That would be Greg. My regular assistant quit, so Greg helped me set up. I did all the cooking and food handling, though. He wasn't here all that long."

"Greg?" Joe frowned. "A little out of his league, isn't it? Since when did he start catering?"

"He and Todd help sometimes when I'm in a pinch." Annie's gaze traveled from her clasped hands to Joe's face. "I know what you're thinking, but Greg didn't do it. He didn't like the mayor—everyone knows that. I didn't especially care for him either—not after what he did to my father and the way he's treated Todd. But I certainly wouldn't kill him." Her voice rose as she did.

"Okay, calm down." Joe's hands closed over her

shoulders. "It's just that I have to consider every possibility."

"Helen." Joe turned toward Gram. "While I'm dealing with the food, would you see if you can find the guest list? Mrs. Ames says there was one on the mayor's desk."

"You'll need a key," Jennie volunteered.

Joe flashed her an exasperated look. "And just how would you know that?"

"Um—I heard someone talking in there earlier." Jennie repeated the conversation and added, "When I checked the door it was locked. Then the mayor and Senator Baker went in. I was going to eavesdrop, but Hawk stopped me."

"A good thing." Joe frowned. "You should have come to me instead of playing junior detective."

Jennie bristled. "I was going to. I only wanted to find out who they were."

"Right."

Jennie told him about the Native American who'd been talking to Mrs. Ames, and Joe wrote the information down.

"You were with the mayor when he collapsed?" Joe asked.

Jennie nodded, trying to recall the details of what they'd talked about and how he'd acted.

For the next two hours, Joe and his deputies methodically covered every inch of the kitchen and Annie's van. They also moved everyone inside when it started drizzling to question the remaining guests—the three artists and Jennie, Ryan, Gram, and Senator Baker. They were all sitting in the family room like suspects in an Agatha Christie mystery.

The senator railed at Joe. "I can't understand why you're wasting precious time questioning honest folks like us while a killer is running loose out there somewhere."

Joe leaned back in his chair. "The more thoroughly we investigate the crime scene, the better our chances of discovering who did it."

"Then talk to that McGrady girl. She was with him—maybe she knows something."

"You were with him, too, Senator—in his office, not ten minutes before—" Jennie sank back when Joe gave her a keep-quiet sign.

Turning back to Senator Baker, Joe asked, "What were you and the mayor talking about in his office?"

"The campaign. We were planning our strategy for coming out against the gambling initiative. I can assure you I had nothing to do with Forrest's death."

No one did, or at least they wouldn't admit it.

Two days later Jennie made a breakfast of blueberry pancakes and bacon. Nick was trying to eat while pretending to read a section of newspaper J.B. had given him. J.B. peered over his paper. "Says here the mayor died from eating toxic mussels found in the cioppino he'd eaten."

"No kidding." Jennie set her piece of pancake back onto her plate. "I ate some of that—it was great. How come it didn't affect me?"

"Good question. Says here Annie had held a portion out just for him. He ate three bowls of it all told."

"Hmm. I had some from the second batch. Maybe the bad mussels were only in the first one. Still, that doesn't explain why no one else got sick."

"No one else was affected?" Gram asked.

"Apparently not." J.B. ducked back behind the paper. "The pathologist says they only found traces of the toxin in the pot."

"What does that mean for Annie?" Gram asked. "They certainly don't still suspect her."

"Not at all." J.B. folded the paper and set it aside. "They found some of the toxin in one of the packages from the processing plant. Which means the supplier may have accidentally gotten some bad shellfish in their stocks. There's a danger of that during the summer months. They're guessing that since it's a naturally occurring toxin that the mayor just got a higher concentration of it than anyone else."

"Does that mean they don't think anyone poisoned him?" The explanation seemed a little too pat.

"That's what it says," J.B. replied. "And I suspect they're right. It would be very difficult to single out the mayor's clams. If someone poisoned the entire batch, anyone could have gotten them. And bivalve shellfish are not generally used as a murder weapon."

"Well, I for one am glad to hear it was accidental." Gram picked up a piece of crisp bacon and waved it as she spoke. "I must say, even one suspicious death in Bay Village is more than enough. And with poor Charlie—Joe still doesn't have any leads on the stabbing. At least Annie's no longer a suspect. She's been beside herself with worry. She already has a full plate with her cousin being blamed for Jessica's death and caring for her father."

"Hey, Papa." Nick lifted J.B.'s paper. "How about reading me the funnies?"

J.B. ruffled Nick's hair. "That's a fine idea. As soon as we finish breakfast we'll take our papers into the living room."

Gram raised an eyebrow at J.B. and smiled. "It might be best if you both set your papers aside and finished your meal."

J.B. winked at Nick. "Your gram's right, lad." They obediently folded the newspapers and concentrated on breakfast.

Something nagged at Jennie, trying to trigger a memory, but it didn't come—maybe later. "Gram? After the benefit when Joe was questioning Annie, she said she didn't like the mayor because of her father. What was that all about?"

"That's something you'll have to ask Annie, I'm afraid. I do know he was injured in a logging accident, but I have no idea how it connects to the mayor."

Jennie finished off her breakfast. The puzzle seemed to

have a lot of non-connecting pieces. She'd already surmised that the mayor's and Jessica's deaths and the attack on Charlie were all somehow tied in to the gambling initiative. In fact, the more she thought about it, the more certain she became. With Todd still in jail, he couldn't have murdered the mayor—or attacked Charlie. That left a killer on the loose—someone who would stop at nothing to get the gambling initiative passed.

Greg remained on her suspect list—especially since he liked to gamble. And he had been on the premises. Hawk definitely went on the list. And Travis—the fired campaign manager. Of course she had to add Senator Baker and the stranger she'd seen at the benefit. Gram seemed to think Annie was innocent, but Jennie wasn't about to eliminate her yet. There were other possibilities as well.

"Jennie?" Gram waved a hand in front of her face. "What are you so deep in thought about?"

"I still think there's a connection to the gambling. Suppose the pro-gambling guys hired a hit man to kill the mayor and hurt Charlie."

"An interesting premise, lass." J.B. leveled a tell-me-more gaze on her.

Jennie went through her list of suspects and ended with Hawk.

"Hawk?" J.B. raised a silver eyebrow and glanced at Helen.

"Yeah," Jennie went on. "The guy is everywhere. He stopped me from going to eavesdrop on the mayor and the senator. He found Charlie—his uncle runs a casino—"

"I don't think that's—"

"No, it's true. You need to meet Hawk, then you'll understand."

"You must stop this line of thinking, lass. It'll get you nowhere."

"J.B.'s right, darling," Gram said. "It's time to let it go."

Jennie folded her arms and sank back into her chair. "That's what Joe said too. But I don't know if I can. I keep thinking about it and—"

"Perhaps you'd better tell her," Gram said. "We can certainly trust her not to say anything, but if she persists she might cause some damage."

In that moment Jennie knew—it didn't take a mind reader to decipher it. She should have seen it sooner. Jennie pictured the tall, lean man—the *chauffeur* who wore a shoulder holster and carried a .38 special like her father's and J.B.'s "You don't have to tell me. Hawk is FBI, isn't he? He's the one Joe said was on the case."

"That's about the size of it." J.B. sounded weary. "He's a good man—one of the best. Thanks to his uncle, he's managed to get himself into a key position."

"His uncle? You mean the casino operator?"

"I can't tell you more than that. Now you need to stay clear and let the man do his job."

Jennie closed her eyes. "I'll try. It's just that things keep happening when I'm there. I can't not think about it."

"Thinking is fine. Just don't act on your suspicions."

Gram's hand closed over Jennie's. "How would you like to go with me today, Jennie? I have a few errands to run, and I'd like to stop and see Mari Ames."

"Sounds good." With Charlie back to work and Ryan working for Greg, Jennie had been wondering what she'd do with herself.

On the way into town, they stopped to see Mari Ames. When they pulled into the driveway next to a black town car, Micky skateboarded toward them, veered off, and hit a makeshift ramp. He and the skateboard went airborne, executed a mid-air somersault, and came down on the board.

Jennie congratulated him on his perfect landing but got no response. His mouth was a thin, flat line on a mannequin-like face.

"Mom's not in the house," Micky finally said when they stepped onto the porch. "She's in her studio—above the garage." He pointed to the exterior steps attached to the two-car garage. "She's been in there since . . . for two days."

Gram glanced at the garage's upper windows, her face a study in compassion. "Has someone been here to care for her—and you?"

"I've been bringing her food, but she won't eat." His lower lip quivered, but only for a moment. Anger replaced the hurt Jennie had seen in his eyes. "I can take care of myself. I don't need her. I don't need anybody." Micky pushed off, rolling toward the ramp again.

Jennie and Gram looked at each other, then headed for the stairway.

16

Gram reached the top of the stairs first. The door opened, nearly hitting her.

The Native American Jennie had seen at the benefit backed out. "I'm sorry for your troubles, Mrs. Ames, but I'll expect you to honor your husband's debts." He closed the door and spun around. If Jennie and Gram's presence surprised him, he didn't show it. His dark eyes assessed them. "Excuse me." He squeezed by them on the narrow landing.

Jennie waited until he reached his car, then nudged her grandmother. "That's the guy who was at the benefit."

Taking a pen and pad from her handbag, Gram jotted down the license plate number. "We'll call Joe. First, though, we'd better see to Mari."

Mari Ames sat at a spinning potter's wheel. Gray, wet clay oozed between her fingers as her hands circled a spinning pot. A bowl, Jennie surmised, viewing the stacks of similarly shaped items already thrown and sitting on shelves. Mari glanced up at them as they entered but didn't seem to see them. Her gaze went immediately back to the wet clay. She inserted one hand into the pot and with the other began at the base and worked her way up. The piece grew wider and taller, then slumped in the middle, like rolls of fat on a sumo wrestler.

The potter's shoulders slumped as well. She pinched her

lips together and squeezed the fallen pot between her fingers, then slung a glob of it into a slush bucket. What had begun as a bowl or a cup now sank into the mire—a meaningless lump. Jennie pulled her gaze from the disturbing sight.

Mari looked up at Jennie, her eyes glazed and unfocused. "Jessica. You've come back. I knew you would." A thin smile curved her lips. "You're just in time to help me plan for the party."

Jennie stepped back. Mari Ames had gone over the edge.

Gram moved behind Mari and took hold of her shoulders, speaking in soothing tones. "You need to stop now, Mari. It's time to go inside and rest."

"No!" Mari twisted away. "I have so much to do. Did you see him? That horrible man is spreading rumors about my husband. He told me Forrest and Jessica were dead and that I needed to face facts. He said I had to pay the bill—"

"Jennie." Gram placed her hands on Mari's shoulders again. "Go call Dr. Hanley. His number is in the book. Tell him what's going on and ask him to come over."

Jennie ran out the door and slipped twice on the damp stairs. The house was unlocked, and Mrs. Ames' once spotless kitchen had been thoroughly trashed. At least that's what Jennie thought at first. Then she realized it was just the victim of neglect.

Dirty dishes filled the sink and cluttered every counter. Leftover food sat in pots on the stove. And it smelled like week-old garbage.

Jennie ignored the mess and hurried to the phone. After rummaging through the phone book, she found and dialed Dr. Hanley's number.

"I'll be right there," Dr. Hanley told her when she'd explained that Mrs. Ames was hallucinating. "Don't try to dissuade her. She might stay calmer thinking you are Jessica for now."

As Jennie hung up the phone, she noticed an empty envelope on the counter from the Soaring Eagle Casino. It was addressed to Mayor Ames. Jennie picked it up. Why would the mayor be getting a letter from the casino? A contribution? Not likely. An advertisement? Jennie folded the envelope, stuffed it in her pocket, then hurried back to play Jessica to the very confused Mrs. Ames.

———————

Dr. Hanley settled Mari down with a sedative and ordered her to bed. Jennie offered to stay and care for her and Micky until Mari's sister in Portland could come later that afternoon.

While Mrs. Ames slept, Jennie made a lunch of chicken noodle soup and a peanut butter and jelly sandwich for Micky. While he ate, she started cleaning the kitchen.

"You don't have to do that," Micky said through a mouthful of sandwich.

"I know, but I want to."

He swallowed. "We have a cleaning lady. Mrs. Olsen comes in once a week."

"Is she coming today?" Jennie grimaced as she picked up a plate thickly coated with dried orange-colored sauce.

"Nope. Tomorrow."

"I'm not sure this place can last that long. Besides, I still owe you for saving my life. Remember?" Having cleaned out one of the double sinks, Jennie plugged it, ran hot water, squeezed in dish soap, then put the grungiest dishes in to soak.

Jennie pulled out a chair across from Micky. "I'm curious about something."

He shoveled in a spoonful of soup and slurped in a couple of noodles. "Like what?"

"Why didn't you tell someone your mom needed help?"

"She told me not to. 'Sides, I coulda taken care of things."

"Right—like you've been taking care of the kitchen?"

Micky's gaze dropped to his half-eaten sandwich. "I fixed us food. I didn't know what else to do."

Jennie chewed on her lower lip. She was being too hard on him. Losing a sister and father within a matter of weeks had to be devastating. Even if he put on a macho act at times and pretended like he didn't care, Jennie knew he did. "It's okay. I didn't mean to criticize you."

"I guess I should have called somebody—I just didn't know who. Mom seemed okay in some ways. It wasn't till she got that letter—" He stopped as if he'd said too much.

Following a hunch, Jennie pulled the envelope out of her back pocket. "The one from the casino?"

His eyes widened. "She tore it up—how did you. . . ?"

"I don't have the letter, only the envelope. I found it on the kitchen counter." Jennie set the envelope on the table. "Do you know what was in it?"

He shook his head hard enough to jiggle the table. "No, Mom didn't tell me. It must have been bad. She tore it into pieces."

"Micky, this could be really important. It might help us find out what happened to your dad and maybe even your sister. What happened to the letter? Did she throw it away?"

"I . . . I think so. She was standing by the sink tearing it up. She yelled at me to get out, so I did. I've never seen her so mad. Maybe she threw it in the garbage can under the sink. After that she went to her studio and wouldn't come out."

"Well, there's only one thing to do." Jennie took a deep breath to prepare herself for the unpleasant task ahead. She got up and opened the cupboard below the sink. After pulling the white plastic bag free of the sturdy garbage can, Jennie lined the can with a new bag. She opened several drawers.

"What are you looking for?"

"Rubber gloves." The words had just come out when she

found a pair beside a stack of dish towels. Slipping them on, she began transferring trash.

"You're not going to dig through all that garbage, are you? What if it isn't there?"

"I have to look." Jennie couldn't explain what drove her to root through the disgusting mess of papers, cans, and rotting food, but she had to know what had set Mari off.

Jennie spotted a scrap of white paper and held it up and waved it. "I found one."

She rescued at least a dozen pieces of the letter, some wet and slimy from food waste and coffee grounds. Micky watched her for a few minutes, then joined her on the floor, methodically sifting through the mess.

When they'd finished, Jennie set the scraps of paper on the kitchen table, wiped off the worst of the garbage, and patted them dry with a paper towel. "There. Now all we need to do is put them together."

Not an easy task. She discarded all the pieces without writing and assembled only those containing type. As the puzzle came together, Jennie began to understand why Mrs. Ames had reacted so violently. Though stains made it difficult to read, the message was clear.

Dear Mayor Ames:

We regret to inform you that we can no longer extend credit to you at the casino. Your current debt of $500,000 must be paid immediately or we will be forced to take legal action. It has become apparent that gambling has become an obsession. . . .

"What are you doing?" Mari Ames shrieked. Her hair stood at odd angles. Her wild gaze darted from the table to Jennie. Jennie backed away.

Mrs. Ames swept the table with her arm, scattering the papers all over the floor. "You had no right!" She straight-

127

ened and pointed to Micky. "Go to your room. I'll deal with you later."

Micky opened his mouth to argue, then shut it. His jaw twitched as he pushed the chair he'd been sitting in to the floor, kicked it away, and left the room. Mari waited until Micky had gone, then turned on Jennie. "I want you out of my house. You had no right to snoop through my trash."

"I thought it would help find out who killed your husband and—"

"I tore that piece of junk up for a reason. That letter was a lie. My husband is against gambling—everyone knows that. Those terrible people are trying to discredit him. It's a conspiracy. They'll stop at nothing to bring gambling into Bay Village. They killed Jessica and now they've killed Forrest." Mari walked to the cupboard near the stove and retrieved a cup, then picked up the teakettle and started to pour a cup of water.

"You need to take the letter to Sheriff Adams. He can verify if it's true or not." The sculpture Jessica had created took on an alarming reality. The Ames family was not at all what they seemed. Jessica's book on gambling addictions. It all made sense now. The mayor had a gambling problem. Had Jessica confronted him? Had he killed his own daughter to protect his dark secrets? How deep was the mayor's deception? Was he really against the gambling initiative like he'd claimed?

And the money stolen from Charlie. Had the mayor stolen campaign funds to pay his debts? But then who had killed the mayor? Too many questions. Jennie needed time to find the answers. She needed to take this new information to Joe. She needed to get away from Mari Ames. "Let's call Joe." Jennie inched toward the phone.

"No." Mari slammed down the teakettle and yanked open a drawer. Pulling out a butcher knife, she raised it over her head and dove toward Jennie.

17

Jennie ducked. The knife crashed into the dishes soaking in the sink. Water sloshed over the rim and onto Mari's clothes. She moaned, sounding like a wounded animal, righted herself, then staggered toward Jennie again.

Jennie backed around the table, putting it between them. She let her gaze leave Mari for half a second, trying to orient herself. Jennie had to get to the door, but the table and the crazed woman blocked her way.

Mari raised her arm again, then staggered and fell against the table. The knife clattered to the floor. Mari slumped onto a kitchen chair, folded her arms on the table, and buried her face in her arms. She reminded Jennie of a toy whose batteries had run down.

"What's the use?" Mari rocked back, her arms hung loosely at her side. "I knew I wouldn't be able to hide it forever."

Jennie swallowed hard. She could escape now, but there didn't seem much point. Whatever demon had driven Mari to attack Jennie seemed to have deserted her, leaving her as lifeless as the clay she'd been working with that morning. Jennie kicked the knife into a far corner for safekeeping and reached for the phone. Her gaze fixed on Mari, she dialed 9–1–1. Jennie doubted the woman would try to hurt her again but had no intention of letting down her guard.

After reporting the incident and asking for assistance, Jennie hung up. When Mari didn't make any attempt to move, Jennie went back to the table but didn't sit down. "It's true, isn't it? Your husband owing all that money?"

Mari drew in a deep, shuddering sigh. "Yes. Jessica tried to tell me about his gambling—I didn't believe her."

"That man who was in your studio this morning—is he from one of the casinos?"

Mari nodded. "Soaring Eagle. His Name is Blake Elan."

"He was at the benefit Wednesday night too."

"He came to talk to Forrest and me. I guess he thought I should know about my husband's gambling addiction."

"Why didn't you go to the police?"

"I didn't think it mattered. Forrest was a good mayor. Why ruin his reputation now that he's dead?"

———

When Joe and two other deputies arrived, Jennie explained what she'd found and how Mari had reacted. Dr. Hanley came as well, insisting that Mari be admitted to a psychiatric hospital.

Joe and his crew gathered up the evidence and put Mari in a squad car to transport her to Meadow Brook, a facility located about thirty miles south. Dr. Hanley had called ahead to have her admitted and planned to meet her there.

Jennie gave her statement but decided not to press charges. Mari Ames had enough trouble.

She stayed at the house with Micky until Mari's sister, Chris Nelson, arrived at two.

"Micky," Jennie called. He'd gone upstairs to get a video a few minutes before. "Your aunt is here."

"I sure appreciate your looking after him, Jennie."

"No problem. He's a neat kid. Um . . . have you heard how Mrs. Ames is doing?"

"The doctor said she's quieted down. She's worried

about Micky—that's a good sign. Mick and I will drive down to see her."

"That's good. Tell her . . . tell her I'm thinking about her."

"I will."

Micky dragged down the stairs carrying a Nike bag. "Hi, Aunt Chris." He stepped into her embrace.

"Are you ready to go?"

"I guess."

They locked up the house and headed for the car. Micky looked at Jennie. "Thanks for all you did."

Jennie nodded, not trusting herself to speak. It hurt to see such a great kid going through so much heartache. "Um, listen . . ." She settled an arm across his shoulders and gave him a hug. "Keep in touch, okay?"

"Yeah." He glanced up at his aunt. "Could you stop by Don's place? I gotta tell him good-bye."

"Of course." Chris took the keys to the house from Jennie. "Can I drop you off somewhere?"

"Thanks, but I'll walk. My grandmother lives nearby."

They left then, and Jennie offered up several prayers for her new young friend and his mother while she walked back to Gram's.

Ryan met her in the driveway. "You look beat. What's going on?"

"It's a long story. Let's go down to the rocks, and I'll fill you in."

After leaving a note for Gram and J.B., they took the familiar trail through the woods. Out on the rocks, the sun was shining, and judging from the few puffs of clouds on the horizon, they were in for a gorgeous afternoon. Jennie just wished she could enjoy it more. Her mind seemed lost in heavy gray clouds, and she couldn't see much of anything. Finding out about the mayor's gambling addiction had done nothing except to complicate matters even more. Jennie waited until they were seated, then filled him in on the letter and Mrs. Ames' breakdown.

When she'd finished, Ryan whistled. "Unbelievable. Maybe that's what Jessica was portraying in her clay sculpture. Her dad's addiction and her mom's denial."

"It explains the book I found on gambling addictions too. Jessica had told her mom, but Mrs. Ames said she didn't believe it."

"I'll bet Mrs. Ames knew all along—even before Jessica—and just kept it a secret. In fact, maybe Jessica threatened to tell, so Mari killed her."

Jennie shuddered. "I can't believe she'd do that. Jessica was her daughter."

"It happens. Mari Ames stood to lose everything if word got out that her husband had a gambling addiction."

Jennie hugged her knees and drew in a deep breath of crisp ocean air. "I feel so bad for that family."

"Me too. What's gonna happen to Micky now that his mom's gone?"

"His aunt is taking him back to Portland with her in the morning."

"That's good." Ryan reached for Jennie's hand and wove his fingers through hers. "I talked to Todd today."

"And . . ."

"He apologized for lying to me."

"Good—so are you friends again?"

"Yeah. I just wish we could prove he didn't kill Jessica. He still swears he didn't go back to talk to her that night. And if he's telling the truth, that means Mayor Ames was lying, or someone stole Todd's car, or it was someone with a car like Todd's."

"That's unlikely—there aren't that many powder blue '57 Chevies around."

"True. And after what you told me about Jessica's

parents, I'll bet anything the mayor was lying—maybe to protect his wife."

"And his reputation." Jennie gave Ryan's hand a reassuring squeeze. "Anyway, I wouldn't worry too much about Todd. The mayor's actions will discredit him and cast doubt on his testimony. I have a feeling Todd will be acquitted."

"I hope so." A wide grin lit up his eyes. "Hey, I have a surprise for you."

"What?"

"Tomorrow you and I are going whale watching."

"You're kidding."

"Nope. You know I've been helping Greg out with his business. . . ."

Jenny nodded.

"Well, Greg said I was ready to take a boat out alone. I can't take a tour yet, but he said it would be okay to bring you."

Jennie arched an eyebrow. "Taking a lot for granted, aren't you?"

"What do you mean?"

Jennie's smile crept through despite her determination to keep a straight face. "I mean, what if I don't want to go?" She did, of course. She just didn't want Ryan making plans without asking.

"Oh, I get it." He chuckled and wrapped an arm around her neck and drew her close, forehead to forehead, nose to nose. "Let me rephrase that. How'd you like to go whale watching with me tomorrow?"

Jennie held her breath and closed her eyes, stilling the butterflies in her stomach. "I'd like that very much."

When Jennie arrived back at the house, she and Gram drove into Lincoln City where they planned to shop for school clothes and meet J.B. for dinner. Since J.B. had some business in town, they'd asked Ryan to watch Nick.

Gram listened with interest as Jennie filled her in on the letter from the Soaring Eagle Casino and her run-in with Mari.

"I'm not sure I even want to speculate as to who did what. This has turned into a muddy mess, and I'm glad I don't have to clean it up."

"Me too," Jennie said with less conviction than she felt. While she'd have preferred to spend more time talking about possible suspects, Gram clearly didn't.

Gram picked up an envelope from the console beside her and handed it to Jennie.

"I talked to Charlie today, and he said to give you this."

Inside was a thank-you card and a check for $350. "Wow! I didn't expect this much."

"Charlie said he was giving you a bonus for a job well done."

"Great timing," Jennie said, sticking it in her handbag. "I know just how to spend it."

———

By the time they'd finished shopping, over $200 of her check had been spent. At six, they trudged back to the car and stashed shoes, jeans, shirts, underwear, and three new mysteries in the trunk.

Fifteen minutes later they walked into the Kyllos Restaurant at "D" River. J.B. had already been seated, but he wasn't alone. Hawk and Blake Elan were sitting with him. Jennie felt a moment's panic. Was J.B. into gambling too? The panic subsided when she remembered Hawk was FBI.

Once Gram and Jennie had been seated, J.B. made the introductions. Jennie was surprised at J.B.'s openness as he told her Hawk's real name was actually John Elan. John didn't fit him—Hawk did. Jennie thought it odd that Hawk and J.B. *and* Hawk's uncle would be together—unless they'd completed the investigation and Hawk was no longer under cover. Maybe now that the mayor was dead, he didn't need to pretend.

"So how are you, Jennie?" Hawk asked. "Heard about your run-in with Mrs. Ames."

"I'm okay." Even knowing he was an agent didn't calm the uneasiness she felt around him. "Have you heard how she is?"

"Not real great. Looks like she may be doing time."

"For what?"

"Killing her husband."

Jennie nearly choked on her ice water. "You really think Mrs. Ames killed him?"

Gram frowned. "I thought his death was accidental."

"So did we until we found a vial of the concentrated shellfish toxin in Mrs. Ames' closet."

Gram shook out her napkin. "Not something most people have lying around the house, is it?"

"No, it isn't. But a shellfish laboratory up north had reported a break-in last week. A couple of vials of the stuff were missing."

Even though Jennie had narrowly missed being stabbed by the woman, she had a hard time seeing Mari Ames as a cold-blooded killer and said as much. "Maybe the toxin was planted." Everyone's gaze shifted to her. She squirmed under their scrutiny and felt her cheeks grow hot.

Hawk leveled his penetrating dark gaze on her as if to say, *Who do you think you are to have an opinion?*

"Tell us what you're thinking, lass." J.B.'s serious response to her question gave her courage to go on.

"Mrs. Ames was trying to hide the mayor's problem. Murdering him would have called everyone's attention to their family. I mean—why go to all the trouble of hiding it, then commit murder?"

"You have a point," Hawk said, "but we weren't supposed to find out."

"Then why would she stash the toxin at her house—and why didn't the police find it before?"

He shrugged. "She's not too rational—you've seen that for yourself. We have an even stronger motive than the gambling. Mrs. Ames blames her husband for Jessica's death. We figured his daughter knew about the gambling and confronted him. Jessica no doubt threatened to go public. He may have felt he needed to silence her."

"Do you have children, Hawk?" Gram asked.

"No, ma'am."

"I thought so. Most parents wouldn't dream of hurting their children. Some do, of course, but to kill a child deliberately . . ." She shook her head. "I can't imagine Mari or Forrest doing that. They adored Jessica."

"That may be, Mrs. Bradley, but Mayor Ames had a lot to lose, and people with addictions don't always make rational decisions."

Jennie's heart hurt. How could one family get so messed up? She focused on her menu, wishing she could forget the entire ordeal. If Hawk was right, it would be over. Todd would be vindicated. Mrs. Ames would be arrested. Unfortunately, it didn't *feel* over.

Hawk paused when the waiter came to take their orders then went on. "Looks like we were right about the gambling initiative, J.B. While Ames was coming out against the gambling initiative publically, privately he had big-time ties in Vegas. Seems he made a deal with a number of casino owners to back his venture. And I do mean *his* venture. He was all set to build the biggest casino on the West Coast."

Blake shook his head. "The man was a phony through and through. If it hadn't been for his gambling addiction, he might have pulled it off."

"Did you determine whether he had any local backers?" J.B. asked.

"I'm still checking out the possibility," Hawk responded. "With the complexity of the case, he must have had at least one person working with him."

"He did," Jennie said. "During the benefit he was in his office talking to someone. I told Joe about it. One guy said something about things being under control. The other guy—I think it must have been the mayor—was worried about Charlie finding out. They must have been planning something because the other guy said there wouldn't be any slip-ups."

Hawk glanced at J.B. "Joe didn't say anything to me about that." His already small eyes turned to narrow slits. "Must have been when Ames sent me to get some papers he'd left in his office at city hall. I was gone fifteen minutes—max."

"Whoever it was," Jennie said, "must have been the one who worked Charlie over and stole the campaign funds."

Blake leaned back when the waiter brought his coffee. "Personally, I think you should check out the sheriff. We had one go bad on us a while back—maybe we have another crook in the bunch. While you're at it you might want to have a crack at Senator Baker. You know what they say about power corrupting."

Jennie thought maybe Hawk should investigate his uncle, too, but didn't say so.

Hawk tossed J.B. an apologetic glance before answering. "With all due respect, uncle, we've investigated both men and there's no reason to suspect them. However, I intend to keep an open mind."

"See that you do, nephew, see that you do." Blake Elan's regal posture and sincere tone nearly erased Jennie's suspicion of him.

By the time their dinners arrived, Jennie felt thoroughly confused. There were too many possible answers to the questions that continued to haunt her, and none of them quite fit. Who killed Jessica? And why? Like Gram, Jennie had a hard time thinking of any parent being bad enough or desperate enough to kill their own child. "I keep trying to make sense of it. I guess I can go along with Mayor Ames killing Jessica to keep her quiet, but I just can't see Mrs. Ames killing her husband."

Gram squeezed Jennie's shoulder. "It is hard to imagine, but we need to remember Mari has suffered a great deal of trauma."

"Not only that, Jennie," Hawk said, "she had means and opportunity. According to Annie Costello, Mrs. Ames oversaw the catering operation and was in and out of the kitchen several times. Annie made two batches of cioppino. The second had no trace of the toxin. Mrs. Ames was there when Annie made the first batch, but not when she made the second."

"Another consideration," Blake added, "is that despite Mrs. Ames' being so upset about the debt, she has plenty of money to cover it."

"I'm afraid they may be right," J.B. added. "Mrs. Ames is a wealthy woman in her own right. She held a million-dollar life insurance policy on her husband. If she discovered he'd been lying and suspected him of killing her daughter, I believe she might consider getting rid of him."

Jennie kept silent for the rest of the meal. Earlier Gram had called the case a muddy mess. So true. *Sometimes,* she reminded herself, *when the waters are too churned up, it helps to leave them alone until they clear.* That's exactly what she would do. Tomorrow she'd forget all about the murders and the gambling initiative and everyone involved and concentrate on whale watching and hanging out with Ryan.

18

Heaven. Pure heaven. Seagulls flew overhead squawking for handouts. Jennie complied by tossing out pieces of bread she'd brought from Gram's. The sun poured down warm and bright. Jennie sat on the bow of the fishing trawler, letting the wind whip through her hair, pulling it free from its braid. Her thoughts drifted back to Dolphin Island off the coast of Florida and the dolphins she'd grown to love. Gram had taken her there for her sixteenth birthday. It seemed so long ago, but it was only a summer away.

Out here on the ocean she was far removed from Jessica Ames and her father. Far away from whoever had murdered them. At least that had been her plan. But thoughts of Jessica buffeted her mind again and again as forcefully as the wind.

"Jennie, look! Off the starboard side!"

"I see them." Jennie tucked her thoughts away and focused on the performance of two gray whales pausing in their southern migration to play. Well, maybe not to play. They would often use the rocks as cleaning posts to rid themselves of barnacles and other sea life that hitched a ride. But it sure looked like play. Whales, like dolphins, seemed to enjoy performing for the people who took the time to watch. The pair breaching not fifty feet from the boat were no exception.

A huge gray whale arched its body as it came up for air. A high stream of water escaped from its blow hole and dissipated. It dove deep, lifting its tail in a wave. His companion followed suit. Just as suddenly as they appeared, they were gone again, leaving no trace of their existence.

"Keep watching. Maybe they'll surface again." Ryan slipped an arm over Jennie's shoulders. "It's great seeing them up this close."

"I love it. Oh . . ." Jennie's heart skidded to a stop when one of the whales rose not ten feet away from them, blew, then rolled, disappearing once more.

"Hold on!" Ryan grabbed for the railing as the boat teetered in the big mammal's wake. "Whoa. That guy has to be at least fifty feet long."

Jennie vacillated between admiration and fear. If the whales got too careless they could turn their boat into driftwood. "I didn't know they'd come this close."

"Awesome, huh?" Ryan shouted to be heard over the engines. He needn't have bothered. The engines sputtered and died.

Back at the helm, Ryan twisted the key. The motor made a sick attempt to start.

"Maybe you're out of fuel," Jennie suggested.

"I'm not out of fuel. I filled up before we came out." Ryan tried the key again—nothing.

"The fuel gauge is on empty."

Ryan's chilly blue gaze met hers. "I am not out of fuel. It probably registers empty when the engine is off."

"Okay, no need to get huffy. I'm just trying to help."

"Well, don't, okay? Just go sit somewhere. I'll figure it out."

Jennie bit into her lower lip, advising herself to keep her mouth shut. He'd figure it out eventually.

Leaving Ryan to mutter to himself, Jennie went downstairs to the galley to get a drink and something to snack on. She rummaged through the small refrigerator Ryan said he'd stocked the day before. She found a couple cans of soda, a chunk of furry gray-green cheese, and a couple of unmarked plastic containers of who knew what. "Give me a break, Johnson," she muttered. "If this is your idea of—"

Jennie's grumbling turned into a high-pitched yelp when the boat pitched and threw her to the floor. The contents of the refrigerator tumbled out on top of her. One of the soda cans split as it hit the floor, spraying its foamy contents into her face. After trying unsuccessfully to plug the leak, Jennie scrambled to her feet and tossed the can into the sink, then grabbed a towel and began mopping it up.

So much for a fun, relaxing day with Ryan.

She put the other two cans back on the shelf and was wiping root beer off one of the containers when she heard another boat approach. Ryan must have radioed for help. Maybe the Coast Guard or another whale watcher.

Well, good. At least they'd be rescued. Not that she'd been all that worried. She wasn't in too much of a hurry to go topside. Ryan wouldn't appreciate her assistance anyway. Apparently he felt taking care of downed vessels was a guy thing.

She wiped off the opaque white plastic container and froze. The message had been facing away from her earlier. There was no fancy scientific name, no professional label. Someone had drawn a crude skull and crossbones beneath the words, *bivalve shellfish toxin*.

Jennie pushed the container back into the fridge, trying to make some sense of its presence. Who had put it there and why? Greg? Annie? Both had access to the boat. Or maybe it was another case of planted evidence. This was Greg's boat. He'd been at the benefit helping Annie. One way or another she had to let the authorities know about the toxin.

She latched the fridge and hurried up the stairs, finding Ryan at the bridge, steering. The engines were still dead. The boat she'd heard was pulling away. "What's going on?" Jennie put her hand on his shoulder.

"Greg's giving us a tow." He glanced at her, his face just short of crimson. "There's a leak in one of the fuel lines."

Jennie watched the cable between the two boats grow taut. She didn't like the idea of Greg towing them, but there wasn't much she could do about it now. She sighed and gave Ryan's shoulder a squeeze. "I'm not sure how to tell you this, but something really strange is going on." She explained what she'd found in the galley.

Ryan frowned. His Adam's apple shifted up and down. "I messed up, Jennie. I was supposed to take the *Lucy S*, not the *Linda Sue*. They look so much alike I just grabbed the first one."

"That explains the lack of food in the galley." Jennie climbed into the passenger seat. "So you want to venture a guess as to why a container of the toxin is on Greg's boat?"

"I don't have a clue. You're the detective. You tell me."

"Maybe Greg is the killer. Maybe he took Todd's car that night and went to talk to Jessica. He was at the benefit helping Annie. He could have been the guy in the mayor's office."

"That would mean he was working for the mayor. Greg wouldn't do that. Besides, why would he kill him? Or Jessica?"

"I don't know. Revenge. To get back at Mayor Ames for what happened to his dad."

Ryan shook his head. "His dad died in a logging accident. Ames owned the company. You don't kill a guy for that."

So that was the connection. "What about Annie? She blamed Mayor Ames for the accident too."

"No way. After all this time? It's like someone is deliberately trying to manufacture evidence on everybody involved. First Todd, then Mrs. Ames. Maybe this whole thing with Mayor Ames was made up too. Maybe he really didn't have a problem with gambling."

"Now that makes no sense at all." Jennie fixed her gaze on the boat towing them. They were picking up speed now and would soon be in Bay Village. She'd get off the boat, thank Greg for the tow, pretend she hadn't found anything, then walk straight to the sheriff's office.

A thread of fear wove itself around Jennie's heart. Something wasn't right. Glancing at her watch, then at the sun behind them, Jennie grabbed Ryan's arm. "What time do you have?"

"Ten. Why?"

"That's what I've got."

"Why all this interest in time? You have an appointment or something?"

"No." Her response came in a pant. "The sun is behind us."

"So?"

"Ryan, don't you see? If we were being towed *in*, the sun would be in *front* of us. Greg is pulling us farther out to sea."

Ryan dragged his hands down his face. "Okay. Let's not panic. There's got to be a reason."

"Right. He's going to kill us."

"No. He wouldn't do that. He's a friend, Jennie."

"You took the wrong boat. Maybe he thinks we saw the toxin. He came on board while I was in the galley, didn't he?"

Ryan closed his eyes and leaned forward, thumping his forehead on the wheel. "Yeah. He wanted to know where you were. When I told him, he got even madder. Told me to hook up the cable so he could tow us in."

"He did it. He killed Mayor Ames."

"Okay, maybe you're right about that too. But it'll be okay. We'll make it. I'll radio for help." While Ryan radioed, Jennie watched Greg lean over something on the back of his boat.

After several tries, Ryan slammed his hand on the console. "The radio's dead. Greg must have disconnected the wires while I was attaching the tow line. Oh, Jen, I'm so sorry."

Jennie slipped off her chair and stepped into Ryan's arms. "Don't give up. We'll make it."

They pitched forward as the boat slowed. "Look!" Ryan grabbed the console to steady himself. "He's lost the tow line. We're drifting again."

"This is bizarre."

Greg had turned around and was coming toward them.

Ryan breathed a deep sigh and hugged her. "It's okay. Maybe the line broke. He's not deserting us."

"He was pulling us out to sea."

"Jennie, relax, will you? I'm sure he has a good explanation."

Greg pulled up alongside the disabled craft and jumped aboard.

"What happened?" Ryan asked. "Why were we headed out?"

"You don't want to know." Greg, knees bent for balance, reminded Jennie of a gorilla. He reached in the pocket of his vest and pulled out a gun.

When confronted with danger, yell for help and run. That's what the self-defense manuals say. Unfortunately, Jennie had nowhere to run. And the only people who would hear her screams would be Ryan and the man holding the gun. *So now what? Okay, McGrady*, she told herself. *Just stay calm and look for a way out.*

"W-what are you going to do to us?" Ryan stammered.

"Believe me, Ryan, I wish I didn't have to hurt you. If you'd taken the *Lucy S* . . ." His gaze swept to Jennie. "You found it, didn't you?"

Jennie didn't answer him. "Killing us would be a big mistake, Greg. Since we went out on your boat, the sheriff will be able to tie you to our deaths."

"Don't count on it. All the authorities will know is that you took the wrong boat. This one needed repairs and had a leak in the fuel line. Unfortunately, it blew up with you two on board."

Jennie gulped back the rising panic. She had to stay calm.

"Why did you kill the mayor?" Maybe if she could keep him talking.

"It's a long story."

"So tell it," Ryan insisted. "If you're going to kill us, at least tell us why."

Greg smirked. "Forrest Ames killed my father."

"I thought that was an accident."

"It didn't have to happen. Over and over the men pleaded with Ames to get new equipment, but he wouldn't spend a dime more than he had to. Used all the money to build his big fancy house and get himself set for when the business failed. The scum deserved to die."

Jennie remembered Greg's comment about people paying for their sins. "What about Jessica? Did she deserve to die too?"

He released a jagged sigh. "Yeah. As a matter of fact she did. She broke Todd's heart. He almost killed himself because of her."

"What are you talking about?" Ryan took another step toward him.

Greg waved the gun at them, warning them to stay put. "That night he came home. I heard him drive up, but when he didn't come in, I went out to the garage. He was sitting in his car with the motor running—crying. Todd hadn't cried since our dad died. I took him in and made sure he was okay, then drove over to talk to Jessica. The ring Todd had given her was on the seat. I wanted to shove it down her throat."

Revenge. Jennie pressed back against Ryan. "I can understand why you'd be upset, but—"

"No! No you can't. I'm sick of people saying they understand. You can't possibly know what it's like to—" Greg's dark eyes turned to pebbles. "You're trying to upset

145

me. Get me to make a mistake. That's not going to happen."

Ryan stepped in front of Jennie. "You're right, Greg. I don't understand how you could kill Jessica in cold blood and let your brother go to jail for it."

Greg shook his head. "He'll get off. I hired a good criminal lawyer."

"With what? You said yourself business was bad."

"Let's just say I got all the money I need, thanks to Mayor Ames. He hired me to steal the funds from Charlie and rough him up a bit."

"Rough him up?" Jennie glared at him. "You nearly killed him."

"Yeah—why not? He was set to put Todd away. Now shut up and give me your life jackets."

"Why?" Jennie managed to talk past the lump in her throat.

"Why do you think?"

This was it. They really were going to die. Being this far out without a life jacket, they'd never make it. Maybe there were more on board, she reminded herself. If they had enough time she could get to them. *Oh, God, please help us.* Jennie and Ryan removed the orange jackets and tossed them on the floor in front of Greg. Greg scooped them up, then climbed back on board the other craft. Seconds later he pulled away. Jennie ran toward the back of the boat to the wooden box where life jackets were usually stored. She heard the gunshot about the same time a bullet tore into the deck in front of her.

Ryan grabbed her around the waist and dragged her back. "What are you trying to do, get yourself killed?"

She struggled against him. "Let me go. If I don't get the life jackets, we'll die anyway."

A gunshot rang out again, this time hitting the back of the boat.

"He's trying to blow us up!" Ryan let her go. "We don't have a chance."

"Yes we do. We can jump clear of the boat." Jennie clambered to the starboard side and grabbed the railing. "Who knows how many shots it'll take to—"

Greg fired again. A split second later an explosion ripped the boat apart.

19

The force of the explosion threw Jennie into the air. As though caught up in a slow-motion scene, she flew some twenty feet, then sliced into the water. Within seconds the bone-chilling cold and the lack of oxygen shocked her into action. Jennie kicked and crawled upward, gasping as she surfaced.

Something dragged her back. Treading water, she kicked off her shoes, then pulled off her heavy sweat shirt to make herself more buoyant. Otherwise swimming or even treading water would tire her out too quickly.

Jennie glanced around. Panic threatened to pull her under again. High swells lifted her up, then down, making it almost impossible to see anything but water. When the water lifted her, she caught sight of Greg's trawler heading out to sea. He hadn't stuck around to make sure they were dead. But then why would he? The boat had been blown to pieces, and they were too far off shore to swim.

She spent the next precious minutes pleading with God and looking for Ryan, swimming in a circle—or what she thought was a circle, but could find no trace of him in the debris floating around her. She was tiring. Jennie looked for a flotation device—a life jacket or board—anything that would hold her. She could tread water for another fifteen minutes—maybe. But the water was cold, and she could already feel her body temperature dropping. Jennie thought she spotted a life jacket in the distance, but by the time she could get to the spot she thought she'd seen it, it had disappeared.

Several minutes passed before Jennie found a piece of wood big enough to hold her. She hoisted herself on it. Pink salt water dripped onto the white plank. It was then she felt the sting of salt on her cheek and noticed a cut on her hand.

Gathering up her T-shirt, Jennie wrung out the water and pressed it to the wound on her cheek. The board she'd managed to secure was about the size of a surf board—maybe wider. She lay flat on her stomach and continued to paddle around the debris, hoping, praying Ryan had made it out alive.

Half an hour later her arms ached from paddling. Her head hurt. Jennie didn't want to give up, but her body refused to cooperate. She didn't want to think of Ryan drowning so she tried not to think at all. Jennie drew her arms out of the water and rested her head on them. The sun had nearly dried her shirt and pants and taken the edge off the cold.

———

Sometime later Jennie awakened to the sounds of seagulls cawing and the flapping of wings. One gull, then two, landed on her back and pecked at her head.

"Ouch!" She covered her head with one arm and waved them off with the other. Her narrow bed shifted, spilling her into the water. She mounted the board again and tried to orient herself. According to her watch it was noon. The sun would be straight up. "Okay, God, which way do I go?" Jennie scanned the horizon as best she could. She spotted a boat in the distance and started to wave.

"You're losing it, McGrady. A lot of good waving will do. No way they can see you from that distance." She couldn't tell which direction the boat was headed. And she didn't know if she'd be moving toward shore or out to sea. Since it was the only option available at the moment, Jennie dipped in one arm, then the other, and headed toward the vessel.

She didn't make it. The boat soon disappeared. Her feet and forearms had grown numb, her lips parched and dry. The sun had come out again, renewing her hopes, then crushing them again when she realized how low in the sky it hung. It would set soon, leaving her exposed and vulnerable.

Don't give up. Keep moving. Come on, you can make it.

"I can't," Jennie argued with the almost audible voice. "I'm too tired, and I don't know which way to go."

The sun will guide you.

Jennie lifted her head expecting to see an angel or that bright light she'd heard about from people with near-death experiences. She did see light—a blinding light on the horizon. *The sun.* Jennie could almost feel the adrenalin pump through her veins at the thought. Spinning herself around, Jennie kept the sun behind her and headed toward the shore. She would make it home or die trying.

———

In the distance Jennie heard a strange thumping sound. A boat? Maybe. At the moment, she was too exhausted to care. She tried to loosen her grip on the board so she could brush her hair from her face. Her fingers wouldn't move. She had no idea how far she'd come, only that she had no strength left. When the swells moved her just right, she thought she could see the shoreline and a light or two flickering in the distance. Jennie opened her eyes, then closed them again.

The sound grew louder. A powerful wind buffeted her around and sent her already precarious craft to spinning. Jennie felt the board slip away from her. "No, don't. I'll drown. I . . ."

"Hey, take it easy," someone shouted. "I've got you."

Arms and legs flailing, Jennie struggled to free herself

from whoever was holding her. *Holding her?* Jennie's eyes flew open. A man in a neon orange survival suit was hanging from a cable attached to a Coast Guard helicopter. Another had grabbed her from behind and had a vise grip around her waist.

Jennie stopped struggling. "Where . . . when?"

"Don't try to talk. Just work with us, and we'll have you out of here in no time. I'm hooking a belt around your chest." Then he attached her to the cable and passed her on to his partner. Jennie sent a dozen silent thank-yous to God and to her rescuers on the way up.

Minutes later, wrapped in blankets and drinking hot cocoa, Jennie sat in the helicopter telling her rescuers about Greg Kopelund and his attempt to murder her and Ryan. "Please tell me you found Ryan. I looked for a long time, but . . ."

The guy who'd hauled her out of the water shook his head. No, they hadn't found Ryan and were getting ready to go in when the pilot spotted her.

"We need to keep looking. If I made it, maybe he did too."

"We'll go out again tomorrow at daybreak." The message written on their faces offered little hope.

"How did you know to look for us?"

"Got a call from your grandmother saying you hadn't come in. The boat was still out, and when we couldn't get a radio response we headed out. Been looking for you since around three."

The Coast Guard chopper landed at the base where an ambulance waited to transport her to the hospital. Gram was there when she arrived. Once settled in the emergency room, Jennie sat up on the stretcher.

"Oh, Gram—it was awful . . . and Ryan . . ." The words caught in her throat.

"There, there." Gram wrapped Jennie in her arms and patted her back. "Don't try to talk, just rest. Joe called before you came in to tell us he'd picked up Greg. He'll be by later to get your statement."

After being warmed, poked, and prodded, the ER doctor stitched up the gash on Jennie's jaw and sent her home. She felt numb—like somebody else was occupying her body— moving and talking while she watched from a distance, trying to make some sense of it all.

J.B. had driven to his office in Portland earlier in the day and would be flying to Las Vegas with Hawk to round up the mayor's backers and put an end to the casino sham. Hopefully it would put an end to the gambling initiative as well.

She spent what was left of the day in a fog—sitting mindlessly in front of the TV with Nick, watching Nick play catch with Bernie, and finally at eight-thirty putting Nick to bed.

Exhausted, but too upset to sleep, Jennie stumbled downstairs and joined Gram in the kitchen.

"I made you some chicken noodle soup," Gram said. "When you're done with that I suggest you go to bed."

Jennie shook her head. "How can I sleep knowing Ryan's out there somewhere? I should see how his parents are doing."

"You need to eat . . . and rest." Gram wrapped an arm around Jennie's shoulder.

"What about Joe? He'll need my statement."

"He can see you tomorrow."

"I'll never be able to sleep. Not with Ryan missing."

"You will."

After Jennie had eaten, Gram escorted her up the stairs. Dutifully, Jennie crawled into bed.

Treating her like she might a small child, Gram tucked her in. "Would you like me to pray with you?"

Jennie nodded, then blinked back a landslide of tears while Gram thanked God for bringing Jennie home safely, then asked Him to bring Ryan home as well.

"Gram." Jennie grasped her grandmother's hand. "Do you think he'll make it?"

Gram pressed her lips together. "I honestly don't know, darling. Miracles can happen. After all, they found you."

Jennie tried to sleep but after an hour of tossing gave up. Over and over the explosion rocked her. Thoughts of Ryan injured and drowning and calling for help haunted her. Finally, Jennie got up, wrapped an afghan around her shoulders, and went to the window. The moon was full and bright, cutting a swath of white across the black sea.

"Ryan Johnson," she whispered, looking out at the horizon, "you'd better not die out there. I'll never forgive you. . . ." The tears came again, and this time Jennie didn't try to stop them. There was nothing she could do now except pray and wait.

———

The next morning Joe stopped by as they were finishing breakfast. "How are you doing, Jennie?" A dark shadow lined his jaw.

"Better. Thanks." Even though every muscle in her body hurt, she did feel better. She'd managed to convince herself that Ryan had survived and that the Coast Guard would find him.

"Would you like something to eat?" Gram set a plate of muffins on the table next to a pitcher of orange juice.

"Thought you'd never ask." Joe settled into the chair next to Jennie. "You up to telling me what happened?"

She nodded and gave him a detailed sketch of Greg's confession. "He must have really hated Mayor Ames."

"Revenge runs deep in some folks, Jennie. All that hate was bound to come out sooner or later."

"I still don't understand how it all fits together." Gram set her teacup on the table and sat down.

Joe smeared butter on his muffin. "It gets kind of complicated. Apparently it all boils down to revenge. Greg blamed Mayor Ames for his father's death and never got over it. When Jessica broke up with Todd, the anger flared up again. He went to see Jessica and apparently fought with her."

"It still seems odd that he'd let Todd take the blame."

"I don't think Greg ever meant for Todd to be convicted. More than likely he was playing out all his cards first. Somehow, maybe from Todd or Jessica, Greg found out about the mayor's gambling and started blackmailing him. He apparently planned to get as much money as possible out of the deal, then kill the mayor off."

"Why would Forrest go along with Greg?" Gram asked. "It seems a rather unlikely alliance."

"The mayor probably thought it was better to have Greg working *for* him rather than against him. I have a hunch he was ready to do anything to protect his name at that point. By the way, Jennie," Joe added, "it was Greg you heard in the mayor's office the night of the benefit. Annie told me today she'd seen Greg go in."

"Why didn't she say something earlier?" Jennie stood and began gathering dishes.

"Didn't think it mattered." The sad look in Joe's eyes showed disappointment.

"You think she might be involved too?"

Joe's head came up. "No. Not at all. She volunteered the information as soon as she heard we'd arrested him. She's pretty upset about the whole thing. Still can't believe Greg's capable of murder."

"I guess I can understand that," Gram said. "It's difficult to believe a family member could be involved in any crime— let alone murder."

They talked more about the case—at least Gram and Joe did. Jennie's mind traveled back to the ocean and the rescue efforts. *Please let them find Ryan, God. Please. I don't want him to die.*

154

20

"He's alive," Jennie reassured herself as well as Ryan's mother. Gram and Jennie had gone over to the Johnson house to offer comfort, coffee, and chocolate chip cookies. "He knows survival skills, and he knows the ocean."

Mrs. Johnson sipped at the amaretto-flavored coffee Gram had made. "I keep telling myself that. But we have to face facts. Every minute that goes by lessens his chances." She gave Jennie a vacant look.

Jennie pinched her lips together. She'd break down and cry again if she sat there much longer.

Gram touched Jennie's hand and as if reading her mind said, "You look like you could use some fresh air. Why don't we all take a walk?"

After rounding up Nick and Bernie, the five of them hiked over to Fogarty Creek State Park and wandered along the beach. Jennie jogged ahead with Nick and Bernie. Gram did much better at comforting people than Jennie did. And Mrs. Johnson needed a lot of comforting. What Jennie needed was to find Ryan. Up the beach she noticed a large form. A body? She left Nick to draw pictures in the sand and ran on ahead.

No, don't even think it, McGrady. It's just a clump of seaweed. It has to be. But it wasn't seaweed. It was a dead seal.

"Oh . . ." Jennie covered her eyes and ran, dropping to her knees a short distance away. "It isn't fair, God. It just isn't fair. Why Ryan? Why couldn't you have taken me instead?"

After a few seconds, Jennie scrambled to her feet again and ran back to the others. The last thing Mrs. Johnson needed to do was see that poor seal. Jennie told them she wasn't feeling well and insisted on going back to the house.

It was three-thirty by the time they got back. A familiar white Toyota sat in the driveway. Camilla was leaning against it, watching them. Jennie groaned inwardly. Camilla was the last person Jennie wanted to see.

"Hi." Camilla pushed away from the car and walked toward them. When she got closer, Jennie could see she'd been crying.

"I need to talk to you, Jennie."

Gram said she'd be upstairs taking a nap with Nick and left the two girls who loved Ryan Johnson alone. When Jennie drew closer she felt a sting of guilt. Camilla's eyes were as red and puffy as her own. Jennie sighed. "Come on inside."

"Actually, I was hoping you'd have a Coke with me in town. I . . . there's something I need to show you and . . . well, the truth is, I don't want to be here so close to where Ryan lives—lived."

"You had it right the first time. It's too soon to give up hope."

Camilla bit into her lower lip and nodded. "So will you come with me?"

"I guess." Jennie folded her long frame into the Toyota, and within a few minutes they were sitting at Charlie's place ordering drinks. Charlie chatted with them for a while about Greg, then excused himself to wait on customers.

"What did you want to talk to me about?" Jennie puzzled over Camilla's clandestine behavior. After all, the mystery was solved. And this was not the time to argue about who should claim Ryan as a boyfriend.

Camilla reached into her handbag and retrieved some

papers. "I wanted to show you these."

Jennie recognized them immediately. The pages from Jessica's diary. "Where did you get those?"

"I took them. I knew where she kept it and . . ." She looked away. "I shouldn't have done it, but when they arrested Todd I had to do something. I knew he'd never hurt Jessica. I thought she might have written something that would prove he didn't kill her."

Jennie scanned the notes. "Only it implicates him."

I broke up with Todd tonight, Jessica had written. *I know he hates me, but it's better this way.*

Now comes the hard part—talking to Dad. I hope he'll listen to me. Mom says I shouldn't say anything.

Sometimes I think it would be better if I could just end it. Here and now. It would be so easy.

Jessica used the rest of the page to write about what she might do and how she felt about her father's betrayal. Then on the next page wrote

I can't believe he'd do something like this. I'm going to talk to him tonight. It's late—almost midnight—but I need to know the truth . . . I hear a car . . . Oh no, he's back.

"I knew it would look bad for Todd," Camilla said.

"So you kept this and told everyone you thought she might have committed suicide."

"She was despondent. She'd been depressed for a long time."

"Well, now we know why. She knew about her father's gambling." Jennie folded the papers and handed them back.

"I think she was planning to commit suicide and that's why she broke up with Todd."

"Could be. But we'll never know that for sure."

"I suppose not." Camilla tucked the pages away. "I guess I should take these to the sheriff."

"That would be wise." Jennie took a sip of her Coke. "You heard about Greg?"

Camilla nodded. "Todd is devastated. He was afraid Greg might have killed her when the mayor insisted he'd seen Todd's car. He convinced himself that Mayor Ames was lying and trying to pin the blame on him. But when he saw the ring, he knew Greg had done it. Greg was the only one who could have taken the ring from Todd's car."

"No wonder things were so confusing. Todd lied over and over—first to protect himself, then to protect his brother."

"The poor guy," Camilla said. "Now he's bearing the guilt of Ryan's . . ."

Death.

Jennie pushed her drink aside. "I really don't want to talk about it."

"Sure. Do you want to go back to your grandmother's?"

"No," she snapped. Jennie needed to get away.

Camilla's eyes had turned as gray as the sky and were threatening to rain.

"I . . . I'm sorry." Jennie stared at the table, then brought her gaze back to Camilla. "I shouldn't be getting mad at you. I was thinking about going for a walk. You can go along if you want."

"I'd like that."

They drove back to Gram's, where Camilla parked her car. Jennie led the way to the rocks, not stopping until she reached their cave. "Ryan and I used to come here all the time." She let her gaze drift over the churning water.

Camilla sat on the ledge, hugging her knees. "He really liked you, Jennie. He told me you were the nicest girl he's ever known—and the smartest too."

"I'll bet that made you feel good."

"It was okay. I like Ryan a lot. I probably always will. He's not only great looking, but he's, you know—kind."

"I know." Jennie closed her eyes, remembering their times together. She and Ryan had spent a lot of afternoons and evenings there, watching sunsets and moons and stars and solving the world's problems.

"It's beautiful out here," Camilla said.

Jennie opened her eyes. "Yeah. There's a cove down below—where we go to hunt for agates." Jennie didn't know why, but it suddenly seemed important to be there. "Want to see it?"

"Sure."

Even before she stepped onto the sand Jennie knew why she'd been compelled to come. Her heart slammed into overdrive. A body had been washed ashore, and this was no seal.

"Jennie, look! It's—"

"Ryan!" Jennie raced toward him, stopping just short of where he lay. So still and white. Forcing her feet to move, Jennie took a step closer and knelt beside him. She had to know. Placing a hand on his shoulder, she turned him over.

"Is he. . . ?"

Jennie felt for a pulse. "He's still alive."

"Thank God." Camilla rested a hand on Jennie's shoulder. "What can I do?"

"Go for help. I'll stay with him." Jennie took off her jacket and draped it over him, tucking it around his shoulders. She cradled his head in her lap, talking to him, urging him to hold on.

He opened his eyes once and tried to smile. "You came," he whispered.

"Shh. Of course I came."

It took less than an hour for the Coast Guard to rescue Ryan and airlift him to the hospital. Jennie refused to leave his side until he was safely resting on a stretcher in a cubicle in the emergency room and under a doctor's care.

The next morning Jennie rose early and hurried back to the hospital. She'd stayed until ten the night before and at Gram's insistence had gone home to sleep. Now with the light of morning, Jennie needed to make sure Ryan's rescue hadn't been a dream. His being alive was a miracle in more ways than one, and she could hardly believe it. Jennie parked in the nearly empty lot and jogged inside. She paused at the door to Ryan's room. Apparently she wasn't the only one interested in Ryan's miraculous rescue.

"I'm not kidding." Ryan's smile brightened the room— or so it seemed to Jennie. Of course the light could have come from the flashbulbs and television cameras. Ryan was being interviewed by all the major television news teams.

"You're telling us a whale brought you in?" The question came from a man holding a Channel 8 microphone.

"I know it sounds crazy, but it happened. I'd been blown free of the boat and was trying to get to the surface. I must have gotten disoriented and gone down instead of up. Anyway, I felt something huge brush past me. I was panicking by then. All of a sudden this whale came back under me and lifted me clean out of the water."

"And it brought you in to shore?"

"Close enough for me to swim. I made it to the cove but couldn't go any farther. Guess I must have broken my leg in the blast. I wasn't about to give up, though. I knew that sooner or later my girlfriend would come out to the rocks and find me. I just didn't think it would take her so long." Ryan reached for Jennie's hand.

Then the cameras focused on Jennie, who for the umpteenth time told her side of the story.

From the Ashes

Patricia H. Rushford

Books by Patricia Rushford

Young Adult Fiction

JENNIE MCGRADY MYSTERIES
1. *Too Many Secrets*
2. *Silent Witness*
3. *Pursued*
4. *Deceived*
5. *Without a Trace*
6. *Dying to Win*
7. *Betrayed*
8. *In Too Deep*
9. *Over the Edge*
10. *From the Ashes*

Adult Fiction

Morningsong

HELEN BRADLEY MYSTERIES
1. *Now I Lay Me Down to Sleep*
2. *Red Sky in Mourning*

From the Ashes

Patricia H. Rushford

BETHANY HOUSE PUBLISHERS
MINNEAPOLIS, MINNESOTA 55438

From the Ashes
Copyright © 1997
Patricia Rushford

Cover illustration by Sergio Giovine

Published by Bethany House Publishers
A Ministry of Bethany Fellowship, Inc.
11300 Hampshire Avenue South
Minneapolis, Minnesota 55438

Printed in the United States of America.

Library of Congress Cataloging-in-Publication Data

Rushford, Patricia H.
    From the ashes / by Patricia H. Rushford.
       p. cm. — (Jennie McGrady mystery ; #10)
    Summary: Jennie searches for the person responsible for
burning down the buildings that comprised her beloved
church and school.
    ISBN 1-55661-563-9 (pbk.)
    [1. Arson—Fiction. 2. Christian life—Fiction.
3. Mystery and detective stories.] I. Title. II. Series:
Rushford, Patricia H. Jennie McGrady mystery series ; 10.
PZ7.R8962Fr   1997
[Fic]—dc21   97-21124
                                              CIP
                                              AC

For Corisa Lester and Jennifer Anderson
and for friendships that last forever.

A special thanks to Evelyn Larkin and Birdie Etchison
as well as the Clark County Medical Examiner's office,
and Vancouver police and fire fighters—
especially to Don Phillips and Don McCoy
for lending a degree of authenticity to *From the Ashes*.

PATRICIA RUSHFORD is an award-winning writer, speaker, and teacher who has published numerous articles and over twenty-five books, including *What Kids Need Most in a Mom, The Jack and Jill Syndrome: Healing for Broken Children,* and *Have You Hugged Your Teenager Today?* She is a registered nurse and has a master's degree in counseling from Western Evangelical Seminary. She and her husband, Ron, live in Washington State and have two grown children, six grandchildren, and lots of nephews and nieces.

Pat has been reading mysteries for as long as she can remember and is delighted to be writing a series of her own. She is a member of Mystery Writers of America, Sisters in Crime, and several other writing organizations. She is also the co-director of Writer's Weekend at the Beach.

1

"Jennie, pull over. Hurry!" Lisa urged. "We have to let them get by."

"I'm trying." Jennie McGrady nosed her red Mustang into the right lane of traffic. Sirens howled and horns tooted through the hot and hazy September afternoon. Jennie's thoughts quickly turned from cooling off in their friends' swimming pool in Lake Oswego to merging with the dozens of other vehicles that clogged the four-lane boulevard.

A hard knot formed in the pit of her stomach as four red fire trucks and two ambulances whizzed by. The heavy traffic impeded their progress, and Jennie hoped they'd make it through in time to wherever they had to go.

"Oh wow. I wonder if that's where they're going. Looks like a huge fire." Lisa, Jennie's cousin and best friend, rolled down the window and leaned out to get a better view.

Jennie scanned the blue sky, her gaze coming to rest on billowing black clouds barely visible over the tree-covered hillside. She eased her car back into traffic, staying in the outside lane in case other emergency units needed by. They had gone only a short distance when sirens split the air again. Police cars this time.

"Oh no." Lisa covered her mouth, and panic filled her green eyes. "What if it's . . . no, I can't say it."

She didn't have to. The billowing fireball seemed to be

emerging from the woods near their church and school. "Trinity's not the only building over there," Jennie reminded her. "The fire looks close, but it could be farther away."

"I . . . I know. Let's go by the church to make sure."

Jennie nodded, turning onto Brentwood Road. The two-lane road meandered up the hill, past elegant homes snuggled between stately evergreens. She could smell the smoke that settled over them like a menacing fog. Neither of them spoke as they watched the fire now only a short distance in front of them. Just ahead, two police cars blocked the road, their lights flashing. Two uniformed officers were setting out flares and barricades. Several cars were parked on the street, and a crowd had already gathered.

"It is Trinity! I knew it." Lisa gripped the door handle.

"At least wait until I stop." Jennie jammed on the brakes, pulled over to the side of the road, and jumped out, tearing ahead of her cousin. The searing fire had bumped the heat up from 90 degrees to at least 110. Still she ran toward the flames, drawn by the choking fear that someone she knew might be hurt.

"Hey, you can't go in there!" one of the officers yelled.

Jennie dodged her and kept running.

"No!" Lisa screamed. "Let me go!"

Jennie glanced back. The other officer had Lisa pinned against him, her arms and legs flailing as she tried to escape. "Let me go!"

Jennie slowed. *What are you doing, McGrady? You just went through a police barricade.*

The officer chasing her caught Jennie by the arm and spun her around. "I told you to stop. You can't go in there."

"It's our school—and church. . . ." Jennie stammered. "I need to help."

The officer's anger subsided. "I'm sorry, but there's nothing you can do. We've got orders not to let anyone in there. It's too dangerous. You need to vacate the area."

Jennie looked at the officer for the first time, letting her gaze drift over the woman's frosted hair, into her dark brown eyes, and down to her badge and a name pin that read *B. Saunders*. Her bulletproof vest made her slender figure thicker, more masculine looking.

"Do . . . do you know how bad it is?" Jenny asked. "Or if anyone was hurt?"

Saunders shook her head. "I haven't heard. Just got orders to keep people out."

"Jennie!" Lisa cried. "Make him let go of me." Her face nearly matched the color of her red curls. Two more police vehicles had arrived.

Jennie frowned at the handcuffs he pulled out. "You're not going to arrest her, are you?"

"Come on, Calahan. Cut her some slack. It's their school," Saunders explained. "And church."

"That may be," Calahan growled, "but we've got our orders."

One of the new officers put a bullhorn to his mouth. "Listen up. We have orders to evacuate the area. Please move back."

An unmarked police car pulled in behind Jennie's Mustang. A familiar dark-haired detective emerged.

"Dad!" Jennie barreled toward him, stopping just short of flinging herself into his arms.

"What are you doing out here?" He didn't seem very happy to see her.

"Lisa and I were headed over to the Beaumonts' to swim. We saw the smoke and thought it might be . . ." A lump clogged her throat. She managed to say, "Dad, it's Trinity."

His arm went around her shoulders as he guided her back up to where Lisa was still being detained. "I know. I heard the call on my way home." Jason McGrady was a homicide detective for the Portland Police.

"Can't we do something?" Jennie asked.

"That's what I'm here to find out."

"Uncle Jason, I'm so glad to see you." Lisa brushed a hand across her eyes. "Make them let me go."

"What's going on?" Jason McGrady showed the officers his badge and introduced himself.

"You know these kids?" Calahan asked.

"Yes, this is my daughter, and the one you're holding is my niece."

"Better get them out of here. We've got a four-alarm fire up there. Doesn't look good."

"Come on, girls."

"Can't we stay here with you?" Jennie pleaded. "We won't get in the way."

"No. Not a good idea," Dad said. "I'll try to get some details and let you know as soon as I can."

Heading back to the car, Lisa mumbled something about Officer Calahan's bad manners. "Uncle Jason should have punched him out."

"Let it go, Lisa." Jennie glanced behind her at the still flashing lights. "They were only doing their jobs. We're lucky they didn't book us—especially you. It's against the law to hit a police officer. The poor guy's legs are going to be black-and-blue."

Lisa sniffed, wiping away the last traces of tears with the back of her hand. "I suppose you're right. I just feel so—so angry. I wanted to see for myself. I wanted to do something."

"Yeah. Me too. But like Dad said, we'll be more help if we let the fire department take care of things. That's the only—"

An explosion rocked the ground. Jennie staggered back.

"Get down!" Dad shouted.

Jennie dove to the asphalt, taking Lisa with her.

Seconds later the hillside sat in stony silence. Debris rained down on them. Jennie felt numb and disoriented. Her elbow burned where she'd scraped it on the rocks. The pungent smell of smoke nearly overpowered the tar from the road. Sharp pebbles bit into her bare legs and the side of her cheek.

Jennie rolled onto her back, sat up, and brushed herself off, staring at the blood oozing out a small cut on the back of her hand.

"This can't be happening." Lisa picked a patch of tar from her knee.

As if to argue the point, a piece of charred paper floated down, landing in front of them. Jennie picked it up. If she'd needed proof, there it was in black and white. Trinity's letterhead with half the page burned. The only words still legible was their mission statement: *A community of caring people serving you.* An embossed cross making up the "T" in Trinity was all that remained of the heading. Jennie swallowed hard, biting into her lower lip to keep it from trembling.

2

Dad and the other officers checked Jennie and Lisa for injuries. Dad dug a bandage out of the first-aid kit in his trunk and carefully placed it on Jennie's hand. "We need to get you two out of here. Can you drive, Jennie?"

Jennie nodded. When he opened the car door for her, she slid in. As if on automatic pilot, Jennie pulled the seat belt around her and buckled it. The scene was like something you might see in a war movie. Not something that happened in an elite neighborhood near Portland, Oregon.

Officer Saunders helped Lisa in on the passenger side, then reached across to buckle her in.

"Are you sure you can make it out of here all right?" Dad clasped Jennie's shoulder.

Jennie assured him she was fine. Fumbling with the keys, she managed to start the car, turn it around, and drive back down the hill.

"I don't know how you can be so calm." Lisa glanced at Jennie, her green eyes still registering shock.

Jennie blinked back a new rush of tears. *Calm?* She was anything but. She'd learned in her life-saving classes through the Red Cross that you can't panic. You do what you have to do, then when it's all over, you can fall apart. "Somebody has to stay calm. Since I'm driving it better be me."

Lisa leaned back against the seat and stared at her watch.

12

"I wonder if it's on television yet."

"Probably." Jennie's gaze lingered for a moment on her cousin. Lisa's copper curls hung in disarray as damp tendrils clung to her cheeks. Black smudges smeared her freckled face and her fluorescent lime T-shirt. She looked as bad as Jennie felt.

Jennie's hands were beginning to shake. *Hold on, Mc-Grady. Just a little farther.* Jennie turned right on Lakeview Drive, then made a left into the Beaumonts' driveway. The castle-like home sat on a hill, surrounded by a moat of luxurious green grass. At one time the Beaumont mansion had seemed foreboding and threatening. Now Jennie felt almost as comfortable there as in her own home.

"I wonder where Rafael and his dad are?" Lisa scanned the grounds, looking for the gardeners. She'd developed a crush on Rafael Hernandez, and they'd gone out a couple of times. Jennie had hoped to see them as well. Mr. Hernandez's brother, Philippe, and his son Carlos had only recently come to the U.S. on a work release. Philippe was the janitor at Trinity.

"I hope Philippe and Carlos are okay," Jennie voiced her thoughts. "They would have been there."

"Oh, Jennie, please don't say anything. I don't even want to think about who might be there."

Glancing back in the direction of the church, they could see the thick columns of smoke still pouring out. What had once been a beautiful complex with a blue-tiled roof was now an inferno. Names and faces of people she knew and cared about moved through Jennie's mind. She blocked them out. Like Lisa, she didn't want to think about the dozens of people who could have been inside. Jennie jerked her gaze back to the house, bringing the Mustang to a stop in the turnaround.

Allison and B.J. clamored down the steps, nearly tripping each other in the process. "Where have you been?"

"Did you get caught in the traffic?"

"Did you hear about the fire? What happened to you?"

"Hurry up—they're talking about it on the news."

Jennie didn't know who had asked what and let Lisa answer their questions. They hurried inside and up to Allison's room on the second floor, where Jennie plopped on the bed and sat cross-legged. "Shhh. They're putting someone in an ambulance."

"There must be a lot of injuries." B.J. scrambled onto the bed beside Jennie and punched the control to turn up the volume.

"Firefighters are still battling the blaze near Lake Oswego today. Residents reported the fire at four this afternoon. By the time firefighters arrived the blaze had consumed much of the facility. And just a few minutes ago we received word of an explosion. Authorities have evacuated the area. We have Brenda Ellis at the scene. Brenda, what can you tell us?"

The cameras shifted from the newsroom to a reporter standing near police cars. "It's utter chaos out here, Mike. As you can see, the fire is still burning out of control. I'm standing in front of the police barricade. No one is allowed in other than emergency vehicles. They are especially wary now because of the explosion."

"Any word on what caused that, Brenda?"

"Just speculation at this point, but one firefighter told me it may have been the oil furnace. I have the pastor of the church, Reverend Dave Wilson, here with me. Reverend, can you tell us what happened?"

The camera zoomed in on Pastor Dave. He brought a fist to his mouth and coughed. His face was smudged with black smoke. "We were having a board meeting this afternoon when the fire broke out. We're guessing it started in the basement—maybe the furnace. It all happened so fast we barely had time to escape."

Allison grabbed B.J.'s arm. "Oh, I just remembered. Daddy was at that meeting."

"I know." B.J. pulled her arm away. "Just listen."

"I understand there were at least a dozen people inside. Did everyone make it out all right?" Brenda asked.

"As far as I know. I'm not sure who all was in the building. It's been so chaotic. Michael—our youth director—went back in to check. I don't know if he made it out before the explosion."

Jennie's heart dropped to the pit of her stomach. "What about Michael? What happened to Michael?"

Michael Rhodes had come to Trinity a little over a year ago and had taken over the position of youth director that summer. He had been engaged to Jennie's mother and they'd almost married. At the time, Jennie's father was missing and presumed dead. Then Dad came home and changed everything. Jennie was thrilled to have her family back together but felt sad for Michael. She'd hated him at first, but she'd grown to love and admire him, as had all the kids at Trinity. He really cared about helping them.

Please, God, Jennie offered up a silent prayer. *Let Michael be okay*.

"Let's hope he did. We have no word yet on how many people have been injured." The reporter glanced at a note pad, then asked, "The complex not only houses a church but a school as well, isn't that right?"

"Yes, the church is the central-most part. It separates the grade school, K through eight, and the high school." Pastor Dave turned away and coughed against the back of his hand.

"Since this is a school day, do you know if there were any students or teachers left in the building?"

He shook his head. "Not for certain." His voice broke. "I'm sorry. This is difficult. It's almost too much to comprehend."

Brenda turned back to the camera. "As Pastor Wilson said, it is almost incomprehensible. No one here can be certain of anything, except that one of the largest and most diverse churches in the area is under siege. The loss to students and to church members as well as to the community will be devastating."

The camera pulled back, showing the newsroom and the live action scene.

"Brenda, is there any word yet on how the fire started?" the anchorman asked.

"No. It's too soon to tell, but because of the way the fire spread so rapidly, they suspect arson."

"Thanks, Brenda." He turned away from the monitor and looked into the camera. "This is the third church fire in the Portland area. Last June, arsonists destroyed the First Baptist Church in the Rosewood district. Two months before that, a fire gutted St. Mary's in Beaverton. No arrests have been made, and both cases are still under investigation. Authorities are not saying for certain, but there is speculation the three fires may be related."

Jennie fell back against the pillow. *Arson.* The ugly word seeped into her mind like the thick black smoke that was once again filling the television screen.

"Who'd want to burn down Trinity?" Allison pushed the mute button when the station went to a commercial break. Tears pooled in her eyes as she spoke.

"I can't believe it." Lisa paced to the window. "It's too awful."

Jennie couldn't believe it either but didn't say so. Allison and Lisa found it hard to envision anyone doing anything that bad. They didn't want to think people had a dark and evil side. Jennie had seen it once too often. B.J. had too. Which is why her response didn't surprise Jennie one bit.

"I'll bet it was a hate crime. Somebody who didn't like what Trinity was doing."

"What could anybody object to?" Lisa swung back around and leaned against the windowsill.

"There have been a lot of changes at Trinity since Michael came on staff, and even more with Pastor Cole." B.J. stared at the television screen as she spoke.

"That's dumb. Having a black pastor on staff is a good thing, isn't it?" Allison picked up a ruffled pink pillow and hugged it. "I like Pastor Cole. She's so . . . colorful."

"Of course it's good," B.J. answered, glancing at her sister, then back at the screen where another stupid commercial with talking pets advertised dog food. "So is the AIDS program and offering our sanctuary to minorities for their church services. But not everybody agrees. There are even people in our church who don't like what's going on. Dad said a couple of the board members were really miffed about some of the changes."

"Sure, but enough to burn down their own church?" Allison flipped the pillow aside and slumped deeper into her chair.

"Well," Lisa said, "if we're going to start listing suspects, we should add that neo-Nazi creep, Jared."

"You mean the guy who came to our youth group Saturday night?" Allison sniffed, then retrieved a box of tissues from her dresser.

"Yeah. Rafael says he's bad news. Jared hates everyone who isn't white."

With her eyes still closed, Jennie pictured Jared Reinhardt. Tall, thin, average-looking, with a pointy chin and chiseled features. What little hair he had was blond. He'd shaved it all off and it was just beginning to grow back.

Michael had been counseling Jared, helping him break free of a neo-Nazi group he'd hooked up with—at least that's what Jared had told her. Jennie felt sorry for him and had accepted an invitation to go with him for ice cream after the youth meeting. That had been two days ago. Though she wasn't interested in him as a boyfriend, he'd touched a cord in her. He seemed lost and scared—almost desperate. Of course, some of the kids at the meeting hadn't helped—Lisa

17

included. They'd been uncharacteristically rude. Now listening to Lisa, Jennie understood why.

"Good call, Lisa." B.J. shifted and nudged Jennie. "What do you think, McGrady?"

Jennie opened her eyes and looked from one to the other. She wasn't ready to defend Jared—at least not yet. But she wasn't ready to suspect him of arson either. "Why ask me?"

B.J. shrugged. "Thought you might have an opinion."

"I think it's too soon to speculate. You don't have any facts to back up your argument. We should wait for the fire department to tell us whether or not it's arson. Then we can talk about who might have done it."

"Jennie's right," Allison said. "Let's wait until we have all the facts before—"

"Hey." B.J. pointed to the television set and pressed the mute button. "They're talking about the fire again."

Cameras focused in on an ambulance. Paramedics were putting someone inside.

"Can you see who it is?" Lisa asked.

None of them could. The ambulance drove off and the reporter came back into view.

"Ambulance crews have taken five people to the hospital so far, but we don't yet know the extent of their injuries. Authorities are withholding names until relatives can be reached."

They pulled back, showing a wide-angle view, then an aerial shot. "The fire continues to burn, though firefighters say they should soon have the upper hand. And we do have some good news. Fire chief Ron Hughes tells me all of the people believed to have been in the building are now out. Back to you, Mike."

"Good news, indeed." In the next breath he went on to report about some senator who was under investigation for fraud.

Jennie let out the breath she'd been holding. Michael had

escaped and so had Philippe and Carlos. She just hoped no one had gone in undetected—that the students and teachers and volunteers were all safe.

The phone rang somewhere downstairs. "Allison, B.J.!" Mrs. Beaumont called. In the next moment she came through the door. "That was the hospital. Your father's been hurt."

Allison shot out of the chair. "Is he okay?"

"Where is he?" B.J. asked at the same time.

"He's suffered some burns and smoke inhalation, but they couldn't tell me how serious it is. He's at the University Hospital." Her gaze slipped quickly over each of them. "Do you girls want to come with me?"

"I do," Allison said.

"I'll come too." Lisa slipped an arm around Allison's shoulders. "For moral support—but, um, I'll need to wash up and borrow some clean clothes."

"B.J.? Jennie?"

B.J. had an odd expression on her face. "N-not right now. Someone should stay here."

"I'll stay too." Jennie wanted to go, to check on the victims and learn who they were and how badly they were injured. She had a feeling, however, that B.J. needed moral support too—maybe more than her sister.

Mrs. Beaumont tossed them a disapproving look but didn't argue. "All right. I'll call as soon as I learn anything."

B.J. didn't respond.

When they were gone, Jennie bounced off the bed. "I need a swim." She grabbed B.J.'s arm. "Come on. It'll make us both feel better."

"What makes you think there's anything wrong?"

"I know. You're worried sick about your dad. This whole thing is eating you up inside. Just like it is me."

"I . . . I should go, but I can't. Not yet." Fear shone in her eyes. Through a bizarre set of circumstances, B.J. hadn't

19

known her real father or her sister and stepmother until just a few months ago. B.J. and Allison's real mom had left Mr. Beaumont and Allison while she was newly pregnant with B.J. She never told Mr. Beaumont about the pregnancy and never told B.J. about her real father. When B.J.'s mom died, the birth papers revealed she had a family. With a chip on her shoulder as big as Texas, B.J. had reluctantly come to Portland to live with them. She was just now beginning to adjust.

"I'm not sure what's wrong. Maybe—" B.J. looked down at her hands. "I just found my dad, Jennie. I don't want to lose him."

Jennie nodded. "Let's swim a few laps to calm down. Then I'll drive us to the hospital."

If B.J. didn't need the exercise, Jennie did. Swimming laps helped her to relax and put things into perspective.

While she swam, Jennie wondered what would happen to the three hundred students who went to Trinity. They certainly wouldn't be able to use the building. Would they send them off to other schools or rent space somewhere? What would happen to their sports program and their weekly newspaper?

Gavin, the paper's editor, would be devastated. He loved journalism. Jennie wondered where he was. Knowing Gavin, he'd be right in the middle of things—probably on the scene, taking photos and interviewing people. Or he could have been at the school working on the paper. He often stayed after school. She imagined him trapped inside the inner room of the graphic-arts department, flames engulfing the walls, blowing out the windows.

Jennie hit the wall of the pool and came up for air, shaking the water from her hair and the images from her head. The phone rang. She pushed herself onto the deck. B.J. was still swimming and apparently hadn't heard the phone—or didn't want to.

Grabbing a towel, she hurried into the kitchen and answered with an out-of-breath hello.

"Jennie? Is that you?" Mom sounded upset, which meant she'd probably heard about the fire.

"Yeah. What's up?"

"The hospital just called me." She hesitated. "About Michael. They've been trying to find his family and . . . he still had me listed to call in an emergency."

"Is he—?"

"It's bad, Jennie," Mom interrupted. "They don't know if he's going to make it."

3

"The nurses felt someone should be with him," Susan McGrady said. "Since he doesn't have family close, I . . . I need to go. I'm leaving Nick at Kate's. Either you or your dad can pick him up on your way home."

Thinking of Nick brought another bout of pain. Jennie's five-year-old brother had just started kindergarten and loved it. There would be no school tomorrow or the next day or the next. . . . Jennie pushed the disappointing thought away and forced her attention back to her mother's request.

"You want me to get Nick right away?" Jennie explained about Mr. Beaumont being injured and her planned trip to the hospital with B.J.

"That's fine, honey. Go to the hospital first. Kate said he could stay as long as we need him to. I'll have your dad pick him up on his way home."

Jennie rubbed the goose bumps on her arms. "I'll see you at the hospital, then." She hung up the phone and leaned against the wall.

Jennie closed her eyes, feeling helpless and uncertain. Less than an hour ago she and Lisa were happy and comfortable and life was just about perfect. School had started after a long and exciting summer. She had looked forward to her classes and to settling down to her studies and taking care of Nick. Since she was part homeschooled, she did most of her work at home and came to school to check in with her teachers and to work on projects that could only be done at school.

Some of the kids thought the plan sounded complicated, but Jennie liked it. Mom had set up the program a few years ago so Jennie could care for Nick while Mom worked. Neither Jennie nor her mom wanted Nick in day care, so the homeschool/private school thing seemed ideal. Only now she might not have a school to go to.

As if the fire weren't enough, Jennie's intuition kicked in, giving her warning signals of even more trouble.

"Who was on the phone?" B.J. pulled the towel from her hair and flicked it at Jennie.

Jennie stepped aside. "Mom. Michael's been hurt really bad."

B.J. bit into her lower lip and wrapped the towel around her shoulders. "I guess it's time to go to the hospital."

Jennie's gaze dragged across the tiled floor, lingering on the drops of water still dripping from their wet suits. "Yeah. I guess it is."

Borrowing clean clothes—white cotton shorts and a tank top—from B.J., Jennie ducked into the outside bathroom and finished toweling off. She slipped bare feet into her white sandals, and after pulling her damp hair into a ponytail, she grabbed her book bag and waited for B.J. in the entry.

———

The St. John's Medical Center sat high atop what some Portland residents referred to as Pill Hill.

The waiting room, with so many familiar faces, reminded Jennie of the narthex after church with members milling around talking with one another. Only today there were no smiles, just dazed faces of people not quite ready to accept the tragedy as their own. Mrs. Talbot's husband had both elbows on his knees and his head buried in his hands. His wife was the school secretary. Jennie swallowed hard, thinking she should talk to him. She started toward him, but the receptionist called his name and he went to the desk.

"Our moms are over there." B.J. nudged her forward.

Susan McGrady was sitting next to Mrs. Beaumont against the far wall.

"I can't believe it's taking so long," Mrs. Beaumont said as Jennie and B.J. approached.

Both women looked up at the same time. Mom stood and gave Jennie a hug.

"Thanks for coming, B.J.," Mrs. Beaumont said, not getting up.

Mom hugged B.J. "Allison and Lisa are down in the cafeteria with Gavin. He was asking about you."

"Have you seen Michael yet?" Jennie asked.

"Just for a minute—to let him know we're here for him." Tears gathered in Mom's eyes and Jennie turned away. She wondered how Dad would feel about Mom's being so concerned for Michael. *He'd understand*, she told herself.

"Can I see my dad?" B.J. asked.

Mrs. Beaumont shook her head. "They're working on him right now. I only got to see him for a minute. He's doing okay. Said to tell you he loves you."

"It'll be a while before we can see any of them," Mom said. "Why don't you join Allison and Lisa. If we hear anything we'll have you paged. There's really not much point in all of us waiting here."

"Do you know who else was hurt?" Jennie shifted her gaze to the man still standing at the reception desk. "Mrs. Talbot?"

Mom nodded. "She was injured before the explosion. Um . . . something fell on her. She's one of the people Michael brought out."

"How bad?"

Mom shook her head. "They aren't telling us much yet.

24

Probably because they don't know for certain."

"Let's go." B.J. turned and nearly ran from the room, down the hall, and to the elevators they'd ridden up on.

Jennie leaned back against the wall next to the elevators. "I still can't believe any of this is happening."

"Yeah." B.J. punched the button for the ground floor. "I know what you mean. It's like a bad dream. Only we can't both be having it."

The elevator stopped and the doors opened. Having been there several times before, Jennie led the way down the corridor to the cafeteria.

They picked up drinks and headed for a table by the window, where Allison, Lisa, and Gavin were engrossed in conversation.

"Hey, Jennie." Gavin pulled out the chair beside him with one hand and pushed his glasses back against the bridge of his nose with the other. "What took you guys so long? Figured you'd be here long before this."

"I had other things to do." Jennie set her drink on the table and sat down.

"So were you there? Did you see it?" B.J. hooked a chair from another table and sat at the end between Allison and Jennie.

Gavin nodded. "I was in the journalism room working on this year's schedule, filling in deadlines for the newspaper and yearbook when I smelled smoke. I figured it was the furnace. Philippe still hasn't gotten the knack of working that thing. I thought I'd better check it out, but when I went to call, the line was dead. I didn't think too much about it 'cause there was no alarm. Figured if there was a fire there'd be an alarm, you know?"

Gavin paused to take a sip of his drink.

B.J. whistled. "No alarm. No phone. That's pretty weird."

"No kidding," Gavin agreed. "I went down to the office

to use the phone in there. Made it as far as the hall when . . . *Boom!* Good thing I got out of the room or I would have been dead meat."

"You weren't hurt?"

"A few bruises on my backside . . . guess I lucked out."

"I'm surprised you're here," Jennie said. "Thought for sure you'd be down there gathering all the facts."

"Couldn't. Soon as I got out of there, the EMTs checked me over and put me in an ambulance with some of the others that weren't as badly hurt." He shook his head. "It was the weirdest thing. The fire must have wiped out the electrical system."

"Or someone disabled it before setting the fire," Jennie murmured.

"Arson?" Gavin's eyes narrowed into slits. "No way." He ran his fingers up and down his glass, wiping off the condensation. "Is that what they're saying?"

"*They* are saying nothing of the kind." Allison leaned back. "No one knows for sure."

"Allison's right." Jennie wrapped her long braid around her finger. "I shouldn't have said anything. It's too soon to speculate."

"Maybe, but now that you mention it, having the phone dead and the fire alarm not working . . . that's just too much of a coincidence."

———

An hour later, Jennie's rear end was getting numb from sitting on the hard plastic chair. Her brain had shut itself off and she was operating on automatic pilot. They were down to four, Gavin having left twenty minutes earlier when his mom came by to pick him up.

Jennie nibbled on one of Lisa's cold French fries.

"You should eat something, Jennie," Lisa said. "Do you want me to get you a salad or something?"

Jennie looked at the limp fry and grimaced. "I'm not hungry." She glanced at her watch. Six-thirty. They still hadn't heard anything from the trauma center. "Think I'll go up and see what's happening. Anyone want to go along?"

Lisa stood. "I'll go. Um . . . maybe you could take me home pretty soon. Rafael is coming by at seven for his tutoring session." Lisa was working with Rafael on his English. "I could call him, but . . ." She glanced at Allison, then B.J. "You guys don't mind, do you? I know I said I'd keep you company, but I didn't think it would take so long."

"No, that's fine," Allison said. "We'll probably head upstairs pretty soon too."

B.J. glared at her sister. "You don't have to answer for me, Al. What makes you think I plan to stay?"

Jennie could have beaned her. Sometimes B.J. didn't have the manners of a pig.

Allison's head drooped as she stared at something on the table. "I'm sorry." Her head came up again as her gaze met her younger sister's. "You're right. It's your choice. I'd like you to stay with me, but if you want to go I'll understand."

After a long moment B.J. settled back in her chair. "I'll stay."

"Honestly," Lisa said when they were out of earshot. "B.J. can be such a brat."

"True. But she's having a pretty rough time with this. Think about how you'd feel if it was your dad that had gotten hurt."

"You're right. Speaking of dads, mine's due home tonight. I can hardly wait to see what he brought me." Lisa's father was a commercial pilot.

"Where'd he go this time?"

"China. And Hawaii. He's been gone for a week."

Reaching the elevator, Jennie pushed the up button. "You don't seem very excited for him to come home."

"I am. It's just that I'm a little nervous. Rafael's coming

27

over and . . . Dad hasn't met him yet."

"So . . ."

"So, Rafael is Hispanic."

"Does Uncle Kevin have something against Hispanics?"

Lisa shrugged. "I hope not. Mom says I shouldn't worry, but after what Mr. Beaumont said . . ."

"What?"

"Well, it wasn't what he said to me, exactly. It's what he told Allison and B.J. when Rafael first came."

The elevator doors swished open, and Jennie waited until they were inside before prodding Lisa to go on.

"He said Allison and B.J. were absolutely forbidden to see Rafael socially."

"Because of his race?"

"Apparently. That and the fact that they're on entirely different social levels."

"I can't believe . . ." Jennie stammered. "I thought Mr. Beaumont . . . I mean, he's sponsored Rafael's whole family."

"All I know is that he threatened to send Rafael back if he so much as caught Allison or B.J. even looking at him."

"Has Mr. Beaumont said anything to you?" Jennie held her stomach as the elevator rose three floors.

Lisa shook her head. "No, but I'm not so sure he knows. It's no wonder Rafael was so reluctant to ask me out."

Jennie tucked the information away. She'd think about it later. Right now she had to brace herself for news about Michael and the others.

Mom was sitting with Mr. Talbot this time. Lisa took a chair across from them and Jennie slumped into the chair next to her. "What's going on? Where is Mrs. Beaumont?"

Mom nodded toward the double doors. "In there. The doctor said she'd be able to take him home. He's got second-degree burns on his hands and arms and suffered some smoke inhalation. Otherwise, he's okay."

"Wish I could say the same for Elsa." Mr. Talbot sighed.

"She isn't . . ." Jennie couldn't finish.

"She's in surgery," Mom said. "Having a hip replacement. She fractured her hip when she was knocked down."

"That's the worst of it," Mr. Talbot said. "There were some other injuries too . . . bruises mostly. I'm just thankful Michael was there to bring her out before the fire got to her."

"How is Michael?"

"I still haven't heard."

Jennie watched a man in blood-soaked scrubs come through the doors and glance around the room. His gaze settled on Mom. "I have a feeling we're about to find out."

"Mrs. Rhodes?"

Jennie winced. She didn't like being reminded of how close Mom had come to being Mrs. Rhodes. "She's not—"

Mom stood up. "I'm Mrs. McGrady. Mr. Rhodes is . . . a friend. How is he?"

The doctor looked at Jennie and Lisa and frowned. "Are either of you relatives?"

"Michael is our youth director," Jennie told him. "Is he going to be okay?"

"I'm afraid not. We'll do all we can for him, but he has first- and second-degree burns on over seventy-five percent of his body."

"Oh no!" Mom covered her mouth and closed her eyes.

"Maybe you'd better sit down." He reached around Mom for a box of tissues and handed it to her. "Does he have any relatives? We should contact them."

Mom dabbed at her eyes and blew her nose. "He has a sister Ashley. She's a missionary in Tanzania. I don't know how to reach her. He should have letters in his apartment." Her gaze shifted to Jennie. "I don't have a key anymore."

"It's okay. We found a set on him. I'm sure the police will find it for us."

Beside her, Lisa sniffled and reached for a tissue. Jennie didn't cry. She just looked at the blood on the doctor's scrubs. Michael's blood.

4

"Can I see him?" Jennie heard herself ask.

"Soon. He's being transferred to the burn unit. It's on the fifth floor. I'd wait for another hour so the staff can get him situated. He'll be in isolation. It's important to keep his environment sterile. I'd suggest you come back around"—he glanced at the clock on the wall beside the reception desk—"eight or so."

Mom wrapped an arm around Jennie's waist. "We should go home. Your dad and Nick will want dinner. We can come back later."

———

Twenty minutes later Jennie and Lisa pulled into Lisa's driveway. Rafael was leaning against an older model Cadillac that looked like it had seen too many accidents and not enough paint.

"Hi," Lisa greeted as she stepped out of Jennie's car. "Sorry I'm late. Did you hear about the fire?"

"I heard." He brushed a hand through his course black hair and came toward them. His dark eyes had a brooding look that Lisa called mysterious. To Jennie he seemed sullen and angry most of the time. She could understand her cousin's attraction, though. Rafael was one great-looking guy.

"I was worried about your uncle," Jennie said. "Was he . . . in the building?"

"Sí, and Carlos."

"They're okay, aren't they?" Lisa wrapped her arms around his waist and leaned back to look at his face. His arms closed around her in a lukewarm welcome. At five-feet ten he was nearly a head taller than Lisa. They were a study in contrasts—Lisa's fair complexion and smattering of freckles on her face and arms; his bronzed skin, made even darker by working long hours in the sun. His sleeveless white muscle shirt did what it was supposed to do.

"No, they are not *okay*." Rafael spoke in broken English. "Philippe try to put out the fire. Carlos is burned as well."

"I'm so sorry." Jennie didn't remember seeing family members in the hospital waiting room and said so.

"They were not badly hurt so taken to Sunnyside." He shrugged. "They will survive, but the burns are not the problem." He dropped his arms to his side.

"I don't understand," Jennie said.

"The policía think the fire was not an accident. They blame Philippe."

"Oh no." Lisa stepped back and glanced at Jennie. "How could they? Jennie, we've got to do something!"

"There is nothing you can do. My uncle admits to being in the basement when the fire started. He tells them it is his fault." Rafael slipped his hands in the pockets of his cutoffs and dropped his gaze to the ground.

"That's terrible. Does he have a lawyer?" Lisa asked.

Before Rafael could answer, the door to Lisa's house swung open. "Jenny," Aunt Kate waved, "don't leave without Nick."

"He's still here? I thought Dad was picking him up."

"No. He called about half an hour ago. He'll be late. Something to do with the fire."

"Does Mom know?"

"Yep. She just called." Kate hesitated a moment, then said, "Jennie, could you come in for a minute? There's some-

31

thing I'd like to speak with you about."

Jennie didn't like the tone in Kate's voice or the strange look on her face. Something was wrong. Had Dad been hurt? She mumbled a hasty "See you later" to Rafael and Lisa and hurried inside.

"What's going on? It isn't Dad, is it? Please don't tell me he's been hurt."

Kate draped an arm across Jennie's shoulders. "No, your dad's fine." Leading her into the living room, Kate asked Jennie to sit down. "What I wanted to talk to you about is your mom."

"Mom?" Jennie dropped onto the sofa and grabbed one of the stuffed floppy-eared bunnies that served as cushions. "What about her?"

"Have you noticed anything odd about her behavior lately?"

"No." Jennie started playing with her hair again. "Not really. Have you?"

"Yes. She seems so tired and run down. And . . . depressed, maybe. I'm wondering if she's working too hard. With you back in school and on the swim team and Jason back home—I'm not suggesting your dad is a burden or that you're not doing your share, but when you think about the extra laundry, meals, picking up . . . all I know is that when your uncle Kevin is gone, there is a lot less work to do around the house."

Kate chuckled, her dark eyes shining. "Don't get me wrong. I dearly love him. I guess what I'm trying to say is that I'm worried about Susan." She shrugged. "Maybe she's just having a bad week. You haven't noticed anything?"

Jennie rubbed her forehead where she was starting to get a headache. "I haven't paid that much attention. I guess I have been pretty busy lately." Jennie's gaze moved from the floor to her aunt's face. Jennie and her aunt Kate shared many of the same features and were often confused for mother and daughter. They had the same dark hair and deep blue eyes. Not unusual when you considered that Kate and Jennie's father were twins. "You don't think she's sick or anything. . . ?"

"I hope not. With remarrying your dad and all, I expect she's had a lot to deal with emotionally as well as physically. I probably shouldn't even have mentioned it. It's just that when she brought Nick over today she seemed so drawn and . . . frail. She'd been crying."

"About Michael. She told you about his getting hurt?"

Kate nodded. "Yes—that poor man. Losing your mother and now this."

Jennie bit her lip. Worry sat like a big lump in the pit of her stomach. "Maybe it's not just because he's hurt. Maybe she's sorry she broke up with Michael to marry Dad."

"Oh no, honey. Susan loves your dad very much. She's concerned for Michael. That's only natural. No, I'm sure it's just stress and overwork."

Jennie sighed. "I hope you're right. Now that Mom and Dad are back together again, I don't want anything to mess it up. I'll try to do extra work around the house."

"I'm sure she'd appreciate that." Kate smiled and patted Jennie's hand. "Oh, and don't tell your mother I said anything. She seemed rather touchy the other day when I mentioned her looking a bit peaked."

"Right." Jennie stood. "I'd better get home."

"Kurt and Nick are in the backyard." Kate stood, too, and gave Jennie a hug. "Sorry to put this on your shoulders, honey, but I thought you should be aware."

Jennie nodded. "It's okay, Aunt Kate. Really."

Only it wasn't okay. The last thing Jennie needed was to be reminded of her mom's weird behavior. Jennie went to the back door and yelled for Nick to meet her at the car. She should have waited for him, given him a bear hug, and carried him to the car. At the moment, though, she didn't feel like hugging anyone. Normally she would have asked him about his day at school and looked over his papers, praising his work. Normally she would have been happy. Only today was not a normal day. The world seemed to have gone berserk, spinning out of control.

Jennie said good-bye and escaped to her car. Hot and stuffy as it was, it gave her something to hold on to. Something tangible and solid. She swatted at a mosquito flying near the dash and killed it. She draped her arm over the steering wheel and rested her head against it while she watched Lisa and Rafael go inside and Nick and Kurt come out. Kurt was five years older than Nick, but not much taller. They were more like brothers than cousins and did practically everything together. Just like she and Lisa used to.

That had changed too. Jennie wasn't much into boys. She did have a boyfriend, Ryan Johnson, but he lived at the coast next to Gram, and she didn't see him all that much. Which was okay. She had no intention of getting serious about guys yet anyway. Jennie's future plans included college, then law school. After that she'd think about marriage and babies. Maybe. The thought didn't excite her like it did some girls. But that was probably because she'd been helping her mom take care of Nick for five years. Not that she minded. She just didn't plan on having kids of her own until she was at least thirty.

She watched Nick run to the car and fumble with the door handle, finally managing to pull it open, climb inside, and close it again. She started the car while he whipped his seat belt on and gave her a wide grin that faded when she didn't return it.

"You mad at me or sumpin'?" He dumped his papers and book bag on the floor in front of him.

"No. I'm just sad today."

" 'Cause of the school?"

"Partly."

34

"I'm sad too. Kurt says it's a 'venture and he hopes we won't have to go back to school at all for a whole year. But I don't want to not go to school. Do you, Jennie?" Nick's big blue eyes were nearly the same color as hers and their dad's and Kate's. It was a McGrady trait. So was the dark hair and being tall and thin.

"No."

"What do you think will happen?"

"I don't know." Jennie glanced at him. "Look, Nick. I don't want to talk about it, okay?"

" 'Cause it makes you more sad?"

"Yeah."

"Can I read you a book?" He reached forward and withdrew a chapter book from his bag.

She nodded. "Sure." Nick's *reading* usually took the form of him looking at the pictures and telling his own made-up story. He flashed her another grin and this time she returned it. His story would take both their minds off the tragic fire, and her mind off Michael and Mom.

She half listened as Nick recited the story about the Little Mermaid.

Jennie pulled into the driveway a short time later, relieved to see Dad's car parked in front of the garage next to Mom's. They were sitting in the front porch swing talking. Jennie's heart did a somersault—at least that's what it felt like. She loved seeing them together like that. Her fears about them splitting up subsided. Nick raced up the walk, dodging Bernie, his St. Bernard pup, and dove on top of them. Jennie watched her parents make a fuss over his drawings, feeling just a little jealous at being too old for that sort of thing.

"I can read, Dad!" Nick petted Bernie, who was still woofing, licking, wagging his tail, and being a nuisance.

"I'll bet you can." Jason McGrady scooted his son to his lap, both their dark heads bent over the book he'd been pretending to read to Jennie.

"Dinner's ready," Mom said, making no move to get up. "Nothing fancy. Just salad."

"Do you want me to bring it out here?" Jennie asked. Aunt Kate was right. Mom looked tired and thinner and there were dark rings under her eyes. Even her beautiful red hair looked different, not as full or shiny.

"That would be wonderful, Jennie. Thanks." Mom gave her a wan smile and leaned her head against Dad's shoulder.

They ate Chinese chicken salad with sesame seeds and crisp noodles, and herb bread on trays. Mom and Dad stayed in the swing, while Jennie stretched out on the chaise lounge and Nick sat in his small wicker rocker. For the first time since she'd heard the sirens that afternoon, Jennie began to relax.

At seven-forty-five, Mom heaved a heavy sigh, gave Dad a kiss, and got up. "If we're going to see Michael, Jennie, we'd better get going. I'd like to at least get these dishes in the sink before we leave."

Dad picked up his tray from the floor where he'd set it. "Are you sure you need to go again tonight? You both look exhausted."

"I'd like to check on him, darling. If he had family here it would be different. But he's alone and . . ."

Dad nodded, drawing a hand down his face. "Go ahead, then. Nick and I will take care of the dishes, won't we, little buddy?"

"Yep." Nick grasped his dad's hand. "Me and my dad will do it."

———

Outside Michael's room, a nurse helped Mom and Jennie suit up in isolation garb—a special cap and booties, and a gown and sterile gloves.

"Have you ever seen a burn patient before?" the nurse asked.

36

Mom said she had once. Jennie said no.

"It isn't a pretty sight. We have most of the deep burns covered, but you'll be able to see some on his face and upper torso."

"Is he in a lot of pain?" Mom asked.

"Unfortunately, yes. But it's the less severe burns that hurt the most. With the more severe burns, the nerve endings are gone."

"The doctor said he might not make it."

"That's true. The most dangerous thing right now is fluid loss and infection. We'll do our best."

Mom nodded. "Earlier, I told the ER people to get in touch with his sister, Ashley. Have you been able to contact her? Does she know?"

"I don't think anyone has been able to reach her yet. Is she his only relative?"

"I'm afraid so."

"Can I go in now?" Much as she wanted to see Michael, Jennie dreaded the visit and wanted to get it over with.

"Sure." The nurse opened the door and led Jennie inside. "You can talk to him, but don't touch him or anything around him. You can visit for about five minutes. I'll be right outside if you need me."

"Hi, Michael." She hesitantly approached the bed, swallowing back a pear-sized lump in her throat. "It . . . it's me. Jennie." Seeing Michael tore a hole in Jennie's heart. It was all she could do not to run out of the room screaming. Draped in white linen, he resembled a corpse. What she could see of his face was raw and blistered. She'd never seen anyone in so much pain or so badly burned. She took a deep breath to hold back the nausea, then focused on the call button beside his bandaged hand.

"Thanks . . . for coming, Jennie," he said in a raspy voice. "Means a lot."

She nodded. Tears streamed down her face and into the

mask. She sniffled but couldn't wipe them away for fear she'd contaminate the sterile gloves.

"Don't . . . cry." He raised his hand a fraction of an inch, then let it fall back on the sheets. "I'll be okay. I'm either—" he gasped, then went on in halting phrases, "going to make it through this . . . or I'll get to see God." Jennie watched his chest rise and fall several times before he spoke again. "Either way . . . I'll have it made."

Jennie wanted to ask him about the fire, how it started and if it was an accident, but talking seemed too painful for him. Instead she said, "I'll pray for you and get all the kids to pray too. Please try to get well, Michael. We need you."

When Michael didn't answer, Jennie moved her gaze up to his shoulder and past the excoriated cheek and nose to his eyes. His warm hazel eyes, glazed and unseeing, seemed to look right through her. She backed away. "Please, God, no. Don't let him die," she whimpered. "Please don't let him die."

5

Jennie ran from the room, pulling off the face mask. "I think he's . . ." She covered her mouth and closed her eyes, then slumped against the wall in the hallway.

"Oh, honey." Mom reached for her. Jennie pushed her away. She didn't want that. Didn't want anything but to get as far away from there as possible. Ripping off the gown and cap, she took off. "I'll be in the car."

"Jennie, wait . . ."

Minutes later, Jennie leaned against the car door. She'd forgotten that Mom had driven and still had the keys in her purse. Hard as she tried, Jennie couldn't stop crying. She pressed the heel of her hands against her eyes to dam the tears. "It isn't fair," she murmured. Michael was one of the kindest people she'd ever known. He didn't deserve this. She tipped her head back and raked her fingers through her hair. Looking at the stars, she gritted her teeth. "Why, God? How could you let this happen?"

She turned around and kicked the tire. "Ow." *This is stupid. Stupid. Stupid. Stupid. You're sixteen years old, for Pete's sake. Why are you acting like such a baby?* Four months ago she hadn't even liked Michael. Now her heart ached as though she'd lost a best friend. Jennie's mind whirred back to when she first met Michael Rhodes. Mom had known him from church and started dating him. With Dad missing for five years and presumed dead, Mom had decided to get on with her life, but that decision couldn't have come at a worse time.

In her heart, Jennie knew Dad was alive. She just needed to find him. Eventually she did, but he couldn't come home and she was sworn to secrecy. Dad worked for the DEA and had gone undercover to protect his family. She couldn't tell a soul—not even Mom. In the meantime Mom, thinking Dad had died, filed for a divorce so she would be free to marry Michael. Jennie hated the idea but eventually came to accept it. She'd even grown to love Michael. Then Dad showed up, and he and Mom fell in love all over again. Their story would have made a great novel. Except novels had happy endings.

She'd wanted Michael to find someone else and fall in love and be happy. Now he'd never have that chance. Even if he'd survived, his life would have been miserable. The fire had burned off half his face. Jennie shook her head to dispel the image. Maybe it was better that he did die.

Jennie placed her hands on the hood and leaned over the car, hauling in long, deep breaths. *You have to get control of yourself, McGrady. You can get through this.* She straightened again, determined not to fall apart. She shivered and rubbed at the gooseflesh on her arms. The hot day had turned into a cool night, and she hadn't thought to bring a jacket. Maybe she should go back inside.

Jennie brushed away the last vestiges of tears from her cheeks with the back of her hand. Hearing footsteps, she glanced up.

"Jennie? Are you okay?" Mom approached with a what-am-I-going-to-do-with-you look.

"I guess."

"I know seeing Michael like that was upsetting, but I don't appreciate your running off. What were you thinking?" Mom pulled the car keys out of her handbag.

Jennie lowered her head and stared at the faded white line

that separated their Oldsmobile from a teal-colored van. "I'm sorry. It's just . . ." She scrunched her eyes together. "He looked so awful. I've never seen anybody die before."

"Oh, honey." Mom wrapped her arms around Jennie. "Michael's not dead. Is that what you thought?"

"But his eyes . . . they were all glazed over and . . ."

"He's on high dosages of pain medication. If you'd taken a minute to check him, you'd have realized that."

"Oh." Jennie stepped away. "Mom, I feel so stupid and mixed up. I guess I should be happy he's still alive, but I was just thinking maybe it would have been better . . . Never mind. Are you ready to go?"

"I'm not going home, Jennie. Someone needs to be here with Michael. He is still alive, but his situation is critical. He may not last the night."

"Why do you want to stay? How can you stand to watch him?"

Mom looked back at the hospital, silhouetted against a red and purple evening sky. "All I know is that if it were me lying in that bed, I wouldn't want to be alone."

Jennie nodded. "I guess I'd feel the same way. How will you get home?"

"I'll call when I'm ready."

"What about Dad?"

"He'll understand." An odd look passed across Mom's face. Jennie half expected her to qualify her statement with an *I hope*. But she didn't.

Heading home, Jennie plugged a LeAnn Rimes tape into the tape deck and sang along with a remake of an old Righteous Brothers tune. She almost succeeded in blocking the images of Michael from her mind.

By the time she pulled into her driveway, Jennie wished she'd stayed with her mother. She could understand why Mom had chosen to be with Michael. What she couldn't understand was the way her stomach hurt at the thought of telling Dad.

Jason McGrady was sitting in the family room watching a news program. Jennie came up behind him and wrapped her arms around his neck. "Hi. Nick in bed already?"

"Yep. Glad you're back." He looked toward the entry and frowned. "Where's your mother?"

"Still at the hospital." At his puzzled look, she added, "Michael's really bad and Mom felt like someone needed to stay."

"What about the pastor or some other church member?" He rubbed the back of his neck.

Jennie shrugged. "No one else was there. She said you'd understand."

He stood and dug his hands into the pockets of his faded jeans. "Did she want me to pick her up later?"

"She said she'd call." Wanting to change the subject, Jennie asked, "Have you heard any more about the fire—I mean whether it was arson or not?"

"No." The frown slipped from his face and he lowered himself back into the chair. "We won't know for certain until it cools down enough to investigate."

"How long will that be?" Jennie straddled the arm of the sofa.

"Not sure. Twenty-two hours maybe."

"Do they have any idea how it started? Or where?"

"No. Probably the furnace room."

"Have you ever worked on an arson case, Dad?"

"Not directly, and I'm not working on this one. Neither are you."

"I wasn't—"

"Then why all the questions?"

"I . . . never mind." Jennie jumped up and stomped into the kitchen.

Mom would have yelled at her to adjust her attitude. Dad

ignored her. Jennie didn't know which was worse. She fixed a snack of brownies and milk, took a helping to her dad, who grunted an insincere thank-you. He'd changed channels and was watching a baseball game. After a few minutes of feeling about as wanted as a skunk, she mumbled something about having homework.

"Jennie!"

She stopped halfway up the stairs and turned around. "What?"

He came up beside her, dragging his hand through his hair like he so often did. "I'm sorry. I'm upset and I shouldn't be taking it out on you."

"Are you mad at Mom?"

He hesitated. "Not exactly." His gaze met hers. The scar on his cheek curved as he smiled. "At any rate, I'm sorry."

Jennie hugged him. "That's okay. Do you want me to stay down here and keep you company?"

"If you want. I was about to shut off the television. Have to appear in court tomorrow so I thought I'd better go back over the case."

Ordinarily Jennie would have asked him what the case was about, but not tonight. It was only nine-thirty, but all she wanted to do was take a hot shower and go to bed. "I'll see you in the morning, then."

———

Something cool and wet touched her hand. Jennie pulled it back under the covers. "Bernie, go away." The St. Bernard pup nudged her again. "You're not supposed to be in the house."

"You gotta get up, Jennie." Nick tugged at her blankets. "Somebody needs to take care of me."

"Where's Mom?"

"I don't know. And Daddy's gone too."

Bernie whimpered, then let loose with a loud bark.

Scenes from the previous day drifted back to her. The fire. Michael. The burn unit. Jennie lifted her head and peered at her digital alarm. Seven.

Nick pushed at her shoulders. "Come on, Jennie, we have to get ready for school."

Jennie groaned and rolled over onto her back, rubbing the sleep from her eyes. "There is no school today, Nick."

"Why? Is it Saturday? It can't be Saturday 'cause yesterday was Monday and—"

"No. It's not Saturday." She patted the bed. "Come up here. We have to talk."

Nick climbed up on the bed and straddled her stomach. "What do you want to talk about? You better make it quick."

Jennie closed her hands around his skinny arms. "Remember what happened yesterday? Why Mom took you over to Aunt Kate's?"

His bony shoulders rose and fell under his green plaid pajamas. "All she said was she needed to go to the hospital to see somebody that was real sick."

Great. Mom hadn't told him about Michael. "Right. Do you know why the people were at the hospital?"

"Yeah. Kurt says they got burned in the big fire. And the school got burned and the church and everything."

"Right. And that's why we can't go to school."

"Why?"

Jennie heaved an exasperated sigh. "Because of the fire. The school burned down."

"But, Jennie." Nick's wide blue gaze met hers head on. "They got it all fixed already."

"No . . ."

"They do. I saw a picture of it on telebision—on the news."

"Oh." Understanding dawned. "That was probably a picture of what it used to look like."

44

"Uh-uh." Nick wagged his head back and forth. "They built a new one."

Jennie lifted him off to the side and scooted off the bed. "Go get dressed and put Bernie out."

Surprisingly, he didn't argue.

Jennie hurriedly braided her hair and threw on shorts and a T-shirt. She didn't know if it was the right thing to do, but having Nick actually see the place was going to be the only way to convince him. Besides, she needed to see Trinity for herself. She could understand why it would be hard for Nick to comprehend the damage. She had a hard time believing it herself.

In the kitchen, Jennie read Dad's hastily scribbled note. *Jennie and Nick. Sorry to rush off, but I had some important business at work. See you at dinner. Dad.*

After a quick breakfast of yogurt and cereal, Jennie called her mother at the hospital. When Mom finally got on the line, she asked about Michael.

"He's about the same. Is your dad there?"

"He left already. Do you need me to come get you?"

She didn't answer for a moment, then said, "Why don't you come at ten. Reverend Cole said she'd try to spell me. She agrees we should try to have someone with Michael all the time."

"Maybe I could take a turn," Jennie volunteered. "Since we probably won't be going to school for a while. . . ."

"That's sweet of you, honey. I'll put you in the schedule."

By the time she hung up, Jennie felt better. Sitting with Michael wouldn't be the most pleasant task, but at least she'd be giving her mother a break. And Dad wouldn't need to get upset.

———

At eight-thirty, Jennie turned up the familiar hill to the school and parked at the top of the driveway. Yellow police tape had been strung between barricades. A security guard leaned against his car watching her. A fire engine and a lone fire fighter stood at the ready near the burned-out building in case fire erupted again.

"How come you're stopping here?"

"The police won't let us go any farther. Besides, we'll be able to see the whole school yard from up here."

Jennie couldn't count the number of times she'd turned into the drive and been greeted by the brilliant blue-tiled roof. She exited the car and came around to help Nick out. Picking him up, she carried him to the side of the road. The bitter smell of smoke and burned wood nearly choked her as she made her way to the ledge. About thirty feet below them the once beautiful structure lay in ruins.

Nick took one look and buried his face in her neck. "I want to go back home. I don't want to be here."

Jennie wished she hadn't brought him. Her gaze swept across the black debris. The only thing left standing was the gymnasium, and that only because it was a separate building joined to the rest of the complex by a covered walkway. The walkway had collapsed. She closed her eyes, remembering the way it had been only the morning before—the roof proudly shimmering in the sunlight like peacock feathers. The building had been built in four stages. The church formed the central-most part of the fan-shaped structure. Members had built it twenty years before. Five years later they added the grade school and day care.

Five years after that they built an expansion on the opposite side of the church to add the high school. And only two years ago they'd built the gymnasium and covered the entire complex with the new blue roof.

Jennie opened her eyes again. Her gaze settled back on a couple patches of blue that hadn't been blackened by soot. "Well, at least it's not all gone," she said. "Look, Nick. The gym is still there." She pointed to the far end of the property.

"And the playground equipment is there too."

He lifted his head from her shoulder. "Can we go swing?"

"Not yet. It'll have to be cleaned."

He sighed. "Oh."

"It won't be so bad," Jennie went on, wanting to wipe the despondent look from his face. "Pretty soon workers will come and clear all the ashes and burnt stuff away. Then they'll bring in lumber and start building. They'll have big bulldozers and trucks and we can come and watch sometimes."

His eyes brightened. "Will they make it just like it was? And will it have a library?"

Jennie nodded. "Sure." Though she said the words, she wasn't certain she quite believed them. It would take millions of dollars to rebuild and replace what the fire had destroyed. She thought about the artwork in Michael's office and the stained-glass window in the sanctuary. The Bibles and the hymnals, the thousands of books that lined the shelves of their library.

She had to get out of there before she started crying again. As she turned away, a movement near the woods behind what used to be the chemistry lab caught her eye. Jennie focused in on the lone figure in army fatigues creeping along the tree line. Crouching down, he ran past the playground equipment and disappeared behind the gym. The cap he wore kept her from seeing his face or making a positive ID.

Jennie had heard somewhere that a criminal always returns to the scene of the crime. She wasn't sure if that was true, but one thing she did know. That guy had no business being there.

6

Jennie put Nick back in the car. "Stay here for a minute. I gotta check on something." Jogging over to the security guard, she reported what she'd seen.

"You sure?" The guard, obviously irritated with her for causing him trouble, scanned the grounds. "I don't see anyone."

"He went behind the gym. He might be trying to break in."

The guard crossed his thick muscular arms, and for a minute Jennie thought he might not take her seriously. Then, apparently deciding he'd better check out her story, he unhooked a cell phone from his belt and punched in a code. After a moment's hesitation he said, "Yeah, this is Chuck Owens. Some kid down here says she saw a guy snooping around the school. I doubt it's anything, but I better check it out." While he talked, he headed down the steep drive.

"Aren't you going to wait for backup?"

He cast her a frosty glare and kept going. Jennie walked back to her car, where she had a better view.

"Can we go home now? I want to see Mom." Nick leaned out the window.

"In a minute."

"Why can't we go now?"

"Because somebody's down by the school who shouldn't

48

be there, and I want to find out who they are." *Besides*, she thought to herself, *the guard might need help.*

Nick settled back in his seat, arms crossed and a scowl on his face. Below her, the guard walked to the far end of the grounds near the woods, then moved back toward the gym. He went behind the building and several minutes later came to the front entrance and went inside. Jennie shook her head. Not a smart thing to do.

A squad car pulled up behind her. An officer jumped out. Hand close to his weapon, he approached her. "I'm Officer Cooper. Got a call from a security guard saying he got a tip there might be trouble—know where he went?"

"He's in the building." Jennie quickly filled him in.

"Did the man you saw have a weapon?"

"I didn't see one. But if I'd been the guard, I wouldn't have gone in there without backup."

A second officer drove up before Cooper could respond. He was just getting out of his car when the door to the gym flew open. The man in fatigues ran out. He was no longer wearing a cap.

"That him?"

"Yeah." Jennie's heart ripped into overdrive. The guy looked straight at her. Jared Reinhardt.

Cooper and the other officer drew their weapons and at the same time shouted for him to stop.

For a second Jared looked like he was going to run. His gaze darted back to the building, over to the trees, and back to the police.

"Put your hands up where I can see them," Cooper yelled.

"Don't shoot!" Jared lifted his hands.

Within seconds the police descended on him, making him lie face down while they frisked him. They yanked him to his feet, pulled his hands behind his back, and cuffed him. After talking with him, the second officer went inside—probably to find the guard. Cooper walked Jared up the hill and ordered him into the back of his squad car.

Jared didn't speak to her, though his cheeks were flushed with anger. She had no doubt his menacing stare was meant to silence her, but Jennie had no intention of being intimidated. She met his gaze head on.

"Do you know him?" the officer asked.

"Not very well. His name is Jared Reinhardt. He's a . . ." Jennie looked back at Jared. He looked more frightened now than angry. She wished she could ask him what was going on. Had he told her the truth of wanting out of the gang? If so, why was he at the school? Had he been responsible for the fire?

"Was he a student here?" the officer prodded.

"No. Michael, our youth director, had been counseling him. Jared told us he was a skinhead and wanted out of this neo-Nazi group he'd been with."

The guard and the officer emerged from the building.

"Good, he's okay. I was afraid . . ." Jennie let her voice trail off. She felt a strange sense of relief, not only that the guard was unhurt but that Jared hadn't harmed him.

"Jennie!" Nick whined. "Please, can we go home?"

"In a minute." Jennie pushed her strange mix of feelings aside and focused on what the officer was saying.

"I need to know how to get hold of you," Cooper said.

"Sure." She gave him her name, address, and phone number.

"McGrady . . ." Cooper mulled the name over. "Jason McGrady's girl?"

"Right."

He nodded and flashed her a grin. "Good man. Looks like we won't have any trouble getting hold of you if we have any more questions."

"Guess not." Jennie opened her car door but didn't get

in. Concern for Jared still loomed large in her mind. "Officer Cooper?"

He looked up from his notes. "Yes?"

"Um—what will happen to Jared?"

"Depends. He claims he didn't know the area was off limits. Says he left something in Michael's office and came here to see if it survived the fire. Wouldn't tell us what it was, though."

"Could you let me know whether you decide to charge him or not?"

"Sure." He raised an eyebrow. "Say, he's not your boyfriend, is he?"

"No. Just curious, that's all."

Jennie ducked into her car, wishing she could forget about the strange attachment she felt toward Jared all of a sudden. She didn't like it in the least. Didn't especially like *him*. He stood for everything she hated. Jared had been running with a band of white supremacists. Likely the same gang that had beat up a man only last week because he was a Jew. She shuddered at the thought.

Jennie started her car and eased away from the wide shoulder onto the road. She had the oddest sensation of being drawn into Jared's life. "You're losing it, McGrady," she mumbled.

"What are you losing?" Nick asked.

Glad for the diversion, Jennie grinned. "Nothing important." *Just my mind*, she added to herself. "How would you like to go visit Aunt Kate and Uncle Kevin? We have about an hour before we need to pick up Mom."

"Yay!" He bounced up and down. "I get to play with Kurt! I get to play with Kurt!"

Jennie grinned. It sure didn't take much to make Nick happy. She wished she could switch moods that easily.

"Kate, Kevin, Kurt, and Lisa. Kate, Kevin, Kurt, and

Lisa." Nick chanted the names six or seven more times. "Jennie?" Nick stopped bouncing.

"What?"

"Did you know all their names start with a K except for Lisa's? How come they didn't name her with a K too?"

"'Cause she was named for Grandma Calhoun, and her name is Lisa May."

"Well, they shoulda named her Karen, then they could've had four Ks. Now they only got three." He giggled and began chanting the names again.

"That's enough, Nick."

"Why?" Nick's blue gaze drifted up to hers.

"Because I said so." She softened her tone. "I'm not in a very good mood right now, so I need you to not talk for a few minutes. Okay?" She caught his hand and squeezed it. "Why don't you sing me a song instead."

He shrugged. "Okay. Ummm. How about the li'l monkeys jumpin' on the bed?"

"Good." While Nick sang about the monkeys falling out of bed and bumping their heads, Jennie thought about Jared and his skinhead friends. She remembered seeing films from the old south where men would hide behind white gowns and hoods, killing and maiming blacks in the name of justice. It was the same justice many early settlers used in dealing with Native Americans. And that Hitler and the Third Reich had used against the Jews. They were all different groups that fell under one ugly word—prejudice.

Jennie shook her head, surprised at how far afield her mind had drifted. Funny how thinking about one thing could lead to another and another. Jared Reinhardt, skinhead, neo-Nazi/white supremacist. Prejudice.

Though she didn't want to jump to conclusions, Jennie couldn't help wondering if the fire had been race related. Of course, the authorities hadn't said for certain if it was arson. All she'd heard so far was speculation.

Jennie ended up leaving Nick at Kate's and bringing Lisa along with her to the hospital. They arrived at quarter to ten. Since Pastor Cole hadn't come in yet, Lisa offered to stay with Michael while Jennie took Mom home. Lisa had already donned the isolation garb and gone inside. She sat next to the bed, talking with Michael, and didn't seem at all affected by his appearance.

Jennie waited for Mom to come out of the room—her very tired-looking mother. Jennie frowned, noticing how much weight Mom had lost. She had been dieting off and on, trying to keep her weight down since she'd been pregnant with Nick. She sure didn't need to worry about losing weight now.

"You look terrible," Jennie said when Mom joined her just outside the room.

"Thanks." Mom lifted her shoulder-length auburn hair off her neck.

"You've lost weight."

"I have?" She smiled as though it were a good thing. "I haven't even been trying."

"Mom." Jennie peered into her mother's eyes from her six-inch height advantage. "I'm not sure it's a good idea for you to stay here so much."

Mom looked away. "I . . . I have to do this, Jennie. I don't expect you to understand, but—"

"You don't still love him, do you? I mean—you married Dad and . . ."

Mom pulled off the paper shoes and stuffed them in the garbage, then slowly removed the gown. Her blouse looked rumpled. "I'm not sure how to answer that. I do love Michael—not in the same way as I love your father, of course, but . . ." Mom's gaze met Jennie's again. "He was my best friend for six months. You can't just turn that kind of thing off."

Mom picked up her sweater and handbag. "You don't have to worry about me, honey. I'll be fine."

"I hope so." Jennie started for the elevator. "You ready?"

The elevator doors opened like curtains on a stage. It wasn't the elevator itself but the person inside who brought the analogy to mind.

The Reverend Marissa Cole stepped out in a flurry of autumn colors—red, brown, cream, and gold. "Susan, Jennie. I am so glad I caught you." Her hands fluttered as she spoke, showing off her slender fingers and long nails. Each nail had been painted a different color to match her dress. "I apologize for being late. What with the press and the police, I'm lucky to be here at all."

As usual, Jennie found it hard not to stare. Whether she meant to or not, Reverend Cole demanded attention. Jennie marveled at the way the brown in her floor-length dress perfectly matched her smooth bronzed skin and deep chocolate eyes, while the tawny gold matched her very short hair. Even her voice matched, Jennie thought. If voices had colors, Marissa's would be ivory—like silky cream. Though she was born in the United States, Marissa had lived in South Africa for the last five years as a missionary. Prior to that, she'd traveled with a Mercy Ship. As a result, she was an exotic blend of culture, style, and personality.

"The police? What did they want?" Mom asked.

"They're questioning everyone who was in the building when the fire broke out. You never heard so many questions." Marissa sighed heavily and adjusted the strap of a huge brown leather bag over her shoulder. "But let's not talk about that right now. How's our patient?"

"I wish I could say he's doing better, but there's been no change. Lisa Calhoun is with him right now."

"Oh good. In that case, I'll run down to the cafeteria and grab a bite to eat. Believe it or not, all I've had today is coffee."

Jennie believed it. Marissa Cole had a Tigger personality, all bouncy and bright. This morning, though, she seemed bouncier than usual.

"Would you two like to join me?" Marissa asked.

"I'd love it. I haven't eaten this morning either." Mom turned to Jennie. "You don't mind, do you?"

"I guess not." What could she say? Actually, she did mind. She was hoping to talk to Gavin. If anyone knew the latest news on the fire, he would. On the other hand, Marissa had just spoken with the press and the police. Jennie tagged along behind them, half listening as Mom filled Marissa in on things she needed to know about Michael.

While Mom and Marissa ordered breakfast, Jennie helped herself to a glass of orange juice, told the cashier her mom was paying for it, and secured a table by the window. Marissa's strong alto voice carried all the way to the seating area. Mom's didn't, which was why Jennie heard only one side of the conversation. Enough to know they'd changed topics.

"The Lord works all things for good," Marissa said. "And this is no exception. That fire was a terrible tragedy, but do you know, people from all over the country are responding with donations? We'll be able to rebuild in no time."

"Has the board met at all to decide what to do in the meantime?" Mom asked as they approached the table and sat down.

"Oh yes. We met last night. As you know, we didn't lose the gym. Praise the Lord for that. A lot of smoke damage, but it'll be as good as new in a week. We'll set up temporary offices there and hold services."

"And the children?"

"That's a problem." Marissa used the pads of her forefinger and thumb to carefully pry open a container of jam. "Mr. Beaumont has some space in one of his plants. He's downsizing. It would take some fixing up, but we might be

55

able to work something out. Otherwise we'll have to integrate the students into other schools."

"That would be terrible," Jennie said. "You can't just split us up. We—" She stopped, realizing it would do no good to protest. Their school was gone.

"I know," Marissa cooed. "It's a terrible thing. But we don't have many options. If by some miracle we got the funding to rebuild tomorrow, we couldn't move into the school until next year."

"What about portable classrooms? Once the rubble is cleared out—"

"It would be too expensive." Marissa hesitated, then added, "But I'll suggest it. You never know."

"I think we'll go to homeschooling completely," Mom said. "At least for Nick. There'll be less disruption that way. It'll probably be best for you, too, Jennie. You wouldn't be able to be on the swim team, but the pool will still be here for you to practice, and maybe next year . . ." Mom held her stomach. "Um . . . I'm not feeling so well. Excuse me." Covering her mouth with her hand, she pushed back her chair and fled.

"Do you want me—" By the time Jennie got to her feet, Mom was already halfway to the rest room. Jennie turned to Marissa. "I'd better go check on her."

The toilet flushed as Jennie entered the rest room. Looking pasty white and shaky, Mom emerged from the stall. "I'm all right, Jennie. Just lost my breakfast is all. You didn't need to come in."

"Maybe you should see a doctor. There are lots of them around."

Mom wet a paper towel, squeezed the excess water out of it, and pressed it against her forehead, then each cheek. "Don't be silly. I probably shouldn't have had eggs. They haven't been setting too well with me lately." Mom looked into the mirror, where she met Jennie's concerned gaze. "All right. If it will make you happy, I'll see a doctor. But not today. I'll call Dr. Cameron and set up an appointment. Now, go back and keep Marissa company."

"You sure you're okay?"

Mom assured her again, telling her she'd be out in a few minutes. Though reluctant, Jennie did as she was told.

"Is everything all right?" Marissa asked when Jennie came back.

"Mom says it is, but I'm not sure."

"You think she's lying to you?"

"No. But I don't think she's telling me everything." Jennie picked up her napkin and tore off the corner. "My aunt is worried about her too. I mean, what if Mom is really sick? Maybe she's got a disease and doesn't want to tell us."

Marissa's warm brown gaze softened as she patted Jennie's hands. "Your mother seems to be a wise and caring lady. I'm sure if there was a problem—especially anything as serious as all that—she'd tell you."

"Not necessarily." It wouldn't have been the first time Mom had kept a secret. Back when Dad was missing and presumed dead, Mom had been seeing Michael for several months before she decided to let her family know.

"It does no good at all to worry, Jennie. You need to trust your mother. But more important, you need to trust God to work everything out according to His purpose."

Marissa's words had meant to comfort. They did anything but. If God would allow Trinity to burn to the ground, Jennie wasn't certain she trusted Him with her mother.

7

"What am I thinking?" Mom ran her hands through her already mussed hair. "We forgot to pick up Nick." Jennie and Mom had just pulled into their driveway after being at the hospital.

"I was hoping you wouldn't notice. Don't worry about it. I'll go over there right after I get Lisa and visit Michael."

"That's sweet, honey." She yawned. "I could use some sleep."

"And don't worry about dinner tonight. I'll take care of it."

"Well, that is nice. Thank you."

After telling her mother again to get some rest and not to worry about Nick, Jennie headed back to the hospital.

Flipping on the radio and not wanting to hear a commercial, Jennie punched the buttons until she found a song she liked by Vince Gill. *I Still Believe in You.* She sang along until it ended.

"More of your favorite tunes to come," the DJ promised. "But first an update on that church fire."

Jennie turned up the volume.

"Police are questioning several people today in conjunction with the Trinity fire, now believed to be arson. Five people were injured in that blaze. One, Michael Rhodes, still remains in critical condition."

"So it *was* arson," she said aloud. And one of the people they were questioning had to be Jared. "I wonder what he was looking for." Maybe she could ask Michael.

———

Once in Michael's room at the hospital, she told him what had happened that morning and asked if Jared had brought him something.

"Yes." Talking seemed painful for him and Jennie wished she hadn't asked.

"If it hurts too much, you don't need to answer. I'm sorry. I just wish I knew if he was telling the truth. About anything."

"I . . . believed . . . him," Michael rasped.

Jennie pulled her chair a few inches closer. "Can you tell me what he brought you?"

"Box. Didn't have . . . time . . . to look."

"It was in your office?"

"Yes." He hesitated again for a long time. "Need to tell you . . . in case . . . I . . . don't make it."

"Oh, Michael, please don't talk anymore." It twisted Jennie's insides to watch him struggle so. "You'll make it. I know you will."

"Jared was . . . turning . . ."

"Miss McGrady?" The nurse came into the room. "We need to change Michael's dressings now. You'll have to step out."

Jennie glanced back at Michael. "I'll be back as soon as they're done."

Lisa was waiting when Jennie stepped out of the room. "Well?"

Jennie told her what Michael had said about Jared. "Looks like he was telling the truth about giving Michael something."

"Okay, but what did he give him?"

"And why did he want it back?" Jennie thought of something else. "Michael said he didn't have time to look at it. Probably because of the board meeting. That means Jared was at the church close to the time the fire started."

"Oh wow. He could have done it. We need to tell the police."

"Not yet. I want to hear what else Michael has to say." Jennie glanced around. "Where is Reverend Cole?"

"Talking to the police again." Lisa sighed. "She never did get in to stay with Michael this morning."

"She isn't a suspect, is she?"

"No. At least I don't think so."

Jennie swung her gaze back to the curtained area where the nurses were working on Michael. "They might be a while. Do you know where Marissa is?"

"Visitors' waiting room."

"Let's go."

Jennie and Lisa slipped into the crowded room. Reverend Cole sat in a corner chair, looking like a foreign dignitary. Her subjects, mostly reporters along with a couple of police officers, hung on her every word. "There is no doubt in my mind who set that fire." Marissa rearranged the folds of her skirt. "I have been getting threats since I came on staff three weeks ago. Trinity was targeted because of me and the people I brought with me. Though Trinity is not a predominantly black church, since my arrival our numbers have tripled and are growing every week."

"So you see this as a racist crime," one of the reporters said. "And you know who is responsible?"

Marissa seemed in her element. "Racist, yes—a hate crime through and through. There are people in this world who would like nothing better than to destroy the black community. You know who I'm talking about. The Northwest has a large white supremacist contingency that openly admits to wanting to eliminate races other than their own. Why, only last week they held a convention on a compound they purchased in eastern Oregon." She shuddered. "Folks out there parading around in their white robes and hoods . . . you all saw them."

Marissa sat up straighter and lifted her chin in an even more stately pose. "I have a message for the people behind this. You can burn our churches. You can maim or even kill our bodies, but you cannot destroy our spirits. We've lost our beautiful building, but the building is not the church—the people are. We will rebuild. We will continue to stand together, united. And one more thing," Marissa's voice softened. She looked straight into the camera. "I want to challenge every one of you to join us at Sunday services."

The room erupted in questions. "Reverend Cole," a woman nearest Jennie asked, "how can you issue an invitation like that? Aren't you angry with them?"

"I am angry about what they have done. I am not angry with them as individuals. They like sheep have gone astray."

"I suppose the next thing you're going to tell us is that you love them." The man who spoke wore a cynical expression.

Reverend Cole's gaze drifted downward, then up again. "No," she said softly. "I am sorry to say that I can't profess to love them. I am much too human for that. And my own personal wounds are too deep. But I know that God does love them—just as He loves all of his children. God is willing to forgive and to love much more readily than I. Eventually He will work that spirit of love and forgiveness into me and into all the people of Trinity who have been hurt by what they have done."

Reverend Cole went on to tell them about God's grace and love and how repentance—turning away from sin— could save the soul. She'd turned the waiting room into a chapel and the press conference into a sermon. Maybe that was why Pastor Dave and Michael had urged the board to hire her.

"You said your own wounds were too deep. Can you tell us what you meant?" a reporter across the room asked.

Marissa pursed her lips, and for a moment Jennie thought she might not answer. "When I was a little girl some men came to our home. My daddy had been called to testify against a known white supremacist who was standing trial for the murder of our neighbor—a man who was running for mayor. The police chief assured Daddy that our family would be protected."

Marissa's lovely brown eyes drifted closed. She touched her colorful fingertips to her forehead and drew them down her cheek. "I believe now the chief may have been a secret member of the Ku Klux Klan. The night before the trial, four men in robes and hoods beat and hung my daddy from the oak tree in our front yard. Then they beat and killed my mother. The police never even found a suspect."

In the stillness of the room, Jennie could almost hear the beating of her own heart. In the awkward moments that followed, no one seemed to know what to say.

Marissa drew in a deep breath. "I find it very hard to love those people. But God was good to me. He placed me in the home of a wonderful family who gave me all the love I could possibly want. They raised me as I believe my parents would have. To be bold and to speak my mind and . . . to do the will of God."

"Have any provisions been made for the children to continue school?" someone asked, obviously wanting to change the subject.

Marissa gave them the same answer she'd given Jennie and Mom earlier.

"Are you aware the police are holding the janitor for questioning?"

"No." She threw up her hands in disgust. "Poor Philippe. He would never do such a thing. He and his son, Carlos, have only been in this country for two months. He is thrilled to have found work. No, I do not for one moment believe he set that fire. To find the real culprits, I suggest the police turn this town upside down and bring in everyone who's ever had an affiliation with the white supremacists."

An urgent message over the intercom drowned out her last words. "Code Blue. Code Blue. Emergency staff report to the burn unit immediately."

Jennie's heart sank, landing somewhere near her feet. *Please, God, don't let it be Michael.* The operator repeated the message several times as Jennie and Lisa made their way back to the unit. Half a dozen doctors and nurses poured into Michael's room.

"What's going on?" Lisa asked. "Why aren't they suiting up?"

"They don't have time." Jennie grabbed Lisa's arm and pulled her back out of the way. "He's coding."

"Coding—you mean his heart?" Eyes wide and teary, Lisa sank into the chair at the nurses' desk.

Jennie stood behind her, absently massaging Lisa's neck and shoulders while she watched the flat line on the monitor above their heads.

8

"God, please let Michael live," Jennie whispered. Behind closed lids she imagined Michael getting out of his bed and walking toward her. He stood in the center of a white light.

"I have to leave now," he said. "God is taking me home."

No. You can't—not yet. Jennie wanted to argue but stood transfixed, unable to speak.

"I wanted to finish working with Jared. God has great things planned for him. He needs a friend, Jennie, to help him through this. I'm counting on you." In the next instant he was gone.

Jennie opened her eyes. "He's dead." The words tumbled out of her mouth before she could stop them.

"He can't be." Lisa pointed to the monitor. "Look! His heart is beating again!"

"What?" Jennie could hardly believe it. The image she'd seen and heard seemed so real. She couldn't have imagined it. Could she?

A nurse came out of Michael's room shaking her head. "We should have let him go."

"Couldn't," a second nurse said, stripping off her gloves. "He didn't have a living will. You know that."

The first nurse turned on the water and began washing her hands. "Sometimes we go too far."

Jennie tuned them out, confused by what had just happened.

64

"Why did you say that, Jennie?" Lisa asked. "Why did you say he was dead?"

"I—never mind." She couldn't very well tell anyone what she'd seen. Not now. What she thought had been God bringing her a message must have only been her imagination. "I didn't think he'd make it, I guess." She sighed, thinking she should be rejoicing and thanking God that Michael hadn't died. Only she didn't feel thankful—just sad.

One by one the team of doctors and nurses that had responded to the code drifted out of the room. Through bits and pieces of conversation, Jennie put it all together. Michael was now on life support—a ventilator that would breathe for him. They'd stabilized him—for now.

Reverend Cole had come in during all the excitement. Now she was getting into the isolation garb so she could take her turn staying with Michael. It seemed a shame Marissa had to cover up her beautiful outfit. The pale green scrubs did nothing for her rich brown skin.

"How long can you be here?" Jennie asked.

"Until two. I'm meeting with the board at two-thirty."

Jennie nodded. "I'll be back. Or Mom will."

"I wish Marissa could stay longer," Jennie said to Lisa on the way back to the car. "I have something I need to do and Mom looked so tired. I don't want to wake her up."

"I could come back this afternoon," Lisa said. "I kind of like being here, watching the nurses and reading to Michael."

"Really?"

Lisa's lips separated in a wide smile. "You don't need to look so surprised. Remember when we did those career-guidance tests last year?"

"Yeah."

"Nursing was one of the careers I scored highest in." She wrinkled her nose. "I thought I'd be too squeamish, but I did okay."

"Much better than me." Though Jennie had some medical knowledge and knew CPR, she had no desire to go into a medicine-related field.

"Maybe I'll be a forensic pathologist and you can be a detective and we can solve murders together."

Jennie chuckled. "I'll believe that when I see it. Sitting in a room with a patient is a whole lot different than doing autopsies."

"Hmm. You may have something there. Guess I should think this through a little more."

While Lisa thought, Jennie opened her car door and scooted inside. The day was another scorcher. Temperatures, according to the weather report on KISN, would reach ninety degrees. It was hotter than that in her car. Definitely a day for air conditioning.

"Do you want me to go back to the hospital this afternoon?" Lisa asked when they were only a short distance from her house. "You didn't say."

"That would be great. I need to check something out."

"What?"

Jennie pinched her lips together. Releasing a deep sigh, Jennie told Lisa about her strange vision—or whatever it had been.

"Wow." Lisa frowned. "Wow," she said again.

"It was so weird. I wish I could forget about it, but—"

"You can't. What if it's a message from God?"

"If that's the case, why is Michael still alive?"

Lisa frowned. "Maybe it's a sign of what's to come. Maybe God meant for Michael to die. You heard what that nurse said about going too far."

"Maybe. Even if it was only my imagination, I feel like I have to talk to Jared. He probably does need a friend right now. And I know it's what Michael would want." Jennie slowed to turn onto Lisa's street. "I wish I knew if I could trust him. I keep thinking about what Marissa said about the white supremacist groups. Even if Jared is telling the truth and does want out, the fact that he joined them in the first place . . ." Jennie shuddered. "It's hard to have sympathy for somebody like that."

"True, but Marissa also talked about forgiveness. If he does want out, we should support him and show him he's better off without people like that in his life."

"I know Michael believed in Jared, but don't forget, he was at the school just before the fire broke out. If he's innocent, why would he have come back this morning? I'm not sure we can trust him."

"I suppose you're right. What are you going to do?"

"Go to the police station. Find out if they arrested Jared. Then I'm going to try to talk to him myself."

Jennie pulled into Lisa's driveway. "Will you need a ride to the hospital later?"

"I don't think so. I'll leave a message on your answering machine if I do."

Jennie started to drive away, then remembered her brother. Lisa met her on the porch.

"Nick's not here, Jen. Mom left a note. She and Dad took the boys swimming out at Vancouver Lake. They won't be back until around four."

"Great. That gives me plenty of time to do some digging."

Driving to police headquarters, Jennie had mixed feelings about talking to Jared. The night before, Dad made it clear he didn't want Jennie involved with the investigation. He wouldn't like her involvement with Jared either. Maybe she should talk to him first—bring him up to date. Unfortunately, if she did that, he might forbid her to even talk to Jared again. Though she felt a strong obligation to Michael to help Jared, she didn't want to go against Dad's wishes. She hated situations like that.

Jennie found a parking spot a couple blocks away from the police station, plugged the meter, and hurried up the street. The morning had already escaped and Jennie hoped she wasn't too late. If Jared had been released, she wouldn't have a clue where to find him.

"Jennie!" Dad came out of the building just as she was going in.

"Hi." Jennie waited for him to join her.

"What brings you down here?" His smile faded. "It isn't your mother?"

"Mom's fine. Sleeping. Reverend Cole is at the hospital with Michael." Jennie dropped her gaze to the steps. "He coded, Dad. They have him on life support."

"I'm sorry to hear that."

"Mom doesn't know yet. She'll probably be mad at me for not waking her up, but she seemed so tired, I thought she should rest."

"Good decision, princess." He rubbed the back of his head. "Um . . . so why did you come down?"

Jennie thought for a moment before speaking. She briefly considered sidestepping the truth but doubted she'd get away with it for long. Besides, she had a lot of love and respect for her father and didn't want to destroy that.

"While you're deciding whether or not to be straight with me, how about some lunch? I'm starving."

Jennie flashed him an embarrassed grin. "How did you know what I was thinking?"

"A father knows these things." He draped an arm across her shoulders. "Lacy's Deli okay?"

"Sure." Jennie fell into step beside him and told him about seeing Jared that morning as well as what had happened in her encounter with Michael.

"That's quite a story." Dad opened the door to the deli and motioned her in. The deli had a large counter where people could buy baked goods and sandwiches and salads to go. It also had a seating area, which was usually overflowing. According to her father, the family-owned restaurant had the best food in town.

After being seated in a far corner in one of the six tan vinyl booths, Jennie said, "The reason I came down here was to find out what happened to him."

Dad scanned the menu and set it aside. "You're not developing feelings for this guy, are you?"

"No. At least not in the way you mean. I just want to help him, that's all—I mean, if he's telling the truth about wanting out." Jennie glanced up at the waiter, a youngish man with curly dark hair and a skull cap. Daniel Goldberg, the owner's son, greeted Dad and gave her a nod.

"Too bad about your school burning. Must be tough." He set two glasses of water in front of them and pulled out his note pad.

"Yeah. How did you know it was my school?"

"Mr. McGrady told me. You'd be surprised at the topics we can cover over a cup of coffee."

"What's good today, Daniel?" Dad asked.

"Mom made a great black bean chili. And we got a special on our Reuben."

"Sounds good. I'll have both—and coffee."

Jennie ordered a shrimp salad and iced tea.

"Okay. Be right back with your drinks."

"Nice kid," Dad murmured when he left.

"I guess." Jennie shrugged and took a sip of water. "So-o-o, you have any idea what happened to Jared, or how I can find out?"

"He was questioned and released."

"Oh."

"Remember what I told you last night about my not being involved in the case?"

"Uh-huh."

"Well, I was wrong. The chief turned it over to me this morning. I first got called in to question the janitor. He's a recent immigrant and speaks very little English."

Jennie nodded. "Philippe Hernandez. I met him and his little boy a few days before school started—over at the Beaumonts'. Philippe's brother Manuel—that's Rafael's dad—works for them. Mr. Beaumont got Philippe the janitor job at the school."

"Right. Beaumont has already set him up with a lawyer."

"You don't think he set the fire, do you? Rafael said he was a suspect."

"What I think doesn't matter. The poor guy's confessing to all sorts of things. It's like he's trying to blame himself."

Dad moved back when Daniel brought the drinks, then after waiting for him to leave said, "I have a feeling he's protecting his son."

"Oh no. Not Carlos. Dad, he's such a neat little kid." Jennie remembered a tragic fire a few months back where police discovered the arsonist was a little boy who'd been playing with matches. "Do you really think he could have done it?"

"I doubt it. Carlos couldn't have disarmed the fire alarm or the phone. We think that's what happened."

"I thought homicide didn't handle arson." Jennie stirred her iced tea.

"We're usually in on the investigation. You'd be surprised at how many people use arson to cover up a murder."

Jennie set her glass down and leaned forward. "Murder—is that what happened?"

Dad nodded. "Forensics found human remains in what used to be a small sleeping room near the furnace. No one seems to know who it is, or if they do, they're not talking."

9

Murder. Jennie's mind spun with possibilities. The fact that no one from church or school had been reported missing only added to the puzzle. Had the victim been the target, or suffered the tragedy of being in the wrong place at the wrong time?

Daniel brought their food and they ate most of the meal without speaking. Dad seemed lost in thought—and no wonder. Questions bounced around in her head like dozens of Ping-Pong balls.

"Jennie, I . . ."

"Was it . . ." They spoke at the same time.

"Go ahead." Dad waved his fork at her.

"The person in the fire—was it a man or a woman?"

Dad shrugged. "Don't know. We're thinking it may have been a vagrant who managed to find his or her way to the basement. We're checking all the members of Trinity, though, in case it's someone who lives alone."

"What were you going to say?" Jennie asked.

"Believe it or not, I was going to ask if you'd like to give me a hand on this case."

"What?"

Dad chuckled. "You heard me."

"Yeah, it's just—" She arched an eyebrow and gave him a skeptical look. "Dad, this is so out of character for you."

"I know. But you have connections that I don't. You've already met Hernandez and his family. All I want you to do is get close to Carlos. Make friends with him—let him play with Kurt and Nick. The boy knows something. I'm hoping you can get him talking. We've already called in a psychiatrist to work with him, but I have a hunch he'll open up faster with you and the boys."

"That won't do much good if he can't speak English."

"Unlike his father, Carlos can speak fluent English. He learned it in a Catholic missionary school in Mexico. But right now he's not talking at all—in any language. Philippe says he hasn't spoken since the fire. We figure he's experienced some sort of trauma—like maybe he saw the person who started the fire. In which case the arsonist might be after him."

"Like Sarah," Jennie mused, thinking back to one of the first crimes she'd helped to solve.

"Who?"

"A girl I met in Florida when I went to Dolphin Island with Gram in June. Sarah witnessed her dad's murder, and afterward she went into some kind of shock where she couldn't talk or even take care of herself."

"Like a catatonic state?"

"Right. She was like that for two years. The dolphins helped her come out of it." Jennie shuddered, remembering how the murderer had tried to kill both her and Sarah by trapping them in a cabin and torching it.

"Dolphins?"

"Yeah—there's this thing they do down there called dolphin therapy. Swimming with the dolphins helped Sarah remember. They are so cool, Dad. It's like they have this sixth sense."

"Dolphins." Dad shook his head. "I'm afraid we don't have the time or money to ship Carlos to Florida to swim with the dolphins. And we don't have two years. Let's hope you, Kurt, and Nick will have a similar effect." Dad smiled, then turned serious again and said, "Since Philippe has confessed, we can't dismiss the possibility that he's telling the truth. We'll probably have to hold him. I . . . um . . . I told him we'd look after Carlos for a few days. Worked it out with social services. Poor kid doesn't need any more trauma. The psychiatrist agrees."

"That's a great idea, Dad. He can bunk with Nick." Jennie slid her plate to the side of the table. "What about Mom? We really should make sure it's okay with her. Having another kid around might not set too well with her right now."

"I'll talk to her. If she has a problem with it, I'll ask Kate. The important thing for Carlos is that he has people around him who care and who can provide some sort of stability."

"What about his family? Maybe it would be better for him to stay with Manuel and Rafael."

"It would, but there's no room. They've already got six people crowded into the two-bedroom guesthouse."

"What about the Beaumonts? They have more than enough room, and B.J. and Allison would love taking care of him."

"They might, but their parents wouldn't. I already talked to Beaumont. He doesn't want Carlos or Philippe anywhere near the property until this mess is straightened out."

"He really thinks one of them might be responsible for the fire?"

"There's still the possibility. After the fire, the nurses at the hospital found a book of matches in Carlos's pocket. Apparently he's fascinated with fire. Beaumont caught him playing with matches shortly after they came up from Mexico."

"Oh boy." Jennie sighed. She cast her father a curious gaze. "Maybe having him stay with us isn't such a good idea."

"Oh?"

"I guess I'm having a little trouble understanding how

73

you could put our family in jeopardy. I mean, what if Carlos did it?"

"We'll just have to make sure he doesn't get a hold of any matches."

"But, Dad . . ."

He wiped his mouth on a napkin and set it aside. "It's a remote possibility, princess, but not likely. My intuition tells me he's an innocent kid who witnessed a terrible tragedy."

"Then what about the arsonist? You said he might come after Carlos."

"I'm hoping no one will find out where he is. He'll be in protective custody." He drew his hands down his face. "Your mother will never go for it. I shouldn't even be suggesting—"

"Dad, I think it's the right thing to do. Mom will be okay with it—especially if we pitch in and help."

"Let's hope so. I'm bringing him home for dinner tonight."

On her drive home, Jennie's thoughts bounced around from Michael and Jared to Carlos. She shifted from being elated about her dad's request for her help to being disappointed about not finding Jared, and then to being excited about Carlos staying with them, and being worried about Michael. And back to Jared again.

Since the police wouldn't cooperate by giving her Jared's address, and since she hadn't seen him at the usual haunts around Pioneer Square, she'd had no luck finding him. Maybe she'd have to wait until he contacted her. And maybe she should just forget it.

You shouldn't be worrying about Jared, she told herself. *You should be concentrating on helping Carlos.* Maybe she'd take him and Nick and Kurt for a walk in the park. They could bring a ball and play catch. They could all go swimming tomorrow. The important thing, Dad had told her, was to make him feel comfortable and provide a safe environment.

————

Jennie pulled into her driveway at two that afternoon. "The first thing I'd better do is decide what to fix for dinner."

The banging of pots and pans in the kitchen told Jennie Mom was up and that she was not in a great mood. "It's about time you got here." Mom slammed a small pan into a larger one and set them in the cupboard, then started in on the silverware. "Where have you been?"

Jennie opened her mouth and shut it again when Mom kept talking.

"I can't believe you didn't call to tell me about Michael. When were you planning to do that?"

"I didn't want to wake you, and I figured there wouldn't be anything you could do anyway." Jennie hitched herself up on the stool at the counter. "How did you find out?"

"I called the hospital when I woke up."

"I don't see what you're so upset about. You act like it was my fault he coded."

"Don't be ridiculous. I just want to know what's going on." Mom threw in the last fork and slammed the drawer closed. "If you're willing to take care of dinner, I can still run over to the hospital this afternoon."

"I told you before I'd fix dinner." Jennie glanced at the clock on the stove. "Lisa's there by now so you don't need to go until—"

"It isn't a matter of needing to go." Mom glanced up at Jennie, her vacant gaze scanning the room. "Where's Nick?"

"Swimming." Jennie explained what had transpired that morning and got as far as lunch with her dad before noticing the pallor on her mother's face. "Mom, I think you'd better sit down. You don't look so good."

"I'm fine. Just need something to eat, that's all." She

grabbed a banana from the fruit bowl and sank onto the kitchen chair.

"Can I get you anything? Some yogurt or cereal? Something to drink?"

Mom shook her head, intent on peeling the banana. The phone rang. Mom looked at it and then at Jennie. Jennie grabbed the phone on the third ring. "Hello."

"Jennie, is that you?"

Relief swished through her. She hadn't talked to her grandmother in way too long. "Gram, where are you?"

"Still in the Bahamas. We've decided to stay another week." Gram was a travel writer, and she and her husband, J.B., had gone to the Bahamas at the request of her publisher.

"Oh." The news disappointed Jennie. "I wish you could be here. Things are kind of crazy."

"Kate told me about Trinity and Michael. I'm so sorry."

Jennie filled Gram in on some of the details when Mom hurried away from the table, looking like she was about to throw up again.

"I'd better go." Jennie briefly explained her mother's odd behavior. "I wish I knew what was wrong. She's too sick to be worried about Michael, but he's all she seems to care about anymore."

"Has she seen a doctor?"

"Not yet. She promised to make an appointment, but I don't think she has."

"Hmm. Do you think it would help if I spoke with her?"

"Maybe."

Jennie took the phone into the living room, but the bathroom door was still closed. "Gram, I don't think Mom's going to be able to talk to you right now."

"I'll try to call her back later, okay? I'd have her call me, but we're on the road. Speaking of which . . . I've got to run, sweetheart. Tell your dad I called and give everyone a big hug from me. Love you."

"Love you too, Gram." Jennie held the receiver against her chest for a moment before hanging it up. She wished she knew what to do for Mom. Worried and frustrated, Jennie hung up the phone and made her way back into the living room. She knocked on the bathroom door. "Mom?"

When she didn't answer, Jennie called again. She heard a faint moan. Pushing down the rising panic, Jennie opened the door. Mom was lying in a heap on the bathroom floor.

10

"Why won't you let me call 9–1–1?" Jennie sat back on her heels beside the sofa where Mom lay.

"Absolutely not. I just fainted, that's all."

"Maybe I should call Dad, then."

"No. I'm feeling much better. I'm going to lie here for a few minutes, then I'm going to the hospital to see Michael." Mom handed Jennie the cool washcloth she'd put on her mother's forehead earlier.

"If you have the flu it isn't a good idea to go see Michael."

"I don't have the flu. I'm upset—too much stress, most likely."

Jennie cringed, partly because if it wasn't the flu it might be something more serious, and partly because of the extra burden of having Carlos there. "Mom, there's something I should tell you." She explained her father's plans to bring Carlos home. "I think it would be really neat if he could stay with us, but you won't hardly have to do anything. I'll take care of him and Nick. You won't even know he's here." Jennie heaved a sigh. "What am I saying? Maybe it would be better if he stayed with Aunt Kate or—"

"Nonsense. That poor child. Of course he can stay with us. It'll be difficult, but we can manage."

"Mom, are you sure? I thought with you not feeling good lately you might not want to."

"Oh, Jennie, I wish you wouldn't worry about me. We'll get through this."

———

Mom left half an hour later to go to the hospital. When she'd gone, Jennie pulled ground beef out of the freezer, deciding to make hamburger stroganoff—a family favorite. She prepared a fresh jug of lemonade and a pitcher of iced tea, then mixed up a raspberry gelatin dessert.

With the dessert made and chilling, Jennie went up to her room. Things had been happening so quickly since the fire, she hadn't had a chance to do much thinking about it. Then with Mom being sick and Michael hanging on to life by a thread, she'd been too worried to try to think about much else.

"It just doesn't seem real," she said aloud as she moved aside her stuffed animals to make room on her window seat. Jennie loved her room with its bay window and Victorian flavor. She sat in the warm afternoon light. Somehow she kept expecting to wake up and find she'd been having a terrible nightmare. Part of her felt numb, like her brain had been shot full of Novocaine. Another part felt like the Novocaine was wearing off. She didn't know what to do about Jared or if she should even do anything.

That afternoon when Dad had asked for her help, Jennie could hardly believe it. The thought of contributing something had left her feeling almost normal. She liked the idea of being involved in the case. Working with Carlos was a good start, but already she wanted more. The detective in her wouldn't rest until she learned the truth and the police had the person or people responsible behind bars.

"So where do I start?" *Where you usually start, McGrady*, she answered herself. *By writing it down*. Jennie retrieved a pad and pen from her desk and went back to the window. On it she wrote: *Trinity Arson Fire*. Using her usual format, she

79

divided the page into four columns across labeled *suspect, motive, means,* and *opportunity*. Moving down the page she drew a line under the labels and started listing suspects. *Jared* took first position, then *Philippe*. And *Carlos*. Though Jennie thought it unlikely that either Carlos or Philippe had started the fire, it was too soon to rule out anyone. And Philippe had confessed.

Another possibility struck her as she wondered about the identity of the person killed in the fire. Why was he there? Had he started the fire? Or had the fire been set to deliberately kill him and cover up another crime? Under suspects she wrote a big question mark. There were so many unknowns, Jennie doubted she'd ever be able to figure it out. There had to be other suspects as well. Anyone in the building could have done it. On a fresh sheet of paper she began listing the people she knew were at the church. *Board meeting: Mr. Beaumont, Michael Rhodes, Reverend Cole, Pastor Dave, John Mossier, Charles Talbot.* There were a couple of other people she couldn't remember. Others who were at the church included Jared, Gavin, Philippe, Carlos, and Mrs. Talbot. She tapped her pen against her lip, wondering if she'd left anyone out.

Going back over the names, Jennie still felt the most likely suspect was Jared. Jared had both the means and the opportunity. He'd been at Trinity prior to the board meeting. He could have easily slipped into the basement, disconnected the wires, and started the fire. Under motive she wrote the word *hate*. Jennie found it hard to believe that people could actually murder someone or destroy a church because they didn't like the color of someone's skin or their beliefs or lifestyle. "But it happens," she said aloud, thinking about what Marissa had told them about her parents. "What I don't understand is why Michael believes so strongly in Jared's innocence."

The doorbell rang, putting an end to her musings. Jennie

tore down the stairs to answer it. Lisa stood on the porch with B.J. and Allison.

"I hope you don't mind our dropping by," Allison said. "We need to talk."

"No, come on in." Jennie stepped back to allow them to enter, then led them to the kitchen. "Um—you guys want a Coke or lemonade or something?"

"Sure, Coke would be great." B.J. hooked her leg over the barstool to watch.

The others opted for lemonade.

Lisa, as much at home at Jennie's as in her own house, took down glasses while Jennie retrieved the drinks from the refrigerator.

"Let's sit on the porch," Jennie suggested. "I haven't cleaned my room since before school started and I'm not sure I have much sitting space."

"No problem." B.J. lowered herself onto the lounge chair. Allison took the new white wicker rocker, curled one leg up under her, and set the rocker in motion with the other.

Jennie sank onto the porch swing and, once Lisa had climbed in, set it to swinging. "What did you want to talk about?"

"Al and I are working on a suspect list." B.J. set her drink on the floor beside her.

"We think maybe the arsonist may have been after Dad."

Jennie nearly choked on her lemonade. "Your dad? Why?"

"He's made a lot of enemies lately." Allison glanced at B.J. as if wanting her to take over.

"One of Dad's businesses has been having financial trouble. He decided to downsize, which meant laying off about twenty people. He's gotten some threatening letters."

"Did he tell the police?" Jennie asked.

"No. He says he doesn't think his employees would burn down his church to get even with him."

"He's probably right," Lisa said. "If they wanted to hurt your dad, it seems like they'd figure out something that wouldn't involve so many other people."

"Lisa's right," Jennie agreed. "Whoever torched Trinity was ruthless. I mean, burning down a church and school doesn't seem like a logical way to get revenge."

"Maybe, but people who lose their jobs sometimes get desperate. Remember the postal worker who went to that restaurant and gunned down a bunch of innocent people? The guy who fired him wasn't even there."

"And there was a man who went into the KOIN building and took hostages." Allison stilled the rocker. "I think we should check out Dad's employees. B.J. and I already started. So far we've talked to four—all of them have other jobs already and didn't seem all that upset. With the four of us working, we could get through the list much faster."

"I'll help," Lisa volunteered. "How about you, Jennie?"

She shrugged. "I guess we should consider the possibility of revenge. But we need to let my dad know. He's working on the case now." She told them about the victim burned in the fire. "The fire could have been set to cover up a murder."

Allison shuddered. "That's so awful." Tears filled her blue eyes. "Don't you just feel like you want to . . . I don't know . . ."

"Hurt someone?" B.J. finished. "I'd like to find whoever's responsible and beat them to a pulp." She clenched her fist.

"B.J., you shouldn't be making threats you can't follow through on," Allison said in her big-sister voice. "The best thing we can do is figure out whether or not someone in Dad's organization did it. I think the police should know, too, but not yet. I'll tell our dad about your father handling the case, Jennie. He might change his mind. If not, we'd better wait until we find some solid evidence. Dad would be furious if the police started hassling people—especially if they didn't do it."

Jennie didn't like the idea but agreed not to say anything for now. Allison reached into her canvas bag and retrieved some papers, then distributed them around. "We made up a list of employees from Dad's files."

B.J. tucked her hands behind her head and stretched out. "I figure you and Lisa can take the first half, and Al and I will take the rest."

Jennie had to smile at the way B.J. had linked up with her sister. Only a month ago she would have preferred anyone's company but Allison's.

Jennie looked over the names. The list included each person's position in the company and their addresses. "Any ideas on how we should approach these people? We can't very well ring their doorbells and say, 'Hi, I'm taking a survey. Did you burn down Trinity to get even with Mr. Beaumont?'"

"Get real, McGrady." B.J. guzzled down the last of her Coke.

"Wait a minute," Allison said. "The survey idea is good. We can develop a list of questions to ask. Like how long have they been in the neighborhood. Where they work, whether or not they go to church, what church they go to—that sort of thing."

"How did you handle the others?" Jennie asked.

B.J. shrugged. "We told them our dad was concerned about them and wanted to know how they were doing. Which is true."

"I like that approach." Lisa glanced at Jennie. "By showing concern for them—which is really the truth—we have a chance to get inside and talk to them for a while."

"Their immediate response will tell us if they're still mad at your father," Jennie said.

"True." Allison tipped her head to the side, letting her shimmering blond hair cascade forward. "The people we talked to thought it was so nice that Dad cared enough to check on them."

"Sounds good to me," Jennie said. "When do we start?"

"We'll probably hit a few tonight after dinner."

Jennie frowned. "I can't go tonight. Dad's bringing Carlos over. I'm supposed to be watching him."

B.J. grimaced. "I heard you were taking him in. Dad thinks Philippe is covering up for Carlos."

"What do you think?"

"I feel sorry for both of them," B.J. said. "Poor kid is scared spitless. So's his dad. Personally I think they're innocent, which is why we wanted to check out Dad's ex-employees."

Lisa shifted around, tucking her legs up under her. "Rafael says his uncle is an honest man. He's pretty upset that the police were so quick to take him into custody. He claims that Philippe's getting a raw deal because he's Hispanic."

"That's not true," Jennie said, jumping to her father's defense. "Dad has no choice but to take Philippe's confession seriously. He's trying to help."

"I'm just telling you what Rafael said. You don't have to get so upset." Lisa bit on her lower lip.

Jennie sighed. "Sorry. This whole prejudice thing upsets me. Rafael is wrong. No matter what nationality Philippe is, he'll be treated the same."

"By Uncle Jason, maybe, but . . . well, never mind. We need to decide when we can go out and check on these people." Lisa took a long sip of her drink, then leaned forward to set the glass down on the floor beside the swing.

"With Carlos being here and Mom not feeling well, I'm not sure when I can. Maybe tomorrow."

"I know!" Lisa exclaimed. "You could bring Carlos and Nick over to my house in the morning. The boys will want to play with Kurt. I bet Mom will watch them for a few hours." Lisa jumped out of the swing. "I'll call her right now. See if they're back from taking the boys swimming."

While Lisa called home, the others took their empty

glasses back to the kitchen, then went back outside to wait.

A few minutes later Lisa came out. "It's all set. She said she'd be glad to watch the boys. Oh, and, Jennie, she wanted to know when you were picking up Nick. No hurry, she just wants to know if she should set an extra plate for him for dinner. I told her I thought you'd probably come get him since Carlos was coming."

Glancing at her watch, Jennie winced. It was already five. "I'd better move it." To Lisa she said, "Are you going with them or do you want me to take you?"

"Might as well ride with you."

B.J. and Allison left, Jennie wrote a note for her parents, and Lisa called home to let her mother know what they were doing.

———

Jennie pulled into her driveway at six and began dinner, which wasn't easy with a five-year-old hanging on her leg. "What's that boy's name again, Jennie?"

"Carlos." Jennie pried him off and pointed to the refrigerator. "Go get me the mushrooms and an onion."

"How old is he?" Nick opened the fridge and nearly disappeared inside.

"Eight." Jennie pulled out the electric frying pan, turned it on, and dumped in the partly thawed hamburger.

Every time she answered one question, he came up with two more. "Why is he coming?"

"Because he needs a place to stay for a few days."

"Why?"

"Because he does."

"Can Kurt spend the night too?"

"Ask Mom."

"When's Mom coming home?"

"Soon. I hope." Growing impatient, Jennie hustled him out of doors to play with Bernie. Five minutes later he was back inside, so she put him to work setting the dining-room table.

Mom finally arrived while Jennie was stirring the mushroom soup into her hamburger, onion, and mushroom mixture. Nick transferred his attention to her, explaining in detail what Jennie had told him about Carlos. Mom didn't seem to mind his constant talking or his questions. She parked herself at the kitchen table and cuddled him.

"How are you feeling?" Jennie asked.

"Better. Wish I knew what was causing these spells. A nurse I talked with today said I might be anemic. I picked up a special vitamin supplement on my way home. Maybe that will help. And yes, I called to make an appointment with the doctor."

"Good. How's Michael?"

"No change, I'm afraid." She gave Nick another squeeze. A car pulled into the driveway. "Sounds like your daddy's home. Better go see."

Jennie, nearly as anxious to see Dad and Carlos as Nick, turned down the heat on the frying pan, stirred the noodles, and followed her mother and brother into the living room.

"Daddy, Daddy!" Nick squealed over and over as he ran to the front door.

"Hey, there's my boy."

Jennie smiled as Dad scooped Nick into his arms and swung him around, then gave Mom a kiss. Carlos, head down and looking frightened, stood just inside the door. Dad took Carlos by the hand and drew him into the room. "Carlos, this is my family—Nick and Mrs. McGrady, and you know Jennie." Dad pulled her into a warm hug, then turned back to his charge.

"Hi, Carlos." Jennie gave him a welcome smile. "Hope you're hungry. I made a big dinner."

Though he didn't say a word, his large dark eyes told her

86

he was glad to see a familiar face. The idea of dinner seemed to brighten his sad features.

Not wanting to be left out, Bernie stood just outside the door and barked. Dad introduced him to Carlos, and for the next few minutes before dinner Nick and Carlos sat on the porch petting Bernie and getting licked in return.

Later that evening, Jennie helped the boys get ready for bed and read to them. Carlos was beginning to respond to her but still refused to or could not speak. She knew it would take a while to earn his trust, but she couldn't help wishing he'd come around quickly.

Mom and Dad came up to tuck the boys in.

"Are you two ready for prayers?" Mom asked.

Carlos jumped up and ran to his bag. He held up a rosary and clutched the cross in his hand, fingering the beads.

"What's that?" Nick asked.

Dad explained the Catholic tradition of praying the rosary.

"Can we say that one for Carlos, Dad?"

"Sure. I don't know all of it, but we can say the Apostles' Creed and the Lord's Prayer. Then we'll let Carlos do the rest."

Dad said something in Spanish to Carlos and they all knelt around the bed.

Afterward, Nick recited his special prayer. "And dear God, please help my new friend Carlos to talk again and please help us be his friends."

With tears in her eyes, Jennie kissed both boys good-night and went downstairs. The dishes from dinner were still stacked in the sink, so Jennie went to work on them.

A few minutes later she heard voices in the living room. "I can't believe you're going out again tonight," Dad said, not bothering to hide his annoyance.

"Keep your voice down. I thought we already settled this."

"Honey, I have no problem with you visiting Michael once—maybe even twice a day. What I don't understand is this crazy notion that you need to be there all night. The man's an adult—he has nurses at his side around the clock. You, on the other hand, have a family."

"But he doesn't. I finally got word to his sister, and she'll be here in a couple of days. In the meantime I *am* his family, and I intend to be with him as much as possible."

"And I'm your husband, or have you forgotten that?"

"Jason, don't—"

"Don't what? You want me to pretend it doesn't bother me? I can't do that. I need you here, Susan. You owe me that much."

"I owe you?!" Mom's voice rose a couple octaves. "Jason McGrady, I don't owe you anything. You disappear from our lives for five years, without so much as a phone call, then you come back and expect me to be the dutiful little wife who bows to your every whim? I don't think so."

Jennie's heart felt tight. She could hardly breathe. *Please don't argue. Please*, she pleaded silently. Jennie squeezed her eyes tight and forced her hands deep into the dishwater, grabbing hold of the silverware and willing herself to concentrate on washing them.

"I'm leaving now," Mom announced. "I may or may not be back in the morning." The front door slammed with a finality that nearly jerked Jennie's heart out.

11

Jennie's hand stung. She looked down and gasped at the pink-tinged water. "Shoot." She pulled her hand out. Blood streamed from a cut on her forefinger. "I can't believe I did that."

"Did what?"

Jennie spun around, slinging pink soapy water all over his white shirt. "Oh, Dad, you scared me. I thought you were still—"

"What did you do to yourself?"

"I was washing dishes and cut my finger on a knife."

He snatched her hand and raised it to the light. "Doesn't look too bad." Grabbing a paper towel, he wrapped it around the wound and applied pressure to stop the bleeding. "Come sit down."

Jennie sank into a chair at the kitchen table. "It's just a little cut, Dad," Jennie said. "It'll be fine."

He unwrapped her hand and examined the cut. "Doesn't look like it needs stitches. You should be more careful. Didn't your mom teach you how to wash knives properly?"

Jennie bristled, resenting his attitude. "Dad, I *know* how to do dishes. I know I'm not supposed to put the sharp knives in the sink with the other silverware. It was an accident, okay?" She lifted her head and met his gaze, swallowing back her anger. It was the first time since he'd come home that she'd said a harsh word to him. "I . . . I'm sorry."

Dad's dark blue eyes shone with understanding. "You heard your mother and me arguing, didn't you?"

Jennie nodded.

"Just like old times, huh? We can't seem to be together for two minutes without a disagreement. Then I come and take it out on you."

"You're not going away again, are you? 'Cause I know Mom loves you. She's just worried about Michael. He's a good friend and—"

"You don't have to defend your mother's actions to me, Jennie. I don't know why her going out upset me so much." He sighed and went over to the coffeepot. Pouring himself a cup, he said, "I have to admit I'm jealous of the time she's spending with him." He took a sip and shook his head. "Don't worry, princess. We'll work it out."

Jennie wasn't so sure. Not wanting to dwell on the problem, she fixed herself a cup of peppermint tea and joined her dad at the table. "How's the case going?"

He fixed a blank gaze on her. "What?"

"The investigation—you know, the fire and everything?"

"Hmm. Not great. Too many people with too many opinions and not enough hard evidence. We did find something today, though, that might shed some new light on things."

"What evidence? Can you tell me?"

"Not just now. All I can say is that we've got to be certain of our facts before we make a move. We can't afford any slip-ups. This is a touchy situation from a lot of standpoints."

Jennie wished he would tell her more. At the same time, she wanted to tell him about the list B.J. and Allison had put together. Instead, she shifted directions and asked, "Is Philippe still in jail?"

"For now. He gave us a sworn statement this afternoon, against his lawyer's advice. Says he set the fire because he was angry about the way some of the board members treated him.

He claims he didn't know anyone was in the furnace room."
Dad rolled his coffee mug between his hands. "I just wish
Carlos would open up. The more I see of that kid, the more
I think he knows something."

They sat quietly for a few moments.

"Heard some good news today." Dad set down his cup.
Jennie looked up at him. "What?"

"Come next week, you and Nick will have a school to go
to."

"Really? Where?"

"Beaumont offered Trinity the use of an empty warehouse he owns. With a little work, it can be converted into a
school. He announced his plans this morning and by noon
had enough volunteers and donated materials to get the project done over the weekend."

"Wow. Do you know where it is?"

"Yep. Drove by it this afternoon. It's in Oregon City, just
south of the freeway. Not much to look at, but it'll do until
they can rebuild."

"That's super. I wonder why Allison and B.J. didn't tell
me. I think I'll go call Lisa. She'll be so excited."

"Ah, Jennie." Dad had turned serious again. "Would you
mind if I went out for a while?"

"I guess not. Where are you going?"

"I'm not sure. I have some heavy thinking to do."

When the front door closed, Jennie stood there for a moment looking at it, feeling like a part of her had gone with
Dad. What would happen next? Her life had been like a roller
coaster lately, up one minute, down the next. Now it felt like
the train had flown off the tracks. Dad had said not to worry
about his relationship with Mom. But how could she not?
She couldn't very well turn off her brain.

But you could think about something else, part of her seemed
to say. With a deep sigh and a prayer for her parents, Jennie
went upstairs to call Lisa. Her room glowed with the rosy

light of a sunset. Jennie loved the warm, comfortable feel of it. She sprawled out on her bed, picked up the phone, and dialed.

"Hi, Jen." Lisa greeted. "I was going to call you. I just hung up from talking to Allison, and you'll never guess what she told me."

"You mean about her dad donating the building for the school?"

"How did you know?"

"Dad told me."

"Isn't it cool? My dad's volunteering to help get it ready. I am so excited. Mom says she's proud of how the entire community is coming together to make it happen."

"That is pretty cool," Jennie agreed.

They talked for the next hour about going back to school and how some of the kids had already transferred to other places. Jennie did get some new information. Only the seventh through twelfth graders would be going to the warehouse. The other children would be going to two different churches in the area, both with lots of room that wasn't being utilized during the week. As they talked, Jennie lost some of her earlier enthusiasm. Going to a warehouse in some industrial area had little appeal.

"At least it's a building," Lisa reminded her. "And most of the students will be back together again."

Jennie heard Aunt Kate call Lisa to get off the phone. "Sounds like she's upset about something," Jennie said.

"What else is new? I'm forty-five minutes over my call limit. I'll talk to you tomorrow."

Jennie smiled as she hung up. The one great thing about having her private phone was that she could use it whenever she wanted. The private number had been Mom's idea. Not because Jennie made too many calls, but because so many of the calls coming in were business related. Mom wanted people to get through and felt there would be less friction all around if she gave Jennie her own line.

Jennie had barely hung up when the phone rang again. It was Gavin Winslow.

"Solved the case yet?" Like a lot of sixteen-year-old boys, Gavin's voice cracked as he spoke.

"What makes you think I've been trying to?"

"You telling me you haven't?"

"Not exactly. What about you?"

He chuckled. "That's one of the reasons I called. Wanted to touch base and pool information. I overheard one of the investigative reporters say the police are getting ready to make an arrest. It's all hush-hush. Lots of speculation. Since your dad's on the case, I thought maybe you might know. Truth is, I'd love to beat the other reporters to the punch. The more news stories I can do, the better my chances of being hired after I graduate."

"Sorry, I can't help you. Dad wouldn't tell me anything. They're being careful is all I know."

"Which probably means they're going after somebody big. Like Beaumont."

"You think he started the fire? That's crazy. Mr. Beaumont is letting Trinity use one of his buildings."

"Rent, Jennie. Trinity is renting it with the insurance money they're getting. It's no secret Beaumont has been having financial problems. He recently closed a plant and laid off twenty people."

"That's no reason to torch Trinity."

"Maybe, maybe not. All I know is he'll come out of this deal with a ton of publicity and a lot of cash."

"I can't believe that of Mr. B. Look at all the good he does. He's on the board of directors at church. He sponsored Rafael's entire family and his uncle and Carlos so they can become U.S. citizens." Jennie paced across her rug, remembering what her dad had said about Beaumont believing that Carlos or Philippe might have started the fire.

"Nice guy or not, Jen, he's got motive."

"I suppose." Jennie dropped one knee onto the window seat and peered into the semidarkness. "But he's not the only one." She went on to tell him about Jared and how she'd seen him on the school grounds. "Any one of those people could have set the fire."

"That's true enough. On the other hand, Trinity was well insured. And guess who was on the board when the policies were set up?"

"Beaumont—and Pastor Dave, and Micheal and—"

"Yeah. There are a lot of possibilities, aren't there." His voice shifted up an octave when he said, "Just a minute." When he came back on, he seemed out of breath. "Hey, listen. I gotta go. My ride is here. Call me if you hear anything, okay?"

"Sure." Jennie pressed the disconnect button and sat back on the cushions. She hoped Gavin wasn't getting himself into trouble again. They were alike in a lot of ways. Much to Jennie's chagrin, they had nearly the same bean pole shape. And they both loved investigative work. He wanted to be a reporter; she planned to go to law school.

Jennie leaned forward to watch a brown van turn from Elm onto Magnolia. It slowed down in front of her house. When it passed under the streetlight, she caught a glimpse of the passenger. A young man—maybe still high school age—looked directly at her through an open window, then ducked back inside.

Jennie scooted away from the window, the hairs on the back of her head standing on end. She'd never seen him before, yet he looked familiar. His shaved head reminded her of Jared.

The van passed out of sight. Seconds later Jennie heard the distinct sound of glass breaking.

12

Jennie's heart skidded to a stop. She picked up the phone intent on dialing 9–1–1, then hung up. *Hold on, McGrady. All you heard was breaking glass. That doesn't necessarily equate with burglary.* As for the car, whoever was in it couldn't possibly have stopped and gotten into the house that quickly. Jennie took a deep breath and peeked out her window. Magnolia Drive was quiet as far as she could tell. Part of her wanted to call 9–1–1, stay in her room, and crawl under the bed. Another more curious and adventuresome part wanted to look around. She crept to the door and stepped into the hall, lighted only by a small seashell night-light.

Except for the hum of the refrigerator, the house was quiet. She checked the bathroom and then went across the hall to peek in on Nick and Carlos, thinking one of them may have gotten up and broken a glass or something. The boys were sound asleep.

Of course, it could have been Mom or Dad, she reasoned. Maybe one or both of them had come home while she was on the phone. She moved to her parents' bedroom and pressed her ear against the door. Being slightly ajar, it swung open.

When she didn't find anyone in her parents' bedroom, she sucked in a deep breath and ventured to the stairs. Hugging the wall, Jennie slunk down them, stopping at each step to listen. She'd heard nothing since the breaking glass and was beginning to think she'd imagined the entire thing. From the landing, Jennie scanned the hallway and the dining room and as much of the living room as she could see. No creepy figures pounced out of the shadows. The only movement she could make out was the slight ruffling of the sheer curtain on the dining-room window. Which would have been fine if she'd left the window open. She hadn't.

Jennie hurried down the rest of the steps and flipped on the lights. A cool breeze was coming through a hole the size of a basketball. Glass shards lay on the hardwood floor beneath the window, spreading under the table and chairs.

"The guy in the van must have thrown something in," Jennie mused. It didn't take long to find out what. A grapefruit-sized rock lay on the floor against the dining-room wall. A piece of paper had been rubber banded to it. Jennie started to pick it up, then stopped. There might be prints. Jennie did dial 9–1–1 then.

After explaining what had happened and giving her name and number, Jennie waited. Seeing the flashing lights of a squad car five minutes later, she ran outside to meet them.

"I'm so glad you're here. Someone threw a rock in the window. At first I thought somebody had broken in, but—"

"You're Jennie McGrady?"

Jennie nodded.

"I'm Officer Carey. Can you tell me what happened?"

Jennie explained what she'd seen and heard. By the time she'd finished, another officer arrived. They methodically searched the grounds and house for an intruder before zeroing in on the broken window and the rock.

"What's going on?" Dad stepped into the entry, glancing from one to the other.

Jennie yelped with relief and ran into his arms, nearly knocking him off balance. She related her story again.

"You think it might have been Jared?" Dad asked.

"I don't know. He looked familiar—and the shaved head, but I couldn't be sure."

Dad's gaze swept to the officers. "Have you looked at the note?"

"We were about to." The officers introduced themselves and shook Dad's hand, then knelt to examine the rock.

Using tweezers to protect the integrity of any prints, they carefully opened the note. Officer Carey frowned. "You'd better have a look at this, Lieutenant," he said to Jennie's father.

Dad moved in front of Jennie. Placing a hand on his shoulder, she tried to look between them. Dad stood up, blocking her view.

"Go upstairs, Jennie," Dad ordered, his voice sharp and edged with anger.

"But I want to—"

"Now, Jennie. We'll talk later."

"That's not fair, I—"

"Go!"

Jennie turned abruptly and stomped away. She couldn't remember seeing her father that angry. She hadn't caused it—that much she knew. The anger stemmed from whatever had been written in that note. *Dad is just trying to protect you,* she reasoned. Now she wished she'd picked it up and read it when she'd first seen it. On the other hand, if it was as bad as Dad and Officer Carey seemed to think, her reading it might have been a mistake.

Still, it made her mad. Jennie stood in front of the mirror, examining her cross features. "Scowling doesn't become you," Mom had said on a number of occasions. She was right about that, but at the moment, Jennie didn't care. Pulling her braid forward, she undid it, grabbed a brush, and went to work on the tangles. The sun had bleached her hair in spots, leaving reddish brown highlights. She hadn't noticed that before. But then, she didn't stand in front of the mirror and examine herself all that often either. When she looked up, the frown had disappeared, but the ocean of emotions churning inside hadn't.

After brushing her hair, Jennie grabbed her latest mystery from the dresser and flopped on her bed. Two pages later she set it down. No way could she concentrate on the story when a real live mystery was going on downstairs. Jennie eyed the phone, wishing she could talk to Gram. Not that it would do any good. What could she say? "Gram, you have to do something about your son. Dad is being mean to me. He wouldn't let me see the note some skinhead threw in our living-room window."

Right. Get real, McGrady. Knowing Gram, she'd agree with Dad. But she'd be a whole lot nicer about it. Turning out the light, Jennie moved back over to the bay window and sat down. She imagined the van again, trying to capture any details she might have missed earlier. Had the guy in the van been Jared? She couldn't be sure, but the resemblance was striking. Yet there was something different about him too.

"Maybe it's just wishful thinking." Jennie picked up a stuffed koala bear and hugged it. "Maybe you don't want it to be Jared because that would mean Michael was wrong about him." Jennie wished she could talk to Jared again. Seeing him face-to-face might help.

She needed to talk to Michael again too. It seemed like an eternity since she'd seen him that morning. Since he'd . . . *died*.

A timid knock on her door brought her out of her reverie. "Come in."

Dad poked his head in. "How come you have the lights out?"

"I was thinking."

"Mind if I turn them on?"

"Go ahead." Jennie would have preferred talking to him

in the dark. She didn't want him seeing her messy room or her.

Nevertheless, the lights came on and Dad came in. He'd taken off his sports jacket and loosened his tie. He looked more relaxed and a lot less angry. "Looks like your room could use some attention."

"I'm behind. Don't worry, I'll get to it." Jennie braced herself for his lecture about watching her tone of voice. The lecture didn't come. Instead, he crossed the room and stood at the window in front of her.

"I'm sorry if I embarrassed you down there, princess. I shouldn't have yelled at you in front of Carey and Sherman."

Jennie shrugged. "I wasn't embarrassed. Just upset. I wanted to see the note. I mean . . . I know you were trying to protect me. Mom would have done the same thing. But how bad can it be?" She shifted over so he could sit beside her.

Dad lowered himself onto the seat, sighed, and hung an arm around her neck. "You don't need to be exposed to language like that. But as offensive as the words were, the worst part of the note was the swastika and the threat."

"So it *was* the skinheads. Did they take responsibility for the fire?"

"No, but that doesn't mean they didn't do it."

"Were they threatening me? Are they mad at me because I turned Jared in when I saw him poking around the fire scene?"

"Not exactly." The expression on Dad's face said it all. It *had* been aimed at her.

She swallowed back a rising tide of panic. "Was it a death threat? I have a right to know."

Dad drew a hand down his face. "I suppose you do." Taking her hand in his, he said, "They've threatened to kill you if I don't release Jared."

13

"The skinheads want you to release Jared?" Jennie finally managed to say. "But you don't have him, do you?"

"No. Like I told you, we questioned him and let him go." The scar on Dad's face twitched as he spoke.

"Well, at least now we know for sure Jared wasn't the guy I saw in the car."

"Not likely. Officer Carey thinks you may have seen his older brother. Carey has dealt with some of these guys before. Rich Reinhardt is the group's leader."

"No wonder Jared has had trouble leaving the group." Jennie jumped up and paced across the floor. "I still don't understand. Why would they think you still had Jared?"

"I have no idea."

"Unless Jared told them that. . . . Dad, suppose Jared is telling the truth and he really does want to leave the gang. He could be hiding somewhere to keep from going back. Maybe he's afraid of what they might do to him."

"Then I guess we'll just have to find him."

Dad stood and stretched. "In the meantime you'd best get ready for bed." He glanced around the room, his expression changing from one of concern to annoyance. "I hope you plan on cleaning this mess up soon."

An all-too-familiar resentment surged through her again. *You have no business criticizing how I keep my room. Mom never did—hardly ever.* Of course, Jennie usually didn't let it get this bad. She clenched her fists and clamped her jaw shut to keep from making the caustic remark. "I'll get to it," she said through clenched teeth.

"Good. It's important to have order in your life, princess. Especially when the world outside is a mess."

Tight-lipped, Jennie nodded. Her anger dissipated some. Dad had a point, but she didn't feel like acknowledging it right now. *You're being defensive, McGrady. Let it go.* Relations between her and her father had been nearly perfect since he'd come home, but in the last few days she'd had feelings of almost wishing he hadn't come back. She didn't want to feel that way.

Jennie shoved the thought aside. "I love you, Dad," she said aloud to reassure herself more than him.

"I love you too, princess." He kissed her cheek and started to leave. At the door he turned back around. "By the way, I stopped by the hospital tonight to see your mother."

"You did?"

"Hmm." The expression on his face indicated the visit hadn't gone well.

Jennie told herself that he might just be tired. "How's Michael?" What she really wanted to ask was: *Did you work everything out? Is everything okay between you two?* But she was afraid to ask that. Afraid the answer might be no.

"No change." Dad hesitated a moment, then said, "I'll be gone by the time you get up in the morning. Have an early breakfast appointment. Your mom said she'd call you around nine."

Jennie nodded and told him about her plan to take Carlos and Nick to Kate's. "Lisa and I have some stuff we need to do."

"Good. Your mother could use the rest." He frowned, looking like he wanted to say more but didn't. "Good night, princess. Sleep tight."

When the door closed, Jennie sank onto her bed. Glancing around her room, she winced at the mess. Dirty clothes lay in heaps where she'd taken them off. Drawers hung halfway open. Her book bag still lay where she'd set it on Monday, unzipped, its contents falling out. Chaos. Just like everything else in her life right now.

Remembering her father's comment about order, she picked up a pair of socks and a shirt that lay at her feet, then scooped up the other clothes littering the floor as she made her way to the closet. She dumped them into the empty laundry basket behind the closet door.

Twenty minutes later the room looked tidy, and Jennie did feel better and a lot more in control. Pajamas on and teeth brushed, Jennie had one more task to do before she could fall asleep. She pulled out the suspect chart she'd started on the fire investigation and added another name: *Rich Reinhardt. Skinhead. Jared's older brother.* Under motive she wrote *revenge.* If Rich knew of Jared's visit to Michael, he could have had more on his mind than prejudice.

Setting the chart aside, she pulled out her diary. She hadn't written in it since the first day of school over a week ago. Reading over the entry brought a smile to her lips.

This is going to be a great year. I'm officially on the swim team. Coach Dayton says I'm the best swimmer she's had in a long time. Jennie stopped reading and leaned back against her pillows remembering. She'd not only made the team, she'd broken a state record.

Friday afternoon after school Jennie had gone to the pool to keep her appointment with Coach Dayton. All the other team members were in place, but because Jennie had been out of town during tryouts the coach wanted her to come in so she could be placed according to her abilities. She'd qualified for nearly everything but the hundred-meter and stood at the ready for the signal to go.

"Come on, Jennie. You can do it!" Lisa yelled from the sidelines.

Bang!

Jennie's lean body sliced into the water and surfaced in the center of the pool. Stroke. Glide. Stroke. Glide. Her long legs kept up a steady rhythm while her arms automatically executed an Australian crawl, her best stroke. While part of her concentrated on staying in her lane and on making turns, another part pretended to be swimming with the dolphins like she had on her vacation with Gram to Florida.

The dolphins were fast and sleek, and when they swam full out, not even the boats could catch them. But for Jennie, they had slowed down as if to give her a fighting chance. Swimming with them had not only made her faster but had more than doubled her endurance. She'd always been a good swimmer; now she was even better.

Jennie came to a stop when her hand raked the side of the pool at the end of her lap. She pulled off her cap and shook her hair free of it.

"Good job, McGrady!" Coach Dayton yelled. She jotted something down on her clipboard. "Keep it up and we'll make state this year. You just beat the hundred-meter record." Diane Dayton, DeeDee for short, gave Jennie a thumbs-up sign. With her trim figure, short hair, and small heart-shaped face, DeeDee looked more like a student than a thirty-five-year-old woman with four kids. "I'm placing you in the hundred-meter freestyle, in the fifty-meter, and in the relay." She grinned and reached down to give Jennie a hand out of the water. "Congratulations, McGrady. Good to have you on the team."

"Thanks." Jennie grabbed a towel. Embarrassed by the accolades from her PE teacher and her cousin and best friend, Lisa, she headed for the showers.

"Come by my office and pick up your schedule," DeeDee shouted. "I want you in here working out with the team every day after school." She ducked into the room near the women's locker room.

Jennie pulled away from the memory. A tear spilled down her cheek. She brushed it away. What would happen to the team now? Had their hopes gone up in smoke too? Jennie hadn't talked to Coach Dayton since the fire. Maybe she'd call tomorrow. Maybe it wasn't too late.

The memory of that Friday afternoon lingered like a familiar tune that wouldn't go away—like something that needed to be repeated. Jennie closed her eyes again and let it play out. "Hey, Jennie!" Gavin Winslow had shouted to her when she'd climbed out of the water that day. "Great finish. I caught it all right here." He held up his camera. "How about one of you standing beside DeeDee."

Jennie swung around. "No more pictures, Gavin."

"C'mon, Jennie, be a sport." Ignoring her protests, he took half a dozen photos. "If you're going to start breaking records, you gotta get used to the publicity."

Jennie made a face at him and walked away. As much as she liked Gavin, she totally disliked being the focus of attention. With all the crimes she'd helped solve lately, Jennie had been in the news more times than the president—well, almost. Gavin was right, she should be getting used to it.

Lisa had stayed in the pool area to talk with Gavin. She shuffled into the locker room as Jennie stepped out of the shower. "Why do you have to be like that?" Lisa asked.

"Like what?"

"You know. Gavin's only doing his job. You were being nasty."

"I know. It's just that I've never liked having my picture taken. I'm too skinny."

"You are not. You're perfect. I'm the one—"

Jennie sighed. "Let's not get into that. Like our moms and Gram are always telling us, we're both just right for who we are."

Lisa grinned. "And don't you forget it. You looked really good out there." She propped a foot on a bench to tie her tennis shoe, her hair shimmering like a new copper penny as it shifted forward. "There is one problem, though. That business with Gavin isn't just because you don't like publicity. You've been acting strange lately. Like you're mad at the world. Mom says it might have something to do with all the adjustments of your mom and dad getting back together."

Jennie frowned. "Having Dad home is definitely not a problem."

"Okay, I didn't say it was. I'm just saying that for five years it was just you, your mom, and Nick. It can't be easy having another parent living with you."

"I like having Dad there. He belongs with us."

"Of course he does. . . ." Lisa glanced at her watch. "Never mind. We need to get going. I told Allison and B.J. we'd be there at five. It's almost that now."

Jennie finished toweling off and pulled on her blue cotton shorts and tank top. While slipping her bare feet into a pair of white sandals, she pulled her wet hair into a ponytail, then grabbed her book bag.

A strong smell accosted them when they reached the hall. "What's that smell?"

Lisa shrugged. "I don't . . ."

Goose bumps broke out on Jennie's bare arms. "Smoke." She sniffed again.

"Maybe it's that old furnace." Lisa wrinkled her nose. "The new janitor still hasn't gotten the hang of it."

"Maybe." Jennie stopped at the coach's office to get the schedule. "We'd better check it out."

DeeDee smelled the smoke too. "It's probably nothing or the fire alarm would have gone off by now." Her concerned gaze caught Jennie's. "Still, we should report it. Better to be safe than sorry." She picked up the phone, punched the numbers to the school office, and reported the smoke. After listening for a few seconds, she cradled the phone. "Just as I thought. Nothing serious. Philippe is working on the furnace. Sure will be glad when we get a new one. The money has been set aside. Just has to be okayed by the board."

Jennie opened her eyes, turning off the memory. That had been on a Friday. The fire had started on Monday. The faint smell of smoke lingered in her mind. The alarm hadn't gone off then. Why? Had Philippe turned it off while he was working on the furnace?

The possibility played in Jennie's mind. What if Philippe had turned off the alarm when it was smoking so it wouldn't keep going off? What if he'd forgotten to turn it back on? That meant it could have been an accident all along. Maybe Carlos had been playing with matches and accidentally set the fire.

"That would explain his silence." Jennie bounced out of bed and headed downstairs to talk to Dad. She stopped at the landing. All the lights were out, which meant he'd probably gone to bed. She retreated back to the hall and started to knock on her parents' bedroom door when she heard her father snoring.

Sighing, she went back to her room. Tomorrow would be soon enough to tell him about the fire alarm. Turning off the overhead light, Jennie used the illuminated numbers on her clock radio to direct her steps to the bed. Twelve-thirty. She crawled into bed and switched on her bedside lamp, then set the alarm for five A.M. That should get her up early enough to catch Dad before he left.

Jennie turned off her lamp and snuggled under the covers. True to form, while her body was more than ready to go to sleep, her mind refused to shut down. It raced with possibilities and questions. Who had set the fire? Had it been an accident? Where was Dad going so early in the morning, and who did he have an appointment with?

Jennie punched her pillow and squeezed her eyes closed, willing herself to go to sleep.

14

The alarm went off at five. Jennie eyed the glaring red numbers, groaned in dismay, and turned it off. She'd managed to fall asleep sometime after one and was definitely not in the mood to get up yet. She did need to talk to Dad before he left. Promising herself she'd lie there just another couple of minutes, Jennie yawned and stretched, then closed her eyes.

————

"Watch this." Nick giggled.

The mattress shifted as he climbed onto it. Barely aware of his presence, Jennie rolled over onto her stomach. "Go 'way, Nick."

"She always does that." Nick giggled. "Sometimes I play horsey on her back, but sometimes I just tickle her."

Jennie rubbed her eyes. "Who are you talking to?"

"Carlos."

Jennie bolted upright. "Oh." She glanced at the clock and moaned. "It's after eight already. Why didn't you wake me up sooner?" Her gaze flitted between the two boys. They were both dressed, and from the stains on Nick's turquoise shirt, they'd already eaten.

"Me and Carlos was watching telebision. He made me breakfast and everything."

"I see that." Jennie tossed Carlos a smile. "Thanks for taking care of him for me."

Carlos's gaze swept to the floor. He still wasn't talking.

"You guys better scoot so I can get dressed." She waved them away.

"You promised we could go play with Kurt. We're still going, right?"

"I think so."

Nick turned to Carlos. "Kurt gots the neatest tree fort. We play jungle and G.I. Joes and lots of stuff."

When they'd gone, Jennie threw her covers aside and made her way to the bathroom. A hot shower, though quicker than usual, revived her, bringing back all the questions she'd gone to sleep with, including the one about who Dad was having breakfast with.

Frustrated with herself for sleeping in, Jennie stood in front of her closet looking for something suitable to wear. Nearly everything she had was in the laundry basket. She definitely needed to wash clothes. With no clean jeans or shorts, Jennie settled on a pink cotton sundress and sandals. She rarely wore dresses, but since she'd be interviewing people, Jennie figured the dress wouldn't hurt.

Mom called at eight-forty-five as Jennie was stuffing a load of white clothes into the washer.

"How's everything there? Are Carlos and Nick getting along?"

"Fine and yes. What's going on with Michael?" Jennie scooped up a measure of soap, poured it over the clothes, and turned the machine on while Mom filled her in.

"He's still on life support. Pastor Dave and Maddie Winslow volunteered to sit with him today. I don't know what happened to Reverend Cole. Anyway, I should be home by nine-thirty."

"We'll be gone by then." Jennie explained her plans to leave Carlos and Nick with Aunt Kate while she and Lisa helped Allison and B.J. with a project.

"This project wouldn't have anything to do with the fire, would it?"

"I doubt it," Jennie said. "Allison and B.J. think maybe one of the people Mr. Beaumont had to lay off might have started it for revenge, but it doesn't seem very logical to me."

"Did you talk to your father about it? Sounds like something he would want to know."

"Not yet, but I plan to. And don't worry. We're going in pairs."

"All right, I suppose it won't hurt. But, Jennie, don't be gone too long. I hate imposing on Kate."

If you stayed home more, maybe we wouldn't have to, Jennie felt like saying, but didn't. "Kate said it wouldn't be any trouble. You know how she likes having other kids around to play with Kurt."

"I know. Plan on being home by four so you can fix dinner."

Jennie agreed and hung up, feeling annoyed and resentful again. It wasn't fair that Mom was gone so much. *Michael's injuries aren't fair either,* she reminded herself. *And Mom's right. Someone should be there for him.* Jennie just wished it didn't have to be her mother.

———

Lisa and Jennie met Allison and B.J. at twelve-thirty at Better Times, a book, gift, and coffee shop in Lake Oswego. Allison had suggested the meeting to talk about how their morning of interviewing had gone.

"Did you find anybody suspicious on your list?" Allison peered over the menu.

"No one." Jennie handed her list of names to Allison. "Dead ends."

"Not for us." B.J. pulled a scrunched-up paper out of her back pocket. "Al and I think we may have a couple leads."

She unfolded the paper and pressed out the creases. "This guy—Gary Stanford—is our best bet. He's an engineer. When we went to his house he was gone, but four of the people we talked to said he'd threatened to *do something* to Dad. One lady said he still wasn't working and that he was staying home with his three kids and not having an easy time of it."

"Okay," Jennie said. "I'll have Dad check him out. You said you had a couple of guys. Who's the other one?"

"Fred Desmond. He was close to retirement and hasn't been able to find a job. And get this—he filed a lawsuit against Dad for age discrimination."

Jennie jotted both names and addresses down.

"I still don't think you should tell your dad yet," B.J. said. "At least not until we've checked them out for ourselves."

"I don't think that's such a good idea. If one of them really did do it—"

"Please, Jennie." Allison wiped her mouth with her napkin. "Dad will be furious if he finds out we turned these guys over to the police without good cause. He made it very clear he didn't want his employees hassled."

"Maybe we could all four go together," B.J. suggested.

Jennie looked at each of them. "I think we'd be too intimidating, but we could all go and two of us could wait in the car while the other two go in. That way if there's trouble, the other two could go for help."

"And," Lisa added, "there's less chance of trouble when the person knows we're in a group."

"Perfect." B.J. crunched a potato chip for emphasis. "We'll go right after lunch."

———

Growing curiosity made Jennie volunteer to go in with B.J. to visit both suspects. Curiosity plus the fact that Lisa and Allison had both turned chicken. Fred Desmond was first on the list. His wife, a white-haired woman who walked with a cane, answered the door, greeting them with a hesitant smile.

"Hi," B.J. introduced herself, then Jennie. "Is your husband in?"

"N-no, I'm . . . afraid . . . not." Mrs. Desmond spoke haltingly. Her head wobbled when she talked, like Grandpa Calhoun, and Jennie guessed she had Parkinson's Disease.

"Could we come in and talk with you for a few minutes, then?" Jennie asked.

"Certainly. Where . . . are my manners?" She led them inside, asked them to make themselves comfortable, and set a plate of cookies on the coffee table before cautiously lowering her small frame into a chair. "Did you say your name was Beau . . . mont? You wouldn't be our Mr. Beaumont's . . . daughter, would you?"

"Yes. I'm really sorry about your husband losing his job." B.J. reached for a cookie. "My father is very concerned about everyone he had to lay off."

"Is he?" She fingered a delicate crocheted doily similar to the kind Grandma Calhoun used to make. "That's very nice of him."

"Yes. Um—has your husband been able to find a job yet?"

"No. But . . . I wouldn't . . . worry about it, dear. He's . . . suing . . . the pants off your father."

"I heard about that," B.J. said. "Dad didn't want to close the plant or lay people off. He couldn't afford to keep it going."

"Oh, I know that, dear. We harbor . . . no hard feelings. It's . . . the only option open at the moment."

"M-maybe I could talk to Dad about hiring your husband in another facility."

"That's not . . . likely. Fred will be able to retire . . . in another year. All we want . . . are the benefits he has coming to him."

Jennie tuned them out and nibbled at a peanut butter

cookie while she glanced around the modest house. Family photos and knickknacks covered nearly every available space. She picked up a gold-rimmed plate and smiled as she read the inscription. The date, written under a pair of wedding bells, read *Married September 8, 1957*. The fire had been set on the eighth.

"I see you just celebrated your fortieth anniversary." Jennie showed the plate to B.J.

"Yes." A radiant smile transformed Mrs. Desmond's lined face. "Our son . . . William . . . lives in Pasadena—he's a lawyer, you know. He flew us down there for a big family reunion. We . . . just got back into town yesterday."

Jennie nodded. "Is he handling the lawsuit?"

"Why, yes, how did you know?"

"Just a wild guess." Jennie started for the door. "We'd better go, B.J." Turning back, they thanked Mrs. Desmond and wished her and her husband well.

"Don't tell Dad I said this," B.J. said as they walked out to the car, "but I hope they win the lawsuit."

Jennie grinned. "Me too."

"I don't understand why Dad let him go like that. Maybe I should talk to him. I'll bet he would hire him back."

"I wouldn't count on it, B.J. I've heard about companies downsizing, and they do whatever they need to save money."

"Dad's not like that. My father probably doesn't know about Fred. Dad has a lot of people working for him. Not everything gets his attention."

The next suspect, Gary Stanford, greeted them at the door wearing a perplexed look on his face and diaper over his shoulder. "Who did you say you were with?" he asked when B.J. introduced herself.

"We're not with anyone—not exactly. My father—David Beaumont—is very concerned about all the people he had to lay off and . . . well, we're just wondering how you're doing. I guess you must be pretty upset."

A baby started crying in the background. He looked inside, then back at B.J. and Jennie. "Um—I'm kind of busy right now. Um—" A loud crash and a scream interrupted him.

Gary left them standing at the door and raced inside. Jennie hesitated only a second before following him in. He stood transfixed as if he didn't know what to do next. The living room was in a shambles. One baby sat on the floor chewing on a plastic ring. A girl about four stood next to a counter that separated the living room and kitchen. She looked ready to cry. "I didn't mean to, Daddy."

Jennie followed the little girl's teary gaze to the tipped-over end table and the shattered glass vase beside it. She spotted the child's head behind the table just as he began wailing.

She and Gary headed for him at the same time. Gary ran both hands through his hair. "Oh my . . . Tiffany, what have you done?"

"I didn't, Daddy. Brian just falleded."

Brian lay on his back, screaming and gagging, his mouth full of blood. Jennie scooped up the child and held him so the blood could drain forward. Without asking, she grabbed the diaper Gary had over his shoulder and dabbed at the wound in Brian's lower lip.

Gary still had that vacant look. "I—we better get him to the hospital."

"It probably isn't as bad as it looks," Jennie yelled over the wailing. All three of the children were crying now. "He must have hit his mouth on the table and bit through his lip. My little brother did that once. Could you get me a cold washcloth?"

Seconds later he came back with one, and Jennie washed off the blood around the mouth, touching the bloody lip tenderly. Brian caught the wet cloth in his mouth and began sucking on it. Little by little the wailing turned to whimpers. B.J. had picked up and comforted the other baby, while Gary held Tiffany. "It's okay, honey," he told her. "It was an accident."

His gaze shifted to Jennie. "Is he going to be okay?"

Jennie removed the cloth and examined the split lip. "I think so. You might want to take him to the emergency room. Sometimes they do stitches. Nick—that's my brother—didn't need them, but it's hard to tell."

"Look, um . . . what was your name again?"

Jennie told him and reintroduced B.J.

"I don't know how to thank you. I'm kind of new at this."

"No problem." After looking at the cut in Brian's lip again, Jennie suggested she go with Gary to the hospital while the others stay with the two uninjured children and clean up the mess.

"Whatever you say, Jennie." Gary reached into his pocket, extracting a set of keys. "You seem to have things well in hand."

Jennie talked to Allison, B.J., and Lisa about her plan. They were more than willing to help and were already cleaning the living room when Jennie and Gary left.

Gary drove his Lexus while Jennie held little Brian on her lap. He was nearly sleeping and had snuggled comfortably against her. "He's so cute." Jennie tenderly brushed a lock of damp blond hair from his forehead. "Are he and Brandy twins? They look so close to the same age."

He nodded. "That was a surprise. We'd only planned on having two kids . . . but life doesn't always follow our plans."

Jennie chuckled. "That's for sure. My friends and I were only going to talk with you for five minutes, maybe ten. And here I am, riding with you to the hospital. Strange."

"Right. What was it you wanted to talk to me about?"

Jennie felt certain Gary was not the type of person to resort to arson but decided to question him anyway—especially now that she had the opportunity. "We've been questioning the people Mr. Beaumont laid off to see how they're getting along."

"Why would you do that?"

"Mr. Beaumont is concerned about you. And—" Jennie glanced over at him and down at the baby in her arms and opted to come right out and ask. "We're questioning everyone connected with the layoffs to see if anyone is carrying a grudge. There's a possibility one of the people who worked for him set fire to our church to get even."

He frowned and shook his head. "I can't imagine any of us doing something like that."

"Several employees said you had threatened to *do something*."

"Oh yeah." Tipping his head to the side, he added, "I'll have to admit I was pretty riled at first. I won't honestly say I didn't plot revenge. I must have put in a hundred job applications. My wife went out and got a great job producing a couple of news shows for a television studio, and well, rather than hire a sitter, I took over her responsibilities at home." He grinned at her. "As you can see I'm still a bit green, but I kind of like it."

"So you aren't still mad at Mr. Beaumont?"

"No. Beaumont was doing what he had to do. Looking back, I guess I'd have to be thankful if anything. I've gotten closer to my kids than I ever would have otherwise."

Gary pulled up to the emergency entrance. "How about you park this thing while I take Brian in?"

Jennie agreed, parked the car, and was walking back to the building when she saw a familiar figure making his way through the parking lot.

"Dad! Hey, wait up."

"Hi." He greeted her with a customary hug. "What brings you down here? Where are Nick and Carlos?"

Jennie briefly explained as they walked toward the hospital entrance.

"I thought I asked you to watch Carlos. I need to know when and if he decides to talk."

"I know. And from now on I will. But I promised B.J. and Allison I'd interview their dad's ex-employees."

"You should have come to me."

Jennie explained that too. "It turned out to be a dead end. Look at it this way, we saved the police department a lot of legwork."

He stopped before ascending the steps leading into the hospital and shook his head. "I don't know what I'm going to do with you, princess." With a sigh he added, "None of that matters much now anyway. I think we've found the arsonist."

"Really? Who?"

"Don't let this get out. We won't be announcing it to the press until after we make a formal arrest, which should be sometime this afternoon."

"I won't say anything to anyone, Dad. I promise. Who is it?"

"Marissa Cole."

15

"You're kidding, right?" Jennie gave her father an incredulous look. But he wasn't kidding. Dad wouldn't joke about something like that. "Reverend Cole?"

"We found evidence at the scene and in her apartment. She was in the building when the fire broke out."

"Sure. At the board meeting."

"No. In putting the pieces together, we discovered that the fire had been set just before the meeting. The board members were just coming in." Putting a hand at Jennie's back, he nudged her toward the sliding-glass doors.

"So it could have been any of the board members."

"It could, but the evidence leads to Reverend Cole."

"Is she here? Did you come to arrest her?"

"No. I came down to tell your mother. Didn't want her finding out on the news or some other way."

"Good idea, but I thought Mom was home."

"She was for about three hours." Dad punched the up button on the elevator with a little more vigor than necessary.

"Why did she come back? I thought someone was relieving her this afternoon."

"Apparently no one else is as committed to this as your mother."

"Dad . . ."

"You don't need to explain. Your mother is doing what

117

she feels she needs to do. Can't argue with that. Humph. I feel bad even complaining about it."

The elevator doors swished open and Dad mumbled, "I'll talk to you later."

Jennie caught her father's arm. "Are you sure it was Marissa? What about the threatening notes she got?"

"That was the clincher for me, princess. Marissa sent those notes to herself."

"But, Dad—" Jennie started to dispute the allegation. None of it made sense. Reverend Cole was a wonderful, giving person.

"I know you have a lot of questions. So do I, but this isn't the time or place to discuss it. We'll talk later—at home."

They parted then, Jennie veering toward the emergency room and Dad taking the elevator up to the burn unit. At the emergency room, she caught up with Gary, who was trying to fill out some forms and hold the squirming Brian at the same time.

"Can I help?" Jennie extended her arms to Brian, who seemed more than willing to escape his father's grasp.

"Thanks. I never noticed before how many hands you need to be a parent." Gary tossed her a wry grin. "I tell you, I have a great deal of respect for moms these days."

While Gary filled out the papers, Jennie took Brian to a corner of the room loosely termed the children's play area. While part of her mind focused on watching Brian, another part drifted back to the day of the fire. The waiting room had been full then. Mrs. Beaumont and Mom were waiting to hear about Mr. Beaumont and Michael. Mr. Talbot had been there too.

Poor Mrs. Talbot. Jennie frowned. In all the worry over Michael and the business with her parents, she had forgotten about the school secretary.

"Brian Stanford?" A nurse stood at the emergency room door, a clip chart in her hand.

Gary, who'd finished his forms, snatched up his son. "Want to come in with us, Jennie?"

"Sure." Jennie made a mental note to check on Mrs. Talbot and pay her a visit soon.

———————

"Watch this, Jennie!" Nick shouted as he stood at the side of the Beaumonts' pool and waved his skinny little arms. "I'm gonna jump in."

"I'm watching." She stretched out on the chaise lounge and sipped on a tall glass of pink lemonade. After such a hectic afternoon it felt good to vegetate and unwind. Upon leaving the Stanfords' home, Allison and B.J. had invited Jennie, Lisa, their brothers, and Carlos over to swim. Jennie hadn't hesitated to accept. She'd called home from Lisa's and left a message on the machine, borrowed a swimsuit from Aunt Kate, and here she was. Lisa was lying on a chaise lounge beside her, and Allison and B.J. were inside fixing a snack.

Brian hadn't needed stitches after all, and Jennie felt relieved that Gary was not the arsonist. All four of the girls agreed that he was much too busy playing Mr. Mom to be considered a suspect.

Jennie didn't believe Reverend Cole was the arsonist either. Yet Dad seemed so certain. And they had evidence. Motive, means, and opportunity. Jennie could hardly wait to talk with her father. She also wished she could tell her friends.

"Come on, Nick. I'll catch you." Kurt stood chest high in the turquoise water, reaching for his younger cousin.

Carlos sat on a step at the shallow end, moving his hands back and forth and staring at the rippling water as though it held a secret.

"He looks so sad," Lisa murmured. "I wish there was something we could do."

"Maybe bringing him here wasn't the best idea." Jennie set her drink down. "It probably reminds him of his dad."

Jennie itched to tell him his dad would be released soon now that the police had another suspect. But that would have to wait until the police made Reverend Cole's arrest public.

"I wonder what he saw that upset him so much." Lisa lifted a hand to shade her eyes from the late afternoon sun.

"Me too."

"Hey, great news!" Allison emerged from the house carrying a tray heaped with fruits and veggies.

"They made an arrest in the arson case and released Philippe?" Jennie piped up.

"No." Allison gave her a have-you-lost-your-mind look. "Dad just called to say they got most of the inside walls framed today at our temporary school. They'll do the wiring and Sheetrock tomorrow. He's really pleased about the progress."

"That's great." Lisa snagged a carrot stick from the tray when Allison set it down.

B.J. set down a plate of assorted cookies. "Aren't you going to tell them the best part?"

Allison raised her eyes. "You mean the gym?"

"That and the pool. It's almost ready."

"Great!" Jennie felt a ton lighter than she had all week.

"Dad just talked to Coach Dayton," B.J. continued, "and she wants us there tonight to finish cleaning the place up, then we'll practice."

"Tonight?" Jennie glanced over at the boys. Nick and Kurt had coaxed Carlos into the water and the three were playing catch. "You going?"

"Of course." B.J. sank into one of the white metal chairs at the glass-topped table and bit into a chocolate chip cookie. "Aren't you?"

Jennie shrugged. Much as she wanted to, with Mom gone there'd be dinner and dishes, not to mention watching the boys. She related those things and added, "I was planning to visit Michael and Mrs. Talbot tonight too. What time does DeeDee want us there?"

"Six-thirty. I was hoping you'd pick me up. I could get a ride, but I'd rather go with you."

"I'll have to check with my parents." The sound of laughter dragged Jennie's attention back to the pool. "Did you hear that?" Jennie whispered, not wanting Carlos to hear. "He's laughing."

Kurt had the ball balanced on his nose. Nick and Carlos were trying to knock it off. "My turn, my turn." Carlos grabbed the ball and set it on his nose.

When Jennie arrived home at five-thirty, Mom was there fixing a salad. The kitchen smelled lived-in and warm. The bread machine beeped three times, letting them know the baking cycle had finished.

Mom hugged Jennie, then Nick and Carlos, and sent the boys out to feed and water Bernie. "He missed you today, Nick. Why don't you take the ball out and play catch."

"Come on, Carlos." Nick took the older boy's hand. "I'll let you put the food in Bernie's dish."

Carlos had retreated again but seemed to like the idea of playing with Bernie.

"I didn't think you'd be home yet." Jennie peeked into the oven. Hot air perfumed with garlic, Worcestershire sauce, and whatever other spices Mom had used on the baking chicken warmed her face. For a moment life seemed almost normal again.

"Maddie offered to relieve me. I thought you might like to help work on the pool."

"I do." Jennie retrieved an apple from the freshly filled fruit basket. "Thanks."

Mom smiled. "So how was your day? Did you get to talk to all the people you wanted to?"

Jennie crunched down on the apple and nodded. "Yep. We could have saved ourselves the trouble." She told Mom about the interviews and her trip to the hospital. "Dad tell you about Reverend Cole?"

Mom gave Jennie an odd look, snapped off a piece of plastic wrap, and covered the salad bowl. "He did." She set the bowl in the fridge and shut the door harder than necessary.

"I take it you don't agree."

Mom's gaze met hers. "You have to ask?"

"Guess not. Did Dad tell you what evidence they had?"

"Not specifically." Mom opened the oven and turned over the sizzling pieces of chicken. "I don't care what your father or the DA or anyone else says, Marissa Cole is not an arsonist."

"You think someone set her up?"

"What other explanation is there?" Mom backed away from the stove, her face red from the heat.

Jennie didn't have an answer but she knew someone who might. "Carlos talked today."

Mom poured herself a cup of coffee. "Really?"

"He didn't say much, but it's a start."

"Why don't you come sit with me at the table and tell me about it."

Jennie straddled the chair, much as one would a horse, and complied. It felt better than good having Mom back home. When she finished telling her about Carlos, Jennie sighed and slouched in the chair. "I haven't asked him about the fire yet. Guess I'm afraid he'll stop talking again."

"It's best not to move too fast. He needs to feel comfortable with us and trust us. Maybe we shouldn't talk to him about it at all. From what I know about these things, it's best to wait until he decides to open up on his own."

The comfortable mood remained all through dinner.

Carlos and Nick giggled like old friends. Dad seemed in a better mood than he had all week. Mom was even looking healthier. Things were definitely looking up. Except for Reverend Cole. Dad hadn't brought the subject up—probably to keep from upsetting Carlos—but while she was getting ready to leave for the pool clean-up party, Jennie caught the story on television.

"The investigation into Monday's arson fire at a local church and school took a bizarre twist today when police arrested Reverend Marissa Cole late this afternoon. The DA's office says they have strong evidence to support the case against the former missionary. Reverend Cole will be arraigned tomorrow morning at nine-thirty. Cole had little to say to reporters this evening. Friends and relatives are shocked. We'll keep you updated on this story as it unfolds."

"Better hurry, Jennie," Mom called from the dining room, where she was washing off the table. "You'll be late."

"But this is important." She sighed.

"We'll fill you in when you get home," Dad said.

Jennie kissed him on the cheek. "See you."

She gave her mother a long hug. "Thanks, Mom."

Tears filled her mother's eyes, but she was smiling. "Scoot."

Outside, Jennie stopped briefly to say good-bye to Nick and Carlos.

"Where you going?" Nick asked.

"To the school. I'm going to help clean up. . . ." Jennie's voice faded as she watched Carlos's expression change from innocent curiosity to fear. "What's wrong, Carlos?"

He wrapped his arms around Bernie's neck. Silent again.

16

"Dad wasn't kidding when he said they'd gotten a lot done." B.J. leaned out the car window. "It hardly looks like there's even been a fire."

"I guess it shows you what people can do when they work together." The first thing Jennie noticed from the top of the hill above the school was the roof on the gym. Workers had cleaned and restored it to its peacock brilliance. Much of the debris from the fire had been removed. The heavy equipment made the grounds look like a building site rather than a crime scene. The only obvious evidence of the fire was a cavernous black concrete hole in the ground that had once been the basement and furnace room. Yellow tape still surrounded the perimeters of the burned-out building, and signs warned people to stay out.

A sign also directed Jennie to drive around to the parking lot on the far side of the gym.

"Looks like a lot of people turned out." Jennie pulled into an empty spot.

"Which means we'll get done faster. Hey, look. There's Gavin." B.J. waved and climbed out of the car. "Hey, Gav. How's it going?"

"It's about time you two got here." Gavin chucked a piece of debris he'd picked up from the still-blackened grass into a dumpster and brushed off his gloved hands.

"We're not that late." Jennie glanced around at the dozens of people busy with various tasks. "What are we supposed to do?"

"DeeDee's got a work detail all mapped out. I think you're assigned to the locker rooms."

Gavin's gaze fell on B.J. "You bring your camera?"

"No. What do I need it here for?"

"This is news. I want us to run a series of articles on the fire and the clean-up efforts. You were supposed to write this one, remember?"

B.J. shrugged. "I'll write it. Just didn't know you wanted pictures."

"If you're going to be a journalist, you always want to think photos." He pushed his glasses back against the bridge of his nose. "Never mind. I'll get some shots today, but you need to get into the habit of carrying your camera around. You never know when a great photo opportunity will come up."

Bewildered, Jennie looked from one to the other. "I didn't know you were interested in journalism, B.J."

"Gavin needed an assistant on the school paper and yearbook, so I volunteered. Thought it might be fun."

"You're still planning on doing a newspaper?" Jennie asked. "I mean, didn't we lose all the equipment?"

"It's been replaced." Gavin's eyes shone brighter than headlights on high beam. "*The Oregonian* went together with some of the other local publishers and raised the money for our journalism and English department."

"Oh, that reminds me," B.J. said. "Dad said someone is donating sixty computers to the school and giving us free online access for a year."

"Who is it? Maybe I can still get the story into *The Oregonian* tonight." He checked his watch. "I can call it in."

"I don't know. He said the donor wanted to remain anonymous."

"Well, tell me what you've got and I'll call it in to the paper. It'll run tomorrow." After getting the details from B.J., he loped off to the pay phone at the gym's entrance.

Jennie and B.J. went in search of Coach Dayton and found her testing the water in the newly filled pool.

"Jennie, B.J." DeeDee rose and greeted each of them with an exuberant hug. "Glad you could make it."

"Where do you want us?"

Putting an arm around them both, she ushered them into the locker room. "In here. The locker rooms weren't damaged by the fire, but everything is covered with soot." Picking up two trays, she handed them each one. "You'll find rags, gloves, and a cleaning solution in these. We already used a power washer to get most of the dirt off, but everything needs to be gone over with cleaner and dried. There are some step stools you can use to reach the top of the lockers. Just wash everything down."

"Hi, guys," Tracy, one of the girls on the swim team, emerged from a shower stall.

The tall, athletic Courtney Evans, Gavin's girlfriend—who used to color her hair a different color every week but now had a natural-looking ash brown shag—peeked around one of the locker rows at them. "About time you got here."

Each of the girls had been assigned a section, and Jennie set to work on hers. She was to do row three of the lockers and the two benches in front of them. The locker room wasn't very big, and within an hour the four girls had finished it.

DeeDee did a quick inspection. "Good work, girls. Go ahead and suit up. It's seven-thirty already. Better hustle."

Jennie shrugged into her swimsuit, still self-conscious about the public changing area and showers that afforded no privacy whatsoever. Maybe if she'd had a figure like most of the other girls, it wouldn't have been so bad. But Jennie had about as many curves as a telephone pole. That was a

McGrady trait, which Gram and Aunt Kate bore witness to. Jennie adjusted the straps of her royal blue one-piece suit and joined the others on the bleachers, where Gavin sat with his camera.

DeeDee outlined her expectations for swim team members, of which there were twelve. Six girls and six boys. One of the guys, Russ Brown, sidled up to Jennie and in a deep whisper said, "Good to have you on the team, Jennie." Russ, a senior, was the team's star diver. More than once Jennie had admired his form as he'd executed his dives in competition. Her stomach fluttered at his open admiration.

"Thanks." Jennie returned his smile. Russ had been part of Trinity since Jennie could remember. His dad was a board member. Jennie automatically added his name to her suspect list. She really should have a talk with all the board members. Since any one of them could have started the fire prior to the meeting, they were all suspect—especially those who weren't hurt. It stood to reason that if they knew what was coming, they'd be able to get out right away.

"Was your dad hurt in the fire?" Jennie asked.

Russ shook his head. "He was late, and by the time he got here the fire was going full blast. Dad's the one who called the fire in on his cell phone."

Jennie nodded and tried to concentrate on her coach. Her mind had ideas of its own. The biggest problem Jennie had with any of the board members was motive. Why would they burn down their church and the place where their kids went to school? It didn't make sense. *And why are you even thinking about it, McGrady? The case is closed. Reverend Cole did it.*

"No," Jennie mumbled. "She couldn't have."

"What did you say?" Russ asked, his voice low and rumbly. B.J. looked up at Jennie with the same question in her eyes.

"N-nothing," Jennie whispered, then turned her attention back to DeeDee.

"I expect you all to be here every day after school and on Saturday mornings. We've got a lot of talent and I can see us going to state."

Several of the team members cheered. Gavin snapped a few photos. Russ whistled in agreement and nudged Jennie.

DeeDee waited for the group to quiet down. "That means daily practice, along with weight lifting, stretching, and endurance swimming." DeeDee went on to give them their placements on the team. Jennie felt tired just listening to the requirements. Swim team would definitely take a huge chunk out of her day. She wondered briefly when she'd have time to work on the case. *You don't have to, McGrady,* an inner voice reminded her. *The case has already been solved.*

A movement by the men's locker room caught her eye. When she looked again, whoever had been there was gone. Jennie rubbed her arms to ward off a sudden chill. *The room is cold, that's all,* she told herself.

"McGrady." DeeDee's stern voice dragged Jennie's mind back to where it belonged. "I don't know what you think you're going to see coming out of the men's room, but I'd appreciate it if you could stay focused on what I'm saying."

B.J. elbowed her and snickered. Jennie started to defend herself, then stopped. It wouldn't help, and DeeDee had already gone on with her instructions. Still, an embarrassed flush warmed her cheeks. She fixed her gaze on DeeDee's clipboard and tried harder to concentrate on what the coach was saying.

"As you know, we lost a couple of students who'd planned to be on the team with us. Shawn Masters and Kelly Dupont transferred out. But we're going to do just fine. We have three newcomers this fall—Jennie McGrady, Katy Anderson, and B.J. Beaumont. I've seen what these girls can do and believe me, we're in for a fantastic year." She paused and encouraged the rest of the team members to give them assistance, encouragement, and to help them adjust to the routine. "Since we don't have a lot of time tonight, I thought we'd have some fun. I've separated you into four relay teams—three members each."

The coach teamed Jennie up with Brian, a junior, and B.J. Brian swam first, then B.J. At the end of the second leg, their team trailed Russ's by nearly half a lap. Russ dove into the water. Jennie followed on his heels. She'd swim hard to catch up, stay even until the last lap, then go all out. Russ had issued a challenge she couldn't ignore. Just prior to the gun, Jennie had overheard him tell his teammates they'd win, no sweat. Well, they might win, but she had no intention of making it easy for him.

While Jennie swam with her imaginary dolphins, she thought about how ordinary things seemed again. Only a couple of days ago the school had been in ruins. Now they had their pool and gymnasium back. And come Monday they'd be back in school. Everything was coming together. She remembered a poster she'd seen somewhere of wild flowers growing among the charred remains of a forest fire. Beneath the photo was part of a Bible verse from Isaiah 61: *The Lord gives . . . beauty for ashes.*

"Come on, Jennie. Go, go, go!" she could hear the other two members of her relay team yell. From the sound of it, they were all cheering for her.

Jennie hit the wall, ending her fourth and final lap. She'd had to work hard to keep up with Russ.

"It's a tie!" DeeDee announced.

Russ leaned on the blue nylon rope that separated the lanes. "Good job, Jennie."

"Thanks." She pulled off her cap, letting her hair cascade into the water, then tipped her head back to wet it and slick it back from her face.

Russ leaned closer, his eyes turning serious. "Um . . . you want to go somewhere after practice?"

"Can't. I have to take B.J. home."

"Tomorrow?"

Jennie shrugged. "Maybe. Give me a call."

Russ pulled himself out of the pool and reached a hand down to Jennie. His blue-gray eyes reminded her of Ryan's, but the resemblance stopped there.

Ryan was blond; Russ had rich chestnut brown hair. Ryan was thinner and an inch or two taller. Russ had the powerful shoulders of a swimmer. Annoyed by the direction her thoughts had taken, Jennie squeezed the water from her hair and grabbed a towel.

"That's it, kids," DeeDee said. "Official practice starts Monday. I'll be here all day tomorrow and strongly urge you to come by. Thanks for all your help in getting things ready. God is turning our ashes into roses."

"How do you do it, McGrady?" B.J. asked as they settled in her car a few minutes later.

"Do what?"

"You attract guys like flies."

"Oh, come on, B.J. You're exaggerating."

"Am not. Russ likes you."

"You think so?" Jennie stuck the key in the ignition and started the car.

"Yeah."

"You're not jealous, are you?"

"No way." B.J. flipped a hand through her curls. "I think it's cool. Russ is a great guy."

"He is nice." Jennie's grin faded. "Too bad. I'm not interested. In case you've forgotten, I already have a boyfriend. Besides, I have more important things to think about than guys."

"Like finding out who really started the fire?"

"What are you, a mind reader?"

"No, I just feel the same way. I don't think Reverend Cole set that fire. Not in a million years."

"Do you have any idea who did?"

130

B.J. sighed. "Not a clue. I mean, it would be really easy to say Jared did it, or Carlos, or Philippe. There are just too many suspects."

"For sure. Makes me wonder why I'm even worrying about it. Part of the time I'm thinking let the police take care of it. And part of the time I'm trying to come up with the answer."

"Yeah. I know what you mean." B.J. tipped her head back and yawned. "Hey, meant to tell you earlier, you did good out there tonight."

"Thanks. So did you."

On the rest of the way back to B.J.'s they talked swimming, and B.J. invited her to the pool the next day to work out.

"I'll think about that. Can I bring Nick and Carlos? Carlos loves swimming, and he's starting to open up. Maybe more time in the pool will help."

"Sounds good to me."

After dropping B.J. off, Jennie drove to the hospital. It was getting late, but she needed to see Michael. The chances of him being able to talk to her were practically zero percent, but she was in her mystery-solving mode again and had to at least try. Michael was probably the only one who could help her track down Jared. She especially wanted to find him. Even if Dad had the real arsonist, there was still the matter of the threat on her life.

Glancing in the rearview mirror, Jennie frowned at the headlights of the car behind her. She had the notion it had been there for a while—maybe since she and B.J. had left the school. When she turned in at the hospital parking lot, the vehicle, an off-white van, kept going. Jennie let out a swoosh of air. "You're way too jumpy, McGrady. Way too jumpy." She shook off the last vestiges of fear and made her way through the lighted parking garage and into the hospital.

"Hi," Jennie greeted the nurse on duty. "How's he doing?"

"No change, I'm afraid." She peered at Jennie over the rims of her glasses.

Jennie wasn't surprised but still felt a surge of disappointment. "Can I go in?"

"Have you been in to see him before?" The streaks of silver in the nurse's hair gathered light and made it look like she was wearing a halo.

"Yeah. I'm Jennie McGrady. My mom's usually—"

"Say no more." She bestowed a warm smile on Jennie. "You know the procedure." While Jennie got into the clean gown and accessories, the nurse went on and on about how dedicated a woman Susan McGrady was.

"Where's Mrs. Winslow?" Jennie asked. "Mom said she would be staying here tonight."

"Oh, she is. I sent her down to take a break while we changed his dressings. She should be back soon."

Suited up and feeling like an alien in all that mint green, Jennie quietly slipped into Michael's room.

"Hi." She sat in the chair. His eyes were closed, his body still. He reminded her of a dead person she'd seen at an open-coffin funeral once. Only the corpse had looked better. Jennie tried not to think about that. Instead she focused on a clear drop of IV solution as it escaped the bottle and dripped into the IV tube. *Drip. Drip. Drip.*

"The police arrested Marissa Cole today," she said. "Thought you might like to know."

If she'd expected some kind of reaction to her news, she didn't get it. Jennie thought again about the vision and wondered about the strangeness of it all. Had Michael really died that day? Was his body just an empty shell and had his soul already winged its way to heaven? She'd heard that in a song once. Was he already up in heaven having a great time with God? Or was he trapped in his body? She didn't know much about such things. Wasn't sure she wanted to know. Maybe no one knew for sure. How could they? You'd have to die to find out, and then you couldn't tell anybody.

"Where are you, Michael?" Jennie sighed. "I wish I knew if you could hear me. I need to know where I can find Jared. I need to know why his brother thinks the police are still holding him and why they want to kill me."

Drip. Drip. Drip. The solution fell like tears.

Jennie swallowed hard, pushed back the chair, and paced across the floor. "None of this is making any sense. Someone is setting up Marissa. They must be. Is it Jared's brother? Rich Rienhardt. Do you know about him?" She stopped and came back over beside the bed and gripped the rail. "How can I help Jared if I can't find him?"

Jennie closed her eyes and tried to pray. No words would come. Her thoughts wouldn't settle down enough to be spoken.

The door opened and another green alien walked in. "Hi, Jennie." Maddie Winslow slipped an arm around Jennie's shoulder. "What are you doing out so late?"

"What time is it?"

"Quarter after ten."

"Ouch. Guess I'd better go." Jennie reached the door and turned around. "Thanks for taking over for my mom tonight."

Maddie nodded. "It's the least I can do, Jennie. You be careful driving home, okay?"

"I will."

Jennie dragged off her greens and practically ran out of the hospital. She hated the helpless feeling she got being around Michael. There didn't seem to be anything she or anyone could do to help him.

Stuffing her hands deep in her pockets, Jennie shivered. It had cooled off again—definitely felt like fall. And here she was without a jacket again. She crossed the street and headed into the lighted parking garage.

Tires screeched and squealed on the pavement. A van ground to a stop in front of her. A truck stopped behind her. Flashes of white from two sets of high-beam headlights surrounded her. Scuffling footsteps. Car doors slammed—two, maybe three.

"Get her!" a deep voice shouted.

Something struck her head from behind. Sudden darkness.

It happened too quickly for Jennie to be frightened. Fear didn't enter the picture until much later when she woke up in a strange bed in a strange house. And even then she was more curious than afraid. The thing that brought on the raging torrents of fear and the feeling of doom was the nylon rope that bound her hands and feet together. And seeing Rich Reinhardt's shaved head and pebble-hard eyes not more than a foot from her face.

17

Jennie jerked back and tried to sit up. Her head felt like it had been used as a soccer ball.

"Hey." Rich smiled. His smooth voice was the kind of tone a guy might use with his date. As near as Jennie could remember, he hadn't asked—and she definitely hadn't accepted. "I'm sorry about the bump on the head. Told the guys not to rough you up too much."

"Where am I?" Jennie's throat felt tight and dry. She pushed herself to a sitting position.

He chuckled and pulled a chair around, straddling it, his arms draped across the back. "Now, you don't expect me to tell you that, do you?"

"Why—?"

"Didn't you get my note?" He rested his chin on his arms. He might have been handsome if not for the aura of evil that surrounded him.

"Jared . . ." Jennie swallowed back a rising panic.

"Right. I want my brother back. No more games." His tone was clipped now, edges hard and sharp as razor blades.

They don't have him, she started to say, then stopped herself, again feeling the need to protect Jared. "You won't get away with this."

He laughed again. "You're funny, Jennie girl." His eyes were the color of blue ice. His features sharp and chiseled.

135

Up close he didn't resemble Jared much at all. Rich was older—by about ten years. Jared had a warmth and sincerity that Rich only pretended to have. "I'm sure Lieutenant McGrady will see the light."

Jennie swallowed hard, forcing back the bile that rose to her throat. "What makes you think the police have him?"

"I have my sources."

Your sources aren't too reliable. "Are you . . . planning to kill me?"

"Maybe." He grinned. "Maybe not. Depends on whether or not your dad comes through for me."

Jennie closed her eyes, debating whether or not to tell Rich that his little brother no longer wanted to be a part of his disgusting organization. She doubted he'd believe her. Part of her wanted to taunt him, to tell him his brother had chosen the higher path. But Jennie sensed he'd kill her on the spot. Her best chance of survival, she decided, was silence and to hope that Dad would find Jared.

In the meantime she'd have to stay calm and alert to any opportunity to escape. Opening her eyes again, Jennie's gaze slid back to her captor. He was still studying her as though some secret code were etched across her forehead. A cold chill passed through her.

He stood and pushed the chair aside. Snatching a knife from a leather holster on his belt, he pressed a knee on the bed and reached for her.

Jennie flinched when he brought the knife down. She bit her lip to keep from screaming. "No need for these." Rich slid the knife between her hands and sliced through the ropes and slipped the knife back in its sheath.

Not daring to speak, Jennie released the breath she'd been holding and rubbed the sore, reddened skin on her wrists.

"Thought you might like something to eat." Rich grabbed her arm and hauled her off the bed. "Don't get any

136

ideas about escaping. You won't. This place is as tight as an army compound."

After feeding her a breakfast of eggs, ham, and toast, Rich gave her a tour. The house was an older two-bedroom log cabin with a loft. The kitchen, living, and dining areas were all part of a great room with high windows that offered a view of fir trees and, in the distance, a mountain—Jennie wasn't certain which one. It wasn't pointy enough for Mount Hood and too tall to be Mount St. Helens. Maybe Mount Adams in Washington State. Outside, half a dozen men in camouflage fatigues milled around—some carried weapons, some seemed occupied with various chores.

"I expect you to earn your keep while you're staying with us," Rich said. "Keep the house clean, do the dishes, and cook meals—you can cook, can't you?"

Jennie stared at him without answering. He wasn't a big man—maybe only a couple inches taller than she. She straightened, teeth clenched. He may have captured her, but she did not plan on helping him or his men.

He laughed again. "Oh, Jennie girl. I can see we're going to have to have a little talk." Picking up a rifle, he grabbed her arm and pulled her across the wood floor and out onto the porch. "Kids are supposed to obey their elders."

Panic spread through her again like a forest fire. Terrified, she hooked her arm around the support beam, jerking them both to a stop. "Where are you taking me?"

"You obviously don't like my first plan, so I'm showing you the alternative." He yanked her to him, nearly pulling her arm out of its socket. "We've got a little prison of sorts—nothing fancy. Maybe a few hours in there will take some of that stubbornness out of you." He snorted. "Sure worked for Jared."

When Jennie dug in her heels and pulled her arm out of

his grasp, Rich yelled for one of the men working on a truck to help him. The ruckus set off a chain of barks and growls from the pen that held four big Rotweilers. One man at each side, they dragged her across the yard. When they reached a small shed, Rich handed his rifle to his buddy and slammed Jennie up against the wall. His face not more than an inch away, he used his entire body to pin her to the wood. "You won't do that again, Jennie girl," he growled. "Not if you want to get out of this alive." He pressed his arm against her throat. "Do I make myself clear?"

Jennie swallowed hard, determined not to cry. Rich took her silence for a yes, released her, and shoved her inside. The force propelled her across the dirt floor. She struck her shoulder and head against the wall on the opposite side of the small room. The heavy door closed and a lock clicked into place.

"Let me out of here!" Jennie tore back across the room and banged her fists against the door.

"When you're ready to cooperate." Rich laughed. Through a pencil-thin opening between the boards, Jennie watched them walk away.

"When do you want us to let her out?" the man who'd helped him asked.

"*I'll* let her out when I'm good and ready. The girl needs to know her place."

"That'll do it. You think the cops will turn Jared loose?"

"Let's hope so. Don't much like the thought of killing a white girl."

"Aarrgh!" Jennie beat on the door again. "You racist pigs."

Settle down, McGrady, she told herself. *Getting mad isn't going to help.* Jennie grabbed the door handle. It slid down but the door didn't budge. They'd used a padlock. She leaned back against it, taking several long, deep breaths. *Defying Rich was a stupid thing to do. You should have gone along with him. At least then you could have scoped the place out. It may be heavily guarded, but you might have been able to find a way out. Now you're stuck.*

As rage melted and terror subsided, a sense of hopelessness washed over her and with that came tears. "What am I going to do now, God?" Jennie whispered. She sank to her knees in the damp black earth, grabbed a handful, squeezed it into a clump, and threw it against the far wall. It smelled musty and old. The wetness seeped into her jeans. "How can you let those creeps get away with this?"

Jennie had asked that question more often than she cared to remember. She'd heard the answer often enough. Everyone would stand before God one day and would have to answer to Him for all the wrong they've done. "Maybe knowing that should be enough, God, but it isn't." Jennie wanted justice now. That's part of why she wanted to be in law enforcement like her dad and Gram. Not that God needed help in rounding up criminals. Jennie believed He used police officers and agents to bring about justice.

She sighed. Sitting there philosophizing about the judgment of evil people wasn't going to get her out of there. Okay, so she was stuck in a decaying old shed. That didn't mean she shouldn't try to escape. Maybe she could pry loose some boards.

She tried them all, but the only things she managed to move were the thick, sticky spider webs that draped the walls and filled the corners. The unpainted building had weathered and every board was hard as stone. Light squeezed in through the thin openings between some of the boards. There were holes in the roof, but no way of reaching them. Except for her and a piece of plywood in the center of the room, the square little building was empty. Jennie suspected it had once been a pump house and that the board covered a well. Her curiosity being what it was, Jennie lifted a corner of the wood. A black hole some two feet across confirmed her suspicions. Grabbing another handful of dirt and pressing it

139

into a clod, she tossed it into the yawning hole and waited. She heard a faint splash a few seconds later as the dirt hit water.

Something tore out of the hole and scurried across the floor. Jennie stifled a scream and dropped the board. *It's a mouse, McGrady.* Jennie backed up to the wall. *Just a little mouse. You are not afraid of mice.*

Oh, great. Now she was hyperventilating. Jennie pulled the bottom of her T-shirt loose and held it against her nose and mouth, then concentrated on taking slow, deep breaths. She closed her eyes, trying to imagine the cute little mouse in the Tom and Jerry cartoons rather than the giant sewer rat her brain had brought to mind. She watched the mouse run around the room, probably more terrified than she.

Jennie lowed her T-shirt, then took pity on the little guy and lifted up the board, just enough for him to run back in. She adjusted the board, making certain every inch of the well was covered. She just hoped the ground around her remained solid and that the mouse and his friends and family hadn't created too many tunnels.

"You gotta get out of here," she murmured.

Grabbing another handful of dirt, Jennie hit on an idea. Maybe she could dig her way out. There was a cement foundation, but with any luck at all she could burrow her way under it. After scoping out the area as best she could, Jennie went to the back wall and began digging. The shed stood only a few feet from a barn. Every once in a while she could hear the snorts and soft whinnies of the horses. She didn't see that many men around. Maybe five or six besides Rich. They all wore camouflage uniforms and carried weapons. None of them had gone into the barn so far. She'd burrow out, then wait until dark to escape. She'd easily be able to sneak into the barn, take one of the horses, and ride away.

Jennie's empathy for Jared doubled over the next six hours as she worked. She wondered how often he'd been stuck in there as punishment and for how long. Unfortunately, the dirt had only been soft for about six inches. Now she was into rocks and soil nearly as hard as the concrete itself.

The hole she'd dug was about a foot across and at least that deep, but she still hadn't cleared the foundation. She leaned back on her heels and wiped her sweaty brow with her forearm. The sound of approaching footsteps sent her heart skittering. Jennie wished God would magically open a door for her to run into like she'd done for the mouse. She glanced at the door, then back at the hole she'd dug. She didn't want to think about what Rich would do if he discovered it.

Click. Rich put the key in the lock. "You ready to try this again, Jennie girl?"

Jennie shoved the loose dirt back into the hole.

Click. Scrape. He pulled the lock out of the metal clasp.

Jennie stepped on the dirt, packing down the mound.

Wood scraped against wood as Rich pulled at the door.

Jennie moved to the side wall and sat cross-legged on the floor.

"What's the matter, Jennie girl? Cat got your tongue? I asked you a question." He struck the rifle against her foot.

Jennie debated answering him. If she didn't, maybe he'd leave her in the shed and she could keep working on the hole. With as little progress as she'd made thus far, she might not get a hole dug for days. If she went along with him, she might have a better chance.

"I . . ."

"I can't hear you." He grabbed a handful of her hair and yanked her head back.

"Don't, please . . ." The pain brought tears to her eyes. "I'll do what you want."

"That's better." He let go of her and, grabbing her arm, yanked her up.

He prodded her with the business end of the rifle as he

herded her into the house. When they got to the porch, he shoved her inside. "Go get yourself cleaned up. You look like you've been sleeping in a pig sty."

I'm not nearly as dirty as you are, Jennie felt like saying. *At least my dirt will wash off.* Instead she said, "I don't have anything else to wear."

"Stupid broad." He leaned his rifle against the door frame, grabbed her wrist, and pulled her across the living room and up the stairs to the loft. "This is Jared's room. He's not much bigger than you. You should be able to find something in here. There's a washer and dryer downstairs next to the bathroom. Figure it out. Then I want you down in the kitchen. There's food in the fridge and instructions on the counter. Screw up and you're back in the pump house."

He dropped her wrist as if she had some kind of skin disease and stomped off. Jennie watched him from the loft until he'd taken his rifle and gone outside.

When she could no longer see him, Jennie dug through Jared's closet. There wasn't much to choose from. Two sets of fatigues, a pair of jeans, and a camouflage T-shirt. She picked the jeans and T-shirt and took them into the bathroom. Locking the door, Jennie took a long, hot shower, washing away the dirt and the crawling places on her skin where Rich had touched her. The dirt came off, the crawling sensation on her skin and the disgust in her heart didn't.

———

For the next two days, Jennie cooked and cleaned, did laundry for Rich and his small army, and fed the horses and dogs. The men didn't socialize much—at least not with her, but she was gleaning some information. Enough, she thought, to testify against them if—no, *when* she could escape. Believing themselves to be the pure race, they sought to eliminate the enemy and actually used the Bible to back up their views. She had learned one thing that could possibly

142

help her escape. Rich actually believed that if she hung around long enough, she'd come around to his way of thinking. Jennie decided to put that misconception to good use.

Jennie set a large platter of roast beef on the table, along with mashed potatoes, gravy, and green beans in an onion bacon sauce. The men made their usual noises about how good the food was, and after Rich asked a blessing, they dug in.

The table prayers had surprised her at first. When she'd asked Rich about it afterward he'd acted like she was some kind of heathen. "We believe in the Good Book and all its teachings. We also believe the government has gone too far in taking away our rights. We believe in the right to bear arms and to own land without all these restrictions. And we think we ought to be able to get jobs based on our qualifications instead of our sex or the color of our skin. We don't think Blacks and Hispanics, or Asians, Indians, and gays should be getting special privileges. It's getting so a white guy can't get a job anymore 'cause the government says you gotta meet a quota. Don't matter if you're qualified—what counts is if you're a minority."

"Maybe some of that is unfair, but—"

"I know what you're going to say. We should take our concerns to Washington." He sneered. "Fat lot of good that does. They don't understand our mission." He'd walked away then, as if he'd answered her question. He hadn't, of course; he'd only left her with more.

Jennie sat at the end of the table opposite Rich, nearest the kitchen. She looked around at the men, each of whom she now knew by name. Rather, by nickname. Bones sat to her right. The tall, skinny man from the Midwest had been a farmer forced off his farm when the government refused him disaster relief after a flood in which his wife and most of his livestock had died. Jennie felt sorry for Bones—for all of the men, actually. She just couldn't understand why they would join an Aryan group like Rich's.

Silver, whose hair would have been that if it hadn't been shaved off, was a member of the NRA. He vowed never to give up his right to bear arms and would go to his grave defending that right. Jennie believed as her parents did in some form of gun control but didn't dare say so.

Next was Jesse, then Rich and Billy. Jesse and Billy were brothers who'd done time for robbing a bank. They hadn't told Jennie why they'd joined, only that they were angry with the system.

Thoreau—so named because of his love for poetry—sat next to Billy. On the first night she'd cooked for them, Thoreau had shared from his journal of poems. He'd been a political-science professor at some big university—she didn't know which and he hadn't said. Nor had he told her what had gone wrong, only that he had been accused of something and arrested. He'd been innocent, he said, but the FBI had released word of his arrest to the press. "My reputation was ruined, Jennie. I was tried and convicted long before the trial. I blame the FBI for that."

"Hey, Rich," Texas, a big man from the same state, drawled. "I'm startin' to think maybe we should forget Jared and move on to Idaho. Take Jennie here with us. She's much better lookin' and—ooowie—can that girl cook!"

Fear lodged like a bone in the back of her throat. She pretended not to notice the way Rich looked at her or the way he seemed to be mulling it over, chewing on his steak like a cow with his cud.

"We'll wait for Jared and take Jennie too," he finally said. "How about it, Jennie girl? Now that you know what we're all about?"

It took every ounce of courage Jennie had not to bolt from the table. It took even more to look Rich in the eye. "I might be interested. But only if you let me carry a weapon."

Texas guffawed and slapped her on the back. "Kid's

tough as nails, Reinhardt. Maybe you ought to take her up on it."

"What are you guys, crazy?" Jesse speared his bloody steak. "She's a cop's kid, for cripes sake. We shouldn't have taken her in the first place."

Jennie went on cutting her meat as though she hadn't heard him.

"Which is why we can't let her go." Rich scowled at Jesse. "Don't matter whether the cops release Jared or not. Bottom line is, Jennie stays with us—or she dies."

18

"Oh, Dad, I'm so scared." She breathed the words, too frightened to whisper lest someone hear. "Where are you? Why haven't you found me?"

Jennie stared at the stars that hung in the inky black sky outside the now dark cabin. She must have dreamed up a hundred escape plans and discarded every one of them. Rich stayed in the downstairs bedroom beneath the loft, his rifle always within reach. Jesse guarded the front of the house—Billy the back. Though Jennie hadn't responded to Rich's ultimatum at the dinner table, he must have known what she was thinking because he had added a third guard, Texas, to stand watch out by the vehicles and patrol the periphery. The other men were in the bunkhouse.

Jennie had hoped that her compliance would make the men more lax. It hadn't. She couldn't make a move outside of the house without being watched. Still, Jennie refused to give up. Nighttime offered the best chance of escape. In fact, she'd worn her shirt and jeans to bed every night, in the off chance an opportunity should arise. There had been none.

The other thing she'd hoped to do was to find out if Rich and his men had burned down Trinity. She'd brought up the subject half a dozen times, and all the response she'd gotten was that they thought Reverend Cole's arrest was hilarious. "Serves her right," Rich had said. The fact that they hadn't bragged about their conquest made Jennie seriously doubt their involvement. On the other hand, they hadn't denied it either.

As she closed her eyes, another plan began to unfold. Tomorrow night she'd stay awake. Then pretending she couldn't sleep, she'd bring a plate of brownies and milk to the night guards. On her way from one to another, she'd slip away. She'd made friends with several of the horses the last two days. They were pastured behind the barn. She'd lure one of them, probably Missy, a beautiful Arabian mare, to the far end of the field. Then would come the tricky part of getting the horse to jump the fence. She imagined herself mounting Missy. She'd grab hold of the mane, lean forward, get her going at a full run, then sail over the barbed-wire fence to freedom.

With that thought, Jennie fell asleep.

———

Sometime later, Jennie awoke with a start. It was still dark, but something was definitely wrong. She'd heard something. There it was again, a faint creaking sound. The kind the stairs made when she climbed them. A dark figure approached her bed. She started to scream. His hand shot out and covered her mouth.

"Don't make a sound," he hissed, then leaned closer. "I'm not going to hurt you."

Jennie squinted, trying to make out his features. Moonlight glinted off his shaved blond head. Rich? No, *Jared*.

He drew back his hand and Jennie scooted up in bed. "What are you doing here?"

"Get dressed," he whispered, "we're getting—"

The living room lights came on. "Get your hands up." Rich cocked the rifle and trained it on Jared. "Turn around so I can see you."

Jared slowly raised his hands and turned to face his

brother. "Hey, bro—what kind of greeting is that?"

"Jared?" Rich lowered his gun. "What are you doing up there?"

"Me? What's she doing up here? This is my bedroom, remember?" Jared glanced back at Jennie, then down at Rich. "The cops finally decided to let me go. I would have been here sooner but it took me a while to lose them."

"You sure you lost 'em?"

"I'm sure. Pretty stupid, if you ask me." Jared started for the stairs. Jennie shrank back into the bed. She felt certain Jared had come to get her. Was he lying about losing the police? Was Dad here somewhere? Her hopes soared.

The front door opened and Jesse came in. "Everything okay in here?"

"Yeah," Rich said. "No thanks to you. Why weren't you at your post?"

"Something spooked the horses. Went out with Texas to check. Didn't see nothin'. Came back and saw the lights was on." His gaze drifted to Jared. "How'd you get in here?"

Jared shrugged and descended the stairs. "Just walked in. Must have been me that set the horses off. I came in on the south road. Sorry about that. Guess I should have let you all know I was back. Didn't want to wake anyone. Figured I'd just hit the sack and talk to you in the morning."

"Good to see you, kid." Rich slung an arm around Jared's neck. "You guys better get back out there. Knowing cops, they may have had more than one tail." He released Jared and walked Jesse to the door. "Get the others up. I want the grounds searched. Use the dogs."

"I told you I lost them," Jared said. "Don't you believe me?"

Rich lifted the curtain and peered outside. "Yeah, I believe you, I just don't trust McGrady. He's going to want his daughter back."

Jared whistled, his gaze moving to the loft. "That's Jennie?"

"Who'd you think it was?"

Jared shrugged. "A new recruit—I don't know. Why is she here?"

"Told McGrady we'd make an exchange. Jennie for you. Didn't the cops tell you?"

"Are you kidding? They just handed me my stuff and told me to get out." Jared rubbed a hand across his newly shaved hair. "I was really careful, Rich. Took the old road and cut off into the woods for a couple miles."

Jennie's heart constricted. What was going on? Had Jared really come to get her out? Or had he just come back? What kind of game was Jared playing? And where was Dad?

"Don't worry about it," Rich said. "If anybody followed you in here, they won't live to see the sunrise."

Jared nodded and looked up into the loft, sending her a warning to play along. Or was it just a look of contempt? Jennie couldn't be sure.

"You want your bed back?" Rich offered. "We can kick Jennie out and give her the sofa."

Jared shook his head. "Naw, leave her there for tonight. Sofa's too close to the door. And to tell you the truth, after tonight I don't much trust the guys to make sure she doesn't get loose."

"You're right about that. I need to get a few more men up here."

"Ah . . . Rich," Jared said as he dropped onto the couch, "now that I'm back, what are you planning to do with Jennie?"

Rich explained the options. "Kill her or take her along to Idaho."

"I vote for killing her." Jared scowled as he glanced up at the loft.

The words ripped into Jennie's heart like a hunting knife. What was he doing?

Rich came back and stood over his brother, arms folded. "Do I detect a little resentment here?"

"It's Jennie's fault I landed in jail. She turned me in for setting that fire."

Another lie. She'd only reported him being on the scene after the fire.

"So you did set it. I wondered." Rich seemed pleased. Jennie felt sick.

"Yeah, I set it. And I planted evidence so that black pastor would take the fall. Went back the next day to finish it up and Jennie saw me. I want her to die, Rich, and I want to be the one to do it."

"Hoowie! You are growing up, boy. I was beginning to think you didn't have it in you." Rich punched his brother in the shoulder. "Okay, I'll miss her cooking, but you're right. She's trouble. Best to get her out of the way."

"Good. I'll take her out in the morning. Maybe one of the guys can ride along to help me dig the grave."

Rich laughed, sending cold chills up Jennie's spine. "You hear that, Jennie girl? Better say your prayers. Looks like to-night was your last supper."

Long after the lights were out, Jennie lay staring into the night sky, trying to make sense of what she'd heard. Was Jared really going to kill her? She shuddered again at their cold, calculating discussion, as if killing her were no more a moral issue than hunting down and killing a deer. She desperately wanted to believe that Jared had come to sneak her out of the compound. Now she was thoroughly confused. If he meant to help her, why had he suggested to Rich that she be killed and why had he wanted one of the other men to come along—unless he really did want someone to help dig her grave?

The sun rose despite Jennie's prayers that it wouldn't. Jared had come in around two in the morning. Jennie slept in snatches after that, awakening again and again to dogs barking in the distance. And once, the sound of gunfire. She practically flew out of bed. Who had they killed? Though the thought it might be Dad waited on the periphery of her consciousness, she refused to entertain it.

She wavered between being terrified and being angry. By morning she felt numb. All through breakfast, Jennie listened and watched and hoped and prayed for the cavalry to ride in and take the camp by storm. Every law-enforcement agency in the state had to know she was in danger. So why didn't they come?

She peered out the window again. Texas and Bones were standing by the victim of the gunshot she'd heard early that morning. Though the sight of the deer hanging in the yard, gutted and cooling, made her want to puke, she was thankful it wasn't a human. Jennie piled the last of the pancakes onto a platter in the oven. She marveled at her acting abilities as she went out to the porch and rang the bell. One by one the guys straggled in. Jennie set platters of pancakes, eggs, and ham on the table, then sat down next to Jared, who'd squeezed in an extra chair.

They all bowed their heads while Rich said grace. Jennie's anger came back full force. "You hypocrites," she said aloud. She hadn't meant to, but now it was too late. She pushed herself away from the table.

"Did you say something?" Rich fixed his icy glare on her, daring her to continue.

Jennie looked around at the men. Texas shot her a warning glance. She'd be nailing holes in her coffin, but what did it matter? One way or another she was going to die. She might as well have her say. "How can you call yourselves Christians? You're nothing but cold-blooded killers. You think God would condone what you're doing? You're crazy." Jennie stepped back. She could almost feel the heat of Rich's fury as he watched her. He said nothing as she continued.

"The Gospel teaches that we are to love one another. You people don't know what love is. And I don't want to spend another second looking at you." Jennie took another step back, then straightened and turned, marched through the living room, and ascended the stairs.

The silence stretched on until Jennie thought she'd explode. Would Rich come after her and beat her senseless? She dropped onto the unmade bed.

"You gonna let her get away with that?" Jesse asked.

Rich laughed. "Don't worry about it. Jared and I are taking her out and burying her this morning."

————

Less than an hour later, Jennie stood next to the Arabian with Jared on one side, Rich on the other. They mounted their horses and grabbed for Jennie's reins at the same time.

"Great minds . . ." Jared flashed his brother a grin.

Rich chuckled and withdrew his hand. "You two go ahead. I'll bring up the rear."

Jared moved his gelding out, pulling Missy alongside. Rich didn't trust him, Jennie could tell. That should have made her feel better, but it didn't. She didn't trust Jared either.

All during the hour-long ride, Jennie imagined herself taking back the reins and spurring Missy on, dodging trees, outrunning her captors. She visualized Jared getting the drop on Rich and giving her a chance to run. She even imagined herself using karate to punch and kick her abductors like she'd seen Gram do once. Only problem was, Jennie didn't know karate.

"Stop here." Rich pulled up his horse.

"You sure this is far enough from the house?" Jared turned his and Jennie's horses around.

"Don't matter. We'll be gone by morning." Rich drew his rifle out of his saddle holster, then unhooked two shovels from his pack. "We'll bury her here."

"Whatever." Jared dismounted and came around to help Jennie down. She was on the ground when he whispered in her ear, "I'm sorry. It wasn't supposed to be like this."

Jennie turned around, looking into his sad blue eyes. He *had* come back to rescue her. Now they were both trapped.

"Start digging, kids." Rich cocked the rifle. "Only, make the hole big enough for two."

19

"W-what are you talking about?" Jared stammered. "I'm not—"

"Save it. Don't you think I know a traitor when I see one? You lied about setting that fire. I thought all along you might have. Figured all those visits there were so you could scope the place out. That's why I made sure the black broad would take the rap for it. I'm the one who planted the evidence." He shook his head. "You disappoint me, boy." He jammed the barrel into Jared's ribs. "Dig."

The grave would be a shallow one. Jennie and Jared had only gotten about a foot down with all the roots to dig around. Her fury had dissipated with each shovelful. Now, except for the raw blisters on her hand, she felt numb again and too tired to care. Jared kept tossing angry looks at her as though his brother's decision to kill them both was her fault.

Jennie leaned against the shovel, tired of the work and the silence and asked, "How could you kill your own brother?"

"I hope you're not going to start preaching at me again, Jennie girl. I know the Bible. In the first book, Cain kills Abel. There's lots of killin' in the Bible, for your information. God did a good portion of it himself trying to purify the earth. That's what we're all about, Jennie. Helping God purify the world by getting rid of the garbage."

"Garbage. Meaning people who don't think like you or

154

have the same color skin?" Jennie closed her eyes. The man was insane.

"There's no use arguing with him." Jared shoved his blade deep into the ground.

"He's right there, Jennie girl." Rich stood and stretched. "You two keep digging. I got to take me a little walk into the bushes. Don't get any ideas about running. I'll have you in my sights the whole time."

Jared watched him until he was out of earshot, then turned back to Jennie. "You need to get out of here. Go as soon as Rich gets behind the bushes. If you run due east of here you'll get to Wind River campground. I was supposed to meet your dad and some FBI agents there."

"You were working with my dad?"

"Yeah. It's a long story." He glanced over his shoulder. "Go—now!"

Ripples of sunlight danced through the trees, making the clearing seem peaceful and serene. Yet none of that peace reached Jennie. "What about you? Rich will kill you. . . ."

"Don't worry about me. Just get out of here. Go!"

Jennie hesitated for a moment, then dropped her shovel and ran. She'd gotten only a short distance when she turned around. *You can't leave Jared.* She debated going for help and directing the FBI agents back here, but it would be too late by then. Rich would be furious. Jared might stand a chance if she could outwit Rich.

A gunshot echoed through the dense forest. Jennie ducked, covering her mouth to silence her screams. Rich had killed him. Shots erupted again. *No, it can't be Rich*, she reasoned. The shots were too far away. "The compound." Maybe the cavalry had come. Maybe Dad and the others had rushed them when Jared hadn't come back. Maybe . . . Another possibility came to mind—that the heavily armed men with the shaved heads might win.

Jennie shook off the thought. She needed to get back to

Jared. As she circled back to the would-be grave site, Jennie picked up and discarded several sticks she planned to use against Rich. She envisioned Jared keeping him occupied while she snuck up behind Rich, using the horses as cover. She'd whack him on the head and they'd both get away.

The horses did provide cover, but as she came closer, they grew skittish and whinnied. Rich whirled around. "Hold it right there, Jennie girl. Drop the stick." He laughed. "And here I thought you were a smart kid. Shoulda run while you had the chance. Not that you'd have gotten very far. Terrain can get pretty rugged around these parts."

Jennie fought to keep her gaze on Rich and not on Jared, who moved toward his brother, shovel raised. "What can I say?" Jennie's voice dripped with sarcasm. "I missed your company." She gripped the two-inch branch even tighter.

"I said, drop—"

Jennie winced as Jared's shovel landed with a crack on the side of Rich's head. Mouth still open, a surprised look in his eyes, Rich dropped to the ground.

"Come on." Jared grabbed her hand and pulled her away. "Let's get out of here."

"No." She pulled her hand out of his grasp and knelt beside Rich, examining the bloody wound on Rich's skull. "We can't leave him like that. He needs medical attention. Help me tie him up. We'll stop the bleeding and put him on his horse."

"He deserves to die. He's—"

"That may be, Jared, but it's not our call. I wouldn't be able to live with myself if I just left him here. Could you?"

Jared sighed. "You're right. I . . . I wasn't thinking."

"Good. Now, give me your T-shirt and see if you can find some rope."

Jennie applied pressure to stop the bleeding while Jared dug a rope out of the saddlebags on Rich's horse to tie him up. Within a few minutes they had him draped over the saddle and were on their way.

"Thanks for coming back for me, Jennie," Jared said.

Jennie shrugged. "No problem. I should be the one thanking you. If you hadn't come, I'd be dead by now—or on my way to Idaho. Either way . . ." Her voice trailed away. "I have to admit, though, you had me going for a while. When you told Rich you started the fire and wanted to kill me."

Jared's lips parted in a wry smile. "I had to convince him. Unfortunately, I never was much of a liar."

Jennie frowned. "You didn't start the fire, did you?"

"No, of course not."

"Then, what were you doing snooping around the ashes the day after?"

"Trying to find the journal I'd given to Michael." He glanced back at Rich who was still out cold.

"The box?"

"Right. My journal was in it. I'd written down the names of all the members of Rich's contingent, along with crimes I knew they'd committed. They burned down those other two churches and were responsible for the cross burnings."

He looked away. "I never wanted to be part of the gang, Jennie. Never. But with Rich, you didn't say no."

"The pump house? Did he put you in it a lot?"

"That was the easiest part. At least in there I felt safe. Rich didn't believe in sparing the rod." His blue gaze met hers again. "He wasn't always like that. After Mom and Dad died, he kinda went off. It's hard to explain. They were in an accident when I was seven. Rich was fifteen. The guy driving the truck that hit them fell asleep at the wheel. He was black. Then this social worker tried to split us up. Rich went crazy. He and I ran away from a foster home one night and came to live with this great-uncle of ours. He was a member of an Aryan group."

"Where's your uncle?"

"Died a few years back. Rich buried him in the woods and kept collecting his pension check. The ranch was Uncle Bill's."

"So you told Michael all this?"

Jared nodded. "Some of it. The rest was in the journals. He seemed so easy to talk to, you know?"

"Michael's like that. Do you think your brother found out that you were talking to Michael about turning him in?"

"There's no way he could have known."

"Don't be too sure. He might have followed you," Jennie mused. "I heard Rich say he was proud of you for starting the fire, but he could have been leading you on. I mean, if he set Reverend Cole up to take the blame, doesn't it make sense that he caused the fire too?"

"At first I thought he might have, but now I don't think so. Rich looked at everything from a military standpoint. He and his men planned their hits down to the last detail. To them, the church burnings and other hits were like war maneuvers. They had maps and everything. I'd have known."

"Maybe. But if Rich thought you were leaking information, he might have kept it secret from you. He may be crazy, but he's not stupid. What if he found out about the journal and knew you were about to turn him in? He and his men could have set the fire, taken the journal, and—"

Jared shook his head. "Doesn't wash. As far as the journal goes—I'm sure Rich didn't know about that. I kept it buried in the pump house in a metal box. Other than me, Michael's the only one who ever saw it. After the fire I thought I'd better try to find it. I wasn't ready to turn it over to the police. I thought the metal would survive the fire . . . maybe it did. I don't know. You caught me before I had a chance to look."

Jennie sighed. She wanted the arsonist to be Rich. She wanted it to be over. "Why did you go to Michael in the first place?"

"Sometimes some of the guys and I would come into Portland and hang out around Pioneer Square and Old Town to recruit men for the cause. I met Michael down there. He was talking to the kids, inviting them to church and telling them God loved them—stuff like that. Something just clicked with him, you know? Hard to explain, but all of a sudden I knew he was telling the truth, and everything he said made sense. Michael gave me the courage to break away from Rich. After a few meetings, I gave Michael my journals, hoping he could help me. He said he knew a police officer we could trust. I think it was your dad. Then . . ." Jared stared off into the woods in front of them.

"Have you seen him since the fire?"

"No. I was afraid to go to the hospital. After the cops let me go that day, I hid out in Old Town. I couldn't go back to the compound."

"That's where Dad found you?"

"Well, he didn't find me, exactly. I saw on the news yesterday that you were missing and that they suspected Rich of kidnapping you. I called your dad and talked him into letting me try to get you out. He didn't want to go along with it at first, but the Feds decided to let me try—they didn't want a big confrontation. We were afraid if we stormed the place with you still there, they'd kill you for sure. The plan was for me to get you away from there. Once you were safe they'd go in."

"What happens now? To you, I mean."

"I don't know. Your dad and the DA said something about protective custody. I'll be testifying against Rich and the others."

They rode along for a while in silence. Michael had been right about Jared. Jennie just wished the youth pastor could see the results of his kindness. She also wished she could figure out who was responsible for putting Michael in the hospital. If Jared was right about his brother, she now had two fewer suspects. Jared seemed certain that Rich hadn't done it, but Jennie wasn't quite ready to cross him off the list. He was cunning and resourceful and a liar.

You're weird, McGrady, Jennie told herself. *Why are you even thinking about that? Dad's probably solved the case by now.*

"Jared?" Jennie turned toward him. "Were you in the building when the fire started?"

He hesitated, a pained expression crossing his face. "I . . . yeah. I was there. I should have stayed to help, but all I could think of was getting as far away as possible. I was afraid they'd think I did it." He looked like he was about to cry. "If I'd stayed, maybe Michael wouldn't—"

"You can't blame yourself."

He didn't respond and Jennie didn't press it. "Did you see anyone when you left?"

He shook his head. "If you mean somebody who might have started the fire, I couldn't say. I saw Michael, of course, and Reverend Cole. On my way out I saw some Mexican guy and a couple men in business suits. I didn't know them. It was pretty stupid of me to run like I did. All those witnesses putting me at the scene."

"Not at the scene. If you were there in the hallway and had just left Michael's office, you couldn't have been down in the basement setting the fire."

"Guess that's why the police let me go, huh?"

They'd come to a narrow gravel road, and Jared drew back the reins. "We're almost there. This road will take us down to the ranger station at Wind River. We should run into the deputies before that, but if not, we'll call from the ranger station." He didn't seem to want to talk the rest of the way back. That was fine with Jennie. At this point she was too tired to think straight.

A couple of sheriff's deputies were waiting at the rendez-vous point. The others, as Jennie suspected, had gone into the compound.

"Sure glad to see you two," one of the deputies said. "Jennie, you have one worried father."

"I've been a little worried myself. Is he okay—I heard shooting."

"No casualties," the deputy said. "Lieutenant McGrady is on his way over here now. I'll let him know you're safe." He radioed the message to her father and while they waited asked Jennie and Jared to relate their stories.

Dad drove in fifteen minutes later. He didn't say much, just wrapped Jennie in his arms and held her like he never wanted to let go. Or maybe it was Jennie who held on.

"Oh, Dad, I was so scared. If it hadn't been for Jared . . ."

Dad released her and shook hands with Jared. After questioning them, the federal agents took Jared with them while Jennie rode back to Portland with her dad.

The compound, Jennie discovered on the long trip home, was nestled in the Mount Adams wilderness area. The men had all been arrested and there'd been only two injuries. Jesse and Billy had both been wounded in their effort to escape. The others had surrendered.

Dad about had a fit when he found out she'd escaped and turned back. But even he had to admit he'd have done the same thing. Of course, he hadn't been too happy about her getting abducted in the first place. She shouldn't have stopped at the hospital on her way home from swimming that night. She shouldn't have gone to the parking garage unescorted.

To keep Dad from lecturing her again on the subject, Jennie asked, "Have you gotten any more leads on the arson investigation? I mean, now that we know Reverend Cole didn't do it . . ."

Dad glanced over at her and frowned. "We're back to square one."

"What about the body? Do you know who—?"

He cut her off. "We're still checking that out."

Jennie sighed. "Has Carlos said anything?"

"No. At least not that I know of."

Knowing she wasn't going to get any more information out of her father, Jennie put the seat back down as far as it would go and slept the rest of the way home. She didn't wake up until they pulled into the driveway.

"Jennie! Jennie!" Nick barreled into her before she had a chance to get out of the car.

She scooped him into her arms and held him tight, burying her face in his neck.

"Why're you cryin'?" He leaned back. "Are you sad?"

Jennie sniffed and laughed. "No, I'm just glad to see you. Where's Mom?"

His deep blue gaze drifted up to the second floor. "In her room. She's sick. . . ."

Jennie shot her father a worried look, but he was already moving toward the door.

20

"When can I see my mom?" Nick tugged on Jennie's hand, pulling her into the waiting room. Carlos, silent as ever, held tightly to her other hand.

"I wish I knew." Jennie had remained behind to shower and change while Dad had literally picked Mom off the floor and taken her to the hospital. Jennie was only half an hour behind him, but worry had stretched it into an eternity.

Nick ran to Aunt Kate, who was already seated near the reception desk, and asked her the same thing. "I'm sure it won't be long." Aunt Kate lowered a *Better Homes and Gardens* magazine and pulled Nick onto her lap. "They're running some tests, so we should know something soon."

Jennie gave Carlos a hug and led him to the chair beside Kate and Nick, then paced the length of the waiting room, spun around, and paced back. "This is all my fault, Aunt Kate."

"Jennie . . ."

"No, it is. If I'd gone right home after swimming and hadn't gotten myself abducted by those creeps, this wouldn't have happened."

"She was sick before all that, honey." Kate got up and wrapped a slender arm around Jennie's shoulders. "She's been trying to do too much." She sighed. "With Michael and family and—"

"Me. How is he?" Jennie asked. "Did his sister come?"

"Yes. She got here yesterday. Ashley hasn't left his side since she arrived."

Jennie glanced at her watch. "Do you think I'd have time to go see him?"

"Go ahead. I'll have you paged if we hear anything."

Jennie raced up to the burn unit, slowing when she neared Michael's room. A woman wearing a pastel blue dress was slipping her arms into the drab green gown. Her flaxen hair was pulled back in a bun, and tendrils of curls framed her tan face. She tucked it all into the green cap. Glancing up, she caught Jennie's gaze and smiled, motioning her inside.

Jennie donned the all-too-familiar green isolation garb and went into the room.

"You must be Jennie." She spoke with a slight British accent.

"How did you know?"

"Oh, your mum told me all about you. We've been praying for you. I'm glad to see our prayers have been answered. I'm Michael's sister, Ashley Montgomery."

Jennie nodded. "I'm glad you're here."

"I wish I could have come sooner. We were in the field and didn't get the message right away."

At Jennie's puzzled look, Ashley went on to explain. "My husband, Brent, and I run an orphanage and a hospital in Tanzania. We go out to the villages and care for the people who are too ill or weak to come to us."

"Sounds interesting."

"It is. You will have to come visit sometime." Ashley glanced out into the hallway. "Where is your mother? She said she'd be by today."

Jennie told her about coming home and finding Mom passed out again. "She's been sick off and on for a couple weeks."

"Oh, I didn't know. She seemed fine yesterday. Worried about you, of course, but . . ."

"How is Michael?" Jennie asked, changing the subject.

Ashley's soft blue gaze shifted to her brother's face. "No change, I'm afraid. I wish I could have come sooner . . . before . . . but then, it does no good to make wishes after the fact, does it?"

Jennie forced herself to look at his permanently scarred face. "You were right about Jared, Michael," she said. "You were right to trust him." Turning to Ashley, she added, "Do you think he can hear me?"

"I wouldn't be surprised." She smiled. "Would you like to tell me about this Jared? I'd like to hear a bit about what my brother's been up to. Your mother shared a great deal, but I'd like to hear more."

"Sure. Michael was counseling him. . . ." Jennie went on to tell her about Jared and the fire and how Michael had been a hero. She also told Ashley about the day Michael had coded. "I thought for sure he'd died. I saw this—" Jennie stopped. "I'm sorry. I shouldn't be talking about that."

Ashley placed her slender hand on Jennie's. "Please, go on. What did you see?"

"I thought I saw Michael die. It was so weird. I didn't want him to—but it was like a movie playing in my mind. He even said good-bye. It was like he wanted to go."

Tears glistened in Ashley's eyes. "Oh, Jennie, I can't tell you how relieved I am. It helps me know what I must do."

"I don't understand."

"As you probably know, the doctors don't offer much hope for Michael's recovery. They've asked me to consider taking him off life support. At first I wouldn't hear of it. Now that I've been with him . . ." She sighed. "I have prayed and struggled and this morning I agreed. Bless you, Jennie. Your story has confirmed to me that I'm doing the right thing.

We'll take him off life support and leave him completely in God's hands."

Jennie barely heard her name being paged over the turmoil of emotions tumbling around inside her. She didn't want Michael to die but knew in her heart that Ashley was right. "I . . . I'd better go," Jennie stammered. "My mom . . ."

"Oh yes, by all means. You'll let me know—about your mother, I mean?"

Jennie nodded.

"And don't worry, Jennie. God will take care of Michael—whether it's here on earth or up in heaven."

Jennie believed that, too, but it didn't make things any easier. Why did things have to be so complicated? Jennie wished more than anything she could go back to the days before the fire. Things had changed so much, she doubted they'd ever get back to the way they were.

By the time Jennie reached the emergency room, Kate, Nick, and Carlos were gone.

"We've admitted her," the receptionist said, looking over her half glasses and smiling. "Room 312. Your father said to send you up."

Jennie went back to the elevator and punched the up arrow. When the elevator doors opened, she stepped inside, immediately recognizing the only other occupant. "Mr. Beaumont. Hi."

"Jennie! What—I mean, I thought you were—I saw on television . . ."

Jennie had to smile at his obvious shock. That and his resemblance to a guppy as his mouth opened and closed. As long as she'd known him he'd never been at a loss for words.

"I'm sorry. The last I heard, you'd been abducted." He punched the button for the door to close on the elevator. It finally did and he pressed four for his floor.

Jennie pressed three and briefly filled him in on her escape.

"I see. I'm glad you're okay—the girls have been very worried. You'll have to give them a call."

"I will." She glanced down at the bouquet of pink carnations and baby's breath in his hand.

He held them up. "For Mrs. Talbot—from the board. I was coming over to see Michael, so I volunteered to bring them."

"How is she? I've been meaning to go see her."

"She's doing much better. They'll be transferring her to a convalescent home soon."

"Why?" The doors swished open and Jennie stepped out.

"With her injuries she'll need long-term care."

The doors closed before she could ask him any more questions. Jennie vowed to visit Mrs. Talbot before she left the hospital, then made her way to room 312. Worry for her mom settled in her stomach like a rock. It had to be serious if the doctor was keeping her there.

"I still can't believe I missed it," Kate was saying when Jennie walked in. "I guess it's been too long for both of us."

Mom laughed. "Less for me." Her face was flushed, her eyes bright.

Dad brushed a lock of hair from Mom's forehead, leaned over the bed rail, and kissed her. "Well, I'm just glad we found out what's been going on."

Jennie looked from one to the other. Judging from the grins on their faces, the news must be good.

"What *is* going on?" Jennie approached the bed.

"Oh, Jennie." Mom reached up for a hug. "Welcome home. I was worried sick."

Join the crowd. "I'm okay, Mom." Jennie pulled out of Mom's embrace. "I've been kind of worried about you too."

Nick bounced out of his chair. "Guess what . . . Mom's—what's that word again, Daddy?"

"Pregnant." Dad fastened his warm gaze back on Mom. She touched a finger to his cheek, then looked back at Jennie.

Tears blurred Jennie's vision.

"That means we're going to have a baby." Nick raised his arms for Dad to hold him.

"I know what it means, Nick," Jennie snapped as she tightened her grip on the bed rail.

"What's wrong, sweetheart? I thought you'd be pleased." Mom reached for her.

Jennie backed away. *What is wrong with you, McGrady? This is the part where you're supposed to jump up and down for joy and dance around in circles. Mom's okay. She's having a baby.*

But Jennie didn't feel like dancing or jumping or anything else. Except maybe getting away.

"Jennie, wait," Dad called after her.

Jennie ran from the room, nearly knocking down one of the nurses. She found the exit to the stairs, flew down them, taking them two and three at a time. Jennie didn't stop until she reached her car. Shoving the key into the ignition, Jennie started the Mustang and drove away. She didn't know what to do or where to go, but she had to get away before she exploded.

Half an hour later, Jennie pulled into the driveway of what had once housed her school and church. Driving past the charred remains, she parked near the gym and went inside. DeeDee sprang to her feet and gave Jennie a hug. "I heard on the news you'd been found!"

"Yep." She struggled to make her voice sound normal. "It's okay if I swim, isn't it?" She'd stopped at her house to pick up her swimsuit and leave her parents a note.

DeeDee gave her a look of understanding. "Sure. Take as long as you want."

Jennie hurried to the locker room, changed, and went back to the pool. The water simmered like an aquamarine gemstone as the afternoon sun streamed through the bank of windows on the west side.

She moved into the sunlight and rubbed the goose bumps on her arms. Taking a deep breath, she dove in.

As always, swimming helped to clear her head. She felt foolish now and frustrated with herself for reacting like she had to her mother's good news. And it *was* good. Jennie still couldn't understand why she'd behaved like such a jerk. She was no shrink but figured it had a lot to do with being kidnapped and with Michael dying and the fire.

While she swam she found herself wishing she could talk to Gram. Gram always helped her through the hard times. She'd suggest they sit at the table or in some quiet corner and have a cup of tea. Jennie imagined herself talking with Gram. Gram would probably say something like, "My goodness, darling, with all you've been through it's a wonder you're not a basket case."

"I am a basket case," Jennie would answer.

Then she might say, "You mustn't try to handle everything at once. Tuck all those problems away in little drawers in the closet of your mind. Then pull them out one at a time."

While she settled into a steady, unhurried stroke, Jennie slowed her mind as well. Piece by piece she picked her thoughts apart and set them in different drawers.

Four laps into her routine and they were all neatly tucked away. Jennie felt a surge of relief.

Now, cautiously, she opened the drawer containing what would probably be the easiest problem to resolve—the one involving her family and her new brother or sister. Why she'd reacted so strangely still upset her. She'd acted more like two than sixteen. Now she would need to apologize—especially to Mom.

Thinking back, Jennie envisioned the day she'd first learned that Mom was pregnant with Nick. Jennie had felt much the same way. Shock, anger. The last thing they needed to complicate their lives was a baby. Turned out Nick had been exactly what they needed. While no one could take Dad's place while he was missing, Nick had made Mom's and Jennie's lives more bearable.

She smiled thinking about Nick as a baby and wondered what this baby would be like. Would it be a girl or a boy? A girl, Jennie decided. Would she have dark hair like the McGradys or red like the Calhouns? Boy, girl, redhead, blonde, brunette—none of that mattered. A baby. Her heart swelled to twice its normal size. This time Dad would be there. *He will, won't he, God?*

Jennie turned, switching from a crawl to a back stroke. It was then she saw him. A figure emerging from the men's locker room, carrying a bucket and mop.

Jennie swam to the end of the pool and pushed herself up. "Rafael! Hi!"

"Hallo, Jennie. I did not see you there." He set the bucket down and came toward her.

"What are you doing with those?"

"Working. My uncle will lose his job if he cannot work. We—my father and I—come and clean for him until he comes home."

"That's very nice of you. Philippe is still in jail, then?"

"Sí. But not for the fire. Señorita Cole is causing that."

He was wrong about that, but Jennie didn't bother to correct him. "Then, why?"

"For killing the man in the basement."

21

"The man burned in the fire?"

Rafael nodded.

"Are you sure?"

"Sí. The policía say José was dead before the fire started. My uncle could not do this. The man was his compadre—his friend."

Jennie shook her head. "This isn't making any sense. If Philippe knew him, why didn't he identify him right away?"

Rafael's Adam's apple shifted up and down. "That is why I know he did not kill him, Jennie. Philippe didn't know his friend die in the fire until the policía tell him. Now it breaks his heart to know."

"That's terrible. How did he die?"

"Someone shoot him in head first, then start the fire to cover up. Lisa says you are a good detective. Maybe you can help Philippe. My uncle should not go to prison for something he did not do. Your father is too quick to judge Philippe and . . . you could talk to him, maybe?"

"I don't see how I can help, but, yeah, I'll ask Dad about it."

Rafael flashed her a wide smile as he thanked her, but his eyes remained dark and distressed. "Um . . . how is Carlos? Has he told you anything?"

"No. We keep hoping, but . . ." Jennie shrugged. "He and

Nick are getting pretty close, though, so maybe he'll feel comfortable enough to talk to us soon."

"I wish Mr. Beaumont would have let us keep him with us. It would have been better." He ambled back to his mop and bucket, then disappeared into the men's locker room.

Jennie turned, then pushed off from the side, gliding under the water, letting what Rafael had told her sink in. The murdered man now had an identity. He was Philippe's friend. And if Philippe hadn't killed him, who had? And why? Had Carlos seen the crime? Had he witnessed the murder? Were the arson and the murder done by the same person, or were they separate crimes?

———

"Those are excellent questions, Jennie," Dad said when she asked him later that evening after a dinner of take-out pizza. The boys were upstairs in bed, and Jennie and her dad were sitting on the porch swing, listening to crickets and frogs and the sounds of sunset. "But if it's all the same to you, I'd rather not talk shop."

"What do you want to talk about?"

Dad smiled. "The baby, what else? You must be feeling better about it."

Jennie nodded. When she'd finished swimming, Jennie had driven straight back to the hospital to see her mother. Mom would hardly let her apologize, just kept hugging her and crying and telling her how excited she was. The doctor wanted to keep her in the hospital overnight to run tests, one of which had been an ultrasound.

Jennie and her father talked for a while about how having a baby would be a big adjustment for everyone. Eventually, Jennie managed to steer the conversation back to Carlos and what would happen to him with his father still in jail.

"He has family, princess. I'm sure his uncle will take him.

Either that or he'll go back to Mexico to live with family there."

"Do you think Philippe killed that man?"

"I don't know. The fire has destroyed so much evidence. Half the time I feel like we're grasping at straws. I've been going over and over it. We're fairly certain now that the killer used arson to cover up his or her crime."

"Her? You don't think Reverend Cole . . . I mean, Rich said . . ."

He rubbed his eyes and dragged his hands down his face. "It's all very complicated. The fact that Rich admitted to framing her doesn't necessarily mean he did. In fact, now he says he didn't. We know she wrote those threatening letters to herself. She claims she was trying to show how terrible these groups were and at the same time call attention to the work she and the others were doing at Trinity. She swears she had nothing to do with setting the fire."

"Did she know the man who was killed?"

"Claims not to and so far we haven't made a connection."

"How do you know for sure he was murdered? Maybe the guy died accidentally." Jennie tucked her feet up under her and settled into the corner of the swing.

"Not hardly. The medical examiner discovered a bullet hole in the piece of skull found at the scene. The bullet apparently went into the back of the head."

"Oh." Jennie chewed on her lip, wondering how long Dad's mellow mood would last and how many questions she could get answers to before he told her to mind her own business. "Dad, does Marissa Cole have a gun?"

"No, but that doesn't mean she couldn't have gotten one and discarded it. She had a purse with her in the hospital, and to my knowledge it wasn't searched that night." He stretched out and set his stockinged feet on the wicker table. Tossing Jennie a crooked grin, he asked, "Why all the questions? I'd think after being held hostage for three days you'd be wiped out."

"I talked to Rafael today, and he told me about the man being Philippe's friend. He doesn't think his uncle did it."

"I know. He told us that, too, but we have to look at the evidence. We figure Philippe was using the church basement to operate a business on the side. He and his friend, whom we now have identified as José Chavez, were bringing illegal immigrants into the country and supplying them with falsified papers and green cards. They would get them jobs and take a percentage of their paychecks as payment. We've tracked down two families who have come in that way."

"Not Rafael's family?"

"No, they're legal. Beaumont had his lawyer check them all out."

"What about Philippe's friend?"

"The immigration office has no record of him even applying. He was working for a Mexican restaurant in Tigard. That's where we found the two illegals. I'm betting José and Philippe disagreed on something and Philippe shot him. Carlos may have witnessed it and is afraid to say anything for fear it will incriminate his father."

"When did you find all this out?"

"While you were vacationing in the mountains."

"Some vacation." Jennie scooted next to him and rested her head on his shoulder.

"I know, princess. I'm sorry." He put an arm around her shoulders and hugged her close. "I shouldn't be joking about it."

"Dad?"

"Hmm."

"If Philippe shot this José guy, what happened to the gun?"

"Another good question and one I'm still puzzling over. He wouldn't have had time to take it off the premises. But we haven't been able to find any sign of it at the crime scene. And if he'd taken it with him, the EMTs or ER staff would have found it."

"Unless Philippe killed him earlier, got rid of the gun, then came back and started the fire."

"Thought of that too, princess." Dad yawned and stretched. "Let's not talk about it anymore tonight. I'm too tired to deal with it."

Jennie said good-night to Dad, then looked in on Nick and Carlos, said her prayers, and went to bed. After an hour of tossing and turning, she got up and crept downstairs to get some milk. She poured herself a glass and was taking it back to her room when a car pulled into the driveway. Lisa.

Jennie stepped out onto the porch and waited for her cousin to join her. "What are you doing out so late?"

"I was with Rafael, and we got to talking about that man who was killed."

Jennie dropped down onto the top step. "And . . ."

"We think we know who did it."

"Who?"

"Mr. Beaumont."

"How do you figure that?" Despite the fact that Jennie had listed his name on her suspect list, hearing Lisa say it out loud made the notion sound ridiculous. Still, in mysteries anyway, it was often the least likely person who turned out to be the bad guy.

"Think about it, Jen." Lisa sat on the second step and leaned against the railing. "Mr. Beaumont has been having financial trouble. He hired immigrants to work for him. Maybe he figured he could earn some extra money on the side by bringing in illegals and blackmailing them. Rafael thinks he might have hired José to work for him and was letting him stay in the church basement."

"That doesn't make any sense. Why would he use the church when he had a vacant warehouse?" Jennie drained her glass and set it down next to her.

"Maybe that's why it's empty. Maybe he thought he could make more money by firing all those people and using his warehouse as a storage facility."

Jennie wasn't certain why she felt she needed to defend Beaumont—maybe it was because of B.J. and Allison. They'd be devastated if their father turned out to be a killer. Besides, while some of what Lisa was saying seemed plausible, some didn't.

"Lisa, think a minute. If Mr. Beaumont was using his warehouse as a holding place for illegals until they could be given phony papers, why would he offer to let us use it as a school?"

"Greed." Lisa shot back the answer without hesitation. "Remember what Gavin said about Beaumont renting the building out? I went over there to help work on it yesterday. The school only takes up about half of the building. There's a full basement and a top floor. And there's something else. Rafael says the police don't even know this, but Beaumont opened a clothing manufacturing plant down in Mexico the first of the year under another name. Rafael thinks they're shipping up truckloads of clothing and probably have a partition or something where they can hide the illegals."

"That's very interesting, Lisa." The door behind them banged shut as Jason McGrady stepped outside.

"Uncle Jason!" Lisa jumped up. "You scared me!"

Dad didn't apologize. "Your mother's on the phone. You were supposed to call her when you got here."

"I forgot. It's okay if I spend the night, isn't it?"

"Sure, it'll probably take you that long to explain what this business with illegal immigrants is all about and why you think Beaumont is behind it."

"I was planning to tell you, Uncle J., but I wanted to run it by Jennie first."

Lisa and Jennie followed Dad inside, where Lisa repeated

nearly word for word what she had told Jennie earlier. Dad thanked her and said he'd take it from there. "Believe it or not, girls, the police can operate without your help. I'm sure we would have eventually found out about the plant in Mexico. I'll admit it does sound like a good lead. How did you find out?"

Lisa grinned. "Rafael said he knew about the factory because his mom and older sister used to work there but didn't know anything about bringing illegals in. When he heard about José he put two and two together."

Dad nodded. "I'll be sure to send him a thank-you note. Now, you two get to bed." He ran his hand through his thick dark hair. "Looks like another sleepless night."

———

By morning Lisa was feeling as terrible as Jennie about Mr. Beaumont being a suspect in the murder investigation. Dad was gone when they woke up, and the boys were still asleep.

"We need to go see Allison and B.J. They'll be devastated if it turns out their dad is guilty," Jennie said. "Maybe your mom will watch Nick and Carlos."

"You're right. But, please, Jennie, don't tell them I'm the one who told Uncle Jason. I hope they won't be mad at us."

"Well, I hope it doesn't turn out to be Mr. Beaumont."

Lisa sighed. "Who else would it be? He's the one with all the money and power. And he's kind of arrogant—like he thinks he's better than other people."

"I don't know about that. Mr. B. can act stuck-up sometimes, but he's a kind man. Look at what he did for Allison's boyfriend that time. And he hired a lawyer for Philippe and found jobs for Manuel and Philippe—" Jennie stopped. There was no point defending him. They'd find out the truth soon enough. Dad would have launched a full-scale investigation by now. It was out of their hands.

Rafael called at eight to thank Jennie and Lisa for their help. "The police arrive a few minutes ago," he said. "They have taken Mr. Beaumont in for questioning. Soon they will see that he is guilty and Philippe will be released."

"How are B.J. and Allison?" Jennie asked. "It must be terrible for them."

"It is a sad day for everyone."

Jennie sighed. "I suppose you want to talk to Lisa."

"Sí. If you would be so kind as to put her on."

Jennie handed the phone to Lisa and headed for the stairs to check on Nick and Carlos. It wasn't like Nick to sleep so late. Jennie was halfway up the stairs when the door to Nick's bedroom opened. He barreled right for her.

"Jennie! Jennie! He's gone. I woked up and I can't find him anyplace."

"Whoa. Slow down. Bernie's here. I just fed him."

"No, not Bernie," Nick wailed. "Carlos! Carlos is gone!"

22

After searching the rest of the house, Jennie carried Nick into the kitchen. "Carlos is gone," she told Lisa, who was still on the phone. "You'd better tell Rafael, then I'll need to call Dad. We've got to find him."

"Oh no." Lisa gave Rafael the information. "Okay, sounds like a good idea. Let us know if you find him." Handing the phone back to Jennie, she said, "Rafael's going to drive back this way—maybe Carlos is trying to get to the Beaumonts'."

Jennie nodded and dialed her father's number, letting him know what had happened.

"I'll get people on it right away. Stay put."

After hanging up, Jennie turned her attention back to Nick.

"Can we go look for him, Jennie?"

She hugged him close. "Not right now. Dad said we needed to stay here. The police will find him. Come on." She settled him on the chair. "How about some cereal and juice?"

"Is Carlos going to jail?"

"No, Nick." Jennie took a bowl and glass out of the cupboard and set them on the table.

"They don't put kids in jail for running away." Lisa pulled out the chair beside him.

"No, not for running away. For starting the fire."

179

Jennie nearly dropped the cereal. "Why would you say something like that? Did he tell you he started the fire?"

Nick shrank back. Covering his mouth, he shook his head. "No, no, no."

Jennie and Lisa exchanged glances. "Nick, this is very important. If Carlos told you something, you need to tell me."

"It's a secret. He made me promise."

"Come on, Nick. Remember what Mom said about secrets? There are good ones and bad ones. If it's a bad one, you need to tell."

"But I don't want him to get in trouble."

Jennie took a deep breath. "Okay, Nick. I'll guess and you tell me if I'm right, okay?"

"Okay."

"Carlos told you he started the fire."

Nick shook his head.

"Did he tell you who did?"

Nick shook his head again.

Before Jennie could question him more, the police arrived. Jennie gave them as much information as she could, and after making a search of the house and grounds, they spread out over the neighborhood, checking with neighbors and combing the area. When they'd gone she returned to the kitchen, where Lisa was still trying to coax an answer out of him.

"Come on, Nick. You can tell us. What did Carlos say?"

He put his hands over his mouth again.

Jennie carried him into the living room and sat him down on the sofa. "Let's try this again. Is Carlos afraid someone will hurt him?"

Nick's eyes grew larger. He nodded.

"Who? Did he tell you?"

"He can't tell 'cause his dad might have to stay in jail forever."

"His dad did it after all?" Jennie felt thoroughly confused.

The phone rang. Lisa ran into the kitchen to answer it. "Yes," Lisa said. Then after a few seconds, "No kidding. That's great. We'll be right there."

Jennie set Nick aside and joined Lisa in the kitchen. "Someone found him?"

"Rafael. Carlos is at the Beaumonts'."

Jennie heaved a deep sigh. "Let's get you dressed, little buddy. We're going to pick up Carlos. Now that he's talking, maybe we can find out who really did start that fire."

"If he even knows," Lisa said.

Jennie called her dad but didn't get an answer, then let dispatch know that Carlos had been found and was safe. Minutes later they were on their way to the Beaumonts'.

Even before she rang the bell, Jennie knew something was wrong. She attributed it at first to the fact that Mr. Beaumont had been taken in for questioning. Allison opened the door, her blue eyes fearful as though she were trying to tell them something. She didn't speak as she stepped back to let them in.

"What's that noise?" Jennie thought she heard someone moaning.

The door slammed behind them. Jennie spun around.

Lisa squealed. "What are you—?" Her mouth moved, but no sound came out.

Jennie pulled Nick close behind her. "It was you. All this time." Jennie wasn't surprised. Just disappointed. She'd read the darkness in his eyes but had never dreamed he'd turn out to be a killer.

"Move." Rafael waved the gun at them, herding them toward the basement stairs. "The others are waiting."

"Why—?" Lisa turned back to look at him.

Rafael had the decency to look penitent. "Oh, Lisa, I did not mean for this to happen. José and I, we bring many friends and families into United States. It is chance for a better life. But José take too much money. We argue and I—"

"You shot him and started the fire," Jennie finished.

"Carlos started the fire. I was going to put it out but saw that it would destroy the evidence, so I left it burning."

"You . . . you—" Lisa lashed out at him, knocking him off balance.

Seeing an opening, Jennie slammed into him. He slipped on the top stair and fell backward, firing a shot as he went down.

Jennie heard a swishing sound and felt something brush by her head. She'd been shot, but it didn't hurt much—just burned a little. Unable to catch herself, she fell forward, landing on her assailant.

Lisa screamed. Someone shouted to get down. Jennie heard voices, but they seemed to grow more and more distant. Then she heard nothing at all.

23

From the familiar scent of antiseptic and the sound of instruments dropping into metal bowls, Jennie knew where she was before she even opened her eyes. "She's coming to," someone said.

"I'm almost done. Couple more stitches."

Jennie's eyes drifted open.

A woman wearing bloody surgical gloves smiled down at her. "Hi. Glad you finally decided to join us."

"What happened?" Jennie vaguely remembered tackling Rafael and falling on top of him on the stairs.

"I think I'll let Lieutenant McGrady answer that." She glanced toward the curtain. "Tell him he can come in."

Moments later, Dad stood over the gurney, his hand gripping hers. "Princess. You and I are going to have to start coordinating things a little better."

"Huh?"

"Never mind." His dark gaze moved over her face and linked up with her own. "How are you feeling?"

"Okay. Did you get Rafael? He's the one who killed José and—"

"I know all about it. In fact, we were on our way to arrest him."

"How did you figure it out?"

"Talked to Jared again. He identified the people he saw

at the scene. Said when you and he were talking, he remembered a Hispanic guy coming out of the basement. I showed him Philippe's mug shot, thinking it was him, but it wasn't Philippe at all. Jared said he thought it might have been one of the kids he'd seen at the youth meeting he went to. We had our artist do a sketch from his description and guess who we came up with?"

"Rafael."

"I should have picked it up when you and I were talking last night. Rafael told you José had been shot in the head. He couldn't have known that unless he'd been there. We didn't release that information to the press until later that night."

"All done." The doctor rolled her chair back and pulled off her gloves. "We had to shave off a little of your hair, above your ear, but you have lots left to cover the bald spot. The wound will be uncomfortable for the next few days. Put ice on it and I'll write you a prescription for pain pills." She patted Jennie's arm and left the cubicle.

Jennie reached up and touched the square gauze dressing and the skin around it.

"It'll grow back, princess," Dad assured her. "The important thing is that you're still alive and that Rafael didn't get a chance to carry out his plan."

"What was he going to do?"

"He was running scared. He figured sooner or later Carlos would talk and that Beaumont would eventually put two and two together. I'm not sure how he did it, but he must have taken Carlos from our place sometime during the night. Lisa says her key to our house is missing, so he probably got in that way after I left and you girls went to bed."

"Poor Lisa. She must feel awful."

"She's more mad than sad, I think. Especially when she realized what he was up to."

"I can just about guess. He planned on putting us in the movie room and starting another fire. I thought I saw Mr.

Beaumont down there. Wasn't he supposed to be in jail?"

"We had him in for questioning and released him. Beaumont said when he came home he started asking Rafael about the situation. Rafael pulled a gun on him and took him back to the house. He had the entire family down there."

"And was waiting for us. I can't believe he'd kill that many people to cover his tracks."

"You know, Rafael isn't that much different than Rich when it comes down to it. Both men were willing to kill to further their cause. They were both prejudiced. Now they are both going to face life imprisonment."

"How is Carlos?"

"He's fine now that he's back with his dad. Told us everything. He had been playing with matches and set a fire in a wastebasket. He'd heard the shot and saw Rafael coming out of the room near the furnace. Rafael set the wastebasket in the room and pulled Carlos out. Told Philippe Carlos had started the fire and they'd need to get out. Rafael told Carlos he'd better keep his mouth shut if he ever expected to see his dad again."

"Poor little guy. No wonder he was so frightened." Jennie yawned. It had been a bizarre case, but thank God it was over. Almost over.

"What about Reverend Cole? What's going to happen to her?"

"She's been released. She'll be seeing a therapist for a while, but she seemed in pretty good spirits. I think she'll do just fine."

———

Two days later, Jennie stood on a hill in Mount Tabor Cemetery with her parents and Nick, Lisa, Aunt Kate, Uncle Kevin, Kurt, the Beaumonts, Gavin Winslow and his parents, Reverend Cole, and Michael's sister, Ashley, along with all the kids from the youth group and dozens of other members of the Trinity congregation. Jared was there as well, flanked by two men, federal agents for protection, Jennie guessed.

They'd all come to pay their last respects to a man they all had come to love. Pastor Dave gave the eulogy, saying how Michael would have been proud of the way they'd come together and that his dream to make Trinity a home to everyone, regardless of race or culture, was becoming a reality.

"As we say good-bye to our brother, let's keep our hearts and minds attuned to the way Michael lived. Let us love God with all of our hearts and minds and souls, and let us love one another as Christ first loved us."

Jennie's watery gaze fell to the rose she held in her hand. Taking her turn, she walked forward and dropped her rose on the casket. "Good-bye, Michael. I'll miss you."

"I'll miss you, too, Jennie," she could almost hear him say.

Dad wrapped an arm around her shoulder and whispered, "He was one of the good guys."

"Yes, he was," Mom said as she, too, dropped her rose. "We'll all miss him."

"Mama?" interjected Nick. "If Michael is in heaven, why are we putting his flowers in the ground?"

Several people nearby chuckled.

Jennie stifled a smile.

"That's a very good question." Mom knelt down beside him. "Would you like to put your flower somewhere else?"

He nodded. "Up in the tree, then Michael can reach down and get it."

Dad lifted him up while he deposited his flower.

Jennie would have given anything if Michael had survived the fire. But as Ashley had reminded all of them, in heaven Michael would experience complete healing and was in a far better place. Jennie was glad about one thing. She'd had the opportunity to capture the man responsible for the fire. In this case, at least, justice would be served.

"Jennie?" Dad's soft mellow voice broke into her thoughts. "Are you ready? We need to get your mother home."

"Sure. Let me say hi to Jared first."

"Don't be long."

"I won't."

"Hi," Jennie said as she approached him. "Um . . . just want to see how you're holding up."

"Okay. I'm staying with a foster family right now. They're nice."

An awkward silence stretched between them as they stood on the hillside looking down at the grave.

"Well," Jennie said finally. "I should go. Mom's going to have a baby, and she tires out pretty easily."

"That's neat. I—I'm glad we got a chance to talk. I want to tell you how sorry I am about Rich abducting you. If I hadn't lied to him about being in jail he wouldn't have—"

Jennie stopped him. "Don't worry about it. I don't blame you. Besides, it came out okay. We're both safe and you're free to live the kind of life you want."

"I'm not sure, but I think I know what that's going to be." He glanced toward the grave. "I'd like to pattern my life after Michael's. When the trial is over, I'll go to college and maybe seminary. First though"—he gave her a lopsided grin—"I need to let my hair grow out."

"Oh," she teased. "I was just getting used to it." After another long pause she said, "I'd better go."

"Yeah, me too." He reached forward and gave her a hug. "Thanks for believing in me."

Jennie smiled. "Thank Michael—and God."

———

On the way home, Jennie leaned back against the seat and

closed her eyes. Her brushes with death, both with Rich and Rafael, might have deterred some, but Jennie McGrady was more determined than ever to become a lawyer. She just hoped the next case would be a while in coming.

Teen Series From
Bethany House Publishers

━━∞∞∞━━

Early Teen Fiction (11–14)

HIGH HURDLES by Lauraine Snelling
  Show jumper DJ Randall strives to defy the odds and achieve her dream of winning Olympic Gold.

SUMMERHILL SECRETS by Beverly Lewis
  Fun-loving Merry Hanson encounters mystery and excitement in Pennsylvania's Amish country.

THE TIME NAVIGATORS by Gilbert Morris
  Travel back in time with Danny and Dixie as they explore unforgettable moments in history.

Young Adult Fiction (12 and up)

CEDAR RIVER DAYDREAMS by Judy Baer
  Experience the challenges and excitement of high school life with Lexi Leighton and her friends—over one million books sold!

GOLDEN FILLY SERIES by Lauraine Snelling
  Readers are in for an exhilarating ride as Tricia Evanston races to become the first female jockey to win the sought-after Triple Crown.

JENNIE MCGRADY MYSTERIES by Patricia Rushford
  A contemporary Nancy Drew, Jennie McGrady's sleuthing talents promise to keep readers on the edge of their seats.

LIVE! FROM BRENTWOOD HIGH by Judy Baer
  When eight teenagers invade the newsroom, the result is an action-packed teen-run news show exploring the love, laughter, and tears of high school life.

THE SPECTRUM CHRONICLES by Thomas Locke
  Adventure and romance await readers in this fantasy series set in another place and time.

SPRINGSONG BOOKS by various authors
  Compelling love stories and contemporary themes promise to capture the hearts of readers.

WHITE DOVE ROMANCES by Yvonne Lehman
  Romance, suspense, and fast-paced action for teens committed to finding pure love.